The Stone Age

Shy, naïve, nineteen year-old Griffin returns one night from the insurance office where he works to his parent's home in the suburbs where he still lives, to discover that he has been drafted. Against the odds, he survives induction into the army where fierce sergeants set about transforming him into their version of a man—without a great deal of success. But he learns what he needs to know pretty quickly once they land him as a combat soldier in the Vietnam war. Faced with the worst horrors of human conflict, Griffin transforms into the most fundamental of humans—hunter-killer—the quintessential example of the most dangerous predatory animal ever to walk this planet. And then, just as suddenly, his time is up and he is dumped back into civilised society and expected to cope. Unable to resume any part of his former comfortable, happy existence, he sets about trying to be someone else—without much luck—until he falls in with radical draft-dodger Lew Sigg. Painfully, Griffin undergoes a 180° turn and becomes an anti-war protestor, more or less, but it solves nothing. Finally Lew, on the run from the law, takes him on a journey that will finally bring him to terms with himself.

By the Same Author

Boss Gull
Aesop's Solon
Shadow Rider
Being Jarvis Kreeg
The Lake Mulga Mob
Pythagoras Dreaming
The War of Immensities
The World Beneath Their Feet
Wandering at Large & Other Stories
A Thousand Thousand Slimy Things

The Stone Age

Barry Klemm

"It is my firm belief that there is nothing in the present situation or in our code that requires us to bomb a small Asian nation into the stone age."

General Matthew Ridgway, US Chief of General Staff

in association with

COLLINGWOOD GALLERY PUBLISHING

The action in this novel commences in November 1965 and ends in December 1972

ISBN 978-0-9807343-2-4

www.barryklemm.com
manager@collingwoodgallery.com.au

Chapter 13 and chapters 18 - 29 were published by Black Pepper Publishing, Melbourne as "Running Dogs". That book was also selected as a book reading by the Australian Broadcasting Corporation.

Contents

PART ONE:

RUNNING DOGS

"Death to the American Imperialists and all their Running Dogs"

-Ho Chi Mihn

A Letter from Pig-iron Bob

Dear sir,

It is my duty to advise you that under article 2/56 of the National Service Act of 1962, that you are required to report for a medical examination at the time indicated on the attached form. This examination is for the purpose of assisting to determine your eligibility for compulsory military service in accordance with the further requirements of the above act. It will be conducted by a qualified medical practitioner appointed by the Department of the Army. Failure to attend is liable to a fine of not more than £2000 or two year's imprisonment, or both...

On the evening when he found this letter—perched vulture like on the empty cup and saucer and looming over his dinner setting on the kitchen table—Griffin had just completed another unendurable day at the offices of the insurance company where he worked in the city. Nightly he would join the legions of commuters marching resolutely to Flinders Street Station where he would catch the 5.17 from platform 10 east, express to Moorabbin, whereon he undertook his nightly battle with the crossword puzzle, and usually lost. From there he would catch the rattling red bus that ran down Merrijig Road, reading the evening news as he went. It wasn't entirely for this reason that his view of current events was always somewhat shaky.

He would enter the house at five past 6, which, since it was a working-class family, was one hour and five minutes after dinnertime. On such evenings the house would at first appear to be deserted—the lights dimmed, a somnolent stillness in the air. But no, if your hearing was up to it you would have perceived a babble of voices from the left where lay the lounge room, thoroughly sealed from draughts and the outside world.

He would sneak down to the kitchen and there find the table set for one person, with no indication whatsoever that the rest of the family had eaten an hour before. Office hours differed from those of factory workers and, since long before he existed, his father's dinner had been placed before him the moment he walked in at five o'clock. Thus for the last three years Griffin had arrived home late for dinner with precisely the same regularity that his father did not, and at no time was it contemplated that there be some change to the natural order of things.

From the next room, muffled sounds that would have been clear to anyone were emitted, even without the occasional eruptions of gunfire and galloping horses, punctuating music and overly dramatic voices.

He would call. "Hello. I'm home."

To which his mother would reply either. "Hello dear. Your dinner is in the oven." or. "Hello dear. Your dinner is on the stove." Her voice came reassuringly through the door, only a little louder than the video mumble. In three years it had never occurred that his dinner was neither in the oven nor on the stove.

On the particular evening of the letter from the *Department of Labour and National Service,* his dinner was on the stove. He peeked—Irish stew, so it must have been a Tuesday, which also meant that dessert would be rice pudding and cream, awaiting his pleasure in the refrigerator. Before doing anything to rescue his dinner, he opened the letter and read those fateful words. It was a mistake—he didn't feel much like dinner after that.

Into his mind sprang an idea that went back to the games he played in his childhood—cowboys and indians, space invaders, pirates and explorers, cops and robbers—all of which had led to appropriate ambitions for his dubious future. When he grew up, he wanted to be at various times a spaceman, a test pilot, a policeman, a US marshal, a buccaneer, quite in the mould of certain individuals—Ned Kelly, Captain Cook, Phillip Marlowe, The Durango Kid. Perfectly healthy stuff for any boy, but there was always one game he never wanted to play which was the game of *War,* and always one sort of hero he never wanted to be, and that was a soldier—not even Audie Murphy.

Now a more serious view needed to be taken. He realised immediately that it was the work of Pig-iron Bob. Just before the Second World War, Robert Menzies, Prime Minister of Australia, incurred considerable profits by selling local pig-iron to the Japanese. Now it probably was *not* the same iron that composed the bombs that the Japanese were soon to drop on Darwin—the Japanese don't have that sort of sense of humour—but Australians do and so everyone said it was. However, Australians also have short memories. Although they called him Pig-iron Bob forever after, they also continued to re-elect him, and he had been Prime Minister for all of Griffin's lifetime, until he recently retired, shortly after deciding that Australian troops should be sent to assist the Americans with a little problem they were having in a place called Vietnam. Conscription was to be re-introduced to aid the nation's flagging military strength. All this seemed very unimportant at the time—after all, Pig-iron

Bob was the person that everyone blamed for everything.

You could not go more than for a few hours into any given day before someone seemed to find cause to mutter 'Bloody Menzies!' or 'Pig-iron bastard!'. There didn't seem to be anything he could not be blamed for—the state of the world, the rural decline, the economy, droughts, late trains, motor accidents, influenza, cups that lost their handles in the washing up water, his father's snoring... Pig-iron Bob, it appeared, kept the nation alert and unified by inventing new things for the populous to complain about, and this business of conscription and *Vietwherever* seemed merely his latest creation. No one realised that this would be his masterstroke, the final gesture before stepping down, to provide his people with something they could complain about more vociferously and determinedly than ever before, for long after he was gone.

But Griffin could stand and brood these things no longer, and so, letter in hand and leaving the Irish stew to its bubbling fate for a moment longer, he crossed to the sliding door that divided kitchen from lounge room and opened it just enough to poke his head through. In the flickering grey-blur of the video, he saw his mother on the couch, pillows propping her troublesome back and her knitting on her lap; his plump housecoated sister and pyjamaed brother on their chairs to the right; his bald and weary father still in his overalls in the chair that no one else was ever allowed to sit it.

But the dominant presence was the television, so completely did it root their attention. There, lantern-jawed Chuck Connors was mouthing platitudes of truth, charity and justice to his extraordinarily well-behaved son, as a humane pause between those times when he ruthlessly mowed down owlhoots with his modified rapid fire rifle.

"Is something wrong with dinner dear?" his mother asked as quietly as she could, if not quietly enough for his brother and sister who immediately hissed like a pair of startled snakes.

"No. No," he murmured, incurring further sibling sibilation and he hastily retracted his head as if in fear of some more dangerous form of venom.

Left alone then to share his unfathomable fate with the Irish stew and rice pudding. And unfathomable it was. His father had been in the war—he went to Singapore to help the British try to stem the Japanese advance until the defences cracked, whereby he was imprisoned in Changi until the end of the war when he came home to immediately set Griffin's life in motion.

But his father, like his uncles and certain other men about the neighbourhood, could never be persuaded to talk about it in any sort of explanatory detail. He would often attempt interrogation. Once a week throughout his boyhood, his father would take the kids to the movies and sometimes combat films would be the fare, but as they walked home after seeing such excellent examples as 'Bridge on the River Kwai', or 'To Hell and Back', he would turn to his father with wide-eyed boyish excitement and ask anxiously. "Was that what it was like, Daddy?"

His father would answer. "No."

That was all.

Just a flat 'no'.

Griffin was left in the dark amongst eyewitnesses. He had only the heroisms of John Wayne and Richard Attenborough to guide his imagination. And even then, he did not like the way it went.

He tried to remember what he knew about this Vietnam place but the truth was that for all his newspaper reading, the matter had not been at all expanded upon since he read about *Insurgents in Indo-China* at school, which he at first translated as *Laundry Habits in the Himalayas*. Apparently, the evil designs of Chairman Ho and his hooligans continued unabated, all these years later. Mostly, he was a little bit surprised to realise that he knew that much about it. Maybe his knowledge of the world was not as slight as he had previously thought.

But he found himself to be dallying—the flurry of gunfire from the loungeroom suggested the demise of *The Rifleman*'s adversary of the evening and paved the way for his own entry to the scene. He gulped down the rest of his meal and then rushed about, washing his dishes, shaking the crumbs from the tablecloth outside, and so was able to creep into the lounge room at the usual time, which was the moment that the solemn fanfare announced the advent of the six-thirty news.

He took up his seat, on the couch beside his mother, just as the newsreader began an account of the day's events. There was a major strike in the motor industry, cyclonic storms in North Queensland, and Pig-iron Bob's successor, Harold Holt, was in America and gleefully declaring that Australia would go 'All the way with LBJ'. With that as a claim to posterity, it was probably for the best that Holt was soon to drown himself at Portsea beach, but such things were not to be seen with any such clarity at the time.

These three items justified an advertisement break, and

there then appeared on the screen a flurry of baby's bottoms—the only sort of people permitted to possess such things on television in those days—all of which lead to an extolling of the virtues of *Sorbent Toilet Tissues*. And his mother, once the matter concerned tissues rather than tots, took the opportunity to look up from her knitting and ask. "Did you get your letter, dear?"

"Yes," he said softly.

He didn't know how to continue and there was a long pause. *Sorbent Supersofts* were superseded by the equestrian heroes of *Marlboro Country*, wherever that was.

"Looked important," his mother said.

Under such pressure, secret information could be suppressed no longer.

"Yes. It was from the Department of Labour and National Service. They want me to..."

But he was robbed. When three advertisements were customary, there were only two, and the persuasive professionalism of the newsreader easily sliced through his stumbling sentence with vital information of the arrival in Melbourne of an American Film Actress.

There followed a number of local items but he was in such a state of verbal strangulation that he could not take them in. Somehow he feared the matter might be complicated by some report concerning Vietnam. Sometimes there were pictures of US troops and helicopters, and there had been much publicity when a noted Test Cricketer had been called up and then, adding insult to injury, a successful pop singer right after him. But the cricketer never left Australia and somehow his leave time co-incided with all important cricket fixtures, while the Top 40 fared no worse for a hero singing songs of war in military green. But no such matter occurred that night—Vietnam had been going on long enough to be a stale story, in the view of news producers at least.

At last the newsreader announced another break, and *Wilkinson Sword Double-edged Razors* slid over a disembodied Adam's Apple while it felt like a hundred blunt ones where scratching Griffin's entire body.

"What did you say they wanted?" his mother asked.

"I have to go for a medical examination."

"Oh? Is something wrong with you, dear?"

"No. It's just routine apparently..." And tried to look as calm and healthy as he could.

But he saw that the eyes of his father had been wrenched

away from the video and planted their gaze upon him with no less fascination—plainly the significance of all this had not escaped him in the manner that it had his wife.

"Bloody Menzies," he muttered in disgust.

Younger brother Michael, who spent the greater part of his life seeking ways into adult conversations, saw a chance now.

"It ain't Menzies. It's Holt."

Wally Griffin, as usual, saw no reason to make any response to this whatsoever.

He looked at his mother and saw a hoard of questions were brewing in her weary brain, but time was running out for her. *Reg Hunt Motors* was being promoted by just that sort of salesman who would one day be immortalised by Richard Nixon posters, and then psychedelic surfers in glorious monochrome were skimming down speckled waves to a frantic rock beat only seconds away from female accompanied gulps of *Coca-cola*.

"I don't see why you need to go to a doctor if there isn't anything wrong with you," his mother said plaintively, and rattled her number three needles in disapproval.

He had to wait again until the gap between the sports report and the weather, and then, speaking as rapidly as he could, eventually managed to convey to his mother the general implications of the letter.

"Oh," she gasped. "So it means that you've been drafted."

"Cos it does, yer silly old moo," Wally grumped.

"It depends on the result of the medical examination," Griffin explained.

"Oh, well," his mother decided. "I s'pose you better go then."

"Mum, he don't have any choice," Narelle cried impatiently.

"Oh, well, I s'pose you better, then. What do you think, Wally?"

Wally Griffin did not trouble to turn in his chair. In a voice as flat as the television screen, he said, "Bloody Menzies."

The final word had thus been spoken, and with that they were able to settle down and watch the rest of the evening's television programs in relative peace.

The Guardian of the Lair

On the morning following the arrival of that fateful letter, Griffin proceeded to the *Australian and New Zealand Insurance Company,* burning with the fires of resolve, and immediately discovered that Mary Stemple had spared no effort in her attempts to quell every ember of them. Of all days, she had chosen this one to exhibit a little blue dress that was plainly her newest acquisition. Dismay overwhelmed him. He was already seated at his desk pretending to organise the documents and purchase orders for a day of industrious endeavour, but really he had eyes only for Mary Stemple as she breezed in and placed herself behind her own desk—immediately outside the office of the Branch Manager—which lay directly ahead of his own allotted place in the world of fire and household insurance.

Mary Stemple, with her flowing blonde hair and radiant smile, wore a blue dress with a plunging neckline and raised hem revealing superb plump thighs. At any time of the day, all he had to do was lift his eyes from his work and there she was in all her splendour, and it might have been for that very reason that Griffin was looked upon as one of the more diligent workers in the office. The honeyed tips of the golden mane swept across her shoulders, the graceful curve of breasts above her eminently leer-worthy neckline, the delicious sheer-nyloned thighs, the pouting lips with their thick vanish of glistening lipstick—surely were you to kiss her you would remain stuck forever.

Now God's grace and office etiquette had combined to fit a modesty panel to the front of her desk and that along with desktop, papers and typewriter formed a merciful barricade from Griffin's perspective; but all that really meant was that there were continual glimpse to be had as vital bits of her appeared suddenly from here and there. It was a game of now you see it now you don't which any lecher knows is the very basis of all eroticism, and it all seemed to be designed with the singular purpose of driving a young man like Griffin to utter distraction as his mind sought to fill in logical gaps and imagine things only just beyond the limits of his vision.

Any interest he might have been able to conjure in miscalculated purchase orders and incorrectly valued office furniture stock would continually dissolve into a cheek-burning oblivion of the most extraordinary fantasies. And then her eyes—blue and, like her tongue, very sharp, would suddenly glance up and apprehend his mesmerised gaze, sending him scattering like startled pigeons back to the proposal forms, not daring to raise his head again for at least half an hour, which was the time it took for the redness that emblazoned his shame-filled face to subside.

However, to think that Mary Stemple was positioned as she was entirely for the purpose of Griffin's personal torment would be to overlook the real reason for which she was paid—to guard the door of the Branch Manager's office and protect Mr Lord for all unnecessary contact with the outside world. And since Griffin had firmly decided that today he must confront Mr Lord and inform him of the fate that had befallen him, it was going to be necessary to somehow find his way into that hallowed chamber, and hence, someway past Mary Stemple. All this the blue dress and its devastating neckline conspired against. It was all completely unbearable.

Of course, he could have resorted to what was laughably described as 'normal channels' which was the means that all matters intended for the attention of Mr Lord travelled about the general office to his ears. This required that Griffin go first to Sprinkler Sampson, the Fire Claims Superintendent who was his immediate superior and occupied the small glass partitioned cage to Griffin's right, which, supposedly, Griffin himself would some day inherit. Sprinkler would then pass the matter to Dozey Dawson, the Staff Superintendent, who in turn would address Bloodshot Biggins, the Assistant Branch Manager, and it was supposed to be he alone who was permitted to pass by Mary Stemple and enter Mr Lord's sacred domain.

Unfortunately, there were a number of blockages likely to occur along the 'normal channel'. Firstly was Sprinkler's fascination with fires—he considered himself the greatest expert on the subject alive and could describe in detail the destruction of every building that ever came to a fiery end—the cause, the characteristics of the spread, the date and time, how long it took for the firefighters to attended and put it out, the number of men and fire appliances in attendance and probably the names of the men. Mention a surprise in last week's football scores and you would be told of how the Fitzroy grandstand burned down in 1935, try to discuss the government's latest scandal and you would be told of the deficiencies of the fire protection system at Parliament House. If it did not concern fires, it did not interest Sprinkler Samson—no point at all in raising vital personal issues with him.

By-passing him would achieve little. Take the problem to the office of Dozey Dawson and he would jolt awake and cry: 'Yes, I'll see to it right away,' and promptly go back to sleep and forget it completely. And even if he did remember and take the matter to Bloodshot Biggins, all he would discover was that Bloodshot wasn't there. To find Bloodshot, you would need to proceed to the back bar of the Francis Hotel where he spends most of every day, but of course, like everyone else who valued their continued employment in the company, Dozey made a point of not knowing that.

Naturally, all of this meant that Mr Lord never actually got to hear about anything intended for his ears. Indeed, had he depended on normal channels, he would have needed to peep out of his office periodically just to assure himself that he still existed, which was an act considerably below the dignity of so important a personage as himself. But there was a second, far more efficient channel through which office information flowed, which took the form of the office gossip. All matters, relevant or trivial, travelled about the building by this means and eventually reached the ears of Mary Stemple, who edited, filtered, and passed it on to Mr Lord.

Griffin shuddered at the thought of information so deep and personal and how pitifully it would fare when swept along the streams of gossip. People would ogle, people would want to express sympathy, people would want to tell him how they knew so-and-so who was or wasn't or might or might not be drafted. The thought of creating such a turgid mess of emotion and fascination was intolerable. The only option then was to approach Mr Lord personally, and to do that he needed to find a way to get past Mary Stemple and her little blue dress.

Innumerable times throughout the day, Griffin would stir up the necessary courage to jump up from his desk and make a step or two in Mr Lord's direction but always Mary would reappear from wherever she was and he would be forced to divert over to the filing cabinets to search for something he didn't need or across to the counter to attend a customer who wasn't there. Didn't she ever pee? Perhaps magnificent creatures like her were above such things. His desk was becoming littered with superfluous documents and office equipment, and Mary was getting suspicious—each time she spent a little longer gazing at him quizzically. He set time limits—eleven o'clock, twelve, straight after lunch—all of which passed without success. He would have to do it. He would *have* to!

Three o'clock passed, and three-thirty. The day was running out with its central purpose unfulfilled. Griffin sweated on four, frustration boosting his diminishing determination, poised like a tiger at the edge of his desk as the sweep hand covered those last few seconds. The hand touched twelve and he sprang forth and booted his wastepaper bin across the office, spewing out clumps of discarded paper as it spun like a top of the smooth floor and crashed against the filing cabinets beyond. Everyone gaped. The whole office, Griffin knew, would be craning and straining to try and make out the cause of the commotion. Dozey awoke, Sprinkler waited for fire alarms, Mary Stemple sat with her hand over her mouth, suppressing laughter. Griffin scurried about, burningly redfaced, bum up, gathering scattered paper, stuffing it back in the bin, and finally shuffling in his shame back to his seat. For the next hour, he was seen checking cover notes with a diligence never observable before, back hunched, shoulders compressed, his fiery red face only inches off the surface of the desk.

Disaster. Tragedy. Hopelessness. These three thoughts swirled about in his head, kicking the remnants of his broken brain to death. Time was running out and soon he would be able to escape home, dragging his humiliation and failure with him. Perhaps tomorrow... And meanwhile, the calculations. *Five class F supervisor's visitors chairs at nineteen pounds per item was ninety-five pounds plus tax is ninety-eight pounds six and six pence...*

"Ken?"

Eight hundred and seventy five gross of steel paper clips at...

"Ken!"

So absorbed was he that he refused to hear his name, emitted with such angelic tones from across the room. How could he face her, speak to her, now. At the third try, her tone became threateningly insistent.

"Ken!"

He could not avoid the impulse to glance up. Mary Stemple sat looking straight at him with her helpless-female-pleading expression that no one in the world would be able to resist. She raised a single index finger straight in front of her nose and bent it beckoningly. Griffin sighed. Was there to be no end to his shame? He slithered out of his chair, eased his way carefully around the treacherous waste paper bin, and teetered when he would have preferred to crawl, over those elusive few yards to her side.

Mary Stemple wore her very sweetest smile as if in a genuine effort to dispel the fears of degradation rattling around inside him. There was a sheet of paper that she was brandishing—*in Mr Lord's handwriting*—she jabbed a red fingernail at it to draw his attention that way but, standing over her as he was, his eyes had to traverse the twin orbs on view down the front of her dress to get there. His stomach churned, his knees quivered, embarrassment coursed through his veins and exploded redness on every part of his flesh.

He could feel his skin overheating. His eyes could not tear themselves from that chasm of loveliness to the point on the page at which he fingernail jabbed. When she leaned forward to try and help him, his eyes glazed and he was sure he would faint. The thick coating on that fingernail matched his complexion rather more than hers as she jabbed with annoyance at the page.

"This word here. Can you tell what it is? His bloody handwriting is atrocious."

Desperately, Griffin wrenched his bulging eyeballs to the true focus of the matter and strove mightily to get them to focus. Finally the scrawled word came into view.

"It looks like pumpkin," he said, to prove he was a complete moron.

She sighed. Griffin continued to stare at the word and so missed the expression on her face which must have been fairly bleak if her voice was any guide. "I *know* it looks like pumpkin, but it isn't. The letter has nothing to do with pumpkins. Read the whole thing and see if you can tell what it really is."

He did so: it took a number of attempts but he finally got through it. "Quantity," he declared. Given the context of the sentence, it could not have been anything else.

"Of course it, is," Mary Stemple smiled appreciatively. "Thank you, Ken."

She lowered the sheet and prepared to get on with her typing, and Griffin should have walked away but he did not. Realising that some sort of paralysis had overwhelmed him, Mary Stemple turned her most delightful smile on him.

"I did say thank you."

"I want to see Mr Lord."

"You what?"

"Nothing."

"You said something about Mr Lord."

"No I didn't..."

"Yes you did."

"No... well, yes... I did..."

"Tell me what you said..."

"I want to see him."

"Do you really? What about?"

"I can't tell you. It's personal."

"Oh, Kenny, come on. You can tell me."

"No. Only Mr Lord."

"Well, I'm sorry but I'm afraid you can't see him unless you tell me what it's about. He doesn't like surprises. He's very insistent on that point."

"It is very personal. Tell him that."

"What is very personal?"

"I can't tell you, but I have to see him."

"I'm sorry. It's quite impossible..."

"FOR CHRISTS SAKE TELL HIM I WANT TO SEE HIM!"

Now if there is a universal law in an insurance office, it is that one never raises one's voice—everything is spoken in hushed tones. It was therefore plain to Mary Stemple that if a person would yell like that, there was no telling what else he might do. All around everyone stopped whatever they were doing and stared, mouths open, eyes bulging, too shocked to move. Mary Stemple gulped and after one last defiant glare, allowed her trembling finger to creep to the intercom button. It was plain that Griffin had scared the living daylights out of her.

Fairly much the same conversation repeated itself with Mary Stemple speaking Griffin's lines and Mr Lord presumably her former ones, although it was rather hard to tell because Mr Lord's replies were so crackly that it was amazing that Mary could understand them. Certainly she had to repeat Griffin's name several times before Mr Lord finally seemed to have some idea who that might be.

"No, he won't tell me what it's about," Mary Stemple sighed.

"Yes. He says it is very important," she declared, when, if Griffin's memory served, he had not.

"But he says he has to see you."

"But he *has* to."

And finally she released the intercom button and looked up at Griffin, smiling a rather flustered smile.

"Okay, Ken. You can go right in."

Grimly, Griffin stepped and opened the hitherto unopenable door, struggling to get his breathing and most of his other bodily functions under control as he did so. He stepped through and found beyond a vast chamber that was anything but what he would have expected. A huge room, quite out of step, he knew, with Mr Lord's status. There was a large desk and executive chair far off in the corner and way over there a couple of filing cabinets and a bookcase with only a few books. The rest was all soft carpeted distance, unless you wanted to count the numerous oil paintings on the walls. No wonder Mr Lord was so careful to keep the minions out.

Mr Lord was seated at the desk with only the shining dome of his well-polished head showing between his hunched shoulders. Spread before him on the desk was the evening newspaper and not a single other document, letter or file and there, poised under his pen-clutching forepaw, was the partly completed crossword puzzle.

Then, suddenly, Mr Lord's dark intense eyes were on him, and Griffin forgot all that, and everything else as well. Half-tiger, half-snake, but mostly, Mr Lord was a giant Sea Lion.

"Ah yes, Griffin, isn't it."

It was the first time in the two years that he had worked for the company that Mr Lord spoke to him and Griffin replied in the way he always responded to authoritative tones.

"Um...well...its...um...."

"Come on, lad. Out with it. Busy man, you know. What's the problem?"

Griffin, however, had anticipated this. So predictable was his vocal breakdown in the face of seniority that he had thought to bring the letter from the Department of Labour and National Service, and now he drew it from his pocket, shuffled forward a few paces, and dropped it on Mr Lord's desk. Mr Lord took it up and only after a suspicious gaze at Griffin, began to read. He stopped, looked a lot hard, and then read on to the end.

"It seems you've been drafted, Mr Griffin," he said, and now his tone was soft and respectful.

"Yes sir. I think so, sir."

"Oh no. You have for sure."

"Yes sir."

"Very unfortunate for you. In some ways."

"Yes sir."

"But fortunate in another, on the other hand."

"Which hand is that?"

"The army. Makes a man out of a boy like you."

Boy?

"Oh yes, I see."

"Still, we must look on the bright side, mustn't we?"

"Bright side?"

"You might fail the medical... or something."

"Oh yes."

"But then, on the other hand, let's assume that you do have to go."

"Yes. Let's assume..."

"Well then, of course the company has an obligation here. At least I think we do."

"You think..."

"Yes. And naturally we'll honour that."

"Yes."

"Of course we must. It's the law, you see. Unless, of course, you decide that you might not want to come back to us."

"Mightn't I?"

"Well, two years can be a very long time. Other fellows, your present contemporaries, will have advanced some way further along in their careers by then. We cannot guarantee that you won't be disadvantaged in that way."

"I wouldn't want..."

"Of course, on the other hand, we wouldn't want you to think that the company won't stand behind you on this, but you must realised that a young man can change a lot in two years..."

Griffin, wondering how many hands Mr Lord imagined he possessed, was slowly beginning to realise what the conversation was about.

"Things might well be different by then."

"They probably will."

"You can't tell."

"No sir, you can't."

"So, what I'm trying to say is, that if, on the other hand, you decide not to come back to us, we will understand."

"Yes. I see."

"And, of course, it will be a great help to us, should you make such a decision, if you were to let us know at the first available opportunity."

"I understand."

And then came a pause. Mr Lord, who seemed relieved now that he had got that off his chest, leaned back and lit a cigar. Gladly, he did not offer Griffin one. Only slowly did Griffin realise that there seemed to be an air of expectancy in the room.

"Um..." Griffin said.

"Yes?" Mr Lord asked, his raised eyebrows offering

encouragement.

Plainly, Griffin was the one who had to speak although he could not for the life of him think of what to say. "Ummm..." he offered.

"Does that mean yes or no?" Mr Lord asked, his patience having run out.

"Yes or no what?"

"Will you be coming back to us after your period of service or not?"

"I don't know..."

Griffin could see that his answer was the worst he could possibly have offered.

"Oh dear. Very well then. Of course, on the other hand, the government has insisted on this undertaking and we will honour it. Indeed we must. Just as long as you're sure."

And he waited again, his hands spread on the desktop as if he was about to leap it and throttle Griffin on the spot. But because Griffin did not know what to say, so he sensibly said nothing.

Mr Lord's expression of disappointment could not have been more pronounced. The truth was that he did have a serious problem. Government policy of the time allowed employers to pay lower wages to junior staff with the result that it was company policy to find a pretext on which to dismiss any employee who turned twenty-one and therefore became eligible for full wages. Young Kenneth Griffin was presently twenty—when he returned he would be twenty-two. But it was too late now—the government was quite firm in its commitment to conscripts. Mr Lord made a mental note to fire Griffin immediately should he fail his medical and not be drafted—otherwise, well, two years from now was another day.

Griffin, of course, was unaware of all of this at the time. Mr Lord rose and came around the desk, putting an arm about Griffin's shoulder until the latter responded to the forces that turned him around and headed him out the door. Which Griffin was glad of, if only to escape the cloud of cigar smoke that presently enveloped him.

"Very well, Young Griffin. Of course if, on the other hand, you do make a decision, don't hesitate to let us know. Good of you to give us such advance notice. All the best, young man."

Before he quite knew it, Griffin was standing beside Mary Stemple's desk and the door to the hallowed chamber snapped firmly shut behind him. As such he was thrust into a world of curious faces with eyes striving to read his mind and not the least was that of Mary Stemple.

"Was it... okay?" she asked.

Since there wasn't any answer to that question either, Griffin shrivelled off back to his desk to bury his head in the documents where at least the world made some pretence of making sense and wait out the final desperate minutes before he could safely scamper off home.

Ways of Escape

Summoned by a bell that operated when Griffin came through the door from the street, the nurse—a gargantuan woman with a permanently diffident look—came swishing up the hallway from the bowels of the building, both of her feet remaining in continual contact with the floor in the characteristic gait of her profession. There was a small counter in the waiting room and a journal laid open in it and, taking up her biro, the nurse leaned over it and prepared to write.

"Name!" she demanded in a piercing voice.

Not at all convinced that he was in the right place, Griffin provided his name dubiously.

"I am in the right..?"

"Did you bring your appointment letter?"

He handed it over and she thumped it on a stack of similar letters.

Apparently it was the right place, or else everyone else had made the same mistake.

"Just take a seat, Mr Griffin. You'll have to wait your turn."

And was already swishing away back down the hallway.

There were four other young men sitting about the waiting room, all of them presumably of precisely nineteen years of age. Griffin took a seat as far away from each of them as he could manage. There were no magazines on offer—someone should have advised him to bring a book.

His doubts arose in that he naively expected that his preliminary medical examination would be carried out in a hospital or at least a doctor's surgery, but these were the offices of the *Department of Labour and National Service,* a small premises hidden away in the midst of the Moorabbin shopping centre where under more normal circumstances the unemployed and otherwise deprived members of the community came to confess their inadequacies in return for meagre social security cheques. In a fairly affluent suburb like Moorabbin with its attending vast industrial estate, such a place was made as unobtrusive as possible with no indicatory signs except the Departmental motif discreetly painted in the middle of the plate glass window. Sheets of brown paper had been stuck over the window from the inside such that the casual passerby would satisfyingly see only their own reflection and never be required to look upon the appalling scenes of life amongst the down-and-outs that would otherwise have been on view. The passerby could proceed, their sense of security unblemished.

Now that he assured himself (more or less) that he was in the right place, Griffin cast an eye over his four supposed compatriots. Two were scruffy looking fellows in grubby shirts, grubbier jeans and filthy desert boots—one large and the other small—who with their long uncombed hair and unsavoury appearance looked for all the world like grown-up bodgies. The larger bodgie was reading a magazine that he had plainly brought with him—'Boxing Weekly'—while the smaller constantly fiddled nervously with his hands, looking all around and sitting on the edge of his seat. The third chap was dressed similarly but looked not so much like a bodgie but a victim of them—he was crumpled in his seat, his face pale and sweating and from time to time would fold his arms across his belly, leaning forward with a grimace and emitting a low groan. He might have been stricken with nerves (as Griffin certainly was) or maybe it was the very uncomfortable nature of the seats.

The fourth guy was, by contrast, a very neat-and-tidy fellow—tall, handsome, in a smart suit and somehow familiar. Griffin had to think for a few minutes before he realised he was looking at Tony Overton, the star centre-half-forward for the Moorabbin Football Team and moreover the son of the most important business and political figure in the community. The hand of fate falls upon rich and poor alike, Griffin smiled to himself. Tony Overton seemed utterly unanxious, occasionally looking at his watch in annoyance and then down the darkened hallway where, Griffin imagined, the doctor and nurse were busy getting their equipment set up.

Griffin had only just settled himself and completed these observations when the bell rang again and the door opened, and through it came a very familiar figure indeed—Lew Sigg, who once cut up Mr Demetre's strap. Lew had grown taller and had thick curly hair and he was dressed sensibly, as Griffin suppose he was himself, in slacks and a white pullover. He strode to the counter and thumped on it, even though the swishing of the nurse's approach was evident. Meanwhile, Lew leaned on the counter the way tough guys did in American movies and surveyed the scene before him.

"Hey, G'day Tony."

"Hi Siggie."

"You be gettin' a game next season, you reckon?"

"If I can keep your knee out of my balls, Siggie."

"Name!" the nurse said, with her pen poised.

Lew ignored her completely.

"Oh yeah, sorry about that. It was an accident, of course."

"Sure it was. How many weeks you got to go on your suspension?"

"Just the first two games..."

"Name!"

"Keep yer shirt on, luv."

"Name!"

"Sigg, Okay?"

"Sigg, O. No. I have a Sigg, L. No Sigg, O."

"'L' will do," Lew grinned, enjoying the joke.

The four young men already waiting were positioned such that Lew would have to sit next to one of them—plainly that wasn't likely to be Tony Overton. He ran his eyes over the rest and the narrowed when they fell upon Griffin.

"Know you too, don't I?"

He advanced and sat into the gap between Griffin and the small bodgie while Griffin mumblingly admitted who he was.

"Ah, yeah. Griffin. I remember. Usta have a lot of accidents."

"Yeah, that was me."

"What are you up to these days, Griffin?"

"Getting drafted, apparently."

"Ah, yes. Plucked from the barrel by the fickle hand of military fate."

"Unfortunately."

"Yeah. Bloody remarkable, isn't it. They pull you name out of the lottery and off you go to get your head shot off."

"They pull dates out, apparently," Griffin corrected.

"Names. Dates. No bloody different. It's a real cunt act."

"If you gotta go, you gotta go."

"No one should have to go, Griffin. Anyway, a piece of piss to get out of this."

"Is it?"

"Sure. I'll be getting a student exemption, myself."

"You still a student."

"Yeah. Gold and Silversmithing at RMIT."

"Oh, right... But if you're getting an exemption, how come you're here?"

"Ah, bit of a fuck up, that. I got chucked out of the course at just the wrong time."

"Now that's the Lew Sigg I remember."

"Yeah, nothing ever changes, does it? But it will be alright though."

"Will it?"

"Yeah. Me mum chatted up the professor and I got a letter. Just show it to the doctor and I'll be in the clear."

Griffin boggled. He was trying to imagine the sorts of mums that chatted up professors, amongst other mysteries. Lew went on:

"Hey, didn't you usta wear big thick glasses?"

"Yeah. But my eyes corrected. I don't need them anymore."

"You shoulda worn them tonight."

"Can't see a bloody thing through them these days..."

"Still shoulda worn them."

Griffin could not see entirely why.

He was still wondering about it when the nurse came swishing back up the hallway. She consulted her journal.

"Overton," she declared.

And swished off. Tony Overton followed, the clump of his alligator shoes punctuating her shuffle into the depths. Griffin was about to ask any of the thousand questions that were herding in his brain when immediately the alligator clump was evident again. Tony Overton reappeared, shooting a wise smirk at Lew before he went straight out the door. He had not even had time to take off his jacket—maybe the hand of fate did not fall quite as Griffin imagined.

"Has to be the shortest medical examination in history," Griffin said.

"With a rich and influential father like his," Lew quietly explained. "All he had to do was hand the doctor a fat envelope and it was all done."

"Really?"

"Sure..."

But the nurse was swishing down upon them again, and this time it was the larger bodgie, who stood, flexed his considerable muscles, slipped his folded magazine into his back pocket and sauntered away with the proud gait those sorts of fellows develop.

This time the examination took what seemed to be regulation time—about fifteen minutes. Throughout that time, Lew asked again about how Griffin earned his living and Griffin tried his best to explain.

"Insurance, hey?" Lew declared. "Then you ought to know someone with a bit of influence."

Griffin was sure he didn't.

Meanwhile, across the room, while the small bodgie continued to fidget, the crumpled fellow began to show no interest in proceedings at all, hunched up in the seat, shivering, sweating, moaning, his face contorting.

"He doesn't look very well," Griffin remarked—wondering if perhaps the doctor ought to be summoned and what the nurse might think of someone going out of turn.

"I reckon he's done something to himself," Lew remarked unconcernedly.

"Done something?"

"Yeah. Taken a dose of something to make himself ill so he'll fail the medical. You know."

"I guess," Griffin thought, faintly shocked. "He sure isn't faking it."

"What about you? Got any good ailments?"

"Not really."

"Then you really should have brought your glasses."

"You mean, you reckon I should try to convince the doctor there's something wrong with me when there isn't?"

"Is that such a bad idea?"

"I don't believe I'd ever be able to live with myself for such an act of cowardice, Lew."

Lew sighed. "No, Griffin, I don't suppose you would."

Soon, footfalls announced the return of the large bodgie, whose body language said it all. His muscles seemed to have sagged and he appeared to be about three inches shorter, and as he sadly traversed the waiting room, he paused, looking bleakly upon the faces there. Plainly his ego insisted that he make some explanation of himself, even if no one wanted to hear it.

"Flat feet," he declared, and flip-flopped out the door.

The small bodgie was summoned. He sprang to his feet and charged after the nurse as if fully intending to tear her limb from limb even though, given their relative sizes, the reverse outcome seemed more probable. Almost immediately, a vociferous discussion began down there. Griffin and Lew listened, and could easily make out the voices.

"Get away from me you bastards," the small bodgie was shouting. "I object on conscientious grounds. You aren't allowed to touch me!"

There was another calm, more patient voice that they could only assume belonged to the doctor:

"The war you can object to. This is a medical examination. You can't legally object to that."

"I'm a Buddhist. My religion says I can't kill anybody."

"Nobody's going to get killed here. It's just a medical..."

"Nor involved in anything that will lead to killing."

"Buddhism is not a recognised religion in this country, old boy."

"It's recognised all over the world. I have my rights!"

"If you belonged to some decent religion you might have rights. A Christian faith. Catholics. Then you have rights..."

"Christians! Catholics! Those are the bastards that started this bloody war in the first place. They started the Commie scare because Communism meant less money in the collection bowls. That's what this war is all about, man!"

"Whatever you think, old boy, either you submit to this examination or else I shall be obliged to call the authorities."

It was the sort for argument that might have gone on indefinitely and probably would have, had there suddenly not been a more dramatic turn of events. This concerned the crumpled fellow who, as if indeed struck down by the hand of some God or other, chose that moment to topple from his chair onto the floor. There he lay, quivering violently, his legs bent up and kicking outward so that his body began to rotate of the polished floor and his right hand beat a tattoo on the linoleum. White froth bubbled from his lips.

"Get the doctor, quick," Lew shouted, and dived across the room to the ailing man's aid.

Griffin, who might have preferred to ignore the whole thing, moved slowly at first, and gained speed in response to Lew's sense of urgency, rather than the situation. As he advanced down the hall, the argument continued ahead. "You just gotta look at the bible, man. *Thou shalt not kill,* but how about Moses and the Red Sea and Joshua and Jericho and David and Saul. All the big names, man! And bloody mass murderers, the lot of them!"

"Clara, call the police," the doctor was saying and Griffin opened the door.

The nurse and Griffin therefore collided in the doorway. Although she was soft all over, it was Griffin who bounced off. After a very embarrassing tangle, the nurse concluded that she was suffering a sexual assault and backed off, and Griffin got into the room.

"Sorry, old boy. You'll have to wait your turn," the doctor said with ludicrous calm.

"But there's this fellow out here..."

"He'll have to wait his turn too."

At this juncture, the small bodgie decided to take advantage of the interruption and make a run for it, but the nurse, her pride dented by the tangle with Griffin, decided to try her luck on the smaller subject and wrapped her arms around the flailing, shrieking lad. "Petty Bourgeois shits! Your supposed to save people's lives, not get them killed."

"Okay," the doctor quietly decided. "You hold him Clara. I'll call the police." and he brushed by Griffin. "Young man, perhaps you might give my nurse a hand."

"But doctor, there's this fellow. He's collapsed. He's dying maybe..."

However, since the doctor, in his search amongst the darkened offices for a telephone, was heading generally in the right direction, Griffin simply had to follow along. They groped about, bumping into desks in the darkness, and the doctor's hand did finally fall upon a telephone, and he began to dial.

"Dying, you say?"

"Come on, have a look for yourself."

He actually tugged at the man's sleeve.

"I see. Well, one thing at a time, old boy. Police? I have a emergency—violent assault, I should think..."

While the doctor gave the details, Griffin backed off and decided to close the door to the examination room, where shouting and crashing of things still emitted. He was sure the nurse would get the upper hand before long.

"Now, let's see to your friend."

Griffin followed along, and did not trouble to point out that the crumpled fellow, now flattened fellow, was no friend of his.

The medico brushed Lew aside and made a five second examination.

"Silly boy. He's poisoned himself."

Lew winked at Griffin and said nothing while the doctor spent a few more moments checking pulses and loosening collars and then he stood, looking at Griffin. "Call and ambulance and stay with him until he arrives," and then he turned to Lew. "And you come with me and help us subdue this maniac down here."

Griffin wondered if Lew would be of any more help than he had been.

Having located the telephone again and called the ambulance, Griffin could do not more than sit and watch the unfortunate who still shuddered on the floor and only occasionally convulsed. Down the way, the dispute continued unabated.

He felt heavily burdened with helplessness and was therefore fairly relieved when the door burst open and after what could only be described as a dramatic pause, two policemen entered. They moved forward and their eyes fixed upon the convulsive blubberer. Their eyes grew suspicious as they turned toward Griffin.

"What happened to him?"

"He's poisoned."

Being inexperienced at dealing with policemen, Griffin was yet to learn the necessity to be simplistically infantile with them. The large, older policeman, who was a sergeant, took out his notebook.

"Better tell us what you know about it, laddie."

"I don't know anything about it."

There is little a policeman likes less than someone who alleges to not know anything about something. Meanwhile the other policeman, a constable, was kneeling over the victim and shaking him.

"Hey, come on, mate, wake up."

"That won't do any good," Griffin told him.

If there is something a policeman likes even less than someone who alleges not to know anything about something, it is someone who alleges that they know what will or won't do any good. The constable decided to stand beside the sergeant, both looming over Griffin and it was becoming very claustrophobic. Griffin stood up.

"Sit down," they ordered, giving him a shove in the chest.

"Look, you've got the wrong bloke."

"Yeah, so you say."

"Not me wrong bloke, him wrong bloke," Griffin explained, pointing to the man on the floor.

"Looks like the right bloke to me," the sergeant said.

But by then the constable had become aware of the commotion elsewhere and drew the sergeant's attention to it. Up the hallway came a procession, the doctor marching proudly ahead of the nurse who had the small bodgie in a hammerlock and Lew wandering along behind with his hands in his pockets. To add to the confusion, the ambulance crew arrived.

The small bodgie was still shouting but pain was rendering his words unintelligible now, the nurse was grunting louder and louder as she tightened her grip and the doctor was preparing to apply his best bedside manner to the situation. Lew had ducked into the background, chuckling furiously, while Griffin was not too far removed from joining the chap on the floor. For all his education, the doctor had no easy time sorting it all out.

"I see," the sergeant said, consulting his notes. "So this fellow poisoned that one."

"No, sergeant. That's not it at all, old boy."

"Then give it to me again."

The doctor sighed and began doing his rounds again. "This man is to be arrested and charged with assault and property damage and refusing to undergo a medical examination in accordance with the National Service Act. And so is this man, only he must be taken to hospital first and treated for self-inflicted poisoning. But there is no connection between the two."

"And this bloke?" the sergeant asked, pointing to Griffin.

"He has no connection either."

"There has to be a connection," the sergeant knew.

"That's right, it's a conspiracy," the small bodgie shouted. "They're all in it together. You won't get away with this. I'll fight you to the end."

"You want a fight, mate, why doncha join the army," the constable smiled.

Eventually, they were gone. The ambulance carried away its grisly burden and the police their frenzied one and the doctor and nurse went down to restore order to their equipment. There was only Griffin and Lew.

"My, what an exciting place Moorabbin is becoming these days," Lew chuckled. Griffin didn't really see anything to chuckle about.

"Mr Griffin!" the nurse bawled and he went forward, armed only with a slap on the shoulder from Lew. The doctor eyed him sternly. "Well, old boy. I hope you aren't going to give me any trouble."

"What? Who. Me? trouble? No sir."

And so he coughed at the right moments, said 'ahhh' just loudly enough, urinated the right amount into the jar, assured the doctor he had a happy childhood and even read the blurry letters on the chart on the wall correctly. It all went so smoothly he completely forgot to mention his ruined knee nor how he had once had a breakdown. Non-smoker. Non-drinker. Not allergic to anything. He was passed fit. At least Ella would be pleased to hear about that.

On the way out, he gave Lew the *thumbs up* and Lew responded in kind, and it was only a long time later that Griffin realised that, under the circumstances, the same gesture had two absolutely contradictory meanings.

Ninety Percenters

Came the day that would dictate the terms to the rest of his life, and Wally drove him to the induction centre. They rose and had breakfast as if it was a normal day and then, because it was somehow 'men's business', he said 'see you later' to Ella, who was tearful, and Narelle, who was warm, and Michael was proud, and went. Almost entirely, his own emotions were confined to absolute terror about the unknowns that lay ahead. Wally seemed to sense this—as they drove he chatted mostly about the state of the car engine and how certain racehorses had run. But finally, if far too soon, they arrived at Richmond Army Barracks.

There, a large number of young men milled about, looking as lost as Griffin felt, and watching over them was a row of army sergeants, waiting with well trained restraint when plainly they could hardly wait to get amongst this lot. A row of buses waited to carry them off to Puckapunyal once the initial paperwork was completed. Wally and Griffin sat in the car for a few minutes, taking this in. Mostly, they regarded the row of sergeants, looking like an unarmed firing squad.

Then Wally said. "Listen. I got just one piece of advice for yer. All army officers and NCOs are fifty percent less important than they think they are and ninety percent less important than they tell you they are. They're just big kids and you gotta humour them. That's the real trick to survival here. The army is ten percent serious and ninety percent bullshit. What you gotta do is take the ten percent seriously and pretend to take the ninety percent seriously as well. But make fucking sure you can tell the difference. Ninety percent bullshit—remember that and they won't bother you much."

Wally reached out and, for the first time in Griffin's life, they shook hands. And then he was out of the car and into the army. They had to queue past desks, sign forms, make declarations and of course there was another medical examination and finally they were loaded into buses, the last few moments of their civilian lives draining away as they went. Griffin saw Wally still sitting in the car, waiting until the bus went out of sight.

On that bewildering first day, they rode in the buses from the induction centre in the city for fifty miles up the Hume Highway and then turned off to a place called Puckapunyal—

aboriginal, they said, for *Valley of the Winds*—it was that all right. The wind tore straight through them when they tumbled off the buses in the middle of the parade ground, awkward and vulnerable in their civilian clothes and carrying bags of things their mothers were sure they would need—changes of underwear, aftershave, pyjamas and slippers, extra food—all of which they would get a good laugh out of later on. There had been a set of instructions that said plainly how none of those things would be required and every mother ignored the instructions, because they secretly knew they were losing their sons to a rival forever and couldn't help but put up a final fight. But the army, the most gargantuan of all mothers, would soon brush such personal sentiments aside.

They stood on the parade ground in a hopeless gaggle, exposed to the relentless wind, unsure what to do and then there was a sergeant who strode into their midst, and was the very manifestation of all our worst fears about army sergeants. And that sergeant was Tiger Braddock.

"I know all about you fucking conscripts. You blokes reckon you're pretty fucking unlucky to be drawn out of the barrel, don't you? Well you are, too. Dead fucking unlucky. But your luck's gonna change from now on. It's gonna get fucking worse!"

Sergeant Braddock, pacing tigerishly back and forth as he bellowed at them, his roaring vulgarity assailing their senses with skin-crawling intimidation, and he seemed twice as big as he really was that day. From the sunken hollows either side of his flat broken nose, his eyes glared ruthlessly from under the brim of his slouch hat, his words spat out over jagged teeth that formed his face into a perpetual snake-like grin. Tiger Braddock, starch-greened, spit-polished, razor-sharp, ramrod stiff, the terror of their lives.

"There's just two ways to learn things around here—the hard way, and the very fucking hard way! I don't give a fuck which way you learn, but you will learn. I am gonna make good fucking soldiers out of you lot of civvy slime if it fucking kills the fucking lot of yer!"

From then on, Tiger Braddock was always about somewhere, striding about as if he had forgotten how normal people walk, bellowing and roaring all the time and often doing so just a half-inch from your ear in a voice that rattled windowpanes a hundred yards away. By this means they were marched through Q store and injections and further medicals and documentation and finally into the barrack rooms that would be their home for the next ten weeks.

It was all Tiger Braddock. Other officers and instructors tried to emulate him but compared to Braddock their efforts at perpetual rage and ceaseless intimidation were puny. Griffin was no less terrified of Braddock than was everyone else, but years of coping with the bodgies of Moorabbin Tech had taught him a thing or two. The best plan was to ignore him completely, to quietly go along with whatever he ordered, never respond and never cower. For Griffin knew exactly what to make of him—he was ninety percent bullshit.

But if he knew how to cope with the tyranny of Tiger Braddock, that was about the extent of Griffin's skills. Even he was rather shocked to discover how completely unsuited to the army he was. His physical awkwardness alone meant that he was in attendance at every punishment detail, and his booming voice, when he dared use it, was invariably used at the wrong time and place. He injured himself nearly every day as the drill instructors strove to make him fit and strong. He could not march straight, nor snap to attention at exactly the same time as others, and when the finally gave him a rifle, couldn't hit any target. It was hopeless. Even his appearance was wrong:

"Am I hurting you, sonny?"

"No sir."

"Well, I ought to be. I'm standing on your hair. GET IT CUT!"

He went back to the barber three times in three days and still the reaction was the same—finally he got his head completely shaved.

"Think you're smart, do you Recruit Griffin."

Whatever answer he made, he knew it would be wrong. If he thought he was smart, he would have his smart-arseness knocked out of him; if he thought he wasn't, he would be punished to wise up. It was a thing, typical of all military, that would come to be called *Catch 22*. Griffin stood rigid and made absolutely no response.

"Well, answer me, laddie!"

Still he did not respond.

"You are bloody hopeless, Griffin. Got it! HOPELESS!"

Griffin stood rigid. And that was the end of the matter. He was getting the hang of this.

Worst were their attempts to get him to salute with the right hand. No amount of training nor punishment could teach him to tell his right hand from his left. Or perhaps it did, for as Tiger

Braddock observed, he did get it wrong *every* time. The trouble was, he was always trying to get it right and always double-guessed himself wrong.

"You've saluted me with the wrong hand, soldier. Do it again!"

He snapped a salute again with the opposite hand to the one he thought was the wrong one so it had to be the right one, didn't it.

"You've done it again, you idiot! Come on, GET IT RIGHT!"

So if that one was wrong this one must be right but since he was always wrong then it had to be the other one.

"No, not that hand, moron. God Almighty, what the hell is the matter with you, soldier?"

When he might have wanted to claim a paralysed arm, instead he made absolutely no response.

"Get out of here!"

Yes, no doubt about it. It was working.

Well, almost. The result was that Griffin ended up on the barrack parade ground, receiving special saluting practice from Tiger Braddock. Tiger began by tying the other arm behind his back. This seemed to narrow the options sufficiently.

"Listen, you deadhead. The clue to getting it right is the slouch hat. You see it is turned up at one side. That should guide you to the correct hand to salute with."

Since the hat was on his head and therefore the turned-up section of brim outside his range of vision, Griffin could not understand how it would help in any way. But he didn't say so. He didn't respond at all.

"Now you will stand here all day and all night and you will salute everything that goes by, officers and civilians, all ranks, all recruits, any passing dogs or cats, birds flying by, planes going over, flies, bees and clouds. If it rains, you salute every fucking raindrop, got it."

Griffin did not respond, which Tiger Braddock understood to mean he had got it.

"By the time your arm drops off, you'll always remember which one to use."

Griffin resisted responding to the logical contradiction.

So he stood and saluted everything and everyone and did so with the correct hand because the other was tied behind his back. Shortly after dinnertime, having stood at attention saluting everything for ten hours, he fainted. The loss of circulation to his secured arm almost caused it to become paralysed. At the base hospital, a minor operation was required and they kept him in overnight for observation. What was being observed was the blue colour fading away and his temperature slowly dropping. At the dawn parade next morning, they let him go.

"Me arm nearly dropped off, they reckoned," Griffin declared, overwhelmed by the need to exaggerate a little.

"Well, that woulda solved the saluting problem," Mick Delaney declared.

"No," Griffin said. "It was the wrong arm..."

Mick Delaney was the gang leader amongst the recruits—the fittest, smartest, cheekiest and with his good-looks and quick wit, the most popular. He was the extreme opposite of Griffin—a recruit who was good at all aspects of military training. And he was the one who organised the protest at the mistreatment of Griffin. Next morning, the company paraded as always before the Major who gave the orders for the day which were usually more running and jumping and climbing and shooting, and at which punishment details were organised. Griffin, only just released from the hospital, was ordered to stand before the men.

"Now," the major declared. "Recruit Griffin is going to show us all how to salute. Salute now, Recruit Griffin."

Since Griffin's other arm was still in a sling, there seemed to be a reasonable chance of him getting it right. He saluted. The assembled company saluted back. Every one of them, as Mick Delaney had organised, with the wrong hand.

The officers responded, only it seemed to them, for a moment of credible doubt, that it was themselves who were saluting with the wrong hand. It took Tiger Braddock and the other instructors a moment to figure it out, until they realised that the entire company had their slouch hats on the wrong way around.

"Okay," Braddock bellowed, while the officers still looked at their hands in bafflement. "Get those hats on right, you smart bastards. And now, the whole company will run up Tit Hill. Get moving. NOW!"

The company jogged off. To run up the steep side of Tit Hill (which with its perfect curve and cairn erected on top was named obviously) was the cruellest of punishments available. The parade ground cleared, but Griffin still stood there.

"You too, Griffin!" Braddock screamed in utter fury.

Griffin said nothing, but he did reach into his pocket as produce his chit for light duties. Braddock, every blood vessel in his face about to explode, grabbed the chit and threw it on the ground and stamped on it. Other men had to restrain him.

"I think this better be the end of this matter, Sergeant Braddock," the Major said and the officers removed themselves from the parade ground.

Tiger Braddock gazed into the relentlessly unseeing eyes of Griffin.

"Griffin, you make me weep."

To this, Griffin did finally respond. He grinned.

At Puckapunyal for the ten weeks of their recruit training, they were virtual prisoners; there was no leave, weekends had no meaning and their spare time each night was fully taken up with preparation of their gear for the next day, and to accommodate the frequent spontaneous inspections. Everything at 2RTB (2nd Recruit Training Battalion) was subject to inspections—bodies, uniforms, equipment and bedspaces all had to be maintained in immaculate condition at all times, a point which was carried to absurdity. Not a crease in a bed, not a speck of dust on anything, brasswork on uniforms mirror-shined, boots, gaiter and belts split-polished, clothing hanging in lockers had to be buttoned and with collars facing the same direction and sleeves hanging perfectly aligned and of course all arranged in a particular order. Punishment was instant and merciless—a hundred press-ups on the floor for minor failings, charges laid in more serious instances resulting in all-night sentry stints or mess duties and a run up Tit Hill was the result of any attempt at protest or explanation. If a fly flew in the room during an inspection, the man whose belongings or person it landed on was doomed to punishment, and any attempt to wave it away despatched the miscreant to the crest of Tit Hill. Inspections could occur at any time—and it was not considered unfair when gear used in training that day was inspected and found unsatisfactory before there had been any opportunity to clean it. So they would sit in their bedspaces, polishing and spitting and buffing away, and the gravest dangers of all lay with those unfortunate souls who smoked or chewed gum—for rubbish bins also had to be found spotless and empty.

Such a night then and they, the members of 17th Platoon, sat about at going through their chores mechanically, cracking feeble jokes, carrying on the banter normal for people who spent too much time in close proximity to each other. Suddenly the door flew open and there stood the looming, malevolent figure of Tiger Braddock. The first man to see him roared "AttenSHUN" and the rest jumped out of their chairs and stood rigidly by their bunks, bracing themselves for yet another inspection, no man daring to glance about and see what minor items of equipment might be slightly out of place. Tiger Braddock stood in the doorway, wearing his Jolly Roger grin, allowing the dread to destroy their minds.

He closed the door behind him and began to move forward slowly, and moved in on Griffin who was the first man inside the room. He stood, glaring into Griffin's glazed eyes, in an attempt to draw the flicker of a reaction. Griffin immediately caught the strong whiff of alcohol. Braddock said nothing, moving on to the next man, and so he proceeded all the way to the end of the hut without saying a word, looking each man in the eye, daring them even to breathe. These were his moments of supreme power. As he went by, Griffin allowed his eyes to follow and saw the horrific sight that was the back of his neck, the redness streaked with the white corrugations of undulating scars that, Griffin had heard, went all the way down his back. The plastic surgeons had done their best, but just to catch a glimpse of the mangled scarring was enough to cause Griffin almost to feel the pain of the hideous wounds that caused them. Tiger Braddock was a decorated hero of the Malayan Emergency, terribly wounded by a mortar shell as he saved other men's lives.

Now he stood in the very middle of the hut while twenty raw recruits sweated with fear.

"Right, every man, get out all the money that you possess and put it on your bunks—do it now!"

It might have sounded absurd but that was what recruit training was all about. None of them questioned it—already it was ingrained to do exactly what they were told without the slightest protest. There was nothing worse than a run up Tit Hill on a cold night like this. Griffin quickly placed his personal wealth in a very neat pile and sprang like a rubber band back to his rigid position.

Tiger Braddock retraced his steps the length of the hut, pausing at each bunk to explore the meagre piles of funds with a disdainful finger. Griffin wondered what was in store—perhaps a run up Tit Hill for the richest or poorest, or maybe an hour's drill on the parade ground for anyone whose banknotes were not folded precisely down the middle. The last currency collection to be examined was Griffin's.

"Shit, Griffin. Where'd you get all that?"

"My mother sends it to me."

"Why?"

"She refuses to believe I have nothing to spend it on."

"Well, let's see what we can do to improve her lot. She must need all the help she can get after giving birth to a hunk of slag like you."

Braddock turned and moved out to the centre of the hut:

"Okay, Spargo, Griffin, Magee, Delaney and Weedman, grab your money and come here. The rest of you, at ease, go about your business. Spargo, bring that table here. Weedman, gimme that blanket, pull up chairs. Do it now!"

They sat around the table, and Braddock grabbed a chair and joined them, adopting a sly grin and pulling a deck of cards from his pocket:

"Okay, gentlemen. I am in a state of financial embarrassment and you have all volunteered to help me out. The name of the game is poker."

"I don't know how to play poker, sir."

"You will play poker, Griffin, and that's a fucking order. Hollis, come and stand behind him and show him how."

"I could play the hands for him, sarge."

"Yes, I don't mind. I don't really like card games."

"It's your money, Griffin, and you will lose it yourself."

"Yes, sergeant."

In fact, Griffin was surprised to find how simple a game it was. He won the first two hands and Hollis was dismissed from his post.

"Now we'll see how you go."

"Is four queens any good?"

Griffin saw that winning was simple. You always pretended that you had a lousy hand, and never bet the same way twice. The trick was to always get it wrong and so play irrationally. For Griffin, nothing could have been easier. Braddock, in turn, was a hopeless poker player and they fleeced him, but that didn't seem to matter—well, not much.

"If you don't stop winning, Griffin, you'll be running up Tit Hill for the rest of the night."

Griffin discreetly played a few hands in accordance with his cards, and lost, but it made little difference to his overall winnings.

But the most surprising thing of all was that while they played, Braddock, sitting wearing his crocodile smile, sucking on beer cans that he provided for the participants, began to tell them stories as amazing as he was himself:

"We were in Penang, see, and there was this bloke called Fiery Finn. Called him that because he did this fucking trick where he would light a fag and then take a mouthful of petrol from his hipflask and breathe out and this long tongue of flame would erupt from his mouth. Fire-breathin' Finn, like a fucking dragon. Usta scare the shitbags outa the noggies. Anyhow, there was this nig-nog owned a bar and got fed up with Fiery singein' his walls and blisterin' his bar and scarin' away the customers so he gets a couple of his noggie mates to hide behind the curtain with a fuckin' firehose and sure enough, Fiery Finn turns up and lights a fag and takes a sip from his flask and he's just about to let go a ten foot flame when wham they hit him right in the belly with the jet of water and he swallows instead of blowin' and he gets the fires of hell roarin' through his lungs..."

And by this time he would be roaring with helpless laughter.

"Jesus, what a way to die," Delaney said in horror.

"Die? Old Fiery Finn? Don't be fuckin' silly. But he did stop doin' that trick after that—reckoned now that everyone was wise there wasn't any fun left in it. And he gave up smokin' too. Reckoned he just couldn't get the same satisfaction from a cigarette anymore."

Tiger Braddock, the terror of 2RTB, would be out there next morning in the fog shrouded predawn darkness, bellowing at them to get out of their fart-sacks and into another gruelling day of pain and childish discipline but now they knew the answer—it was all bullshit. For next night he would return again to draw from his bottomless supply of tall stories of extraordinary characters and money to lose. As far as Griffin could tell, he never told the same story twice, nor did he ever tell the one about his own heroism and how he received his medal and his wounds. Tiger Braddock, fierce disciplinarian, ninety percenter, and as he played Griffin looked at the scars on the back of his neck and knew that was the ten percent that wasn't bullshit.

"Private Hollis, do you want to go to Vietnam?"

"Yes sir."

"Really?"

"I have a wife and child to support. All those extra allowances will come in handy. We're saving for a house, you see."

"Not exactly. But aren't you a conscript?"

"Yes sir. The only married conscript in the entire army."

"You seem to have lost out both ways, Private."

"Are you going to let me sign the bloody thing or what?"

Hollis had come to the army from a clerical job in Benalla and was indeed the only conscript to be married, since it was law that only single men could be drafted. With an outstanding display of bad timing, he had been married just ten days after he was drafted. Every night, Ten Days jumped in his car and drove a hundred and fifty miles across the border into New South Wales and the town of Wakool to visit the wife for an hour or two and drove back again in time for parade at six in the morning. No one knew when he slept. To try and obviate his continual exhaustion, Ten Days went AWOL in Sydney with Mick Delaney but immediately headed for Wakool like a homing pigeon. They collected him a few days later and after he got out of Holdsworthy, sent him off on a medical course and, unfortunately, when he had completed that, returned him to the battalion. The idea was that when anyone hurt themselves, they would always know where to find the medic—in his bunk asleep. If he wasn't in Wakool...

Nigel's Honour

Toward ten o'clock—which Griffin refused to learn was really 2200 hours—on a bleak icy night in August 1966, two carloads of soldiers came cruising quietly along the highway and into the town of Seymour. A fierce wind lashed through the night, fresh from the snowy mountaintops beyond the Goulburn River Valley and the light rain, the aftermath of torrential downpours throughout the day, cast almost horizontal slits of brilliance through the headlight beams. It was a grim reminder that the all but expended might of a cruel winter was far from willing to succumb to the warmer days to come. The two cars eased their way along, past the long row of heavy-laden semi-trailers parked along the side of the road, those huge juggernauts awaiting the dawn when they would plunge onward in their great journeys to places hundreds of miles to the north. The highway did not pass through Seymour itself but only the edge of it and at this point the town possessed a second centre—the traveller's centre. Here the road was brilliantly lit and lined with cafes, garages and pubs. It was to the second of these pubs that the cars were headed.

The first car was an immaculately polished FJ Holden in an extraordinary shade of green, which belonged with loving pride to diminutive Alfie Magee; the second was a pile of junk which, they were assured, had once been a Ford, and it was no less proudly owned by Ernie the Weed. Griffin, with all due respect for his continued existence, rode with Alfie in gentle comfort although it was not without its risks for Alfie Magee had as little control of his car as he did all other aspects of his life. But if Alfie drove timidly and constantly dodged invisible obstacles and never seemed to be going directly down the road, still it was to be preferred to riding with Ernie Weedman, which was always an adventure, usually nightmare-ish, for Ernie was never sober and his car impossible for a sober person to drive anyway.

There were five soldiers in Alfie's car and four in The Weed's. Griffin had carefully placed himself in the backseat where Snowy Spargo's bulk cut out most of the forward view; he gripped the seat covers with white-knuckled determination and was thankful for many things not seen.

When they had reached Seymour, Bugsy Norris, who was driving Ernie Weedman's car, cut the pace to a slow crawl, oozing along, and they were all on the lookout, or supposedly so. Ernie the Weed wasn't driving because he was lolling on Griffin's right shoulder, having drunk himself to oblivion earlier that evening as he did by this time any other evening—from time to time he snored.

To his left Ten Days Hollis was tense and silent, gazing nervously out the rain-splattered window of the car, flexing his fists anxiously as they approached the town.

"I wish we weren't doing this," he said edgily. Griffin could only agree.

"Gotta be done," Snowy Spargo grunted from the front seat. "It's a matter of military honour. We're a fighting unit now."

"I still wish we weren't doing it," Ten Days insisted.

The two cars approached the second pub and Griffin saw what he was hoping to not see, even before Snowy spoke.

"There they are."

Yes, there they certainly were.

"How can we be sure they're the right ones?" Alfie Magee wanted to know. But they were seeing what they expected to see, exactly where they expected to see it. Up ahead, Bugsy made a slow U turn and Alfie followed and they drew to a halt. Good position in case they needed a fast getaway, Griffin thought but didn't bother to say.

Snowy Spargo sprang out of the car with bounding enthusiasm while the rest followed along with varying degrees of reluctance. From the other car, Bugsy Norris, Mick Delaney, Mumbles Dorset and Greyman Goolie emerged similarly. Ernie Weed was almost comatose and needed to be supported—Griffin had one armpit and Hollis the other.

"We shouldn't have brought him," Mick Delaney declared with a scowl.

No one answered. They had been through it earlier when they had to go to the toilet block to drag Weed out. They were a unit and it was a unit matter. They all had to go and all together. It had been argued that Magee, Hollis and Dorset were hardly suited to such a task and Griffin would have liked to put himself in that category, but it was a matter of honour. They were a unit of fighting men and they would fight as a unit. It was as simple as that.

And so they stood in a line at the edge of the road that rainswept night, facing the Prince of Wales Hotel on the far side. They were Ned Kelly and his gang awaiting the arrival of the trainload of troopers at Glenrowan; they were the Earps heading down to meet the Clantons at the OK Corrall; they were Leondias and his three hundred Spartans gazing coldly on the advance of Xerxes vast slave army toward the pass of Thermopylae. The enemy, in this case, was just across the road, or at least tangible evidence of them. Eight motorcycles stood at the kerb in a row, parked outside the POW pub. The members of 4 Section, 11th Platoon, Training Company, 7th Battalion, Royal Australian Regiment stood facing those motor bikes and no one bothered to suggest that it might be a good idea to get over there and out of the rain.

Greyman Goolie was an aborigine and he had done a bit of boxing in his time. Now he pranced about, throwing short jabbing punches, sparring with the raindrops.

"We gonna take 'em, are we Bugsy? We gunna take 'em."

"Yeah, sure, Greyman," Bugsy said wearily—for him this might have been one fight too many in his life. "We'll take 'em. Don't you worry."

He didn't sound too sure.

Mick Delaney was their nominal leader and he stood tall and focused on the target. The rest of them tended to cringe somewhat, especially when cars went by throwing up huge swirls of spray.

"I'll go check 'em out," Delaney said and when there was a gap in the traffic, jogged lightly across the road.

"All this fighting is stupid," Alfie Magee declared adamantly. Again no one answered. They were all busy watching Delaney as he moved about over there, peeping in windows of the pub to see what he could see.

"Silly bloody Nigel," Ten Days declared.

It was all the fault of Nigel, as they called him, who had been their section leader for just two days. Corporal Robert Naughton was his real name, a veteran of the British army in Ireland, Malaya and Cyprus, with a big moustache twisted to spikes at the end to prove it, who had alienated himself completely with his Pommie accent and abrasive humour, but that didn't matter. Earlier that evening, Nigel—the name had been immediately coined by Snowy Spargo and was regarded as in all senses derisive of all matters British—had been in this pub and, for reasons unknown, fell foul of the gang of bikies therein. The result was that Nigel now lay recovering in the Puckapunyal Base Hospital, and it had taken less than an hour for word of the matter to travel to the 4 section barrack room.

"But we don't even like the Pommie bastard," Greyman

Goolie protested.

"Doesn't matter," Mick Delaney insisted. "We're a unit and he is our leader. We gotta stick together and back each other up. If we don't do that, we ain't gonna last ten minutes in Vietnam."

It was disputed for some time, but really there was never any doubt. It didn't matter how they felt about Nigel—what mattered was that he was one of them, and his misfortune had to be avenged. So they stood there in the rain, and prepared themselves for what would be in a strange sense their baptism of fire.

Delaney came plodding back across the highway and stood before his soggy and bedraggled troops.

"They're in there, alright. Mean looking bastards, too—right in the middle of the bar. Couple of them are playing pool. The others watching. Otherwise, there's a few truckies and a couple of locals and the barman. None of them seem friendly with the bikies so I reckon they'll with us."

Griffin regarded Delaney doubtfully—fights in Seymour pubs between soldiers and all comers were legendary—once they got in there, he was sure no one would be liking anyone much.

"Okay," Delaney went on. "Here's the plan. Me, Snowy, Bugsy and Goolie go right in the front door and straight up to them. Griffin, you take Magee, Ten Days, Dorset and Weed in through the saloon door on the side. There's a door that connects to the main bar so you'll come up behind them. No pissing around—we tell them why we're there and then we hop into them."

He glanced around the faces for approval of the plan. It was the old catch-em-in-the-crossfire trick they'd learned a week ago. Sounded good.

"Let's go," Delaney said.

Divided then into their two detachments, they crossed the wet glistening highway and headed for their respective entrances. Griffin led his bunch—his first moment of leadership of anything—around to the side where he presumed he would find the saloon door. Gladly, it was there. He looked back. He had already outdistanced his troops. Ten Days and Mumbles had Ernie Weed between them with his lifeless arms across their shoulders, and further back, Alfie Magee had slipped over in the mud and groped in search of his glasses. All in all, his first command was not entirely an impressive one. He went back and was still in time to see Delaney leading his troops—*the main assault group*—as they passed by the row of motorcycles which, from this angle, showed themselves aligned in a perfect regimental rank. Tiger Braddock would have been delighted at such an orderly bunch of big, black, oily, powerful monsters—the bikes themselves looked fearfully—Griffin strove to avoid imagining the owners.

Griffin's mob—*the cut-off group*—went in through the saloon door and were at least out of the rain. Griffin saw the connecting door and headed toward it and arrived just as the main assault group closed on the target. There were eight bikies, as expected, all of whom had plainly never recovered from the image of Marlon Branflakes. There were two basic sizes—big fat ones with missing teeth, broken noses and vast muscles under their sleeveless leather jackets which exhibited all manner of badges, studs and burst stitching; and thin, evil-looking ones with severe acne, missing teeth, broken noses and tough wiry muscles under their sleeved and optimistically oversized jackets. Every one of them had the skull and crossbones tattooed on him somewhere, along with every other imaginable emblem on every square inch of exposed skin.

The locals and truckies, summing up the situation, immediately reached a universal desire to head for the dunny, taking their beer glasses with them. The barman jumped up as if he had been shot and darted from behind the bar and out the door into the street. Meanwhile, Delaney engaged the largest of the bikies in conversation.

"There was a soldier in here before. A corporal with a Pommie accent. You done him over."

The leader of the gang glanced over the enemy force and decided he was well pleased with the situation. He hadn't yet seen the cut-off group but Griffin doubted that would have mattered.

"What's it to yer," the leader grunted.

Delaney punched him straight in the face, removing the remnants of his teeth and sending him pitching backwards to the floor and there he stayed.

Snowy Spargo and Bugsy Norris shaped up in proper pugilistic stances and each took on one of the larger opponents. Snowy and his man pranced all about the room, throwing punches that all seemed to miss, while Norris and his man slugged it out with successive body blows. Two more of them ran at Delaney, one wrapping about him from the front and the other jumping on his back and so they lurched about the bar, until Delaney finally fell and they rolled together on the floor.

Greyman Goolie looked like he knew what he was doing, handing out a left-right-left that despatched one smaller bikie to dreamland but immediately another came up behind him and belted him over the head with a lead pipe. The Greyman, Griffin always thought, was generally a bit silly in the head and he was a lot sillier from that moment on. He staggered all around the room, throwing punches at no one in particular, finally slumped against the bar with his fists still going and at last slipped to the floor, hurling punches madly at the ceiling.

All this happened in the seconds before the rest of the cut-off group finally caught up with their leader, colliding with his backside and sending him bravely forward into the fray. In fact they had only two of the smaller bikies left to deal with between them. The blinded Alfie Magee ran straight into one of them immediately, and the bikie grabbed a bottle, necked it on the bar and sliced the jagged end through the air at Magee. Magee had already fallen and the projectile went on toward Mumbles who let go of his half of Ernie Weed, lost his footing and they went down in a heap, but spared having their heads cut off. Magee jumped up and fled to the toilet where he had to battle truckies to get in and the door before they all finally locked themselves away in the cubicles.

Griffin saw he had his own problems now as the guy with the lead pipe lined him up and charged. But gladly, the charge came to an abrupt halt when leadpipe tripped over the sprawling Ernie Weedman and crashed heavily to the floor, winding himself. Griffin knew that the right thing to do now—if Wally's brief instructions and stories of such matters served—was to run in and start kicking the guy to death before he recovered and got up. Gladly, Ten Days arrived to fill that role. Further over, Mumbles had head-butted the bottle-thrower and they had jointly vanished under the pool table. Griffin stood helplessly—there was no one left for him to fight. Just when he was getting the hang of it.

At the same time, something quite singular was happening. Ernie Weedman, contrary to a basic human condition that hitting the floor and loss of consciousness are inherently connected, did the opposite. Being already unconscious when he hit the floor, he immediately regained his senses and sprang to his feet, looking every whichway in bewilderment. All about him, he saw only madness. Worse, he discovered that his hipflask, the joy of his existence, had been ruptured and flattened in the fall, its sacred contents spilling out over his buttocks and down his thighs. Ernie, confused beyond imagining, flew into a complete rage and went screaming off, running blindly amok, out the door and into the night, crying out to the world for revenge.

Griffin, watching all this, knew he ought to be doing a little more than he was. The opportunity arose when Delaney, with his red-faced appendages still attached front and back, came to his attention.

"Get these bastards off me, will you, Griffin?" Delaney screeched.

Griffin had that very thing in mind, if he knew how. Ten Days, having kicked one bikie half to death, rushed in to show him how. Unable to bring himself to such actions, Griffin contented to seize the other by the hair and pull with all his might. Thus Delaney was freed, and jumped to his feet, fighting mad. The flow of the conflict had turned the soldier's way decisively.

On the pool table, Snowy wrestled one guy, each trying to shove balls down the other's throat. Mumbles was stuck under the table with another. Norris and his opponent were entangled behind the bar. Appearance suggested Norris was losing out and Delaney decided to go that way first, and thus made a grave error. On the way he passed the coolroom which the publican, in his hasty departure, had left open. At that moment, the fellow that Griffin had previously been holding by the hair broke free, swung at Griffin and missed, but then charged Delaney and into the coolroom they went. In the chilly interior, Delaney's boots could find no traction on the icy floor and he went down, whereby the bikie darted out, closed the door and shot the bolt. Two of his friends joined him guarding the door. Bikies, plainly, are not as dumb as some people think.

With the loss of Delaney and the otherwise depletion of the military numbers, the issue was quickly resolved. The three loose bikies descended first upon Snowy Spargo and hauled him off their colleague, off the table, and threw him through the doorway. Spargo, fighting mad, would have returned but out there two burly policemen—summoned by the deserting barman—waited to take him in hand. Spargo was locked up in the divisional van before he knew what was happening. The policemen awaited the next outcome—they had called for reinforcements and had no intention of entering the bar before they arrived. But then, they didn't need to—the bikies, the balance of numbers now constantly running their way, next grabbed Ten Days and hurled him out, whereby he followed

Spargo into the back of the van.

Griffin reviewed his situation carefully. He awaited the return of his exited friends in vain. Three soldiers—Norris, Goolie and Mumbles, lay dazed on the floor in various parts of the bar. Weedman, Magee, Spargo and Ten Days had vanished. And five bikies remained on their feet and between Griffin and the coolroom door where Delaney could be heard thumping inside. He was alone and trapped. He would be murdered, slashed with knives, sliced with glass, choked with chains and generally kicked to death. There seemed no alternative. The only thing to do was resort to reasoning.

"Umm... now... look, fellas... Let's talk this over, shall we? I'm sure it just a little misunderstanding... That Pommie corporal—we don't like him anyway..."

The five bikies continued their advance.

Then suddenly he was saved. The two policemen came through the shattered doorway and stood there smiling.

"Hey, you blokes," one of them called. The bikies stopped their advance on Griffin and turned, buoyed by their apparent victory and quite happy to accommodate a couple of policemen as well. But the policeman went on:

"There's a bloke out here who says that if you blokes don't give in, he's going to set fire to your bikes."

The bikies gasped their horror and ran to the windows to peer out on a scene that might have been their worst nightmare. It was Ernie the Weed, bent on revenge for his crushed hipflask, who had turned one of the motorcycles on its side and opened the petrol cap such that the gushing fuel made a great puddle under the remaining seven bikes. Beside it, The Weed stood swaying precariously and smoking a cigarette.

"You've gotta stop him!" the bikies shrieked. "Don't let him do it."

"Now," the policeman said with a grin. "You blokes better call this off or this fella will blow your bikes to smithereens. He's pissed enough to do it too."

The policeman was braver now, because he could hear the sirens approaching on the highway.

The bikies were taken to the local lock-up and run out of town next morning, or so they said. Ambulances arrived and did some general patching up on the soldiers, on everyone except Griffin—unless you counted Alfie Magee who made his own escape back to the barracks later. To avoid the possibility of their gaolhouse being utterly wrecked, the police loaded the soldiers into their vehicles and were good enough to convey them back to the guardhouse at Puckapunyal.

There, an hour later, Tiger Braddock found them.

"You idiots. You absolute fuckin' useless lot of dickhead morons!" Braddock raged. "The bloody lot of you will be charged and get the full fuckin' treatment for this."

"Arr come on, sarge," Delaney, still shivering in a blanket, protested. "The bloody bikies started it."

To which Braddock thundered. "You ain't bein' charged for AWOL and you ain't bein' charged for fighting. And you ain't bein' charged for makin' a public nuisance or property damage. You blokes are trained to fight a fuckin' war and you let the civvies kick shit outa yer. I'm chargin' you because you fuckin' got done. Got it! Because you got fuckin' done!"

"Private Weedman. Do you want to go to Vietnam?"
"They tell me beer is ten cents a can in Australian bases, sir."
"I understand that is the present price."
"Where do I sign?"

Boys' Games

There can be little dispute that the best method of studying the wonders of nature is at point-blank range. You go to some bushland setting, make a camp, build a fire and with childlike curiosity, poke your nose as close as you dare to the subject creatures that happen by. So Griffin was thinking, although not on his own behalf.

For there was no mistaking that in this particular instance, he was the subject creature and the one doing all the exploring and studying was giving him the eye from an decidedly unhealthy distance of three feet. Griffin stared. The monster stared right back and then hissed as it's long black tongue slide forth from its cruel mouth and then retracted again. There was absolutely no doubt about who belonged in this wild bush setting and who did not.

"Ummm. Hullo there," Griffin said sheepishly.

The monster replied with another more forceful hiss that unquestionably demanded 'back off'.

Now this was a moment of crisis. Griffin's mug of coffee had just come nicely to the boil and it was sweetened with the last of his condensed milk. It wasn't something to be given up easily but his little hexamine stove was positioned exactly half way between himself and the invader. He reached for the handle of the mug and immediately the monster advanced a pace and opened its hideous jaws. There was no evidence of teeth, but those lips looked rock hard and to boot, its feet exhibited sizeable claws. Griffin backed off, sliding along on his bum until his back ran up against a tree. The monster nodded its satisfaction and advanced to the stove.

Griffin's knowledge of reptiles was barely up to the occasion. Of course, he knew all about dinosaurs as any self-respecting lad did and whereas this creature undoubtedly bore all the appropriate silurian characteristics, he knew it couldn't be because the dinosaurs were all extinct. At first glance, crocodile came to mind but they were way up in North Queensland and he was sure that crocs only inhabited river regions. But, in any case, it was a giant lizard of some kind, and an utterly fearless one. At least five feet from head to tail and able to stretch its head to knee height. It looked vastly old, indeed Jurassic, and those glassy eyes had not the slightest difficulty staring him down. Griffin would have run for his life had he not suspected that it could probably propel itself faster on its four legs than he could on two.

"Hey!" he called frantically. "Hey, everybody. Come here quick."

The beast seemed satisfied at this display of terror and so dismissed Griffin and turned its attention to its true purpose. Griffin was able to realise that the beast was not intending to devour him at all, but in fact was after his precious mug of coffee. For, to his astonishment, the great ugly muzzle reached over the edge of the mug and the darting black tongue began to lap up the fluid. It paused for a moment—perhaps the Nescafe was not to its taste—and it lashed its tail furiously. Then it tried again—paused again—lashed some more and made another attempt. Griffin began to realise that the only problem was that the coffee was too hot—a problem in the process of solving itself because the hexamine tablet had burned itself out some time ago.

Other men had gathered, keeping well back.

"Jesus, look at the bloody thing. What a monster."

"Aincha never seen a goanna before."

"Too big for a bloody goanna."

"It's a fuckin' goanna, alright."

"Cook up real good on the barbie."

"No need to hurt it."

"Why not? It'll bite the fuck outa yer if you let it."

"Nar they don't. They run up yer and sink those bloody great claws into yer."

"Why do they do that?"

"Cos they're real short-sighted and when they get a fright, they run up the nearest thing they reckons a tree. Right now, you're the nearest thing."

"Bullshit."

All this nature study was fine, but Griffin, who in fact was closest and backed up against the nearest tree as well, could see there was little danger.

"He just wants the coffee."

"Goannas don't drink coffee."

"Nar. They prefer tea, good and strong."

"This one is drinking coffee," Griffin insisted hotly.

"I reckon that skin will look great stretched on the boozer wall," Snowy Spargo said, feeling the edge of his razor-sharp machete.

"You leave it alone," Nigel Naughton ordered. "That is one

beautiful creature."

"You must have a real weird taste in women, Nigel," Ernie the Weed chuckled.

"It's my coffee and my goanna," Griffin insisted. "You leave it alone."

In any case, the crisis was passed. The goanna, trying to get its muzzle deeper into the mug, overturned it and the remains immediately soaked into the sandy soil. With a final hiss of disappointment, the goanna turned and started away. With its awkward swaying gait, it passed into the foliage and could be heard for some time after it disappeared.

"Fantastic," Nigel declared.

"I have never been so close to any wild animal that big," Griffin breathed—there was, he noticed, still a trill of excitement on his voice.

"Most people wouldn't be dumb enough to let it get that close, Yogi Bear," Bob Sutches grunted.

"Well, better make another coffee," Griffin said, retrieving his mug.

"Maybe you'll get a bunyip this time," Daryl Leyton chuckled.

By then, Griffin was beginning to realises the true situation.

"Anyone got some coffee. I've run out."

"No bloody wonder if you go feeding it to all the fuckin' wildlife."

"And some condensed milk as well."

The State of Queensland had been invaded by an imaginary enemy army and the fledgling Seventh Battalion sent to hunt them down and drive them out. Exercise Barrawinga, it was called, which meant six weeks of patrolling steep mountain ranges and dense jungle. Which made plenty of sense since rumour had it that the region of Vietnam that they would eventually be operating in was a flat place of paddy fields and open rubber plantations. The QTs, as the fictional enemy were called, were composed of a bunch of US marines on visitor's permits, the Pacific Island regiment, a detachment from the British red berets and some veterans of the First Battalion who had recently completed their tour of Vietnam.

The first four weeks had been spent without a trace of the so-called enemy, although their initial attacks were expected nightly as the Seventh prepared an airstrip and base from which to operate against the foe. Griffin had passed the night of his twenty-first birthday in a bunker beside the airstrip, quite alone except for a bunch of small green frogs and a rather huge cane toad that inhabited a stump beside his overhead cover. He had stolen some chocolate and a can of coke and sang 'Happy Birthday' to himself before blowing out the flame of his zippo and wishing he could go home and stay there.

Now the base was ready and so were they and they had taken to the mountains to track their invisible enemy down. The goanna that hi-jacked Griffin's coffee, a lot of snakes and venomous spiders, and a weird array of biting insects were the only resistance they had encountered so far. In fact, they were assured that it was very realistic—in Vietnam they would expect to do and awful lot of patrolling without finding anything.

They moved along the ridgeline and came to a wide plateau of boulders and long grass. Griffin found his boot had become entangled and jerked it free and lo!, straight behind him there was a sharp crack. He turned to see a mystical plume of purple smoke rising out of the grass. While he and the others stood gazing in puzzlement, a short tubby RSM came galloping onto the scene, followed by a couple of men armed with what seemed to be pots of paint. They all wore armbands with the letter U on them, which, apparently, designated *umpire*.

"Stay where you are, you men!" this RSM umpire was yelling agitatedly. "We got him! We got him! Don't move, any of you."

Griffin stared incredulously. By all indications, one of the 'yous' who had got got was him.

"What do you mean, got?"

"You, lad. You've been hit. Tripped an anti-personal mine."

"Don't be silly. It's just a smoke grenade."

"Simulated mine, sonny. They got you good."

Really, Griffin was sure he was feeling just fine.

The RSM took to pacing from the purple apparition and stopped one pace short of Griffin.

"Fuck it," he cried. "Only wounded. Spotter here! This man! At the double."

One of the chaps with the paint pots ran over.

"Drop your pants," he ordered Griffin.

"Drop me what?"

"Your daks. Down with 'em."

"But I'm wounded. You can't treat me like this."

He lowered his greens and the spotter daubed heartily at the place where the RSM pointed.

"Shrapnel wounds to the left buttock."

The red paint that was lavished there ran all the way down

his leg and into his boot.

"Lie down. You're unconscious for twenty minutes."

Meanwhile, The RSM was doing more pacing.

"This man too," he bellowed jubilantly, pointing at Nigel Naughton. "Shrapnel to the lower back and both buttocks."

"You useless fucking dickhead, Yogi," Nigel was growling as he too was daubed from behind.

"Hey. That tickles."

"Shut up and lie down. Has someone called for the medics?"

Nigel and Griffin sank to the ground in defeat.

They lay face down in the grass with their bums bare to the sky while the medics rushed to the scene and many a raucous joke was exchanged—plainly this was to be only the beginning of the indignities that must necessarily follow from such a situation. Field dressings were applied and non-existent sedatives given and soon both wounded men were placed on stretchers, ready for evacuation. Meanwhile, Alby Dunshea had assumed section command and the company moved on. Now that they were abandoned to the excited medics, things really started to get out of hand.

It is no pleasure to be carried, strapped to a stretcher, belly down, over gullies and rocks and fallen logs by a pack of over-enthusiastic quacks with the ground and the heels of someone's boots often only inches from your nose. They protested, Nigel especially, and threatened and pleaded and bribed and cajoled and begged that they might be allowed to walk or at least be turned right-side up—that is, face upward. Their captors would have none of it. Although to carry them in such awkward circumstances was no small difficulty for the medics, still they were a prize, a symbol of achievement for them and hence no burden at all in their moment of triumph.

Soon Griffin's mouth and eyes and nose was completely clogged with dust and debris and his leading edge, which is to say the top of his head, was bramble-scratched and battered from bumped rocks and accidental kicks. His chest and stomach ached unbearably from cramp as much as the innumerable times they dropped him as they relieved each other, a fumbling ritual they needed to perform at increasingly shorter intervals. If they were not real casualties before, they certainly were by the time they were brought to some flat open country from where they could be transferred to a truck for the remainder of the journey to the hospital at Base Headquarters.

There they passed the days in Porky's Infirmary, the very

first combat casualties of the exercise to be brought in which made them objects of considerable attention. They lay on camp-cots, face-down with their backsides bandaged, their dressings changed at appropriate times by the medics, drugs administered, meals served, bedpans cleared.

"The army is a mother to us all," Nigel said.

Soon they were joined by other men with arms in slings, heads swaddled or legs in splints. All of these were more fortunate, being about to sit or lie upright rather than on their bellies as Griffin and Nigel had to do—it lead to much unofficial rolling over and a great deal of complaining. Daily the doctor came by to examine their injuries.

"Coming along nicely," he declared.

"When the fuck do we get out of here?" Nigel demanded.

"When your wounds heal. You ought to be fit to return to duty in three days."

"Why three days?"

"Because that's when the Brigadier will have completed his tour of inspection."

So there it was. All for show to impress the brass. They could not have been more disgusted. Except it wasn't all—the doctor had moved on to a man whose arm was in a sling and had spent his time looking very disconsolate.

"Medic, get here," the doctor roared.

Don Bergen happened to be the medic on duty.

"This man has a broken arm," the doctor raged.

"Yes sir," Bergen replied coolly. "That's what it says on his tag."

"No, you fucking moron," the doctor seethed. "He has a real broken arm. Get him to the real infirmary immediately."

"Real infirmary?" the man with the broken arm wondered.

No one dared answer.

"But if this isn't the real infirmary, what are you blokes doing here," he persisted.

"Can't understand it myself," Nigel moaned.

Finally the day came and the Brigadier arrived, a weedy bald man escorted by a dozen officers with bright polished brass. Griffin caught only the merest glimpse of him for of course he was face down, his backside bared and upward in a splendid display of the fine works of the medical corps.

"Here we have shrapnel wounds to the buttocks. Two anti-personnel mine victims from Delta Company, sir."

"I see. I see," a deep authoritative voice murmured. "How is it going, soldier?"

"Fine, sir, just fine," Griffin said, assuming it was he being spoken to.

"That's the spirit," the Brigadier declared. "My goodness, what is that smell?"

For indeed, everyone was sniffing and there was some clearing of throats and they were shuffling on in some haste. Nigel, Griffin noted, did not sniff.

"Did you do that?" Griffin asked him in horror.

"Let me remind you that as an English gentleman, such an accusation is greatly offensive."

"Jesus. What have you been eating?"

"Been saving it for him for days," Nigel chuckled. "Come on. We gotta get outa here."

Their escape from the infirmary followed immediately, and was very unexciting. They ripped their bandages off and pulled their pants on and walked out to the airstrip where a number of helicopters stood with their rotors running.

"We gotta get out to Delta Company," Nigel told one of the pilots.

"Get in," he said. "They're just getting ready for the big push out there."

The helicopter landed them in the middle of Battalion Headquarters and they knew right away that the jig was up. Standing right there was a big man in US camouflage jacket, deerstalker hat, sunglasses and smoking a cigarette through a long holder. It might have been the Prime Minister of some remote and warlike British colony but in fact it was the Battalion Commander—Porky himself.

"You speak," Nigel gasped, keeping his head down. "He knows me."

Griffin gulped and decided the best thing to say was the only thing he could think of.

"Hey, buddy. Which way to Delta Company?"

Porky's mouth fell agape and immediately filled with swirling dust from the helicopter rotors, such that he was only able to offer a wave in a vague direction.

"Thanks mate," Griffin called as they strode away.

Nigel was almost helpless with laughter. "I see you're developing some skills in the area of handling senior officers," he mused.

"With your fine example to follow, how could I miss," Griffin chuckled.

So they were reunited with their friends, and the rest is sad to relate. They rejoined the company at just the time when they were preparing to attack a QT position just along the ridgeline. There was barely time for Griffin to brag about easy times in the infirmary and how sexy the nurses were and Snowy and the others to moan about the innumerable mountains they had climbed during that time.

Hatrack gave the command to attack and Tiger Braddock ordered Nigel's men to lead the assault, straight up the guts. They charged along the exposed ridge uttering wild war cries and brandishing weapons and managed to get about thirty yards in their frontal assault before the entrenched QTs opened fire. Immediately, an umpire raced in shrieking.

"Right. You men. You're all dead. The lot of you."

The whole section was wiped out but they knew they had died bravely. The spotters came with their red paint pots and lavished blood on their chests and faces and they retired a little way down the slope to watch the rest of the company storm by in continuation of the attack.

"I only hope we do a little better than this when the real thing comes along," Griffin sighed.

"You sure got a way of bringin' us bad luck, Nigel," Snowy Spargo complained.

"Ah well, at least this time we're dead," Nigel grinned. "It could have been worse. We might only have been wounded."

"Corporal Naughton! Do you want to go to Vietnam?"
"I don't want to, sir. I have to."
"Are you implying coercion, Corporal?"
"No sir. I have a lot of debts to pay. A tour of Vietnam is the only means I can see of satisfying my creditors, and keeping them off my back while I raise the necessary funds."
"Then you want to go to Vietnam."
"No sir. I have to."
"That is not the right answer to my question, Corporal."
"Would be if you asked the right question, sir."
"Bugger you, Corporal. Sign the bloody Affirmation!"

Temporarily Misplaced

A group of Australian soldiers became temporarily misplaced during a simple navigation exercise in the Victorian countryside—*temporarily misplaced* mind you, since in the military parlance *lost* describes a condition far more serious than merely not knowing where you are.

It occurred, in the first instance, because Hatrack, their Company Commander, became agitated about a certain lack of basic map and compass skills amongst his NCOs and rightly so, not only in the light of the following incident but because within two months his troops would be seeing active service in South Vietnam—all this happened in 1967. It has to be added that the bulk of his troops had little idea of where on earth this South Vietnam place might have been either.

He chose a small range of low but rugged mountains and arranged for his troops to be deployed in a wide circle, divided into its nine section groups, with the notion that each group would navigate to a central Rendezvous Point (RV) by the evening of the following day. Each soldier was burdened with full combat gear, each section a radio, and an officer to observe and assess the NCO's abilities, and to complicate matters the RV was relocated several times throughout the exercise. The result was that none of the groups arrived at the final RV on schedule; several went to wrong RV's, two others were found bewildered and somewhere in between, and one group, from 11th Platoon, did not turn up at all. This was Corporal Naughton's group, supervised by Lt Hollingsworth.

Now Nigel Naughton was a very experienced soldier. He had been with the British army in Northern Ireland and Cyprus and later joined the Australian army during the Malaya Emergency. In the interim, he had made several attempts at marriage and civilian life, all of which failed and forced him back into the army. As a result he was one of the most experienced men in the battalion, yet held the lowly rank of corporal, reputedly a result of a tendency to express his views in the presence of officers. His name wasn't really Nigel—it was just what they called him because he drank tea incessantly, had a pronounced Pommie accent and a moustache waxed to points at the ends—'like every other Nigel in the world' as Snowy Spargo put it.

By contrast, Lt Peter Hollingsworth was very much a short-timer, and he had come directly from his graduation—

an honours degree in Psychology at the Duntroon Military College—to be involved in this fiasco. With a frail build and an effeminate voice, Holly had to contend with the difficulty of asserting his authority when he was the shortest and most youthful-looking man in the platoon. The rest of the group were rather grumpy conscripts.

From the outset they were in trouble. The day was ferociously hot and the terrain proved to be far more impassable than Hatrack had assessed. As the blazing sun numbed their skulls, they scrambled up and down the shaly slopes, thrashed their way through savage tracts of brambles and teetered desperately along sheer cliff-faces. Holly was certain that there had to be a mistake for surely no responsible senior officer would deliberately plan for his men to negotiate such dangerous country. Nigel Naughton knew that they most certainly would have, and Hatrack more so than any. Constantly the two men disputed their position while the rest struggled and cursed their way along, unbalanced by their top-heavy gear, every knee and elbow skinned, daubed with red streaks as the brambles slashed their flesh.

Hour upon hour they battled on, seemingly getting nowhere and it was all the more frustrating because this exercise should have been so easy for men of their experience. The six conscripts had been in the army for nine months by then, surviving the rigours of two long wargame exercises in the heat and mountains of North Queensland, and had endured the cruelties of the Jungle Warfare Training School at Canungra—thought by many to be the toughest course in the world. Now, as their time in Vietnam neared, Hatrack ensured their fitness with a ten mile forced march before breakfast every morning, with full equipment and two bricks in their packs to replicate operational weight. The mentally and physically unsuitable had been weeded out of their ranks. They were drilled relentlessly, day after day. These were tough hard lads, ready for war, and in a sense that was their downfall; the route they followed would have been completely impossible for men of normal fitness and it was only their superior condition and tenacity that allowed them to penetrate as far as they got.

It became apparent that at their present rate of progress they would be fortunate to arrive at the RV within a week, let alone by the next day. In the end, for there had to be an end, they could go no further and it was plain that some justification was needed to bring the expedition to an immediate conclusion.

It was the gunner, Snowy Spargo, who contrived to do so, by promptly twisting his ankle and falling off a cliff.

Snowy was a big fellow, immensely strong, a rugged shearer from out West and when he fell the earth shook. Down he crashed, cascading amid a small avalanche that included Nigel Naughton and Ernie the Weed, both of whom had been unable to get out of his path, each tumbling over the other until they reached the flatter ground fifty yards below. Up above, the survivors stood, staring in horror, until they perceived that there had been no loss of life since the torrent of abuse, swearing and placing of the blame that arose from that dusty tangle of bodies and limbs and gear and bushes and rocks was distinctly emitted by three voices. But the radio was smashed, and the compass lost and, worst of all, Snowy's ankle sprain was about as serious as they get.

"Good!" the gunner muttered in bitter jubilation. "Now you bastards are gonna have ter carry me!"

That wasn't likely—a man of Snowy's weight could never have been carried any distance over such difficult terrain. In addition, there was nowhere sensible to carry him to since by then it was apparent that they were undoubtedly lost.

"Temporarily misplaced," Nigel corrected grimly.

Obviously they needed a new plan and it was only after lengthy altercation that Nigel and Holly agreed upon one. It was pointless continuing west, but southward lay the main road connecting two small towns—just across the next ridgeline according to Holly, or three ridges over if you preferred to believe Nigel. But the point was that by dead reckoning, they would have to strike the road sooner or later, and from there civilisation, a telephone and arrange a helicopter rescue for Snowy. So they left Ernie Weedman to look after the injured man and set out on their mission of mercy. It was then late afternoon but it took them a full night of hopeless scrub-bashing before, fifteen hours later, they eventually scrambled up onto the ridgeline along which ran the asphalt road.

There they rested for a time and tried to hitch a ride—it was not the most promising possibility. In midmorning on a weekday, the road was rarely used but even had some stray motorist happened along, that they might have stopped was improbable. Here were six men in what was left of military green, each man's clothing ripped to tatters and the remaining fragments black with sweat. They were unshaven and ruffled and filthy dirty, and each bore visible cuts and abrasions, open wounds arrowed by dried or drying blood. They had rifles and machineguns and bandoliers of ammunition—admittedly blank—slung about their bodies and from their belts hung bayonets and machetes. And if that wasn't enough, each of them wore the most savage expression in proper reflection of their misfortunes. In short, they were as fearsome, dangerous-looking and disgustingly dirty a bunch as you would ever hope not to see, so it was probably just as well that no motorist passed for he would hardly have dared pick them up anyway.

There was nothing to do except pick themselves up and walk and it remained only for Holly and Nigel to argue whether their best option lay east or west. Ultimately, Holly pulled rank, demanded east, then decided west might be a better idea, and the exhausted men dragged themselves to their feet, gathered up their gear, and staggered off in the nominated direction. As they went they were taunted by the chatter of a distant helicopter, far out across the ridgelines. Probably it was searching for them, but doing so entirely in the wrong places. Once or twice it did come toward them, but then banked away again. Plainly, no one at headquarters was able to imagine just exactly how far off course they might have got.

At last they came upon a farmhouse, set well back from the road in a clump of pinetrees. No one said anything for no one had any breath left for saying things. Nigel, who was in the lead, simply veered off onto the rutted track and opened the gate. The house was two hundred yards up the rutted track from the gate by which stood a sign—*Trespassers Prosecuted!*—but men carrying guns need pay no heed to signs, although they were careful to fasten the gate behind the last man.

They trudged through, heads down, but eyes firmly planted on that house. Help could be found here, and more immediately, water and perhaps some shade to lie in. They staggered on, fearing that to pause would have meant loss of their blind stumbling momentum which was now all that kept them going.

The house was an old weatherboard structure with a rusted iron roof and all manner of tumbledown outhouses. There were two watertanks and these the men eyed thirstily while around the vicinity of the house white blobs wandered that had to be chooks—food! Up the track they strode in what was, by force of habit, good tactical formation—spaced well apart, each man on an alternate side of the track—and a small dog emerged and began to bark at them, though it was careful to keep its distance. The heat and their exhaustion, the lethargy of their senses and the reluctance of their muscles to respond, permitted none of them to observe that a front window opened a few inches and through the gap poked a long tubular object that to men of their training ought to have been unmistakable. There was a puff of smoke and the heavy thump of the blast, at which a single word fell from the lips of every man.

"Fuck!" they all said.

Hatrack would have been delighted with their response. In an instant, they went in all directions, leaping, diving, rolling, as Nigel bellowed, "Contact front!"

When they came up, they were in a line abreast the house, lying prone with weapons levelled, each man ten yards from the next. Like lizards they slipped and slid until they found good cover, their pulses racing, their eyes squinting at the target and in one second flat they were perfectly deployed for contact response. All that training at *instantaneous reaction* bore fruit in that moment. Each man now slipped a round up the spout.

From the springboard of such an excellent deployment, to take the house would have been elementary. Bugsy Norris and Greyman were well placed to lay good covering fire onto the front while Nigel and Gibson could easily outflank the assailant on the left. Holly was not placed so well but he could cover their backs, while the remaining man had gone to the far right from where he had the whole backyard in his sights should the enemy try to *bug out*. Nigel, backed up by Gibson, could then dart from shed to house and onto the verandah without undue risk, and once there creep along crouched below window height and lob in a couple of grenades. Elementary stuff—they'd rehearsed it a hundred times.

"Go Nigel! We'll cover you!" Bugsy Norris even roared.

"Don't be fucking silly," Nigel roared back.

This reply was not to be found anywhere in the tactical manuals and caused each of them to hastily reassess the situation, and much the same picture occurred to each. There was a simple farmer sitting quietly in his lounge room on a sunny afternoon when he hears his dog barking so he goes to the window and looks out. There, bearing down on his house, he sees half a dozen men of the most menacing demeanour, men so dirty and ugly and tattered that they might have been through both world wars on the same day, men armed to the teeth with state-of-the-art weapons technology, men with no respect for private property. What the farmer did next was what many might have done in such a situation—he called to his wife to get under the bed and went for his trusty shotgun.

This threw a somewhat different light on the matter, and it became apparent that diplomacy, rather than tactics, was going to be the best approach. With that, Holly plucked himself up and dashed forward, crouched low, to drop down beside Nigel in a position behind the rusted remains of an abandoned plough.

"Hey. You in the house! What on earth are you doing?" Holly called plaintively. Nigel regarded the heavens—clearly he would not have phrased it quite like that.

The imagined farmer, doubtless interrupted in the act of reloading, had to think about that for a moment, before he replied in a croaking voice that very much confirmed their guesses at his antiquity. "Well. Wadda yer reckon you're doin'?"

Given the circumstances, it was not the easiest question to answer.

While Nigel and Holly whisperingly disputed the best reply, the farmer helped them out by deciding to elaborate. "Reckon yer can come walkin' inta a bloke's place and take ova without a fight, do yer? Yer ain't in bloody Yankeeland now, yer know. I'll show yer what a fight is!"

While this might have been the sort of challenge not easily overlooked by men of the fighting disposition, there remained the fact that the farmer's shotgun was loaded, whereas their weapons contained only plastic blanks.

"We don't want to fight," Holly sighed dejectedly.

But the farmer was het up now and more intent on talking than listening. "Walkin' inta a bloke's place with yer bloody guns. All the bloody same, you Yanks, with yer bloody guns."

It was becoming clearer. Here was a man who suffering the effects of watching too much television.

"We aren't Americans, my friend. We're Australians." Holly offered.

"You don't sound like an Aussie to me."

"Orr, come off the grass, mate. Fair dinkum. We're as true blue as you are," Holly attempted, but like all well educated middle class Australians, his attempt at the indigenous accent was a pathetic parody.

"Bullshit!" the farmer guffawed.

Such being the case, it was plain that from here on, the less Holly said the better.

Nigel Naughton, on the other hand, considered his own accent no impediment whatsoever. "Listen, you fuckin' pea-brained cowcocky. Put up your fuckin' gun or we'll come in there and jam it up your arse so hard you'll shit through your ears for the rest of your life!"

"Oh, nicely handled, Nigel," Owen Gibson chuckled.

The farmer thought it through and realised that such strong words could only be a bluff. "Yer don't reckon I'm gonna fall for that one, do yer? I didn't come down with the last shower, you know."

Obviously deeper heritages were going to have to be called upon. Now Billy Goolie was a halfcaste aborigine although he looked more like a fullblood. Apparently he was more white than black only in the farseeing eyes of bureaucracy, since it was illegal for fullbloods to be conscripted. Billy was a man in conflict with himself—his black half still declaring itself free and roaming the dreaming and hating his white half for getting drafted and dragging all of him into this mess.

They called him Greyman because the issue of his blackness and whiteness still remained disputed and officially undecided—and he should have been the perfect answer to this problem, except Greyman was never the perfect answer to anything.

"Awright, Greyman," Nigel called. "Stand up and show him how Australian you are."

"Get fucked, Nigel," Greyman growled back. "I ain't standin' up with that trigger happy yokel in there."

"Hey, in the house. Hold your fire while this bloke shows himself. He's an abo. What could be more Australian than that?"

"Orright, give us a geek at him."

Greyman crossed himself though he was not a Catholic, jumped to his feet, stood for less than a second and then dropped down again.

"Come on, Greyman. Give him a good look," Nigel urged.

"No need," the farmer called. "I saw enough."

"Well?"

"Ain't necessarily Aussie," the farmer pronounced.

With that, Greyman jumped to his feet again, seething and roaring with the rage of forty thousand wasted years of unwanted heritage.

"Open your bloody eyes, you stupid old dag. Don't ya know a fuckin' abo when ya see one?"

"Might be one of them American niggers," the old voice croaked back sagaciously.

Had not Bugsy Norris and Owen Gibson been on hand to

restrain him, Greyman would have stormed the house then and there in the very best VC winning style.

Possibilities were diminishing. Gibson, who was short and skinny and redhaired, was a Tasmanian and with his soft-spoken ways could not have persuaded anyone of his Australianness, while Bugsy Norris was a Scots-Italian mongrel and therefore no more appropriate. All eyes then turned on the last hope—the extra man out on the far right. This was a fourth generation Australian from the grassy Melbourne suburb of Moorabbin and no one could have been more typically Australian. This person, it must be shamefully admitted, also happened to be Griffin.

"Righto, mate. Do I sound Aussie enough for you?"

"Yep. Not much doubt about that."

"So what makes you think we're bloody Yanks?"

"Cos yer look like bloody Yanks."

"Take it from me, mate. We're ridgy-didge Diggers."

"Oh yeah? Then where's yer bloody slouch hats?"

In an age of crumbling traditions, nothing could have been truer. Soldiers were soldiers but Diggers wore slouch hats. It was their distinguishing mark, and if the changing trends in jungle warfare fashions had forsaken it for the more practical bush hat, still it remained true. On those occasions when they wore slouch hats—on parades—they could not help but feel Australian, whereas at other times, they might have been anything.

The man on the right undertook to explain:

"Things have changed, cobber. The Aussie Army is catching up with the world. New clothes. New equipment. We only wear slouch hats on parade these days."

But the farmer wasn't having any of that—he'd been on the Kokoda Trail and knew for himself what was and what wasn't.

"Diggers wear khaki—not green like you got. And slouch hats. You can't fool me. And I seen yer bloody helicopter—a Yankee helicopter just like on telly. You bloody Yanks have been tryin' ter take over this country fer years. And them fancy rifles, and all that junk you got. Yankee rifles!"

"Belgian actually."

"Yer come walkin' inta a bloke's place and reckon yer can jest take over with yer bloody helicopters and big guns. Well yer can't. Yer bloody can't!"

"But our rifles aren't even loaded."

"Bullshit! What's the bloody point of walkin' round the place with bloody empty rifles!"

There are some questions to which no sensible answer is possible. The man on the right, after a pause, decided that the matter might be better approached in less academic terms.

"Look. We were out on an exercise. We got lost. And here we are. That's all there is to it."

"Aussie Diggers are bushmen. They don't get lost."

"Only temporarily misplaced," Nigel Naughton moaned.

Since it would have taken a far greater intellect to get out of that one, the man on the right gave up with a groan of dismay.

There was no doubt about it, logic had failed, might had been defeated by right, and the only saving grace was that when the last domino fell and the Yellow Peril swooped down from the north, they might find this country a little harder to capture than had been previously supposed. The cycle was completed, and it all fell back into the hands of Holly.

"Fair enough, my friend," he sighed. "So whether we are Australians or Americans or bloody Afghans, it doesn't matter. You have the best of us. What do you want us to do?"

Again the farmer only answered after the most careful consideration—plainly his planning had not extended this far.

"You mean you surrender?"

"If you must put it like that."

"Do yer bloody give up or don't yer!"

"Yes," Holly groaned.

There was one dissenting voice.

"No fucking way. I'll kill the bastard," Greyman bellowed, but fortunately they were still pinning him to the ground.

"Yes. We surrender," Holly called defeatedly.

And with defeat, of course, there is always humiliation. The old farmer knew what to do. They had to throw down their weapons and stand in the open with their hands clasped on top of their heads. One by one they had to strip off their packs and equipment belts in case of booby traps or hidden weapons and then walk forward to the broad open space directly in front of the house. Only then did the victor emerge from his seclusion.

He must have been more than sixty, bald and wizened and grinning jubilantly with his yellow teeth. His skin was brown and spotty and his thin hands with protruding veins as thick as fingers clutched a very old and very rusty shotgun. His gumboots and overalls were still thick with the mud of last winter and perhaps a few before that.

"Mabel. Get on the phone and call the coppers," he called

back into the house, not taking his eyes off his prisoners for a moment.

They stood about for a while then, the captives with their heads bowed in disgrace, the farmer surveying his achievement. Soon his floral-clad lump of a wife appeared on the verandah, standing directly behind him and peeping around his shoulder, to report that the police were on the way. The farmer nodded, still alert, but his taut expression was beginning to mellow. He was beginning to realise that his victory was perhaps not as considerable as it might at first have seemed.

"Hey," he said softly. "You blokes look to be in pretty bad nick."

It was Holly who found the strength to reply. "Do you think we could move into the shade? We've had little rest for two days and no water since last night."

"Orright. But no tricks!"

And then burst forth the whole tale of woe. The difficult exercise, the two abandoned comrades, the failed rescue mission. It was far too pathetic a yarn to be entirely disbelieved.

"Oh Horrie," the farmer's wife said. "The poor things. And they're all so young!"

"Maybe we could give 'em some water," the farmer said through gritted teeth, but he was weakening.

"Or perhaps I should make a nice pot of tea," Mabel proposed, chubby cheeks shining at the prospect. "Would you nice young men like that?"

"Dear lady," Nigel Naughton sighed. "Tea would be a miracle."

By the time the two policemen from Blackwood arrived in their divisional van, the surviving members of four section, 11th Platoon of the Pig Battalion were sitting on the steps of Old Horrie's house, sipping tea from dainty cups with saucers balanced on their knees, spotted with the crumbs of a cream spongecake that was a mandatory part of afternoon tea. The police had received a report earlier to be on the look out for missing soldiers, and a rescue helicopter was on the way.

"Your other two blokes got picked up yesterday afternoon," they were able to report. "They couldn't figure out what had happened to you. What the hell are you doing in this part of the world anyway?"

"Just getting some rough country practice," Nigel said.

"We're off to Vietnam in a month or so," Holly told them.

Old Horrie listened to all this, and slowly it dawned upon

him that all he had been told was true. He broke his shotgun and removed the cartridges and walked back into the house.

"God save us all," he said.

"Lieutenant Hollingsworth! Do you want to go to Vietnam?"
A little man with a giant family tradition of military careers to uphold and an educational debt to pay—what choice did he have?
"Yes sir!"
"Thank you, left-tenant. Sign the Affirmation please."

Uncle Sam's Jam

It is probably no slight reflection on the Australian character that Melbourne's most primary arterial road—Swanston Street—is dominated by a huge shrine built to honour the fallen soldiers of both world wars at one end, and an even huger brewery at the other. Traversing between these two iconic edifices, Swanston Street neatly bisects the centre of the city.

If you stand in front of the brewery you can gaze down the hill where the thoroughfare runs straight as an arrow between the offices and department stores that rear like canyon walls at the foot of which thousands of hurrying pedestrians mill about in a jumble amidst the cars and trucks and trams, all under an amazing suspended lattice of electric tram wires. At the bottom of the hill, Swanston Street bridges the Yarra River and then broadens into the beautiful wide boulevard of tree-lined St Kilda Road, which finally veers away a mile in the distance. But at the point where it veers, there is a grassy knoll upon which the enormous mausoleum of the Shrine stands grey and dark and foreboding.

Conversely, you can stand on the steps beneath the towering doric columns of the shrine and take in the same view in reverse, across the broad parklands on the south side of the Yarra, back up the commercial canyon to the top of the hill where the massive red-brick building blocks the horizon, attendant with it's gigantic oval festoon sign with the letters CUB—Carlton and United Breweries. Where, you ought to know, the very finest beer in all the world is brewed to the eternal delight of all Australians.

On the morning of the third of April 1967, the Prime Minister of Australia—one John Grey Gorton, the successor to the fortuitously drowned Harold Holt—stood on the steps of the shrine taking in the latter view and—if the newspaper stories regarding his drinking habits were to be believed—considered the distant aspect with reverent appreciation. Certainly, as he spoke, he kept his head aloft and eyes straight ahead and his tongue did seem to lap thirstily at his lips at every pause in his speech. Where he did not look was downward where, had he looked, he would have seen the green conglomerate of the 692 man compliment of the Pig Battalion, standing rigidly in ranks of three in company groups, spit-polished, at attention, weapons tucked under their arms in perfect alignment, starched and slouch-hatted at their military best.

They stood on the tarmac before the shrine, placed sensibly with their backs to the distant brewery but because it was a hot dry morning, that image of the red-brick and oval sign did not need to be seen to be firmly imprinted on every one of the 692 minds. But they looked directly ahead as good soldiers should, seeing nothing really and certainly not hearing a word of what John Grey Gorton had to say—but then, according to later news reports, neither did anybody else.

Had they been listening, they would have heard at tedious length of the long and great tradition of Australian fighting forces. In fact, it is neither long nor great. It began in 1900 when the first Australian soldiers became part of the British Army and went to fight a bunch ill-trained, ill-equipped dirt farmers in South Africa called the Boers and lost. They again became part of the British Army in the First World War, and most notably comprised the greater part of the British attempt to take Gallipoli—another comprehensive defeat. But it did provide the first military hero in the form of Simpson who with his donkey plucked the wounded from No Man's Land consistently until the Turks picked him off; to which must be added the gaining of their identity both as Anzacs and as *diggers*—the result of the remarkable tunnel systems they built to protect themselves from the Turkish artillery. In World War II, still under British command, they perpetrated the most magnificent defeat yet when they refused to surrender to Rommell's superior numbers and firepower at Tobruk and became *The Desert Rats,* holding the Germans up for months while the allies regrouped and regained the upper hand. Meanwhile, the bulk of the Australian fighting force was handed over to the Japanese when the British decided to abandon Singapore. At last, as the Japanese bore down on their homeland, the Australians broke free of the British penchant for defeat and alone halted the southward advance of the Imperial Emperor's forces on the Kakoda Trail through the mountains of New Guinea and drove the Japanese back into the sea. The fact that the Japanese supply-lines were hopelessly over-extended and most of them died of starvation or disease is hardly worth mentioning. Finally they took their place in the UN forces in Korea, which was at least a draw.

Throughout all this, the Australians had developed a reputation for dogged defence and effective guerilla fighting—not to mention legendary insubordination and drunkeness—and a less-popularised fame for cruelty and ruthlessness.

Now this new breed were to be given the opportunity to add to this frightening record—which was something none of the conscripts that faced John Grey Gorton that day could have looked upon with particular enthusiasm.

John Grey Gorton finished off pointing to the shrine behind him and pleading with the young men to follow the example of the men in whose honour it had been built. But since those men had gone off to their various wars and got themselves killed, it was an example that no member of the Pig Battalion desired to follow to any great length. Twenty-six years of continuous conservative government had given them John Grey Gorton; seventy years of spasmodic involvement in other people's wars had given them their fighting reputation; thirty-five minutes on the hot tarmac in front of the shrine gave them the most collective thirst that the city had seen from some considerable time.

The Pig Battalion stood in spit-polished magnificence, the result of a fortune in bribes paid to the new recruits at 2RTB, for few of them retained the appropriate skills for properly polishing their brass and boots. John Grey Gorton took the salute and set off for the nearest pub while the CSM's took over the parade, roaring orders that set the battalion in motion for a final march through the streets of Melbourne.

In broad ranks, they marched to the beat of the military band, down St Kilda Road, past the green parks and over Princess Bridge into the city. To the tune of *Waltzing Matilda* the Pig Battalion marched with its bayonets fixed and slouch hats perched at a cocky angle, their boots clumping on the tram tracks, men on the brink of supposed glory. Huge crowds of people lined the kerb watching, kept safe by rows of policemen who held up long queues of traffic at every intersection. They crossed Flinders Street and the drunks came out of Young and Jackson's to raise their beerg lasses in a toast to the soldiers and shout they were once Anzacs themselves. And the soldiers glared hotly at those frothing amber glasses.

As they wheeled around the wide corner from Swanston Street into Bourke Street, there stood in quiet anxiety the ladies from *Save Our Sons*. There were two dozen of them, all women, mostly in their thirties and forties although there were a couple of young girls and a couple of grandmothers—not a great number but in the circumstances more than enough. All of them had troubled to don their Sunday best, high heels, ridiculous hats with veils, white gloves. They might have gathered for a

Tupperware Party or a meeting of the Mother's Club—indeed the thermos's of tea were present—except they stood silently, rigidly in their ranks, and each carried a white card about a foot square that they clutched in front of their breasts. Each had been neatly inscribed with a message—'Thou shalt not kill', 'Stop Conscription', 'Keep our boys home'—but mostly they emblazoned a common message—'Save Our Sons'.

But, as the soldiers went through their exacting right wheel, a bunch of workers came down from a construction site to see what the fuss was about. Large men in overalls and singlets, they advanced in a line to confront the ladies from *Save Our Sons.*

"Go home, yer bloody dumb broads," one of the bawled, and the others flexed their muscles in support.

The ladies stiffened and flapped their placards in annoyance.

"Don't you men have some work to do somewhere?" a woman in a silly red hat said reasonably.

"Pretty bloody obvious you wimmen don't," a big bricklayer said.

"You wouldn't think so if it was your son being taken away to prison," another women in an even sillier green hat offered stiffly.

"If my boy showed that kinda cowardice, I'd soon kick it out of him," a welder declared.

"I'd rather have my son in prison," a chubby woman in a purple coat said shrilly. "than allow him to mix with the likes of your sons in the army."

"Lady, the army ain't gonna want your sons, if they're the sort that need their mothers to do their fightin' for `em."

That brought a laugh from the onlookers, and red to the faces of the ladies, and the policemen could see now that it was time to break things up. And the soldiers wheeled and marched on, stoney-faced and unheeding.

Up the hill they marched and into Spring Street and the State Politicians broke off their petty squabbles to come out on the steps of Parliament House and take the salute from the marchers; and the soldiers hit them with a smart 'Eyes RIGHT!' and burped and farted and poked out their tongues. Around the block and into Bourke Street they went, and the trendy ladies emerged from boutiques with their gaudy shopping bags and waved and smiled patriotically. The cars trapped at crossroads bleated; parties of schoolchildren brought from their classrooms to boost the crowd numbers waved flags and cheered; the office workers munched on their sandwiches and asked each other what the hell was going on; overloaded mums came out of the department stores and saw the soldiers as a chance to take a breather before rushing home in trams and taxis. Masses of people waving and cheering and the policemen stood guard lest some small child or old person should run out and be trampled by the relentless tramp of the troops. The Pig Battalion sweated and laboured because in spite of their supreme fitness they were unused to marching so formally for such distances. They stepped out, swinging their arms to regulation height, their bayonets fixed and rifles locked into their sides, and even if those rifles were not loaded, they were enough to bring the city to a stand-still that day.

They marched in ranks eight men abreast and the ranks were arranged according to height, the tallest at the ends and shortest in the middle, which placed Griffin at one end and Mick Delaney at the other. Griffin marched as a good soldier should, eyes straight ahead, unmoving from his course even when the crowd spilled out into his path. He knocked a foolish little woman off her feet at one stage but brushed by without missing his stride nor even glancing at her fate—it simply remained to haunt him later—and less so a moment when he almost took the nose off a policeman with his bayonet. At the front of each platoon, its two leaders marched. Holly and Braddock, the latter the very thing the people had come to see, the former looking like a young boy who had slipped into the parade.

And so the Pig Battalion came to the end of its march, and the eight men of Nigel's section were, like the others, assembled and ready to go. They marched right to Spencer Street railway station and onto the train that would take them to Sydney where the troop ship waited to carry them off to Vietnam. The train was dry—a necessary precaution—which meant that they had packed plenty of beer into their packs. Griffin didn't drink but even he felt moved to try one.

"Okay you fucking dickheads," Tiger Braddock was bellowing. "Put those fucking cans under the seat until the fucking train moves out, you morons. D'yer want the fucking civvies to think we're a pack of fucking drunken animals or something?"

Civilian dignitaries and mothers and fathers on the platform shrank away in horror, and Spargo got out his guitar and they sang their theme song to the tune of John Brown's body:

When I get out of the army I'll be joining up again,
When I get out of the army I'll be joining up again,
When I get out of the army I'll be joining up again,
Like pig's fuckin' arse I will!

And the train rumbled out of the station on the first leg of their journey to Vietnam.

"Private Norris. Do you want to go to Vietnam?"

"Yes please, sir."

"Your enthusiasm is refreshing, Private."

"If you knew the alternatives facing me, you wouldn't say that sir."

Just a year before, almost to the day, Bugsy Norris had been in a pub in Sydney's western suburbs and talked to a pretty girl who had a jealous boyfriend. The girl proved to be a flirt and the boyfriend unwilling to meet Bugsy toe to toe, and if you'd seen Bugsy's bent and flattened nose and sleepy evil eyes and scar twisted lips and bulging muscles, you might have been equally unwilling. On the other hand, it is best to think you aren't the sort of person to lie in wait in a dark alley with three tough mates to ambush Bugsy when he teetered out of the pub later on.

Bugsy had done some boxing and made quite a fight of it, to the extent that the brawl was still proceeding when the police descended upon the scene. Bugsy was by then in a fighting frenzy and flattened both policemen before he realised what they were. He had been around long enough to know the unforgiving ways of the constabulary, and so he appropriated their divisional van and fled through the suburbs, finally wrapping it around a telephone pole and continued his escape on foot. Despite innumerable minor injuries and a considerable loss of blood, he managed to get home to his dear old mum who tended his wounds and fed him broth and fretted about his lack of fatherly discipline since 'that bastard' walked out on her fifteen years before. The moment he fell asleep she telephoned the police and turned him in. For his own good, of course.

Consequently on the run, Bugsy faced a life of crime that, given his upbringing, had possibly been inevitable, but the scales of fate were already rebalancing. Some weeks earlier the Department of Labour and National Service had informed him that he had been conscripted. He had considered the possibilities, none of which included surrendering himself to military discipline. The choice seemed to be between becoming a draft dodger and staying in hiding until the government changed which, since it hadn't for two decades, seemed improbable; or else fighting them in the courts with the almost inevitable result of the next two years in prison.

Now the balance of options had swung back again. The long and the short of it was that Bugsy wound up in the army where he was subject to military, not civilian, law. When the police finally caught up with him, it was too late—the military authorities pointed out that as long as Bugsy stayed in the army, civilian law could not touch him, and sent them away empty handed. The Crown Law Office disputed the matter, arguing that because no one with a criminal conviction was eligible to be drafted, Bugsy had no right to the protection of military law. Anyone could have seen the flaw in that position: the alleged offences occurred after he had been conscripted, and anyway, he had not been convicted of anything yet. Bugsy and the army decided that they should be friends.

"I don't want to know about your alternatives, Private Norris. Just sign the Affirmation please."

Soft Option

Griffin was sitting in Anzac Square, goring the worst hamburger of his experience, when he gradually became aware of a disturbance farther down the street. At first he barely noticed—disturbance was the order of the evening. Moored down the hill at Garden Island Dock was the HMAS Sydney—*the Vung Tau Ferry* as it was affectionately known—aboard which conditions had been so cramped that they were impeding the loading operations and the only solution was to give the soldiers one final night's leave. It was not as hard a decision as might have been imagined.

One thousand drunken combat-readied troops on their last night of freedom might well have been apocalyptic in most places, but King's Cross could accommodate them with a shrug of indifference. The narrow streets were jammed with expensive cars, elegant-looking ladies and smart foreign gentlemen, rubbing shoulders with pimps and thieves and derelicts. The whole place had an air of blatancy in the brilliant neon lights that somehow seemed to deepen the shadows rather than illuminate, hiding the tiredness in the faces of the young girls leaning in the doorways, offering the gaudy shopfronts a rather gothic appearance, easing a certain anonymity onto each of the hundreds of faces of the thronging crowds on the footpaths.

Out there somewhere, mates were roaming between the brothels and bars of The Cross. Mick Delaney, Ernie the Weed, Tiger Braddock and Bugsy Norris had invited him to a dive they knew, but Griffin had declined. Nigel and Snowy Spargo were trying to drink themselves into oblivion in a nearby bar before the midnight curfew when every man had to be back on the ship, but Griffin wanted to stay sober and alert. Greyman had a mother living in the gritty back alleys around here somewhere, Alfie Magee would be praying in a church somewhere, and Dunshea and Gibson were working themselves up into exploring the wonders of Stripperama. But Griffin was playing it cool in Anzac Square.

He sat on the rim of the fountain, a sort of peacock arrangement that apparently had something to do with the victory over Rommel at El Alamein and the immortalisation of Australia's glorious warriors. But this particular warrior was losing his battle with that awful hamburger, with its meat indistinguishable from the bun and the tomato sauce escaping all over his hands—like blood, he supposed. And still the vast crowds of people marched by, people of all known kinds, men from every walk of life, women of every possible shape, children of every breed, trudging by in the multi-hued neon, weaving about the spruikers outside the strip joints. Everything was going on, but nothing was happening, Griffin thought, but prematurely, for suddenly, insidiously, strangely, almost imperceptibly, something was...

Arising from the rumble of traffic and babble of voices in that dazzling world of constant movement and noise, he became aware of a particular sound and movement, singling itself out in his wary brain for special attention. He listened. There was a sharp shrieking voice coming from somewhere farther down the street, the source invisible, the words indistinct, but the message completely clear. It was trouble.

At first, all he could see was a lot of other people looking that way too. Accident? Brawl? Something such. He tried to shrug it off. Whatever it was, he did not want to know about it.

The crowd was moving, as crowds do, all rubber-necking or avoiding the focal point of the action, so that, when the object of their attention finally emerged, it possessed a broad area of vacant footpath fore and aft. It seemed to take the form of four soldiers, all drunk, none of whom Griffin knew, stumbling along in the direction of the square but on the far side of the road. They in turn seemed concerned by something happening behind them for every few yards they would stop, turn, shout unintelligible abuse or jerk arms or thumbs at their antagonist further back who was, evidently, the source of the high-pitched voice. Griffin listened—the actual words carried by that fierce female voice remained indistinct but for one, which seemed to be her favourite, for it was given a little extra gusto every time she gratingly uttered it:

"Murderers!" she screeched.

Then, finally, he saw her. It was like a Disney cartoon he once saw where the hero waits outside the dragon's cave, listening in horror to the grumbling and growling in there, but when the dragon finally springs out you see that for all its roaring and firebreathing, it is in fact a rather comical and endearing creature. So it was here.

The woman waddled into view with her fist upraised and her mouth wide open, as wide as she was high with fiery red hair standing on end, although not so red as her round gleaming face. She flopped in thongs and wore a loose floral dress and tended to wobble along more than anything, her masses of flab quivering about her such that it might have been hard to tell exactly which direction she was going in: what was certain was that not all, or even most, of her was going in the same direction at any given time.

Griffin had to laugh. The idea of this little blob of a woman terrorising four husky soldiers was enough to break him up, and he rolled on the seat with mirth as the woman continued her tirade and the soldiers beat their ignominious retreat.

"Bloody murders, that's what you are. Hired killers for the fucking Yankee deadshits. Why don't yer let 'em go and fight their own fucking war? No need to send our blokes ter die fer the fuckin' Yanks. What'd the fuckin' yanks ever do fer us anyway? Bloody murders for the fuckin' Yankees!"

So this miniature procession continued, but the soldier's long strides and the woman's blobberations meant they were gradually outdistancing her, and directly across the road from Griffin's position they finally escaped into the crowd. The woman halted, physically though not verbally:

"Let the fuckin' Yankees fight their own fuckin' battles. Ain't nothin' ter do wif us. Why don't yer all go home instead of goin' to their fuckin' war. Bloody Yankee murderers!"

By this time Griffin's laughter had subsided, as he watched the woman catch her breath and cast her eye about in search of a new target for her venom. It was almost disappointed that they had eluded her, until suddenly she spied Griffin sitting on his bench. Her mouth flew open doubly wide as she put everything into what might have been a jubilant cry and pointed right at him.

"Murderer!" she shrieked.

As she started across the road toward him, Griffin saw that he had outlived his usefulness in the vicinity and with what might have been an apologetic smile toward the woman, he rose and began to stroll away as nonchalantly as he could manage. He would have preferred to run, but there was an inexplicable need in him to go with dignity. Out on the road, there was a screech of tyres, but he was not so lucky as to be saved by a careless motorist. The woman slammed her fist down on the bonnet of the car, and the metal did seem to buckle:

"Fuck off!" she roared.

The motorist made his tyre-squealing escape and Griffin continued with his, glancing back to see that she was still after him:

"Hang on, you murderin' bastard. I'm still talkin' to yer..."

Griffin was certain that they had little to discuss, but because he was marching forward and looking backward, he collided with a telephone pole. Which gave the woman the edge she needed.

You wouldn't have called it running, but the woman did make a mighty effort to propel herself forward, mostly by casting her obesity in Griffin's direction and allowing it to drag the rest along behind. Griffin got around the pole but pedestrians got in his way as he heard her rubber thongs flip-flopping right behind him. He turned to assess what evasive action was necessary, but she had borne right down upon him, hurling a mighty round-arm punch that, for all its lack of pugilistic finesse, caught him squarely in the side of the head and sent him crashing into the gutter between two parked cars.

"Got yer, yer bastard!" she wailed in triumph.

Got, indeed. Griffin was dazed and flat on his back, between the blurred canyons of looming bumper bars. The wild redhaired woman appeared to him as a fuzzy giant as she blotted out his view, leaping between the cars with a clear intention of trampling him to death. Griffin went crabwise, under the back of a car with its still hot exhaust searing his hands, while her rubber feet pounded his torso.

"You won't be doin' any murderin', I'll see ter that. I got yer. No fuckin' Yankee murderin' fer you, yer bastard!"

Apparently the best means to prevent someone committing a murder was to murder them first.

Griffin tried to crawl further under the car but his shirtfront caught on something and tore. He felt the jab of her long toenails in his ribs and thighs, and heard the painful chunks of her shins against the bumper bar that did not deter her in the slightest, but only made her cries all the more frenzied.

Then the avalanche of kicking suddenly ceased, and Griffin could see long dark trouserlegs in place of the woman's flailing fat calves. There seemed to be some sort of scuffle going on.

"Come on, luv. Take it easy," came the voice of authority from up there somewhere.

Hands poking out of blue uniformed sleeves were then reaching to help, or perhaps drag, Griffin from his decidedly undignified position, and when he was straightened to his feet, he saw that his rescuers were, however improbably, a contingent of policemen. Three of them had hold of the woman, although Griffin wondered if three was enough.

"Wadda yer grabbin' me fer! He's the bloody murderer!"

A large sergeant stood by, regarding Griffin and then the woman.

"Now Matilda," he was saying. "We warned you about picking on the soldiers."

"Get yer fuckin' hands off me, mug coppers! Fuckin' Yankee assassins, that's what they are!"

While most of the policemen busied themselves in what appeared to be a futile attempt to calm Matilda down, the sergeant confronted Griffin, who strove to regain composure. His shirt was torn and his whole left side doubtless covered in scratches and bruises, and his left eye throbbed and seemed to have lost its vision.

"That's one hell of an eye you got there digger," Griffin did not need to be told.

Matilda was dragged off to the Divvy Van, still bellowing rage and apparently just as happy to say the same things about 'mug coppers' as she did about 'Yankee murderers'. Even when the vehicle was taking her away, she could still be clearly heard.

"I'm okay now," Griffin told the sergeant.

"You better get that eye seen to, soldier."

"I will. Back on the ship."

"You can come down to the station and lay charges, if you want."

"Nar. What'll you do with her?"

"Matilda's harmless most of the time. We'll let her go once you blokes have sailed."

"Doesn't like soldiers much, huh?"

"She's a local painter. Well known, I understand. But she has some odd ideas. Gets on the juice and goes real funny."

"Yeah. Barrel of laughs."

"Just a bit queer in the head. Reckons the Yankees are plotting to take over the world. Well, if you're okay, I'll be moving on. All you chaps about isn't making for an easy night."

"No worries. Thanks for your help."

"Yeah. And good luck, digger. With the war,"

Griffin was getting the impression he was going to need it.

Of course a sizeable crowd had gathered by that time to watch the show and as Griffin made his sorrowful way through them, there was another woman—perhaps Matilda's sister.

"Animal," she hissed at him.

Griffin departed at the double.

He made his way to the nearest pub and had a beer, but that

didn't make him feel any better. He went to the dunny and examined his eye—it was bloated and blackening already and completely closed. His tattered shirt was also splattered with blood. He was limping and listing to one side in deference to his aching ribs. He looked more like he had just come back from a war, rather than about to go to one. All things considered, the only thing to do seemed to be return to the ship.

And so with his tail well and truly between his legs, he made his way down the hill, turning his back on the bright lights and chaos of the Cross, and prepared himself to face the ignominy of being the first man to return to ship. He dawdled, hoping someone else might pass him and spare him that dubious honour, and for a moment it seemed that was about to occur.

Up ahead, he saw through his one good eye, there was a figure making his way along the footpath in the finest drunken soldierly manner, zig-zagging back and forth, hardly making any ground at all. He hit a fence, reeled to clutch a light pole as his knees sagged, straightened, lunged on, only to topple against a parked car and fall to the ground. Griffin stopped to contemplate the matter. The outcome was already clear to him. He would go to this fellow's aid and somehow get into still more trouble. Therefore, Griffin crossed to the other side of the road and hurried on as best he could.

But the stumbling fellow wasn't finished yet. Somehow he regained his feet and staggered out into the middle of the road, heading for Griffin's side. But he didn't make it. Deprived of artificial support, he fell, right in the middle of the street. Griffin looked up the hill and of course there had to be a car coming. He looked at the fallen fellow and of course he showed no sign of saving himself. With a loud curse, Griffin hobbled into the middle of the road and dragged the felled man to safety.

In the performance of this rescue, surely not the most heroic you've ever heard of, two things became evident to Griffin. The first was that there was something familiar about this unfortunate, and the second was that as he gripped the man's shirt, he found his hands covered with a tacky fluid that had to be blood. Griffin rolled the fellow over to look at his face, or what was left of it. There were a pair of ruptured lips swollen as fat as witchetty grubs, a nose flattened and bent that pointed vaguely toward his left ear, and a pair of black eyes that made his own seem trivial. The face was covered in blood, but for all that rearrangement, Griffin was still able to recognise how it had once looked. Not much better, Nigel Naughton would have said.

"Bugsy Norris," Griffin breathed.

He dragged him across to prop him up against a brick fence. Bugsy was still conscious, more or less, although his head lolled about in a very rubbery manner.

"Whodat! Whodat!" he was able to grumble through his ruined lips.

"It's me, Griffin. Take it easy."

"Arr, Yogi, Yogi. Yer gotta help me, mate."

"She's right, Bugsy. I'll look after you."

"Good old Yogi Bear. Big trarble, Yoges."

"What happened."

Bugsy sighed sadly and shook his head—a figure of utter tragedy. "We went to this knock-shop. Me, Delaney, Tiger Braddock and Weed. Then Tiger starts this big foit—real big foit. Coppers bust in, and Delaney downs a couple of 'em, and its really on. Got the shit kicked outa me, but we gave some too."

"Glad to hear it."

"They got me. Got me good. Delaney and Tiger got me out. Then Delaney pissed off. Jumped a cab and away. Tiger brung me here then he pissed orf."

"They left you here?"

"Thought I could make it back to the ship meself. Only a few hundred yards..."

"I'll get you there, mate. Let's go."

There was truly little choice. The police had not given up in their attempts to apprehend the infamous Bugsy Norris, the Pig Battalion's only known criminal. There was a matter before the courts as they strove to extract Norris from the army and try him on civilian charges that would put him in gaol for a long time. But as long as he stayed in the army, he was safe from them. For him, like no one else, the sooner the ship sailed, the better off he would be.

Griffin dragged Bugsy to his feet and got an arm over his shoulders and they began to continue their painful journey, the one good eye they had between them picking out the route. Ahead the great bulk of the HMAS Sydney, floodlit, blocked out the skyline. They shambled on awkwardly, and finally came to the gate of the dock.

"Hey, you blokes. Hold it there," a voice assailed from their blind side.

"Shit!" Griffin breathed.

They stopped, and Griffin swivelled his head to bring the speaker into his range of vision. There were two of them actually, both large fellows, and both Military Police.

"What's the problem, Sergeant?" Griffin asked amicably.

The sergeant came to stand directly in front of them.

"Well, you ought to know. It looks like you're the one who's got it."

"No problems sarge. Just heading back to the ship."

"Ah-huh. Had a good night, did you?"

"Yeah, sure, sarge. Just great."

"That's one hell of an eye you've got there, sonny."

"I got hit by a little old lady."

"Ah-huh. And your friend here. Same old lady?"

"Same old lady."

"Who was she? Cassandra Clay?"

Assuming that was a joke, Griffin had a good laugh about it. Then the sergeant stopped smiling and looked to his companion. "Corporal, call out the medics. You two better come inside and make yourselves comfortable until they get here."

"It's okay," Griffin protested. "We can make the ship. We're nearly there."

"Inside!" the MP sergeant snapped.

Inside that building by the gate was, of course, the guardhouse.

They clumped across the wooden floor and the door of the cell clanked shut behind them. While Griffin laid the barely conscious Bugsy on the bunk, the sergeant stood by the bars. "You know, we just got a report from the civvy coppers. They're after a couple of blokes who escaped from a stoush in a knock-shop in Darlinghurst Road. One big blonde one and one dark ugly one. That wouldn't happen to be you guys, would it?"

"Not us, sarge."

"Ah-huh. I'd stick to that story if I were you, sonny."

The Navy medics came and, only after a lengthy argument, got Bugsy Norris moved into the infirmary on the ship. They just glanced at Griffin's eye and chuckled when he told his story and didn't even offer him a painkiller. Griffin was rather glad about that—the pain in his head stopped him from thinking too deeply about the possibility of being handed over to the civilian police and ending up in Long Bay Gaol. It was just too cruel.

Out there, as the hours passed, the men trooped back to the ship. The MP sergeant, having made his one joke for the evening, now contented himself with the occasional *Ah-huh* as he assisted the even less communicative MP corporal to sort the regathered leave passes into alphabetical order.

The guardhouse was an equally uninteresting place, a single brick rectangular room divided in the middle by a strong wire grille. The only difference between Griffin's half and the MP's was that theirs had a desk and two chairs and a cupboard and a sink with coffee brewing equipment and, most importantly of all, a door to the outside world. Through that open doorway, Griffin could see the dazzling lights of the city on the far side of Woolloomooloo Bay. In Griffin's half was a double-bunk, an open dunny and a small barred window through which he could look across the wharf to the vast grey bulk of the HMAS Sydney, just one hundred yards away. On the ship he would be safe, but here, in this small brick structure at the gate to Garden Island Dock, the dividing line between the military and civilian worlds was all too tenuous.

Soon he heard distant wailing sirens and he knew they were coming after him. The MPs stopped playing with leave passes and peered at the blank wall at exactly the same spot Griffin was. None of them needed X-ray vision to see police cars—two of them—screaming down the hill from King's Cross. No one moved. The sirens eerily died at the gate and there was the clump of footsteps outside.

"Lock the fuckin' door," the MP sergeant said and the corporal jumped up, fumbling keys, but far too late—the door swung violently back against the wall and six burly Sydney policemen came thumping into the room.

They were lead by a Senior Sergeant with an enormous belly, florid face and narrow suspicious eyes—they all carried guns and had their sleeves rolled up to show off their bulging biceps. Griffin's two MPs seemed frail by comparison and looked as though they might have preferred to have been on Griffin's side of the iron grille right then.

"Right, he's the one, is he?" The Senior Sergeant pointed a thick finger at Griffin.

Griffin smiled and shook his head faintly while the MPs exchanged a desperate glance and the MP sergeant said 'Ah-huh' but whether that was affirmative or just one of his customary mutters was hard to tell. The senior sergeant handed him a document:

"Right. You gotta hand him over to us."

The MP sergeant read the document with great concentration, sweating from the effort, and did not seem to understand a word of it. He passed it back but no one took it—it just quivered in his shaking hand:

"Ah-huh. Um...I'll have to talk to my superior officer about this..." he ventured in not much more than a whisper. The Senior sergeant positioned his bulbous red nose one inch from the decidedly less bulbous and red nose of the MP sergeant:

"You turn him over to us or we bust him outa there, pal."

"You can't do that!"

It was perfectly obvious to Griffin that they could.

"He did one of me blokes," the Senior Sergeant went on. "And he ain't gonna get away with it."

The MP sergeant backed off, nearly falling over a chair and finally retreating into a corner. 'Ah-huh. Ah-huh. Ah-huh' he was saying. The Senior Sergeant grabbed him by the shirtfront and shook him:

"Give me the keys, pal, or we'll kick the fucking door down."

Griffin, by this stage reduced to cringing in the fartherest corner of his cell, had convinced himself that he was doomed when for the second time in a matter of minutes, the door of the Guardhouse flew open violently at the insistence of a heavy boot and five more uniformed men walked into the room. But these five wore military green—the cavalry had arrived, as all cavalries should, in the nick of time.

There was Hatrack, fierce commander of Delta Company, and his bulldog henchman CSM Doyle, and there was Sergeant Tiger Braddock with a huge grin and a wink for Griffin because he knew who should really have been in that cell, and Nigel Naughton armed with a cricket bat, and a rather incongruous bald rotund fellow who turned out to be the Battalion Adjutant and therefore its legal representative.

Hatrack, that craggy, fearsome, eagle of a man, stood with his hands on his hips and seemed to pin the blue uniforms to the walls with the menace of his gaze.

"Okay, what the hell's going on here?" he demanded.

The Senior Sergeant loosed his hold on the MP Sergeant, causing the latter to almost sag to the floor, and returned the malevolent gaze of Hatrack.

"That man is our prisoner, Major," the Senior Sergeant said angrily and snatched the document from the MP's hands to wave it under Hatrack's nose. Hatrack snatched the document and passed it straight onto the Adjutant who adjusted his spectacles and began to read. But Hatrack didn't wait for it, he turned stony eyes on Griffin for a long withering moment and then said, rather quietly for him. "He is also one of my men, Sergeant, and I seriously doubt that I am about to let you have him."

"We got a court order," the Senior Sergeant cried. "You gotta hand him over."

Now Hatrack waited until the Adjutant had frowned and puzzled his way through the document.

"Well, what about it, Adjutant?"

The Adjutant scratched his bald head and handed the document back to its owners:

"Well, Major, it's all quite legal and in order, as far as it goes. But since we are a combat unit under orders, it is of questionable relevance. I should think, given the extraordinary circumstances, that it is entirely up to you."

Hatrack nodded—it was the sort of answer he liked best. He smiled his best smile—the sort of smile that snakes and crocodiles have.

"You can't have him."

The temperature in the room dropped about four degrees.

The Senior Sergeant took a moment for consideration. Plainly he was assessing the athletic ferocity of Hatrack, the muscular bulk of Bulldog Doyle, the wiry toughness of Tiger Braddock. He was probably not too deeply concerned by Nigel Naughton's cricket bat nor the rotund bespectacled Adjutant, but both MPs did seem to have grown in stature these last few minutes. All in all, they looked the equal of his own men—he allowed his posture to relax and sought negotiation. "Major, one of my men is lying in hospital with a fractured skull."

"One of my men is in the infirmary suffering multiple injuries, Senior, and I understand another is in North Shore Hospital."

"Other people have been injured and are making formal complaints, and a premises has been severely damaged."

"People, and premises, of dubious repute, I understand."

"Major, my man was seriously injured in the performance of his duty by this drunken mad animal!" the senior Sergeant roared.

That raised a few eyebrows. Hatrack even repeated: 'Animal' and everyone in the room took a moment to gaze through the bars at the object of the dispute. The drunken mad animal—Griffin would not have been surprised if someone had thrown him a peanut.

Hatrack approached and eyed Griffin from under lowered

brows. "Come here, Private Griffin."

Griffin advanced as near as he dared.

"Did you assault a policeman this evening, Private Griffin?"

What a wonder it was to be asked a question you could answer honestly.

"No sir!"

"How do you assess this, CSM Doyle?"

"The story is he got slugged by a little old lady."

"Your thoughts Sergeant Braddock."

"Hard to tell which story is less believable," Tiger grinned. There were few people who could tell a lie like Tiger Braddock.

"Corporal Naughton, he's your man. What do you think?"

"Griffin couldn't beat up a cop if it was a cardboard replica," Nigel smiled.

"Thanks very much," Griffin groaned.

Hatrack nodded and returned his gaze to the Senior Sergeant. "The man denies the charge, Senior."

"Ask him how he got the black eye."

"I have at least thirty men on the ship who scored similar injuries tonight, Senior. But, in any event, even if this man committed the alleged offence, what would you consider suitable punishment."

"Put the bastard in gaol where he belongs."

"Hmmm. But as it happens, Senior, this man, Private Griffin, will in a few hours embark for Vietnam in a combat unit. Out there, in your city, there are quite a number of young men who have made it plain that they would rather go to gaol than Vietnam. In other words, they consider imprisonment to be the soft option. What do you say to that, Senior."

"It's a civilian offence, Major, and should be punished by civilian law."

"If he goes to prison, he will eventually be set free. In Vietnam, he may be killed or seriously maimed. A possible death sentence as opposed to a year or two behind bars. Which would you regard the soft option, Senior?"

"When you put it that way..."

"It would seem to me that it would be all too simple for a man to commit a civilian offence in order to avoid his military responsibilities. Would you like to see someone get away with something like that?"

"When you put it that way..." the Senior Sergeant repeated.

"That is the way I am putting it, Senior."

It was Griffin who was shocked. He had never really thought

about it like that before. Could it really have been that he had it the wrong way around. Griffin shivered as the possibility engulfed him. He had been so busy running away that he had never once looked at where he was running to. What a fool...

Meanwhile the Senior Sergeant readopted his gorilla stance and said what Griffin himself might have said:

"I don't like the way you put it, Major."

"Then let me put it another way for you," Hatrack smiled. "Either you leave quietly or else we will throw you, your men and your fucking police cars in the fucking harbour."

Now, finally, Hatrack had said something that the Senior Sergeant clearly understood.

"Oh yeah. Let's see you try."

Hatrack smiled. "Corporal Naughton—get your men in here."

Nigel did not need to say anything—they were right outside the door and heard it all. In lumbered Snowy Spargo whose great bulk left little space for anyone else in the already overcrowded room, but Alby Dunshea could be seen over his shoulder, and there were Greyman and Gibson trying to squeeze by.

"Shit," the Senior Sergeant said.

"Why don't we all step outside where there's a bit of elbow room," Nigel Naughton proposed.

Out there, Griffin could hear them, carrying on for a bit when obviously it was all over.

"You won't get away with this," the Senior Sergeant was shouting, even though car doors were being slammed. "I'll be making a formal complaint."

"Deliver it personally, why don't you? Nui Dat is very interesting at this time of the year."

Finally the police cars roared away and the MP corporal came and let Griffin out, leading him outside by the arm and handing him over to Hatrack. Griffin looked at the ship and shivered.

"I hope you appreciate this effort on your behalf, Private Griffin," Hatrack said as he turned to march away.

For Griffin, the final monumental proportions of his mistake loomed as large as the aircraft carrier. He swivelled his head toward the departing police cars. "I've changed my mind," he said. "I want to go with them."

"Too late, Griffin."

"Let me go. I've been wrong. I don't want to go to Vietnam."

"You had your chance, Griffin and you blew it."

"But I don't want to go to Vietnam."
"Private Griffin, get on the fucking ship."

"Private Griffin. Do you want to go to Vietnam?"

"You mean I have a choice?"

"If you go, it must be of your own volition."

"And what happens to me if I don't go."

"I imagine you will continue general duties here at Puckapunyal."

"God no. Anything but that!"

Griffin, after all this time, had no idea what he thought about it really. Army life in Australia was so awful to him that he could only assume Vietnam would be better. This, Nigel suggested, was a slightly flawed assumption. But what was the point of losing two year's out of your life for the purpose of fighting a war if you didn't then go and fight that war? Similar assumption, Nigel thought. The truth was one that Griffin would have been less willing to admit to. Several times when he had returned home, he saw something that he never expected. There was a look in Wally Griffin's eye and, if Griffin was not mistaken, it was pride. Wally never said anything and, when asked, said these decisions were up to him. But it was that look of pride that pushed Griffin forward when he knew only too well that he was not fighting soldier material in any way. He just couldn't bring himself to disappoint Wally in the end.

"Sign the Affirmation please, Private Griffin."

The Rustchipper's Lament

There were several different stories of how Hatrack and his gang rescued Ernie the Weed from police guard at North Shore Hospital and returned him to the ship and the bosom of the Battalion Headquarters clerical staff. Under the circumstances, it was not too difficult for Griffin to imagine how it went. There were quite a few things left up to his imagination over the next few days for he spent the time in solitary confinement in the brig, deep in the bowels of HMAS Sydney.

The brig was just a steel cupboard, only long enough to hang a hammock from the hooks at either end and wide enough to allow it to swing normally without bumping the walls. You could either lie in the hammock and sleep or else take it down and roll it up and sit on it. Otherwise, the room possessed an air-conditioning vent and a single light bulb in a cage. You had to thump on the door to be taken to the dunny by an armed Petty Officer and were similarly escorted to the canteen where you were served minimal meals. The latter was no cruelty, for throughout his stay, Griffin had little inclination toward food.

Exhausted by his night of adventure, he hung the hammock and slept a long time, wakened only once when the medic came to examine his eye and determined that nothing could be determined until the swelling subsided. It was fiercely hot and stuffy and he slept in a lather of sweat, suffering nightmares that were nearly as bad as reality. The onslaught of illness was his only indication that they were underway. There was a deep throbbing sound that for a long time Griffin thought was inside his battered head but was in fact coming through the walls from the engine room. All around, vast objects the nature of which he could not guess at creaked and groaned gigantically. He dreamed of laughing Mick Delaney's rising up out of toilet bowls and mad women tearing down grilles to grab him and hurl him off the top of Sydney Harbour Bridge as it swayed wildly in the wind. Then he would be hammering frantically on the door and Petty Officer Braun would help him to the dunny that was just part of the ongoing nightmare.

On HMAS Sydney, they made marvellous hot bread rolls which were the only thing Griffin found edible. Petty Officer Braun forced him to eat because it was the rules—in fact he was a decent chap who chatted happily while Griffin chewed lethargically on the rolls and by turns heaved them up in the toilet.

"It was really quite a show. All your blokes were up there, lined up on the deck and thousands of people down on the docks waving and yelling, and the band playing *Waltzing Matilda* and all that stuff. Hundreds of yachts and powerboats escorted us out of the harbour, all blowing horns and people on them cheering. Quite a show. They never give us send offs like that. Bet you're sorry you missed it."

Griffin gurgled that he was.

He lost all track of time but on the third or maybe fourth day, someone finally seemed to remember he was stuck down there in his steel cocoon. Petty Officer Braun opened the door and assisted the sweat-soaked, bile-ridden, wretched remains of Griffin out along the corridors.

"You're allowed on deck today."

Up and around through a maze of grey tunnels and doors they went until suddenly he was popped outside. Sunlight savaged his eyes. Fresh air stuck him a physical blow in the chest. His lungs took in that strange stuff warily at first, then in frantic gulps. He was feeling better. This was okay, he thought. Of course, he should have known better than that by then.

The great flat deck of HMAS Sydney seemed like a sponge-rubber mattress beneath his feet as Braun led him to join a group of other men, wretched as himself, also assisted by Petty Officers. These were other miscreants like himself and all looked about equally devastated. They were completely out of sight of land now, just the undulating table-top of the ocean except rearward—sternwards—where the destroyer escort HMAS Vampire sliced neatly through the waves. She seemed to be staying well away from the bow lest Sydney develop some of the treacherous tendencies of her infamous sister.

Petty Officer Braun looked at Griffin's face and knew the signs. He led him to the side where the morning's ration of breadrolls were despatched to the deep. Griffin felt like following them himself. He was going to die. Here and now. He would never get the chance to be killed in Vietnam.

But he had not been brought up onto the deck for purpose of sight-seeing nor utilising a broader version of the toilet bowl. Along with the other defaulters, he was handed a cold chisel and a hammer and knelt down on a well-chosen patch of the deck. Under the grey paint were several layers of rust that bubbled the plastic surface and cracked away in ugly holes. Griffin began to chip. Each blow removed a section about the size of a cigarette ash. Eight such men working constantly ought to clear the whole flight-deck of rust in about three million years.

It wasn't so bad. It was better, for instance, than the bottomless nightmare of confinement to the brig. On the butt end of the chisel, he could see clearly the face of Mick Delaney sneering at him and he could hit it—whack—gotyouyoubastard! Mick Delaney—whack. Tiger Braddock—whack. Delaney—whack. The time passed very pleasantly that way.

For three days he chipped on with fervour and enthusiasm, interrupted only for twelve hours of sleep through the darkness, unless you countered trips to the dunny, meal-breaks and the continual need to rush to the side and yodel his stomach contents into the receding waves. His hands became mass of bleeding calluses, his knuckles and wrists bruised from mis-hits, his knees unable to straighten properly from kneeling on the cold hard deck and his head floated out all over the Coral Sea. He wished mightily that the Senior Sergeant of Police had been allow to have his way and he crunched again and again the Tiger bones of Delaney and Braddock.

One day he saw the real one. Tiger Braddock. Not under the blade of the chisel either but over there, walking the deck with other men. Griffin's one good eye tried to thrust right out of its socket and the rest of him propelled off in the direction it stared. 'Yaaaaahhhhh!' he roared like a Watusi warrior as he ran down the deck with chisel and hammer raised and Tiger Braddock owed his life to the fact that Petty Officer Braun was a pretty good rugby player and brought him down in a flying tackle.

"I kill him! I'll kill him!"

"He's gone troppo," witnesses cried, and they carried raving Griffin back to the brig.

Throughout this time, Nigel Naughton had been making determined petitions to the relevant authorities to try and get Griffin freed. The army knew the brig and its contents were navy jurisdiction, while the navy thought the army should control its own men. Once gossip concerning this incident spread around the ship, it gave weight to Nigel Naughton's continual protestations, but really the matter was resolved when Ernie the Weed regained consciousness.

Next morning. Griffin was led up to the area of the ship occupied by Delta Company and a cabin which Hatrack was using as an office.

"March the prisoner in, CSM," Hatrack bellowed from

within.

CSM Bulldog Doyle began to roar from the immediate vicinity of Griffin's right ear. "Prisoner, right turn! Quick march! leproitleproitleproitleproitleproitleproitALT!"

Almost automatically, Griffin was standing before Hatrack's desk.

"Read the charges against this soldier, CSM."

"No charges, sir."

"Then why is he here?"

"Case of mistaken identity and wrongful arrest, sir!"

"How do we know this, CSM?"

"Confession from Private Weedman, sir. It was Private Delaney, not Griffin. Verified by Sergeant Braddock who was a witness to the incident, sir."

"Then why is Private Griffin before me rather than Private Delaney."

"Private Delaney deserted and did not rejoin the ship, sir."

"You mean, CSM, that you want to make this a matter of record. Is that it?"

"Private Griffin has received five days hard labour for no reason, sir."

"Very well, CSM. It is so recorded. Case dismissed."

The clerk made the note in the official record and Bulldog left-righted Griffin on his way.

The rest of the voyage was relatively uneventful. The sea was like glass, the ship and aircraft carrier but Griffin's sea-sickness remained completely unabated. Whenever he was well enough, he escaped the infirmary and went up on deck, watching the rust-chippers chip on. One day Nigel Naughton joined him there.

"You don't suppose the army owes me anything over this, do you?"

"You mean compensation?" Nigel said, gazing at the waves in the broiling wake of the ship. "No. I don't think so. You got beat up by a little old lady, so they say. Unit morale insists that some effort be made to toughen you up a bit."

Griffin turned his back on the flight-deck and he too considered the wake, arrowing back toward Australia and civilisation and decent folk.

"Another week and we'll be there," Nigel said.

"It won't be so bad," Griffin assured him, or perhaps himself.

"Couldn't be worse than it's been," Nigel admitted ruefully.

"It won't be so bad."

"Bloody pushover after all this."

"It won't be so bad at all."

It was a bloody lot worse than they thought.

"Private Delaney, do you want to go to Vietnam?"
"I might."
"Do you or don't you?"
"We'll see what I think on the day."
"Are you prepared to sign the Affirmation then?"
"Sure, why not? It's just a bit of paper."

Mick Delaney first went AWOL at Puckapunyal rather than face the consequence charges arising from the fight in the POW pub. He got as far as the gate and they brought him back and he spent two weeks in the guardhouse. But the experience he gained was invaluable. When they went for their six week course at the brutal Canungra Jungle Warfare School, Delaney took one look at nearby Surfer's Paradise and made the easy choice between the options, taking Ernie Weedman with him. They sunned and surfed and sozzled themselves for a fortnight while the rest of the unit slugged and slaved its way over endless obstacle courses and endured ceaseless bastardisation and had to run everywhere they went. They were caught when Mick had to admit The Weed to Tweed Heads Hospital with alcoholic poisoning, whereby Delaney did a month in Holdsworthy Prison which apparently differed from Canungra only in that when he ran everywhere he had to carry a bucket of sand in each hand. But Sticky Micky never did go to Canungra.

Soon after he was restored to the unit, they set off for the long exercise in the Shoalwater Bay area in Queensland but Delaney wasn't keen and slipped off the train in Sydney. They picked him up in a raid on a brothel in King's Cross a month later and this time he got three months in Holdsworthy. Except in an unprecedented way, his sentence was shortened by a month to allow him to join the march through Melbourne and the ship to Vietnam that would follow immediately.

But when the ship sailed, they found that Sticky Micky had slipped through their fingers again.

"Lance-corporal Dunshea. Do you want to go to Vietnam?"
"R and R is guaranteed, right?"
"Quite so, Lance-corporal."
"All them gorgeous slant-eyed horizontals in Bangers. No probs, hey?"
"Assured, Lance-corporal. Sign the Affirmation, please."

Nui Dat

Dawn: a portrait in grey. The grey of the sky eroded from black that stretched over their heads like a vast opaque cupola, unbroken and unblemished from horizon to horizon, and if it might have been whitening in the east, that wasn't noticeable yet. The grey of the sea beneath the sky, the one a mirror reflection of the other—a smooth silver serving dish under its domed lid. Closer at hand a slight rise and fall could be seen on the surface of the water but farther out it appeared as smooth and flat as a glass pane, a sheet of sheer perspex stretching away to the end of the world.

Grey too, but darker, almost black, the forbidding tongue of the headland splitting sea from sky, piercing the horizon ruthlessly, its menace enhanced by the huge circular lattices of the communication dishes that lined the crest of the ridgeline.

And the grey of the tired and battered old ship, its throbbing engines muffled like a harkened voice as it steered its way fitfully into the harbour, running a winding course to stay well clear of the other warships and steamers anchored randomly about. With the first light of dawn, HMAS Sydney nosed its way into Vung Tau harbour, and the men tumbled from their bunks and lined the sides to gaze upon the scene—a bleak, foreboding scene which they could do nothing other than regard with intimidated silence.

And that silence pervaded the world, and seemed to grow heavier as the old warship drew closer to land, deeper into the harbour, nearer to the terrors that every man knew lay beyond those headlands. Closer in now and the surreptitious junks bobbed about on the swell of the bow wave—the vessels of the enemy, they could only assume, with the nets and boxes on their decks concealing guns and bombs. The men gazed down upon them, gripped in a private dread that all of them shared yet none of them wanted to share. The last hope, dream, fantasy that each of them held that it might not come to this, that they might turn back, that it might all go away, was gone itself. They had arrived.

And then, almost magically, everything changed. The silence, other than the rhythmic thump of the engines and the swish of the parting water, was suddenly shattered as the anchor clattered over the side and crashed into the sea—and with that the malevolent spell was broken. The sun immediately appeared as of accordingly summoned, to cast forth not fearful fire but a rather soft pastel pink and yellow across the sky, the land and the water. The hills lightened and out of the diminishing darkness materialised gentle wooded slopes and flat rice paddies. The fishermen emerged in their now innocent junks and began to mend their nets and spread their sails to dry, and they smiled and waved and called in unintelligible ringing voices, as did other men on the larger ships, all pointing and waving and echoing a welcome across the harbour.

The men responded as best they could, striving to shrug off the weight of their dread, their enthusiasm growing unsteadily. Along the shore they saw houses dotted and the grey-green agglomeration beyond that was the seaport, hazily besmudged by the languid wisps of smoke that rose comfortingly from the morning fires within the chunks of buildings. Suddenly the world was bright and seagulls drifted and called to each other like half-remembered friends, and even a huge jet plane—perhaps a bomber—seemed to float across the sky, leaving its phantom vapour trail. The men shook their heads in bewilderment and wondered at their initial misapprehension of this placid scene, amazed that they could have taken fright as this gentle seaside vista. Although when they thought about it, they knew why only too well.

And then the officers were calling and the men scattered and bustled about the ship, gathering up their already packed gear and bundling and tumbling their way onto the deck. The broad platform of the flight deck of this one-time aircraft carrier rocked only slightly as the men gathered in their units and stood to one end, orderly, anxious, waiting. They looked, and out of the dawn came the huge Chinook helicopters, airliners of their class with their long tubular hulls and great rotors for and aft. They chattered out of the sun, unsteadily descending, and one by one they set down on the deck in an orderly row, like massive insects, touching on their hind wheels with their noses slowly settling after.

The black gunners in their vulnerable compartments along the sides and the white pilots in their perspex cockpits waved to the men and took out their cameras, as indeed the men did in turn and they all photographed each other and waved and smiled while the chopper engines roared deafeningly and the gales from the rotors swept across the deck.

The American loading marshall roared. "Go, Group One, Go!" and dropped his arm and the groups of men indicated jumped up and ran toward the chopper, knees bent, heads at hip level, hats in hand, the way they had been taught. They rushed to the rear of the Chinooks and onto the ramps that lowered from the tail, redfaced and grinning the fire-fighter's grin as the hot exhaust fumes hit them and then inside, dumping their gear and rifles on the floor, flopping themselves on the seats with their backs to the walls. The engines roared all the louder and the Chinooks lifted off and carried them away and they craned and peered out of the windows or over the tail ramp while the old aircraft carrier fell away behind them, befuzzed by the heat haze. And as the old ship became a mere toy amidst the other toy ships in the harbour, they felt a severing stab of pain as the chopper banked and cut it from view, cruelly slashing their umbilical cord to their mother country.

Out they went across the swampy peninsula of Cape St Jaques toward a place they knew only too well although they had never seen it, a place they dreaded and despised although they had not yet experienced it, a place that was only heat and horror and insects and known to them as Nui Dat—a hell on earth that was about to become their home, their world, their lives, themselves.

Nui Dat: cunt of a place. As the shuddering chopper banks toward it, there is just the scrubby hill that gives it its name and beside the bumpy asphalt airstrip in the midst of the foliage; an old rubber plantation completely obscures the rest of the base from the air. Australian Task Force Operational Base Nui Dat straddles the highway, Route 2, at the point were it passes onto Cape St Jaques, protecting that vital link between Saigon and the important seaport at Vung Tau. Four thousand men live down there, in rotting four man tents scattered in groups of three all throughout those dying, decaying, disused rubber trees, and they make Cape St Jaques and Vung Tau the safest place in all of Vietnam.

The men sit in the chopper all atangle with their gear, relaxed and calm, waving to each other, shouting inaudible comments, smiling and laughing, jostling each other playfully, precariously reckless, heedless of any danger.

Nor is any apparent two thousand feet below, where the terrain is mostly flat paddy fields with the occasional geometric square of a plantation. Groups of mountains stand straight out of the plain strangely without the forewarning of foothills. Villages dot the countryside everywhere, as do the specks of peasants out in the fields with their oxen, or whizzing Lambrettas or wheeling carts along the rough roads. Down there and up here as well, it seems that someone has forgotten to mention there is a war going on. All that changes when you land at Nui Dat.

Along the bumpy runway, the chopper touches down unsteadily, throwing up a blinding storm of dust. The men come spilling out, clutching their gear, hats off, bending double, scuttling clear. All along the airstrip, choppers touch down, men scattering away from both sides, the skittish choppers lifting off and immediately racing away.

Out on the airstrip you are exposed to the sun and the heat strikes like a hammerblow; you will never get used to it no matter how long you are here. You reel along, squint-eyed, almost blinded by the dust and dazzle, gasping unbreathable air and lathered in sweat, but everyone sweats continuously and copiously, for all of the year they are forced to live in this bastard of a place.

The men are gathering into groups and moving away toward the road that runs parallel to the airstrip, from which they will disperse toward the company lines. There is a lot of shouting of orders, most of it drowned out by the roar of the rotors or choked off by flying dust, and no one seems to be responding anyway. The men have their heads down and are heading for home, and they pause only for the Sally Man who will always be there, offering free ice-cold cordial which, like everything else at Nui Dat, is either green or yellow.

You head for the Delta Company lines, on the rise at the north end of the airstrip, an acrid, insect-ridden place, befouled by the smell of rotting things—dead rubber trees, leaves, rubbish, people's armpits. Here, no less than in the jungle, the world seems bleak and uninhabitable, utterly hostile, and the tension, the strain, that you've brought with you continues to hover about you like an extra sense, an aura surrounding your sweat-soaked skin.

The moment the choppers are clear, the guns on Nui Dat hill begin to roar, crushing the eardrums as they blast their whistling shells out all over the province. The guns thump away, constantly, day and night, but after a few hours you get used to it and hardly hear them at all. Still, you will have to reacclimatise to those earth-shaking detonations, and the heat, and the smell, every time you return to Nui Dat, after days in the cold chilled quiet of the jungle.

You live in decaying four-man tents called hoochies with their rotted duckboard floors and walls of sandbagged mud—

the bags now hang in tatters, the mud hardened to bricks. All the metal around is rusted and pitted, all fabric and rope frayed and shaggy. The rubber trees themselves are diseased and will drop boughs on the hoochies while you sleep, and crawling all about the earth infecting the carpet of decomposing leaves like a malignant virus is a knee-high bramble that tears viciously at the trouser-legs. Everywhere, red dust settles, swirling suffocatingly at the slightest touch. A place utterly fetid, and always the savage heat and the roar of the guns. It is as if the environment itself is saying; go away, you aren't wanted here...

After a week of acclimatisation and preparation of the base and their gear, they made their first trip outside the wire. It was the most tentative expedition imaginable. Through the maze-like gap in the three layers of barbed wire entanglement that was the particular part of the perimeter of the base that Delta Company guarded, out five hundred metres, and back again. Mostly it was to give them some idea of the terrain that lay out there, beyond their hoochies, under the continual watchful eye of the men on picket duty in the platoon bunker, at which everyone got a turn on a rostered basis.

The bunker was an underground room with a slit facing the wire. There, an M60 and an M79 grenade launcher were always at the ready and the man stood guard with his finger on the trigger. A second man kept him company—which made sure he stayed awake—and listened on the radio for the periodic perimeter radio checks from BHQ. You did two hours per shift, one on the gun and one on the radio, every third day since there were three sections in the platoon. From the bunker, you could only see as far as the wire and fifty metres of cleared land until the dense foliage began. There, too, began enemy territory.

The bunker had already seen action, so to speak. On the third night at Nui Dat, when the battalion was in repose and Magee and Gibson on picket at the bunker, distant pinging sounds sent soft-whistling objects falling out of the sky. Griffin, his nerves way ahead of his brain, was out of his bunk as the first percussion filled his ears but there were three more explosions before he advanced any further than snatching his rifle.

"Mortars," he heard Greyman whisper in the darkness—in fact he spoke loudly but Griffin's ear-drums—like those of everyone else—had momentarily lost all sense of proportion. Griffin and Greyman ducked outside, still keeping themselves below the line of the sandbag wall of the hoochie.

"They're coming from a long way out," Greyman breathed.

"North-East, I reckon."

"*The Horseshoe*?" Griffin wondered aloud.

"Could be. Fell about a hundred metres outside the wire."

Because that was his first assessment too, Griffin did not answer.

But it was hard to tell how close they were. The eruptions numbed the ears, shook the ground underfoot, set the heart beating at a frighteningly erratic pace. Six more blasts split the night and this time they could see the brief flashes of detonation and knew they were at a safe distance. Then silence. They waited. Someone was running up the path from the bunker.

"We're being mortared! We're being mortared!" Alfie Magee was shouting as he ran.

Greyman chuckled. "Alfie to the rescue."

In the total darkness, Magee actually collided with Snowy Spargo, who stepped out of cover to grab a handful of his shirt.

"We're being mortared," Magee explained, though somewhat least emphatically.

"We know that." Spargo muttered grimly. "We got ears. They're a bit away from us yet."

The whole section had gathered, except Alby Dunshea who somehow managed to sleep through the whole thing. Nigel Naughton was taking charge.

"What are you doing here, Alfie. Aren't you on picket?"

"There's mortars," Magee gasped, his panic subsiding.

"I know there's fucking mortars," Nigel erupted. "So why the fuck aren't you on the radio telling someone about it."

"Gibson's on the radio."

"Fine. And since a mortar attack often precedes a ground attack, who is manning the gun in the bunker?"

Magee sagged, his knees almost giving out.

Nigel looked around shaking his head in dismay.

"Okay. So the attack begins and we all stand around like Brown's cows. Fucking terrific. Snowy, get the gun and position it there. Norris with him. Yogi, Greyman—down to the bunker and help Gibson out. And you, Alfie, go find a bed to hide under. I'll go and see if I can find out what's going on."

In the almost total darkness, Griffin followed the path down to the bunker, partly from dead reckoning, partly because his feet were bare and able to determine between bare dirt and ground foliage. Gibson sat on the floor of the bunker, holding the radio. "What's happening?" he asked.

"You tell us. What were the whiz-bangs?"

Griffin took up position looking along the sights of the gun, toward the wire, just in case there did happen to be an enemy attack going on. All was quiet out there.

"A message just came through. Believed to be drop-shorts from niner-five. They are confirming. Meanwhile the whole base is on stand-to."

"Niner-five, I presume, is *The Horseshoe*?"

"It is."

"Meaning they're our own."

"It does. What happened to Alfie?" Gibson asked with genuine concern.

"Still running," Greyman replied.

Apparently it happened all the time and they would get used to it. Just a little mix-up with the co-ordinates. So Nigel later explained.

"And we gotta do something about Alfie Magee," he added helplessly when in private with Griffin and Spargo.

"And Alby Dunshea. He was so pissed he missed the whole thing," Spargo grumbled.

"Yeah, him too."

"What do we do?" Griffin asked. "Shoot them?" Thinking it a joke.

"If we have to," Nigel replied, knowing it wasn't.

"Jesus, Nigel," Snowy despaired. "At this rate we'll have wiped ourselves out before the Cong even get a go at us."

The bunker, then, was the proverbial *sharp-end* which might have been perceived as expanding and contracting as they went out and returned from operations, but even that first short excursion outside the wire was unable to prove uneventful. Two men needed to remain behind to man the bunker and Nigel had no trouble choosing Dunshea and Magee, while the rest of the company made their way out and thrashed through the dense foliage for five hundred metres.

There, they happened to encounter a passing stray dog.

"Contact left," someone shrieked and they all hit the deck on opened fire furiously. Various authoritative voices screamed at them to stop.

"You fucking idiots! You're firing back at the base!"

Back at Nui Dat, cooks and clerks and drivers were diving for cover in all directions. And Alfie Magee was on the M60, determined to make amends for his previous mishap. He opened return fire, about a kilometre wide of the Delta Company patrol but that was for the best. As it happened, it was an historic moment, for it was the only time throughout the decade of its existence that Nui Dat was ever subjected to ground attack.

Griffin's role in that moment of dubious posterity, however, was to be denied. His SLR jammed at the first attempt to fire it. The second round simply refused to fit properly into the breach. He took it to CSM Bulldog Doyle, who was the company armourer. Doyle poked around the workings with a stick and soon found the problem.

"Dud round," Bulldog gruffed. "Discharge pushed the first round just a fingernail up the barrel and then she stopped. Metal cooled and she expanded, blocking the barrel. Nose of the second round run up the arse of the first and there wasn't room for her to fit in the breach properly. Lucky for you, Yogi. Cos if that first round had gone a fraction further and allowed space for the second round to slot in, the whole damned thing woulda backfired and taken your head clean off."

To all this, Nigel Naughton had a simple explanation. "It's all perfectly normal," he said.

"How the hell can you describe this sort of thing as normal?" Griffin protested.

"Seventy percent of all casualties in any war are inflicted by their own side," Nigel explained.

"Oh, I get it," Greyman grinned. "It ain't the Viet Cong I gotta worry about. It's you blokes."

"That's right," Nigel said. "The most dangerous enemy you'll ever have to face is yourselves."

The world is always in the greatest trouble when such simplistic philosophies begin to become self-evident.

But at least one problem was solved. A few days later, the Battalion Padre asserted his rights and demanded that his batman—Alfie Magee—be returned to him. Though it left them with a section comprising only seven men—three short of full strength—still neither Nigel Naughton nor anyone else could manage to raise the slightest protest.

"Private Goolie. Do you want to go to Vietnam?"

"No sir. I don't want to even be here."

"But here you are, Private. And Vietnam is the next logical step."

"Logical for you whiteys, maybe. Have you thought about the consequences of someone like me getting killed over there. An aborigine? Think what the newspapers would do with that?"

"It doesn't say you're aboriginal here, Private."

"Have a bloody look at me."

"Oh. Oh, yes. I do see your point, Private. Could be very awkward..."

"You bet."

"All right, Private. I'll follow this up and see what can be done. Meanwhile, we'll just put the Affirmation aside, and I'll query it to Task Force."

Whether the Adjutant of the Battalion did so or not soon became irrelevant. All along the issue of Greyman's aboriginality had been a contentious matter. Greyman, half black, half white, was an eternal battle for dominance by the two halves and it was Mick Delaney who finally brought the matter to an abrupt end.

Even while other men queued for their little chat with the Adjutant and another man whom nobody said was a psychologist, Greyman's outcome was on all lips. Should he be killed in action, the possibilities were too horrible for officialdom to contemplate—should he make a hero of himself, the advance of the aboriginal cause would be immeasurable—to leave him behind solely on the basis of his skin-colour would be purely racist. But of course, officialdom always errs on the side of safety and probably would have this time too, had not, as Greyman passed by, Mick Delaney said:

"I bet you didn't sign. You bloody boongs are all alike. A bloody pack of spineless bastards. We didn't take your country off you, you gave it to us because you were too fucking gutless to fight for it."

Little Greyman flew at Delaney but Tricky Micky had the sense not to hit him, instead taking evasive action and allowing the rampaging Goolie to do himself an array of minor injuries against the wall and in the bushes. Delaney did what he did best, he pissed off, leaving his laughter ringing in Greyman's ears with the result that Greyman stormed back into the Adjutant's office and signed the Affirmation.

The Patriotic Pig

Delta Coy
7th Batallon
Nui Dat
Phouc Tuy Province
South Vietnam
30th April 1967

Chao anh!

It's the only Vietnamese I've learned so far—it's the informal greeting to a male friend, or at least I bloody well hope it is. You'd better not check. It might mean we're engaged.

I have been in war-torn Vietnam for ten whole days and already it feels like I was always here. War is hell, believe you me. We almost got beaten at volleyball this morning.

We are pretty well set up in a base camp called Nui Dat—bugger of a place but we inherited the old 5RAR positions which means we didn't have to build hoochies or dig bunkers. Then the wonderboys up top decided everything should be moved, by us and by hand. Mostly we carry sandbags around making neat little stacks to hide behind should we be attacked, a possibility that seems about as likely as snow on Ayres Rock.

So far the most terrifying incident was a dog with rabies that attempted to penetrate our perimeter. We had orders to shoot it on sight but after about five assaults against the terrible beast, it lives on and continues to appear in the same place.

On the 8th and 9th of May, the Pig Battalion went out on its first operation against the Viet Cong. Operation Puckapunyal, it was called, with doubtful overtones of all those months of yapping RDIs and brass monkey parades, and I suppose it was a training exercise really. *Acclimatisation and Orientation*, they call it. The battalion would fly out eight miles by chopper and after searching and clearing an area, walk back to Nui Dat.

The initial enthusiasm for receiving our first full supply of real ammunition soon wore off when we discovered how heavy it was. My job in the section was 2nd scout which simply meant that should something happen to the forward scout—like death for instance—I would take his place. While he lived and led the way, I would be no more than general pack mule.

My gear consisted of a web belt with three bottles of water across the back, two large pouches at front containing 140 rounds in magazines and a grenade in each, machete one side and bayonet the other, and of course, my rifle. My pack contained two days' rations (on most ops, they said, it will be three) mosquito net and ground sheet and entrenching tool hung on the back. In addition, to provide the big warrie touch, two 100 round belts for the M60 machine gun were slung around my shoulders, Mexican bandit style. 'El Tougho' rides again, I joked, but it took about five seconds in full regalia to realise that two days under that weight was going to make me a lot shorter and rounder.

On the morning of the 8th, they dragged us out of the fartsack at 5.30, not because we were in a hurry but because that's the way the army is. We had pill parade, showers and breakfast and went back to bed until 8.30.

Around here, birds are out of fashion unless they have horizontal props on top. Whirlybirds are all the go, and everywhere. Ours came in flocks of twenty in two perfect files, landing simultaneously, all dust and noise. Six men per chopper dashed across the airfield, piled in and away they went, all twenty together, still in files. Meanwhile the next flock approached. Very pretty.

Six men, plus gear, in a chopper resembles the 5.17 from Flinders Street seconds after the driver hit the brakes, and with the lack of doors and safety belts, those on the outside do some solid thinking, especially when the chopper banks 50 degrees. 2000 feet straight down stares you in the face, and there's nothing to hang onto except your gear which goes if you go. It seems impossible that you don't fall out but you don't. The shit sticks you to the floor, they reckon.

Landing in a battle zone is tricky. The side gunners open up as you approach, blasting away at the invisible enemy waiting in the jungle. It does nothing for the confidence. The pilot touches down, waits four seconds, and goes regardless. If you take six seconds to get out, the first step is the longest and last you'll ever take.

Within minutes of landing, we moved away from the clearing, passing through the fires caused by the artillery that pounded the area before we arrived. In those oppressive conditions, the full weight of our gear was knee-weakening—we staggered along, bent forward, gasping for air, fearful of unknowable dangers, our shirts black with sweat before we'd gone ten yards.

We moved into the jungle—well, bush really—the trees were a type with long prickly tendrils that reach down and scratch you everywhere. Sap-brothers of Triffids, these characters. They love to pluck your hat off your head and suspend it twenty feet in the air, or hang you by the neck with spiny nooses. One branch lifted my machete right out of its sheath and carried it away—I never saw it again.

Leaving the scrub, we crossed onto flooded rice paddies, stumbling along the raised mounds feeling frightfully exposed. The rounded embankments were uneven and with the weight and the heat and the exhaustion, men tended to lose their footing and topple into the slime below. Everyone was sure it was only knee deep but I found a place where I went down to the waist. During my rescue, I got stuck in the mud at the bank and they had to haul me out on a rope. Terribly undignified. Wars are never won, only lost by varying degrees.

Then came the real jungle, a soggy place forever shielded from the sun, hopelessly entangled vines and snaking trees and outcrops of bamboo, fierce brambles and rotting boughs, moss-layered exposed roots and mangroves. We tumbled and tripped and cursed and crawled our way along, all the time trying to watch out for enemy, but the jungle seemed devoid of life. No birds—it's so strange once you realise it. No small animals scurrying. Only in the swampier sections did insects of all imaginable varieties abound, but otherwise there were only the snakes, scorpions and spiders. It was as if *Nature* knew humans were making war here and so withdrew to safer regions all but the hardiest and most ferocious of creatures. Like us, for instance, and the Viet Cong—except that even they seemed to be missing.

As indeed they were—little did we know that this region had been completely cleared by the veterans of 6RAR the day before, and that the track on which, at the end of this exhausting day, we laid our overnight ambushes was in fact a short-cut between two perfectly innocent villages and guarded at both ends by MPs, the locals being warned to stay home that night. We set up our ambushes in section groups along the track, totally unaware that we were the victims of a tactical practical joke. We tied our communication cords and settled down to wait skittishly for an enemy that couldn't have got near us if it tried.

Communication cords were one of those ideas that commonly occur in the army—great in theory but no practical use whatsoever. Normal ambush procedure, the way we learned it back in Queensland and the Victorian State Forest, required that each man be secluded along the track five yards from the next and one would stay awake and alert while the others slept on a rostered one hour basis. To remain still and quiet was the essential characteristic, so a strong nylon cord was run from first man to last, tied to the wrist of each man along the way. You could send messages—one tug was acknowledgment, two meant *wake up and take your turn at watch*, three meant enemy coming.

There were some obvious difficulties with this: the problem of messages sent to the nearby shrubbery rather than the man hiding behind it; of restless sleepers sending inadvertent messages or else strangling themselves; of sleepers like me who wouldn't awaken to a Force Ten earthquake, much less a few tugs on their wrists. But, as usual, we went ahead undeterred.

The cord passed down the line from wrist to wrist and ended with me. Greyman passed it on, an amused expression on his dark face.

"I jest worked out what these things are really for," he said, his teeth glowing as the night matched his darkness. "If we're all tied together, none of us can run away."

Undeterred by that thought, I attached the end of the cord to my wrist.

As night descended, the jungle came alive—it was amazing how it could go to work on the mind. Out there, things unspeakable creaked and crackled and the communication cord was jumping and jolting like someone was performing tightrope tricks on it. On the other hand, it did serve a purpose—it let me know the others were still there, and as the darkness became total I needed to know that.

"That is a branch falling," I told myself.

"That is the wind in the canopy."

"A small animal ferreting over there."

"That is Snowy farting."

I finally settled down beside a tree trunk—I knew it was not thick enough to stop any of the projectiles that we or they used but still it seemed a protective friend—and tried to sleep.

It came, stomping and rustling through the jungle and no one did anything until it was right on top of our position. I jerked awake, praying it was only a nightmare. It was right there somewhere! Immediately, the communication cord sprang to life as seven people all tried to pull it three times simultaneously, but it was far too late. The menace was in our midst. My first reaction was to clutch my trusty tree trunk the way I once wrapped around Wally's leg when I was a small boy and imaginary dangers approached. There was nothing imaginary about this. My senses strained for clues, hopelessly impeded by my quivering flesh, erratic heartbeat, frantic breathing and throbbing pulses. Something of generally human proportions was coming straight at us through the jungle, and not out on the track where it was supposed to be either but back there, behind our ambush position. We were surrounded!

But there was something wrong with that. It did not seem to be trying to make any secret of its presence, and as it came it was making a very deep grunting sound. With a desperate thrust I peeled myself off the tree and snatched my rifle, trying to figure exactly where to point it. Sweat dripped in my eyes, my heart wanted to burst the prison of my ribcage and run away and take the rest of me with it. But hang on... It was going wide. Heading more for Snowy than me. Then it turned again and came back. It was stomping up and down in a line parallel with our ambush, maybe five to ten yards in—it knew we were there and it wasn't afraid of us in the slightest. Back and forth it went, those grunts becoming more pronounced and, I suspected, more irritable all the time. But by then all the clues were in place for Nigel Naughton, our section leader, to make his assessment of the situation.

"Awright," he said very distinctly. "Take it easy, you guys. It ain't nothing."

"Bloody noisy nothin'," Owen Gibson said.

"Just some sort of animal," Nigel pronounced.

That didn't help a lot. People like me with overwrought imaginations had little difficulty attaching physical form to the creature. Too small for a Tyrannosaurus, for instance. No crocodiles or alligators here. Maybe a giant Monitor Lizard. Or was it the supposedly legendary

Vietnamese Tiger, seen by many despite official assurances that it did not exist. In any case, I might have preferred the Viet Cong, and maybe Alby Dunshea had reached the same conclusion.

"Might be one of those dirty Viet Cong tricks," he offered.

"If it is, it deserves to work," Norris chuckled.

But Nigel, the wouldbe zoologist, had run his mind through the available evidence much as I had, although he came up with a far more probable answer.

"It's only a pig," he deduced.

'Only a pig'—apart from being a considerable understatement—struck a profound chord. We were The Pigs. We had been ever since The Beast first arrived to take over as RSM of 7RAR and while inspecting the Officer's Mess, raged in his impressive voice that they were a 'pack of pigs' so loudly that all the rest of the battalion heard it, and instantly immortalised it. Colonel Smith was thereafter branded Porky and his namesake sprang up on all the battalion insignia—the MPs were Porky Pig in Wild West garb with sheriff's badge and six-shooter, the RAP had him mummified in bandages, even The Beast's quarters were identified by a huge tusked boar at full gallop, and it was this image that immediately leapt into my mind when Nigel spoke.

"Maybe he wants to sign up as unit mascot," I suggested, thinking that was a pretty humorous thing to say. Nobody laughed.

Certainly not Snowy Spargo who, being a country lad, knew more about wild pigs than any of us and promptly picked up a heavy rock and hurled it at the creature.

"Piss orf, you fat bastard," he growled spitefully.

Miffed by this insulting rejection, the pig immediately took the only self-respecting option available if honour was to remain intact—it lowered its head, aimed its tusks, and with a mighty bellow of rage and anguish, it charged!

"Shoot the bastard, quick!" Nigel screeched, but it was too far late. While we fumbled safety catches, the roaring monster thundered into our midst. I raised my rifle over my head without thought of how futile butt-stroking might have been, but fortunately the pig went through our ranks between Dunshea and Gibson, touching neither, and carried on roaring out onto the track. Which would have been the end of the matter, had it not become entangled in the communication cord.

Gibson and Alby Dunshea were uprooted from their positions and with cries of dismay dragged out onto the track, and me and Greyman would have gone with them had I not been slammed hard up against the trunk of my faithful tree and anchored there, the cord tightening on my wrist and trying to pop my left arm out of its socket. At the other end of the cord, Bugsy and Nigel both went sliding forward until their weight combined with the considerable bulk of Snowy Spargo, pinned down that end. The entangled squealing pig, brought to a sudden halt, was tearing up huge clumps of dirt from the track as its trotters strove for traction, while behind it the helpless flailing forms of Gibson and Dunshea flopped about like fish on a line. Frantically, Snowy whipped out his razor-sharp machete and slashed the cord, then dived over the rapidly departing Nigel and slashed again. At the other end, my Boy Scout failings allowed my inadequate knot to slip and the cord separated from my wrist, and Greyman was able to take up the slack and free himself from the tangle.

The pig by then had been swung around in its berserk efforts to escape and was now facing straight down the track toward the other ambush positions where seventy men in eight well spaced groups waited with shattered nerves and itchy triggerfingers.

Freed of two thirds of its drag-weight, it was making good progress with surging, grunting thrusts of pure porker energy, and dragging the hapless Gibson and Dunshea along behind. Snowy was on the track and after them, brandishing his machete like a pirate, and I too found my footing and ran onto the track and, like Nigel, dived on one of the abducted victims. I heard the air go out of Gibson as my full weight came down on his upturned belly. Behind, Bugsy Norris jogged with his rifle, seeking with worrisome desperation to get a clear shot at the pig. But Snowy did the job in the end—when his machete sliced the cord between Dunshea and the pig, the latter finally broke free with a partial somersault and then tore off snorting with jubilant liberation, straight down the track.

We, the vanquished, remained as we were for a moment, gazing in bewildered astonishment, and then all hell broke loose down there. There was an almighty burst of gunfire, a brief silence, then another barrage, and a third, and so on, each occurring further away than the last. With each eruption, our heads sagged lower in shame. Then the final, most distant barrage stopped, echoes of echoes diminishing into the night.

"Eight," Nigel said, unnecessarily for we had all been counting. "I'd say he got through the lot of 'em."

Finally, peace returned to the night.

Defeatedly, we picked ourselves up, covered in dirt and humiliation. Each had minor injuries to examine and all of us now had left arms decidedly longer than our right.

"Well, that went well, didn't it," Bugsy chuckled.

But Nigel was frantic and serious. "Whatever happens, we tell no one about this."

"That ought to save a lot of embarrassment," Greyman chortled.

"Most of all Hatrack," Nigel went on. "We know nothing about pigs. We did not see it. It did not pass us. Got it?"

"Pig? What pig?"

"Was there a pig?"

"I didn't see any pig, did you?"

I settled back against my tree, and everyone else resumed their places. The ambush was reset. And as the night passed, you would suddenly hear one of us, when it wasn't myself, begin to snort and giggle and then be overwhelmed by laughter which would infectiously spread from the one to the rest.

"Shut up," Nigel giggled. "Ambushes are a serious business."

I can tell you that had any unsuspecting Viet Cong come our way, they would have concluded that we, the dreaded Uc Dai Loi, for all our fearful fighting reputation, were a very merry bunch of chaps indeed. And so we should have been for the story has a happy ending. Nigel's estimation was correct—they all missed and the pig got away.

So here I am, safely back at Nui Dat. The sandbags feel lighter than before, probably because we know that tonight we will sleep with several barbed wire fences around us to keep out patriotic pigs.

And the Viet Cong? Yeah, we've read about them in the papers. I guess we'll get around to meeting them sooner or later. We thought we already had for a minute there. On the way back to Nui Dat, two platoons surrounded three perfectly innocent Vietnamese woodcutters and took them without a fight. The Intelligence Officers returned them to their village and offered profuse apologies and asked us to please leave the locals alone in future. The noggies didn't seem to mind, evidently they are used to Aussies who think all slant-eyes are Charlie (short for Viet Cong—VC—Victor Charlie—get it?). They just went along quietly when we ran them in and then went home quietly—the sappers later delivered them a load of firewood to make up for the time and labour they had lost.

'All very well,' we protested, 'but how do we tell which are Charlie and which aren't.'

'Charlies are the ones that shoot at you,' the IO answered. Great system. Don't shoot anyone that doesn't shoot you first. Things are pretty quiet now and I think I'll go to bed and have a few pleasant nightmares about that.

Such letters Griffin wrote weekly to his family. He always tried to keep them light and cheery. But this was to be the only time he ever attempted to describe an operational incident, or tell them anything even vaguely resembling the truth. He knew his father would understand, that his mother would ignore what she didn't want to hear, his sister would giggle at the vulgar bits, but the one he didn't think about was his younger brother, Michael, in whose vulnerable adolescent mind the beginnings of a legend was being created. He knew that the less he told them, the more they would imagine, but that didn't matter. Even their most terrible nightmares would never be able to approach the way it really was.

"Private Spargo! Do you want to go to Vietnam?"

"You've got to be joking, sir."

"This is no joke, Private. Answer the question, please."

"No sir. I don't want to go to Vietnam."

"What are your reasons, Private."

"You bastards will get me killed."

"What you'll get is an insubordination charge if you're not careful, Private."

"Who gives a fuck! At least I'll still be alive."

"Private Spargo, please take this matter seriously."

"Up your arse. I didn't ask to be in your fucking army and I don't want to go and fight your fucking war!"

"We aren't interested in your opinions, Private. We just want you to sign the paper?"

"Are you serious? We're all conscripts here. Do you seriously expect any of us to sign this thing?"

"The others all have."

"You're lying."

"Have a look. See. All of them."

"Fucking idiots, what's up with them?"

"You won't want to be the only man in the unit not to sign, would you?"

"No bloody way."

"Sign the Affirmation, please, Private Spargo."

Perfect Timing

Tail-end charlie again, bugger it all. Down the arse-end walking backwards, counting fucking paces for navigation. There's fuck all here anyway on this dead loss operation: Operation Broken Hill they call it—they name them all after towns in Aussie—and not a hill to be seen, broken or otherwise. Just this dead flat, scrubby jay in lightly forested country with occasional bamboo outcrops. No fucking Charlies either, fuck all. The company has propped for muck-arm but there's this bit of a track and you get to go check it out. Just five hundred paces down, a listening post, in case the Charlies are coming. Fat fucking chance. Nothing's been along this track for years—the ground is soft and wet from the constant rain dripping from the forest canopy. No tracks. Why do they fucking bother?

Owen Gibson is forward scout, with Armalite and sawn-off shotgun slung and a couple of Claymore Mines in his pack, and a bloody poofta in most opinions but really loves machines better than people. You all reckon Greyman, being an Abo, oughta be scout but Nigel sticks with Gibson.

Nigel Naughton is next in line, a corporal many times busted, section commander, and a good bloke even if he's a whingeing Pom. Long and skinny with a huge waxed moustache, he has that sort of humour that keeps you going but gets you all the shit jobs when he turns it on the officers. He carries an American Armalite, a Luger on his belt, and the compass and map for navigation, every so often looking back to get the pace count from you, and then signalling the line of march forward to Gibson.

Next is Snowy Spargo, backcountry shearer and section gunner, yellow-haired of course. Snowy carries the M60 machine gun and bandoliers of ammunition slung Mexican bandit style off each shoulder, two more in his pouches, two more in his pack. Enough to stop a fair sized army. He's a fucking fanatic about that gun, calls her Mabel, mad jealous of inferring fingers, spends all his free time cleaning her, sleeps with her they reckon. For sure when he fondles her foresight or caresses her butt, you'd reckon there's weird stuff going down.

After Snowy comes his back-up—Bugsy Norris with his bent face and cow-eyed look, with three belts of ammo for Mabel, a standard SLR for himself and carries slung the section M79 grenade launcher.

Then the Greyman, Greyman Goolie, half-caste aborigine, except he can't be because they aren't allowed to be drafted—a privilege reserved for Australian-born single white males. Trouble is, Greyman looks like a full-blood abo, and all the confusion that caused gave him his name. He carries SLR and our M72 collapsible rocket launcher, and two more belts for Mabel, and he'd carry the radio if they had one but they don't. Won't need one on this short routine patrol, they reckon. They reckon...

Then Alby Dunshea, Section 2IC, big ugly prick and he hates everybody. He's one of them agros who need to beat up someone every so often to prove they exist, and you are just the sort he likes. Just because your big and not a fighter, or so he reckons. You can ignore him. It's just a pain in the fucking arse, that's all. Annoying, like scorpions. Dunshea is a lazy bastard and travels light, just an Owen Gun and a few grenades, to give anything he encounters a bit of a fright. With that twisted pockmarked puss of his, he'd give 'em a fright all right.

And Yogi Bear, down the back, covering their arses and checking the distance travelled.

You've come just one hundred and twenty-seven paces from the company perimeter when Gibson, who is half that distance again ahead of your position, reaches the apparent end of the track. Could be the shortest fucking patrol in history. There's this huge wall of thick bamboo, fifteen feet high and too dense for a fucking rabbit to squeeze through and it goes out of sight left and right. The track runs up to the wall and stops. Gibson stands, regarding the obstacle, looking like Ali Baba trying to remember the right words. Dead end, but if nothing goes any further, how come there's a track? Nigel gives him the signal to look around.

Down low he finds a hole. Maybe wild pigs made this track and forced an opening through the bamboo to the other side. Nigel nods and Gibson gets down on his knees and crawls through. It is like a tunnel in there, just big enough to fit a man on all fours but the bamboo has barbed runners that catch on everything and hurt like hell if you get one in you. It's only six feet to the other side but Gibson has to fight and jerk and thrust every inch of the way, muttering ceaseless curses under his breath. Then he emerges, and is unsure of his next move.

The rest of them are back on the other side of the wall, standing, waiting, but there's no reason to bring them through the hole if there's nothing on the other side. Gibson finds himself in a wide area of sparsely treed ground, flat and open and with a slight up-slope. Too flat, too open, but that doesn't click at first. He's looking for where the track goes next but there isn't any need for a track here—you can go any way you like. Ahead to the right there is a small clump of undergrowth and Gibson wanders that way, looking around, trying to make up his mind what to do. He's made over confident by reports that there are no Charlies within miles of this place. Safe ground. Routine check out.

Ahead, thirty yards away, he sees a mound of hard red earth, about two feet high. He looks at it and frowns. What could have made that? Then he realises there is another nearby, and another, maybe half a dozen in visual range all in a line... There's only one sort of creature could have made those mounds in so precise a geometric pattern... but Gibson doesn't realise that yet. But what he does get is a pungent odour on the air, sharp and distinctive, and when his nose detects that, then he gets the picture.

His next instinctive reaction saves his life. Instead of going back toward the hole to report or escape, he goes forward, leaping like a panther and hitting the deck beside that clump of undergrowth, rolling into the ditch out of which it had sprung. As he does, the five 30cal machine guns, one in each of the bunkers behind those mounds, open up. They blast their evil abrupt chatter, and worse is the whiplash sound of the bright-sparked tracer-rounds as this torrent of gunfire pours straight over the top of him...

... and straight at the blokes on the other side of the bamboo wall. There's the frozen moment of horror as they realise they're in the shit, and then the instantaneous reaction—they scatter. Nigel and Snowy go to ground by the hole; Norris backs off the track and takes cover behind a fallen log and is out of the action; Greyman and Dunshea both dive for a ditch at the base of the bamboo and collide there—unknowingly they have placed themselves right in the line of fire from the bunkers to Gibson's position and will not be able to get their heads up.

A huge gap has opened up along the track between your position and that of Nigel and Snowy, fifty yards away. In your mind a single idea, impressed upon you in all those months of fucking training—if in doubt, go straight up the guts. And away you go, running flat out, from one side of the field of fire to the other. Halfway there, a long strand of barbed bamboo reaches down like a skeletal finger on the hand of God and plucks your hat clean off your head, and there it dangles, prancing like a puppet on a string—for a moment you think of dashing back to get it. It's the sort of shitwit thing that goes through your mind at a time like this. But you keep right on going and the hat dances in midair behind while you slide in like a baseball player, behind Nigel and Snowy, stripping off your pack, ready for action, almost entirely unaware that you have just done the most amazing thing of your life.

In fact your run across the field of fire isn't as brave as it seems. The downslope from the bunker position works against them and the silly fuckers are firing too high. The brilliant lizard tongues of tracers come shattering through the bamboo wall about ten feet up, showering you in a fog of dust and splinters. You're pinned down, but not in any immediate danger, but you don't realise that just yet. The downslope works for Gibson too, flat on his guts and digging-in with his finger and toe nails. They are ripping the foliage above him to shreds but they can't get him unless one of those gunners is prepared to expose himself and stand on tip-toe to get the downward angle required.

Which one of them might have done, had Gibson not started screaming. "Jesus, you blokes! It's fuckin' murder in here. Get me outa here! Get me fuckin' outa here!"

No one troubles to answer him, and he goes on yelling the same thing, over and over, but it does have two effects. It lets the others know he is still alive; and tells them exactly where he is. He is wide; to the right of the line from their position to what is to them the mysterious source of a hell of a lot of shooting. Which gives Snowy a go. He opens up with a long burst from the M60, shooting blind straight into the bamboo wall. His only concern is to miss Gibson, and that he does, until Mabel jams on him.

Snowy goes down on his knees, snapping the breech open in a fury and hurling the belt with the bent round aside savagely.

"Fuck fuck fuck fuck fuck..." he utters as he digs into the jammed shell casing with his razor-sharp bayonet. But his burst has worked—there won't be any Charlies standing on tip-toe to have a go at Gibson after that.

The Charlies are forced to revise their plan. Since they can't get the necessary down-elevation they launch a few grenades, while still keeping up the barrage of 30cal fire from their five gunposts to keep the Australians where they are. The grenades lob into the top of the bamboo wall and the tree canopy above and explode up there, four, five, six of them, like someone belting your eardrums with a hammer. Fragments of godknowswhat fly everywhere... But they're too high up, the rangefinding is bad, and then there's the dud that falls right beside Greyman.

The fire from the 30cals whiplashes overhead, the grenades erupt in the canopy. Gibson is screaming. "Jesus Christ, Nigel, get me outa here!" Snowy working on the breech of the M60. "...Fuck. Fuck. Fuck..." You are bellowing at Nigel. "Come on, Nigel. We gotta get him outa there!"

And in the middle of it all, from the platoon just back down the track, the plaintive voice of Lt Hollingsworth can somehow be clearly heard. "Do you need a medic up there?"

"Nar. Send shit paper!" Nigel retorts.

You have to laugh, you can't help it. Maybe it's some sort of hysteria arising from sheer panic, but you're on you knees, doubled up, giggling and burbling. And Snowy too bows his head over the jammed breech, his frenzied repairs abandoned to mirth. Nigel looks pretty pleased with himself. Gibson has heard it too, stops screaming for help and lies being steadily blanketed under a heap of leaves and branches, his face buried in his hands, chuckling madly. Back at company, they are all shaking their heads and guffawing away. Had the Viet Cong gunners been able to understand it, they probably would have been laughing too. He's like that, Nigel. Perfect comic timing.

Then the moment is gone and it's back to business. Gibson is screaming again. "Will ya stop cracking fuckin' jokes and get me fuckin' outa here! It's fuckin' murder in here!"

"Come on, Nigel," you are yelling. "We gotta get him out!"

Naughton knows it. "Okay, you guys, come on! Let's go! Straight up the guts!"

Snowy is still frantically prising at the jammed shell, with his bayonet now, and he digs it out, slaps in the new belt, slams down the breech...but it all takes too long. You've launched your way forward and you go right past him and down on all fours into the hole. You scramble madly, barbs tear your shirt and your skin but you pay it no heed, grunting like the wild pig that made this hole, clawing your way through. You hear Snowy behind you, dragging the gun, growling like a tiger, and the others are coming too now, Greyman has barrelled out of the box he was in with a tribal roar and Dunshea is right with him, and Bugsy too—heads down, showered by splinters from the ongoing barrage, all queuing behind Nigel to get into that hole.

You come up on the other side, the open ground, get on your

knees and start firing wildly until Snowy is there beside you, and opens up with Mabel. That'll keep 'em down, and you go. You're guided by Gibson's continued screaming, running flat out across the ground, pumping off the remaining rounds in your mag as you go. You hit the deck rolling, tumble again, and come up beside Gibson who is almost completely buried in a carpet of shattered leaves and branches.

"G'day, Gibbo. Havin' a bit of trouble?"

He looks at you blankly, and then pure joy spreads over his freckled and mud-splattered face. Plainly he's never been so happy to see anyone in his entire life.

"Jesus, Yogi. What took yer so fuckin' long?"

The rest of them are through and deploying, but you realise the incoming fire has stopped. They've gone. They've seen you giving them the fuckin' charge and reckoned there must be hundreds of you, instead of just this six man patrol, and they've pissed off quicksmart. Nigel rushes one of the bunkers and lobs in a grenade, and then another and does it again, but there is no longer anyone at home.

"Okay, you guys, cool it," Nigel says. "Stay where you are."

And he looks at you. "How far did we come?"

"Hundred and twenty-seven paces," you somehow miraculously remember. What silly things brains are!

Nigel grins and turns to the others. "Alby, go back and guide the platoon into here. Rest of you, spread out and hold ground."

You lie beside Gibson, a man at the bottom of a compost heap.

"Jesus, look at this place," he says grimly.

Everything, trees, bushes, bamboo, is shorn off at a height of about three feet. The wood is completely splintered and the whole lot dumped on Gibson—like a kid's game in the heaps of autumn leaves. Next day the newspapers back in Aussie will have his picture and tell how he was trapped under a tree trunk that fell on him—all bullshit as newspaper accounts usually are. There's nothing left of this mess that anyone would call a tree trunk—it's just a tangle of mangled and splintered foliage. You haul him out. Both of you are a little weak at the knees.

The rest of the platoon comes up, men hack the bamboo wall to increase the size of the hole, and they pass by you and the bunkers and check the place out. The platoon commander, Holly, is amazed by what he sees. He calls up the Company. He calls down airstrikes and artillery on the far side of the camp. The Company arrives, and Hatrack is all the more astonished, and calls in the Battalion, Engineers, Intelligence and more airstrikes.

The reports come back. The camp is huge—large enough to harbour a thousand people. They are finding caches of food and weapons, documents and equipment. It seems they were all at home when Naughton's section hit them and went running out the other side of the camp; men, women and children, fleeing into the jungle where now the Phantoms and B-52's are pounding the living daylights out of them. Poor bastards. Five or so men stayed behind to man the 30cals and keep the attackers at bay until they got clear. They were never really trying to hit anyone, they were just trying to slow them down. There were no blood trails—nobody got hurt. There were no officers present—nobody got any medals.

Months later the ARVN found a mass grave in the area beyond the camp, presumed to hold the victims of the airstrikes that befell them as they fled the camp that day. There were conflicting reports as to the number of bodies—between fifty and two hundred and fifty. No one confirmed it. No one bothered to try. It was already ancient history. In the grave there were women and children and well as men—nobody knew what to think about that and so didn't think anything.

You'll never to do anything half so brave again, if brave was what it was. They left your hat dangling from that overhanging bamboo runner as a sort of shrine to what took place that day—maybe its still there. It's not the sort of place people go to often. That was why the camp probably thought itself safe.

An hour later you and the others sat leaning on a tree trunk, still shaking, soaked in sweat, smoking. It was the fifth cigarette of your life, all of them lit of the end of the previous one. Owen Gibson came by and grinned at Greyman Goolie. "Hey Greyman," he calls. "If you want the forward scout job from now on, it's yours."

"No thanks, mate. Somehow I seem to have gone right off the idea. You're better than me anyway."

It really hurts Greyman to say it, but he's gotta, and that's that.

"Better at leading us into trouble, maybe," Gibson laughs.

Nigel sees the need to pass judgement. "But you knew they were there, Gibbo. That's what matters."

"Yeah," Gibson says, headbowed with a humility that probably isn't false. "It was when I smelled `em. That's when I knew."

Nigel laughs. "Then it's your nose I want up front, so you can keep on sniffin' `em out for us."

Maybe it was a massacre, maybe it was a great victory, maybe it was a trivial skirmish in which no one got hurt. No one could ever tell. There's a painting purporting to depict *The Broken Hill Contact* in the Canberra War Museum, but really it doesn't give too clear an impression of what happened. Books on Australia's involvement in Vietnam see no reason to mention the incident; there was no bodycount so nobody cared. For them the only tangible evidence that it ever happened was that thereafter Owen Gibson was renamed *Sniffer*, and the only part of the whole damned thing to make its way into military history was Nigel Naughton's immortal joke.

"Do you need a medic up there?"

"Nar. Send shit paper!"

"Private Gibson. Do you want to go to Vietnam?"

"Dunno."

"You ought to have made up your mind by now, Private."

"Haven't."

"Any reason why you shouldn't go?"

"None that I can think of."

"Then you might as well go, don't you think?"

"I s'pose."

"Sign the Affirmation, please."

The Chi-com Man

Five miles east of Nui Dat was a hill formation that appeared on the map in the rough shape of a horseshoe and so, unremarkably, it was called The Horseshoe. This imaginative name was matched by that of Nui Dat itself, which had been mistaken on the maps by the wise masters at Task Force as the name of the location, when in fact it merely indicated an unnamed hill—Nui Dat meant 'hill of dirt'. At The Horseshoe, Task Force had established a permanent Secondary Fire Support Base, with the notion that the artillery of each base was at the ideal range to cover the other.

Now there was a new plan. The Great Minds considered the Long Hai mountains, lying southeast of both bases, which they assured everyone was the headquarters of Viet Cong operations in the Province. All other terrain in the region was flat and dotted with villages except to the north where it was mountainous and difficult and thinly populated. The idea was that a barrier should be made running due south from The Horseshoe to Phouc Hai, a village on the coast eleven miles away, and so limit the ability of the Viet Cong to move from their stronghold in the Long Hai mountains to points west, including Vung Tau, Saigon, and even Nui Dat itself.

The barrier consisted of two parallel barbed wire fences and entanglements running a good drop-punt apart for the whole distance, straight as an arrow through the countryside, the ground between completely cleared and patrolled from the sky by spotter aircraft. Between the fences antipersonnel mines were planted like cabbages in rows one yard apart, twenty to a row and all linked by trip wires -these could be exploded either by the trip or being stood on. Then, to prevent the Viet Cong from digging the mines up and replanting them elsewhere, each mine was set on top of a hand grenade with the pin removed, so that if anyone dug up the mine, the moment they lifted it from the ground, the grenade beneath would fire and the whole caboodle explode in their faces.

There were several problems with this grand concept. The first was that such a minefield was extremely difficult to lay, and very expensive-some 60,000 mines with their trip wires and grenades had to be planted by the Sappers, no small task, especially since the slightest mistake could prove disastrous. And it did. Frequently during their assignment, there was an explosive accident-some poor sap of a Sapper would forget where he was and step backwards, or tighten the wrong trip wire, or just get a little fit of the fumbles when priming the grenade, and whamo!-scratch one Sapper. One day a dog got in and ran amok, setting off dozens of mines which it survived because it ran low and fast but four men were wounded by the shrapnel. The Sappers were losing about one man dead and a couple wounded a week, but still the mad construction continued undeterred.

Now, Delta Company of the Pig Battalion, had been rostered for ten days to guard those unfortunates as they laid that minefield, and all the time the men of Porky Delta wondered if the Charlie could ever have dreamed of wreaking such destruction upon the Sappers as did their own commanders. But there were other things to wonder at as well.

If you weren't a Sapper and inside the wire being blown up on a regular basis, this job was really the safest in the world. The immediate terrain was flat and wide open, with just the terraces of rice paddies and some low scrub and the moon was full and the sky clear. Safest place in the world. That was what you were thinking, that night, out on picket while the rest of them slept. You were wide awake—you would have sworn to it. You remembered it plain as day... except it was the middle of the night. In the day the Australians controlled the Phouc Tuy Province, but at night they crept back within their perimeters and it was theirs.

You sat with your back against a tree, rifle across your knees. Thirty metres out in front of you were a couple of Claymore mines, the plungers for which hung dangling by their cables over a branch beside you—even in total darkness, a sweep of your hand would gather them up. Claymores are a tin of metal shrapnel backed with a strip of PE (plastic explosive) enclosed in a tight case about the size of an average book. You stand them on little retractable legs for stability and detonators are plugged into the PE. After that, it's no different to the method the baddies use in Western movies to blow up trains on trestle bridges; you run connecting wires back to a safe distance where the mine is exploded by a hand plunger. Anyone within twenty metres cops a rain of scrap metal. It is rather like being shot from close range by a giant shotgun with a six inch bore and pellets the size of peas. Of course, this being a war of escalation, the Viet Cong had their own version of this weapon, called the Chi-com mine.

You could only imagine how it went, but your imagining would haunt you for years afterward, as vividly as if you had seen it all. While you sat there, peering into the soft moonlight, listening and watching for any trace of movement, the very thing you were listening and watching for so intently was closing in on you. You didn't see him, didn't hear him; your 'sixth sense' early warning system failed completely. You had no idea that you were not alone, but the visitor knew you were there.

He probably watched for a long time, to judge how alert you were. He probably smiled as he decided to proceed. He was just twenty feet away, staying on a line close to you rather than distant, so that he would know the moment you detected his presence-know when to abandon his plan and run. But you never detected him and he moved on by, careful with each step to ensure that his bare feet avoided dead twigs that would crackle and give him away, moving through the foliage without allowing a single leaf to scrape against another. He had to move bent over, keeping below the line of the scrub, and would have carried a heavy shoulder-bag, all of which made his task so much more difficult, but his powers of concentration must have been incredible. He would have gone painfully slow, and entered their camp, alone, in the dark, anxious and afraid, but never hurrying.

He closed in on Nigel first. Probably he could have cut the corporal's throat while he slept but his plan was more ambitious than that. Instead he planted a Chi-com mine, no doubt with detonators and wires already fitted, just one inch from Nigel's nose. Then, trailing the thin wire cable, he moved wide to the next position, ten yards away. There Bugsy was minding Mabel for Snowy—and wider, Sniffer, snoring fitfully. Perhaps Sniffer stirred in his sleep, dreaming of Wendy Titmus, and the little man had to squat there, still and silent, for several minutes, waiting for the dreamer to settle again. He then placed a second Chi-com neatly between those slumbering forms and now trailed a second wire. His risks were increasing. Those trailing wires could catch anywhere, touch people, make noise, but still he went for a third target. He found bedding and gear in a heap and assumed there was a man sleeping in there somewhere, and placed the third Chi-com directly in line with the head.

Chi-com, the standard abbreviation of Chinese Communist, referred specifically to a particular type of anti-personnel mine-a more primitive version of the Yankee Claymores. Based on the Russian POMZ-2 stake mine, it is round with a grenade-like shrapnel skin about a PE core and has a spike at the bottom that you push into the ground. At the top a ring pin prevents the striker from hitting the percussion cap and it only needs a 10kg tug on the wire to remove that pin.

This then was his next task. Running out those three strands of light wire without applying too much pressure nor allowing them to tangle. He had to return the way he had come in, again right past your sentry position, every footstep placed in exactly the same place as before to avoid any surprises. He went by you and out into the scrub to the extent of his shortest cable and there stopped, squatting, took up the slack on the other two wires, and then jerked them in rapid succession. And ran like hell...

The sudden explosion floored all your senses, and the rest of you as well: the shockwave hit you in the middle of the back like a fist. You bounced back onto your knees, looking everyfuckingwhichway. Went off right behind you, but you couldn't make out what was fuckin' happening. Too close to be the minefield. Artillery dropshort? Enemy mortars? Yankee airstrike? None of those. You'd have heard the incoming shells whistle, or else the departing aircraft. Whatever it was on the ground, and right here somewhere! You jumped to a squatting position, muttering incoherently to yourself, trying to talk your panic under control. There had to be something out there to be heard, if only you could bring your erratic heartbeat and frantic breathing under control and stop that bloody ringing in your ears.

You liked to imagine you heard someone out there, running away in the scrub, but really there was nothing that distinct. Still it was enough. You grabbed the first Claymore plunger and pressed it. Nothing happened! You grabbed the second plunger-twenty yards too far to the right but what the fuck-and pressed it. The explosion joined the echo of the first one, stalking away into the night, the shrapnel whipping through the scrub, but too late, and too wide, you knew. Wasted effort, but you felt a bloody lot better for it.

Then Bugsy screamed:

"Chi-com-nnn!!!"

And there were people going in every direction in the darkness. Wider, Sniffer was on his feet and running:

"Look out, she's goin' this way," and he threw the dark object deep into the scrub.

"One here too," Nigel said coolly. Carefully, he unscrewed

the plug and removed the detonator.

You shook your head, baffled by all this unexpected activity.

"Yogi!" Nigel roared at him, "What the fuck's going on?"

It took a little while to figure that one out, but once figured out it became an indelible memory. He had come out of nowhere, insidious as the night itself, soundless, assured, like the invisible monster in The Forbidden Planet. The only trouble was that he was not the workings of the imagination nor the Id. He was fuckin' real!

If there is something good to be said about Chi-com mines, it is that they are very inefficient—even worse than the Claymores of which only about half work. This time he was unlucky. Only one of the three went off, and that the one well placed to blow your worldly goods, but not your person, to kingdom come.

"I was awake I fuckin' tell you," you tried hopelessly to convince everyone in turn. They all scowled at you.

"I don't doubt it, Yogi," Nigel said, the way he said things when he didn't believe a word of what he heard.

"Jesus. I've shit meself," Greyman uttered. He had too. Even that seemed to be your fuckin' fault.

"I didn't hear a bloody thing. He came right in here. Right past me. And I heard fuckin' nuthin!"

Nigel was holding one of the dud Chi-coms, looking it over ruefully: "His equipment isn't worthy of him. If one of these others had functioned, we'd all be on parade in JC's basement right now."

"The one that did blew your bedding to the shithouse, Yogi," Bugsy wanted to remind you—really he was babbling hysterically, as everyone all was.

They sat around, in the darkness, talking about it, trying to understand—each of them just the lighted end of a cigarette in the blackness, quivering like fireflies.

"I've heard of this guy," Nigel said, "The Chi-com Man. He's been sneaking into Yankee bases and planting these things for quite some time."

"Yeah," Snowy observed, "But getting into Yank bases is easy. Knocking us off is a fuckin' lot harder."

They were talking far too loudly for the blast had rendered them all deaf but nobody cared about security anymore.

"This bloke was just twenty feet away from me," you were still saying, still shaking your head in disbelief, "And I heard nuthin!"

"Two fuckin' duds outa three. A bloke oughta buy a ticket in

Tatts," Sniffer muttered.

"Maybe there's more than one of them," Greyman proposed,

"Maybe they're breedin' whole bunches of Charlies that can do this sort of stuff."

"I'd prefer to believe there's just one, if you don't mind," Nigel said with a chilled shiver.

And still the enormity of it all would not take hold. Still they floundered to grasp what the evidence made all too plain.

"I'm telling you, Nigel," Sniffer said finally, "If the fuckin' opposition's really this good, I don't wanna play anymore."

Within a few months of its completion, the Phouc Hai minefield was stripped of its mines by Charlie working at night; the only effect of the little surprise underneath was that they got a perfectly good hand grenade as well as a mine. They replanted the mines all over the province and for the next five years Australian soldiers stepped on them with great regularity—the greatest proportion of all subsequent Australian casualties resulted from those replanted mines. Perhaps though, the worst insult was that, within a year, the local villagers were using as vegie patches that land between the remnants of barbed wire fences that had been so thoughtfully cleared for them by the Royal Australian Corps of Engineers.

"CSM Doyle, do you want to go to Vietnam?"
"Yes Sir!"
"Very good, CSM. Sign the Affirmation please."
"What? I already volunteered, sir. Why do I need to sign?"
"To prove that you volunteered, CSM."
"Good grief."

Ninety Percenters Revisited

It was mere coincidence that caused Tiger Braddock to travel with them all the way to Vietnam. Slowly over the year the faces changed as the conscripts were dispersed from 2RTB to army units all over the nation, their officers and sergeants and instructors returned to the various units from which they had been seconded. As what would become the Pig Battalion began to form from scratch at Puckapunyal, there were a small bunch of them who never went anywhere and it seemed that the Battalion formed itself around them. Snowy Spargo, Sniffer Gibson, Tiger Braddock and Griffin. All the others had 'blown in on subsequent drafts' as Tiger put it. Holly had arrived fresh from Duntroon to take over the platoon from Tiger, Nigel Naughton transferred in from a clerical unit and Hatrack, of course, had risen up from Hell itself. But those four originals—Snowy, Gibson, Tiger and Griffin—had been there all along. They were never friends particularly, but there was some affinity between them which none of them would have dared to attempt to explain. Somehow that seemed important later on.

It was a simple incident really. They were on their third operation in Vietnam and Holly halted the platoon on the low ridge—the area was declared clear but they were short of water and the map said there was a creek in the gully right below them. Tiger Braddock, as platoon sergeant, was responsible for selecting a detail to collect the water bottles and take them down to be refilled. Griffin and Greyman went with him, each with twenty bottles on a cord slung over their shoulders. They scrambled down the steep slope and found the creek, trickling in its yellow murkiness through the jungle. Shit water, but better than none—there were decontamination pills they could drop in each bottle. They'd almost finished when the shooting started—it was away to the flank, further up the ridge.

Three Charlies had been following the platoon all day and, failing to notice their objective had halted, had run into the tail section. Shots had been exchanged but all three Charlies escaped, no doubt determined to remember next time that the Uc Dai Loi were inclined to stop for ten minutes every hour for a smoke-o.

Down at the creek, they heard the shots, a fair distance away and for sure not coming in their direction, but that didn't mean it didn't scare shit out of them. Greyman fell in the creek with astonishment and Griffin dived for cover and nearly strangled himself on the bottle cord before he got hold of his rifle and into a firing position. One second later they realised there was no immediate danger and Greyman started chuckling at their foolishness, but Griffin wasn't amused. He was nearest Tiger and saw what he did—Tiger ditched the water bottles, threw away his weapon and ran for his fucking life.

They went after him and found him wedged in under an overhang, eyes bursting from their sockets, mouth fixed open, froth at the corners.

"Take it easy, Tiger. It's okay."

But it wasn't okay, not for some time. They lead him over to the water and chucked him in to try and revive him from the shock, and he finally lay, saturated and panting, flat on his back, sightless eyes staring at the heavens.

They discussed it.

"He's fucked," Griffin said.

"Maybe he'll come good in a minute," Greyman hoped.

"He's fucked," Griffin repeated.

There was no way they could carry him up that rugged hill. In the hope that he might recover shortly, they filled the remaining bottles, found his Armalite, stood him up, slung weapon and bottles over his shoulders and tried to encourage him to climb the slope with them. Gradually, Tiger seemed to comprehend what they were doing, but his body refused to respond. Only with a mighty act of will did he force himself to climb, but even then they needed to drag him much of the way. Finally, they encountered a patrol sent down to see what had happened to them.

"He fell," Greyman said. "Hurt himself."

The presence of other men stirred something in Tiger Braddock's pride and he finally got his legs under him and working properly and by the time they regained the ridgeline, Tiger was his old self and it was as if nothing had happened. But something had happened. Griffin and Greyman took themselves aside and spoke in whispers, observed by a suspicious Nigel Naughton. Greyman's tribal heritage assured him that you never spoke badly of another man, but Griffin's urban childhood offered no impediment to dobbing others in.

"Just let what happens happen," Greyman whispered.

"Can't do that," Griffin grunted. "They gotta be told."

"Then that's what happens," Greyman said.

Griffin told Nigel what he had seen. Snowy Spargo and

Sniffer Gibson, because of that strange affinity, were let into it too. It posed a very special dilemma for them. In the end, when the platoon took up its overnight position, they sought Tiger out and stood around him.

"What happened, Tiger?" Nigel said coldly.

"Happened?" Tiger grinned incredulously. "What do you mean, what happened?"

"You know what we mean."

"No I don't."

"You shat yourself, Tiger."

"Bullshit. Who says so?"

"I say so," Griffin uttered.

"You always were a dickhead, Yogi. You imagined it."

"Greyman saw it too."

"Greyman saw fuckin' nothin'."

"That's right," Greyman said. "I saw nothing."

"Then it's up to you, Yogi," Nigel said grimly. "I'll take it higher if you want,"

"No. Maybe he'll be okay next time."

"What are you fuckin' blokes on about?" Tiger protested.

"Let's just forget it, for now," Nigel decided.

"What do you mean, for now..." Tiger asked.

Snowy Spargo simply clicked the safety catch of his weapon off, and then on. In the still night, it could not have been more resounding.

Back at Nui Dat, Tiger Braddock, the terror of 2RTB, hero of Malaya, took to his hoochie and consoled himself with two bottles of Johnny Walker a day. He reported to the RAP with various complaints and although they found nothing wrong with him, they gave him chits for light duties.

"What do you think went wrong?" Greyman asked Nigel.

"You ever seen his back?" Nigel answered.

"Once, I walked in on him in the shower..."

"Then you know why he never takes his shirt off, and always showers alone."

"Yeah. Fucking horrible."

"Bones mend. Skin heals, or gets stuck back on by plastic surgeons. But you never recover from wounds like that."

"But if his nerve was gone, what's he doing here?"

"I guess he didn't know it himself, until yesterday."

Every morning at first light, the platoon was tumbled from its bunks and lined up outside Tiger's hoochie for their daily anti-malaria pill—but Nigel took over even that minor duty, as he did all Tiger's other duties. Lt Hollingsworth, who occupied the hoochie next door, could hardly fail to notice these things and several times entered Tiger's hoochie to offer him lectures on the evils of alcohol but the subject paid him no heed. He asked Nigel what was happening, and was told, as everyone else was, that nothing was happening. Still, when they went out on their next operation, Holly had the sense to leave Tiger Braddock behind.

Whenever they went out on operations—which was most of the time—the company left ten men behind to man the base perimeter: the sick and injured and any men going to or from leave and then, if that was an insufficient number, others on a rostered basis. Rear Party duty was a privilege jealously observed. Even Platoon Sergeants could be left behind for one operation, but two in a row was more difficult to manage.

Tiger Braddock saw Nigel Naughton passing on his way to the shower, wearing only a small towel about his waist. There was no one else about—the boozer had been open for an hour. Tiger took the opportunity. "Corporal Naughton—a moment please."

Ordinarily some sort of protest might have been expected—this time there was none. Nigel diverted and entered Tiger's hoochie without comment. In there, he could smell the whisky and the staleness of constant occupation for two weeks. Tiger Braddock never left his hoochie, not even to attend the Sergeant's Mess. He lived off rations cooked on the hexamine stove on the floor.

"Yes Sergeant?"

Nigel stood at the entrance, allowing the evening light in. To Tiger it was virtually blinding and he stood with his back turned.

"Have you prepared the picket rosters for tonight, Corporal?"

"Yes, sarge."

"All right. Thanks for helping out, Corporal. I'll take over now."

But even as he said it, he weaved unsteadily and had to sit down on the bunk. Sweat dripped from his brow and chin to the floor and he was quivering all over.

"No good, Tiger," Nigel said.

"I have to," Tiger croaked. "Holly has ordered me out on the next operation."

"Don't go."

"Maybe it will be alright..."

"You know it won't."

"Jesus, Nigel. Help me. What can I do to put it right?"

"Get a transfer, Tiger. Somewhere safe. I'll get the papers for you."

"I can't do it. I can't just walk away. If I do, they'll all know..."

"You can't stay holed up here forever, Tiger."

"Just one more op, Nigel. Just to see how I go. You can be platoon sergeant. I'll take over your section. That way, Griffin and Gibson and Spargo can watch how I go..."

"I can't ask men to risk their lives like that. You know that."

"They're tough. They can handle it."

"I'd be setting up a situation where they'd have to shoot you if it went wrong, Tiger. I can't ask them to do that either."

"Suggest it to them. They know me."

"No. I won't even do that. It's just far too risky. I'll get you those papers, Tiger. That's all I can do."

The transfer papers were prepared—there was little difficulty convincing Holly to sign, but Hatrack knocked it back.

"Too good a man to lose," was the reason.

On the morning of the next operation, Tiger Braddock was irretrievably drunk and they left him behind again.

"Are you going to tell me what's really going on?" Holly asked Nigel.

"No," Nigel answered. "If I do, you'll have to do something about it, and whatever you do will be regrettable. Better we just say Sergeant Braddock is ill."

The third operation loomed—one predicted to be more complex and difficult than those that went before. Tiger Braddock made his way over to the OR's mess and sat down in the midst of Nigel Naughton's section. Naughton himself was not there, busy with acting-sergeant's duties.

"I want a word with you blokes," Tiger Braddock said.

He was ghostly pale and shaking.

"Good to see you up and around, Sarge," Norris joked. No one laughed. Everyone except the three—Gibson, Snowy and Griffin, got up and moved away out of earshot. They knew there were things that it was better to know nothing of.

The three conscripts looked at this man that they had both feared and loved, and could barely see anything recognisable. They remembered his words though—this, they knew, was doing it *the very fucking hard way*.

"What happens," Tiger asked them. "if I go out on the next op?"

"You won't come back," Griffin said.

"The Americans have a word for it. It's called 'fragging'," Sniffer added.

"You know it has to be that way," Snowy said.

Tiger Braddock knew it—even so, he was desperate enough to plead. "Come on, you guys. Give me a break. We've been through a lot together. There's got to be some way."

They thought about it. Finally, Snowy spoke without consulting the others. "Maybe there is. You tell everyone in the company exactly what happened. Admit everything. That way, if there's a contact and some bloke has to shoot you, he won't have any doubts that he's doing the right thing."

"I can't do *that*."

"It's the only way I can think of, Tiger."

"And what happens if I just go."

"*You* will be the first contact."

The day before the operation was a shit-kicking day at Delta Company. Hatrack had arranged his hoochie with the flaps rolled up so that he could sit at his desk and survey the entire area. He saw the men working all about him. The major project was a huge drainage hole, twenty feet deep, being dug by Corporal Naughton's section beside the toilet block. Other men were sandbagging hoochies and digging bunkers. Hatrack busied himself with his paperwork, all the more so when he saw the boyish figure of Lt Hollingsworth approach. Lt Hollingsworth, five foot six with his boots on and with no physique whatsoever, wore a pair of ridiculously baggy shorts, but he was all formality when he stomped into the tent, flashing a precise salute and stamping to attention.

"Good afternoon, sir." All very Duntroonish.

Hatrack was so unused to being saluted these days that he almost forgot to return it. Then he left Hollingsworth standing for a moment, finishing off notating some document.

"At Ease, Lieutenant. How is the work going in your area?"

"They'll have that drainage hole completed by tonight, sir, and will have begun filling it with stones and gravel."

"Very good, Lieutenant. I'll come around for an inspection shortly."

Hatrack went back to his papers, obviously hoping the interview was over. It wasn't.

"Er...sir?"

"Yes, Lieutenant, what is it?"

"A rather difficult matter, sir. A serious problem, in fact."

Hatrack lowered his pen and looked up, waiting.

"It's Sergeant Braddock, sir. He's been worrying me for some time now. I believe he's a very sick man, sir."

"Are you sure he isn't merely annoyed that I refused his transfer to a soft job in Transport?"

"No sir. I believe, with all due respect sir, that the transfer should have been approved."

"I hope you can back that statement up with some facts, Lieutenant."

"I think I can, sir. Mind you, I have nothing against the man personally. In fact I find myself in a very awkward situation."

"I can see that Lieutenant. Go on."

"Well, like I said. He's sick. In no fit condition to handle his duties."

"Perhaps he'll get better, Lieutenant."

"Sir, he is drinking very heavily."

"Everyone here drinks heavily, Lieutenant."

"I had to leave him behind on the last operation because he was too drunk to stand."

"One instance..."

"Corporal Naughton has been carrying out Sergeant Braddock's duties for almost a month, sir."

"Truly? If so, why wasn't this reported sooner?"

"There was the transfer..."

"I doubt that Transport would appreciate us sending them our alcoholics..."

"Sir, I believe that Sergeant Braddock is unable to stand the strain of combat duties. Elsewhere, he may be all right."

"The man has an excellent record. Decorated in Malaya..."

"He was also very badly wounded. I believe that might have had a more serious effect on him than anyone realised."

"I see. And do you consider your opinion expert, Lieutenant?"

"No sir. I just hoped he would settle down. Come good. But he hasn't.

"Are your sure you are not being extreme, Lieutenant."

"No sir. I am not. The man is useless to me. And drinking himself to death. Something must be done."

"That much I agree with, Lieutenant. But a man with Braddock's skills and record must be given every opportunity to prove himself. It is only fair. Take him out on the next operation. See how he performs. I want a full report."

"Sir, I really don't think that is appropriate..."

"I know what you think, Lieutenant, and now you know

what I think. That's all."

"Sir, I really think..."

"Take him out, Lieutenant. That is an order."

At the drainage hole, the men at the top hauling up the buckets of soil saw Holly on his way back. Nigel Naughton climbed the ladder and peered over the mound of red dirt to watch the diminutive platoon commander stride by. Even from a hundred yards away, the expression of anger and frustration could not have been more evident.

"Well, that's it then," Nigel said, and returned to the bottom of the hole.

Operation Ballarat began at dawn next day. Holly, having appraised Braddock of Hatrack's orders the night before, went to the sergeant's hoochie and found him missing altogether. No one would ever find out where he had hidden himself. Griffin had an infected toe and was justifiably left behind, but there was nothing wrong with Snowy Spargo—it wasn't even his turn to be rostered off but Bugsy Norris did not protest.

"If I get killed on this operation, I'll hate you blokes for the rest of my life," he said resignedly.

Sniffer and Snowy had drawn straws, and Snowy won.

Griffin returned to the Delta Company area long after dark on that first night after the Company went out on Operation Ballarat—he had been to the RAP for treatment and stayed on drinking with Ernie Weedman at BHQ. It was a starless, moonless night and the company area was a void of blackness—the base lighting was always minimised when the company was out. He groped his way toward the only source of light he could see, the boozer.

Delta Company boozer—OR's Wet Canteen is the official army expression—was the most rudimentary of places. There was a huge coolroom with an inexhaustible supply of beer that stood inside a shed with a hatch such that one man only could stand in there and collect the money and hand over the cans. Adjoining was a concrete slab with a roof, but no walls, and scattered about were tables and chairs. The one hundred and fifty men of the company could all find a chair, or else stand under the roof if it rained. There was a notice board where messages had to be pinned on the various anatomical appendages of Playboy centrefolds, and a dart board with Hatrack's face at the centre. That was all. Each section had territorially claimed a table and chairs, and on those evenings when the company was in, every square inch of tabletop and much of the ground about was littered with empty beer cans.

But not tonight—tonight everything was neat and tidy and only a few isolated groups of quiet drinkers, all lit by a couple of kerosene lamps hanging from the poles. And stranger still was the four section table which had only two occupants—Snowy Spargo and Tiger Braddock.

"Hey Griffin, come here and wrap yer piss flaps around this," Snowy called as he slapped a can of beer into Griffin's hand. Griffin almost fumbled it, so busy was he staring at Tiger Braddock.

"What's he doing here?"

"Just havin a drink wif me old mates, Snowy and Griffin..." Braddock snorted.

There were all sorts of regulations and traditions that forbade Sergeants and Officers from drinking in the OR's boozer.

"He's my guest," Snowy explained blearily. "It's okay. Sit down."

Tiger was thumping the table with his empty can—and then Griffin saw that the top had been cut away to allow it to serve as a glass. Into this, Snowy was pouring straight scotch.

Tiger Braddock took a great gulp, wiped his mouth with the back of his hand, and then leaned toward Griffin as if drawing him into a conspiracy. His breath at that range seemed highly flammable.

"The soldier is the most fundamental form of man," Braddock said so unexpectedly that both listeners sat back in astonishment. "Right from the fuckin' start, Man the hunter-killer, stalking his prey in the jungle. Maybe these days it's M60s and slant-eyed nig-nogs instead of clubs and stones against woolly mammoths but the principle is the same. Them civvies with their soft lives have forgotten where they came from, and they all wonder why they have heart attacks and ulcers, but the soldiers, the soldier is man instinctual, man natural, the essence of man.

"But the weak civvies have taken over, dominated by their naggin' wimmen's mad craving for comfort, and they've become a disease, a plague, a syphilis of the Earth that eats away the good and leaves only rot and evil and corruption. He kills off all the other animals and puts men and more men in their place. He cuts down trees and replaces them with his own stark concrete structures that corrupt the very dirt on which they stand. His cities spread like an ugly rash and devour all that is beautiful in the world. And yet they reckon war is bad because it kills off men. Wimmen talk. Men are meant to die fighting, to die hunting. That is their destiny. And war is man's ultimate creation, ultimate glory."

The oration ended as abruptly as it began.

"I gotta have a piss," Braddock said as a footnote.

Snowy and Griffin watched as he thumped and stumbled his way out into the blackness.

"What the hell is he doing here?" Griffin immediately demanded.

"I invited him," Snowy said sublimely. "You know he gets this boozed every night, except that usually he does it flaked out on his bunk. I thought he'd like a change of scenery."

"You know the shit will really hit the fan if the Staff Sergeant finds him here in this condition."

"The shit is already in the fan, mate, and nobody gives a fuck what Staff-sergeant Modlin or anyone else thinks about it. Get with it, Griffin. You know the score."

Griffin knew the score—he just couldn't see how it was going to be worked out, but even as he pondered it, scowling at Snowy Spargo's jubilant grin, there came the sound that signalled the next stage. Out there, there was some swearing and cursing and the unmistakable sound of Tiger Braddock taking a fall.

"Right, let's go," Snowy said, pocketing the whisky bottle, grabbing his own torch and thrusting Tiger's into Griffin's hands.

They went out into the darkness and found Braddock down and baffled by the task of buttoning his fly and trying to stand simultaneously. Roughly they pulled him to his feet.

"Come on, sarge, time to go."

"Go? Go where?"

"Back to your hoochie to finish the bottle, of course."

"I like it better in the boozer..."

"Boozer's closed, Tiger. Come on, follow us."

Torches flashing in the darkness, they made their way along the road toward the Delta Company lines, Tiger Braddock reeling along behind.

"Hey fellas, wait for me."

"Come on, sarge. Just follow the lights."

Several times he fell and they had to wait for him to pick himself up, but as they neared the shower block, Snowy went back to help him.

"Here you go, Tiger. Not far now."

Griffin noticed that he shone the beam of the powerful torch right in Tiger Braddock's eyes.

"Right, come on, this way."

But he did not go toward Griffin—instead Snowy went wide, around the far side of that huge drainage hole they had so laboriously excavated, and then stopped on the far side.

"Griffin. Get beside me, quick."

Griffin did as he was told, and they stood together with the chasm between them and the staggering sergeant.

"Keep the beam off the ground," Snowy said and then called. "Come on, Tiger. Head straight for the lights."

Blinded, drunken Tiger Braddock groped his way forward, past the mounds of soil removed from the hole, past the temporary wire safety fence that Snowy must have removed earlier, and then came the stumble and the gasp, and Griffin had only a glimpse of a gaping mouth and bulging eyes as Tiger vanished down the hole, ending with a heavy thump on the stones in the bottom.

"Jesus, you've killed him," Griffin gasped.

"I hope not," Snowy Spargo murmured.

As if in reply, a feeble voice arose piteously out of the earth:

"Gawd Jesus Christ, I've broke me fuckin' leg!"

The break proved to be perfect, just half way between knee and ankle—had it been only meat damage they might have patched him up in Vung Tau hospital and sent him back to Delta Company. The break meant he would be going home. The story was that he had lost his way and fallen down the hole in a drunken stupor. It was a totally unbelievable story that everyone believed without question. Even Tiger Braddock believed it, they were told. They never saw him again.

Hatrack did not believe it. He stood the whole platoon in a line next morning, shaking his craggy head in horror and glaring at them with his gunmetal eyes.

"You men aren't fooling me," he said harshly.

No one moved or answered. They just glared right back at him, and he couldn't think of anything else to say. Maybe they didn't fool him but there was nothing he could do about it, and he knew it, and they knew it. The look he gave them said he would never forgive them for that, but that was okay. They would never forgive him either.

"Sergeant Braddock! Do you want to go to Vietnam?"
"Not another war, is it sir?"
"Yes sergeant. I see you've done service in Korea and Malaya."
"Yes sir."

"Man of your experience, sergeant. Good record. Another tour of duty could well see you right to apply for a commission."

"I should bloodywell hope so, sir."

"Thank you, sergeant. Sign the Affirmation please."

The Chi-com Man's Last Stand

All through the night, Fire Support Base Cactus Jack flamed and thundered. From more than a dozen points on the far side of the perimeter, the 50 cals and M60's yammered away incessantly, while artillerymen pumped shells and mortars off into the night at a furious rate, blasting them high in the sky to come whistling down again at what must have been minimum range. Then a pause and the choppers would return refuelled and rearmed, the slim Huey Cobras streaking through one after the other with their rocket assaults, lighting up the sky with red daylight. The glare of the fires over there cast giant shadows on this side of the base, stretching and flickering as the red balls of explosive fires bounced upward to immediately dissolve into the acrid fog of the smokefilled night. At one point, Phantoms seared the sky deafeningly, dropping napalm frighteningly close—not the sort of thing you wanted to think about too deeply when the night was dark and nasty little mistakes were all the more justifiable. And still hour upon hour, the gunners blazed away and their artillery thumped and roared. The earth shook under you and your ears rang to the point of pain and the eyes were dazzled by the flashes to near blindness. The men of Delta Company of the Pig Battalion sat on the edges of their holes on this side of the base and muttered their disgust.

"Silly fuckin' cocksuckers," you grumbled.

It started up just after dark and carried on unceasingly until way after midnight, and although it might have sounded like the entirety of Ho's hordes were descending upon Cactus Jack all at once, you found it hard to be concerned. Although temporary, FSB Cactus Jack was about twice the size of Nui Dat and vastly better equipped and over populated, and after all, they were fuckin' Americans who like to be noisy about everything and anyway, it was all happening on the far side of the base, half a mile away over the low ridgeline. And finally explorations of the surrounding jungles had made it pretty clear to you that if there was an enemy force in the area, it could not have been particularly large. Certainly, there was nothing happening on this side of the base, except a whole bunch of dreaded Uc Dai Loi losing a full night's sleep and becoming exceedingly grumpy about that.

From time to time, Nigel came down the line with nothing to report and they all grumbled at him:

"We're gonna spend a few quiet days resting in this Yank fire support base, you said," Snowy moaned.

"They'll be movies every night and free booze and colour television, you said," Alby Dunshea complained.

"And real food cooked in real kitchens and women to do our washing and real beds in real barracks with walls and floors, you said," Sniffer protested.

"Well, you've fuckin' got all that, haven't you?" Nigel responded.

"You didn't tell us we wouldn't be able to get any fuckin' sleep with all that fuckin' racket going on over there!" Greyman savaged.

"Ah! You've noticed, then, that our American friends are in contact on the far side of the base."

"Are they?" you cried, "I thought it was the fuckin' Fourth of July."

This then was what came of getting to play with the Yankees in the so-called big time. They established this massive base for just three weeks to support a major drive against the enemy and The Pigs were invited to fill a gap in the perimeter and run ambush patrols outside the wire. Unfortunately, someone had forgotten to invite the Viet Cong, and ultimately the whole shebang would be abandoned as a total failure, but then, most operations were. When The Pigs arrived at Cactus Jack and saw for themselves the equipment and facilities that the Yanks had and they didn't, they could have cried.

It wasn't just the luxury items. Cactus Jack was like a small city, with bulldozers and graders making roads about solid buildings that housed their colour TV's and pinball machines and pool tables and proper beds. They had bricklayers to build fortifications and even a machine that filled and stacked sandbags. While you toiled with shovels to dig-in to four feet, they did the same in minutes with a few sweeps of their mechanical trench-digger. They even had a tractor-towed vehicle for laying barbed wire. At Nui Dat the water was supplied in jerry cans or collected as run-off from the hoochies; here they sank a bore and laid plumbing and all they had to do was turn on a tap—or faucet, as they called it.

"I wouldn't want my blokes getting too used to this sort of thing," Hatrack was reported to have said.

The Yanks tried to be friendly. They offered their machines to dig your holes, they offered cooked food, movies, inflatable mattresses and beer.

"One can per man," Hatrack ordered.

It was awful Yank beer anyway, weak as piss, and you drank it with distaste and felt utterly contaminated.

You didn't like it there. Inside the base the Yanks employed large numbers of Noggies for their domestic chores—at Nui Dat such slackness was not countenanced. Didn't anyone tell them that they were fighting against the masters of infiltration? They moved about the base unarmed—doubtless they had firearms somewhere but could laugh at the Aussies who took their weapons everywhere they went: "Even to the can," the big negroes laughed. Since it was an operational base, they were mostly negroes and they stood laughing and joking and dancing as black men do, in large groups making easy targets. All over the base there was continual noise of machines and voices and music, uncamouflaged targets that moved openly. At night Cactus Jack was lit up like an ocean liner. To you they had no sense of security and you were rapidly losing yours. You liked it best when Hatrack took you back out in the jungle where you all too obviously belonged.

One day the children from a nearby village came down to the perimeter to sell watered down Coca-cola through the wire, and you fired over their heads to drive them off. The Yanks were appalled by this brutality—they began to see you as what you probably were: animals let out of their cages.

"D'yer want them kids to hate us or somethin'?" they protested. But that night when Viet Cong mortars rained down on Cactus Jack, those mortars all fell on targets carefully ranged during the day, in every part of the base except that occupied by The Pigs.

And now this dreadful tumultuous night when all hell broke loose on the far side of the base as the Yank's turned on a display of their awesome firepower, and you shrivelled in their dazzling light like vampires exposed to the sun.

"Gentlemen, I have news," Nigel said, at around three in the morning when you were so cold and sleepless and dishevelled and shitty-arsed that you didn't care anymore.

"Piss off, Nigel."

"Now, now, Greyman, don't be ungrateful. I am now able to confirm that Fire Support Base Cactus Jack is definitely under attack and has been for some hours now."

"How many million Charlies are there?" Snowy wanted to know.

"Not millions. Not thousands, nor even hundreds. Just one,

in fact. And an old friend of yours, Yogi Bear, at that."

And suddenly you were all interested and knew exactly who he meant.

"The Chi-com Man!" you chorused.

"Yes indeed, our old China, the Chi-com man, is back."

"Been missing for a while," Sniffer said, "I wondered what had happened to him."

"Probably been on his annual leave," Greyman remarked.

"How did he score?" Alby Dunshea wanted to know.

"Not bad," Nigel said, "He got in through all their super defences, planted six mines, two of which went off. Four dead—three while they watched telly. One sleeping it off under a truck."

"One of his better days," you considered.

"Could have been better. One of the duds was in the moviehouse. Fifty men in there at the time."

"He really doesn't have a lot of luck, does he?" Sniffer lamented.

"Nope. And what little luck he does have seems to have run out. The Yanks reckon they've got him trapped this time. It's pretty open country over there, and down in the valley there is—well, was—this old stone house. When he was making his getaway, they reckon he ducked into that, and so they've hit the place with everything, including the kitchen sink."

"Fuckin' Yank whackers. He'll be long gone by now."

"Apparently not. In spite of the heavy bombardment and the fact that the house has been completely reduced to rubble, he is still in there. This they know because every time they ease up on their firing, the cheeky little bugger takes a pot shot back at them."

"Oh come on," Bugsy chided, "They could have wiped out Tasmania with the amount of firepower they've laid out there."

"It's the old bombardier's lament. Easy to flatten a city but bloody hard to hit the shithouse door."

Yes, well, you could all have a good laugh about that, but Nigel's attitude, the gleeful delight with which he related all this, was unmistakably suspicious. Somewhere along the line, all this was going to have something more directly to do with you. And you weren't going to like it.

"I see," Alby Dunshea said, "So we have to sit it out all night until they run out of ammunition over there."

"Not at all," Nigel grinned, "First, it will be dawn in three hours. Second, the Yank commanders assure us that they have enough ammo to keep up this rate of fire for about three weeks. And third, an alternative plan has been come up with, which brings us to the point of this little discussion."

"I was afraid of this," you groaned.

Nigel held on to a pause, the final pleasure of savouring secret information before it was shared.

"Well then, a little while ago, our thoughtful and beloved leader, Hatrack, got as fed up with his loss of beauty sleep as you are, so he paid the Yanks a little visit and—in a manner I'm sure you can easily imagine—told them to fucking shut up!"

"A wonderful man, our Hatrack," Greyman chuckled.

"Awright. So then, in the ensuing discussions, Hatrack made a deal. They cut out the racket and his blokes will go down into the valley and flush the little bugger out."

"His blokes being us blokes?" you figured out.

"Well, yes and no, Yogi. Us blokes being you and Greyman."

"I don't get it."

"The plan is that Kinross's blokes will actually do the job. We get to cover them. We circle wide while it's still dark and Snowy, you will put covering fire onto the house from the right flank while Kinross and his boys will come in from the left and grab him by the scruff of the neck and hand him over to the Yanks. Simple stuff."

"So?"

"Only needs four of us to go with Snowy—me, Bugsy, Alby and Sniffer. And Kinross is short a couple of men and those he has are a little inexperienced. He wants Greyman up front, and he wants you, Griffin, because after all no one knows as much about this bloke as you do."

"Being fuckin' nothing."

"Exactly. The point being that you know how little you know better than anyone else."

"Kinross is a dickhead," you muttered, "I don't want to be in his section."

"You won't have to do much, Yogi," Nigel smiled evilly,

"The one he really wants is you, Greyman."

"That's just cos he thinks us abos can see in the dark," Greyman muttered in disgust.

But he was right. It was simple stuff, even though the little fucker was still armed and might have had God knows how many Chi-com's left. But things like that were better not thought about. So you thought about something else instead, "Can I ask a silly question?"

"Certainly."

"Why don't the Yanks go down and flush him out themselves? I'm sure they are just as able to do it as we are."

"Cynics might dispute that, but why should they bother? If they've got the time and ammo, sooner or later they will pulverise him out of existence. It's us that's in a hurry."

"I'm not in a hurry," Bugsy said, but then he never was.

"Look at it this way. Task Force like the idea because it will give us the chance to show the Yanks how useful we are. Hatrack likes it because it'll boost, by one, the company body count. I like it because I will rest a bloody lot easier known that little bugger is finally out of our hair. And everybody else will like it because all that racket is giving the whole base a collective headache. We'll be very popular for this."

"Showing off to the fuckin' Americans, what next?" Bugsy muttered.

"Well, I'm not going," Snowy said adamantly. It was a certainty that if he wasn't, then Mabel wasn't, and without them, you weren't going either. But Nigel faced the crisis bravely.

"Why not, Snowy?"

"If you reckon I'm going over there and put meself in front of the guns of them trigger-happy cocksuckers, you're out of your fuckin' mind."

Nigel patted him firmly on top of his great head, "A wise attitude, Snowy, but the remarkable Hatrack has thought of that too. Thinks of everything, he does. He plans to take the entire company over there, and place one man in each Yank position. The Yanks will be told that if any of them so much as touch a weapon while we are out in front, our bloke will butt-stroke him. Fair enough?"

"He does think of everything, doesn't he."

"Awright. So saddle up and let's get over there and get it done."

For all that assurance, you crossed to the 'hostile' side of the base with considerable reluctance. It wasn't that you were really averse to showing off to the Yanks—it was because the whole exercise was so bloody unnecessary; a pure object of Hatrack's zeal. Body count—that was what it was all about. In a guerilla war where there was no such thing as territorial gain or capture of property or people, the only way to gauge whether you were winning or losing was to count the number of enemy killed. This, in turn, reduced every contact to a grisly game of body snatching, both sides trying to cheat the system by carrying off their dead before anyone could add them to the official score sheet. To date, Delta Company had wreaked considerable damage on the Charlies, but their efforts went unrecognised because, there had not been a single corpse left behind to prove it, much to Hatrack's chagrin. But out there now there was an easy body to be had, and Hatrack was not about to pass it up.

You arrived at the embattled edge of Cactus Jack—the Sharp End as these sorts of places were called. You and Greyman peeled off and went over to where Kinross's blokes had gathered. Kinross was a slim and laconic fellow with a big hose nose and he was a real good bloke. The one thing no one never wanted for a leader was a real good bloke; everybody knew they always lost out. His blokes were Mule Skinner, Fat Leyton, Sailor Simpson, Ron Patches and Stickdick Collins, and they were real good blokes too. Slow in the head and well as on their feet. You were really hating this.

The order was given for the firing to stop and they stood on the perimeter amid the rows overheated machineguns.

"Ain't you guys worried that now that we stopped firing, he might crawl outa there and git away in the dark?" asked the US Army Major who was in charge of that part of the perimeter. Kinross smiled at him reasonably: "If he does, he won't get far, and he'll be easy to follow. But anyway, if he was able to go, he would have long ago."

And from down in the valley there came a single gunshot. Kinross offered the Major a superior smile.

"Waal, goddamnit to hell, he's still there," the Major uttered.

You could all smile, but even so, something was odd. You picked it up immediately. When a shot is fired toward you, it makes an extended percussion whereas when it was fired away, the detonation was short and sharp. A man called Albert Einstein once had a theory about that sort of thing.
You walked over to Kinross:

"Notice something?"

"He fired away from us," Kinross said without hesitation.

"Strange?"

"Very. I don't know what it means. All I do know is that when we get there, he'll be waiting for us. I want you right with me, Yogi."

You nodded to reassure him, and then turned again to the scene before you. What you saw was hard to believe. You gazed out on what might have been a scene of purgatory, bathed in hazy moonlight. It was flat, open land sloping downward from the base, and spot fires burned everywhere, the ghostly smoke drifting away on the slight breeze. In the centre of it, tiny flat surfaces of stone caught the moonlight—a small pile of smouldering rubble about two hundred yards from you—what was left of the house. All about, the blacker patches of bomb craters honeycombed the area.

"The big worry is unexplodeds," Hatrack worried, "Keep well away from any metal object you find."

You knew you would.

"Hadn't yer better git movin'," the American Major said, "It'll be comin' on daylight mighty soon."

Hatrack took him aside to explain, and you were glad to be rid of both of them.

There was no hurry. You were waiting for Nigel's blokes to get into position on a small wooded slope that was beyond and half-right of the house. They had left almost an hour before and had a radio. It would only take you five minutes to get down there. There was plenty of time too, even though the eastern sky was lightening. It was better, in these instances, to have a little light to work by.

From down in the valley, another outbound shot rang out. It sounded almost plaintive, as if the little man was saddened to think that his American friends didn't want to play anymore.

"Hang on, sonny. We're coming," you said softly.

Almost immediately came the radio message from Nigel.

"Four three bravo for four three alpha. All set. Over."

Stick carried the radio for Kinross:

"Roger four three bravo. Wait. Over."

Hatrack, who heard the message, came over as you made final adjustments to your gear.

"Make it count, Kinross."

No one answered. You just went.

You made your way out through the maze of barbed wire, and walked down to the house. There was no need for security—the smoke from the grass fires and the darkness were your cover. You just went easy, quiet as you could. Greyman was out in the lead where he belonged, then each man ten to fifteen metres from the next, Kinross, then Stick with the radio, Mule with Bessie, Leyton as back-up on the gun, Sailor, Ron Patches and you, as always, bringing up the rear.

You walked down into the valley heading slightly wide of the house, zero-ing in on a set of bomb craters lying fifty yards left of the house. Down in the valley, the air was thick from the burning, and the charred remnants of grass crunched underfoot, but the crackling of the fires covered that. You reached the area of greatest proliferation of the craters, a frozen sea of crescent waves where they overlapped each other—seething metallic smells choking the lungs, smoke watering the eyes. You weaved along the mounds of powdered soil thrown up on the crater rims—footing was variable and it was hard to maintain balance, especially for the last man who has to walk backwards mostly.

Finally you reached the nominated craters and deployed. Kinross indicated a large crater about twenty metres from the house. You nodded. The others took up covering positions as you rushed forward, scrambling through the black snowdrifts, and leaping into the chosen crater, crocodiling up the other side until you bobbed up to cover the house. Stick came next, stumbling over the uneven ground, unbalanced by the radio and dropping down beside you. Then Sailor, who did fall into a crater, scrambled up, jumped into the right one, and took up a position on the other side, covering one flank, while simultaneously Ron Patches went the other way. Mule and Leyton dropped back, Bessie facing outward covering your backs. When it was all to his satisfaction, Kinross bounded over and joined you and Stick. All very smooth.

You gazed upon the pile of jumbled stone that, they assured you, was once a house. It was impossible to see anything in there, but still you watched it intently for some sign. There was no need to speak. You waited out the final moments, lying on the inner slope of the crater, body pressed against the hot pulverised soil. Waiting a few moments. Just to be sure. Nothing happened. Okay.

Kinross nodded to Stick who spoke softly into the radio: "Four three alpha for four three bravo. Do it now. Over."

Immediately, the M60 opened up from its remote location, the long tongues of tracers streaking into the rubble, with the bright flashes of ricochets spinning away from the stone. Snowy Spargo doing it nicely, right on target. Close enough to the house to keep the target's head down, far wide enough to allow you and Kinross to come in from the side. Kinross touched your shoulder and you were off.

You had to really think about this. Spargo's cover would keep the Charlie's head down alright, but it also sent ricochets whiplashing overhead, but you were determined not to worry about that. You went and went, scampering a winding course along the interlocking crater rims. You slipped once—had to happen—and went rolling down to the bottom but that didn't matter, up and on, keep moving, that's the thing. You'd already picked the spot you were heading for, and never took your eyes off it, careful too to keep the muzzle of the SLR out of the dirt and finally you were longstriding into that last crater, through the bottom and up the other side to your chosen position. And slammed straight into Kinross who was heading for the same spot. You looked at him and he at you and then you both chuckled and shook your heads. Not very good, both being together like this, but you both picked this spot because it was the best. You lay for a moment, letting your breathing settle, then both crept up and peeped over the rim. No sign of anything. You looked back toward Stick. He shook his head. Maybe the little bugger got away after all.

The house—just a jumble of broken stonework with the odd fire smoking in its midst. There was nothing left upright enough for anyone to hide behind. In the background, a fiery sunrise began to glimmer through the smoke. Kinross gave the sign to Stick who spoke on the radio and Snowy Spargo's covering fire stopped. Kinross and you, lying side-by-side, coated with the white powdered ash from burnt grass. You were behind what used to be the outer wall of the house.

You moved up now, both together, slowly, weapons raised, ready for anything. But the house was so completely flattened that no one could be hiding behind anything. Your eyes pierced the darkness, moving in a sweep, studying every object in turn—nothing—go a few paces forward, nothing. Now you were actually up on the stone and the ankles complained at the angles of the footing. Place each foot, look around, place the next. Work on staying balanced. Kinross going wide, ten yards away now, moving and stopping, looking and listening, as you did. Then he looked at you and you at him. You both shrugged.

More paces, deeper into the remains of the house. Then you saw something. An irregular shape, a shadow that didn't look quite like the other chaotic shadows. You went down on one knee and lined up the sights on it, whatever it was, then made a low, brief, whistling sound. Kinross looked your way, and followed your line of sight to the object. Both peering through the smoke, but for a moment the smoke cleared and you saw it clearly. A hand poking upward out of the rubble, holding a pistol, like a modern Excalibur. It was pointed straight up in the air.

Kinross was closer. You maintained your aim while he

moved in. The hand and pistol pointed straight at the sky, showing no indication of moving. Kinross crouched and moved forward slowly, his eyes fixed on the hand. As he closed in, he lowered himself closer to the ground. He lay for a moment, the pistol a few feet in front of his nose. Then he lunged, and easily wrenched the pistol from the hand. There was no resistance. The hand remained, clutching at the lightening sky, the fingers opening and closing in a convulsive reflex action.

Kinross sat on a stone, regarding the pistol, the hand, looking back at you.

"Come here," he said bluntly.

Then he set the weapon aside and began removing the rubble, stone by stone, excavating what must have been the man buried beneath the rubble. You moved in, still covering. It was like defusing a bomb, but finally you gazed upon the fabled Chi-com Man.

It was hard to tell what was man and what was rubble. He lay flat on his back, completely buried, and the arm of the hand that held the pistol was jammed under a large stone. Fixed thus, he could only ever have been firing straight up in the air. Another mystery solved. The rest was like a man made of blood-stained dust and shattered pebbles, but you could see his eyes moving as you dug him out, removing stone after stone until he was completely exposed. His body was mostly stripped of its clothing, scorched black all over by the fires and explosions and here and there were ugly wounds of sizzling red flesh. His eyes were defiant, his teeth slightly bared, but he could neither assist nor resist. His pain must have been unbelievable. Finally, Kinross had cleared enough stone to raise the man's head slightly, and you stripped out a water bottle, passing it over, and Kinross put it to the man's mouth. Most of the water spilled, discolouring the dust that had become his very flesh.

You stood, facing the base, and raised the rifle high over your head to signal the *all clear,* turned to the others and gave the same signal, and then toward Nigel's mob on the hill and gave it again. They began to gather toward you while from up at the base a detachment of medics came running with a stretcher. You left them to complete the job of digging him out.

The yellow light of dawn began to creep across the black seething plain as you walked back toward the base. Nigel and the others came jogging and you and Greyman blended back in to where you belonged.

"Good cover, was it?" Snowy Spargo needed to ask The

Mule.

"Red hot, Snowy. Fuckin' spot on," Mule said. Words of praise from master to master. No one else needed to say anything at all.

As you reached the barbed wire, the Americans came out of their bunkers and tents and began to cheer and applaud, as if you'd just made a ton in front of the Members at the MCG. Their Delta Company watchdogs followed embarrassedly.

"That was great, boys," the US Major was saying as he greeted you, "Just great. You guys are really something to watch."

"Was he dead?" Hatrack wanted to know.

"No," Kinross said, "But he can't last."

You did not pause to acknowledge the applause, you just kept right on going, and the two Majors had trouble keeping up.

"Tell you what," the Yank one said to the Aussie one, "Your guys did so good down there that, even if my men caused his wounds, when he dies, you get credit for the kill. How about that?"

"How about that..." Kinross echoed flatly.

"That's very good of you, Major," Hatrack was saying, "We really appreciate that..."

You walked straight back to your side of the base, hoping only for sleep.

Moral Grounds

Ancient history. Way back in training days in Oz, at Pucka. The platoon is out on the firing range for a yippee shot where it was observed that not one of the sixty rounds Magee fired had hit the target, human sized, fifty metres away. That wasn't the problem—Griffin only managed about five hits himself and no one cared.

"It'll be a jungle war and rapid fire will be the go," Nigel Naughton pointed out. "You'll never have to aim at anything."

Griffin prayed nightly that it was so, but Magee's total miss raised Tiger Braddock's suspicions. He had never seen a completely unmarked target before. That was because Mick Delaney and Ernie Weedman were AWOL at the time, and everyone else forgot to put a few rounds into Alfie's target as had been the habit in the past. Tiger Braddock stood on the range and towered over the diminutive bespectacled Magee.

"Private Magee, reload."

Magee fitted a new magazine from his pouch.

"Private Magee, at the target, ten rounds, fire at will!"

Alfie Magee, lying prone, while the rest of them stood behind him helplessly, took careful aim and squeezed the trigger.

"Bang!" he said.

Lt Hollingsworth observed this scene with utter astonishment, and came to stand opposite Braddock, with Magee between them. Holly was probably delighted for the chance to loom over the one man in the platoon shorter than himself.

"Private Magee, remove your magazine."

Magee handed him the magazine.

"You silly bugger, you forgot to load it," Holly gasped shrilly.

"No sir."

"Show me your other magazines, Private Magee," Tiger Braddock persisted.

Magee did so without shame.

"Private Magee, why are you not carrying any ammunition?"

"I don't want to shoot anybody, sir."

"It's only a wooden target, Magee," Braddock said bitterly.

"I don't want to learn how to shoot anybody either."

"Are we to assume," Holly assessed. "that this is some form of conscientious objection on morally pacifist grounds?"

"No sir. I just don't want to shoot anybody."

Holly looked about, seeking an appeal to reason.

"Corporal Naughton, what is your assessment of this matter?"

"I have been saying for a long time that Private Magee is complete unsuited to combat duties and indeed, military service," Nigel replied firmly. "I just can't believe that he's still here."

"I did not ask for a philosophic argument, Corporal. I sincerely hope that you were unaware of Private Magee's unarmed condition."

"Completely unaware," Nigel said coldly. "But it doesn't surprise me and it ought not surprise you either."

"I'm not bloody surprised," Tiger Braddock said.

The outcome, after Nigel and Tiger persuaded Holly to drop any charges he intended to lay was that Alfie was transferred. They gave him a job as Padre's batman, which seemed a suitable solution to everyone except Hatrack. Far too many men were being weeded out for acne conditions and other ailments in those last weeks before they left for Vietnam and he was not going to give up even someone as essentially useless as Alfie without a fight.

Hatrack argued that the Padre was not a field officer and could shine his own boots, run his own errands and make his own tea. The Padre, a suitably magnanimous religious man, could only agree—and the final decision was that he would not need an assistant until they reached the war zone. So Alfie Magee—still officially transferred—was returned to the section to make up the numbers on temporary loan until a replacement could be found.

"I'm not sure whether we won or lost that one," Nigel Naughton remarked.

You saw him sitting there with a silly look on his face, clutching an FN that wouldn't hurt anyone even if it did have any ammunition in it. They were short of numbers as usual, but this time it had prompted someone to remember Alfie Magee. Worse, they did so in the middle of an operation so there was no chance of leaving him on rear party. Alfie at the sharp end—it was your worst nightmare. But since there was nothing to be done about it and the company was ready to move out, you could only try to be friendly.

"Padre must be lonely," you smile at him.

"I'm just on temporary loan," he said softly.

"You got any bullets in that thing?"

He simply shook his head slightly.

"Bugger it, Alfie. It's a fucking war. You gotta carry ammunition. It's the rules."

"I don't want to kill anybody."

"And what happens if you get someone else killed because you couldn't shoot to save them?"

"I won't," he sighed.

"Alfie, if we get into trouble out there, we gotta be able to depend on you. Remember what happened to Tiger Braddock?"

"Yeah, I know."

"If it gets bad enough, we might have to shoot you."

"So shoot me. You'll be doing me a favour."

You didn't dare ask Nigel if he remembered—how could he have forgotten? But anyway, it hardly mattered in the end. On the first night out, Alfie was rostered first on the overnight picket. As you sat on a log eating beans straight out of the can, Magee came by on his way to the picket post.

It was almost dark, and Alfie would have hardly settled in his position when the shots came—one, then two more, outgoing. And then Alfie started screaming.

"Contact front," you screamed. "Watch out—Magee's out there."

Snowy came charging by with the M60 and you snatched your rifle and went with him, zero-ing in on the point of Alfie's screams as they pierced the night. As soon as you were level, you both hit the deck and started firing wildly off into the jungle ahead. You already knew you were shooting at nothing.

Alfie quietened. The echoes of your gunfire echoed away through the jungle. Nigel and, further away, Holly were yelling, wanting to know what was going on. What was going on was that Alfie Magee had most of his left hand shot off. You hunted the vicinity for the missing fingers but only found two of them. Might be able to sew them back on, medics reckon.

The dust off chopper came within the hour and Magee was carried away—poor silly Alfie who should never have been there in the first place. He said nothing, and offered no explanation, but at least he agreed when you and Snowy invented a story that you hoped might fit the facts. Alfie, the story went, heard a movement in front of him and parted the foliage with his hand and there was a Vietcong pointing an AK47 at him. At the last second, he grabbed the muzzle and deflected the shots. The Charlie ran. Good story. You almost believed it yourself. You had already grabbed the FN and cleaned it immediately. At least there was no blood or bone caught in the muzzle. As long as no one counted the rounds in the mag, the story would hold.

"Do you seriously expect me to believe that yarn, Private Griffin?" Holly protested.

"I don't give a fuck what you believe."

"Try telling that to Hatrack," he protested.

You did. He stood tall and craggy and listened to your story, shaking his head all the while.

"Private Griffin," he pronounced at the end of it. "You weary me. Go away."

"Private Magee. Do you want to go to Vietnam?"

"No sir."

"Why not, Private?"

"I don't want to kill anybody, sir."

"Conscientious objection on religious grounds?"

"No sir. I just don't want to kill anybody."

"Hmmm. Well, let me see. Ah! It says here that you have been assigned to the battalion padre as his batman."

"Yes sir."

"In that capacity, it is hardly likely that you'll be called upon to deal with combat situations, Private."

"But I might."

"The padre recommends you highly, Private Magee. Do you really think you can let him down like this?"

"I suppose not, sir."

"Well, then. How about you sign the Affirmation and then it will be alright."

"Very well, sir, if you say so."

River of Gold

Even before Sniffer came back too soon, you knew you were in the shit. You got it in the fuckin' neck—early warning system: it happens like that sometimes. Not always: that's the fuckin' trouble. Just sometimes.

You're sitting there, back up against a tree with your nose stuck up a stick book—thumb in your bum and your mind in neutral—when all of a sudden you're rubbing the back of your neck, like some fuckin' insect bite only it don't sting. Just tingles. You rub it and then, you realise.

Trouble...

Now the tingling gets into them hairs at the nape and you know it's on. You look up, the last words you read already forgotten.

Nothing...

Nothing...

You look toward the way Sniffer'll come but he ain't there yet. Look the other way. You can see Snowy through the light-speckled shadows, twenty feet away, flanked by the gun, and Alby Dunshea further over. Nothing there. You know the others are beyond. No sign of them.

Nothing.

Fuckin' nothing.

Swing back round. Bugsy lies beside you with his hat over his eyes, sound asleep? Nope. He's absently rubbing the back of his fuckin' neck! Now he lifts the hat an inch off his eyes and peeps out to see if you've got it too. Yeah, Bugsy, I got it too. Has to be Sniffer. Has to be. You peer back that way. A few clear feet of shadow under the canopy of the jungle and then a hell of a tangle of green shit, but there's a gap you can see through at this angle, right down. Not so far as the sentry post, but far enough. Wait for it. Wait for it. There he is!

Sniffer comes creeping back through the greenshit, real quiet, well in from the track. He stops, bends, peers—he's trying to spot you. You move your arm a few inches—all it needs. His eyes pick it up, and he stoops a little more so you can see his face but in all that shadow and shit you can't make it out clear—he's still twenty yards away. But that's enough. Very methodically, Sniffer holds his fist right in front of his face with the thumb pointing upward and then turns it over, slowly and deliberately, so the thumb points down—just like the Roman

Emperor does at the Colosseum and it means the same fuckin' thing too! Sorta. It's the signal for enemy approaching.

You give the same signal back, and keep watching him close, while Bugsy is watching you and sees the reply. He immediately offers the thumbs down signal along the line to Snowy and Alby Dunshea—they aren't fuckin' looking. Bugsy finds a small twig and throws it their way. Now he can pass the signal and they will pass it, on to Nigel and Greyman who are further over that way somewhere. All this you are only vaguely aware of, sensed at the periphery rather than seen—you are concentrating on Sniffer.

When he sees you've got the signal, Sniffer, very emphatically, shows four fingers on one hand, then one with the same hand. Four of them, maybe one more. Okay. You pass that signal on to Bugsy who sends it down the line. There's another possible signal that doesn't come—a pumping of the fist like someone in the latter stages of wanking a giant prick. It means they're right on top of you and you're in a hurry. But Sniffer makes no such signal. Plenty of time. Sniffer now settles down where he is, ten yards in from the track. Time to move.

Carefully, you slip your stickbook into your pack and fasten the clips—set to bug out fuckin' quicksmart if necessary. Then you shove off the tree, pick up your SLR and crocodile crawl forward a couple of yards to a place aligned with Bugsy but about five yards toward Sniffer's position from him. Check it carefully. Clear view of Sniffer from here, clear the other way to Bugsy, and beyond the vague outlines of Snowy and Dunshea. Moving slowly, you check your SLR—full mag, one up the spout, safety off. Check your pouch for extra mags, the other for the grenade if that's needed. All set. Let's have yer, you little slant-eye bastards!

You settle into your prone position, the ground is cold on your belly and thighs but that's alright. Bare earth means not much fallout from the trees to crunch and crinkle. Means you can see any fuckin' snakes or scorpions coming too, thank fuck! Means you've got good footing if you have to move. You manoeuvre again, a few positioning wriggles to get comfortable, get your elbows onto smooth ground so the nerves won't be jarred, and all the time ensure clear view of Sniffer one way and Bugsy the other. From Bugsy's direction comes the common 'okay' signal—thumb and forefinger pulled into a circle. Everyone ready. No probs. Sniffer is settled, Bugsy is settled—time to concentrate on the track.

The track is narrow and winding through the greenshit, at this point ten yards directly up front. Here the jungle is dense, dank and dark, but over the track the canopy is breached and sunlight comes through illuminating the track so that it kinda flows through the dimness like a river of gold. Out there, you can see everyfuckin'thing that moves—it's like a lighted stage waiting for the actors to walk on—and just as an actor on a brightly lit stage can't see the audience, so too from the track, we are completely fuckin' invisible.

You tried it yourself earlier—stood out there and looked right where Snowy was, and saw fuckin' nuthin. All we have to do is stay still and no one would ever know we are here. That's the skill of an ambush, to see without being seen. They could never detect you in a million years, but we will have a bright clear unobstructed view of them. They've got fuckin' buckley's.

We're good at this. Watch how surely it is done. You look back toward Sniffer: he is down and motionless, watching the track—for sure he expects them to appear right away. At some distance now, you hear the ringing sounds of what might be bird-calls, but they ain't. No fuckin' fear. They are the voices of people calling light-heartedly. It sounds like a discordant song. Definite Vietnamese. You lie there, sweating it out.

There is a tremulous feeling rippling through your body, a feverish anticipation, like a child about to receive a Christmas present. The sweat breaks out on your brow, your neck, the palms of your hands, that same cold sweat that comes with nausea. Your belly dislikes the hard contact with the damp earth; you need to shift your knees slightly, you tense and flex the muscles in your legs and back to keep them supple, tighten the buttocks and free them. It's like fucking the ground itself. You have to remember to breathe as well, for the tendency is to hold the breath. You seem to have slipped your entire body into manual drive. Nothing happens unless you consciously will it. And it is all focused, channelled, into the eyes and the ears. You must concentrate on that track. Nothing else matters.

The ringing voices are nearer. You are locked in, the trap straining against itself to be sprung. Check back with Sniffer—he's watching for you. Again, he raises four fingers—a confirmation. You pass the signal to Bugsy—rugged, rough Bugsy, but now his florid face is pallid and strained as, you must suppose, your own is. Certainly the four fingers you display are trembling. Back to the fuckin' track, concenfuckingtrating. Where are they? Where the fuck are they? There!

They are visible for just a few seconds, but at such moments, time slows down and you see and hear and feel everything in minute detail, like a slo-mo replay only it's for fuckin' real. They come hustling along in their short-stride gait, chatting in sing-song Noggie as they go. The actors, entering stage left, each weighed down by a disproportionately ponderous load. Actors never really work that fuckin' hard.

The man in the lead is barechested and barelegged, with rice tubes looped about his torso and he has an enormous bundle of straight sticks on his back, longer than he is tall, bending him forward as he moves. He carries an AK47 cradled on his forearm. You can pick it from the curved magazine and your eyes light up. Nasty little buggers, them.

A woman, his wife perhaps, follows in black pyjamas and straw hat. She too is stooped under a huge bundle wrapped in black plastic and carries a .303 slung on her shoulder. She grins sweetly as she chats with the two younger men behind, her cherubic cheeks etched by shadow.

The younger men are lightly built and sinewy—maybe her sons. Both labour under the weight of US ration boxes lashed to their backs. One carries a shotgun, the other a US M1.

All that you see in the first second. You absorb it from a single fleeting moment, and you will never forget it. The first second passes since they hustled into view, and in another second they will be gone. It must be now. And yet, for all their speedy gait, they seem to pass so slowly, caught in a time warp, waiting for death. Without missing a stride, the lead man turns and says something and they smile at his comment, thinking it funny. They will die with those smiles on their lips.

The last man in line is yours. Yours and Sniffer's. Your SLR is at the shoulder but you don't use the sights. You'll start behind and walk the tracers onto him, while Snowy hits them in the guts with his beloved Mabel, taking them all on while we pick off individual targets. Sniffer, accurate shot, will go for one killer hit on your target, while you blast all around him, giving him nowhere to go. Now! Do it now! Go Snowy...!

Snowy lets Mabel have her way. At the moment they draw level with him, he gives them a solid fifty round burst. All four are hurled to the far side of the track as if struck by a great wind, crashing to the ground in a flurry of flailing limbs. Bright horizontal streaks of tracer sear across the track and into their thrashing bodies, showering the track with a hail of twigs, leaves, splinters, dust and smoke. All is obscured, mercifully, except that the woman's piercing scream can be heard above the thunder of the gunfire, until she stops as if cut off by a knife.

The barrage ceases as suddenly as it began.

It is all over in three seconds flat. You've fired a full mag into that last guy, although you saw little of him after the firing began. Everything vanished momentarily in a frenzied fog of smoke and dust and leaf fragments and splinters, and when it cleared they were down. You knew where he was and sent your bright stream of tracers zeroing into the spot, until the mag ran out. It takes a moment to remember to stop squeezing the trigger. Take a breath of air. Quick change the fuckin' mag, fuckwit! Whip it off, whip it out, whip it on, click! One up the spout, whack, whack! All neatly done in spite of numb and trembling fingers. Okay. Now check upfront. All you can see out there is your target, down and thrashing on the ground. That's all you have to see.

As the echo of the gunfire stalks away through the jungle, there is a brief lull. Then come the voices of the victors: sharp, callow voices, all calling at once.

"Aw, you bloody bewdy, Snowy..."

"We got `em...we got `em..."

"You fuckin' balltearers..."

"Bowled `em right arse over tit..."

"Did yer see `em drop..."

"That'll take their fuckin' minds off sex for a while..."

Then, the more mature voice of Nigel. "Awright, awright, shut up, you dickheads!"

The dreadful lull returns. Hate this. But you gotta be sure. No point taking chances. Everyone stays where they are, weapons trained on the bodies, waiting for something, anything. Nothing moves now. The death throes are over.

"Awright, take it easy. Watch `em," Nigel is saying unnecessarily—his voice has that same hysterical edge to it.

"Sniffer, that the lot?"

Nigel is invisible at this distance, calling just loud enough for Sniffer to hear him.

"Yeah, just four."

"You okay?"

"Fine, Nigel."

"What's up with you, Alby?"

"Got a heap of shit in the face but I'm alright."

"Can't make you any fuckin' uglier."

"Stick a dick in it, Yogi Bear!"

"I take it you're still with us, Griffin."

"I'm here, Nigel."

"Bugsy."

"Yo?"

"Gun clear, Snowy?"

"Gun clear, Nigel."

"Greyman!"

"No problems, Nigel."

"We got four victor Charlie down. Who can count `em."

"I can count `em," Bugsy calls. "Four Charlie down and out."

"Awright. Check weapons. Reload. Stay where you are."

Oh gawd, is he gonna ask me? Please, not me. I don't like this, never want it. He reckons I'm good at it, but I don't feel good at it. Just don't shit myself if it goes wrong.

"Griffin, wanna have a look?"

Oh, fuck it!

You groan in response. You let that be the answer. There's a snort of amusement from Bugsy, and then Nigel. "You don't have to do it, Yogi."

Oh, sure you don't! Then some other poor fucker goes out there instead and goes cunt up and it's all your fault. Fuckin' wonderful.

"I'll do it."

"Play it cool, Yogi Bear. We got all day."

Like fuck we have. Every Charlie within ten miles in any direction now knows exactly where we are, and there are no sentries. When you're out there, you're all on your own, baby.

You roll onto your side—have to anyway because you've got a bloody erection and it's getting fuckin' uncomfortable under there. You bring your SLR around where you can check the mag, ensure the spout is clear and there's one up there, make sure a spare mag is ready. The SLR is a good gat but the barrel's too long for this sort of job—some blokes lop the muzzle but that kills the accuracy and increases the muzzleflash—no win situation. Maybe you oughta carry a pistol on your belt, except someone'll think you're an officer and you'll end up getting fragged. Right now, the SLR will have to do.

You look at Bugsy but he concentrates on those inert forms out there, his rifle trained. Take your hat off—dump it on the ground, check the machete on your belt. Slide it in and out. Set to go.

You take your time. Slowly you get to your feet, and then look toward Sniffer down the way. He gives the thumbs up.

Okay. No fancy stuff now. You stand full upright, and walk slowly, straight forward, and straight away that fuckin' long barrel tangles in the vines. You pull it free, steady your nerves, and all the way you watch those bodies, nothing else. As long as they don't move, there's no problem. At the edge of the track, you pause, wait, watch. Then, finally, you step out in to the sunlight.

This is the hardest moment—when the sun hits your eyes you are blind for a few moments, and have to wait for the eyes to adjust. You do that, standing stock still. It's not enough to just get reasonable vision, you wait until it is completely clear. That's good. Here we go.

With carefully measured strides, you walk forward. It's like a slow march—one step, pause, next step. Ten paces at one every second, and you arrive at the first body. No need to worry about the other three—your guardians will shoot if any of them moves. You keep your nose out of this as well. On the air is the dank smell of their rice—something about the way they cook it that is so distinctive—and that of lingering cordite, and gusts of the odour of excrement—one of them has shit themselves but who could blame them for that—and the sickly stench of exposed intestines that you remember as a boy when your father used to skin rabbits.

The young man. The one you went for. The weapon lies thrown clear. The M1—butt splintered by a bullet. Good, stand between man and weapon. You slide out your machete and bend, and the muzzle of the fuckin' SLR catches on the ground. Stupid fuckin' thing. But you don't want the M1 either. You just flick it with the machete down the track a way, out of reach. That'll be far enough.

Now, the man. He lies on his back and there are three huge holes in his chest—exit wounds coming through from his back. Good grouping. Check his hands—you can see both of them, his arms thrown wide. But he's fuckin' wrong way up!—think about that. Maybe the impact sent him diving nose first into the ground, but he hit with such fuckin' force that he bounced over onto his back. Only explanation. He wouldn't have been alive long enough to roll himself. This was your target. You probably made a few of those holes. Somehow the image of the brilliant glowing tracers searing through the body is more awful. Check his eyes. You can see them, the rounded lids half-closed, vacant black pupils staring, and mouth gaping open—shouting a warning maybe that he never completed, carrying the final syllable away with him to eternity. No problem here. With those one per second strides, you walk around him and on to the second body.

The other young chap, lying half off the track, upper torso in the bushes. Makes it tough. Nasty leg wound, hidden by fabric but it bled excessively. Bleeding has stopped now. Good sign—for that much blood in so short a time it would have been spouting jets of blood like a stream of piss when you continually squeeze your prick and interrupt the flow. Wouldn't mind a piss right now yourself, or even a pull. The hard knob of your prick is rubbing on the fabric of your pants when you move, exquisitely irritating. Makes it fuckin' hard to keep your mind on the job. Yeah, so, you can see where the spray squirted to, a blood-puddle a yard from the wound, but now there's no heartbeat to pump it out. Good indicator, but not enough.

You'll have to move him. You look around but you can't see that fuckin' shotgun anywhere either. Might have thrown it way off into the bushes when he was hit. Might also have it under him, finger on the trigger, waiting to give you a little surprise when you roll him over. You go forward until you are standing with your toes right up against his hip, the SLR trained at the middle of his back. The slightest flicker of life and you'll fire.

This is very fuckin' dangerous, and very fuckin' awkward. You slip your left toecap under his hip, and raise him slightly. His empty left hand appears. Now you put the SLR in his earhole and reach down and grab a handful of his shirt under the armpit to hurl him over. But the fuckin' geometry is all wrong—length of your arms and SLR barrel, and for a vital terrifying moment, you are off balance, ill-prepared for whatever. Do it quick. Lift him and peep underneath, ready to drop him again if necessary. You haul his upper torso off the ground for a moment. His arms fall limp. Good. No muscle resistance. You glimpsed that other hand and it was empty. No shotgun, no hidden grenades. Okay to roll him, but you straighten first, get that muzzle levelled back at his head, and use your foot. Slip the toecap under his hip and flip him—over he goes. His head comes into view under the bush. His mouth is twisted remarkably, and then you see why—everything from his ear to his collarbone and corner of the mouth to the back of the neck is completely missing. Goner. Good. Can't see that fuckin' shotgun but...

"No weapon here, Nigel," you call—your voice astonishingly croaky.

"It's alright, Yogi. He threw it this way. We can see it. Keep going. You're doing fine."

Doing fine. Now the woman. She's right in the middle of the track, on her side, curled into the foetal position, her arms tucked in across her belly. No problem there. Her head has split open like an axe through watermelon and you can see the porridge of brainmatter splattered everywhere like dropped scrambled eggs. You move by her. The .303 is under her, still slung on her shoulder. She must have taken Mabel's burst full on—her middle part that she tried to defend with her arms is just a mincemeat mess. Her blouse has been torn right off her, and there is the delicate curve of a small breast. That doesn't help. You'll cream your daks in a minute if you don't keep your fuckin' fuckwit mind on the job. But you can still remember what she looked like, in those fleeting moments before... Pretty woman, sweet smile, nice lithe body. Now a blob of offal. But even thoughts like that won't make that fuckin' erection go down. The pain is almost doubling you up, crippling now, your bladder and balls and intestines, all ready to burst. Get on with it, before you explode, like she did.

The man, father, leader. The weapon lies under him and so does one hand as he lies, face down. There's plenty of blood about him but no obvious wound. Stand still. You can feel what seems to be a scorpion clawing and scratching its way up your spinal cord, but that is only imagination. You want to be sick, to piss, to shit, to shoot your bolt. Bodily functions running riot. Watch him! Let it all flow but don't take your eyes off this fucker. There is, you are sure, the barest hint of movement. Perhaps a muscle flexing, a final reflex spasm, who knows. But movement. That's all you need. Without taking your eyes off him, you speak, very distinctly.

"This one's still kickin'."

Out of the void of silence, Nigel speaks. He is still back in there—covering you, watching your every move, but when he speaks it seems that he is right there, his lips at your ear.

"Finish it."

You don't need to move. From where you are there is a clear view of the back of the man's neck and the wet slicked black hair beyond. All you need. Your SLR remains at your hip, pointed downward and all you have to do is raise the muzzle a few inches, instincts tell you how far, and squeeze the trigger.

The abrupt single shot is deafening. You actually see the bullet hit, as if an invisible axe has crashed down on the man's neck and the entire body jolts, and when the skin jumps back to its proper place, there is a jagged hole, not round at all, and from the side of the neck a brief geyser of blood shoots out. You watch with sullen fascination, until it stops.

"The rest are cactus."

"You sure?" Nigel asks.

"Yeah. Real brush and shovel jobs."

"Awright, you guys. Let's tidy this up."

Time to look to yourself. You step a few paces into the jungle on the far side of the track and unbutton your fly. There is a dark shiny stain all down the thigh of your greens—erk! Probably a few down the back as well. You try to piss but your bladder has nothing to offer, and the erection retracts even as you hold it. The bile had risen to your throat, but now it recedes. The crippling pain fades. All bullshit. Your body has been lying to you about what it wanted. Bloody stupid fuckin' thing. You button your fly and step back onto the track.

There is a lot of movement in the jungle behind you and the men of the section come through the foliage at various points and onto the track. Nigel, Snowy, Alby Dunshea, Bugsy, Sniffer and Greyman. They stand in a line, solemnly regarding their handiwork. Frozen in time and space. Their faces are lined with shock, with faint disgust, pale and drawn with strain. Nigel breaks the trance.

"You alright, Yogi?"

"Fuckin' marvellous."

"Awright. Bugsy, Alby—sentry posts right and left. Rest of you, get the gats and search the stiffs."

Bugsy and Dunshea move off to right and left. Nigel, you, Sniffer and Greyman will take one body each while Snowy, with Mabel cradled lovingly in his arms, stands protectively over you all like a old mother hen.

"Four kills, hey. And bodies to show for it," Snowy chortles with great pride—this is his best effort yet.

"Won't Hatrack be thrilled," Nigel says. "We'll be number one boys for this."

Greyman, eternally curious, prods at his body—the woman—with his bayonet.

"Hey, look at this! Her brains are gone and you can see right inside the skull."

Sniffer scurries over excitedly. "Yeah, mine's got an arm blown clean off. Aw, shit yeah. Get onto it. Like a passionfruit after yer've ate the guts."

"Awright, awright," Nigel is saying, though only because he

must. "Cool the fucking biology lesson."

He stands away from his corpse, clutching the shotgun and going through some papers in a wallet he has found. You approach him, like Oliver Twist wanting more only it is you with the offering. The weapon the father carried, a Russian AK47—now that you've wiped the blood and chunks of skin off the butt, it is a real prize.

"This an AK47?"

You know it is.

"Yeah. Beautiful, aren't they. Better than our bloody shitsticks."

"Can I keep it?" you ask, almost pleadingly. "Give it a try?"

Nigel looks it over. It has the firepower of your SLR but it's half the length—a real advantage, for doing jobs like the one you've just done.

"Sure. If you can keep the ammo up to it," he says.

"No probs. Standard stuff, by the look of it."

You strip the magazine to show him. That magazine, so exotically curved, like a cruel piratic cutlass. Nigel nods his approval.

A prize. A real treasure. Something to show for it all when the story is told and retold back at Nui Dat. This is the irrefutable souvenir of your finest moment. Excitedly you search the body for extra magazines and ammunition, and maybe best of all, the cleaning kit. And then Nigel is calling. "Awright, get yer shovels and let's get this lot under. Then let's go and see if we can find some more..."

Hoa Long

Just another of these shambled thatched dwellings on yet another village search. This time it's Hoa Long—the closest village to Nui Dat but that doesn't make it any safer than any of the others. The troops go in at night, surround the town, close in at dawn and go methodically from house to house in section groups, searching, searching, fuckin' searching and finding fuck all. Except sometimes. Sometimes the inhabitants of the town are rounded up and gathered in a central location where Intelligence Officers examine identification papers and interrogate suspects while the men search the houses, going through all their belongings looking for weapons, unofficial documents, or large accumulations of food supplies. That's when they really think the Charlies are using the village at night. Other times, you just go in, bail up the people in their houses and have a bit of a look around. That's just a show of strength, to put the wind up 'em and discourage co-operation with Charlie. This one, this search of Hoa Long, is of the latter type.

"How many of these houses have you seen with a ceiling, Nigel?"

He doesn't answer you. He just looks upward and frowns. None is the answer. In the open-style living of your average noggie, a ceiling can only be for hiding something.

There is a manhole up there, and Nigel circles on the floor, watching it carefully, eyeing it from every possible angle. The house is one room, but ten people live here—they are easy to count because you have them bailed up in the corner. One old man with traditional goatee beard, two old women with lips cherryroot red, a younger woman who might be the mother of the six children of varying ages and degrees of nakedness. The adults all wear the sheening black pyjamas. They all face one way, looking very concerned.

"What's up there?"

The gesture with the muzzle of your SLR makes the meaning plain, but they choose not to understand, and say nothing.

"Better have a look then," Nigel sighs.

You'd like to offer some sort of warning to the blokes outside, but you can't afford to take your eyes off this fuckin' lot. There's Spargo and Sniffer manning Mabel at the front of the house, Alby Dunshea and Bugsy to either side watching the back, Greyman searching the grounds. At moments like this, the manpower shortage is fuckin' critical.

Nigel begins to build a construction under the manhole. He drags the heavy table into place, heaves a smaller table on top, then a wooden trunk atop that. Looks pretty fuckin' rickety but it will have to do. The old man and young woman begin to murmur at each other and look very unhappy. Perhaps they are concerned that he will scuff the furniture, but that is unlikely. These bare floor houses are a mess anyway. Every morning the women sweep attentively the square in front of the house, but inside it's a rug on the bald earth and all their belongings piled upon it in utter chaos. It is impossible to tell where in here the ten people actually do their sleeping.

"You're being frowned at, Nigel," you say softly.

He starts making his way up toward the hatch. He leaves his Armalite on the tabletop and takes from a holster the Luger that is his own property. 'If we're gonna act like Nazis, we might as well look the part,' he commented on it previously, but it is jobs like this he was referring to. Now your hostages start muttering at each other with some urgency.

"Watch yourself, Nigel."

Nigel attains full height, lifts the hatch with the muzzle of the Luger, very slowly. He peeks over the edge but the opening faces the wrong way to allow a good view. Now he gives the hatch a heave and it flops over on the inside. He ducks, but nothing happens. Nigel raises himself and pokes his head up through into the ceiling...

Then ducks again...

There is a single shot!

Nigel comes toppling down, his whole rickety construction collapsing under him. The Noggies all scream and yell and dive for cover, as if they expect you are about to mow them down on the spot. Forget them—you're going sideways, one eye on that manhole, the other on the felled Nigel, who threshes about madly in a tangle of overturned furniture.

"He's going out through the roof!" Nigel roars.

Instincts take over. There are too many things to think about at once but you've stopped thinking anyway. It's all reflexes from here. Nigel's head is still attached to his shoulders—forget him. You've searched the house and there are no concealed weapons—forget the rest of the family. Nigel's problem anyway. There's a man on the roof—get him! That's all. You go charging like a wild animal, out of the house and into the sunlight.

Out there, people are everywhere. In these moments of action, time seems to slow down absurdly, while your mind races through everything you see, feel, sense. You glimpse Snowy on his feet, swinging Mabel around at the hip, the long trailing belt of ammunition flailing like a metallic snake. He's moving in slow motion, and he doesn't know where to look; staring at you with a quizzical expression. Wide of him, Sniffer on his knees, pointing his rifle all directions. In these confined jumbled places, a sound like a gunshot seems to come from everywhere at once.

"He's up on the fucking roof!" you scream wildly.

You can see him too. The afternoon sun throws the shadow of the house to the front and there a figure appears fleetingly, going left, jumping from the eaves into the alley at the side. You go that way, knowing full well that you are heading into Snowy's line of fire, but you also know that Snowy has seen you, knows where you are. Leading him onto the target, you bound to the front of the alley. The man, barechested, barefoot, black shorts, carrying what might be a .303. He's landed heavily, fallen, comes up on his feet, not knowing which way to run. Then he sees you, and bolts the other way.

Now there's the moment of crisis. You're in Snowy's line of fire and know it—either you get out of the way and give him a clear go at the target or else you go after him yourself and risk getting a burst from Snowy up your bum.

"Yogi! Get outa the fucking way!" you hear Snowy roaring behind you, and you don't need to look—best not to anyway—to know he is on line down the alley. Just dive out of the way and leave him to it, all your instincts shriek. But no. There's other people moving up there!

One of them, you realise, is Dunshea who has moved in to block the other end of the alley—no shot for Snowy now. The target charges the astonished Dunshea and hits him full in the chest with a shirt-front any rugged half-back-flanker would be proud of; the shoulder right into the middle of the chest—whop?—and you actually hear the air expelled from Dunshea's lungs by the impact. He goes down flat on his back and the little man goes over the top and tumbles. Now you're the only opportunity and you race down the alley at full pace. The target comes up dazed, shaking his head, swinging that .303 wildly. He goes to take a pot shot to the right, toward Bugsy who must be over there somewhere, and then looks back and freezes when he sees you coming.

You roar like a charging elephant and the target's eyes widen as he sees you bearing down upon him. Three more strides and you'll have the little fucker by the throat and shake the fuckin' livin' daylights out of him, but you have to hurdle the fallen Dunshea, who is coming up dazed, your boot catches his shoulder and over you go—whacko!—flat on your face. The perfect bellywhacker on the hard ground.

When you glance up, the line-up is perfect. Straight between the target's legs you see Bugsy, down on one knee, his SLR at the shoulder—you're looking straight down the barrel and know how he's itching to have a go with it. The target quickly realises his good fortune. He probably can't believe the Griffin-Dunshea slapstick routine, much less that Bugsy hasn't cut him down yet. But Bugsy holds his fire and starts prancing sideways, going wide, fifteen metres away, looking for a line on the target that doesn't include you. By now Snowy and Mabel, and Sniffer and the pathetically hobbling Nigel are coming down the alley. The little man is up and off, limping, running for his life, straight past Bugsy and toward the houses beyond.

You bounce and come up on your knees, swinging the AK around. You'll get him before he's made twenty yards and he needs thirty to any cover. You bring the butt to the shoulder, line him up, death narrows the gap...but no! Fuck it! *There's people back there.*

"Shoot him!" Nigel is roaring. "Splatter the little bastard!"

You're stumbling wide, lining up again, but always there are unsuspecting people beyond, standing, staring, and others moving about, still unaware of the drama. You realise now what Bugsy's problem was. Too many people. Innocent bystanders... You keep moving, searching for that clear line...too late.

By now the trampling herd has caught up and you join in. The target runs between two houses and you go after him, but when you emerge, you find you are in a wide marketplace, stalls all about the perimeter and a twenty yard clear circle in the middle. And about a hundred people, mostly women and children, all standing like an audience, wondering what street theatre they are watching.

The target has charged straight out into the middle and now darts this way and that, unsure of where to go. You come bowling through for another moment of confrontation, Snowy and Co. right on your heels.

"Get outa the way! Get outa the fucking way!" Snowy is

bellowing and heaves the heavy gun to the shoulder. You get out of the way, but the target is running across the face of the crowd on the far side of the circle. Suddenly, they know the danger and a unified scream goes up.

It's only a moment but that's all it needs. Snowy, Sniffer, Nigel and myself, all with weapons aimed, twenty yards from the running man, easy shot. But behind him, frantic terrified people scatter. You'd get him all right but these high powered weapons don't stop at one body. A 7.62mm round will go straight through him and five other people as well, the less controllable Mabel even in the mighty hands of Snowy will down a dozen or more.

Nigel throws his Armalite away and has the Luger out again—only 9mm single shot. Sniffer has abandoned his SLR and is after the man flailing his machete, but it is all too late. The target plunges through the wave of panicking onlookers, ploughing through screaming women shielding children hopelessly, others on the ground with their hands over their heads, still more running this way and that with their heads thrown back and the whites of their eyes and bared teeth showing. Too late. You run forward after Sniffer, but the target is gone, vanished, the chance lost.

Nigel is furious. He is red-faced with rage, bellowing at you all from a few feet away. "You let the fucker get away. He fuckin' near blew me head off and you let him get away!"

"Too many people," Snowy groans lamely. "We'd of wiped out half the fuckin' village!"

Nigel, in sheer frustration, looks about for someone else to blame, and finds the easiest target.

"What fuckin happened to you, Yogi? You had him, right here!"

You just give a hopeless shrug and let that be your answer.

But Bugsy can't be so sensible. "Calm down, Nigel. There's no fuckin' way we coulda got him."

"Try telling that to fuckin' Hatrack!" Nigel thunders.

It was right then that Greyman wandered onto the scene, his puzzled black face wondering what the commotion was all about.

"Where the fuck were you!" Nigel roars at him.

"I missed the whole thing," Greyman says cheekily. "Musta been fuckin' hilarious."

"But where the fuck were you!"

"I was having a shit, awright?"

"Yeah," Dunshea says laconically. "And so was everyone else."

Fifteen minutes later, the section is standing in a pathetic line in the middle of the village with the Noggies looking on and trying to pretend they don't know what's happening, and Hatrack, mood as black as thunder, laying into his men and all jutting angles—nose, ears, jaw, elbows, shoulders, hips. They call him Hatrack because of the way these bits stick out, perfect for hanging things on, except you think they meant *hat-stand*, but who cares. To them, the word Hatrack can be spat out in a way that says exactly what they feel.

"How the fuck did you all miss? It's wide open here!" he raged, and the Noggie audience all stepped back a pace to show how wide open it was. Hatrack was a most unreasonable man at any time, and all the more so when he was right.

"There were people, everywhere..." Nigel tried to tell him.

Hatrack stepped forward to hang the blame on individuals—it was his favourite technique.

"Come on, Snowy. You're the hottest M60 man in the outfit. Thirty, forty yards at most. How the fuck did you miss?"

"There was dust, people, sir," Snowy said lamely. "I never even saw him clearly. Closest thing I came to hitting was Bugsy."

Bugsy rolled his eyeballs with appreciation, but Hatrack wished only to offer him the slightest glance as he passed along the line. "Might have known you'd be in the way, Norris, as per fucking usual. What about you, Sniffer? Crack shot. What happened?"

"Like Nigel says, there was people everywhere. It woulda been a massacre, sir."

He arrived at Dunshea, who by then was sporting a splendid black eye from his collision. "Where'd you get that one, Dunshea?"

"I zigged on a zag, sir," Dunshea managed.

Hatrack, a man utterly devoid of a sense of humour, could never have grasped a concept like that.

"Greyman the Greyman, away in the Dreamtime again were we?"

"I wish I was, sir."

You are at the end of the line.

"One of these days I'll wipe that silly grin off your face, Yogi Bear. Where were you? In hibernation?"

"No," you said softly. What you didn't say was *'no, sir'* but they had long since given up trying to get you to do that.

Truly, Hatrack could think of nothing further to say, and turned away, shaking his head in dismay.

"You owe me a body, Nigel. Make sure I get it."

They all wondered if his own might have filled the bill.

Buddha's Day Off

An old man lay dying on a low, narrow cot in a musky darkened room. You knew he was dying the moment you parted the long veil hanging over the doorway and peered into the dim interior. You can smell it when people are dying like this—a particular odour of human decay that permeates these places, these so-called villages where so-called people lived. Human beings they might have been by species, but the RSPCA would not allow animals to live the way these people do, or have to. In this damp tropical heat everything rots immediately, and what these people—these villagers—possess; their houses, their belongings, their children, their lives, all reek of active decomposition. The odours of rotting things fill the land, reaching into even the remotest parts of the jungle—it turns your stomach until you get used to it, and then you, like them, don't care anymore. But the smell of rotting human flesh is different to all the other rotting smells, different even to that of decomposition after death. As soon as you parted the curtain, and even before your eyes became accustomed to the darkness, and you could make out only the vague form of the cot, you told yourself: a man lies there and he is dying.

You slipped the safety on your AK and raised the muzzle carefully until it pointed at the figure—you could make all the assumptions you liked on the basis of the best possible evidence, but that didn't mean you could be careless. You made no movement, waiting for your eyes to adjust to the dimness, to sharpen their focus. A dying man hidden in a darkened room might well be Charlie, having crawled here in his agony to await a sad, ignominious death in the stifling darkness. Such a dying man might see you as a last chance at glory, attained by a pistol or hand grenade hidden under the pillow. You waited, until you could be sure. There were no chances left worth taking.

Slowly, too slowly, your eyes began to make him out. Both hands were visible, one draped across his belly, the other dangling off the edge of the cot, almost touching the floor. Skeletal, withered hands. But he was clear. You looked quickly about the room for hiding places in case he had friends, but it was solid plaster, three paces wide, seven long, with no cupboards or alcoves, nowhere to hide. There was only you and the old man—you slipped the safety and lowered the AK and quietly paced to the side of the cot.

He was old, very old and thin, an emaciated torso threaded through a loincloth, with the sash of a bandage on his gaunt, prominent ribs. His head lolled over the end of the cot—he wasn't seeing you, or anything. His stomach moved slightly with his faint breathing, eyes open and gazing at a precise point on the ceiling. He was so thin that his ribs stood out like curved pickets on a fence, and the bandage, six inches wide and wrapped right around his body, bulged where cotton wool had been stuffed in on the right side of his ribcage; got him clean through the lung, you reckoned. The old man's eyes wobbled around to look at you for a moment, his head lifting slightly from the mattress, and although he saw you, no expression registered on his face. Then his head fell back, teeth bared, nostrils flaring in his struggle to breathe.

He was an old man like so many old men in these villages, needed now to do the work because there were no young men. In these villages all the young men and young women had been drafted into one army or the other, or were dead, and old men like these were the strength of the community, with their big smiles and goatee beards, offering the soldiers rice wine, squatting in clusters and nodding knowingly. The children ran about in the mud and squalor between the shanty buildings, splattered with the slime of the streets, crowding about the soldiers begging for Salem—their preferred mentholated fags—and chop-chop—food of any kind. In return they offered their sisters, who were all under thirteen or else their mothers and over forty. The 'sisters' in question stood tittering in doorways and looked as nubile and enticing as they could. And the old men squatted, nodding their wisdom, paying no heed. In a world ridden with poverty, there was no generation gap. The old men squatted with their bare feet in the shit, sucking their cherryroot pipes, watching the soldiers go by as they had all their long lives.

This old man was a priest, you assumed, for the room was in a temple. One of those shaven-headed Buddhist priests in bright orange robes who sat in city squares and doused themselves in petrol and went up in a ball of flame. No one really understood why they did that. No fiery death for this old bugger though—just this scungy mattress on a sagging cot.

There was a robe, white not orange, by the bed. You leaned the AK on the cot and picked it up and rolled it into a ball and placed it under his bald cranium. The flesh was clammy to touch, repulsive, but at least that allowed his mouth to close, sparing you his rotten teeth, black where they weren't yellow. Now you reached for the bandage, to see what you could see, and saw his eyes widen with horror, but you needed to examine that wound. You raised the cotton wool a few inches and promptly let go again as a pungent smell of gas gangrene gushed up at you nauseatingly:

"Jesus."

There was a hole under there all right and it was huge—how huge you didn't need to know. The old man gazed at you with his expressionless expression. You sighed, picked up the AK and pushed through the thin woven veil back to where the brighter light of the temple interior savaged your eyes.

It was a Buddhist temple—the squatting gentleman, surprisingly thin in effigy, occupied that space where altar and cross would have been in what you had experienced as a church. There were no pews—the faithful knelt directly on the mosaic stone floor—wobbly knees like yours would have been tested here. It was a massive stone building, of French influence, layered with pink plaster that was riddled with bullet holes and chunks exploded away. It was the largest building in the town except for the Catholic Church. But that was why you were here, wasn't it.

In this main interior of the temple, Greyman drifted, his heritage baffled by the symbols and effigies and artefacts of devotion that, to atheistic you, was the same nonsense in different clothes.

"Hey Greyman. Go get Nigel, quick."

Greyman turned quietly and with all due reverence made his way outside. You looked back toward the veil, but there was no reason to return in there. Because it seemed the natural way to go, you walked slowly toward the Buddha, squatting upon a pedestal more than a man's height above the level of the room. An angelic ray of sunlight reached down to touch the exulted face, and your eye traced it upward. There, high on the gables, was a hole—three or four tiles were missing, the terracotta fragments scattered on the floor. Following that line led you to the step at the foot of the Buddha where there was a patch of dried blood. Someone should have cleaned up by now, you would have thought.

Yesterday Charlie rocketed a convoy of trucks just outside this village and brought an airstrike of Phantoms down upon themselves. Those big 50 cal shells could bounce and go for miles and still hit with sufficient force to turn those roof-tiles into shrapnel. That was the answer, for sure. The poor old bugger was still probably wondering how he had provoked the Buddha to strike him down so savagely.

"Whatever he said, he didn't mean it," you remarked to Buddha's fat-lipped smile.

That attack had brought you here—too late since any Charlies worth catching would have been long gone, but orders were orders. Hatrack's men descended upon the village and went from house to house, searching through everything, checking everyone. It was all to demonstrate that the Uc Dai Loi did not take lightly their men and equipment being mistreated so.

"Uc Dai Loi Number One. Vit Cong Number Ten," the Noggies told you incessantly. It was harder to believe every time you heard it.

This was a village under constant pressure from Charlie and the search was thorough and complex its planning. Near Nui Dat the Sappers were building a complete town surrounded by barbed wire, and many of these people would be rehoused there where they could be guarded or protected, out of Charlies' reach, and forcibly moved if necessary. Intelligence officers would come and interview or interrogate all families, and your job was to clear the way for them, to ensure they got no nasty surprises.

A temporary hospital had been set up in the marketplace, offering medical attention in return for 'hearts and minds'. There they were to dispatch any sick or injured people, but already the unexpected proportions of that task was overwhelming them. Everywhere they went there were people with missing limbs or foul sores, children bloated with malnutrition, women with hideous skin infections, old men so deformed that their hands touched the ground when they walked. Disease dominated this place; it was as if the town itself was a festering wound. Even most of their mangy dogs were three-legged. Ten Platoon found two young men with gangrenous legs turned black and as thick as their bodies—undoubtedly Charlies too ill to escape the cordon. But there were also many wounds on women and children, caught in the crossfire. Every one of them had to be escorted or carried to the Medical Area, and this old man just another.

The plod of Nigel's rubber-soled boots resounded in the chamber of the temple as he came in, tailed by Greyman.

"What's the go, Yogi?"

You jerked a thumb toward the room with its cobweb veil

and Nigel strode on in without hesitating and came right out again.

"Holy fucking mother of Siddhartha. What a fuckin' pong!"

Obviously he had not had time to examine the wound.

"Copped a ripper." Your voice reverberating across to him from where you stood on the steps. "Right through the lung. Looks like a 50 cal. Come in up there and zapped him while he prayed to the enlightened one."

"The bolt from the blue, hey? If he was Catholic, they'd make him a saint for this."

You smiled, but Nigel looked about bleakly, helpless and hesitating—these sorts of days were the worst of all. The natural environment of the Uc Dai Loi was the jungle—you felt awkward and vulnerable in these urban situations.

"Greyman," he said finally. "Go down to the Medical Area and bring back a doctor."

Greyman, who had also gone in for a gander and been driven out by the stink as swiftly as Nigel had, did not respond. You knew why, and looked firmly at Nigel.

"He's fucked," you said.

"I know that! But we can't just leave him there."

"Why not? He's probably supposed to die in there. Part of their religious mumbo-jumbo. Why not just leave him to it?"

"If you wanted to do that, Yogi Bear, you wouldn't have called me in," Nigel said slyly.

"I just thought you might be interested."

Nigel didn't answer, turning to Greyman. The buck passed.

"Go get the quack, mate. Take Sniffer with you for backup."

Greyman nodded sadly and went off. You followed.

"I need you here, Griffin," Nigel said fiercely.

"I'm just going outside for some fresh air," you said.

Wisely, Nigel let that happen.

You stepped through the columned portals of the temple where once great doors had hung—the rusted hinges were still there, the bolts still clinging to fragments of shattered timber. Walking forward on the stone forecourt chipped and scarred by explosions and bullets, you stopped one pace short of where the line of shade ended and the dazzling area exposed to the sun began. The Temple had a high wall around it, topped with upright shards of jagged glass—the poor man's barbed wire—and a broad area of carefully swept dirt lay between the building and the wall. In front of every building in every town in Vietnam the ground was swept every morning, and the bare dirt surface rendered smooth as concrete. The footprints of the soldiers showed clearly here. No one else, you could see, had done any walking that morning.

Snowy had set up Mabel over by the wide gateway in the wall, facing outward through the opening toward the village. He and Bugsy made use of the shade of a huge tree that grew outside but extended branches over the wall. Snowy was brewing coffee, but Bugsy was facing back into the courtyard, rifle across his thighs as he sat propped against the wall, and when he saw you he motioned toward the area to the left of the building. You nodded, and, keeping in the shade, moved along the raised forecourt in that direction.

Inside the compound were several other buildings; those to the right of the temple seemed to be a school of some kind, and behind that was a barn or storehouse, to the left and behind the temple was what might have been a low prison cell block, most likely the quarters of the monks. They had split their forces—yourself and Greyman into the temple proper; Nigel and Sniffer down to check out the school and barn; Dunshea on his own but covered by Snowy and Bugsy, to search the quarters. This last stage of the plan had not worked out, you saw as you reached the right side of the temple. About thirty monks with their orange robes, bare feet and shaven heads, were standing in a line outside their quarters, murmuring to each other and looking very unhappy and each carrying a tall wooden staff. Dunshea stood before them, wondering what to do next.

"Hey, Alby, what's up."

He looked around edgily; plainly he did not want to turn his back on his tormentors.

"They won't let me in."

"Maybe you didn't ask politely enough."

Dunshea snorted through his thick nose and backed up until he was level with you, never taking his eyes off the gathering. Maybe it was his great ugly puss that was bothering them, but you missed the chance to say so.

"Where's Nigel?" he asked.

"Inside. We got a sickie."

He nodded, keeping his eyes on those monks. So did you. They didn't look any happier now that their antagonist had moved away. There was about forty yards between them and you now.

"These blokes won't let me in," Dunshea explained. "Being right nasty about it."

"Probably because of your winning smile," you offered.

"Nigel know about them,"

"Yeah. He saw them."

"They probably think we're invading sacred ground or something," you proposed, though you really didn't know anything about it. "Keep an eye on them."

"I'll keep both eyes on them, I'll give 'em somethin' to chant about."

You nodded. He sat on a parapet in the shade of the temple, facing that unmoving line of orange.

"Better not let them get hold of any petrol drums," you added and immediately regretted it; the images accompanying that remark were better not conjured.

"Piss orf yer iggle-headed pooftas," Dunshea growled. "Yer give me the creeps."

You walked slowly back toward the temple entrance, but paused when Snowy signalled from the gate. Moments later, Greyman and Sniffer came through, followed by Ten Days, who as medic might prove useful, and Lt Hollingsworth, who certainly wouldn't. All four pulled up short when they saw the gathering of monks.

"What's with these chaps?" Holly wanted to know.

"Fan club," Dunshea said dryly. "We seem to have lost their hearts and minds."

Holly gave Dunshea the bleakest of looks, and then, because officers have to give orders now and then to prove to themselves that they are officers, he turned on Snowy. "Why haven't you turned the gun around, Private Spargo, to face the threat from these hostiles?"

"Buddhist monks are pacifists, sir. They aren't allowed to be hostile."

"They don't look in a pacifistic mood to me, Private Spargo," Holly determined.

"Maybe it's their day off," Greyman mused.

We all chuckled until Holly, reddened with fury, snapped his final word. "Turn the gun around and watch them, Private Spargo. This is a war zone. No such thing as a pacifist here."

You turned, shaking your head, to lead them into the temple, knowing that Snowy would leave Mabel exactly where she was.

The cooler air inside was a relief after the unbreathable rancid stuff out there—still Sniffer and Greyman saw the sense in not following and took up places near Dunshea. It was always wise to keep out of the sight and mind of officers, even harmless ones like Holly.

Nigel sat on the steps below the Buddha, brewing a mug of tea right there on the floor of the holy chamber.

"I thought I asked for a doctor," he said, eyeing Ten Days with disdain.

"The doctors have their hands full at the Medical Area," Ten Days explained. "House calls just aren't on."

Holly had vertical lines to either side of his mouth that worked like fish gills when he was irritated. "What have you got for us, Nigel?"

Nigel looked at you.

"Old man with a six inch hole punched through his ribs," you pointed in all the appropriate directions. "Looks like a 50 cal came in through the roof and got him while he prayed to the big fella."

"A sign from Nirvana, I imagine," Holly remarked. Only the eternal smile of Buddha could endure the same joke for a third time. But God, in any religion, was definitely not an American pilot.

Ten Days went in through the veil and Holly followed, took one gasping breath, and came right out again. To justify that little embarrassment, he turned sharply on Nigel. "So what are you doing about the situation outside?"

"What situation outside?" Nigel asked, stirring his tea assiduously.

"The monks seem to be agitated by our presence here."

"And rightly so," Nigel said. "I saw them as I came in. They won't bother us if we don't bother them."

"They look in a fairly dangerous mood to me."

"Not half as dangerous as I bet we look to them."

"I did not come here for a philosophical discussion, Corporal Naughton."

Neither Nigel nor you bothered to ask why he had come, making his superfluous presence all the more evident.

Ten Days saved what might have been a regrettable confrontation by reappearing through the veil. The fierce gust of pungent air that came with him said that the bandage had been changed. Fat lot of good that was.

"He's rooted," Ten Days pronounced solemnly. "Buggered if I know how he's still alive."

"We already know that, clown," Nigel bit at him, wearying now.

The tirelessly formal Holly said. "What do you suggest,

Corporal Hollis?"

"We'll have to take him to the interrogation area, I guess," Ten Days proposed with a helpless shrug.

Nigel was shaking his head. "I suspect our friends outside mightn't like that. That's why I wanted the doctor brought here..."

Holly bristled. Ten Days continued to tread the tightrope between them. "Prob'ly nothing the doc could do even if he did come."

"So what's the point of taking him down there?" Nigel seethed.

"Well I don't know," flustered Ten Days.

But Holly did. "Orders state specifically that all ill and injured are to be removed to the Medical Area for treatment. The major was quite adamant about that."

"Fuck Hatrack!" Nigel bellowed.

And we were all happy to allow that to echo about the chamber for a few moments.

Throughout all this you had shown the good sense to keep your thoughts to yourself, but now Nigel had negated himself with anger and Ten Days with confirmation of the obvious.

"Why don't we just leave him here to die in peace," you suggested, as if you'd just thought of it.

"We can't do that," Holly said. "It's inhumane."

"So's moving him," you countered. "Even if we get past the orange hordes outside, he probably won't survive the trip."

"If we get him down there," Ten Days put in. "They might be able to give him something to ease his pain...or...something."

"He's not in any pain," you debated. "They have this meditation stuff that causes them not to feel a thing."

"What would you know about it, Private Griffin?" Holly interjected.

He was right. You had no particular knowledge of such matters, but you didn't need to know much to work this out.

"Obviously he is supposed to die in there, right where he is."

Holly glared at you angrily. "Well what do you want to do, Yogi Bear? Go in there and belt him over the head and finish him off?"

You looked at Nigel. For both of you that seemed a remarkably sensible suggestion.

But it had developed into one of those situations where Holly could see that all this arguing was eroding his sense of authority and self-importance. You were merely a diversionary tactic, and now he turned on Nigel and made his stand as fiercely as so small a man could manage. "You will move him, Corporal Naughton, to the Medical Area, and that is an order. If you don't have him down there in half an hour, it'll be your stripes, and I mean it. I'm going to round up some more men in case those chaps outside decide to make trouble. But you get him down there, and do it now."

He turned on his heel and marched away, getting out before anyone could raise further dispute. You slept better, knowing that your leaders were strong and wise.

Nigel, still seated on the steps, dashed the dregs of his tea at the feet of the Buddha.

"Alright Ten Days, how do we go about this. Pick him up, bunk and all..."

Ten Days was pained by the need to think about it. "No. Too bumpy and awkward. Best if you just pick him up in your arms and carry him that way."

Nigel looked at you from under his heavy brow. "You found him, Yogi. He's yours."

You didn't want to be looked at, though it was fair enough. You had, after all, started all this. Nigel continued looking, and finally you handed your AK to Ten Days. Still, you could manage one final attempt at sanity.

"Aren't we gonna wait til Holly brings the extra men?"

"Fuck Holly!" Nigel roared. Somehow, his name did not resound half as much as Hatrack's did.

You returned to that abysmal room. The old man lay as before, unmoved by all this moralising on his behalf. Nigel and Ten Days took up position to either side, to render what assistance they could, but they weren't needed. You slipped one arm under the old man's shoulders, the other under his thighs and started to raise him.

"Shit, he doesn't weigh anything," you breathed.

The expressionless expression and bulging eyes fixed on your face, but there was neither resistance nor cooperation. You cradled him against your chest as best you could, then turned and headed out into the temple proper.

"When you get outside, head straight for the gate, pronto, no matter what," Nigel yelled urgently, and darted ahead of you while Ten Days scurried along behind.

You carried him easily, maintaining a balanced brisk stride without jolting him around too much, and so you proceeded out of the temple and into the sunlight.

Nigel went bolting across the courtyard ahead of you. "Snowy! Grab the gun, get behind Griffin, cover him. Rest of you, form a line, here, right now."

Given its unexpectedness, the response was like lightning. As you came out with your pathetic burden and the fussing Ten Days at your heel, Snowy was already running into position with the bulky Mabel, and Nigel was hastily gathering the others into a line facing the monks, blocking their access to the gate. Immediately a cry went up from the monks, and you glanced over your shoulder to see them running forward in a tight bunch, awkward in those orange robes, waving their staves over their heads.

"Keep going Griffin, whatever happens," Nigel was yelling above the din. "Awright, you guys. Back up, real slow, and for fuck's sake don't shoot anybody."

You had about thirty yards to make across the courtyard to the gate, Ten Days running ahead now, Snowy walking backwards behind you. The monks broke their run just short of the line of soldiers, and they levelled weapons at each other, the men with guns backing off, those with staves coming on menacingly. Nigel and his band were brandishing their rifles and shouting abusive threats at their adversaries, while the monks jabbed at them with the staves, uttering angry chants and fearful cries.

You reached the gate and glanced back—the converging forces were just twenty yards away and closing. Then one monk lashed savagely at Nigel with his stave. Nigel parried the blow easily, swiftly reversed his Armalite and, stepping a pace against the traffic, brought the butt down firmly on the monk's shining dome. The plastic butt of the Armalite cracked from one end to the other, and the monk took a nosedive into the dirt.

Everything stopped then. And you had stopped too, right at the gateway, realising that there was no reason to go any further. At precisely the same instant Nigel struck the monk down, the old man in your arms jolted violently, as if the blow had struck him. The convulsion was so sudden that you almost dropped him, and then you immediately wished you had.

The soldiers, frozen in various combat postures, realised that something had happened, and turned toward you as you turned toward them. Blood had exploded out of the old man's every orifice, gushing from nose, mouth and earholes and gurgling out from within his bandage and loincloth to splatter in a ghastly puddle at your feet, splashing onto your boots.

You just stood in horror and repugnance, the old man dangling lifelessly in your arms.

Staves and rifles were lowered. The monks halted their advance and gathered about their felled comrade, and Nigel and his men turned and walked to join you at the gate. The monks did not give chase. They helped the dazed man to his feet, murmuring to themselves, not even looking the way the soldiers had gone.

The men of four section gathered around you, and most had to turn their backs.

"Well, that's it," Ten Days pronounced unnecessarily.

Nigel bowed his head and then looked back to where the monks had gathered. Then he hurled his cracked weapon across to Dunshea who caught it deftly. "Give him to me," he said solemnly.

You were thankful to obey.

Slowly, reverently, Nigel carried the old man back toward the monks, walking right up to them and lowering the body to the ground at their feet. Any one of them could have belted him over the head, had they wanted. Nigel straightened, paused as if he intended to say something to them but did not, and then turned and came back toward the gate.

He went straight by you, snatching his weapon from Dunshea's hands as he passed. The others sullenly followed along. Behind, the monks fell upon the ground and began to wail for the lost soul of their dead companion. You wiped the blood from your hands on your greens, took your AK back from Ten Days, and followed after Nigel.

Riders on the Storm

...fading in again... Remember the rain beating down directly on your face, torrential rain sharply pummeling your cold flesh. Seems strange to be lying there like that, flat on the back, face upturned into the rain, making no attempt to defend yourself from it; you can feel it running in tiny rivulets—across the hollows of the eyes, down between the nose and cheeks, splashing over the lips... open those lips slightly to take some in... nice, cool, refreshing... Yet you feel so cold... got to open the eyes and see what's happening, but the rain pounding the eyelids won't allow it... can't do it... raise a hand to shield them and try... that's better... You open the eyes slowly but they immediately fill with the water... close and squeeze to get rid of it then open again... it's still a watery blur and even when that clears there is only blackness... the back of your hand barely distinguishable from the dark wet world beyond... Rain pouring down and you can hear the wind howling out there... but it's all blackness and then intermittent flashes of blinding light that are only momentary whiteness... Nothing can be seen... there is no anchor for your senses... just the storm... oh yeah, you remember the storm. The storm rages in the night and is no dream, no nightmare, or else the nightmare is real. You remember the storm.

*

Nigel warned you about the storm. A typhoon no less, brewing out in the South China Sea, heading toward the coast of Vietnam. Not this far south though. Way up north. Ho in Hanoi, they'd really be copping it. Still its effects even at this distance were powerful enough...

You saw it coming as you flew in the chopper, one of a row of a dozen in two files, flying across the face of a massive brooding cloud formation in the shape of a giant anvil that filled the sky in that direction—the advance forces of the raging monster behind. You watched it closing in with sullen silent faces, the sunlit billows atop ranging downward through deepening shades of increasingly troubled grey to the dismal streaky downpour on the jungle beneath. Even in the chopper you could feel the new sharpness, the chill, on the wind. In all these months of heat you had forgotten cold, but that didn't mean you sweated any less. You sat in the rattling chopper taciturnly observing the approaching cold front, silently cursing it as one more hardship to overcome.

You sat on the lurching metal floor with feet dangling over the side, along with Snowy who clutched his beloved Mabel to his chest and Nigel, both watching the storm as you did, teeth gritted in disgust. Out there the other choppers, flying westward over the central mountains to the flatter country in the fartherest reaches of the province. No Man's Land. The choppers slid up and down like pistons in an engine, shaken constantly by variable turbulence, dropping into sudden air pockets, the rotors flapping frantically for purchase in the gusting air, quivering with vibration, twisted continually from their relentless course by the irrational wind.

At the head of the line, the two gunships peeled off and banked toward a distant clearing and went racing back and forth while you circled, waiting, at two thousand feet. The gunships skipped about the clearing at treetop height, guns blazing into the forest on both sides, until they decided it was clear and one dropped a red smoke grenade, and then your choppers banked around and began the descent, shuffling into single file, anxiously bouncing and thumping their way toward the earth. And all the time the gunships zipping back and forth, holding the ground.

*

"They say there's a camp at this place called Ap An Quai and the SAS reckon its brim full of Charlies," Nigel had said. "We're going in to clean the fuckin' joint out."

"Oh sure," Snowy answered in flat monotone. "I reckon we'll be sweepin' the gutters and emptyin' the rubbish bins. There hasn't been a Charlie within miles of one of these camps yet."

"Be that as it may," Nigel said, not smiling at all as he sipped from his mug of tea. "Our wondrous leader Hatrack has decided we haven't earned our pay this week, so in we go to have a geek."

He jabbed an indicatory finger at the flat green continuum of the map he had laid out on the ground before you. "We fly in to this point here and then march five thousand metres to this Ap An Quai place. That's it there."

"Five thousand metres!" Greyman cried. "Shit, what do we do after breakfast?"

Nigel smiled flickeringly now: "We have breakfast first, but we are in a hurry. We want to get in and out by nightfall. There's a big storm on the way and they reckon it might turn into a typhoon by tonight. We have to get there, check the camp out, and get back to Nui Dat before it hits."

"Nice to have an easy day for a change," Sniffer said dully.

*

...yes, it is night and the storm has hit with all the expected force, but you never got back again... You were still here, in the camp, in the storm, in the rain, lying flat on your back and helpless.

"Is someone there?"

"Yeah, Yogi. I'm here, mate."

A dark shape looms over you, a blacker area amid the general blackness. Lightning flashed and you can see it is the head of a man with a soggy fag dangling from his lips and a voice that itself is low and grumbling, like the storm. Knew him...

"That you, Bugsy?"

"Who else?" he chuckles. "How you feeling, Yogi?"

"Pretty fucking shithouse."

"Any pain?"

"Nar. Didn't bring your umbrella, did you?"

"Sorry, Yogi. There just isn't any place out of the rain around here."

"Guess we didn't make it back to The Dat, huh?"

"Not even nearly. You'll be there soon though. The choppers are on the way to take you sickies out. Us poor healthy bastards will have to stay out here all night."

"Tough titty. I wish they'd fuckin' hurry."

You seemed to have been lying there forever, for all your known life.

"Lucky to get them out in this," Bugsy ruminates. "All aircraft are grounded but a bunch of RAAF cowboys said fuck that! Pinched their own choppers to run the dust-offs in unflyable conditions. They can probably only do it because they'd all be pissed to the eyeballs at this hour..."

But it is fading again, his voice drifting off into the distance as if he is walking away as he speaks. Come back Bugsy don't leave me like this, only it isn't him who is leaving....

*

It should have been scrubbed from scratch. When the choppers had gone and left you in the clearing and the company began its trek in the pouring rain, it could have been said that there was ample time. On the drawing boards back at Nui Dat where the Task Force masters laid out their tactics, everything said it could have been done. Fly in, five thousand metres, cordon and sweep enemy encampment, mop up and back to Nui Dat. A good solid day's work. Perfectly feasible in theory. But even as you began the march, the world closed in on you. In the shadows of the storm clouds, in the pounding cascades of rain, in the dense shrouded jungle, you walking into a dim narrowing world.

"Any chance of an appeal against the light?" Nigel asked grimly.

It was clear after the first hour that you weren't going to get there in time.

*

Visions of men trudging in the deluge, teeth bared, eyes squinted, constantly troubled by their footing on the uneven sloppy ground. Your clothes and gear were saturated, utterly waterlogged, doubling the weight. Even under the roof of the jungle, the curtain of rain was so heavy that visibility was often restricted to a few yards, and you wondered how anyone could possibly know where they were going. You had walked through heavy rainstorms before, the sudden torrents that hit daily, at a predictable time, flooding everything in a matter of minutes, then just as suddenly stop, the sun would reappear, steam would rise and in no time it would be as hot and dry as if the rain had never happened. This was different. The rain went on and on, thunder erupted almost continually and lightning streaked the sky—a flickering florescence in the murk. The jungle was all instantaneous shadows and indefinable shapes that kept the nerves on edge. The thunder rang in your ears and set your hearts beating at an erratic pace.

"The Great War Gods are angry," The Greyman said forbiddingly.

In the third hour, they ran into trouble—a swamp with trees so dense that you had to cut your way through. The maps were unclear—there was no way of telling what might be gained by attempting to go around this watery forest and the fear of navigational errors that might be induced by such a detour left no alternative but to chop a path straight through. There was the advantage that these soft water trees could be sliced through with a single blow of a machete and most blows lopped several at a time. In a wild frenzy, the lead section hacked away at the wall while the rest of you stood waiting in the green and yellow tunnel they created, up to your calves in slime and boughs and giant leaves, fighting a ceaseless war with the leeches.

The leeches were mostly a minor irritation except that they had a nasty habit of entering the channel of the prick and rendering the owner a screaming wreck until he was got to hospital and a tiny umbrella device was employed to extract the invader. You shuddered at the thought of that dreadful contrivance, and the waiting men needed no encouragement to light a cigarette every ten minutes, lower their daks and burn off the dozen or so new infiltrators on their legs. The cigarettes were regulation issue with the US ration packs, and, like the Vietnamese children, the company's handful of resolute non-smokers also had a preference for Salems. But most gasped Chesterfields and Camels.

There was too, a dread of being bitten on the bum by the watersnakes...

You took your place at the head of the line. Under Hatrack's impatient urging, Nigel, Bugsy and Sniffer chopped frantically until exhausted, you, Greyman and Alby Dunshea took over, and then the mighty Snowy had a furious session all on his own since his huge backswing allowed no space for anyone else. You got to hold Mabel for those few minutes—a rare concession. Snowy swung and slashed way beyond the strength of the other men and then, as if in divine acknowledgment of his effort, daylight suddenly appeared through the broad leaves. Snowy sheathed his machete and hurled his whole body at the wall and ploughed right on through, disappearing out there somewhere with a massive splash. They broke through behind him, Hatrack clawing his way past you, and his momentary jubilance was quickly swamped by gloom.

"Ohhh no," they moaned.

There, spreading away before you in all directions was a vast shallow lake, dotted with clumps of weeds and water trees, stretching ahead of you to the horizon.

"We'll have to go through it," Hatrack gritted, mostly to himself in his despair at the soggy mess the expedition was becoming.

"We can't," Nigel protested. "We don't know how deep it is."

Hatrack flared with fierce impatience. "That's tough. We'll just have to find the shallow parts. We're way behind time already. Nigel, get your blokes together and lead us off."

"Which way?" Nigel asked, staring in frustration at the drowned world ahead.

Hatrack eyed him bleakly and cast a firm directing hand. "Straight across."

Hatrack ploughed back through the tunnel to consult his SAS guides and officers, while Nigel, grimacing angrily, turned toward you.

"Awright, saddle up, you guys. It's bath time!"

In single file, you weaved your way through that lake of foul mud like a huge snake, up to your knees and sometimes your waists in the odorous slime, struggling forward at the point of exhaustion, pushed on by the knowledge that when you stopped you immediately began to sink even deeper. There were the roots of the mangroves and reeds down there just below the bed of mud and that was all spared you from sinking to God knows what abysmal depths. Sniffer led the way until it was discovered that, lightly built, he was able to traverse ground over which heavier men could not follow.

"We need a bigger bloke up front," Nigel said and looked at you.

"What about Snowy. He's twice my size."

"Need him here. Away you go, Yogi."

It was tricky stuff in the lead. You stayed as close to each outcrop as you could, edging around it and then crossing to the next. Every step had to be tested first, probing with the boot for something to put your foot on, giving it a bit of weight, if it held, begin the next step. Directly behind, Nigel puzzled over your true course—at every turn you looked back and he checked the compass and offered the direction you should go, but you were rarely able to go that way. His attempts to make corrections for the constant deviations could only be guesswork.

After Nigel, Snowy struggled along with Mabel, following your footsteps exactly. Mabel was giving him hell—normally he carried her the way most men carried a rifle, but now her bulk was a major problem and he teetered along at the brink of collapse, worn down by his effort with the machete, frustrated by the number of times Mabel's bipod tangled in the mangrove vines, irritated by roots which had tripped him up, exasperated when the uneven footing bogged him down. Sniffer and Bugsy spent half their time gripping Snowy by the armpits to try and keep him afloat.

"He's a genius, that fuckin' Hatrack," Snowy thundered angrily. "No wonder we fuckin' love him so!"

Nigel looked back toward him, his own humour completely worn: "What the fuck are you bitchin' about now?"

"Wadda yer fuckin' reckon!" Snowy savaged back. "First he has us clearin' a fuckin' highway through that crap, now he navigates us into this fuckin' slop! He needs his fuckin' balls cut out, if he's got any!"

Nigel eyed his gunner with despair—it signalled the end of all reason.

"Bugsy. Give Snowy a break with the gun for a while."

Bugsy, a receiver of life's cruellest blows, only nodded and stepped forward and Snowy, so obsessively jealous of Mabel, this time gave her up gladly.

"Hungry for fuckin' kills, that's what he is," Snowy continued to rage. "Couldn't give a shit what happens to us poor fuckers as long as we get him some fuckin' kills and thrill the bigwigs back at Task Force."

Soon, Bugsy was equally wretched.

At the front of the line, you suddenly found that all strength was gone from your legs and you began sinking, slowly at first, then rapidly as you floundered about, and finally sucked right up to your chest. You could find no air to cry for help, and kept on silently going down until Nigel, turning from the Bugsy-Snowy distraction, saw your plight and plunged forward. You felt him grab you by the collar: you could only flail in no reasonable attempt to save myself whatsoever, and Nigel, unable to pull against the suction, could do no more than hang on desperately until Greyman and Alby Dunshea surged forward and helped him drag you out. They propped you up against the trunk of a mangrove and left you gasping and helpless.

"Why didn't you say something, you dill?" Nigel muttered. Still, there was no air available for speech.

"He was tryin' to drown himself," Snowy snarled. "Only fuckin' way out of this fuckin' mess."

"You bastards spoil all your fun," you gasped feebly.

"Awright, Alby. Take the lead."

"You know I always lead us into trouble..." Dunshea warned.

"We are already in trouble, dickhead," Nigel growled.

They moved on, Alby Dunshea taking the lead with a glance

that knew that soon your condition would be his, and you leaned for a while as they went by. Soon after, Kinross's section came through and took the lead and you slipped back down the line but it wasn't any easier there.

*

...now forever later and your can still smell that slimy lake. For hour upon hour you have been soaked by continuous rain yet still the stink of the mud prevails, as if it has permeated your whole body. You seemed to wander in that vile morass forever, now forever ago. Now lying in the rain and the darkness and still the storm raging on. But you can hear voices and sounds, the ring of machete's clear and sharp as men cut away at the trees. Sure, making a chopper pad, or at least clearing the canopy enough to allow one access overhead. Fuckin' useless. Couldn't fly in this shit anyway.

Other men moving, talking, but it is as if it is all going on around you and you were not there to be seen or noticed; a fish peering out of its aquarium, unable to penetrate the glass by word or deed.

"You there, Bugsy?" that voice that is yours but somehow not part of you calls croakily.

"Course I'm still fuckin' here."

"What time is it?"

"What do you want to know the fuckin' time for?"

"I dunno. I just..." but no, that isn't what you meant to ask, something different, not the time, but it's faded now, like everything else.

Then Bugsy says, perhaps as an afterthought: "You were out again for a while there, maybe fifteen minutes."

"Yeah. It keeps coming and going. But it was today, wasn't it, that we were in the swamp."

Bugsy chuckled: "Yeah, Yogi. About seven or eight hours ago. Seems a bloody lot longer, doesn't it."

"Pity we ever got out of it."

"Well, that's one way of looking at it, I suppose."

*

Finally you stumbled up onto firm ground, men dragging themselves free of the slime and collapsing without even the strength to help their struggling mates up the bank. All, that was, except Hatrack, athletic and maniacal, who came bounding out of the swamp like The Creature from the Black Lagoon and was amongst them in a fanatical frenzy. "Come on, come on, you men! Get off your bums! We're running out of time! On your feet! Come on, let's go! Let's go!"

You barrelled through the scrub for now the ground was flat and the scrub light and the going suddenly unbelievably easy after what you had been through. There was a long gentle upward incline that went on for miles, the footing was firm in spite of the rain, and the lead sections could open up and rush along, a long striding desperate pace that had you tail-waggers struggling to keep up. All that you knew of tactics and security was abandoned now—caution, quietness, alertness, these things so inherent to your lives, were forsaken in the blind rush to reach the objective while there was still daylight. You heard that Hatrack himself was now in the lead, along with other more reckless section leaders, for certainly he would never have persuaded someone like Nigel to travel at this pace, charging through the forest, desperate amid so many desperations to make up time as you ran with the day toward its end. And the storm too, seemingly apace with you, strove toward a new intensity—the rain streaking through this more open canopy, the lightning ripping open the dense grey sky, the thunder erupting about you like shell bursts. It was, Nigel said, like a cavalry charge without the benefit of horses; and they came swooping down like riders on the storm to unleash a manmade ravage of your own that rivalled the violence and anger of the typhoon and tore men's lives as the wind lashed the trees...

*

...still feeling the strain of that forced march too, in the weary leg muscles in spite of all that has happened since. And the pain that isn't really pain in the numbness that secretes it. It's the drugs, of course, setting your mind wandering, drifting in a maze of visions real and imagined but the worst ones are real. But for it all, you can still feel the exhaustion that wracks your entire body—neither pain nor numbness nor drugs could completely overwhelm the stress of a body where every muscle, every bone, every joint, seemed to ache, strained beyond all of its limits.

"You still there, Bugsy?"

No answer!

Panic immediately sweeps through you. That dread feeling that you have been left alone, deserted, maybe dead... It is so cold, so void, although there is the rain that is somehow a comfort, contact with life. So helpless, to be left like this. But hang on, there are sounds, men calling, moving, chopping, but they are all so far away, so remote.

"Hey Bugsy, where are you?"

"I'm here, fuck you Yogi. It's alright."

Not exactly here. He is a little way off still.

"I thought you were gone..."

"I was just having a piss, do you mind?"

You hear the rustle as he returns to his place, kneeling beside you, you can almost make out his darker form.

"What's going on?"

"It's alright, Yogi. Don't worry, mate."

"I was out of it again, huh?"

"Just for a few minutes."

Then there are other figures, looming over the top, and Bugsy stands to talk to them. You listen to the distance voices that are right there, as if you are at the bottom of a well.

"Private Griffin, is it?"

That is Bulldog Doyle.

"Yeah," says Bugsy. He doesn't sound too happy. Not at all encouraging in the circumstances.

"Leg," Ten Days' voice says. "No break but he's lost gallons of blood and still losing more. He'll have to be one of the first to go. Is he still conscious, Bugsy?"

"Keeps wandering in and out."

Sounds so strange, listening to people talk about you as if you didn't exist anymore.

"Very well, Corporal Hollis. Do what you can for him," says a different voice. You know that one too. It belongs to that bastard Hatrack...

"Piss off, Hatrack!"

That voice belonged to Yogi Griffin.

There is a shocked silence. Then Hatrack says. "Now, Private Griffin. Just because you're wounded doesn't mean..."

"Get lost you great ugly pile of shit or I'll get up and kick you to death you rotten shithead bloodhungry bastard!"

The second stunned pause is longer.

"I don't think you'll be kicking anybody for some considerable time, Private Griffin," Bulldog Doyle says coldly, but then, further away. "We'd better be moving on, Major."

"I want you to take disciplinary action, CSM..."

"Just move on, Major, before this gets out of hand."

And they are drifting away, or is it you. Test it out. "Bastard! You bloodthirsty killhappy bastard!"

Them drifting away this time.

It is amazing just how much better you suddenly feel, and Bugsy is chuckling as he gets down beside you. "Nicely handled, Yogi. Discreet. Charming. Tactful."

"I thought so."

"I bet you got yourself wounded just especially to be able to get away with that."

"It was almost worth it, Bugsy. Almost worth it."

*

It was Hatrack's fault. It was his fault for going on with the mission when conditions went so heavily against its chances of success. He could have called it off at any time, and should have, but his desperation to succeed would not allow that. And when they arrived, there was too little light left—although much lost time had been made up in that final frantic rush, the storm had brought darkness prematurely and there was simply not enough light. But Hatrack was determined to go on with it, and he did. Ten Platoon was despatched in a wide arc to lay ambushes on the far side of the camp. The rest of the company would sweep through and Charlie, should they be there, would bug out as was their custom and be caught in those Ten Platoon ambushes. Good enough in theory. But there was no time to recce and try and determine what they might have been up against. It was all done with maximum haste on the principle that the sooner you got in there, the more light you would have to see what you were doing. In those last seconds before darkness was complete, you went into the camp, tired, frustrated men, reflexes dulled, minds slow to respond to their senses

Peering through the gloom, you trudged unevenly, and could never have explained how you knew your senses were trying to tell you something. Mute senses, unable to get their messages through, could only raise your awareness until you knew you were looking for something in particular, something odd, something that did not fit, without knowing what it might have been nor even what caused you to look. Every nerve-end seemed exposed, nakedly outside your body like antennae.

Your eyes bulged as they strove to fit visual form to sensation, and then you could see it too, something alien amid the tangle of branches and leaves. You moved on, holding your place in the line, concentrating, confounded by the failing light.

There was a straight vertical edge of blackness in there—man-made. With every step it became clearer—a thatched hut, so perfectly assimilated into its surroundings that you were ten yards from it before you knew it was there. Ears strained now, but nothing could be heard over the rain and the rustling tread of the men either side of you. You wished they could be quieter now, and looked that way. Sniffer it was, and he was touching his nose with his finger. And that was it, that distinct pungent odour that prevailed whenever they were around. The hut, the smell, the sixth sense too—yes, you had it in the neck alright—all of which told you what you and everyone else should have know minutes before. They were there. The bastards were in there!

But the long tedious journey had taken its toll, numbing senses, slowing reflexes, disallowing the sluggish brain to respond. You wondered how many other men knew Charlie was in there waiting in those last crucial seconds when something, anything, done or spoken, might have made others more prepared, might have saved lives. There might have been many who knew, like you did, but couldn't get their exhausted bodies to react. So they just went on in and the trap closed about you, and your dulled reactions allowed it to happen uncaringly.

The sharp, sudden flash and with it the twin detonations, and your brain screamed: rocket! The most terrible of your fears yet three or four more were launched and hit in that instant between recognition and reaction. You hit the deck fast—and there were more white flashes and bursts of yellow light, each sandwiched between the blasts, launching and striking. More of them, bloody tons of the bastards, but hang on. The danger is wide, well wide. Perhaps a safe distance. Relatively... The attack is on Twelve Platoon, a hundred yards away to the left, and even as you realise it, the first splatterings of gunshots can be heard in response, rising swiftly to a crescendo.

You start to get up, looking toward Nigel even though you already know what his instruction will be. "Keep moving," Nigel breathes softly, more an expelling of air than real words, but every man immediately responds. You stand, returning your attention to the huts. They could be in there too, waiting with the fuckin' rockets.

Now all of Eleven Platoon was on the move again, fanned out —no groups for easy targets. All eyes and ears are intent on the shadows and silence directly ahead, shutting out the unseen horror away to the flank. Those bloody rockets—just to hear them was terrifying enough but now, had you listened, you could have heard the cries of men too, their screams of pain, their warnings to each other, orders shouted and reshouted as the clamour of gunfire drowned them out. Pitted against the barrage of rockets, the desperate gunshots of Twelve Platoon sounded pitifully inadequate. And you and the rest of Eleven Platoon are so near and yet so uninvolved, your body heavy with helplessness. All you can do is push on quietly into the camp.

And then you have gone too far, and the camp is all around you. In front is an area cleared to ground level. A dozen small stilted huts stand threateningly in the open. No cover in there, and no going around it either, but it would be suicide to go further if they were waiting, You stop, uninstructed, as everyone stops, eyes and ears straining for some sign, some warning, of movement, of danger. But there is only the dreadful tumult away to the left. Shut it out. Think about this. Eleven Platoon is too far forward, you are sure, and the gap between you and the stricken Twelve Platoon too wide. Hatrack and the support group, coming up behind Twelve Platoon to back them up, are probably equally pinned down, and that leaves you and this open ground and these huts. The next move is with Holly and the little man is in a quandary. The instinct is to rush down to Twelve Platoon's aid, but you must clear this area first, or you'll have rockets up your bums. If you get pinned down too the whole company is fucked. Holly dithers, looking at his section leaders who glare back silently. Finally, it is left to Nigel. "Awright, fuck you Holly. Do you want me to fucking go in there or don't you?"

There really wasn't an alternative. Twelve Platoon and Company were crippled, outgunned and pinned down at the edge of the camp while you were unopposed in the middle. Charlie was staying and fighting back, perhaps a rearguard group with a good supply of rockets providing the superiority they always angled for. In any case, it was in your hands to solve the problem. Hit this area hard and fast and clear it, then strike right down through the middle of the camp and assail its defenders from the flank. A reckless plan but if it all went wrong, bad luck. All the men around the lieutenant glared, putting the pressure on, and he had no choice. "Okay, let's go," he said belatedly. "Straight up the guts."

There is no need for anyone to relay the order—they were away like sprinters, bursting into the open, going straight at those huts. Four section automatically split into three, Alby Dunshea and you to the left, Nigel and Greyman right, Snowy, Sniffer and Bugsy staying where they were, giving cover. It is that blind run again, to make ground for there is no cover except the huts and you go straight at them. If you hit trouble, you sort it out there and then, but in any case, there isn't. One man moves, the other covers, until finally you're under the huts and still no shooting.

"Nobody home," Nigel bellows to Holly, and immediately wheels around while his section falls into line abreast and the other two sections either side, facing toward the savage battle over there in the dark jungle, striding down through the camp at a furious pace.

It is harrowing to go through the camp like this, past so many huts and bunkers that should be explored, cleared, blasted with grenades, but there is no time. With you goes the knowledge that sooner or later you must be fired upon—the camp is huge, you can see, several hundred population, but most are gone. There's just this stubborn rearguard force, concentrated in one part of the camp and you go swiftly, foolishly bold, defying all tensions. It is an aggressor's game now, and all you can do is hope that when the firing starts it will be someone else in their sights.

And when it does happen—when suddenly the white light blossoms ahead and sends the rocket screaming over to strike somewhere behind, it is mostly relief you feel. You plunge to the ground, far too late, showered by flying bits of bark and dirt as another rocket hits closer. Someone begins swearing loudly as you do yourself, but this is better—the nerve-wracking anxiety of the unknown is past and action will come striding into its place.

You begin firing, adding to the torrent of tracers streaking into the base of the hut from where the rockets were given their brief deadly life. You see Snowy flat on his belly, quivering all over as he lays down a deluge of fire from Mabel, and further wide, Alby Dunshea, changing magazines with swift, shaking hands. There are no other men within your range of vision, but the flashes and brilliant yellow slits of tracers tell you they were there. You empty your mag and grapple another out of your pouch, clip it on and slip the empty away. But don't fire again for a moment—don't waste the ammo. Who knows how long this will go on? After that initial outburst, the shooting eases off. There were four or five rockets, all fired immediately—they probably don't have any more. Some incoming gunfire, but maybe even that is really coming from Twelve Platoon. You hug the ground, waiting and watching for more specific targets. There are none. Calmer now, and you notice, or re-notice, that the rain is pouring down again and you are wet and uncomfortable. Steam sizzles from the barrel of your rifle. You take a breath and wait two or three seconds—a year at a time like this.

Something dances by—a bright spirited tracer bouncing off the ground and spinning away, glowing pink. It catches your eye only momentarily but you ignore it, even though you know it could have torn the life out of your body. There is a glimpsed shadow down by that hut—perhaps a shadow, perhaps a man, you pump a few rounds off at it. Three, four, keep count now, don't get caught short, the thump of the butt against your shoulder a reminder of numbers. Over there, a muzzle flash—three four five rounds at that, nine down, half mag. The incoming is depleting—they are losing their taste for the fight and bugging out like they were supposed to do in the first place.

Someone is screaming! Right beside you and you look that way. Alby Dunshea! He's rolled onto his back, muddy hands slapped to his face, white teeth bared. That long, awful scream and then he stops for breath and screams again. No, no, not Alby Dunshea, not poor slow-wit Dunshea. Crabwise, you slither over to his side and pounce upon his body as he begins to convulse, threshing maniacally on the muddy ground. Blood bursts through his fingers still clutched to his face.

"Medic!" you bellow at the top of your voice, without any real hope of being heard amid this racket. Grab him by the wrists and get the hands away from his face, get a look at it. A great hole there, right on the cheekbone. Shit! No time for sympathies though. He's screaming again, mouth stretched wide eyes open staring, body in fierce spasms. Screaming, screaming but your ears are numbing to it. Screaming means still alive. Your fumbling hands and useless fingers tear at his breastpocket and drag out the shelldressing, rip the wrapper away with your teeth. Your hands covered in blood, washed away by the rain, bloodied again as you press the padding to his face, and he twists and tries to get away as if you were smothering him with a pillow.

"Easy Alby easy," you gasp and grab his neck roughly, winding the trailing gauze around his head again and again.

"Medic!"

Figures racing past you, got to get on, don't waste time on wounded and dead, Snowy lumbers by, Sniffer behind like a faithful hound.

"They're bugging out, we got `em running," voices are yelling.

"After them! Keep moving!" Nigel's voice roars.

Dunshea is down, and that scream you no longer hear ripping through to your spine and then suddenly he is silent and still. You kneel there, paralysed yourself, staring in horror. Scream again, Alby, scream again. Someone comes sliding like a baseball player, and hands attack your hastily applied dressing.

"I've got him," Ten Days says.

"Is he dead?" you gasp.

"I've got him. Piss off Yogi."

But you can't move, can't go, not like this, you have to know.

"Is he dead, fuck you?"

While Ten Days frantically hunts for pulses.

"No. He's alive. Now fuck off and let me do my job."

You drag yourself to your feet, backing away. Take it easy, Yogi Bear. You're panicking. Cool it. A long, last glance. You can see Alby Dunshea's chest moving while Ten Days works at the dressing. Poor Dunshea. Then turning, and onward in pursuit of the battle...

*

...poor Alby Dunshea. Too slow; too awkward to get out of his own way. And that screaming lodged in your brain, as if it was your own.

"Hey Bugsy, you still there?"

"Yes, bugger you, Yogi. I'm still here."

"Thought you went away again."

"I'm still here. What do you keep waking up for? There's nothing to see."

"How's Alby?"

"He's alright..."

"You sure. Looked bad."

"He's alright. Better than you are."

"In the face. He got it in the face."

"Bloody lucky, actually. They think it was a bullet that bounced right off his cheekbone. Just a glancing blow..."

"I thought he was dead."

"No. Just a little bit uglier, if that's possible."

And then someone, Dorset, CHQ signaller, calling.

"Choppers are in the area now!"

"Fire the flares!" Bulldog Doyle roars and instantly there is light and movement and giant shadows everywhere. That black world is suddenly as bright as daylight, huge monstrous shadows looming as the brilliant phosphorescence of the flares pierce through the jungle and the storm.

"They see us!" Dorset yells. "Dust-off locked in!"

But the brilliance of the light is too much for failed eyes like yours, you turn your head away and closed it out.

"Won't be long now, Yogi," Bugsy says.

But there is no longer any such thing as time.

*

Running toward the battle from the rear, you are confronted with a scene that seems unrelated to the death and destruction it is supposed to convey. With the night fully descended and the rain almost horizontal before the force of the wind, the white flickers of muzzle flashes, the elongated sparks of tracers, the blossoms of explosions, all seem from your detached position more like a carnival fireworks display. Your ears are now oblivious to the detonations and the fever of action is in full command of your senses—you are no longer inclined to duck and flinch, instead running forward boldly, the yells of the men, screams of pain, of warning, of instruction, all seem to have lost their impact and urgency. It might just as well be the joyful shrieks and laughter of a distant funpark. Over it comes the thunder and lightning, indistinguishable from the explosions of artillery summoned in support, all so continuous that it blends into a meaningless babbling eruption. Toward this madman's monstrous orchestration, you run on, your eyes and ears listening for one thing only, the voice and movement of Nigel, to guide you to where you ought to have been...

Flying through the air, suddenly, inexplicably, upended in midair and hitting the ground in a flurry of arms and legs.

"Jesus Fucking Christ Almighty!"

There seemed to be a heavy crunch behind you, or did you trip, or what. Doesn't matter. You bounce up virtually landing on your feet and still running. No time to think about it—if hurt you wouldn't be running, you're running therefore not hurt. Your skinned knees and elbows remain with you as a reminder of the spill though it will be some time before you realise that you have just been floored by an explosion that must have been pretty fucking close.

"Snowy have a fuckin' look to your right!"

Nigel! His voice hoarse and quaking, but it's him alright. The long slits of tracers so numerous they must be Mabel, streaking across your path ahead. You drop to one knee and see the momentary image of fleeing figures at the end of Mabel's fiery tongue, and pump off a few shots that way yourself. Seven. Give 'em the last two. Change mags. Your breath is completely gone from the hectic run but you can see Nigel now, over there appearing fleetingly like an apparition in the flashes, directing traffic.

"Keep moving, keep moving, keep moving," he is yelling.

Back to the fold.

Something streaked by and splattered mud in your face, but you can't see anything to fire back at. The incoming is almost non-existent now.

"We gotta get closer," Nigel shouts excitedly. He too can see the opposition is lessening.

"Awright, Snowy, give us cover. The rest of you, let's go!"

And you are away, stumbling the first few strides as your boots strive for traction on the slippery ground. Running, hunched forward, over to that post, stop, look, shadows, fire at them, keep count, across to that hut, go, go, go! Other men running, firing, dashing here and there, until there's only you and the firing tails off.

"We got `em running! Look at `em go. Give `em something to go on with!"

Then you can hear other voices, different voices from further wide. Holly, calling urgently. "Don't go any further, Nigel. We're right on top of Twelve Platoon. Prop and hold ground." You go to ground and lay there, watching, waiting, changing mags again. And a lull—inexplicable really—suddenly hangs over you as if Holly had commanded it. Waiting, waiting, something must happen and does. Firing way to the flank, off in the direction, you realise, of the Ten Platoon ambushes, transferring the battle to a new location.

You lay in the rain and sudden cold, shivering uncontrollably. The weather seems to be turning worse or maybe you are becoming more aware of it. Greyman's Great War Gods, as if angered by the brief but violent conflict, have whipped up this fierce barrage of their own, the wind leans on the trees and roars through the jungle like an enraged animal; and the driving rain and the thunder and lightning rendered sight, sound and a cruel chill factor as evidence of their wrath. You lay on the ground and remembered then the things you had seen and done, and for the first time that day, you were really frightened.

From miles away at Nui Dat and The Horseshoe, they blasted shells into the air that streaked overhead and pounded the jungle all around in a one mile radius, adding further, you imagined, to the troubles of the fleeing Viet Cong. Down in the camp, the victors lay with frayed nerves, jumping at each explosion and then cursing their own edginess.

You got a fag alight and it was better then, and then the voices again, even more comfort: there was Nigel, calling toward his men as the other section leaders were doing, but strangely the only voice you heard was his.

"Awright, anyone hurt?"

And you remembered and answered. "Alby Dunshea was hit. The medics picked him up."

"Alive?"

"Yeah. Nasty one but."

"Snowy. Sniffer."

"We're over here. We're okay."

"Greyman. Bugsy?"

"No worries, Nigel."

"Awright. Check ammo."

You settled down. Greyman and Bugsy were right behind you, just a few feet away and you turned toward them. "Did we win?" Greyman asked.

But there was a puzzled look on Bugsy's face, glimpsed in the flashes of light.

"Hey Yogi. What's wrong with your leg?"

Now that he mentioned it, there did seem to be something strange about it. You rolled over, reaching down to grope about. There was a clamminess in your boot like someone had filled it with mud and it felt as if someone was holding you firmly by the calf muscle. When you tried to do the same, your hand went right in amid a mess of warm spongy stuff.

"Hey, hey!" you were yelling. "I'm fuckin' bleeding."

Bugsy came scurrying over, squatted there and seized your trouser leg, ripping it open. He looked at you and you looked at him.

"Hey Nigel, Yogi's been shot."

"What by?"

"A fuckin' bullet."

"I mean what happened, dickhead."

"I'm buggered if I know," was the best you could manage. You were beginning to feel strange, nauseous. It was probably the shock, more than anything. Nigel sprang across and had his pencil torch alight.

"Fuck me dead. You dumb bastard. Why didn't you say something?"

You wanted to explain your unlikely story that you didn't know anything about it, but your lower jaw did not want to assist with speaking. All of a sudden, nothing seemed to be working properly.

"Greyman," Nigel was saying from a million miles away.

"Go find a medic. This is fuckin' serious."

Serious it might have been but you didn't know and didn't care. Just let it all fade away, and fade away it did...

*

...rising up again, floating on an invisible ocean, lurching out of one nightmare into another. This is a frenzied world of shifting dazzling lights, of unbelievable noise and shattering furious violence as a huge monster with one brilliant eye seems to be hanging magically, terribly, overhead, dancing awkwardly against the backdrop of a rainswept sky, intermittently illuminated by the lightning. The one fiery eye of this dreadful flying dragon, more brilliant and more directed than the lightning, seems to be searching the earth for its prey, and you are that prey.

All about you can see silhouettes of men moving in the light of that great eye, men moving in desperate, frantic haste, their hair and clothes lashed by the forces of two different winds—the horizontal gale of the storm and the vertical downdraft of the monster.

You move your head to try and gain some comprehension, some sensual foothold amid this berserk scene of trees and men thrashing in the grip of some massive attacker. You want again the peace of waking up and finding Bugsy there. Instead there is only this hellish madness and sharp stinging pains from your leg to let you know that this is real, that this is really happening.

"Alright Bugsy, let's have yours."

Two figures, one Bugsy, the other possibly Sniffer, lean over you head and foot and somehow raise you up—only then does it occur to you that you have been lying on some sort of makeshift stretcher.

"Jeez, he's a heavy bastard," you hear Sniffer groan.

"Coulda been worse," you hear yourself answer. "It coulda been Snowy."

"Oh no, he's awake again," Bugsy groans.

"You sure you don't wanna sleep though this, Yogi?" Sniffer asks. Sleep through what?

They move you across to a point directly below the wobbling chopper with its single dazzling landing light, hanging in the sky just above treetop height. The wind chills right through your clothing, and there is a great sloshing puddle of water with you in the indentation of the stretcher—all of a sudden you cannot shake the idea that you are drowning. In a sea of blood...

If only you could be warm, it is so cold. They lower you to the ground, fully exposed to the sleet blasted downward by the chopper blades, and other men rush in, brushing Sniffer and Bugsy aside. Without consideration for your condition, these panicky fellows heave you from the rudimentary stretcher to another with a steel frame.

"Hey, take it easy. I'm a casualty," you cry but no one heeds you.

Straps fastened about your body, hooks being clipped to cables, everything double tightened, and all done to a chorus of fumbles and curses while rainwater drips from the chin of someone you don't know, splattering disgustingly in your unshielded face. The speed and unexpectedness of it outpaces your brain—before you can protest, it's all done and you're jerked rudely off the ground. You look around desperately for a friend.

"Hey Bugsy, you there?"

"Don't go pissing the bed, Yogi."

And you're swinging wildly away and he was gone.

Now you are in full possession of the giant hovering cyclops, swinging about in midair and being unsteadily drawn toward that overpowering eye at the centre of a world that is beginning to revolve faster and faster. The rain slices across your face and the downdraft squints your eyes and you spin around and around with the clawlike branches of the trees lashing out at you hungrily. The cable bows and tightens with each jerk, surely it will not stand this strain and snap and send you plummeting to the ground. Trussed up like a roast pig, tied down and helpless while every wrench of the cable pulls you closer to the chopper which means further from the ground, where death yawns should that cable snap.

Heaving upward and upward until there is nothing but the rotating black underbelly of the chopper that by now seems to be spinning as fast as its own rotors. Everything is quivering and shaking. You close your eyes and are instantly gripped by nausea—the horror is worse unseen. What a bloody ridiculous thing to let them do to you!

Then you are right under the chopper—you could reach out and grab one of the landing struts and assure your safety if you had a free arm. Two more jerks of the cable and your stretcher clatters over the strut, and a helmeted head bobs out of the cabin, an arm stretched to steady the cable. You are drawn alongside and the crewman hauls the stretcher in, sliding it across the floor and snapping its feet into the locking grooves on the floor that you always noticed but never realised what they were for.

Once there you find the constant jolting of the chopper no better than that of the cable; the machine unbalanced by the high winds and the need for constant hovering. Choppers aren't supposed to be able to fly in these conditions. Maybe they can't... You are sure that if the floor tilts far enough, you will slide out, stretcher and all, into the empty air and there will be nothing you can do to save yourself, all trussed up like this.

But then they are away, the rotor blades developing that frenetic flapping sound and the whole machine bumping wildly as it strives for altitude against the buffeting wind. Beside you, another stretcher locked in the floor grooves, and several men seated, wearing bandages impossibly huge. No one you can recognise under these circumstances.

Otherwise there is only the twin domes of the pilot's helmets as they struggle to keep flying, and outside the murky, saturated sky when lightning illuminates it, and otherwise black nothing. You leg begins to pain—the drugs are wearing off. It would be nice to be unconscious again, but even that doesn't seem to be working. All you can do is lie there, and try to think of how good it would be when the fear and discomfort ended and you would be safely tucked into bed in Vung Tau hospital.

Streetscene in Saigon

You felt utterly ridiculous but so, you supposed, would anyone else who possessed a shred of dignity. The place was a busy street in the bustling heart of the Cholon district of Saigon where stood the Australian billet, a former hotel converted for the purpose of housing those diggers lucky enough to be posted to that city. Immediately to the left of the wide portals of that edifice was a sentry box, looking rather like a country dunny with the walls missing, except that it had been sandbagged up to chest height. Inside the sentry box stood Yogi the Bear, looking straight and stern, complete with rifle and radio and wearing not only a steel helmet but also—heaven forbid—a flak jacket. All in all, it was a fine spectacle of Downunder ferocity.

And piteously, that was exactly why you were there. Large signs in Vietnamese at either end of the building warned passing pedestrians and motorists that under no circumstances were they allowed to pause or halt outside this building, and that anyone who behaved in a suspicious manner would be shot. You were to ensure that these rulings were properly observed by the indigenous population and, if it came to it, do the shooting. Great fun. Although, in reality, your orders did not match the certainty of the signs. If anyone stopped on the street within your range of vision, you were to call upon them to move on at once, and had even taught you the Vietnamese expression—*Di Di Mau!* and if not obeyed immediately, level weapon and shout menacingly *Mau lên không tôi bán!* which they assured you meant *Quick or I'll shoot!* If they still did not comply immediately, you were to fire a shot in the air, high above the line of the buildings across the street. This would effectively break out the other five members of the guard, presently lounging about inside the building, who would deploy to meet any threat. You were not allowed to shoot anyone unless you positively considered there to be a life-threatening danger.

So far you had got to fire just once, but it was worth it. A car, one of the innumerable yellow and blue Renault taxis that plagued the street along with a sea of bicycles, motor-scooters, rickshaws and pedestrians, had halted directly across the way. A man got out and you bellowed at him. The man looked at you in faint surprise. You roared your second instruction to which this cheeky little Vietnamese offered the Frenchman's shrug. Blam! The shot echoed around the rooftops deafeningly and in one instant, the street was completely clear. By the time the members of the guard burst into the street, you were crippled with laughter. They were just in time to see a man push his Renault around the far corner, giving substantiation to your action. Otherwise, the street was devoid of life.

The logic behind all this nonsense was that not unreasonable thinking that city-based troops were not capable to defending themselves and hence, every week, a bunch of infantrymen were collected from reinforcement groups or the convalescent centre or even Nui Dat, and rostered on this duty. After four weeks in the hospital at Vung Tau, you were glad of the break. The duty roster was twenty-four hours on, twenty-four off. Those twenty-four hours freely roaming the city made it all worthwhile. And in addition, it offered acceptable light duties to test out your leg. You hardly even limped any more.

So you stood at your guardpost like a chocolate soldier and mused on the fact that in less than an hour, your duty would be finished for the day.

"Go on, you silly old bag. Keep moving."

What you needed least of all was someone you knew to catch you in the midst of all this absurdity.

"Do you reckon the sign says *Beware of the Dog!*?" Bugsy Norris asked.

"*Beware of the Bear,*" Sniffer Gibson corrected.

Oh gawd!

They came with their huge grins to lean on the sandbags to either side of the sentry box.

"Go on, piss off you two," you protested. "Can't you read the sign?"

"Vietnamese is all Greek to me," Sniffer laughed.

"It says if you don't move on, I get to shoot you."

"Must be worth gettin' shot if you end up doing important jobs like this," Bugsy chuckled.

"And what, may I ask, are you two yahoos doing here?"

"You hear that, Sniffer. We risk our necks coming halfway across the war zone to visit him and he calls us yahoos."

"Bloody terrible business, Bugsy. Certainly won't be winning many hearts and minds with nasty types like him around."

An hour later, you were sitting in the bar, all three now in civilian dress, and explanations were being offered.

"So there we were," Sniffer was saying. "with three day's leave in Vungers and getting bored already. Thought we'd go visit our old mate Yogi Bear in hospital. We arrive, but lo! he's not there. We find out he's living it up in the wilds of Saigon. So we dumped the flowers and ate the chocolates and headed for the nearest bar."

"Where," Bugsy picked up the tale, "we happened upon a chap who was a Yank pilot and feeling lonely and he said all we had to do was go to the airport and walk out on the tarmac and ask around until we found a plane going to Saigon and go and ask the pilot for a ride. Which we did, and here we are."

"Mad bastards," you shook your head in disapproval when in fact you were very pleased. "To tell you the truth, the only difference between Vung Tau and Saigon is that Saigon is bigger. And it doesn't have a beach."

"If it's bigger, then it has more bars and more women to choose from," Bugsy declared. "Which makes me wonder why we're wasting time sitting around here."

"You got a one track mind, Bugsy," Sniffer chuckled.

"Yeah man, but it's the only track worth following."

There were other things that they knew they must speak of, once the raucous edge was off their voices.

"How's the leg?" Bugsy eventually asked.

"Bit of a scar. Itches sometimes. It was really just a flesh wound."

"Heard it hit an artery."

"Just nicked it. Really, I'm fine."

"Pity," Sniffer mused. "Just a millimetre more and you might have scored a homer."

You laughed, but it wasn't funny. That extra millimetre and you would have been dead before you reached the hospital. Instead, you were ready to be returned to the unit, only slightly worse for wear. But at least you didn't have to lie about it any more.

There were the hurried letters home to assure family and friends that you had survived—the panicky newspaper reports you had seen made the facts look relatively tame. Then you had lied, just a scratch from a twig, not even a wound to speak of. You carried a piece of metal that looked like a squashed and shredded sixpence, added to your dogtags on the cord around your neck.

"Alby didn't make it," Sniffer said quietly.

"Never regained consciousness," you could confirm. "I thought he was going to be okay but he was dead in the chopper."

"Poor bastard," Bugsy mused. "Musta pissed him right off

knowin' the last thing he ever saw was your smiling face, Yogi."

"Yeah," and you needed to think, to strive to find what little you could feel for Alby Dunshea. "Y'know, I always hated the guy. Despised him. But somehow, now he's dead, I wish I'd known him better."

"You woulda liked him even less, Yogi. He was a flatout arsehole," Bugsy said coldly. It shocked you. Though you might have agreed, Alby was one of your own. And he was dead. The truth was you didn't know how to feel about it, since your emotions had nothing genuine to offer and your intellect didn't care.

"Well," Sniffer chuckled. "The world will be a much prettier place now that his ugly puss won't be around any more."

The joke freed you from thinking things that were better not thought. The saddest thing was that was probably the last time anyone thought much about Alby Dunshea.

"Okay, so, where's the sheilas?" Bugsy demanded.

"Everywhere," you grinned. "And the jack rating is around 95%."

"I'm willing to risk it."

"If you do, next time you have a piss your prick will come off in your hand."

You took them to a nearby bath-house for sauna and massage, so called. Softened by the incense and steam, you drifted to such an extent that when the girl jerked you off, you hardly even noticed. And that after all your warnings to the others to save it for later. Then you took them to a bar where you knew the prices weren't quite as outrageous as most places.

"If you stick to the beer," you warned. "And don't, under any circumstances, buy the girl a Saigon Tea, no matter how convincingly she pleads."

"What's so special about Saigon Tea?"

"It's a thimbleful of warm water at two bucks a throw."

"Thieving hounds."

"Exactly. But you will find that once you've downed a few scotch and dry's and the little lovely with her boobs pressed up under her chin has been playing with your prick for a while, the urge to give her the one thing in the world she desires, namely a Saigon Tea, is rather difficult to overcome."

"And how, wise leader, do we meet this hideous threat?"

"We keep moving from bar to bar. By the time the little sweeties realise all their coaxing is to no avail, you've had a hard drink and a nice feel and on we go to the next one."

It worked well for a while. They dappled in various women without succumbing to a single Saigon Tea and generally managed to avoid all other ways of being ripped off as well.

"Gotta hand it to yer, Yogi," Bugsy laughed. "You sure know how to handle these slopeheads."

But by late afternoon, your leg began to stiffen and all three were drunk and tired and you finally bogged down in a bar named Honolulu and began allowing the time-honoured traditions of the local culture to overwhelm you. The girls seemed nicer than average, the booze less heavily watered down and anyway, you had given them a good run for their money.

"You buy me Saigon Tea, Uc Dai Loi, and I make you wery happy."

"Yeah, sure, Brighteyes, but only one."

"Okay, uney, only one."

They deteriorated swiftly once they had stopped. Sniffer was soon going to sleep and the girl he had contracted had to keep prodding him to produce his wallet. You seemed to be failing to describe to the young thing on your knee exactly what a kangaroo was. Perhaps they had been doped, or was it merely the unfamiliar softness of womankind.

Bugsy, on the other hand, seemed to be descending into belligerence. He sprawled on the chair and brushed aside the girl in a minimal green dress who had been holding his attention for almost an hour.

"You buy me nother," she persisted.

"Go buy your own, you greedy bitch," Bugsy growled.

The girl tried not to understand him.

"You buy me nother Saigon Tea, Uc Dai Loi. You number one. You buy me nother."

Bugsy swept her away again.

"Gowan, piss orf."

With his ruffled hair and day's stubble, Bugsy looked ferocious indeed, but still the girl managed somehow to decide that he was only teasing her. She pushed herself toward him, smiling sweetly.

"Oh baby, uney. Wassa matter?"

Bugsy grabbed her by the throat and heaved her across the room—she landed on her backside with a thump. She immediately sprang to her feet and began to remonstrate angrily, in which she was joined by an older woman in black pyjamas who bulged very severely at the middle. When the older woman opened her mouth, everything was red with the cherryroot she chewed such that it seemed somewhat to add the necessary heat to the fierce but unintelligible words she uttered. No teeth nor tongue nor any other feature was discernible, but merely a pulsating red hole of fury. So vociferous was the tirade that it woke up Sniffer Gibson.

"What's going on?" he wondered.

"Once more we seem to be losing hearts and minds."

While the woman and the girl continued to voice protest, some sinewy men started to appear in the background, and you decided it was time to be moving on. You grabbed Sniffer and Bugsy by their respective sleeves and dragged and they came along but as Bugsy passed the older woman, she spat, or spluttered possibly, with the result that a blob of the hideous red muck appeared on Bugsy's shirt like a bullet wound.

"You bitch!" Bugsy thundered, and swiped at her.

A small crowd was gathering, joining in the chorus of protest, to which Bugsy rose to his fullest height and let out a roar that would have impressed any randy lioness. It impressed the crowd too, who backed off five paces and fell silent for a moment. Sniffer loved it, bursting into laughter that you tried to share, but immediately the crowd regrouped and resumed their abuse. Bugsy roared again, this time charging a few paces toward them and so created a panic when they all fell over each other as they backed off.

"Dirty foul-smelling little bastards," he seethed as he marched back and the three invaders turned to the door. There, a tighter band of the small men was jammed.

"Oops," Sniffer said.

But Bugsy was fighting mad and undeterred. He strode straight at them, reaching like a giant amongst dwarfs and, seizing one of the most vocal by the shirt, propelled him backwards into his supporters. The result was that the path to the doorway was cleared as the defenders tumbled out into the street. But when you stepped to the doorway, you immediately saw it was a trap. The crowd surged back, blocking every escape, and directly ahead, a young man stood on the pavement brandishing a very large knife.

Bugsy responded without hesitation, picking up a wooden table and hurling it at his antagonist. The crowd shrieked again and back off once more, clearing enough space to allow them a beach-head on the footpath. But Bugsy wasn't finished in the bar yet—he emerged with another table that he thrashed several times on the concrete before inverting it and using his foot to detach a leg. Swung to hand, it made a formidable club.

The street was full of people, all chattering and whining loudly in their sing-song voices. Wielding his waddy, Bugsy forced them back until it was clear to the middle of the road and you and Sniffer took up your places behind him.

"They tore me bloody shirt," Sniffer muttered in disgust.

Now the crowd encircled them, forming what might have been a cock-fighting arena. But they were keeping back, out of range of Bugsy and his waddy.

"Which way?" Bugsy asked through gritted teeth.

"I think there's a Yank MP post down this way somewhere," you said uncertainly. For sure, it was too far to go back, toward the billet.

"Do you think we'll make it?" Sniffer asked dubiously.

"I didn't think we'd get this far," you replied grimly.

But you found you were allowed to move in the direction you had indicated, the pliable mob oozing around as you went until everyone was at your back and the street before you was completely deserted. Bugsy walked to the fore, beating the rhythm of the march with the waddy on his hand, while you and Sniffer took up wide positions either side. Like the bad guys in a western, you walked the street with the very vocal crowd accumulating behind—you could only hope that the plan was to escort you from the vicinity.

All along the street, people were hiding in their shops until you passed and then emerging, swelling the crowd behind. Every few paces, Bugsy would stop and raise the waddy menacingly and the crowd would try to halt but those at the back pushed those before them forward, often into the range of Bugsy's arc.

"Keep moving," you shouted at him.

But Bugsy persisted in stopping and flourishing his club, creating chaos in the mob whose voices rose to a frenzy.

Several times, people were thrust too far forward and might have be tempted into making and assault. You rushed at them a couple of paces, roaring furiously as Bugsy had done, and they hurled themselves back against the wall of the oncoming mob in terror.

You had to admit it was great—the sense of power you had over all these people, merely at the sound of your voice. Inside you, hatred of the Vietnamese, their country and everything it stood for welled amidst the alcohol and that sensation of power and control began to overwhelm you. You saw some people waiting in ambush in a fruit shop ahead and charged them, roaring, in fine imitation of a rhino. The people threw up their arms and fled screaming out the back of the shop. You returned to the street, chest-swelled, ferocious and seething with race hatred bred in a year of indoctrination.

So the rampage continued, Bugsy terrorising the mob behind, you and Sniffer by turns roaring and rushing those lurking ahead. You could feel the fear you engendered, all of your apprehension and discomfort had gone now and you were the predator, roaring and thundering, stalking terrified prey, no longer capable of speech nor rational thought. You were your basic, original, animal self, without any of the bullshit that had kept you tamed all your life. Now you had broken out, and never had you so completely felt at one with yourself. The exhilaration was intoxicating. The sheer power and strength of naked, unarmed hunter-killer, the terror of the jungle. Your instincts, for just those few moments, had finally completely overcome the years of civilised conditioning. This was who you really were, hunter-killer, master of the earth, the most dangerous predatory animal that ever lived.

And then the moment passed and with it the exhilaration, to be replaced instead by a numb dullness, silent and desperate. On the road ahead, a white landrover had parked, blocking the roadway. Three men climbed out in their white calico uniforms, small Vietnamese policemen—the notorious White Mice. They stood defiantly, barricading the road.

"Us or them?" Bugsy called.

"Them. Definitely," you shouted back.

As if to confirm your assessment, the three White Mice each drew their revolvers.

Now you were trapped. Continue forward and the three armed men might consider themselves attacked, stop and you risked being grabbed or trampled by the mob behind. You looked at the indifference on the faces of the three men and it gave no sign of their intentions.

"Bloody MP's," Bugsy muttered. "Never around when you fucking want them."

"*Dung Lai!*" one of the White Mice bellowed, holding his revolver aloft and, as ordered, everyone stopped. You were about ten metres away from them and the crowd the same distance behind. And all voices were silent now.

"Just look friendly," you said.

Sniffer looked his friendliest.

One of the White Mice, the leader if the embellishments on his uniform were any guide, began making utterances in sing-song Vietnamese that made no sense at all until he motioned with his revolver toward Bugsy's right hand. Bugsy did a dumb act, pointing at the club; the policeman nodded; Bugsy looked blank and shrugged; the policeman repeated his commands more loudly. Bugsy smiled and half-turning, raised the club once more to the crowd. They gasped and cowered.

At that same instant, further down the street behind the White Mice, there was a squeal of tortured tyres and a US Army jeep darted into view, bearing four US MPs.

"Here comes the cavalry," Sniffer grinned.

But you were watching Bugsy who was so caught up in his final moments of Neanderthal existence that he could not let it go. He stood, again brandishing the club over his head and again the crowd cowered and the policeman bellowed his commands. Then Bugsy threw it away. He discarded the club into the gutter and turned back toward the policemen with a wildly defiant look. The MPs in the jeep were yelling and blasting on their horn, the policemen were bellowing commands, the crowd were shrieking with anger and Bugsy was roaring in primal fury, and then suddenly it was as if all these sounds were gathered and drawn together into one single louder, sharper, greater sound that absorbed and obliterated them all. In the next instant there was only the report of the revolver, echoing away amid the tall buildings.

Bugsy went sideways as if in pursuit of his discarded club but he only made a few staggering paces before he stumbled and went over sideways, hitting the roadway and sliding into the gutter. His teeth were fiercely gritted, you saw, and his hands seemed to be trying to hold the top of his brow in place. Then the blood exploded between his fingers and he stretched out and his whole body convulsed violently while the blood gushed into the gutter.

The jeep screeched to a halt, three of its occupants deploying while a third stepped up onto the bonnet, aiming his carbine straight at you. A second grabbed Sniffer as he attempted to rush to Bugsy's aid and gripped him around the neck. The third covered the White Mice, the fourth the street.

"Stay where you are, sonny," the man up on the jeep shouted. "Lessen you wanna end up like your friend here."

You stood with your hands at your side, no longer capable

of direct movement anyway. Sniffer was wrestled to the ground and then the White Mice holstered their revolvers and climbed into their landrover and drove away. Bugsy had finally come to rest with his back turned, a small spout of blood bubbling up from within his hair and running in tributaries between the corrugations of the roadway. A negro MP stood over Bugsy, shaking his head.

"You guys. You guys. You never learn," he murmured.

Otherwise, the street was completely deserted.

Turnover

Operation Tumbarumba—sounds like a belly ache and that's what you've got. The platoon has stopped for lunch, back there in the greenshit, after four days of futile thrashing about in a place where no one has ever been, but there's this track. No footprints or other signs. Not worth an ambush. But you get stuck out here on picket, covering their arses and starving to death. Picket. Silent watching. No eating. No smoking. Alone. An hour of solid self-deprivation.

You're propped in behind the root of a big kapok, and the tracks runs away downhill in a remarkably straight line for about a hundred metres—an enormous distance to be able to see in this part of the world: far enough for it to disappear in a misty haze that hovers ghostlike in this rain forest country. There are no sounds. There is nothing but you, constantly talking yourself out of lighting a dangerous fag.

Alby Dunshea was dead but everyone hated him and no one cared. Bugsy Norris was dead but everyone loved him and no one cared. You tried to care but every time your thought about him it immediately converted into hatred and thoughts of vengeance on the Vietnamese. All you could do was share in the jokes.

"I told him he'd of been better off in gaol."

"Pretty good shot to hit someone like Bugsy in the brain."

"If that's the soft option, what's the hard one?"

If they were jokes.

Before long, it was as if he had never been one of them, as if he had never existed at all. At least he had volunteered so it was his own silly fuckin' fault. Hoo Roo Bugsy. Hoo Roo Bogface. The only real effect was that it made you feel luckier to have survived.

There were times, though, deep in the night, when a weird surge of emotion rose unexpectedly in your body and forced tears into your eyes. You fought such weak moments and suppressed them before anyone noticed. Fortunately, they only happened when you were alone and allowed your mind to drift. Like now...

Fuck you, Bugsy. Think about yourself. There's a fuckin' great scar on your calf muscle that itches a lot and the muscle itself has a hollow and has wasted somewhat—you limp when you get tired, which is just about all the fuckin' time. Wounded war hero—what a fuckin' joke. All it did was scare the living daylights out of Wally and Ella when the telegram arrived.

You returned expecting a hero's welcome, but no one seemed to notice. You were one of the last wounded men to be returned to the unit—they all thought you got a homer, but you only went as far as Saigon. Thirty other men had preceded you back to Delta Company, showing off their scars and telling all the hospital horror stories. There was nothing left for you.

And anyway, they were preparing for their first operation since the battle and when you arrived there was a strange air of apprehension about the place. What had once been routine was now anxious and no one wanted to talk much, especially about getting wounded.

"I bet I'm happier to see you than you are to see me," Nigel said by way of welcome.

He offered to leave you on the rear party but you had already rested too much.

Greyman handed you the AK.

"I was just keeping it for yer," he grinned.

"Yeah, I bet."

Reinforcements have finally arrived, two new conscripts. Daytripper, whose real name you would never learn, is another whingeing Pom except maybe he's got a right to because he came to Aussie on a tourist visa, overstayed and ended up drafted, poor blighter, as he puts it; and a quiet little guy named Mickey Wright who you don't know anything about because you haven't had a chance to talk to him yet.

Everything was the same and yet everything was different. When next morning you flew out into this apparently safe region, these men who once sat recklessly on the landing struts of the choppers and hung out the sides boldly and chiacked each other dangerously now cringed inwardly toward the centre; a tight little huddle of men, contracting more each time the chopper banked, clinging to one another with a shameless intimacy that had never been there before.

"It's as if we've collectively lost our nerve," Sniffer muttered when the nerve-wracking ride was gladly over.

"Maybe we've finally realised this war business is fucking serious," Snowy remarked.

Big black soldier ants march along the ridge of the kapok root. These are the sort that can bore straight through tin cans—they always go straight, through anything, and bite like fuck too. You watch them pass within an inch of your arm with morbid fascination, but they never move off the line. Over trained, snappy little bastards. If you don't do something, take some risk, you'll fall asleep. If you do those little fuckers will bore a hole straight through your skull. That keeps you awake...

It all feels strangely insecure with the tight-knit original group now broken. The two new boys stick together, as do the six old hands, but that will sort itself out. A few shots in your general direction makes an old hand of anyone.

Then you are suddenly peering down the track. You don't know why. You just are. Ants forgotten. Fag forgotten. You tighten your grip on the AK. You are peering right down to the end of the track, as far as you can see, into the murk of the haze. Wait. Wait. Something moves.

Impossible to say what it is. Just a fleeting glimpse of movement, and some sort of specific sounds and rustles amid the faint background cacophony of the forest, but it was something, rather than nothing. You wait and watch, eyes wanting to be zeroed in on the exact spot. There he goes! A man, or the silhouette of one, passes through your perception in one tiny instant and then is gone, as if it never was, only it was. Now you know where and what. Wait on it. Few more seconds. Wait. Wait. There he goes. Another figure briefly glimpsed only this time you've seen black clothing, a rifle held level, the curved magazine of an AK47, just like the one you carry. Charlies!

Waiting, waiting, watching, watching, but that's it. The sound has stopped. They have stopped. Down there, by the track. Nothing else happens. You might have imagined it, so completely has any trace of it passed. Might have nodded off and dreamed it. Like fuck you have!

Hold on a moment. Think it through. Get the fuckin' story straight before you go creating a panic. No immediate dangers. They're a hundred metres away and going nowhere. Crossing the track from left to right. Four of them. And there was something else. Something nags. Let it go. It'll come. Four of them. The first caught your attention; were there more before you detected him? No, not a chance. You picked the signs clearly. He had to be the first. The second zeroed you in on the spot; or was it the first man seen twice? No again—there was a definite pause between your apprehension of the one and the other. Two men. You glimpsed the third; no doubt about that, and then saw the fourth with his AK. Or was it an AK? That's what nags. Looked a little bit large in proportion to the figure. Maybe a larger, similar weapon, there's a Chinese Bren Gun with a curved mag under. Might be one of those... Stopped by the track. One hundred metres down. Okay. That's it. All you know about it. Here we go.

Slowly, quietly, you haul yourself to your feet. Your leg is cramped and has gone to sleep—silly fucking thing. Silly fucking you for not keeping your limbs nimble, that is. You go real careful, real quiet. Reasonable to assume that if you could hear them, they can hear you. You head back quietly, in no hurry, toward the platoon. Spargo's there, sitting by the gun, eating those Ham and Lima beans that no one else can stomach. He looks up and sees you standing there, twenty metres away. You give the thumbs down, and the signal goes through the camp in a matter of seconds.

You drop down beside Snowy, wave Sniffer over, and light a cigarette while he approaches. That one fag a day that you really need. Sniffer was out there on picket earlier—you relieved him, so he knows the terrain.

"There's four Charlies down the track, bottom of the hill. They stopped there. Out of sight."

No further explanation needed. Sniffer nods and heads off to take up your position at the picket post, while you sort this out.

In moments, Nigel and Holly are there with puzzled looks. You repeat the statement, edited for their benefit.

"Four Charlies. Armed. Hundred metres down the track. Stopped on the right side."

Holly sees it as his job to doubt everything.

"You sure there's four?"

"Certain."

"Hundred metres. Long way. You sure they're Charlies."

"Weapon with curved mag. AK47 maybe."

"You carry an AK, Yogi."

"They were small."

"Stopped, you say."

"Came in left to right across the track and went no further."

"Ambush," Nigel said flatly.

"You think they know we're here, Yogi."

"You bet. I reckon they're waiting in ambush for us down there."

Holly sighs. Life is a worry to great doubters.

"We have assurances from SAS and the Yanks that there are no Charlies in the area."

"They're wrong."

But he moves back to his radio man and speaks to higher

authorities. He asks around. Does any unit have men in your area?

"What's he fuckin' pissin' around for?" Snowy Spargo complains. "Why don't we just go down and get `em, while they're still there."

No one answers. Best to play it safe. And if they are lying in ambush, they'll wait for you to get there, just like you would.

"No friendlies around," Holly says. "So you may be right, Private Griffin."

Maybe... No one dignifies that with an answer either.

"How many weapons did you see?"

"Just one. Others were indistinct. And the one seemed too large for an AK47."

"Bigger, similar weapon, you mean?" Nigel asks. It's best to know what you are up against.

"Yeah, maybe," but there is a doubt there. What's wrong with this? You don't believe your answer now. Still it nags.

"Or a very small man," Nigel proposes.

"Or else you've got the distance wrong, Griffin," Holly pipes in. "And they were further away than you thought."

"No. Distance is right."

Holly deliberates. What he deliberates is obvious, and finally he realises that.

"You want to take them, Nigel?"

"Sure."

"Heavy weapon in ambush. Very tricky."

"We can handle it."

"You'll be relying on Griffin's guesswork."

"If Yogi says that's what's there, then that's what's there." You spend the next few minutes getting your suddenly inflated ego back under control.

But Holly continues to fret. "He might have imagined it."

"He might not have too. We're wasting time. Let's go."

"I'll move the rest of the platoon over to the track as back up. You happy to walk your blokes into this?"

The spider is in its web and the little fly leader says 'Head for the centre.' And he asks if we're happy...

"Yep," Nigel says with false confidence.

"Okay, let's go."

You don't wait for the platoon. You move straight out onto the track. No one needs to say anything. This all depends on you having got it right, but it's best not to think too deeply about that. Just get on with the job. You go to pick up Sniffer at the picket post.

"See anything?"

Sniffer shakes his head.

"Lead it, Yogi."

This time Sniffer doesn't complain about surrendering his forward scout role; it's your hand and you have to play it. You will lead them down the track and get as close as you dare, then point to the spot where the ambush is placed and you blow the shitbags out of it. Simple. Unless you go a few paces too far, walk into the trap, and wear it. You lead, and Snowy follows with the M60. Usually Nigel, navigating, comes second, but now you want the firepower up front. Your biggest problem will be getting out of Snowy's way, and you've buggered that up in the past. Then comes Nigel, Sniffer with Daytripper and Mickey Wright tucked safely down the back. They'll run the flank if they know how—Nigel patiently explains what that means.

"When it starts, we wheel right, into the jay and then go straight down through `em."

And bloody Greyman's in Vungers rooting himself silly, lucky bastard. A Bangkok smile passes glowingly through your memory and your whole body tingles for a delicious moment... Keep your fuckin' mind on the job, you dickhead!

You start down the track. There is the place they went in, and just ahead of it a sapling leans out onto the track. That's the spot you're heading for. You go easy, careful with each step, watching and listening all the while. You don't look back but you can sense them behind you. Snowy right on your heels—you can hear him breathe—then a gap to Nigel, another gap to the other three.

It seems to take forever. That sapling is a light year away. Time has slowed down again, even before the shooting starts. You want to run down there and get it over with, but you gotta play the game. One step, then the next, eyes fixed on the place where they went down, ears stretching on the sides of your head such that you can actually feel them. There isn't a sound. There's nothing to work with. Just a memory to guide you which, as the man said, you might have imagined, or got wrong. But you can't afford to think wrong now. The sapling is five paces away and ten paces beyond that the track turns sharply left. You didn't think of that. They came up the track, not across it, and set the ambush at the corner—the best possible place. An ambush works better if you can hit 'em head on. Now that you are down here, nothing looks the way it did when you saw it in the haze. It's all wrong, you are sure. They might be to the right—smarter if they were straight ahead. You can't tell. But they went right. You said they went right. They went right.

Three paces to the sapling. It's not close enough to the corner. You need three, maybe four, more paces, before you hit the right spot. Or will that be too many? They are in there, pointing their weapons at you, waiting, ready to mow you down. How many more paces are they waiting for? You reach the sapling, and stop. No, stick to the original plan. This is where you thought it was. This is where it is. Here. Do it now!

You look back at the men behind you. All eyes are on you as they stand there, tense, intent. You turn and point to the place at the right and then dive away to the left.

Snowy opens up with a long murderous burst, standing right in the middle of the track like the Colossus of Rhodes, firing from the hip. The area of jungle you indicated explodes in a fury of flying dirt and leaves and splinters as you hit the ground on the far side of the track, roll and bring the AK around to bear. Snowy is spraying the whole area but you must look for a specific target, as Sniffer, hanging back with the rocket, waiting to see the right spot to hit. The other three have gone right, straight into the jungle where they will come charging down three abreast, hitting them on the flank. Nigel, directing traffic.

"Go, you blokes, go! Hit `em hard! Come on, son, fire that fucking rocket!"

Look for something, anything! And it's there! Muzzle flashes in through the scrub. You fire straight at them. Something hits the dirt on the track beside you and dances brilliantly as it does a dazzling momentary back flip before your eyes. Tracers. They're firing back, the bastards! You rip off a mag into the spot those flashes came from and then do a quick change. Then there is a double crunch—deafening: Sniffer has seen the flashes too and lets them have it with the rocket. Everything then is lost in smoke, as you eardrums scream in painful protest.

Now Snowy seizes the chance to drop flat on the track, ready to fire from the prone position, and Nigel is going wide, bent double, hunting some cover. Deeper in you hear the flankers blazing away as they descend, but that's all, that's all. No one is firing back now. Zero incoming.

"Hold your fire, hold it! Stop where you are!" Nigel is shouting.

It stops. The gunfire echoes away, sounding like other, more distant battles, far off in the jungle. You wait. There is a sound. It is a sort of whimpering noise, like a dog left on a chain. In there. A tremor of joy runs through your body. They were there, where you said they were. You picked the spot, dead on. Got it right. You fuckin' balltearer! You'll be a living legend around Nui Dat for this and everyone will want to buy you a beer. Yogi Bear, who turned over a Viet Cong ambush. What a fuckin' hero!

"You okay, Yogi?"

"No worries, Nige."

"Snowy, how's the gun."

"Red hot, Nigel."

"Daytripper?"

"I got killed but I died game."

"Dickhead. Sniffer?"

"Two Charlies down right in front of me, Nigel."

"Okay. And the other bloke...what's your fuckin' name?"

"Mickey Wright, sir..."

"Don't fuckin' call me sir you moron. Just tell me whether or not you're fuckin' dead."

"I'm not dead, Corporal."

"Dead right, Wright. Sniffer's got two Charlies down. Anyone else got anything?"

"There seems to be a bit of a clearing there, Nigel," Daytripper was saying. "And they were all in there. Nothing moving now. But someone's alive. I can hear them."

There is that pathetic whimper, softer now.

"Want to have a look, Yogi?"

Oh shit!

"Haven't I done enough?"

"You're having a big day, Yogi. Might as well wrap it up proper."

"Yeah, sure."

"Daytripper says one of them is still alive."

"Yeah, I can hear it."

"We'll give `em another burst if you like."

"No. I'll have a look."

"Hold your fire, boys. Yogi Bear's having a look."

"Good old Yogi," you murmur.

You are about to move, when suddenly a voice can be heard way up the track. Holly. "What's going on down there, Nigel?"

"Shut up. We're busy."

But in the moment of distraction, something happens for

which your senses cannot account. Suddenly, there is someone standing on the track before you. All of your reflexes spring to level the AK and blow the living daylights out of the figure, but nothing like that happens. What you see is too arresting, too horrifying, for that.

She is ten or eleven years old and stands in a trance at the edge of the track, staring vacantly into space with her huge child's eyes. She is completely naked—perhaps the blast from the rocket had stripped away her clothing—although she does seem to be wearing a red cloak cast over her right shoulder and running down to her knee. But it isn't a cloak; it is a great stream of blood, gushing from a wound high on her chest. It is from her that the whimpering sound is emitting.

For a moment, you just stare, and she stares right back at you with those great eyes pleading with the world for pity, for help.

"Good God," you hear Snowy breathe, and his face falls into his hands.

You cannot accept what you are seeing. In utter disbelief, you stand and walk over, all notions of safety and security abandoned now, and as you approach those eyes lock upon yours and follow until she is looking up at you pleadingly when you stand beside her. What have you done to me, they seem to be asking in her child's innocence. You are reaching out to touch her, perhaps wanting to assure yourself that she is real, has substance, but the very moment your fingers contact her arm, she collapses as if you have unsettled the faint equilibrium that held her there. Like a house of cards in the breeze, she drops at your feet and flops about there like a landed fish and you stand, powerless to move.

"What's happening?" Nigel asked, for he can tell it has all gone horribly wrong.

"A kid...she's just a bloody kid..."

"What?" Nigel cries uncomprehending.

But then comes the awful pronouncement from Sniffer who has done some investigating of his own. "There's three more of them in here."

By then you were on your knees and raised her to a sitting position, her head lolling against your shoulder. All the light seemed to have gone from those eyes. They no longer riveted you with accusation. Nigel stepped onto the track, shaking his head, quivering in horror.

"Holly! Holly! Get the fuckin' medic down here. Now!"

There was nothing Ten Days could do. The girl had died of

shock the moment that you touched her. In the small clearing was a boy of eight with his face completely blown off, and two more youths of about thirteen, shot to pieces. The platoon came down and took over, while each of you moved away, trying to find a place where the world made some sort of sense. There was no such place.

"Kids. They're just kids," Snowy was murmuring, over and over, as he wandered around on the track. Mabel, a love betrayed, is abandoned forever. And nearby Sniffer lay flat on his back in the middle of the track, staring up at the canopy above.

"No one touch me. Don't anyone come near me."

You don't know what happened to the others, and at the time you didn't care. You went down the track a way and found a log to sit on. You didn't bother to take the abandoned AK along with you—if someone came and killed you, that was probably just as well. By the time you'd smoked three cigarettes, Nigel came down and brought the AK.

"It wasn't your fault, Yogi."

"Oh no? I said they were small. Remember? I said they were fuckin' small, didn't I."

"You couldn't have known."

"But I did know! I knew it was wrong! Too small, I said. I just didn't think about it enough."

"No one could have thought of that."

"It's wrong, Nigel. We did not come here to kill children."

"They were Viet Cong children."

"They were just fuckin' kids!"

"We were doing the job the government pays us for."

"If the government pays us to kill children, then it has to be wrong."

"Yogi, they were armed. They were lying in ambush for us. They fired back. If you hadn't sprung 'em, they'd have wiped us out, just like their mums and dads would have."

"Are you seriously trying to justify this?"

Your shrill outburst causes him to draw breath. Placatingly, he tries again. "What about their parents? Don't you think they bear some responsibility for their kids..."

"Nigel, when I was a kid, I used to play games with guns. Cowboys and indians, gangsters, wargames. Sometimes I'd pinch me old man's shotgun and go out and play Great White Hunters. Nobody came along and shot the shitbags outa me for that."

"Yogi, these people are into total war. They train their children for it. You don't understand how primitive they are..."

"Maybe. But we are supposed to be civilised human beings. And civilised human beings don't gun down children. Not for any reason."

"Don't do this to yourself, Yogi. It wasn't your fault."

"Words, Nigel. Just fuckin' words."

You walked away, again leaving the AK behind. They say that Nigel sat on the log and wept, but you don't know whether that was true. You had to do something. Words were nothing. What you did counted. You went across to where Kinross's blokes were digging. You walked right up to them and shoved them all out of the way, then grabbed an entrenching tool and held it aloft, menacing anyone who tried to come near.

"I'm doing this," you snarled.

You dug the hole good and deep and square, while the other men looked on. From time to time, one or another would offer to relieve you and you didn't answer. You just dug.

"Right, bring them over."

Bulldog Doyle carried the girl and Ten Days the boy. The two youths were apparently being put in a hole somewhere else. They laid the two small corpses beside the hole in which you still stood in your mad defiance.

"Why aren't you blokes helping him?" Doyle asked.

"You try and get near him," Kinross said.

"Come on, Yogi. Get out of there."

"Piss off, Bulldog."

"That's an order, Griffin."

"Stick it up your arse."

His bulldog tactics failed, Doyle tried a gentler tone.

"Hey, Griffin. Come on. Let someone else do this bit."

"Get away," you growled at him.

"Yogi, we're getting a chopper to take you and the others out. Give it to someone else."

"Don't come near me or you'll wear this."

"You'll miss the fucking chopper."

"Fuck the fuckin' chopper."

"Alright Griffin. Get on with it."

"Let's get them in the hole, shall we?"

At least someone had closed the girl's big eyes, and the boy was turned mercifully face down. Lying in the damp red soil, the girl's naked body was so appallingly white.

"At least someone could have spared a fuckin' hoochie,"

you savaged at them. Quite a crowd had gathered and no one moved. You stripped off your shirt and draped it over her.

First the girl, then the boy. You laid them carefully, gently, in the bottom of the hole and then climbed out and began to fill it in. You shovelled furiously, heaping the dirt onto any part of their bodies still exposed but somehow it seemed that no matter how much dirt you hurled in there, some part of them still remained exposed. A tiny white hand, part of a foot, and more than thirty years later you're still shovelling and you haven't quite managed to cover them yet.

Pumpkins

Next there's a flying cow. Fair fuckin' dinkum, a real cow, about fifty feet above the ground, going moo madly, swinging helplessly in the air. All it needed was the fuckin' moon for it to sail over... but this is no nursery rhyme. The poor bloody animal was suspended in a giant sling connected to the belly of a hovering Chinook with US Air Force markings, oscillating wildly in the gusty air.

"Poor cow," you said sadly.

The cow would trapeze its bovine way across the treetops for three kilometres to where a convoy of trucks waited, guarded by Armoured Corp. That was as close as they could get to this village; it was all narrow muddy jungle tracks from there on to here. The village, without benefit of a name, has a population of a few dozen but a vast storage of produce and area of crops. Far too fuckin' vast. It's a Charlie supply base, no fuckin' worries about that.

But the villagers aren't Charlies. They're just plain folks whose hamlet is under the Charlie's thumb—keep up the supply of food or you get a bullet in the brain. Nice and simple. Even dumb peasant dirt farmers understand it perfectly.

So all the stock and equipment gets lifted out by choppers, and the people are rounded up but they have to walk out to the trucks, escorted by Ten Platoon. They'll be rehoused in what is called the Engineer's Village, built by the Sappers near Nui Dat, surrounded by barbed wire and guarded by MP's so the Charlie's can't get at them. No one says what that place really is.

Twelve platoon has thrown a perimeter around this hamlet in case any Charlie patrols get hungry at this inconvenient time, and you're in the middle to do the rest—burn the houses and wreck the crops. Search and destroy operation. Nice day's work in sunny Vietnam.

"Picture this, Snowy," you are saying, now that the cow has passed from view. "You are sitting on the verandah of your farm out west there, the wife in the kitchen, kids playing in the yard. Then a bunch of soldiers come along, round up you and your family and march them off to a concentration camp, steal your stock, burn your house down, wreck your crops. How would you feel about that?"

"You think too much, Yogi," Snowy grumbles.

"You reckon there's any way you could be convinced that them fuckin' soldiers were doing you a favour?"

"Yogi Bear, what are you fuckin' on about?"

"This! I'm on about this! I've seen movies. John Wayne movies. Richard Attenborough movies. There's the way the good guys behave and then there's the way the Rotten Nazis and Dirty Japs behave. And this? This relocating populations, burning farms, destroying crops. It's the way the bad guys carry on."

"Which only proves you watch too many movies, Yogi."

"But don't you see, Snowy? Don't you see?"

"Yogi, will you piss off and earbash someone else for a while. You're giving me the shits."

Snowy Spargo just wasn't any fun since he broke up with Mabel. He has simply refused to carry her any further, and declared himself an ordinary rifleman. You all had to go down to the firing range and be tested for your M60 skills. You were good and big and strong enough but Nigel had made you his 2IC in place of Alby Dunshea. The only other possibility was Daytripper who wasn't so big but he has a lot of gumption, so he got the job. Meanwhile, Snowy watched grumpily and refused even to join the practice. Back in the middle with an SLR, he somehow looks smaller, less significant, and anyway is constantly in a black mood. Every morning, first time you see him, he tells you how many days he has to go. You and Greyman and Sniffer have the same number of days and everyone keeps count, but he tells you anyway. He is pissed off with you and everything, but then, so were you all that day.

There was a Thanksgiving party going on at Bein Hoa base and the Yankee pilots didn't appreciate being dragged out to give Delta Company a ride to this hamlet. They fumbled their choppers maniacally, playing chicken with each other, wandering all over the sky in no formation whatsoever, and landed right in the middle of the hamlet with guns blazing into the surrounding jungle, and tumbled you out with your shattered nerves.

"This is stupid, Nigel. Why fuckin' destroy the place? Why not set ambushes on all the tracks and wait until the Charlies come in to try and collect their supplies."

"This is easier."

"But stupid."

"Since when did you expect better than stupid from Task Force."

Soon the people were gone and the cattle and goats with them and all that remained was a friendly-looking dog on a chain.

"Here, doggy. Nice doggy. Come on, boy," Nigel said encouragingly.

The dog bit him and he had to be evacuated for fear of rabies.

This little mishap brought the rage of Hatrack amongst them.

"Bloody bloke his age and rank oughta know bloody better. Did you get rid of the fucking dog?"

"No. It was..." you mumbled, directing a hateful gaze at the departing chopper that carried Nigel away and saw you suddenly promoted into the direct path of Hatrack's tirade.

"Oh Jesus," Hatrack moaned, contorting his craggy face in purest anguish. "Well for Christ's sake shoot the fucking thing before some other fuckwit decides to feed it a finger!"

Only the callous farmboy Snowy Spargo could be persuaded to undertake so foul a duty. You buried the dog at the side of the road with a barbed wire cross at its head and a large old bone at its feet.

Hatrack was soon obliged to return when Mickey Wright and Sniffer discovered the disadvantages of setting fire to a thatched house from the inside. Dorset and Sergeant Lawson rushed to their rescue and the result was four men overcome by smoke and coughing their guts out. Ten Days asked for a chopper to evacuate them, which was why Hatrack exploded once more in your midst, hotter and more redfaced than any of the victims.

"If you cannot control this mob of juvenile delinquents, Mr Hollingsworth, then I will replace you with someone who can!"

While Holly was relaying much the same message to you, Ten Days was silly enough to ask about his dust-off helicopter.

"Fuck the dust-off," Hatrack roared. "Make the stupid bastards walk out!"

The four smoke inhalation victims immediately saw good reason for miraculous recoveries.

Holly led the platoon away from the blazing village, and just over the hill they came upon the most enormous pumpkin patch any of you had ever seen. Truly, it was out of all proportion to the probable needs of the entire Viet Cong army, and although they were the small round Asian pumpkins, still they were plainly very ripe and ready for the harvest.

"Shit, look at `em all. It's a bloody plague!" Daytripper gasped.

"Today Phouc Tuy, tomorrow, the world," Greyman foretold.

With the fires in the houses now dwindling, it remained only to destroy the pumpkins but so massive did the task appear that Eleven Platoon could only stand along the ridge, gazing in a paralysis of astonished intimidation.

"Bloody good pumpkins too," you were muttering. "Better than the muck we get back at the Dat, if we get any at all."

In the greasy flyblown kitchens of Nui Dat, potato was always mashed, cauliflower similarly; turnips, parsnips and baked custard all had exactly the same texture and taste, carrot was the same stuff coloured red, pumpkin merely dyed with saffron.

Holly, though, faced the vast yellow hoard without compunction, machete raised like a cavalry officer, and ordered in his shrill voice. "Right men! Draw machetes! Charge!!"

The men waded into the field, following their bold leader, slicing and hacking. It was a massacre and more than you could stand.

"This is disgusting. So wasteful."

"Shut up, Yogi Bear, or I'll mistake you for a pumpkin."

"But Jesus, Snowy. It isn't right."

"I've forgotten the last time we did something right," Snowy answered and hacked on.

The platoon moved through in a great sweep, flailing their weapons and those plump round shapes were swiftly reduced to seedy pulp. You strode forth, spying a big healthy specimen and down upon it you swept, slashing a mighty blow, not into the yellowness, but through the stem. Sheathing your machete, you picked up the pumpkin and carried it out of the field to a small flat area beyond, setting it down gently, and then returned to the fray to rescue another. You toiled on, liberating pumpkin after pumpkin, until you had accumulated twenty-six of them, which was exactly the number of men remaining in Eleven Platoon. Except you'd forgotten to count Mickey Wright.

The men now came down the hill, wiping the yellow pulp from the blades and sheathing their machetes. The slaughter was ended.

They came to the place where you stood proudly by your pile of survivors.

"Good on yer, Yogi Bear," Ten Days was laughing. "So what do we do with them. Eat `em before we go back?"

"How can we, as decent human beings, condone such

wastage..." you cried to the mob.

"We ain't decent human beings—we're soldiers," Greyman interjected. But you could ignore the heckling of the rabble.

"Look, at Nui Dat, vegetables are scarce. Take these back with us, and the cooks will go out of their minds."

"So, I reckon, will Hatrack," Dorset observed.

"Oh come on. Even Hatrack will see merit in something like this."

Holly, of course, was looking most distressed about it all.

"We should ask him first."

Dorset wasted some time trying to get a radio message through, but the major had already returned to Nui Dat.

"So he probably won't even find out. And if he does, he can't help but approve."

Holly decided to try and point out impracticalities. "Maybe, Griffin. But how do you plan to get these back to Nui Dat. Stuff one in each pocket?"

But of course you had thought of that. "We can put them inside out shirts. Plenty of space. No trouble at all."

This was true. An army-issue shirt, like an army-issue anything else, was always several sizes too large, and except for Snowy, they all found they could accommodate a pumpkin and still fasten all the buttons.

"Initiative *and* imagination," Sergeant Lawson groaned.

"You'll never make an officer, Yogi."

It was such a simple plan, so foolproof, so worthy, so very public-spirited that there could only have been one possible outcome—it had to fail. And the point of failure was, of course, the obvious one, for while it was true that Hatrack had returned prematurely to Nui Dat, it was also true that he had taken up a perfect ambush position at the side of the airstrip. When the choppers carrying Eleven Platoon arrived, the men jubilant and their shirts bulging with the knowledge that something good had been done that day, they disembarked and saw Hatrack standing there and knew it was undone. It was plain from his expression that twenty-six soldiers in an apparent advanced state of pregnancy was by no means what he had been expecting to see. His mouth dropped open like a giant cave in the cliff of his rockhard face, and the dragon in that cave bellowed in just the manner that had achieved for him his wide-spread fame.

"You men! Stop where you are! Lt Hollingsworth! Step forward!"

Eleven Platoon halted in a tight little group on the tarmac, everyone trying to hide behind someone else. Holly wandered forward, striving to look like he was there entirely by mistake.

The only advantage in Holly's position was that he was not carrying a pumpkin himself. Hatrack, in true tactical form, held the high ground and had Holly squinting into the sun, squirming with the knowledge that his earlier roastings were about to be enlarged upon.

"Well, Mr Hollingsworth. Let's hear it!"

"Sir, those are pumpkins. The men are trying to aid the mess situation. What with good vegies being in such short supply..."

But Holly ran out of puff, and anyway was completely drowned out. "Don't give me that, Lieutenant! When I give an order, I expect it to be obeyed!"

"But sir..."

"No buts, Mr Hollingsworth. I'll be talking to you later, understand?"

"Yes sir..."

Holly, helpless, defeated, downcast, wandered aside.

Hatrack now redirected his meanest gaze to the rest of the you, and you strove to meet that gaze with one of equal ferocity.

"Alright, you lot. Pumpkins, is it? Well, let's see them. Come on, out and on the ground in front of you."

You unbuttoned your shirt and lowered the pumpkin to the ground—it was a telling point that most men had already given up hope, opening their shirts to let their pumpkins fall incriminatingly at their feet. You bastard, Hatrack, you breathed, and might have made a charge right there and then, had Snowy not been holding onto your belt from behind.

"Steady, Yogi Bear," he whispered in your ear.

Hatrack came down from the embankment and moved toward you, his eyes blazing, his mouth twisted, jaw jutting ruthlessly. "Right, you pumpkin-eaters. You are going to have to learn something and it is called discipline. Got it? DISCIPLINE! When I give an order, I expect it to be obeyed. I do not expect it to be treated as some sort of joke..."

You lowered your head sadly. The fuckin' rotten smallminded shitheaded bastard. All he fuckin' knows is discipline—the sort of fuckin' mindless discipline that has nothing to do with common sense.

"As it stood," he went on. "had you wanted to keep the pumpkins, all you had to do was ask. That's the system—ASK! I like pumpkin too, you know!"

All eyes turned toward Holly. This was his moment, his

chance to explain the efforts made to do just that. But the little runt, standing headbent, was going to let it pass. Fuckin' little gutless freak! Bear gave an extra jerk on your belt. Tell him, for god's sake, Holly, tell him. But the runt's nerve failed him, and Hatrack carried on regardless. "But no, not you lot. You have to go behind my back, sneaking about like thieves. And that is exactly what's wrong with this outfit. Well you are not going to get away with it this time. You are going to learn..."

And you sagged defeatedly in Snowy's grasp. That was the end—the chance was gone. When Hatrack said someone would learn something, all reason was overwhelmed, no matter what was said or done afterward. "...you are going to learn what discipline is and you will learn it now!..."

Yeah, yeah.

"...Right! Every man, draw his machete! COME ON, GET THEM OUT! NOW! MOVE!"

You knew what it meant—the old put-things-back-the-way-they-were routine, no matter how ridiculous the consequences. Fuckin' army was getting sillier and more childish by the day. Useless fuckin' dickheads, and you whip out your machete like a Saracen warrior about to charge...

"Right!" Hatrack roared. "NOW CUT UP THOSE PUMPKINS!"

Other men stood staring in disbelief, but not you. You only had to glance down at that pumpkin at your feet and it turned into Hatrack's head, with its great nose, sneering lips, cold narrow eyes, jutting lower jaw.

"Come on, you heard me!" Hatrack was bellowing. "DO IT! NOW!"

But you didn't need it spelled out. Hatrack's severed head lay at your feet and you flew to the task. With a cry you lifted your machete aloft and brought it slicing downward to cleave that evil face into two neat halves, and you saw the brain spill out and the blood explode all about. Cop that you bastard Hatrack and struck again and again, slash, slash, slash, and other men, perhaps capturing the same image, began going at it like demons too. Kill Hatrack kill. Die you bastard die!

"GET INTO IT!" Hatrack was screaming in an utter frenzy.

"FASTER YOU MEN! SHOW YOU MEAN IT!"

Hatrack, striding back and forth, livid and crazed with the madness of the moment, and the men slashing and slicing furiously, until those pumpkins were chopped to the right size for the cooking pot and then more and more. But with every blow you struck, the divided head of Hatrack became two smaller heads that each need be sliced to two smaller ones, little bloodied heads of Hatrack die you bastard die...

"Alright, STOP!"

And you slashed and slashed at the hundred head hydra of Hatrack, kill, kill, kill them all, slash, slash...

"I SAID STOP, ACTING LANCE-CORPORAL GRIFFIN!"

Snowy shook you and you stopped, panting madly, machete dangling from your hand, your face burning with sweat, glaring straight at your tormentor. Still alive but I'll get you, you bastard. From his high vantage point, Hatrack's face was taunt and his eyes narrow with murderous intent. And the fifty-two eyes that met his gaze were no different.

There was a lull in the fury, and time for more Hatrack speechmaking. "You men are irresponsible and you are also thieves. THIEVES! You are also undisciplined, childish and damned poor soldiers. Good soldiers follow orders unquestioningly. So let's see if you can do it. Ready? Every man, one pace forward—MARCH!"

In perfect drill order, the men stomped one pace forward, which brought them to stand right in the middle of their respective piles of chopped pumpkin. Daytripper slipped over in the goo but nothing could be funny now. You stood exactly in the middle of your mangled yellow pile.

"Right, now...ready for it...Platooooon...Mark TIME!"

You began to march on the spot, grinding pumpkin into the loose gravel at the edge of the airstrip.

"ON THE DOUBLE!"

And you ran and they ran, up and down on the spot, squashing and splattering the orange goo like some idiot tribal ritual, the muck and pulp splotching all over the boots and lower part of the trousers. And the orchestrator of the madness leapt about on his stage and raged and rampaged in accord with his creation.

"FASTER! COME ON, FASTER, YOU THIEVES! GET THOSE KNEES UP! HIGHER! HIGHER, YOU THIEVES, HIGHER!"

The mad wardance continued until the individual puddles of crushed pumpkin became one great one. And Hatrack came down from his high ground to inspect the handiwork.

"Okay, HALT!"

You stood panting, all of you, from the exertion, faces fiery as much from anger as effort. Hatrack advanced to point blank range—easy pumpkin throwing distance were you still armed.

"Good, good. See, you can follow orders after all," he said as if gently scolding a mischievous child. "But look at the mess you've made. We can't go leaving a mess like that all over the airstrip, can we? Of course not. So you'd better pick it all up, hadn't you— every seed and morsel—and since you like carrying pumpkins around inside your shirts, you'll better put it all back where it came from. Got it?"

You didn't get it. It was too unbelievable. But Hatrack could be patient. "I want to be sure you learn that carrying pumpkin around inside your shirts is not such a good idea after all, so PICK THIS FUCKING SHIT UP, YOU THIEVES, AND PUT IT BACK INSIDE YOUR SHIRTS! I WANT THIS AREA LEFT SPOTLESS!"

The men hesitated for one more incredulous moment, and then slowly knelt and began to scoop up the muck in their hands and place it inside their shirts. It oozled horribly in their fingers and quickly stained down the front of their greens. You were the last to kneel, and Hatrack stood, hands on hips, glaring maniacally, until you went down too.

"You will take it back to the company area and there dispose of it in an orderly manner. And you will march back to the area in proper formation. Lt Hollingsworth. CSM Doyle. You will see that this is done. Now get on with it!" And he silenced the murmur of protest with a savage. "And there's no need to talk about it! Your parade, CSM."

It can hardly be supposed that you have ever experienced carrying about ten big serves of uncooked mashed pumpkin pressed coldly against your bare belly by your fastened shirt buttons. It was an exquisitely unpleasant sensation. Every man bent forward slightly, trying to contain the gruesome bundle in his shirtfront, looking like he had just been gutted and was striving to hold his insides in. The shirts bulged with the saggy soggy mess that ran down the thighs, puddling in the crotch and the boots, and soaking clammily through the fabric. It was like wearing back-to-front a nappy that some giant baby had shat in. A rather shamefaced Bulldog Doyle lined you up in three ranks and marched you up the road in a decidedly awkward bandy-legged waddling gait.

"Ah, well," Greyman sighed. "Could be worse. I don't like pumpkin much anyway."

"You're on mess duties for a week, Goolie," Holly screeched in exasperation.

"No use crying over spilt pumpkin," Greyman grinned.

"Two weeks!"

The platoon puddled along like a giant snail leaving a yellow sheening trail behind. Holly was thinking about it.

"And a week for you too, Yogi Bear."

"That'll teach me to mess with Viet Cong pumpkins."

"Two weeks!"

It was, however, a very different Lt Hollingsworth who, later that evening, wandered over to the kitchen where Greyman and you were dixie bashing—scrubbing at the hopelessly stained pots and pans burned black by the useless cooks. The rest of the platoon were relieving their embarrassment in the boozer, while the rest of the company, and indeed the entire Task Force were gurgling mirthfully into their beer. The humiliation of one of the supposedly toughest outfits around was the only subject worth discussing that evening. And this demeanour extended even into the Pig Battalion Officer's Mess, the orderly, white tableclothed impeccable uniformed domain of the high and mighty where, according to Holly, this small scene had just been witnessed.

Porky, the rotund, pompous-looking Battalion Commander, approached Hatrack the moment formalities ended.

"I heard you nearly managed to capture us some nice fresh pumpkins today, Major."

Hatrack, according to Holly, went a most peculiar pale shade. "Not quite, sir."

"Pity. Fancy a spot of pumpkin myself."

To which Hatrack, uncharacteristically, could find no answer. before he walked smilingly away, Porky added. "It's good that the rank and file appreciate the critical food shortfalls, don't you think Major? I do hope you'll personally thank the men responsible for today's attempt. You will do that for me, won't you Major."

"Of course I will, sir."

And, of course, he never did.

The Chi-com Man's Revenge

You are the Chi-com Man. He lives on in your body as well as your mind—the true hero of Vietnam. No good role for John Wayne here—he's too big and nowhere near subtle enough. More like Peter Lorre, before he bloated and died, but no, too villainous. Someone small and quiet, friendly and brilliant. Humphrey Bogart and Clark Gable and Alan Ladd were all runts but they were photographed to look tall—that's the American way—bigness. They know big, understand it, can match big with bigger, but they know nothing about small. They think small means insignificant and ignore it, and that is their greatest mistake. They don't realise that everything big is made up from things small—ignore the small and the big constantly erodes, fails, falls apart, often inexplicably. Or at least, inexplicably to those who ignore the small. The Chi-com Man is Charlie Chaplin with a bomb. And it is because they cannot imagine that character that they can never defeat him, for you cannot defeat something you cannot see, and so they watch their empire falling apart, eroded by the invisible for no reason they can comprehend. You are the Chi-com Man. You can feel yourself diminishing in size, and growing in stature at the same time. You are the Chi-com Man and the Chi-com Man is invincible.

Yogi Bear, it was, as they once knew him, who ran with Greyman to the boozer when their dixie bashing duties were done, to tell the tale of Hatrack and Porky and Pumpkins, retelling it over and over as they drank from the cool cans with feverish excitement, each version slightly more embellished with detail of Hatrack's acute embarrassment, but there were unbelievers.

"No officer and gentleman should ever be caught admitting a mistake nor apologising to his men," Nigel sermonised.

"Then he should be made to," The Chi-com Man said.

But no one heard him nor knew he was there.

"I think we just had one of our better days," Sniffer was laughing.

"We did," Greyman roared. "We had a win."

"Don't often get one of those," Snowy laughed.

"Strange, isn't it," the eternally sober Nigel pontificated. "How the days when we win somehow seem worse than the days when we lose."

"He must be made to apologise," The Chi-com Man said again.

This time Nigel heard the anger and determination in that alien voice, and looked toward you coldly. He did not like people who could not face up to the facts.

"And how, exactly, would you go about doing that?"

"I don't know, but fuck it, Nigel, he's a soldier too. Doesn't he have to follow orders like anyone else?"

"He doesn't have to do anything," Nigel said. "As regards us, he can get away with anything he likes."

And of course, that was it. You knew it was the answer the very moment that Nigel said it.

"Then we must make sure he doesn't get away with it," The Chi-com Man cried.

"There's fuckin' nothing we can do," Nigel insisted.

But The Chi-com Man knew it wasn't so. There might have been nothing they could do, but The Chi-com Man wasn't one of them. The Chi-com Man was a lone wolf, a solitary hunter, who made his own decisions about what could and could not be done.

"So this just gets buried," Sniffer said. "Like everything else."

Like everything else, your brain screamed, like everything else. Like Ap An Quai, like Skull Braddock, and all of his other little acts of bastardry.

"Buried and forgotten," Nigel said sadly.

"It won't be forgotten," The Chi-com Man swore. "I won't forget."

He wouldn't either. He knew that then. The Chi-com Man would have his revenge, but the first thing, the most important thing, was that they would have to know who it was. When it was done, they would have to know that it was the work of The Chi-com Man.

But other people could come up with own ideas. Greyman, his eyes as foggy as yours felt, leaned across the table. "What we need is volunteers to crap in his bed every night, so that he really fuckin' knows how we feel about him."

"And twice on Sundays," Sniffer roared in approval.

What it lacked in originality, it made up for in enthusiasm.

"What a lot of bullshit!" That was Nigel.

"We should tie him down and forcefeed him twenty-six pumpkins," Daytripper offered, swinging his arms in wild excitement at the thought and bowling over a pile of empty beercans.

"A lot of bloody codswallop," Nigel responded.

"Sign him up as a Buddhist monk," Snowy guffawed. "And let him burn himself in the streets."

"I'll sell him the petrol and matches," Greyman laughed, and fell right off his chair.

"Why not just transfer him to the Yanks," Mickey Wright said ruthlessly. "No-one lasts more than a week with them."

"He'd change that to three days," Sniffer cried.

"You're all up yourselves," Nigel wailed.

On and on they went and through it all, the Chi-com Man said nothing. The Chi-com Man was a man of action, not of words. There were no words to be spoken, only deeds to be done. They were all so full of bright ideas and all the while Nigel waved about his dog-bitten paw in protest and telling them that they were all talking nonsense which of course they were. It was just a game to make them all feel better, to let off a bit of steam, destroying the dreaded Hatrack in a ferocious onslaught of imaginings. But in the morning, they would wake up with their hangovers and it would be forgotten, like everything else was always forgotten. Only this time it would not. This time The Chi-com Man was amongst them, laying in wait for the time when the ranting and raving was done, and they were sleeping, the quiet time, his time.

Yet you could not stay completely silent. Not only was it important that this was done, but also that everyone knew who had done it. The Chi-com Man.

"I'm gonna go get him now!" The Chi-com Man roared.

Someone, Nigel probably, had you by the arm.

"Sit down and shut up, you fuckin' dickhead! Haven't you got in enough fuckin' trouble for one day?"

"I don't care. I'm gonna get him. I'm gonna get him."

You were too. You allowed the madness to well up in your body and completely overwhelm you.

"What'll you do, shoot him?"

Anything, anything. Say anything. Shout it, scream it, let yourself go!

"Yeah, that's it. Shoot him, shoot the bastard."

"Don't do that. You'll wake up the cooks."

By this time, they had you down to the floor and you were being sat upon by someone so large that it could only have been Snowy.

"Poor bastard, he's blown his fuckin' mind."

"We gotta get him out of here."

And while such things were being said, you were being utterly crushed to death, but that didn't matter.

"Where's that fuckin' Hatrack. I'll fuckin' get you Hatrack!"

Then they were manhandling you out into the night, Snowy's huge forearms wrapped so firmly about you that it was difficult to breath. There were visions of faces of Nigel, Greyman, Daytripper and each of them seemed to be holding onto some part of your anatomy—they were dragging you to your bed but just for the benefit of the exercise, you put up one hell of a fight. Twisting and squirming, making it hard for them, kicking out savagely, they were big boys and could take it. Forcing an arm free and throw a punch at that face. Take that, you bastard!

"Shit, he hit me!" Sniffer wailed, and fell behind, the victim of a savage haymaker.

Some of the images of that journey are clearer than others. Greyman moving up ahead carrying the case of beer for the after hours party that would be in Nigel's tent, and to which, apparently, you were no longer invited. Nigel to the flank, out of flailing distance, giving orders like a traffic cop.

"Get hold of that arm, Daytripper. Don't let him swing. Lift him, Snowy, keep his feet off the ground."

"You fuckin' try doin' it!" Snowy grunts back in your ear with his hot beery breath.

"Hey you, what's-a-name. Get hold of his legs."

"Mickey Wright, sir."

"Just fuckin' hold him, will ya?"

But mostly it is indistinct shapes struggling in the darkness like a berserk monster of many arms and legs. Whenever Snowy's crushing arms permit you sufficient air, you unleash another outburst in spite of the efforts of Daytripper who, dodging your flailing free fist in deference to Sniffer's misfortune, strives to slap a hand over your mouth.

"Hatrackkkkkkk! I'll fuckin' get you, Hatrackkkkkkk!"

In your ear, you can hear Snowy constantly grunting with effort—that alone is a considerable achievement, but he manages to maintain his mighty grip until the end of the journey. The others fare less well, as your efforts cast them off on the end of a lashing foot or haymaking fist sending them sprawling and tumbling and cursing into the brambles from where they would immediately spring up and rush back into the fray. Finally, the whole shebang reaches the hoochie you share with Sniffer and Greyman and they force you inside.

Of course, the fight is far from over, but you allow your efforts to lessen now. They thrust you down on the bunk and Snowy sits on you, while the others pant and gasp from the strain of battle.

"Shit, he's gone completely mad," Snowy coughs, you can hear the scratch as he lights that one fag a day that he reckons he actually needs. Wouldn't mind a fag yourself after that effort, but you'll have to settle for Snowy's residual smoke. Take it easy, for a bit now. Out of earshot of CHQ, there's no longer any need to blaspheme the name of Hatrack.

"Do you suppose we should tie him up? " Greyman proposes, when you have always thought him to be a friend.

"Good idea. " Nigel grunts. "Get some rope."

The Chi-com Man thinks it not such a good idea. The only course open now is to play dead.

"Hey. He's stopped," Snowy perceives through his vast buttocks. He removes himself from your decidedly flattened form.

They stand around for a time, pondering this outcome. You have your head turned away, lying still and limp. Nigel, you suppose, is the one checking your pulses.

"Out like a light."

"Pity," Sniffer laments with his bruised jaw. "I was looking forward to improvising a strait-jacket."

"Do we still need to tie him up?" that arch-enemy Greyman asks with altogether too much enthusiasm.

"Nar," Snowy snorts. "The poor bugger's pissed right off the planet. He won't wake up for days."

"Awright, let's go have a beer," Nigel says. "I need one after that."

"Near broke me bloody jaw," Sniffer is mumbling as they stomp outside and head up the way to Nigel's hoochie. To kick on, no doubt about it. You lie there, very still, eyes firmly closed, and listen, to make sure all of them have gone. Only then do you risk a smile.

"Fooled the bastards," The Chi-com Man says softly.

For a time, you do not move. Discipline and self-control—that's what it's all about. You hear the sounds you are listening for—the faint sound of music, the murmur of voices, the soft pop of the puncturing of beercans and the gulping of their foaming contents. They will be in there with the tent flaps closed, playing poker as always, staying quiet since drinking after boozer hours is definitely not allowed. Ordinarily you would have been right in there with them. A beer would be good right now, after all that struggling. Or a cigarette... But no. The Chi-com Man does not need these earthly indulgences. The Chi-com Man is strong and fully self-controlled.

Fairly soon now the generator will shut down for the night and the lights will go out. It is a matter of remaining exactly where you are until then, just in case. Once the area is plunged into darkness, your time will have come; but not before. Nevertheless, it is not easy to lie there like that, perfectly still and eyes closed and with the bumps and bruises of exhausting effort and a gut full of grog: those minutes swell to apparent hours, and sleep knows that it is well overdue. You grit your teeth against the beery fog in your brain, and wriggle your toes to prove to yourself that you are still awake. Several times, you jolt—fearing that you have in fact fallen asleep. As Snowy said, once asleep under these circumstances, there would be no waking for many hours. Too many hours. You would have to hold on. Control, Chi-com Man, control.

Finally, the light flickers out. The area is plunged into blackness. The Chi-com Man opens his eyes. It is his time, the time of darkness when he sees most clearly. Wait a moment, let it settle. There are only the sounds you expect to hear—Nigel and his poker game. You sit up in the bunk, and grapple out a fag. The Chi-com Man will allow weak Griffin this one small risk. You light it carefully in cupped hands to hide the light. All these handy little tactics they have taught you, and now they can be put to good use. You sit there, waiting, waiting. Time is on your side.

It takes about fifteen minutes for the eyes to fully adjust to the complete darkness. There is no moon, but the stars are bright—everyone else will be blinder than you. Sit there dragging with unshaking hands on the cigarette and listening, but there is nothing to be heard that you do not want to hear. You smoke the cigarette right down to the butt—until you can feel it begin to burn your fingers—and then stub it out. Good enough—that is all you need. Just enough time to let them all settle down over there. Now to begin.

You edge your way around to the end of the bunk and fumble about in your gear until you find what you want; a cool, metallic cylindrical object about the size of an aerosol can, but under the circumstances, in fact something far more sinister. Slip it into your pocket. Now go to the tent flap and wait there, have a listen, then crouch down and unlace your boots, pulling them off quietly and placing them beside your bunk. Roll up your trousercuffs a couple of turns—you don't want them flapping when you run, making noise, and now you are ready. Here you go.

Outside, your feet feel the cold hard earth. You follow the path worn along the side of the three four section hoochies, keeping wide of the guy-ropes, until you have reached the line of the front of Nigel's tent. They are getting pretty cheerful and raucous in there, and you spare them a momentary smile. Listen to them, talking in there, keeping their voices down so Bulldog Doyle won't hear them, but The Chi-com Man hears all. They are talking about someone you used to know.

"Poor old Yogi. Ain't like him, goin' fuckin' mad like that," Sniffer is saying.

"Remember the nice quiet shy bloke he usta be?" Greyman asks.

"Nobody can remember back that far," Nigel says.

"It's really fuckin' got to him, ain't it," Snowy declares.

"But he just isn't the same bloke he was before he got shot," Greyman persists.

"Who would be?" Snowy wonders.

"I dunno," Sniffer says. "Yogi always took everything far too fuckin' seriously."

"They should never have sent him back," Nigel says cruelly.

Good friends. Good men. But they waste their breath. Griffin is dead. There is only The Chi-com Man. You sway a little as you stand there, but to be truthful you are almost sober by now—the cold sweat on your face and the adrenalin pumping through your body has seen to that. It's all clear, Chi-com Man. Move on to the next stage, nice and easy.

You take the path to the toilet block, safest, surest leg of the mission. Innumerable journeys past, nocturnal and otherwise, make it surest—you can move along smoothly with the assurance of its well worn familiarity, and your exposed feet tell you when you are on the cool bare dirt of the path or if you stray to the edge. That horrible low bramble is already regrouping its forces all over the area, and its sharp little spines turn your toes into antennae. It is also safest because, should it happen that you are intercepted on this stage of the journey, you will be able to make easy accounting of yourself. Ahead you can make out the dark shape of the dunny and you go directly to it and stand at the door.

"Hullo? " you call quietly, just to make sure that there is

no-one in there. Take your time. Over to the piss-o-phone and take a leak. You need it anyway. Get settled. Look all around. Then go around to the other side of the structure, the CHQ side, and prop against the cold galvanised iron wall. God, it stinks in there—something you aren't inclined to notice when on official business. From this position, you can survey the entire CHQ area; the dark outlines of the rows of four-man hoochies. There is no light to be seen, nor sound to be heard. Final leg. You move around to the other side of the dunny and pick up another path, the one worn in accordance with the bowel movements of CHQ.

There is no margin for error from here on—to be found will arouse instant suspicion, and now you slip along almost on all fours, crouched right down, stopping to listen between each stride. It is slow and awkward and your rumbling belly and fuzzy head are both in firm disagreement with so awkward a posture: still you persist, and finally reach the edge of the rubber plantation, or at least the point where the road up from the airstrip had been cut through. Directly across the road is the company office, and the next hoochie beside it is the one that serves both as Hatrack's office and sleeping quarters. The company office, you know, would be as empty as any self-respecting office at such an hour. You wait again and listen—there is no movement anywhere—not even, disappointingly, the sound of men snoring peacefully in their sleep. In five swift strides, you cross the road and drop down beside the sandbags that surround the company office. Keeping very low now, you move along the edge of the sandbags like a Red Indian, you supposed, or slithering like a snake. You had, as punishment duties in the past, aided in the laying of these sandbag walls and so know this little spot of ground like the back of your hand. Never could you have imagined that such knowledge would actually become useful.

You slip along under the guy ropes to the corner, and go around and most of the way down to the back of the office. Right beside you now, is Hatrack's hoochie, just six feet away. You reach into your pocket and feel the cold reassurance of the canister. All is quiet. You can even, you think, hear the deep, even breathing of Hatrack inside, the breathing of a man sleeping as peacefully as a babe. Sleep on, Hatrack, sleep on. You are sweating heavily, panting a little not so much from effort as from the effects of your earlier debaucheries. You run the cool metal over your sweating brow. It feels good. And then carefully, with your nerves outside your skin and your senses constantly scanning the area like a radar sweep, you inch across those critical six feet. You are now placed just the width of the sandbag wall from Hatrack in his bunk. You have laid a great number of those sandbags too. You can distinctly hear his somnolent breathing now. Very carefully, you hold the canister up in front of your face, wrapping a firm thumb over the lever on its side, and looping a forefinger through the ring, gently easing the split pin free. You take one deep breath—the moment has come, and from now on it will be speed rather than stealth that will count. In a single movement you rip off the lever, and reaching in over the top of the sandbags, lob the canister into the hoochie. There is the sharp thwack of the cap coming down, firing the charge, and in the same instant, the thump and rattle of the canister on the duckboards. But even as that happens, you are on your feet and away.

The important thing now is not so much to make your escape without detection—they will all know who it was, but The Chicom Man cannot allow himself to be captured in the act. Go quickly, but not so quickly as to allow the chance of mishaps, such as tripping over guy ropes, falling down holes, or running into rubber trees. You must retrace your steps exactly, when the temptation is to run like hell: you scamper back around the sandbag wall of the company office on your hands and knees and dash across the road at exactly the same place and at precisely the same angle. This provides your line of march back through the trees. You have covered all that distance before the first cry goes up, presumably from the victim, but once within the cover of the trees, you immediately halt and take to walking instead, and sticking to the path. The darkness is on your side—searching eyes peering out from CHQ might well be able to spot a fast moving object inside the plantation, but never a slow moving one. You walk carefully to the toilet block without succumbing to the desperate urge to look back behind you; only when you are safely behind the galvanised iron wall do you pause to survey your handiwork.

You see little, though there is someone back there moving and calling, and strange things seem to be happening to Hatrack's hoochie. The last likely point of discovery is the possibility that someone might have occupied the toilet in your absence—no-one had. You walk with long, careful strides, down toward Nigel's hoochie, and it is only over the last couple of yards that your will finally cracks and you burst into a sprint and so come charging in through the tent flaps to the great shock and consternation of the men gathered inside.

"I got him! You got him!" you gasp triumphantly.

The members of four section sat about the table, drinking and playing poker by secretive candlelight. With the sudden incursion of this maniac figure into their midst, someone immediately doused the candle in a splash of beer to provide everyone else time to hide their incriminating cans, for in that first instinctive instant, they were sure that it was they who had been got, caught out by Bulldog Doyle on a nocturnal raid. There followed a pause of one full second while everyone sat or stood in the sudden darkness and wondered what to do next.

"I got him! I really did!" you cried again, though only half as excitedly as the initial outburst.

They recovered immediately from their panic, and were more or less able to recognise the invader for who he was.

"Got who?" Nigel's voice came at you from out of the blackness.

"Hatrack! Got him a fuckin' bewdy."

Nigel stood up then, and walked to where he thought you stood, possibly staring at you in complete horror.

"Did you kill him? " he asked and then pushed his way past you to look outside.

"Don't be silly. I got him with a smoke grenade. You should hear him out there, coughing his guts out. Got him a ripper."

Indeed, at that very moment and even at this distance, someone could be heard coughing in terrible distress. Others were now on their feet and also wanting to have a look.

Over there, a dozen strong torches were flashing all about, and you could soon compile the illuminated fragments into a complete picture. Great billows of smoke plumed out from under the flaps of Hatrack's hoochie and rose into the night, if some gigantic spiritual being had taken possession of it. Out in front the figure staggered about, doubling up with each lung-wrenching bout of coughing, while other men, all of them shouting incomprehensibly, were coming to his assistance. Still more men seem to be blindly panicking and going in all directions. Chaos. It was terrific. And then amongst the bewilderment came the strength of order, as the figure of Bulldog Doyle made himself apparent, if only through his roaring voice.

"What the bloody hell happened?" he demanded of the world in general. "Get a medic, you men."

The voice of Doyle was enough to bring those watchers from

four section back to reality. Nigel turned and grabbed you by the shirtfront, giving you a solid jolt. "You dumb fuckin' idiot. He's not going to like this. "

"He's not supposed to," you said—quite logically, you thought. You were, to tell the truth, a bit disappointed in Nigel who suddenly seemed bereft of his sense of humour. But Nigel was not a man to dither, and his tactical mind went swiftly into action. "Awright, quickly now. Everyone undress and into bed and look like you've been there all along," and he was already tearing off his own shirt. "They'll be out in a minute looking for the bloke who did it, and you can bet your balls this will be the first place they'll look. "

But of course, you were not concerned in the slightest about that: "Let `em come. We've got plenty of smoke grenades. "

"Snowy! Grab him!"

Wham went the mighty bearhug around you from behind.

You would have liked to have told him that all this wasn't necessary and that it wasn't you who had done it anyway but the Chi-com Man, but Nigel was a man in a hurry. "Awright, let's get him to bed. Greyman, you got that rope?"

"Hey, take it easy, you guys," you were gasping with what little air Snowy's python arms allowed you. "I don't care if they..."

"You might not, but we do. Right, get him down."

Down you went and the metal springs screamed their agony, and you could hardly resist the desperation with which your hands were tied to the bedhead and your feet to the end. Amid that flurry of action, just as you attempted further protest, a firm sweaty hand was clamped over your lips. Then Nigel's mouth was inches from your ear. "Now you get this, you fuckwit. You are unconscious. You stay still, you stay limp, no matter what happens. One peep out of you and I'll belt you over the head with a shovel and make it true, got it?"

You shrugged. Since Nigel had decided to take such a strong view of the matter, it was probably wise to play along. But it was disappointing—no-one seem to be enjoying the game the way you'd hoped they would.

Bulldog Doyle led the posse over from CHQ and came, as Nigel had predicted, directly to the four section area.

"Right-o Nigel. Get `em out here. "

"On parade, four section," Nigel echoed, in a very sleepy voice.

And they came out wrapped in blankets and towels and, as

Nigel put it later, you never saw such a gang of bedraggled, newly wakened, bewildered men in all your life.

You lay there listening to a scene so easily imagined, right down to the stern look on Bulldog Doyle's face.

"What's the go, Charlie?" Nigel ask innocently.

Doyle did not trouble himself to answer. You could hear him pace along the line, eyeing each man, and stopped when he came to the place where you weren't standing.

"Private Griffin seems to be missing, Nigel?"

"Oh, shit. I forgot. He's still tied to his bunk."

"You don't expect me to believe that, do you?"

You braced yourself for it. Immediately came the thump of heavy boots on the duckboards behind your back, and the torchlight showed bright red through your closed eyelids. Hold firm, Chi-com Man, hold firm. This will be the final test of strength.

"He went fuckin' gaa-gaa on us. We brought him back and had to tie him down..."

"How long ago?"

"About an hour."

"Bullshit, Nigel."

There was a pause. And then came a mighty blow to you shoulder—God knows what he hit you with. But The Chi-com Man is tough and can take it and didn't even flinch.

"See, he's right out of it," Nigel said confidently.

There was another menacing pause. Then you could feel hot breath right on your ear. At that range, Doyle's roar could be fatal, but instead he mercifully offered a grumbling whisper.

"Had a hard night, have you, Yogi Bear?"

The Chi-com Man was fearless and stayed limp.

"I don't believe you, Griffin. I reckon you've been out and about, having a bit of a wander."

You wouldn't have called it a wander.

But Nigel intervened: "He'd of needed to be Houdini to get out of that lot."

"Houdini, hey? Well maybe he is. I don't know how he did it. All I know is that he did."

"Did what, Charlie?"

"Someone just snuck over to CHQ and chucked a smoke grenade into the boss's hoochie. Bloody near suffocated him. "

When he put it like that, it did sound like something well worth doing. And indeed, a chuckle arose from the others outside. This was the truest test of The Chi-com Man's willpower, but not the slightest ripple of mirth touched you.

"And you think it was Yogi?" Nigel asked incredulously.

"I know it was," Doyle said coldly.

Another pause. The Chi-com Man could take it, whatever it was going to be. Suddenly you were airborne as Doyle seized the whole bunk and over-turned it on the floor, sending you sprawling. Things bumped and bruised but you went like a sack of spuds and allowed no reaction. Doyle grabbed you by the hair and bumped your face on the floor a few times, then shook your head, dragging hairs out by the roots, but you stayed limp and even a dribble of saliva ran from your lips, or was it blood. No matter; The Chi-com Man could last forever. Doyle gave up then, and let you flop back to the floor.

"We've bred you blokes too tough," he said.

He was as right about that as he was about all the rest.

"I don't believe any of this, Nigel," he said finally.

But he had no choice but to lead his posse off in search of other likely suspects.

Nigel and Greyman uprighted your bunk and lifted you back onto it. Still you stayed limp. Had you responded, it would have been with cries of pain. Keep up the game, the strength, let The Chi-com Man see it through to the end.

"Jesus. Maybe Charlie really hurt him," Greyman fretted.

"Who cares," Nigel replied ruthlessly.

They didn't even bother to untie you, just left you there in your pain and grief to suffer until sleep or was it unconsciousness finally came. And the Chi-com Man vanished back into the night from whence he came.

Rightful Places

The hot morning sun stretched a finger of light under the hoochie flap to strike a point directly between your eyes and pierce fiercely through the skull to broil your brains and incinerate your dreams. You groaned and moved across the bunk, seeking a shadowed spot on the pillow, without daring to open your eyes lest they be burned from your face. Morning, you thought, a new day, and everything peaceful and calm and generally alright. Go back to sleep, and you should have too, had it not been for your foolish mind which then troubled to cast itself backward a number of hours to the last time that you had been awake. It was mostly a blank but what little remained was too unbelievable to abide. You could feel the rope burns on your wrists, and your lips seemed thick and sore and tasted of blood. Shit!

There was no doubt, however much you might have wished to ignore it. Everything was anything but alright! No peace and no calm. You closed your eyes, desperate now in the hope that sleep would restore itself, but it was a hopeless cause. The shock of realisation itself was enough to ensure that sleep would never return. Pretty soon now you were going to have to get up and face up to this, and that was a prospect that could only be regarded as daunting. The only thing to do then was to pull the blanket over your head and pretend to be asleep, and not only for your own benefit either, but that of others. Just try and savour these last few moments of peace before the inevitable disaster struck.

But there was no escape, not under the covers nor anywhere else. Morning had arrived and with it a fate that was utterly unbearable. Bravely you opened your eyes and looked out at the world. Everything was still and quiet—there were no screams of torture to be heard, nor the tramp of the boots of firing squads. In fact, there seemed to be no-one around at all. From where you lay, you could see the bunks of Sniffer and Daytripper, and it was plain that there was no-one under their mosquito nets. But some Good Samaritan had untied the ropes, and arranged you properly under blanket and mosquito net. Under the circumstances, it was helpful to know that someone cared...

Outside, the brilliance of morning began to gush through the tent flap, and your eyes objected to having to process light in such volumes. What you were doing was deciding was whether you were in any condition to move; carefully, you lifted your head, pulled back the thin blanket and diaphanous net, and shifted your feet around and onto the floor. That went alright. Not too bad at all. Maybe you were feeling just fine. Then your head fell on the floor and shattered in a thousand pieces.

"Ohhhhhhhh."

They came and stood about the entrance to your hoochie, peering in at your earthly remains.

"He lives!" Snowy said, far too loudly.

With very nearly sightless eyes, you peered up at them. They came tramping into the hoochie and stood over your ruined, bowed form.

"Ohhhh," you said again.

"He remembers," Sniffer chuckled.

"Ohhhhh, gawd!"

"He does remember," Nigel snorted.

If only to break the monotony, you attempted speech.

"Shit I must have been really pissed."

"Oh, you were, you were," Greyman laughed.

You gazed up as best you could to study their faces, but not one of them seemed to show any expression at all.

"So, what happens now?" you decided to ask. In fact, you had no choice.

"I should imagine," Nigel answered. "That the shit will shortly hit the fan. "

"And me with it," you knew.

"You'd better get your boots on," Nigel said quietly. "I should think there'll be a company parade any minute now."

The surprising thing about that, was that it had not happened last night, right then and there. You began making the effort of pulling your boots on, and discovered that you needed to pull off a pair of green army socks first. Socks were something you never wore and certainly not the itchy army issue type. You frowned with the effort of making sense of that as you removed the woolly things, held them up by the toes, and Sniffer claimed them.

"We put `em on you to cover up your dirty feet," he said. Thought of everything, these blokes.

"I appreciate it," you said, between grunts as you hauled the boots on. "But I'm going to have to own up to this eventually."

"No you won't," Snowy said.

The boots were on but your brainmatter was swirling like a

maelstrom and you had to straighten up. Greyman got down on his knees like one of Christ's disciples and began to lace the boots for you.

"You don't need to do that," you lied.

"We haven't got all fuckin' day, you know," Greyman answered.

"Look. I don't want you blokes getting into any more trouble over something I did."

"We already are in trouble," Snowy grinned. "Have been ever since fuckin' Hatrack took over this outfit."

"We've been over to CHQ to recce the damage," Daytripper said, and could not resist a chuckle. "You really did it nicely."

You were puzzled: "Did I?"

Sniffer had to laugh then: "Fuckin' terrific," he chortled.

"Couldn't have done it better myself," Mickey Wright abetted.

You gazed at their reddened grinning faces in amazement.

"Is that what you really think? "

"We've done a whip around," Snowy said. "Everyone knows who did it, but they're all pretending they have no idea."

Nigel reached out—you flinched because you were sure he was going to hit you, but instead he tousled your hair. "Yogi Bear. What you did was the best thing done around here in an awful long time. "

And they all went quite silly then, thumping you on the back and shaking your hand and slapping you about the shoulders and laughing and all that over-emotional stuff. You weren't really up to all that manhandling yet, and managed to fight them off. "Hang on, hang on. Look, I know you blokes are trying to help but I won't be able to stand by and see other men punished for what I did. I have a fuckin' conscience, you know."

"No-one gives a tuppenny fuck about your conscience," Snowy was saying. "The point is that everyone reckons that what you did was terrific."

"That doesn't change anything."

"Yes it does," Sniffer said. "You just did what we all would have liked to do, if we'd had the guts."

"Yeah," Greyman added. "You said: Hatrack, we ain't gunna take your fuckin' shit no more."

"So it wasn't really you who did it," Sniffer said. "It was the whole fuckin' company."

"And we don't see any reason why you should take all the credit for what we all feel we did," Mickey figured.

You shook your head. But you knew where the final arbitration lay, and looked directly at Nigel. "Do you agree with this?"

"I'm here, aren't I?"

"But do you agree?"

"We are here fighting for democracy, remember? If that's what everyone wants—and it is—then I want it too."

You really wanted a better answer than that, but right then the throaty voice of Bulldog Doyle rose up from CHQ. "Okay, Delta Company, on parade, right now. Let's see yer move, you bastards!"

They had to help you to your feet, and steady you as nausea and dizziness swept over you, but then you were set to go.

"Well," you said. "This is it."

Nigel grinned and landed a soft punch on your jaw. "Yep. Come on, you fuckin' outlaw, let's go."

And you tumbled outside and ran toward the thundering voice of Bulldog Doyle...

...who, it has to be said, was at his bulldog best, in the manner that had not been seen since the days when he made his fearsome reputation on the parade grounds of the training units.

"Come on, you arseholes, get those fucking ranks together, quick smart. Think, laddie, think. Don't tell me you've forgotten how to make three ranks. Right fucking marker. That's the way, boys. Now get ready for it..."

It was awkward in its unfamiliarity but you were ready for it.

"Okaaaaay... Properly at ease... Now... Companeeeeee... Atennnn... SHUN!"

Clump went the boots on the gravel.

"That was fucking awful! Hideous! I've heard you bastards fart in the mornings in better synchronisation than that! Now GET WITH IT! Standaaaaa... TEASE!"

"Steady...."

"Companeeeeeee... Attennnnnnnn... SHUN!"

Crunch!

That time it was perfect, but Bulldog put you through it three more times, just for the sheer bastardisation of it. And every thump of the boots sent shock waves right up through your body to quake in your ruined brain.

But from the corners of your eyes, you could plainly see the scene of the crime, the hoochie opened up to show the musky red splotching of the chemical, and the ground and the trees about it all lightly burnished. And more so Hatrack himself, who stood quietly to the flank as you assembled, his starched greens blotched with the red chemical, his eyes bloodshot, his complexion pale, and in his hand a handkerchief with which he constantly attended his inflamed nose. Perfect, the ghost of The Chi-com Man whispered on breeze that rustled the surrounding rubber trees.

Now that he had completed his preliminary torment of the assembled company, CSM Doyle marched over to Hatrack, stamped to attention and snapped a fine salute.

"Your parade, sir."

"Thank you, CSM."

It was fortunate that, right at that moment, Hatrack was overwhelmed by a bout of coughing, deep and lung-wrenching, and as a result had to make his address in subdued tones, his voice croaking and constantly breaking, and without any of the fire and ferocity with which these things were normally tempered. The men could see what had been done and what were its effects, and decide for themselves how they felt about it. And perhaps it was that Hatrack conjured so pathetic a figure, that they could see for themselves that some sort of difference had been made, however transient it might have been. That, alone, made it all worthwhile.

He walked on unsteady feet to stand before them, and stood, running his eyes along the ranks. Those eyes stopped when they located yours, but you maintained firm focus on a tree branch in the far distance, directly ahead.

"It has come to my attention that we have a dangerous maniac in our midst—a psychopath with the mind of a child, who has forfeited his right to stand amongst you. This individual has perpetrated a cowardly attack, foolishly irresponsible and infantile. This man, and I use the term loosely, is a danger to us all. Last night he placed my life in jeopardy for had I not awoken immediately, I might well have suffocated. Next time, it might well be yours. I now give that man the opportunity to step forward..."

You hesitated, but really there wasn't any choice. You would have to step forward, to own up. It could not be any other way. But even while you were thinking that, everyone moved. The whole company, in near perfect formation, took one perfect military stride forward. You and a bunch of stragglers were left behind, the stragglers shuffled into line until you were last man to move, when you meant to be first. You stepped forward into your proper place in the line.

Over to the flank, Bulldog Doyle needed to put his hands over his face and turn away.

Hatrack, astonished that his order had been so badly misunderstood, only slowly realised what it meant. He looked for help from Bulldog Doyle but the CSM was teetering on the brink of a complete collapse into helpless mirth. Hatrack looked back, his face dissolving into despair. Grimly he strove to force himself toward a fury, but his health was not up to it, and he could only manage a pathetic sigh. "I see. So it's like that, is it. You fools. This man is a coward. He is probably even stupid enough to be proud of his idiotic prank. But worst of all he is prepared to allow all of you to suffer to hide his own guilt. Because that is the only alternative he leaves me..."

But at that moment, a violent convulsion overtook him and while he coughed heavily into his handkerchief, the men all looked at each other, smiling proudly. You turned to Nigel.

"You bastards. You set that up," you whispered.

"Cors we did," Nigel grinned.

"Quiet in the ranks," Bulldog Doyle growled.

Hatrack, was still doubled up by his convulsions, and his handkerchief stained red, perhaps with chemical, or maybe blood. No one cared which.

Finally, he regained control and fought on, his voice even weaker now. "Alright. If that's how you want it... I have no doubt that there are those amongst you who know the identity of this mad animal, but are reluctant to name him out of some false sense of loyalty. Let me tell you that any man may come and see me at any time and name the culprit—your own identity will be kept secret, I assure you."

He wiped his mouth again, and then, after a glance at Doyle who again had to look away, continued. "Until then, I must take the following action. Because of one moron who cannot hold his liquor, all of you will be deprived. The supply of beer is withdrawn herewith and will stay that way until the culprit has confessed, or has been pointed out to me. That is all. CSM, your parade."

Charlie Doyle told you quietly that they were dismissed.

You walked quietly back to the lines and sat on your bunk while the other men set to the task of cleaning and preparing their gear, but you had no enthusiasm for the task.

"Don't talk about it," Nigel said. "Don't do anything about

it. Just get through the day and let it all ride until boozer time tonight."

"But the boozer is closed," you murmured.

"Just let it ride," Nigel insisted.

Before long, Sergeant Lawson came strutting over to your hoochie, looking unusually sergeant-like with his clipboard under his arm. He stomped formally on the duckboards and consulted his notes. "Private Griffin."

"Yeah, Henry."

"I was checking my records, Yogi," he said with his slyest grin. "And I noticed that after the last operation, you omitted to hand back one canister, grenade, smoke, red colouration, signalling for the use of. I wonder if I could have it now?"

You felt a shiver of guilt run through your body. One more lie was completely beyond your scope.

"I don't think I have it, sarge," you said.

"Of course you have. You probably just forgot it—left it in your pack or something..."

"I didn't..."

"Let's have a look, shall we?"

He indicated the pack lying muddy and unopened at the end of your bunk. But you couldn't move, so instead Henry laid the clipboard aside and knelt on the floor and opened the pack. From it—impossibly—he withdrew one red smoke grenade.

"Ah, here it is," he said, sounding all the more dramatic now that you realised it was all a charade. "Good, Private Griffin. That completes the records..."

He marked it off with a tick, and then stood, slipping the canister into his pocket.

"I'll just backdate that to yesterday afternoon, Private Griffin. Can't have people thinking I'm slack in my job, can we. There." Still playing it very formal, clipboard back under his armpit, he turned, but hesitated before he went through the flap. "Private Griffin, I knew I could rely on you to see to it that everything is put in its rightful place."

The Delta Jack-up

At sundown, the world is at peace, even in a place like Vietnam. It's a sensation that you feel of everything taking a quick breath at the end of the long and tiring day, before rushing on into the activities of night. For the things of nature, there is that pause between the time the day creatures bed down and the night creatures come awake, in the human world it is probably because everyone is indoors having dinner. And the same applied at Nui Dat, where that too was the hour when the men went to mess. The airstrip was devoid of life, no aircraft moving, nor people either. The guns on Nui Dat hill were silent, there was no traffic moving along the distant Route 2 by-pass. In fact, the only thing moving around down there was you, heading on back to the Delta Company area after a day of punishment duties filling jerrycans at the waterpoint. You wandered along the road beside the airstrip, taking your time in spite of the fact that you would miss dinner and have to hassle the cooks to whip up some leftovers. The silence and stillness was everywhere, and you savoured it; enjoying most of all, you supposed, the relief of being away from Delta Company. For away from Delta Company was a good place to be at the time.

The *Delta Jack Up,* as it was called, was now entering its third week. That wasn't what everyone called it. At Task Force they were steadfastly not calling it a *Mutiny,* fearing the complications that entailed—instead it was passed off as 'a transitional period of reorganisation', called TPR, of course. Others, especially Americans and civilians, suggested it was a *Rebellion,* a *Revolution* even, but that was far too grand a term. It was a jack-up, pure and simple. You had checked a dictionary—'collective refusal to comply with authority' it said. That was it, spot-on.

What that amounted to was an endless game of cat and mouse being played out between Hatrack and his men which had by now settled down into a routine. Every morning, the men were summoned to the parade and the same questions asked, the same lack of answers given, and the next batch of men, chosen alphabetically, were despatched to Task Force punishment duties. This posed a problem of how to deal with genuine miscreants, who were simply shunted to the head of the list, which must have created an administrative nightmare for someone, keeping track of who was on how many weeks extra duties. Soon, the alphabet was forgotten, and there were more men available for punishment than there were duties for them. Tasks needed to be invented. The RSM got a new brick blockhouse, and all of the Delta Company bunkers were filled in and re-excavated.

You had copped your share—filling jerrycans was one of these—and it was notable that the workload was not evenly distributed over the company. Of course, the whole adventure was common knowledge around Nui Dat, if only because the other units could not have helped but notice that they were no longer being rostered for the punishment duties. They would ask how the jack-up was going and you would say you were jack of it. Most men of other units thought it was a great joke—an opinion that would not have been shared at Delta Company. Task Force too, plainly knew about it, for Hatrack's men had remained virtually non-operational—eight weeks had passed since Ap An Quai, five since the disaster of Operation Tumbarumba, and three since the one-day fiasco of the 'Pumpkins' operation. While they licked their collective wounds, all that inactivity was preying on their minds.

The boozer, naturally, remained closed, for the smoke grenade throwing fiend had yet to confess though he was daily extolled by Hatrack to do so. The men's personal supplies of grog had quickly dried up, but they were not to be defeated that easily. Each night, in twos and threes, they would disappear from the area, and by late evening, Delta Company's hill was virtually deserted. Where they would go was not too difficult to figure out—there were more than a hundred units in the Nui Dat area and each was equipped with an individual boozer, and most of the men in Delta Company had friends in other units.

There were no regulations against men visiting other boozers, but Hatrack felt the matter was covered by the fact that the men of his company were confined to barracks. Bulldog Doyle led a nightly CHQ patrol around the inner perimeter but there were too many ways in and out of the Delta Company area, and under cover of darkness, the men found their training a great asset and could easily evade the patrol. A threat to count heads in the area during boozer hours was to no avail—there were over a hundred men missing the first night, more the second, and Bulldog was not about to go writing out that number of chargesheets.

Mostly, Hatrack relied on the fact that every boozer had only a certain ration of beer available, and that the Delta Company men would put too much pressure on the supplies of the other units, causing a limit to the tolerance of their consistent visits.

But the men of Delta Company were careful to remain thin on the ground at most locations, and anyway, were more than welcome in most places because they had become cult heroes of a sort. Hatrack wrote to the other unit commanders asking that Delta Company men be banned from their boozers, but received almost no co-operation, not only because most of the other commanders did not particularly like Hatrack, but more so because, since boozers were off-limits to officers, such an order would have been difficult to enforce. To attempt to police something like that, the various commanders knew, might well result in a similar jack-up in their own areas: something they were not prepared to risk, especially since Hatrack was not faring all that well with his own.

Naturally, Hatrack laid a huge number of charges against individuals, but that too was quickly reduced to a fiasco. The various sections erected scoreboards, and the number of charges against their various members were recorded and boasted about in serious competition.

HATRACK'S CHARGE SHEET SCOREBOARD
FOUR SECTION
Nigel 0
Griffin 11
Mickey 6
Snowy 9
Greyman 4
Daytripper 4
Sniffer 2
Total: 39

OTHER SECTIONS
Andy's section 43
Wally's section 41
Nigel's section 39
Lane's section 28
Dooley's section 17
Jimbo's section 13
Lou's section 13
Abel section 12
Parker's Slack Lot 5
GRAND TOTAL 211
KEEP UP THE GOOD WORK, BOYS.

When the boozer was re-opened, there would be a prize of a night's free beer for the section with the most charges against it, and a month's free beer for the individual with the most offences recorded against him. At this point, Andy Kinross's section was holding off the rest and although you and Snowy were vying for the individual honours, four section was running an undistinguished third. This was considered the fault of Nigel, who might have been the only man in the company to retain a clean sheet. Your own impressive tally arose mostly from guilt, primarily insubordination such as protesting that you were given the shitcan run two day's running and one refusing to obey an order not taking part in an inner perimeter patrol. You still felt a bit pissweak about not owning up despite the continued solidarity of the company, and perhaps you were trying to make up for it by keeping yourself on almost constant punishment duties, but really you found all this behaviour just slightly undignified.

While these things had now become a matter of routine and an accepted part of daily life, there were other aspects of the jack-up that were not so. On the second night of the ban, a group of men who remained anonymous staged a raid on the Q-store and made off with the company's reserve supply of beer. Doyle was given the task of making a search for the cache but it was never found. The inner perimeter patrols were extended to cover the CHQ area generally, but were rendered inefficient by a lack of sufficient loyalty to Hatrack by the participants.

On the third night, the next smoke grenade was lobbed into Hatrack's tent, this time yellow, but Bulldog Doyle was on hand to kick it outside.

"Not so funny the second time," Doyle was reported to have commented. Which remark, after he thought about it for a moment, apparently received the sternest of gazes from Hatrack. Three more were thrown, but they were to no effect for Hatrack had now switched quarters and moved in with Doyle. No-one wanted to gas Bulldog, however inadvertently, and Hatrack learned the wisdom of keeping someone popular in his proximity at all times. Like carrying a cobra around your neck to keep the flies away, Bulldog commented.

The raids on the Q-store and kitchen continued unabated, and Hatrack, with the few men he could trust, took to employing his officers and personal staff to maintain the interior patrols. On the first night, the kitchen was raided and when Bulldog Doyle arrived on the scene, he found the patrol, comprising

Lt Haig who was commander of Ten Platoon, Quartermaster Tom Modlin and Payclerk Martin, all bound and gagged in one of the cool rooms, and each with the word 'scab' painted on his chest.

"I don't suppose you recognised any of them," Doyle asked as he untied them.

"Not a chance," Haig said. "It was too dark and they were too quick for us. "

Doyle grinned: "These blokes have been chasing the Cong so long they've become like them themselves."

Now Hatrack was forced to embark upon another change of plan. For the interior patrols, he selected for his 'favourites' on the if-you-can't-lick-'em-join-'em basis. The idea was that if offences were committed and the culprits not found, the men on guard duty at the time would face the punishment. That didn't work either, mostly because charges now scored valuable points, or else the raiders merely waited until someone they did not particularly like was on guard before striking. This ludicrous condition still prevailed, with people like Snowy and Greyman volunteering for the interior patrols in their desperation to try and gain the lead. Someone had calculated that it would take two hundred clerks a month to process the paperwork arising from Delta Company charges, and ten officers a year to hear them all.

If Hatrack was having trouble quelling the activities of his men, he fared even worse in his efforts to defend himself. He might, at any time, find something like a dead rat in his pocket, and all manner of foul objects in his bed. Every snake, scorpion and spider found was transferred to his quarters, and there was graffiti slandering him all over the area. Someone, quite disgustingly, actually laid a turd on his pillow. But the coup-de-grace came one day when a gunshot was heard in the vicinity of his tent, and Hatrack rushed into his quarters to find his own Browning pistol lying, still smoking, on the bed. He foolishly picked it up just as Doyle arrived on the scene, along with Holly and Sergeant Lawson as witnesses. Doyle walked up and took the pistol from him.

"Somebody fired that, CSM," Hatrack said.

"So I see," Bulldog said, and looked around. "I don't see anyone."

"CSM, it was not me," Hatrack growled. "Someone crept in here and..."

But Doyle was gazing at the bullethole in the roof of the tent.

"Accidentally discharging a weapon in the base area is a serious offence, sir, irrespective of rank. I'm afraid I must report the matter to the RSM."

"I did not fire that weapon, CSM!"

As a result, the CHQ charge scoresheet gained an extra statistic. HATRACK 1

It was all a bit childish really, schoolboys defying their strict headmaster, and by now you were decidedly weary of it. You found you were ashamed from both points of view—as perpetrator, but also because you were a participant. You wished they would stop, that the company would become operational again, and you could get back to whatever passed for normality. You felt uncomfortable, caught up in something that there was no way out of, and thus obliged to play along, fulfilling your role as unit martyr. You had other misgivings, especially because you had retained your close relationship with Nigel, and talking to Nigel about such things did little to raise your enthusiasm.

Nigel was a man left out in the cold. No-one talked to him much, and he didn't particularly want to talk to them either. His eyes had grown cold, his expression dark. The spring had gone from his stride, and his moustache no longer bristled with excitement. He was, you could tell, extremely disappointed in you, and that hurt deeply. You owed, you were sure, a great deal to that man, and he was your friend as well as your leader. Now, it seemed, he regarded you as a betrayer.

"They should never have sent you back, Griffin," he said to your face, in just the way you knew he said it to others. And if you might have perfectly agreed with that sentiment, you still did not much like the reasons behind his saying it.

You would visit him in his hoochie where he sat alone, sipping from his battered tea mug, rubbing his troubled brow.

"All this anti-Hatrack bullshit," he said grimly. "They just don't have a leg to stand on."

You had to admit that you were surprised at first that even Nigel could reach that sort of conclusion.

"What about that bullshit with the pumpkins?"

Nigel shrugged: "Hatrack had to take the action that he was did because he was worried about the morale of his men. He knew if he let them get away with that, others would try similar things. It's hard, you know, but true enough. What we're seeing right now shows pretty plainly that these bloke's capacity to stay in line is very fragile. He knew, all along, that he had a rebellious mob of reluctant conscripts on his hands, and that he would have to take the tough line to keep them under control. We thwarted that. Like we thwarted everything else he tried."

"And what about Ap An Quai?" you asked. It was the burning question.

"Yes," Nigel said sadly. "Ap An Quai lies right at the bottom of all this. This rebellion is in fact a direct reaction to that battle. But what did Hatrack do wrong? He had orders to hit the place before nightfall, and he had to follow them."

"If possible," you said.

"Yep. And it was possible. We took the fucking place, didn't we? Sure, we got knocked around a bit, but how much do you blame that on Hatrack and how much on the conditions at the time? The truth is, we went in there slack and got barrelled. Hatrack's plan was good because it worked, even in the adverse circumstances. And the task was feasible because the job got done. This is a bloody war, Yogi, not a Sunday school picnic. People are supposed to get hurt from time to time, and other people are supposed to learn to live with it."

You felt a bit ashamed at hearing all this. "So it isn't really Hatrack that's to blame. It's the whole fucking war, the fucking system."

Nigel could smile. He looked at you as if you were a young, wide-eyed boy, anxious to gather in whatever enlightenments a father could pass on.

"The real trouble, Yogi, is conscripts. Conscription does not work. It makes for slack and fairly useless armies. You weaken an army by drafting people. Without the draft, your army would be much smaller, but they would all be professionals and they'd do far better. "

He regarded your expression of dismay and offered a sympathetic smile. "Now, I'm not saying that conscripts themselves aren't any good. You're tough enough, got the guts and got the ability. Ap An Quai proved that. But you conscripts think too much about what you're doing—you're still civilians at heart. It doesn't matter to you blokes that you won the Ap An Quai battle, that it was in fact a major victory. All you can think about is that we got plastered, and you've never got over it. And I don't think you ever will."

Words of that sort can ring in your brain on still evenings. Walking along the elevated embankment of the road beside the airstrip, you neared the Delta Company area with a sense of dread. You did not want to be there, to be a part of all that, and you were dawdling, suspending as long as possible your arrival.

Up there, the madness would still be going on, and you did not want to be a part of that madness, did not want it to be a part of you. It had become like a disease, a disease that ate its way into every corner, every part, of the body. The very inescapability of it all, and the futility. You knew there was only one thing in the world that you wanted, and that was to go home. You still had three months to go before your time would be up. It was bad enough to know, as you had always known, that you would remain a prisoner for those three months yet. It was worse to be sure, to know only to well, that the coming three months were going to be the very worst of your life, far worse even than the nine months that had gone before. You were a dead man, still walking, awaiting his rebirth, but that rebirth, you could see, remained forever away. It was just like Skull Braddock said: no matter how bad things had got since the day you had entered the army, they steadily got worse. It had become a pattern now, far too clear to be denied. It was hard to imagine things being worse than this, but no longer was it hard to conceive the idea that the unimaginable worse condition would very soon exist. You could be pretty daunted by thoughts like that.

And already, it seemed, the movement toward that disaster was underway, if the things you heard were true. Some of the men you had been working with that afternoon at the water point had been from BHQ, and they had a story to tell. The word was that Porky had offered Hatrack an ultimatum and done so in the strongest possible terms. "I don't care how, Major," the Battalion Commander was reported to have said. "but I want Delta Company returned to an operational condition immediately. The other companies are complaining about their extra work in the field and rightly so."

"The punishment doesn't work, sir," Hatrack protested. "They just make a mockery of it."

"You must dispose of the sources of the trouble, Major. Pick the ringleaders—I don't care who or why—and throw them out of the company. You name them, I'll remove them—no questions asked."

"Yes sir."

"But major, make damned sure they are the right ones. Because after them, the next man to go will be you."

What it amounted to, then, if the story was true, was a purge, and it would not have been good, the relaters of the story thought, to have been in Hatrack's boots right then. You could not help thinking that there might have been a number of pairs of boots that it might not have been good to be in around Delta Company at the moment, and you suspected that one pair of those may well have been the very ones you were wearing now.

You reached the Delta Company perimeter just on nightfall, and indeed, the signs were plain enough. The first thing you noticed was that there was no one at the gate to check you in, a practice that had been adopted since the beginning of the jack-up. In fact, there wasn't much sign of anyone. You walked in along the road through CHQ, looking about, quite puzzled. No sign of the guards on the Q store, nor the kitchen. No trace of the interior patrol. And then, it occurred to you that something else was different. There was a sound that was distant, both physically and in terms of memory, but very familiar. Voices, many voices, jovial and raucous, over there, that way, in the direction of the boozer. You turned that way to investigate, but then remembered that you were still carrying your rifle, and rifles were never at any time allowed in the boozer. You would drop it off in your hoochie... but it did seem that the Delta Company boozer was finally open again.

Arriving at the four section lines, you could see that Nigel was still about. Stepping into his hoochie, you pulled up short. The place was in a terrible state of disarray, and in the midst of it all stood Nigel in the process of packing his belongings into his trunk.

"What's going on, Nigel?"

"I'm going places," he muttered, mostly into the interior of his trunk where he was carefully laying his neatly folded greens.

"Where?" Though it had already occurred to you what the answer was.

Nigel stopped what he was doing and turned to look at you. You had the distinct impression that you were interrupting something, and that you were the last person that he might have wanted to be standing there. He stood up, arching his back to ease the stiffness and answered whilst still locked in that posture. "Out of this fucking company, that's where."

"Out.... ? "

You were frowning, far from willing to believe what was only too plain: "Are you serious?" you asked, when it was ridiculously obvious that he was.

Nigel looked at you—his great moustache seemed to be

askew, certainly his face looked crumpled. He sighed, and plainly decided that people who asked such moronic questions did not deserve an answer.

"Why don't you go over to the boozer and have a beer, Yogi. It's open again, you know."

"I noticed," you said. But couldn't for the life of you think of anything else to say.

Right at that moment, two figures came in the rear entrance of the hoochie. Snowy and Greyman, and both looked pretty grimfaced as they stomped in and sat themselves on Nigel's bunk, a matching pair of toy soldiers who looked like they had just been outgrown.

"Thought you might want a hand, Nigel," Snowy said flatly.

"Don't," was all Nigel answered.

But they sat there, and seemed to be suffering that same helpless paralysis that you were. You felt cold, and quite ill. Things were, you knew, badly wrong, and the sorrowful expressions of Snowy and Greyman only served to confirm that.

"What the bloody hell is going on?" you demanded.

Nigel looked as though he was about to jump up and hit you then, but instead he went on with his packing, and refused either to speak or hear you.

"Nigel's been sacked, Yogi," Snowy said solemnly.

"Sacked? But why?"

"For being in charge of the wrong fuckin' section, that's why," Nigel erupted, his hostility intensifying rapidly.

"Nigel has been blamed for the jack-up," Greyman said, and sounded no less exasperated with your stupidity than Nigel. "Hatrack's ripped his stripes off him and chucked him out of the company."

Anyone you like, Porky had said, no justification needed. But this was nonsensical.

"But how can he do that?"

Nigel slammed down the lid of his trunk and glared at you in extreme irritation. "Because fuckin' Hatrack, contrary to current beliefs, happens to be in charge around here and like I told you blokes, time and again, he can do any fuckin' thing he likes."

Shrivelling under that heated blast, you reeled over to flop into Nigel's deckchair, largely because your knees seemed to be sagging under the weight of comprehension.

"But that's fuckin' stupid. Shit, Nigel. You're the last person he could rightfully blame."

You were probably, you realised, the hundredth person to make that statement in the last few hours, but what else could you say.

"Try telling that to Hatrack," Nigel said.

There was suddenly no longer anger, but resignation in Nigel's voice, a muffling of his tone that said it was all too late. Gracious defeat rather than hopeless conflict. But you were far too agitated, shocked, incensed, to accept that.

You sprang to your feet: "I will too!"

"Don't you think you blokes have caused enough fuckin' trouble, Yogi!" Nigel bellowed at you.

And because he could see that he had knocked a pretty sizeable dent in you, Nigel calmed, softened, became sympathetic. While the best you could do was try to convince yourself that this was all some sort of monstrous joke .

"Awright, listen," Nigel was saying. "He said that I was the instigator of all the trouble—that ringleader I was telling you about. He said I was a troublemaker not fit to run a section and that he had to make an example of me. And he whipped off my stripes and threw me out of the company, effective immediately."

Your stomach felt as if it was being twisted on a skewer. "I seem to have heard it all before," you said. "But damn it, Nigel, he's dead fuckin' wrong."

Even you could see you were making a scene about an issue that was resolved, no matter how unsatisfactorily. Nigel had just about finished his packing, and that would be that. Hatrack was an officer in the army and under no obligation whatsoever to be right or fair.

"He's not, you know," Nigel was saying to the contrary. "Hatrack's assessment of the situation was that the trouble generated out of this section, and as the leader of the section, I was responsible. All of which is quite true."

"It doesn't matter. Someone should go to him—tell him that you didn't play any part in what happened..."

But Nigel shook his head. "Not the point, I'm afraid. The fact is that it was not enough for me to ignore the situation. As section leader, it was my job to keep you blokes in line—that's what they were paying me for. I stopped doing it, and they've stopped paying me. Simple as that."

Simple as that. You shook my head, but the disbelief was fading now.

"Are you the only bloke he sacked? "

"At the moment," Nigel said. "He re-opened the boozer and said that if there is any more trouble, more blokes would go. And he'd keep chucking them out until there was no-one left if necessary. But I don't think there'll be any more trouble."

And all too soon, he was packed and ready and the vehicle came up to transport him and his gear down to BHQ. He shook no hands, nor did he make any other sort of parting gesture. You helped him load his gear taciturnly, and the other members of the section appeared and gathered about. And then, he climbed in the vehicle carrying precariously his mug of tea that he had just now brewed. Finally he looked up and said in a bitter tone. "Well, you're in charge now, Yogi Bear. You can take responsibility for these dickheads. Me? I'm glad to be out of it."

You had to look away. You could find no answer to make either. Nigel chuckled then, and for a fleeting instant, his old self reappeared. "Well, I hope you guys appreciate me getting the boozer opened for you. Have a nice war," and then to the driver: "Awright, let's go."

And he raised his mug to you, and was whisked away. You stood watching the vehicle pass from your view in a cloud of dust.

"Well, that went well, didn't it," Snowy said.

"That isn't even nearly funny," you bit at him.

"Nar," he said. "Same old jokes but they just aren't funny any more. "

Within an hour of Hatrack's decision, Storeman's Clerk Private Robert 'Nigel' Naughton reported for duty at the Battalion Quartermaster's office.

Charlie on the Line

There is this ringing sound which, fair fuckin' dinkum, sounds for all the world like a fuckin' telephone. All over, Red Rover, your poor fuckin' brain's completely rooted. Sniffer, forward scout, is fifteen yards up the track, and he stops and turns to offer you a baffled frown. It is a relief to see that he has heard it too. He holds his fist to his cheek, just like someone talking on the phone. You nod. Then you point at several imaginary spots on the track in front of you—find it. You look back toward Daytripper, touch your hand on top of your head and he keeps coming forward, in long careful slow strides, lugging Mabel, until he reaches your side.

"Do you hear that ringing? " you ask in a whisper.

"Of course I hear the fuckin' ringing," Daytripper grunts, a little louder than you would have liked.

"Sounds like a telephone," you say, to make a complete dickhead of yourself.

"Telefuckingphone," Daytripper snorts in disgust.

You wave him through, to back up Sniffer.

Absurd? You bet, but you were willing to believe anything these days. You were, after all, in the remotest part of the jungle in the remotest part of the province, following a small narrow track that showed no sign of being used for a very long time. Hatrack had halted the company when the track was discovered, and while the rest of them had a nice rest and some lunch, you were instructed to take four section five hundred metres down the track and see what you could find. It is just about the turn around point now, when you checked with Mickey Wright a few moments ago, it was four twenty. But now there is this ringing that has to be investigated.

You squat at the side of the track while Sniffer goes forward, very slowly and very carefully, sticking right at the edge of the track, and Daytripper with him, Sniffer head down, Daytripper head up. That's the way boys. The rest of the patrol moves through. Snowy is carrying the radio, a luxury for such a small patrol. When he is with you, you whisper. "Tell them we're checking out a strange ringing sound."

Snowy speaks softly into the handset, and then looks at you, grinning.

"He said to get your ears flushed out."

You just nod. What more could you expect? You keep Snowy

at your side and wave the next man, Mickey through.

"How many paces, Mickey?"

"Four six three."

"Help Sniffer find that fuckin' thing."

"Sounds like a telephone."

"I know. But you can bet it wasn't installed by the PMG." The last man is Greyman. You wave to him to stay where he is, a turn around signal to tell him to watch your backs. All set. Now to find that bloody telephone.

It stops ringing, but by then, Sniffer is waving excitedly and pointing his rifle into the scrub nearby. You go forward, Snowy at you heels with the radio like a faithful hound. You look where Sniffer is pointing and, finally, see the thin black wire stretching low down through the scrub. You follow the line, and there it is.

It is an old field telephone with Chinese markings, wedged down between a couple of giant exposed roots. It looks like it has been there for quite some time, but there are greasy marks in the centre of the handpiece. Someone has used it very recently. It is probably a listening post for a larger Charlie camp on the other end of that cable. And since it has been ringing, it poses in your mind probably the very same question that is in the mind of the Charlie soldier on the other end of the line: what the fuck has happened to the bloke who is supposed to be here answering the call? You look around very edgily, and sneak along in the scrub a few metres following the telephone wire. Yes, someone has passed along here before you, there are broken stems, very fresh. Someone in a hurry. The scenario constructs itself in your mind. The sentry has been sitting here when he hears you coming, has lacked the nerve to stick around, pick up the phone and tell the base, and has instead run off to deliver the warning in person. You look over at Daytripper, and give him a thumbs down signal, then toward Sniffer. That will keep them alert. Because by now, you can be reasonably certain, the Charlies in that camp will know exactly where you are. Crouched down then with Snowy behind the tree, you take the handset of the radio and speak into it, keeping your voice low.

"Four Two Bravo for zero-alpha."

"Zero-alpha," crackles the reply in your ear. Mumbles Dorset.

"Four Two Bravo. Fetch Sunray. Over. "

Zero-alpha Sunray is the general code for whoever is in charge, which in this case meant Hatrack. His voice crackles on the line.

"Zero-alpha for Four Two Bravo, Sunray speaking over."

"Four Two Bravo. We have located a telephone of...."

"A what?"

"Four Two Bravo. A telephone, people, ringing up, for the use of. Definitely Victor Charlie. Operators are definitely in the vicinity, over."

There is a pause on the other end while Hatrack thinks that through.

"Zero-alpha. Your call sign is now Four Two. What is the relationship of the track to the telephone cable, over?"

"Four Two. Not really parallel but in the same general direction, over."

"Zero-alpha. Right, Four Two. Leave a man to indicate position of telephone, and then continue your patrol for another five hundred metres. We will be backing up behind you, over."

"Four Two. Roger wilco, out."

"Zero alpha. Be careful, Four Two. Out."

"Four Two. Affirmative. Out."

That 'be careful' is not really an expression of concern for your personal safety, but an indication to you that Hatrack knows only too well the possible danger he is placing you and the others of four section in. What it means is that you could have disputed the instruction—that you do not have to follow the orders any more than you want to. His plan is quite plain. He will bring up the rest of the company and see where the telephone cable goes to. In the meanwhile, you will be placed five hundred metres ahead of the company. The cable is not likely to be any longer than that, and when the Charlies abandon their position, as they surely will when the company swoops down upon them, there is every chance that they will use a track to do so, perhaps this track, and four section might be able to catch them in an ambush. If it does place four section in considerable danger, it is, on the other hand, not an unreasonable plan.

And that call-sign change? Four Two Bravo is a section patrol, Four Two is platoon sized. Just in case the nasties are tuned in, he's trying to kid them that there's more of you than there really are.

You look around at the others and quickly outline the scheme.

"Greyman, you count the paces. Mickey, you stay here and show them where the telephone is. Keep out of sight. Let's get going."

You could see them looking a little bit nervous and you couldn't blame them for that. But the danger is not as great as might be imagined, at least not if things go true to form. If your original scenario is correct the Charlies at the other end of that telephone would already know that the Uc Dai Loi are about to descend upon them, and have abandoned their position and be long gone before you get close enough to be in any danger. On the other hand, if they did not know the Uc Dai Loi are coming—the sentry having been struck by lightning or perhaps a deserter—then it would be the company following the telephone line, rather than four section, who would contact them. All quite reasonable, except that to rely on such suppositions, no matter how likely they seem, is a sure way to get into trouble.

"Hatrack says be careful."

"I'll bet he did," Greyman says. "The bastard's still trying to get us wiped out."

You grin, and signal Sniffer to lead off.

"Take it away, Sniffer. Straight down the track, nice and easy."

This was the Chinese New Year—Tet, as they call it—and with it the long outstanding promises of Chairman Ho regarding the destruction that they would wreak upon their enemies were put into effect. Nearly every major town and base in South Vietnam was attacked in the space of a couple of days—for Charlie it was a staggering effort, an aspiration far beyond their capabilities, and yet so outrageously ambitious, this mighty unified attempt to seize control of the country and drive the American Imperialists and all their running dogs into the sea. A do or die effort. They died mostly.

From all over the country came reports of massive battles. The Americans were content to sit within their defences, using their enormous firepower to mow down wave attacks, while the South Vietnamese Army was employed as a strike force to try and break up the invading Communist forces pouring down from the north. The Americans established a giant base right on the powerline that led from the Ho Chi Minh Trail into Saigon; it would be necessary for the invading force to capture that base before they could proceed, and the Americans were defending it grimly. But that sort of fighting was not what the Australians were good at, and they dealt with the situation the way they knew best—the only way they knew.

In platoon and company sized patrols, they combed the area about the base, continually striking the leading edge of the Communist forces whenever and wherever they might.

These contacts came thick and fast—Delta Company alone was averaging three daily. In daylight, they were the fast, frantic, hit-and-run contacts, by night it was Charlie running into Australian ambushes. All over the country, an incredible carnage was taking place and the dead being counted by thousands daily, but the Australian casualties were minimal. Another cat and mouse game—you were getting to be pretty good at this.

Sniffer creeps along the track at the slowest of slow rates, and you are happy to follow suite. A pause after each carefully placed step, looking about all the time, listening intently, then the next careful step. Five hundred metres can be a long distance at this speed, but you are in no hurry. You do not want to get any further away from the rest of the company than you have to. The order of march is altered now, with Snowy sticking right beside you with the faintly hissing radio headset pressed against his ear.

"They've linked up with Mickey," he whispers.

You nod. You wish Mickey was here. Your patrol is only five men—he would add better balance. But someone had to stay to direct them to the telephone. Five men, out on a limb, while behind them someone might be sawing it off.

It is for Sniffer to spot any trouble up ahead. You are busy enough keeping your eye on him, watching the compass to try and keep track of the bearing, spasmodically tuning in to Snowy. Behind you, Daytripper has the job of keeping the patrol in formation, for with Mabel, he possesses three-quarters of the section firepower, and so has to keep every man within his range of vision at all times in case they might suddenly need his covering fire. Not far behind him is Greyman, counting the paces and practically walking backwards as he covers your rear.

Sniffer, edging along, stops every couple of steps and looks back at you. There would be a log that might be hiding something, a bend in the track, anything at all. Although on every occasion you signal him to continue, he never fails to check each time he encounters a variable, and neither should he. Finally you raise your hand, signalling a stop. You reckon it is five hundred paces, and look back at Greyman. He holds up five fingers.

They do not need to be told to deploy. Daytripper and Greyman go off the track a couple of paces to cover the area ahead of you, Sniffer backs up to join you and Snowy, retiring into the bush between you, and an ambush is automatically laid. Snowy, without any instruction from you, speaks into the handset: "Four Two for zero-alpha. Task accomplished, over. " The radio is tuned to so low volume that from only two yards away, you hear nothing except an interruption in its normal faint hissing as the reply comes through.

"We're to wait," Snowy says.

You are gasping for a cigarette, but it is too risky. You looked one way toward Sniffer and Snowy, then the other toward Daytripper and Greyman. They sit silently, watching and listening, their faces lined with strain, as no doubt your own is. You will wait. You do not allow yourself to think beyond that point.

Then Snowy is grinning broadly and looks at you. "The phone's ringing again," he reports, and hugs the handset closer to his ear to get a better picture of what is going on. You already have your picture—blank-faced men standing there and looking down at the jangling instrument.

"What do we do?" they would ask each other.

"Answer it," Hatrack, that master tactician, would say.

"Ky is answering it," Snowy reports to you. Ky is the company's Vietnamese interpreter, a bouncy jovial little man who speaks a perfectly eloquent pidgin English.

"It is the Viet Cong, sir," Ky reports.

"Ask him where he is?" Hatrack orders brilliantly.

"He says, you must come try to find him."

"You tell him," Hatrack says hotly. "Many Uc Dai Loi will come and shoot the shit out of him."

Ky smiles: "He say, many Viet Cong there. They shoot shit at us too. They not afraid."

You smile. It is a challenge that cannot be ignored. But really there is nothing to smile about. What it means is that the Charlies are still in their camp, and now they will leave. And that is where you and your undermanned ambush will come in. Snowy hands the handset to you: "Hatrack wants to talk to you."

The hissing black instrument on the end of its spiral cord might well be a viper, such do you handle it.

"Callsign is Four Two, not Four Two Bravo," Snowy reminds you. You nod, and speak softly into the mouthpiece. "Four Two for zero-alpha. Sunray speaking. Over."

"Zero-alpha. What bearing are you on? Over?"

"Four Two. Two seven four, over."

"Zero-alpha. Accurate? Over."

"Four Two. Inaccurate. The track winds a lot. But close. Over."

"Zero-alpha. Roger, Four Two. Go another five hundred metres. As long as the bearing does not decrease. Over."

"Four Two. Roger. Out."

"Zero-alpha. And be double careful, Four Two. They might have you tagged. Out."

"Four Two. Roger. Out."

You pass the handset back to Snowy. Yes, Hatrack, double careful. This is getting pretty dicey now. They might have you tagged, Hatrack says. What he means is that a smart Charlie who could speak English has his radio set tuned in on your frequency would be able to figure out exactly where you are, for he would know the original position of the telephone, and that you have proceeded five hundred metres on a bearing of 274 degrees and are now about to go five hundred more on the same bearing. You continue to pretend to be thirty, rather than five men, but that is the name of the game—confusion of the enemy—but if the telephone operator is no mere braggart and there are many Viet Congs to shoot shit at you, they are all going to be in an awful lot of trouble.

There are a few other things that bother you. Hatrack and the company now would set off following the telephone wire, which appears to run on a bearing of about 270 degrees, which means that you are now placed wide of the camp by four degrees over a thousand metres, in other words, probably less than fifty metres to the flank of the camp, probably a lot less. And the Cong are still there, preparing either to bug out or else stay and fight. Which means that you would have to be pretty bloody close to them. Desperately trying to keep your voice calm, you point these little matters out to the others before you move off. There are no smart answers to report: they take it in silently.

Sniffer goes along even slower, and checks back to you more often. But the tension is on at the rear of the line as well, where Greyman, walking backwards, knows only too well that if the Charlies are a bit slow leaving the camp, they might well come hurtling along the track straight up your bum. Thus you creep along, mere faint shadows in the patchwork shade of the jungle, barely there at all. After two hundred and fifty paces, you raise your hand to Sniffer to stop and summon Snowy and his radio over.

"Four Two for zero alpha. Bearing is now two seven two. Over."

"Zero-alpha. Wait. Over."

It is bringing you in too close. Too close to everything.

"Zero-alpha for Four Two. Roger your message. Proceed. Over."

"Four Two, roger wilco. Out."

"Zero-alpha out."

It is no longer Hatrack but Mumbles Dorset to whom you speak. Proceed, Hatrack has told him to say. You wave Sniffer on again. What you are noticing now is that your sixth sense is not operating, which you would have understood to mean that there weren't any Charlies anywhere around here. You are feeling very tense, and so you ought to be, but that strange calmness that usual indicates impeding trouble is not present at all. Yet you are sure, have been assured, that there are Charlies about. But that was the fuckin' trouble—it only worked sometimes. In any case, you weren't about to rely on such nonsense. Still you are sure. There are no Charlies around here. And in being sure, it convinces you of something else. That something is going badly wrong.

Then Sniffer stops, and looks back and his expression says that he has the same feeling. He raises his hand slightly, and you pass the gesture back on down to the others. You stand there on the track, stockstill, immersed in listening. The faint rustling comes to you, barely perceptible, but it is all you need. Movement, over there in what would have been the most logical direction for the camp. You turn swiftly and give the signal to deploy into ambush. Quickly, yet without haste, you drop off the edge of the track to the left, placing it between you and the movement. And there you lay prone, weapons cocked and thrust forward, five metres apart, and strive to get your thumping heartbeat under control in order that you could better see and hear and know what it is out there. Getting the breathing right, getting the firing position comfortable. Snowy murmurs into the handset. "Four Two for Zero Alpha. We have movement. Out."

Daytripper snaps up the sights on Mabel and nestles the butt into his shoulder, while Greyman arranges the spare belts of ammunition. You check the AK over, and slip the safety catch. And you wait. Oh, they're there, alright. Not the slightest doubt about that. The rustle of men moving through that dense jungle is all too plain. A lot of men too, and not going to a great deal of trouble to be quiet about it. You can distinctly hear the twigs snapping under their boots, the brushing of the leaves and branches on their clothes, the occasional clunk of a metal weapon striking a tree trunk, the thump of a boot on a root. The question is, where are they, or at least, how far away and which direction they are going. Visibility is at best twenty-five metres—less from your prone position beside the track. You have to lie there listening, trying to figure direction, distance, number, collecting all the sounds you hear into a single picture. It seems that they are off the track and not coming directly toward you, but will pass you by at a point about fifty metres into the scrub. Perhaps...

You look at Snowy who is next to you, and indicate with your hand a line running parallel to the track. He nods. You show him five fingers with your hand reversed. He nods again. Your assessment, you can only assume, is correct. They will pass fifty metres from you. The next question to be answered is whether you want them to pass by or not. It is a matter of how many of them there are, and what sort of people. To hit a force from ambush is not necessarily an advantage. You can all too easily picture a force of two hundred well-armed North Vietnamese regulars who know they are being pursued by fifty Australians, and, when ambushed, know the ambushers number only five or six men. They would go straight through you—it would be suicide. On the other hand, if you were to hit them, it should be done before they begin to pass you, thus driving them back onto the company which, you have to assume, is coming up hard behind them but still about five hundred metres away. On the other hand, they might not know anything about you. They might only be women and children evacuating while the men stay behind to meet Hatrack's threat. The possibilities are endless, and you figure you have about one minute left in which to make your decision.

You need to know more, and there is only one way to do that. The risk has to be taken. You look at Snowy and your fingers do a mime of going for a walk, then play a little boys game of looking through imaginary binoculars. Snowy nods. Daytripper raises his arm to indicate the extent of his arc of fire—you will have to keep yourself beyond that line if you want to stay out of the crossfire. You slip off your pack and web belt, load three pockets with magazines, and offering the others a rather helpless shrug to which they either wink or smile, you set off.

Over the track first, the most exposed part, easing along on your belly like an alligator. And then into the jungle on the other side. Wait and listen. They are still coming on, but still a safe sort of distance, as much as any such short distance can be safe. Slowly, you raise yourself onto your knees and look about. That twenty-five yard maximum visibility opens up to you now, but that is all. They are still further away than that. You can go, the sounds of their movement tells you, another twenty metres away from the track—half the distance between their apparent line of march and the ambush. That should take you close enough to see something. You will have to make your decision then—if you are going to attack, you will simply start shooting yourself and Daytripper and the others will follow suit. If you are not, you will probably have to lay low until they pass, for there will be little chance then of sneaking back to the others without being detected. For that reason, you pick a good hiding place over there, and begin to creep toward it, crouched very low. It is that old one step at a time trick. You look at the ground and spot a place where your boot can be placed without making any sound, put your boot there, then look toward the approaching men, see nothing, look for where to place your next step. You get about halfway to your hiding place, and that is all.

All you see is a fleeting shadow, momentarily glimpsed, and nothing more. But that is all you need. You are caught in the middle, and duck down, but it is already too late. As the figure pumps off his first instinctive shots, you dive forward, throwing yourself prone and swing the AK around into the firing position. You can no longer see anything and aren't looking anyway—you simply expend a complete magazine in the direction of the shadow. The AK pummels your shoulder as the bullets rip away on their brilliant streaks of tracers, and at the same time, other tracers flash over your head. There is an absolute deluge of gunfire for about a second and a half, from other men with the shadow, and from Daytripper and the others to the flank. The trees and bushes about you are splintered, their fragments flying everywhere and more dirt and shit fly up in front of you from bullets falling short. But really you are aware of none of it. You are ripping off the empty magazine and about to reach into your pocket when, in spite of the deep thumps of shots and the fierce whiplash crack of them streaking over your head, all those individual sounds so numerous that they are in fact one single deafening one, still you hear something else quite distinctly. A human voice that should have been utterly drowned out, and yet somehow pierces its way through to your senses.

"Holy shit, fucking Jesus," someone over there yells.

Your reaction is instantaneous—there is no time to be horrified yet. You roll your head toward Daytripper and the others and bellow at the top of your voice. "Hold your fire! Hold your fucking fire!"

No more than five seconds will have elapsed by now since those first shots, but in those five seconds, probably two hundred rounds have been expended in that small area. And then, through the duration of the next second, stops. Though it is only partly due to your command. Snowy has been saying on the radio. "Four Two in contact."

But then he heard Dorset saying. "Zero Alpha in contact."

Snowy immediately pounced on Daytripper and stopped him, for Daytripper, blazing away with Mabel could never have heard any mere human voice. Then other men, everywhere are calling ceasefire, and it stops. You all lay there, the echoes of the gunfire stalking away from you, far out into the jungle. And then silence. From ahead of you, a single, unrecognisable voice rises up. "Is that you, Yogi?"

"My fuckin' oath it is."

"Ohhhh, fucking hell!"

You drop the AK and close your hands over your face. Oh fucking hell is right. And then, with some desperation, you jump up, quite unarmed and start forward. You only make about three strides before you see it. A thin, dark line, etched along the jungle floor—the telephone cable. You can only stand there staring at it in dismay. One more second and you would have seen it, and this would have been averted. But that extra second has been denied you, and that is all.

Standing there, small tremors of disbelief running through your body, when the truth is all too plain. It is carried by the voices calling with hysterical urgency for medics, by the curses of anger and anguish of other men, and by one voice that screamed intolerably. That screaming man, the single piercing monotone broken every so often for a new breath upon which to scream again. And that screaming might have been your own, but wasn't. You are paralysed, standing, staring at blank jungle through which no more than moving shadows can be seen, and yet the disembodied voices make what is happening in there all too clear. Again and again, a new voice will gasp: 'Fuck, they're your own blokes,' as the realisation dawns upon one and then another. And still the doomed man screams on and on. As you strive and fail to shut that screaming out of your brain. There is no doubt about it—you are going to have to go over there.

"Snowy? You blokes okay?"

"Yeah, we're alright. But they fuckin' ain't."

You know that. You turn back toward the company and call, louder now. "Hey, you blokes. Hold your fire," you call. "I'm coming in."

"Stay where you fuckin' are, Griffin," Bulldog Doyle booms back at you. "You and your blokes, stay away from here."

Those two voices, yours and Doyle's, so remarkably calm amid the panic that engulfs the other voices. You feel cold, shivering, covered with goose-flesh. Your entire body feels a dull ache from top to bottom. You rise and walk unsteadily, on feeble legs, across that fatal twenty-five metres. And slowly, as you advance, the scene opens up before your eyes. First the blood, splattered everywhere, and bits of other things that you will not want to investigate too closely. The men, gathered in three groups, huddling over those on the ground, and other men arrive on the scene, their faces pale with shock, while Bulldog Doyle tries to hold them back.

Your eyes are drawn first toward the screaming. The man lies on the ground, his mouth and eyes open to their extremities as that screaming went on. It is impossible to tell where his wounds might have been, such is the quantity of blood that has spilled out over those sections of his body that you can see between people's feet, and over the men bending and squatting about him, frantically striving to staunch the blood flow, to pump air through his lungs, to thump his heart back to life... Ten Days is there, up to his elbows in the redness. But the face, the face...

"For fuck's sake, shut him up," Ten Days screeches at no-one in particular. That face, that screaming face, so distorted by its efforts, and yet, for all its unrecognisability, you suddenly know that it is Mickey Wright. You turn away. It can't be true. Not poor silly Mickey left behind to point out the telephone or else he would not have been there... Close it out of your mind. Close it!

Calmly, or so it seems to you, you walk over to the next group of men, and like any ghoul at a motor accident, strain to peep over the shoulders to see what is what. The ashen face of Mumbles Dorset gazes back at you blankly, meeting your eyes and yet they look straight through you. Without changing that expression, he turns his head away. He is sitting upright, sitting on his pack as if it is a dunny seat, while men are fitting a dressing to a gaping wound in his back. He looks back then, and recognition pushes the glaze of shock from his eyes.

"You rotten bastard! You rotten bastard!" he is grunting over and over, but it is his wound he is talking about, not you. So violently does he fight his tormentors that he did not even know you are there. And the final group of men, and suddenly one of them detaches himself, and strides toward you, while other men try to hold him back. Andy Kinross, with his face fixed in its most frightening sneer, bellowing at you in utter rage. "You fuckin' idiot, Yogi! I'll fuckin' kill you for this."

And you watch dumbly as he raises his SLR and points it directly at you, and make no move to defend yourself as the weapon jerks. But nothing happens. Then you can see why, for down where the pistol grip and trigger of the rifle should have been are only a few scraps of twisted metal and splintered wood, and even if the rifle had been workable, he still could not have used it, for he no longer has a right hand, just a stump of bloody goo that jerks convulsively as he pumps off each desperate imaginary shot. And then they had him and dragged him away.

"I'll kill you. I'll fuckin' kill you, Yogi!" he continues to roar.

Now someone bumps against you, and a hand falls roughly on your shoulder.

"Fuck you, Griffin. I told you to stay there," Bulldog Doyle roars. You turn your face toward his—to say something if you can think of something to say. And then Hatrack appears in the middle of it all and stands pointing his finger directly at you. "Get him out of here," he roars. "Get him out of here!"

Bulldog Doyle is already towing you away, his hand gripping your bicep and you are jolted into following him along. He tows you back through the jungle a little way, and again it closes around that chaotic scene and there are only the voices, all blurring in together. There is a log, or something, and Doyle sits you down upon that. You don't know how long you sit there. You remember the shape of Snowy Spargo coming at one point to stand over you, while Doyle sits alongside.

"We're all okay," Snowy murmurs, and then waits. You want to say how pleased about that you are but no words will come.

"Shock," you hear Bulldog Doyle say from a long way away. "Get something off one of the medics, will you?"

The bulk of Snowy disappears. Shock? You really don't feel

that bad, not hurt or anything, not like those others guys, poor bastards, poor fuckin' Mickey...just feeling a little tired that's all. At least he's stopped screaming now, or maybe that's bad. Your head goes forward to rest upon the broad chest of Bulldog Doyle. Just for a moment, Bulldog, hope you don't mind. You can feel him put his great arm about you and there you remain until another figure, maybe Ten Days, maybe Snowy, blots out the light again. They tug at your sleeve, and you feel, vaguely, the prick of the needle going in. You stay there, your head still resting on his chest, his huge arm around you, and slowly it is all fading away. The voices further and further away, the bodies of Snowy and Doyle closing in about you and then they have closed around you completely and there is nothing at all...

The Last Card Game

It was the last card game, and the remnants of what was once four section of eleven platoon of Delta Company of the Pig Battalion sat around a wonky table built of dismantled packing cases in what had once been Nigel's hoochie, playing by the light of a kerosene lamp. The game, always poker, began at ten when the boozer closed and would continue through until dawn, and this time all of them had no option, no matter how drunk or tired, but to see it through to the end.

There was Snowy Spargo, retired gunner, the shearer from way out West somewhere, a simple honest hard worker but a lousy poker player because he just could not help looking pleased when he got a good hand.

"You're bluffing, Yogi."

Yogi Bear eyed him from under his ponderous brow and everything about Snowy's hand was obvious, just as everything about Snowy Spargo always was. It was Snowy who was bluffing.

"Of course I am," Griffin smiled at him cruelly.

Snowy raised the bet a couple of times but Griffin went with him without compunction. Sweat ran copiously from his brow and over his huge round shoulders, discolouring the edges of his green singlet, but the others sweated inside.

"What do I do?" Snowy asked the others.

"Give up. You can't beat him," Sniffer advised in disgust.

Snowy sighed and threw in his hand, two pairs. As a future warning, Griffin allowed them to see his full house.

"I hate you, Griffin," Snowy grumbled.

There was The Greyman, Greyman Goolie, who was apparently half-white but you wouldn't have known it to look at him, and Greyman's white half cheated at poker whenever he could, but his black half would invariably look guilty and give him away.

"Three queens, I win!" he cried and his dark little hand hurled his cards into the pile before anyone could see them properly. As he tried to seize the money, Snowy slapped his wrist and then carefully extracted the cards.

"One of your Queens seems to be missing."

"Of course it fucking isn't. They're the wrong cards.

Griffin then showed his own hand—the other two Queens.

"Oh," Greyman sighed.

There was also a pair of Aces.

Fuckin' white man's magic," Greyman muttered.

There was Sniffer Gibson, the freckled lad from Tasmania whose affinity with machines was stronger than with men, and he played every hand mechanically, exactly on its merits, and always lost because no one ever won at poker that way.

"It isn't fair. I reckon if I've got the best cards, then I oughta win."

"Exactly right, Sniffer," Griffin's deep voice grumbled. "So you oughta."

"Then why don't I win when I've got a better hand than you, Yogi?"

"Ain't what you got, it's what you do with it that counts."

"Poor old Sniffer," Snowy Spargo grinned. "Been fightin' the Viet Cong for a year and still hasn't got the point."

"What's the fuckin' Viet Cong got to do with it?"

"They taught me to play poker," Griffin grinned.

"Bullshit! Charlie don't play poker."

"What he means," Snowy said patiently. "is that although our American friends have infinitely superior firepower and equipment, they are losing the war."

"Sure. No doubt about that. But what's that got to do with playing poker!"

"Just deal the fuckin' cards, Sniffer."

The fourth man was Griffin, alias Yogi the Bear, who frightened them at first the way his usually florid face was bloodless and sallow, his eyes sunken hollows and his heavy forepaws shook ceaselessly as he played, and yet the great booming Bearman was still inside there somewhere, and he had become totally unbeatable at poker.

"Arr, shit, Yogi. You are the arsiest bastard I ever met."

"Not arse, Sniffer, just skill."

"Come on, Griffin," Greyman insisted. "Nobody could be this much better than everyone else at a game like poker. You are really lucky."

"If I'm so lucky, how come I got drafted?"

"I think he's got a point there," Snowy sighed.

"I've also got a king-high straight."

"Arr, shit!"

The Company had gone out on an operation that morning, but these four had been left behind. In just six weeks their time would run out and they would be returned to Australia and discharged from the army, but everyone agreed that they'd had enough, and they became permanent rear party—they didn't even really belong to a section anymore. Daytripper had been promoted to corporal and was section commander now, because he was the only experienced man left.

"Bloody Poms. Come over here and snatch all the cushy jobs," Greyman suggested.

Daytripper sighed. "And to think I might have been back home living it up in Leicester Square and missed this great career opportunity."

It became Daytripper's mob and a whole bunch of new faces filled out the numbers, for the Pig Battalion itself was not due to complete its tour for three months yet. It was as if Nigel Naughton's mob had been wiped out, but that was only on paper. The surviving members, it had been officially decided, had had enough. Snowy, Sniffer and Greyman would sit out the next three weeks like this, but Griffin would be leaving on the mail plane in the morning. It was only for him that this was the last card game.

He had returned from the hospital that morning, that ghostly quivering figure only vaguely reminiscent of his former self, and they'd kept him so drugged for all this time that he didn't really know how long it had been himself.

"I slept through the whole thing," he explained.

They knew it had been fifteen days.

He had packed and labelled his trunk and done the final paperwork at CHQ, and amongst other things, his money had been changed—that was important. In an attempt to control black market operators, the Americans issued their own currency—called scrip—for use only on its bases. Each man could carry only ten Australian dollars in or out of the country, and the US scrip had no value outside the war zone. This posed a problem for Griffin, because the money he was winning in that last card game was all US scrip and the moment he got on the plane in just a few hours, it would become worthless. Monopoly money. Each of his opponents eyed his growing pile of winnings with increasing concern.

"What are you going to do with it all?" Snowy grumbled at him.

"Take it with me," Griffin said ruthlessly.

"But it won't be worth anything," Greyman protested.

"So I'll burn it when I get home."

"Fuck you, Griffin," Sniffer lamented. "You'll send the whole base bankrupt."

"When I'm home, I won't care."

"If you get there," the others chorused.

Griffin eyed them in disgust; it was a running joke, but really they all knew that nothing could be relied upon. The mail plane could be blown out of the sky as it lifted off Nui Dat airstrip. Neither Griffin, nor any of them, could sensibly regard themselves as safe until they were actually standing on Australian soil.

The very room was pervaded by evidence of the obstacles that still lay in his path. The hourly reports from armed forces radio on Sniffer's huge transistor told them of the continuing mortar attacks on Ton Sinh Ut—Saigon International Airport—where in a matter of hours Griffin would transfer to a Qantas 707, should that still be in one piece. Ostensibly the Tet Offensive was over, but there were still pockets of resistance to be mopped up all over the country. From elsewhere came reports of hundreds more NLF trapped and slaughtered. US Armed Forces Radio took you to the spot, provided only that the US forces were winning.

"There won't be any Charlies left after this," Greyman said solemnly.

"Don't bet on it," Snowy declared. "A few hundred thousand dead is a drop in the ocean to them. They breed faster than the Yanks can kill `em."

"Do you suppose," Sniffer wondered. "if sooner or later the Yanks are gonna stop pissin' around and step on them?"

"I doubt it," Griffin said. "They just sit back inside their bases and pick them off by the hundred between their favourite TV programs. They aren't trying to win."

"Then what the fuck are we doing here?" Sniffer puzzled.

"Arse-lickin'," Snowy said emphatically. "Showin' the Yanks what good mates are, not that they give a stuff. In just one year we have cleared out Phouc Tuy Province almost entirely. Nui Dat is the only base in the whole country that they didn't attack during Tet because they didn't have enough forces left to try. And what's happening in all them other Yankee Provinces? Fuck all. They ain't tryin' to win, mate. They're just tryin' to keep the war going."

"But that's stupid!"

"Not to them," Griffin said. "Remember those terrific profits from the Arms contracts to US industry."

"Not to mention a solution to the US unemployment problem," Snowy added.

"And they get a nice handy excuse to build some enormous bases within striking distance of Russia and China."

"And then there's all that good old Yankee patriotism back home."

"This war will go on forever," Griffin said. "It might change location from time to time, but it will never end."

The Chi-com Man lived on. When they were sure that Kinross's blokes had put an end to him, he bobbed up again a few weeks later, and continued to make his deadly nocturnal raids on a regular basis ever since. Maybe they got the wrong guy, maybe there was more than one of them, or maybe, like The Phantom, each death induced an immediate new incarnation—the ghost who walks. In their minds, all things considered, only the final possibility was likely. The Chi-com Man, and his war, would indeed go on forever.

As would this night, and the last card game. To have all the money in the world wasn't everything, Griffin was rapidly discovering.

"Anyone got any fags?"

Sniffer offered him one.

"No, I mean a packet. I'll buy it."

"I'm running a bit short meself..."

"Ten bucks."

"Ten bucks? Jesus Christ. They way I'm losing, that ain't nothin'."

"A hundred bucks."

"You'd pay a ton for a packet of fags?"

"I can afford it. Two hundred."

"It's a deal."

Sniffer handed him a packet of Camels that were suddenly worth a dollar a puff.

"I like to get value for my money," Griffin smiled.

"How many cards do you want, you capitalist bastard."

"I'll play these."

"Arrr, shit!"

When they let him out of the hospital and he walked back into the Delta Company area—strolling with his hands in his pockets, utterly unarmed—the first person he encountered was Bulldog Doyle. The CSM sat in the Company Office with huge bandage on his hand, trying to beat himself at chess.

"Good afternoon, CSM Doyle."

"Jesus fucking Christ, Griffin. What the fuck are you doing here?"

"Nice for a bloke to feel like he belongs..."

"They said they sent you home."

"Then they know as little about where I've been as I do. What happened to your hand?"

"Got bit by a fuckin' scorpion."

"Bit of bad luck."

"No it wasn't. I was scratchin' me balls at the time."

Griffin laughed—it was the first time in as long as he could remember that he did that. His chest muscles seemed troubled by the unfamiliarity of it, and reduced him to a fierce coughing fit.

"You look awful, Griffin."

"I got a bit of paper here says I'm medically fit for release."

"We'll fix up your papers later," Doyle said—plainly it was all too much bother for the moment, and he waved his bandaged paw toward the four section lines. "Your blokes are over there."

"Not my blokes anymore," Griffin said, and started to walk that way. He got about three paces before Bulldog Doyle cracked.

"Griffin."

"Yeah."

"It wasn't your fault."

"Who says so, CSM?"

"I said so, in the report I had to write for Task Force."

"I appreciate the gesture, but it had to be someone's fault. Two units hit each other when they are supposed to be five hundred metres apart. Someone had to be in the wrong place."

Doyle considered his answer a long time before he made it—he was saying things that he knew he was not permitted to say. "You were in the right place. Hatrack was over-excited by the chase—you know what he was like when he was on the scent. He over-shot, that's all."

In Griffin's mind were numbers that had run through his brain a million times. "The company's bearing was 270 and I was on 274..."

But Doyle was shaking his head. "The cable changed direction—to 277 at least."

"And he didn't tell me?"

"In the heat of the moment, he didn't realise how much difference that could make. It was just an accident, Griffin."

They had an expression for it—Friendly Fire. Only the military could make so perverse a use of the word Friend. Did Mickey Wright feel better, knowing he had been killed by friends? Andy Kinross, they said, had returned to Australia where surgeons hoped to fit a hook to replace his missing hand—he didn't bother to say 'good bye' before he left. They said Mumbles Dorset lay in his hospital bed with a Browning under his pillow in case you should appear. Waiting for a friend...

"Yeah," you said. "Just an accident."

Doyle returned his attention to the chess board, and you started to walk on, but this time it was your turn to call a halt to it.

"Hey, Charlie. What was at the end of that telephone line?"

"Fuck all," Doyle said. "The little bugger cut the cord, stuck his phone under his arm, and pissed off. Couldn't have been more than two or three of them."

You breathed at the final, dismal irony of that.

"We're getting done, Charlie. These blokes are too good for us."

"Done like a dinner, Griffin. Done like the Sunday roast your old mum usta make."

"My mum," you remembered. "still does."

Four in the morning. In two hours you were going home.

"Your deal, Yogi."

Home where there was real fresh food not muck prised out of cans by cooks too drunk to tell peaches from pumpkin; home to beds with soft mattresses and clean sheets and you didn't spend the whole night sweating and listening to other men farting and pulling themselves. Home where you could take a bath, when you could go to the pub and talk to women with real breasts, not skin forced up into tight brassieres; home where the milk wasn't powdered, you craved a malted milk more than anything, and where you didn't have to carry a rifle everywhere you went.

"Hey Griffin. Deal the fuckin' cards, will ya?"

You didn't know what had happened to the AK47, your most prized possession, and hadn't troubled to ask. You didn't care. They were all here playing this last card game and no one was bothering to man the platoon picket post against enemy attack. No one cared. Everything that had been important was dissolving into inconsequence. Everything used to matter didn't matter anymore.

You took up the cards and distributed them lethargically about the table, lit another ten dollar cigarette, and looked at your hand. Three aces. There were times when you couldn't lose, just like there were other times when you couldn't win.

"Shit, Griffin," Sniffer said. "How's your mum gonna cope when she sees the way you're always suckin' on a fag?"

"And how you're pissed out of your brain all the fuckin' time," Snowy added.

"And all yer fuckin' swearin'," Greyman put in.

It was just a tactic to try and put you off your game—although you had to admit that these thoughts had crept through your mind once or twice.

"The whole of fuckin' Moorabbin will hang its head in shame when they see what you've become," Snowy chortled on.

Griffin forced himself to grin. "I'm a war hero. They'll forgive me for everything."

Maybe not everything. There was once a simple insurance clerk from the suburbs, a good clean-living lad—didn't swear or smoke, went to church on Sundays, virginal though not for the want of trying, nice bloke. Then the army got him and turned him into an animal—hunter-killer, child-murderer, the taste of blood on his lips forever. Civilisation was bullshit—this was real. This was how those original ape-men lived, these were his most basic instincts. Kill, maim, rape, pillage. Greed and torture were the forces that drove him. Now he knew the true state of man—the most deadly predator of all, lying in ambush, waiting to slaughter the next victim. And just when he got to be good at it, they were sending him home. Try and live your nice suburban life again after this, sonny. What his nightmares saw mostly was this appalling blood-crazed primeval monster, stalking the silent leafy streets of Moorabbin.

"I have to admit it is a bit of a worry," Griffin admitted with a shiver.

"Bit of a worry, he sez," Greyman laughed. "Like the joke about the digger who arrives home first night and sits at the dinner table: Pass the fuckin' salt, he sez. Poor mum melts in shock and he realises what he's done and sez: Sorry mum, didn't mean to make a cunt of meself!"

Nobody laughed, but not because it was such an old joke, but because it wasn't a joke at all.

"Alright," Griffin declared. "No more swearing. Got to practice. You each get ten bucks every time you catch me."

"Fair enough," Snowy said. "It's your deal."

"I just fuckin' dealt, you dickhead."

"Gotcha!" they shrieked and held out their hands.

"At least this way we'll have some money to get on with the

game," Sniffer laughed.

It was easy to forgive them their envy. Some men had shot themselves, others prayed for wounds that would take them home, or diseases, or just for the days to pass and their time to run out. To be going home was the most important thing a man could do at Nui Dat, and that was why they were sitting there with their bloodshot eyes and exhausted bodies, just trying to share a little of what you had.

What could you say to them when you got home. How could you explain how it was? Could you really, in a pleasant suburban lounge room or the pub in Queen Street near the insurance office, tell any of them of what you did? How could you give it a context by means of which they could understand? Tell them you were a primitive predator, good only at ambushes except usually you fucked it up. Tell them about fragging and not fragging? Tell them about dead children and friendly fire? What could you say that they would understand?

Tell them a funny story maybe. About the patriotic pig, perhaps. Well, that one might be alright for your mum, provided you didn't explain too deeply the true purpose of an ambush. Good for a laugh. Was that all it was? The context.

No doubt you'd tell the workers in the pub about Holly's masterstroke. Early on in an operation in a very swampy region and they were losing a man a day to leeches up the prick channel, each one winched into the dust-off (really slop-off) chopper and evacuated in screaming agony, to face the even greater agony of that dreaded umbrella gadget. Too many men; but then Holly, in his naivety, came up with the solution, and ordered in on the next ration resupply, thirty gross of condoms. That would keep the little buggers out, he was sure. And so the scene of a platoon of tough combat soldiers in full fighting order, standing in a circle with their pants around their ankles, trying to fit condoms to flaccid penises, and all of them asking: "How do we get them to stay on?" and Skull Braddock stalking the circle roaring: "Use your imagination!"

But what of the real stories. How could you explain? They all thinking you were having a terrible time, forced to confront the horrors of war. But that wasn't the problem at all. The problem was never what they did to you, the problem was what you did to them. It wasn't the horror of war you confronted, it was yourselves.

There had been eight of you at the beginning, and now just four and only Alby Dunshea could have been attributed to the enemy. And maybe Bugsy Norris. Certainly not Alfie Magee. And even you four no longer existed. It had been, all agreed, a hard run. Just one dead and two wounded of the original eight yet none got through to the finish. They, the survivors, fighting off the overwhelming urge to sleep a sleep that never came anyway these days, playing out this last fiasco of a card game. The survivors, or maybe they were the ones who hadn't survived.

There was a chill that told them it was first light—long familiar from their earliest army days. Just as the first light shows in the sky, the temperature drops noticeably. It was the sort of atmosphere in which the birds would have begun their morning song, had there been any of those. In their absence, Griffin detected a far off hum that was what he had been waiting for.

"Here it comes."

"What comes?"

"Can't you fuckin' hear it."

Even after the payout, it was still a few minutes before they could hear it too. The Caribou aircraft, twin-engined cargo plane, approaching Nui Dat out of the dawn. Wallaby Airlines...

"Don't crash you bastard," Griffin murmured.

Down on the airstrip, they heard the engines reverse as it touched down safely. All four had sat still and silent, waiting for that. Now there was time for just one more hand.

"Last chance, fellas. Do your worst."

Snowy dealt the cards and Griffin glanced at his—three kings. He pushed his entire winnings into the pot. They looked dismayed. Even after all this beating, they could still look dismayed. Griffin grinned.

"I would have done that no matter what you dealt me," he said.

"You mean we've got a chance?" Greyman asked.

"Don't be silly," he grinned.

They bought their cards with whatever they had left. Snowy laid Griffin's two face down in front of him. Griffin wondered which one was the other king—he looked at the one on the left—ten of hearts—so it had to be the one on the right. It was.

"Fuck me dead, Griffin. You are the luckiest bastard that ever lived."

"Yeah. I know."

The tent flap lifted and the feeble daylight greyed the hoochie—just enough to wither any vampires that might have been present. Bulldog Doyle stood there.

"Hullo? What's the go here?"

"G'day, Charlie. Just gettin' a few hands in before breakfast."

"You get breakfast in Vung Tau, Griffin," Doyle said. "Plane's in. Get going."

In front of Griffin was more money than he would ever again see in his life, but it was without the slightest concern that he pushed it all back into the pot.

They stared. So did Bulldog Doyle.

"I think I might just sit in for a hand or two," he said and was in the vacated chair in a stride. Griffin gathered his things while they dealt.

"Hoo Roo, boys," he called.

"See yer, Yogi," Sniffer called off-handedly.

"You won't, you know," Griffin chuckled.

"Feel free to drop in any time you're in the neighbourhood," Greyman grinned. "We're always here."

"Just make fuckin' sure you're on that plane," Snowy menaced. "We don't want to see your ugly puss around here again, got it."

"I'll take three," Bulldog Doyle said.

Griffin walked away, listening to the sounds of the last hand of the last card game, haunted by his own ghost. He walked in his new slouch hat and new starched greens and new shiny boots, carrying an overnight bag, and somehow feeling a little sad. Out over the mountains, the first rays of the rising sun showed. Down on the airstrip, men were loading the Caribou. And over to the left, a lean figure stood, familiar even if it hadn't been for the battered mug of tea in his hand. And unfamiliar too, because he had shaved off his huge moustache.

"Morning, Griffin."

"You're up early, Nigel."

"Like to get as much work done as I can before it gets too hot," said Storeman's Clerk Robert Naughton. His upper lip looked bare as the Sahara.

"Get caught in a bit of BHQ hot air," Griffin asked.

"No shortage of that, mate," he said, touching his vulnerable lip. "Against regs, you know. I heard what happened. Bastards."

"Yeah," was all Griffin said.

They stood there for a moment, two people with nothing to say to each other. This was not the Nigel you knew—not even a reasonable facsimile of him. It wasn't just the moustache, nor the BHQ clean greenness. It was as if the spark had gone, the very force that generated him, the magic that made him what he was then, but not now. Something like that. And you realised then that he probably saw you exactly the same way. Two walking dead men, standing still.

"Got a bit of news for you," he finally said.

Griffin waited on it without comment.

"They sacked Hatrack."

"They what?"

"They've kicked him upstairs to a desk job. He's already been replaced."

"Who by?"

"Donleavy. Know him."

"No."

"Worse than fuckin' Hatrack."

Griffin allowed a pause. He was going home and didn't give a stuff about Hatrack or anyone. But something worth saying finally came to mind.

"I can't understand how that man didn't get fragged."

Nigel thought about it. "He didn't because he didn't deserve it. It wasn't him we were after. It was the whole damn structure. Them politicians and arms manufacturers and fucking lying media moguls. But we couldn't get to any of them. Hatrack was as high up as we could get. That was all."

"You must have a lot of time for postmortems at BHQ."

"No matter what else happened, you used a smoke grenade, Yogi. You might have used a real one, but you didn't. Smoke grenade was right, real one was wrong. Simple as that."

"Just a fuckin' game, isn't it."

"You better watch your language when you get home, Private Griffin."

The plane was loaded. It was time to go. But you didn't. There was one more thing to be said, and at last you knew what it was.

"How was it, Nigel, that after all that trying, we got that ambush right just once, and then buggered it up every time after that."

"Yeah, thought about that too. I guess maybe that after we got it right once, we never wanted to get it right again."

"That's pretty deep, Nigel."

"Get outa here, Yogi."

"Still, we did alright for a bit there."

"You sure?"

"No. You're right. It was a fuckin' fiasco, wasn't it."

"The whole bloody thing's a fuckin' fiasco, Yogi."

The pilot was calling, and a helmeted crewman running over to direct Griffin onto the plane. He turned and jogged through the dust blasted up by the engines. The crewman found him a seat on a box and he could look out a porthole and see Nigel standing there, still clutching his mug, and then he raised it to Griffin and Griffin waved back. The engines roared louder and the plane swung around and he watched the rows of rubber trees go by until they blurred and then began to fall away below. He might have felt a little sad, but he felt bloody good as well. At least no one would call him Bear names anymore.

PART TWO:

INNOCENT BYSTANDER

The Answer to Everything

He clambered up out of the nightmare like a man scaling a vertical precipice, clinging on with his finger and toe nails, his muscles agonisingly exhausted, screaming his desperation to escape the horror below. Down there in the abysmal darkness were the percussions and flashes of the detonations, the streaks of traces and the frantic voices of men screaming his name in terrible agony, but he could do nothing to help. It was, as always, all he could do to escape himself. The detail of the horror was already forgotten—his mind would blot it out completely if only he could make himself awake. He strained to force his eyes open, to end the dream before he fell and it swallowed him forever.

Then the face appeared, as it so often did—the right half shot away, a gaping hole from nose to ear and eyebrow to mouth, the one remaining eye glaring at him in pure malevolence. He knew this was the end, but that didn't mean it scared him any less. The face hoovered gigantically, and then leapt at him, engulfing him in its ghastliness. And he was awake, and safe.

He was sitting upright in the bed, sweating profusely from every pore, shaking like a vibrating engine. All this was normal. Exhausted by the dream, he flopped back on the bed, but immediately the nausea provoked by the fear, by the sheer terror of it all, gripped him, and he swung his feet onto the floor and sat on the edge of the bed, his head in his hands. The nightmares, he was sure, were always different but the way that they frightened him was always the same. In his throat he felt the scratchiness and knew that he had been screaming.

He needed a fag, and a beer, to get himself past this.

The cigarette could be provided instantly, from the bedside table, but his hands were shaking so that he dropped it twice and then had trouble getting to flame of the lighter to its end. Finally, the smoke oozed through his respiratory system, and began to do its work, calming him.

Fucking nightmares! When would they end?

Then he finally noticed that it was daylight. Bloody terrific! You'd think nightmares would have the decency to confine themselves to the night. He remembered then that he had been having just one more with Lew until about 4am, and that had happened because he knew the spooks were about, lurching in the darker corners, waiting in ambush for him to close his eyes and try to sleep.

He listened for a moment to the traffic noise of the city about him, and blearily judged the way the light stretched in through the bay windows before him. He assessed it to be midmorning—about 10 maybe. So he had managed to drink himself into such a stupor that it had taken about five hours for the spooks to get their grip on him. He might have regarded that as some sort of improvement.

Biological needs got him moving at last. He pulled on the shorts that lay right at his feet where he had dropped them last night and trooped from bedroom to bathroom along the upstairs hall, and then, while the cistern jubilantly hummed another successful functioning, he stalked downstairs, to wreck something if he possibly could. No one had brought the paper in, nor the milk, nor the bloody rubbish bin. Slack bastards! He thumped down the hall and threw the door open so violently that the Monster, who was leaning dozily on the other side of it, jumped up in mortal fear and rushed off yelping to some point out in the middle of the street. Only from that safe distance did the dog dare look back and, recognising its Human Being, return bounding and with tail wagging frantically for the customary spring all over the human caper that invariably accorded its return from a hard night's pounding the pavements of Fitzroy.

"Get down, you silly fucking mongrel!" the Human Being growled, but the Monster knew that he was always pretty grumpy on days when he got up late.

The Human Being collected the paper, milk and bin and thudded back into the house; the Monster barely had time to scamper through before the door slammed resoundingly, and then was wise enough to follow at a safe distance, down to the kitchen to be fed while the kettle boiled. After that, they went upstairs together and to bed to read the paper, sip coffee and smoke cigarettes—the human that was—meanwhile the Monster crawled wearily into its chair; a dog needed all the rest he could get when he had to nightly patrol a suburb with such a high population of telephone poles, territorial dogs and savage feral cats.

Midday passed and the postman made his delivery—Griffin heard the metal flap set in the front door shriek its stiff joints loudly and the falling letters flop on the floor in the hallway. The Monster lifted its head, knowing another chance to savage a postman had passed him by. He settled again. So did Griffin.

There wouldn't be anything for him. Not interesting, at least. In all his life he had only received one letter that had made any difference, although that difference was devastating. There he was, a particular person on a particular path through life, and then that letter came and instantly he was no longer that person and that path was now closed to him. Although it took him a little longer than it should have to realise that.

And there it was. That whole way of life over with in an instant—poof! It was as if the person that he had been so assuredly had died and a new one was born into his place. Six years ago now, he realised, from the moment of his first death although two years after that, he was still not quite reborn. He went off to their war as ordered and came home again and didn't get killed, but then how could he when he was already unknowingly dead? In any case, as he preferred to put it, all the people who shot at him missed. Only it wasn't him who returned, but someone else. Someone his own mother couldn't recognise.

He had read all the news, comics and resolved most of the crossword puzzle when the grumble of a motorcycle engine that bespoke engineering tragedy signalled that Lew had returned. That engine thankfully shut down and there soon followed a scrambling and scraping on the front verandah that was all too familiar. The silly bugger had forgotten his key again.

Not wanting to be caught so obviously doing nothing, the crossword solver sprang out of bed and had managed to pull on a pair of jeans before a figure appeared at the window hauling itself up over the balcony, and still wearing the white fullface helmet in case he fell while negotiating the awkward climb up the front of the house.

"Hey Griffin, you slack bastard! Come and see what I've found!"

The head encased in fibreglass poked through the window, followed by the elongated body in its tight torn jeans and grease-smeared T-shirt, bedecked as always in the old leather jacket that had split its seams in a dozen places. Griffin glanced about desperately but he could see nothing that could prevent him from being wrenched from his boredom into some harebrained adventure that might rate a mention in the pub that evening but be of no further consequence after that. Not that Lew Sigg lacked enthusiasm; the helmet opening was filled with a grin so huge that there was barely room left for the shining cheeks, burnished by the slipstream, and those eyes—normally vague and floating—now glistening with the enthrallment of a wonder yet to be shared.

But Griffin had seen it all before. Although the source of this abrupt ecstatic intervention into the inertness of his day could only be guessed at, there was nothing new about the form it took. Still, as with all adventurous quests, the treasure could never hope to match the epic of its discovery. In spite of that, Lew was thrusting the oft-scarred spare helmet into his hands.

"I need a coat," Griffin protested, stalling when all hope was lost. Outdoors a day reminiscent of Summer shimmered and dazzled but precautions needed to be taken and the protruding parts of the body given every chance. He pulled on shirt, desert boots and dufflecoat lethargically.

"Come on, come on," Lew gasped as he lurched about in the hallway, "This is the answer to everything."

His impatience, Griffin supposed, was quite understandable. These things had to be done with spontaneous immediacy if they were to be of any worth.

"I hope this isn't gonna take long," Griffin muttered defiantly.

But Lew could not be daunted; "You can't fool me, you old bastard. You're too grumpy to be doing anything useful."

"Am I now?"

"I bet you got out of bed without the foggiest glimmer of an idea between your ears."

And because that was only too obviously true, Griffin decided it was better left unanswered.

Meanwhile, the Monster could see that something was on the go and was all set to be in that.

"Stay there, you silly bloody canine," Griffin barked at him, whereby the dog shrivelled into a pathetic heap with eyes drooping and only the last centimetre of its tail wagging. Cruel human, but no way could the dog follow the bike.

Tightening chinstraps and fastening clips, they shuffled their way downstairs—by the more conventional route this time—and out across the footpath to the upright oilslick that Lew's old Triumph had become these days.

"You sure it'll take the weight of both of us," Griffin quipped, for they were a couple of rather large fellows and it was a very old and very rusty motorbike.

"Poor old girl's just about fucked," Lew muttered distressfully. But when he threw his leg over and kicked the starter, it immediately burst to life.

The grumble of the engine resounded from the stark factory

wall opposite and rattled the windows in the terrace houses on this side of the street. Griffin, already sweating in the helmet and coat, skipped onto the pillion and they were off.

"Where we going?" Griffin shouted at where he imagined Lew's dome-obscured ear might be.

"You'll see," Lew jubilantly laughed.

Down the road to Nicholson Street anyway—there the narrowest of gaps in the traffic, trying to sneak past a trundling tram, momentarily appeared. Lew hurtled them into the left turn narrowly ahead of the onslaught—first heartstopper! But Griffin was always a nervous passenger. Presently pedestrian; previously, secured within the shatterproof glass and metal skins of Fords and Holdens; the thrill of the outdoor life for him was only a battle for survival. Griffin was one of those people who swam for no other reason than to save themselves from drowning.

Up the hill past the tumbledown convent and the old apartment houses—once classy, now home for the most alone and most forgotten, and across the road the papier-mache monstrosity of the Exhibition Buildings. The sharp left turn into Gertrude Street had Griffin leaning the wrong way and sent them stutter tyred over the tram tracks.

"Get with it you fuckwit!" Lew roared.

But that turn was unexpected—it would have been shorter to take Brunswick Street rather than Nicholson to go this way, but perhaps, Griffin reasoned by way of justification, Lew was taking the longer route to protect the old bike from the bumps.

Still, it wasn't easy adjusting to this. Griffin's face had forgotten how the gritty slipstream slapped at the cheeks and squinted the eyes; his reflexes had not wanted to remember it was lean with the driver and forget the machine underneath. The world was mostly Lew's vibrating helmet one inch in front of his nose, but still Griffin overcame his nerves enough to allow himself to glance from side to side and explore the terrain, even though it had all been familiar for decades.

Down to the tight intersection of Brunswick Street where the Rob Roy and Champion Hotels—as much evil and degradation as this city could manage at one try—faced each other on the diagonal. There, ponderous aboriginal women and their lanky men with bloodshot eyes—the heritage of a nation—and the sagging ragged drunken whitemen—inheritors of the heritage—drifted aimlessly on the curbs. This was the part of the city where it was left to the ethnic peasant class to provide the area with what little respectability it had; otherwise the scene was a plague of modern civilisation. 'Bring out your dead!' but the dead could still walk and brought themselves out, and the local garbage men refused to pick them up like anything else not wrapped in paper and properly put in a bin.

On they went past the dole office—Fitzroy CES—without which aspiring writers like Griffin would have long since starved to death. And now they took the flying right turn into Smith Street and at least Griffin was ready for that one. Here the blue-walled gaudiness of the Last Laugh Theatre Restaurant and Zoo outraged the drab surroundings, to where the young suburbanites came to get staggeringly drunk and ripped off by the meals and thrilled by an indoor highwire act or a vulgar risque revue, and all the time wondering where the zoo might be without realising that it could only be seen from the performer's point of view.

They took the short run on Smith Street before bursting out onto the wide boulevard of Victoria Parade. There a bus wished to assert its dubious right of way—Griffin ducked but Lew wasn't having any of that, roaring the engine and flashing them through a minimum gap and gone in a wail of horns. And all Griffin's guesses at their possible destination were utterly thwarted now. They were heading in the direction of Richmond or beyond, where only working class uncles, God and Lewis Bartholomew Sigg could have possibly found anything of interest. Down the six lane rollercoaster, past the Carlton and United bottling plant and Joe White Maltings—may their good works go on unhindered forever.

And Lew threw a wild glance over his shoulder and weaved his way across the traffic deftly for the side street detour that would take them around into Hoddle Street. There they ran the amber light—Lew, if not Griffin, was bursting with confidence today—and they raced up the hill lined with the elegant terraces of East Melbourne—the rich in smoggy congestion. At the top of the hill they were stopped by their first redlight for the journey—it had been a remarkable run give or take a few amber lights and hair-raisers. They oozed their way forward between two lines of waiting cars, their hands touching the hot panels of this one and that as they made their way to the front of the line. The change! and they were first away and clear, skedaddling down the sharp hill in the direction of the Yarra.

Zooming down, down, the wind plucking at the sleeves and burnishing the eyeballs. Lew was determined, plainly, to catch the already green light where Brunton Avenue pops out at the bottom, and Griffin, not wanting to know anything about that, gazed across toward the parkland on the right, watching the gums and green grass blur by, and through the trees the vast concrete hulk of the Melbourne Cricket Ground. They shot through the lights and under the viaduct where multi-platformed Richmond Station loomed darkly over the top, and where, on wintry Saturdays with his siblings, the snowy-haired Griffin would play the game of being run over by the trains on the way home from the football. Now, raging through with Lew, the thunder of the bike rebounded from all sides, even more deafening than the trains.

Clear of the bridge, Lew veered sharply to the far left lane and took the bumpy right turn into Swan Street. A sudden burst of pace for about thirty yards, and then he stopped, signalling for Griffin to get off. As Griffin walked clear and Lew spring-footed the bike backwards into the kerb, there was a sudden lull with the ears still ringing from the now extinguished engine. Griffin dragged off the helmet and unfastened his coat and stood on the footpath looking around. Plainly they had arrived—but where?

This part of the city was squalid and awful, but worst of all, utterly without interest. It was a little triangle of Richmond wedged in between Hoddle and Swan Streets with the stark concrete wall of the elevated railway along the hypotenuse. Several used car yards, a couple of old factories abandoned or turned to warehouses, the drab Greyhound Pub over there, the station entrance and a handful of shops that surely could not sell anything of note. And that was all. But here, apparently, the answer to everything was to be found. Griffin eyed the nearest used car lot suspiciously, and dread!—Lew was heading that way, pulling off his helmet and grinning his broadest.

"This is it," he said, to crush Griffin's last glimmer of hope.

Griffin tagged along. Classy Autos, the place was called, for god's sake. And worse, full of lean sleek Porsches and tartish phallic GT's. They stepped over the low chain fence and moved between the mudguards of a burgundy Ford Mustang and a yellow Fiat fastback, Lew leading, Griffin still dragging his feet, their helmets tucked under their armpits like spare heads.

The dealer slithered out of his office, straightening arrogantly in front of the Le Mans hoarding and squinting disapproval at the unlikeliness of his prey. With greased black hair neat parted in forties style and shaved to chickenflesh on his swollen neck, he glared out of a face reddened by too many sales-talk lunches, his loud tie angling outward over a huge paunch from too many beers at those too many lunches, his modern beige suit made baggy by his uncorresponding shape. Still, he seemed to decide, you never can tell with young people these days, and so he re-adopted his momentarily displaced business smile and began to rub his hands eagerly as he approached; giving the invaders every chance or perhaps just determined to get rid of them as quickly as possible before their influence devalued every item in the yard.

"Good afternoon, gentlemen," he cheerily called.

The gentlemen, a pair of Martians, halted in a stride. Griffin hovered guiltily in the background while the bolder and less respectful Lew stepped forward, scratching his nose and hip.

"We want to look at one of your cars," Lew said brightly.

The dealer spread forth his hand to guide their eyes over the kingdom of his wares.

"Which one, gentlemen?"

"The Jag."

"Which Jaguar?"

Jay-goo-arr, he pronounced it; it must have taken years to perfect such a word with so heavy an ocker accent. But he could look hopeful—there were two gleaming E-types in the yard and a more prestigious model further across.

"That one," Lew said flatly.

"Oh," the dealer might have known, "That one."

Griffin turned himself in the direction that Lew so adamantly pointed, and his expression exuded a dismay that might well have rivalled that of the dealer. But there it stood, more a small locomotive than a giant motorcar, appropriately battleship grey where the rust didn't show through, shrinking away in the back of the yard as much as something so huge could in its uncared-for and unpolished shame amid the shiny late-model pre-owneds. A sign, pasted obliquely on the windscreen and declaring the price to be one hundred and sixty-five dollars, might have been intended as a final insult.

But it was a Jaguar; even Griffin could recognise that. A car of distinction, or would have been several panelbeaters ago. For all that, it did manage to exhibit that hoary pride of the impoverished aristocrat as they advanced toward it.

"Bout a fifties model," Lew was guessing.

"1955," the dealer overcame his disgust sufficiently to remember, "Mark VII, I believe."

"Complete with sunroof," Griffin observed, although such a car would have to have at least one redeeming feature even if it did constitute a hole in the roof.

"A remarkable car in its day," the dealer told them.

It was, Griffin decided, no less remarkable now, although for entirely different reasons.

The trio then took up their rightful places around the car; Griffin to the driver's door, Lew down on his knees looking underneath, the dealer standing back a little, looking from one to the other and trying to decide upon which of them he would be more likely to unload this pile of oily scrapmetal. Lew straightened; his face betrayed that he was not entirely pleased by what the underworld had revealed.

"Start her up, Griffin."

Griffin got behind the wheel, gave the accelerator a few pumps, turned the key, pressed the starter button.

Nothing!

"Battery's flat," the dealer remarked—it might have been a guess. Lew tilted his head to gaze at him from under the lower extremities of his eyebrows, while Griffin confirmed the diagnosis by checking the horn.

"Do you have a battery?" Lew asked patiently.

"Of course."

"Need a heavy duty job for this."

"Oh."

"How about jump leads?" Griffin contributed.

The dealer was hesitant, as if the thought of connecting this beast with any of his fine fragile machines was totally abhorrent to him. But since there was no alternative, he wandered off to see what he could do.

"Pull the bonnet catch, Griffin," Lew asked.

Griffin found the white knob and pulled; the bonnet showed not the slightest indication of unlatching despite a knob that came away fully two feet on the end of its wire.

"Fantastic," Griffin sighed.

"I'll get a weapon," Lew muttered, staying remarkably calm through all this. He headed off toward the bike—to get something to finish the old bitch off, no doubt.

Griffin was left sitting in the car, looking around. He was discovering, not entirely to his satisfaction, that he was beginning to mellow; perhaps it was sympathy inspired by the degradation to which this fine old car was being subjected. Not that he was a man for mechanical things—that was Lew's domain—but even he could tell, with the aid of one dirty fingertip, that under all that dust was a genuine woodgrain dashboard, and that the seats were like those old armchairs that you could really sink into, even if the stitching in the fair dinkum leather had erupted open in some places. And the sunroof—he reached up and slid it open and the sun did pour in upon him—wonderful stuff! He looked in the back—even people his size could sleep in there. Little winders for the vent windows. A built-in clock that—Holy Moses!—had the right time in spite of an apparent lack of power. Griffin relaxed and played a boy's game of driving for a bit; it wasn't hard to imagine skimming over the highways in this, with every passerby pausing to watch you go. What it all amounted to was an absolute bargain for some enthusiast to buy and restore to its original condition. What he could also see was that neither he nor Lew were likely to undertake a task like that.

They returned; Lew armed with a screwdriver that he poked through the grille to release the bonnet catch, and the dealer with the jump leads that he hooked across to the Mercedes alongside.

"God..."

Griffin was there to peer in with them. In there was an engine you could imagine running a jumbo jet or a powerstation but surely far to vast for a mere motor car. Griffin discerned eight cylinders and twin carburettors but most of it completely confounded his small crop of automotive knowledge. Not that there was much of it visible, for most was utterly lost in a vast swamp of oil and grit.

"Bit of a mess," Griffin commented lamely.

"Hmmm. Probably fix that with a few seals here and there," Lew said.

On some spare Sunday afternoon.

The jump leads were connected.

"Give her a try," the dealer called, not without a certain doubtfulness. Griffin was back behind the wheel and started the engine—it did start this time if only after a lot of shuddering and stuttering, and while the old car creaked and rocked a thick cloud of black smoke arose from underneath.

"Well, at least it does go," Lew smiled.

"Sort of..." Griffin muttered. How could he have doubted...

The dealer looked jubilant—perhaps there was some chance of sealing the deal after all. He went quickly into his spiel, telling them how much registration it had (two months), four wheels, two fuel tanks, eight cylinders (hasn't it?), the one side mirror that wasn't cracked but not the one that was. What a bargain!

"We want to discuss it privately," Griffin said, mostly to shut him up, and met the gaze of Lew Sigg. The dealer nodded obligingly and shuffled off toward his office, to take something for his ulcer or perhaps try to read their lips through binoculars.

Griffin switched off the motor and got out of the car, putting on his most surly expression. Lew decided it was better to look naive for the moment.

"It goes," he said.

"The engine goes. We don't know about the rest of it yet."

"We can take it for a test drive."

"Not until you explain."

"Explain?"

"Explain to me, Lewington, how this is the answer to everything."

For so large and well muscled a fellow, Lew was able to cringe in the manner of all the best introverts. With his copious mass of tight curled black hair and beard, he looked for all the world like a colossal golliwog, whereas a warrior tribesman of the New Guinea highlands was the more usual effect, except, of course, that his skin was officially white.

"Well, Griffin. You did say you were interested in buying a motorcar."

Griffin was, eternally, one of those people who were only ever taken seriously when they did not want to be.

"Maybe. But really, Lewington, this wasn't exactly what I had in mind. It'll cost a fucking fortune in petrol, another fortune to get into a respectable condition. Come on. Be a bit practical."

"You just don't appreciate what we've got on our hands here Griffin."

"I appreciate it only too well. Explain to me just exactly how you plan to get a roadworthy for this thing."

"A what?"

"A roadworthy certificate, as required by law. There won't be a mechanic anywhere either stupid or corrupt enough to pass this monster as roadworthy, and without that, you cannot transfer the registration. You know very well what I'm talking about."

"We can go to Queensland," Lew said benignly.

"Queensland!?!"

"Yes, Griffin. Queensland. They don't have those sorts of

paternal laws up there and the cops are as crooked as all get-out. You can register a car up there without a roadworthy. So we drive to Brisbane, re-register it there, then we bring it back to Victoria and transfer the registration, which, due to the most fortuitous loophole, requires no local roadworthy. Bingo! Problem solved."

"Lewington, you're joking!"

"Fair dinkum, Griffin. It'll work. I checked up."

Griffin had to pause to gather his wits. To be sure, if there was anyone in the world who knew about such things, it was Lew. It would undoubtedly work. But then Griffin realised that he was being sidetracked, and he began to realise which sidetrack he was being sent down.

"Are you sure, Lewington, that there isn't some other reason why you want to go to Queensland?"

"Other reason?" Lew said with an amazement so convincing that all Griffin's fears were confirmed.

"You wouldn't at all be thinking about a certain young lady of our mutual acquaintance who, I seem to recall, just happens to presently reside in that part of the world, would you?"

"Who... Oh, you mean Dell. Oh, come on. That's all history. Never crossed my mind."

"Just a really big coincidence, huh?"

"That's right."

"How could I have thought otherwise."

"How indeed. Especially when you've been saying that we have to get out of town for a while."

Griffin shook his head in disbelief. It was one of those moments that often happened when talking to Lew, where you were made to wonder if your own life was entirely different to the way you normally thought it was.

"Lew, it's *you* who has to get out of town. I don't. It's not *me* they're after."

"They will be, when they discover you've been hiding me."

"I haven't been hiding you, Lewington. Not from them or anybody."

"But how are you going to convince them of that?"

"Lew, you are the fugitive. I did my time, remember?"

"Yes, I know. And therefore how can you, in all conscience, allow me to fall into their clutches."

Griffin again had to shake his head to clear it. It was the most astonishing lot of nonsense he had yet heard from Lew Sigg. Hiding him... Then he realised. It was only Lew bamboozling him again with irrelevant notions to steer him away from the true subject of the conversation. Deftly, Griffin steered them back again.

"Lewington, this old heap of junk won't make it to Queensland. It probably won't even make it back to Fitzroy."

"Of course it will. It's a great car. And it'll be a great trip."

"Lewington, I don't want to go to Queensland."

"But you said it yourself. You need a car, we need to get away. What could be more perfect than this?"

"Lewington, I don't want to go to Queensland!"

Warrior's Homecoming

"This is your captain speaking. We are just now passing over The Great Dividing Range and on our descent towards Essendon Airport. I've put the seat belt warning on—there's a good deal of turbulent cloud beneath us and our approach might be a little bumpy. We expect to be on the tarmac in fifteen minutes. And I am sorry to tell you that it is pouring rain in Melbourne and the current temperature is a nippy 47 degrees Fahrenheit."

That sounded right. It was early Autumn in southern Australia and the driest time of the year; but Melbourne's weather, he remembered with a faint smile, had a habit of being contrary. The only consistent thing about it was its inconsistency. The Summers were not all that hot—compared for instance with the boiling tropics that he had finally left behind him—and the Winters never cold enough to induce the snow and ice of Europe and North America. It was officially classified as a moderate temperature climate—and therefore very nearly perfect—but that could only have been some sort of meteorological joke. The trouble was that weather typical of all four seasons could all occur on the same day and often did: it was thought that nervous breakdowns amongst Melbourne's weather forecasters rated highest in the world. And so there was Griffin, sitting in his seat at the back of the crowded DC9 that was the early morning flight from Sydney, wearing his army greens and no underwear and with his sleeves rolled up. He did not have any sort of coat, nor even a blanket. Someone who had lived in Melbourne for twenty-odd years ought to have known a bloody lot better than that.

As the captain had promised, the descent was very bumpy but that didn't bother Griffin much. It was, for him, only the final moments of what had been a pretty rough trip anyway. It began at dawn the day before when the morning mail RAAF Caribou lifted off the short airstrip at Nui Dat and he sat amid the packing cases with gritted teeth while the wind whistled through what the crewman had cheerfully informed him were bullet holes.

"We got a bit close to the ground on the way in," he laughed. "Scared the shitbags outa me."

That thought was doing much the same to Griffin—all he would have needed at this stage was to be picked off by some overly optimistic potshooter on the ground two thousand feet below to make his year complete. It might have been appropriate, romantic even, but he had long since given up any hope of finding poetry in his life. All he knew was that he was going home. All he wanted was to bloody get there.

Vietnam, March 1968, was a good time to be anyplace else. Naturally, Saigon Airport was under attack at the time the mail plane arrived as the final pockets of fierce resistance arising with the Tet Offensive fought out their last ditch stands. The surviving Viet Cong forces were entrenched a few miles away and amused themselves all night dropping mortars on the airfield. The Qantas Boeing 707 stood on the tarmac looking hopelessly out of place—if ever an aeroplane could have been said to look nervous, that one did. By then the danger was long past—the Charlies fading away with the night and would not return until sunset—or else the 707 would not have been there at all. Still, it was all too conspicuous in its red and white colours while all about it was military green: the ferocious Phantom fighter bombers low to the ground and bristling with rockets, the huge camouflaged-painted Hercules and Starlifters, or the Huey gunships bustling back and forth as they raced off to make airstrikes on fighting clearly evident six or seven miles away. Here and there, carcases of devastated aircraft still burned, the smoke rising to blend with that of the fires raging out of control beyond the airport perimeter. There were still fuming craters rent in the concrete of the tarmac itself and holes blasted in all of the buildings. There were thousands of troops, Americans, moving as they indulged the respite in the fighting to undertake the grisly but safe task of searching the wreckage for bodies. In such surroundings, the Qantas jet could not have looked more vulnerable.

Griffin joined the queue of other Australian soldiers going aboard, many of them wrapped in bandages. If the Boeing was all too plainly a civilian, still it had not escaped unblemished, with its firstclass seats removed to make room for stretcher cases, while the cargo holds were being loaded with a number of hermetically sealed aluminium cases that were all too obviously six feet long. Qantas, being a conservative organisation, had taken into account the deprived nature of the passengers and so had carefully avoided crewing any of their pretty female hostesses, instead the cabin was adorned with a bevy of bright young male stewards, one of whom stood at the door as Griffin entered, edgily peeping outside at the evidence of the recent carnage.

"Must be awful out there," he breathed to Griffin in his effeminate voice.

"Nar. Routine," Griffin muttered back grimly.

Knowing therefore that Griffin was the toughest man he'd ever met, the steward smiled at him in awe, cringingly embarrassed by his own scented sweat.

"Bloody poofta," the man behind Griffin growled, and then, as he looked about the cabin. "Hey, look at this. They've put a pack of pooftas on the plane. Where's the fuckin' molls?"

"I think you just answered your own question," the steward responded sweetly.

The soldier leaned toward him menacingly. "Don't get smart with me, yer pillowbiting cocksucker, or I'll flush yer down yer own fuckin' dunny."

No longer the toughest man on earth, Griffin eased the aggressor back.

"Take it easy, Weed. I reckon Qantas was pretty lucky finding anyone to crew this flight."

The steward smiled appreciatively, although that smile slowly faded as the broader implications of what Griffin had said sank in.

The pack of pooftas might well have disappointed in being the palest imitation of what the soldiers might have hoped for, but they soon redeemed themselves once the flight got underway by keeping up what must have been a bottomless supply of beer. This was called a Champagne Flight and indeed champagne was provided to toast each of the milestones as the pilot announced them—passing out of the war zone, passing over the equator, passing onto the Australian mainland, by which time the journey was only half over and the men otherwise guzzled beer furiously.

Sometime after midnight—Griffin had no idea when—Sydney International Airport was treated to the spectacle of nearly two hundred extremely intoxicated soldiers spilling out of the aircraft and into the terminal building. Many could not stand unaided, fights were breaking out everywhere, vomit and urine splattered in all directions and in this fashion they roared and thundered home. All civilians had been evacuated to safer ground, and the customs and military administrators faced their task with remarkable tolerance while the men behaved like what they probably were—animals let out of their cages. In normal circumstances, the army would have heaved the whole bloody lot of them in the clink and hosed them down, but these were not normal circumstances. To try and stand between two hundred hardened war veterans and their final freedom at this penultimate moment would have been the most disastrous folly. So the forces of authority, like the soldiers, strove to get this lot processed and on their way, while the men chainsmoked in no smoking zones, swore with raucous profusion, burst into unrecognisably out-of-tune songs and frequently, when asked, had trouble remembering their own names.

Griffin was carrying an envelope that had the army bureaucrats puzzling and studying documents and generally trying to convince themselves that he was not a Vietcong spy infiltrating the country. There seemed to be no record of him, no discharge papers available, in fact he didn't seem to exist when they could see for themselves that he certainly did and was very obviously what he claimed to be. Eventually he was issued with a leave pass, two hundred dollars out of his paybook and a ticket on the first flight to Melbourne in the morning.

And now, as the DC9 banked across the northern suburbs of Melbourne, he shifted painfully in his seat, his head numbed by a monumental hangover, his body stiff from an uncomfortable night sleeping on a lounge in Sydney terminal, his extremities sore from the number of times he had rolled over in his nightmarish sleep and fallen on the floor.

He gazed through the rainswept window at the broad expanse of the city. Under the grey curtain of the sky, the redtile roof-tops stretched away to the horizon in all directions, interspersed with the green patches of backyards and dark blobs of trees, the wide black streets slicing through forcing the houses into military formations. Here and there were the blue patches of swimming pools, and the larger white rectangles of drive-in movie screens. Away in the murky distance stood the cluster of tall buildings at the centre of the city—the tombstones of commerce—and beyond them the wide flat mirror expanse of Port Phillip Bay. It might have been any city but as it happened, it was his. It might have been known as a rather flat and boring place but he didn't care. Down there, he knew, everything he ever dreamed of awaited him. Down there, he knew, his every fantasy was poised to be fulfilled.

There was a large crowd waiting in the rain to welcome the soldiers home. Griffin came off the plane and immediately the cold air bit into his skin—the same sensation as when he arrived in Sydney last night when the local staff reckoned it was pretty warm. Plainly the war hadn't toughened him at all, but weakened him—he never used to feel the cold. The civilians burst through the barrier and rushed onto the tarmac, swarming amongst the soldiers like a wave attack. Girls threw their arms around necks, fathers and friends shook hands warmly, mothers clasped their sons in rib-crushing embraces, splattering tears down the front of their shirts. There were shrieks of joy, there was laughter, and desperate sobs of relief. Griffin eased his way through them, knowing that the Griffin family were not given to partaking in minor riots, and indeed there they stood, properly beyond the barrier, patiently waiting. Griffin saw them and quickened his stride—he could see already see that two of them had changed and two had not.

The two that had changed came galloping toward him—his sister Narelle and brother Michael—to grip his arms as if in his exhaustion he might not be able to make it any further by himself. Narelle had discovered henna in his absence, and had softened her whole appearance somehow, he leeringly observed. She beamed the hugest of smiles at him, altogether different from the one he remembered, the supercilious one when he was in trouble with Wally because she had dobbed him in.

"Hullo soldier," she smiled cheekily and gave his arm a squeeze. Griffin flushed red. Narelle the Dragon had turned into a sexy sheila. It was unbelievable.

On his other flank was another soldier, or at least a reasonable facsimile of one. Little brother Michael had grown a foot taller and acquired a face full of pimples, but it was his army uniform that really threw Griffin. He racked his brains and remembered Ella's weekly letters saying something about Mickey joining the cadets. Following in big brother's footsteps. It would have been churlish to point out that having been drafted, big brother's footsteps were rather reluctant ones. Still, for the moment, Griffin had to try and pretend to be impressed. He flipped at Michael's breastpocket. "Hey, what's this?"

"Been in the cadets for ages," Michael declared proudly. "It's great."

Inwardly, Griffin was dying. Everything, he knew, was great until it got real. To try and show enthusiasm he definitely didn't feel, he noticed the pair of stripes on the boy's arm.

"Hey, you little bugger. You've outranked me."

Michael roared with laughter while Narelle shook his arm and whispered in his ear. "Hey, watch your language."

This was going to be tough.

They were towing him now, these people he was obliged to believe were once his brother and sister, towards the two that had not changed, as well as having not managed to get themselves through the gate and onto the tarmac like everyone else. Ella's bad back, of course, prevented her from any sort of haste and so she stood wobbling with tears running down her quivering cheeks and her arms extended toward him in the faith that he would finally arrive. Behind her was Wally, who was totally embarrassed by all this over emotional bullshit, his face fixed in an ironic grin.

Ella, he was sure, was wearing exactly the same dress she had when she had seen him off, and the same scent for all of his life, he noticed, as she wrapped her arms around his middle and thrust her teary face into his chest.

"Oh Kenny, Kenny," she was saying in not much more than a moan. "Oh, thank God, thank God."

With Michael and Narelle pinning his arms, Griffin could only stand and look helpless, until she did lift her face, blinking the tears from her eyes, her soggy cheeks shining.

"Oh Kenny, thank God you're safe."

He was sure that God was getting far more credit for this than he deserved.

"Cors I'm safe," he said firmly, and kissed her lips. She buried her head in his chest again—he was getting the impression she intended to stand hanging onto him forever.

Wally stepped forward now, extending his hands over his wife's shoulder to shake Griffin's firmly. That ironic smile was still there.

"How was it?" he asked flatly, as if he did really expect Griffin to give an account of it all in one sentence. Then he realised that he could and grinned. "Ninety percent bull...er... nonsense."

At this point, Michael and Narelle set about the task of prising Ella away from his middle section, although she showed no sign of allowing it, still quite definitely sure that God was responsible for it all.

"Yer back early," Wally said abruptly. "Though yer mighta got wounded agen or somethin'."

Oh yes, Griffin could imagine how that thought might have scared the living daylights out of them. Certainly, Ella threw herself back and tried to look at every square inch of him at once, searching for missing bits, as did Michael in who's glazed eyes you could see the blood flowing.

"Nope. No bulletholes," Griffin said to try and make a joke of what wasn't funny.

Wally continued to eye him with the utmost scepticism. "Thought somethin' musta happened..."

"No. They just sent me back early. I'm owed a month's leave anyway which will see me out until I'm discharged."

Having unleashed himself from his mother, they began to gravitate through the Arrivals Hall. Narelle remembered to collect the baggage that didn't exist, Michael was concerned about Customs procedures that occurred the night before, Wally was rolling himself a cigarette that Griffin eyed greedily. Ella, he was sure, had completely crushed the Camels that were in his breast pocket. They were drifting through the terminal building, and Griffin was wanting to get rid of a couple of involuntary gestures that he had suddenly acquired—one of continually adjusting his hat, the other of feeling the pocket wherein the Camels lurked. All this, he knew, was the result of nerves and the need to examine every word before he spoke it. He hadn't slipped so far, or at least hoped not. All in all, this was becoming fucking difficult.

Like a bold warrior chieftain, he led his little tribe out into the car park. All the way, Ella, who had now been restored to her proper self, had begun to gabble on about who was in and out of hospital, which relatives wished to be remembered to him, how she had bought new curtains for the lounge room and a lot of other things she had already told him in her letters. Beside her, Wally strode in his overalls—on the journey back to Moorabbin he obviously intended to be dropped off at the flour mill for a normal working day. And Narelle, of course, would also be getting out as they passed the city office where she was a secretary. Michael had the day off school. Ella didn't drive, and suddenly new dangers began to appear. Griffin tried to remember Ella's letters saying anything about Michael getting his driver's licence—surely he was old enough now.

"Yeah, but for a motor bike, not a car," Michael said proudly.

"I did write and tell you," Ella insisted.

Griffin gulped. In such circumstances, embattled with the language, desperate for a smoke and frantic for a beer, driving seemed a gigantic risk. The least he could do was allow his mother to get used to her new son gradually. But because Ella was still full of her information about the Griffin world, and Wally still regarding him suspiciously, and because he did not want to be caught perving on this wonderful thing that had once been his sister, and trembled with fear at the thought of where his example was leading Mickey, Griffin discovered that they had arrived at the car with nothing decided. His own car, in fact, FJ Holden, dog-vomit green where it wasn't rusty, shiningly clean like it never was when he drove it. Wally confirmed his worst fears by throwing him the keys.

"Maybe I've forgotten how to drive," Griffin gasped.

"Some things you never forget," Wally said pointedly.

Narelle, Michael and Ella piled in the back while Wally took up the passenger seat beside him where, presumably, he could aid Griffin's memory on the fundamental principles of controlling such machines. A glance in the rearview mirror showed the three faces in the back, attached to bodies that would have been far less cramped in Wally's larger, later model. This, then, he had to regard as a special treat they were willing to suffer for his benefit—with all options closed, he started the engine, crunched the gears and kangaroo-hopped all the way out of the carpark.

By the time they were out amongst the inbound peak hour traffic on Mt Alexander Road, Griffin was generally getting the hang of it. The heavy GP boots with their metal plates vulcanised into the rubber soles did not make it easy to feel the pedals and the traffic snarled and bleated at him—there seemed to be a lot more of it than he remembered—and he knew that Moorabbin lay twenty-five miles across the city from here. They passed a pub that he found himself eyeing desperately, even though it would not have been open yet. His fingers still darted to his breast pocket and there was a dry feeling in his throat on both accounts. It was getting tougher by the minute. But, as it happened, resolution was at hand as they headed down to an unexpected showdown at Moonee Ponds Junction.

It took the form of a furniture van attempting to force its way through the traffic, the driver plainly smug in his dubious claim to right of way on the basis of size. Griffin was overwhelmed by the urge to demonstrate his superior knowledge of the road laws and so brought both vehicles to a halt in a screech of tyres and blast of wailing horns. Quite before he knew what he was doing, Griffin had the window down and his head sticking out. "Have a fuckin' look where yer fuckin' goin', you great lumbering' shit-for-brains arsehole!"

"You're not in fucking your tank now, digger," the driver replied.

"Get your fuckin' licence, cuntface—out of the Weeties

packet?"

The furniture van driver, seeing he was intellectually outgunned, put his head in and drove on in a squeal of rubber. It was only then that Griffin retracted his own head. In the rearvision, he could see his mother's mouth hanging about as far open as it was able. Narelle whipped out a handkerchief and giggled into that, but Michael was utterly unable to control himself and doubled up on the seat with laughter.

"It isn't funny," Ella barked at him, boxing his ears because she had to hit someone. It wasn't either. Griffin's nerves were so jangled he had the cigarette alight before he knew it, as if by magic despite a shaking hand.

"Shit, I need a drink after that."

His mother's eyes were now as wide as her mouth. And then, as the smoke helped him regain composure, Griffin looked to Wally for guidance. His father still wore that bemused, ironic grin.

"You want me to drive, son?" he asked quietly.

"No. I'll be okay."

And if there might have been a few more near-misses after that, not a further word was said on the subject—in Ella's case, not on any subject—for all of the rest of the journey home.

Outbound

Roaring north on Highway 31, the ancient Jaguar in delight after decades of suburban bottlenecks, used car yards and indifferent ownership: now at last in the hands of people who would turn it to the wind and let it show what it might have been.

And they in much the same mood, Lew keeping the speed up as they blurred through the sprawling suburbs on the way out of the city, heedless of traffic laws, anxious only to run clear of congestion, complexity and cops.

The big motor positively boomed and the experienced well-tuned ears of Lew carefully studied each sound and vibration individually. It was done in the manner of an orchestra conductor at practice, his brain sorting through the cacophony to mentally separate the one violin with a mistuned string, or the single woodwind fractionally out of time. So Lew absorbed each sound, locating, categorising, diagnosing and passing the findings on to Griffin.

"We'll definitely have to check the valves at some point," he would murmur, frowning at the thought of what that might lead to.

"What's that big rattle back there?" Griffin asked, pleased to be able to contribute.

"Most likely have to replace an exhaust bracket. Or else there's a panel, or mudguard, or something, coming adrift. But that's much less probable."

"With this old bitch, nothing is improbable," Griffin remarked, although not without a certain tone of reverence, "I thought you said you fixed everything?"

"She's in good enough shape to get us there," Lew smiled with jubilation, "And that's all we need."

But for Griffin it was almost a duty to remain sceptical, and so he did.

In the soft blue lights of the instrument panel, they were checking and rechecking the astonishing array of dials.

"Oil pressure's dropped," Griffin observed from his side.

"Not surprised," Lew muttered grimly, "The way its been pissing out under the rocker covers. We'll get some comparison figures later and see what sort of drop we're getting."

"Burning a bit too."

"Yeah. You can smell it."

The oil loss constituted their major problem—'check the petrol and fill 'er up with oil!' they would joke with petrol attendants. Only it wouldn't be so funny over a trip of this distance. Twenty-two litres of oil it took in that motor, and if it was capable of disposing of that over a short distance, the expense would be staggering.

But that was a problem for later, Griffin supposed.

They had gone forward, hunched over the controls like a pair of chopper pilots—The Monster, an eternal opportunist, nestled between them, trading fleas for warmth. In the backseat was an immense pile of belongings hastily thrown in, the boot key being lost, in the frenzied rush that preluded the launching of the expedition.

Out through Broadmeadows they went between the gruesome parade of giant industrial complexes they lined both sides of the highway until they lurched up over the Craigieburn Overpass and it could be said they were clear of the city. For all the years he had lived in Melbourne, Griffin saw this as a favourite landmark—outbound it meant you were really going places, inbound that you were nearly home. Although he had come this way innumerable times, that sensation never left him, and it was there again, and he was becoming more awake.

And the car, and Lew, were settling down too—The Monster had been settled since Nicholson Street—and the whole mood became more relaxed. They were speeding on the highway across the coastal plains, slipping little towns that dotted the undulating hills; weaving around treeless crests.

Then they were climbing Pretty Sally hill and Griffin spared a moment to reflect upon the fate of Alfie Magee. Tonight there was no traffic to render into chaos and no ice on the road, and Griffin wanted to say something to Lew about all that but couldn't think of anything. Leave the past in the past, he decided. The plains began to fall away behind as they rushed into the broad curve up the face of the low mountains that stretched unceasingly from top to bottom of the continent—the Great Dividing Range. And the city was a sea of fallen stars behind, while before the black continent stretched away until the end of night.

It was two o'clock on a Wednesday morning, and at such an absurd hour they had the road to themselves. Absurd hour for Griffin, although perhaps not for Lew who might have planned it that way all along, when Griffin was too tired to resist and sufficiently drunk and irresponsible to be sucked out of his deeply ingrained conservatism and into spirited and foolhardy adventures.

"Come on, let's go! Right now!" Lew had cried, and his enthusiasm swept Griffin and dog and their belongings into the car and away.

They passed the turn-off to Puckapunyal and Griffin again suppressed his memories, but this time Lew was on to him.

"Bit of history there," Lew said softly.

"Bit too much," Griffin said.

"It must have been like home for a while though," Lew persisted.

"Pucka was never anything like home."

"Still bitter then, Griffin?"

"I always will be, Lewington."

And through the edge of Seymour and the first hour of the journey gone, and they passed the Prince of Wales pub where, for Griffin, the first of many battles was lost. Griffin could almost have talked about that—Lew would have loved the story, he knew, but again he stayed quiet—it was a time for leaving all that behind. Here the heavy laden semitrailers lined either side of the highway, waiting it out for first light when they would lunge onward in their ponderous journeys. They stretched out across the flatlands of the great rift valley, bouncing over the railway tracks at Mangalore, skating down the long sweep to the narrow stone bridge at Avernal, zooming through Euroa.

"Soon, Euroa won't exist either," Griffin remarked. Even in the darkness, he could see the evidence of the bypass in progress.

"Good thing too," Lew murmured.

"But these places. All that history."

"And history is what they are."

Better their history than his own.

In two hours they reached the large town of Benalla where not one of its 9000 inhabitants was to be seen. And on to the historic town of Glenrowan where the bushranger Ned Kelly walked godlike in his suit of armour from the blazing hotel where his gang was besieged to do singlehanded battle with an army of troopers. A hundred years ago. They say the hills still ring with the sound of the trooper's bullets ricocheting off his suit of moulded ploughshares—the stuff of only the greatest legends, and Australia's sole fragment of mythology even though the house where he was born was demolished a few years before to make way for another sheep paddock.

"Disgusting," Lew muttered, "That shack would be worth an awful lot of bags of wool these days."

Griffin nodded: "Did you hear they pinched his statue, Lewington?"

"His what?"

"There was a statue of Old Ned in his armour back there. The government didn't think it ought to go about erecting monuments to ruffians no matter how famous and revered they were, so the local townsfolk passed around the hat and erected one themselves. Then one night, person or persons unknown snuck into town and set him free."

"Set him free? A statue?"

"Well, they had to cut him off at the ankles. There was uproar in the community. But, even in effigy, he eluded them for a time until he finally turned up on a street corner, in Carlton, would you believe. Not far from the Old Melbourne Gaol, where they hung him."

"Where else. But why would they hang a statue?"

"No, no. They hung the real person. The statue they put in the Carlton lockup for the night, for safekeeping they said."

"Nothing ever changes," Lew Sigg laughed.

Onward, onward in the blackness, cruising easy and the Jag finding its momentum now, devouring the hills and bends. Around the next, Griffin knew, the mountains would come into view, had it been daylight, away to the right.

And they did anyway, haunting moonlight touching the snowcapped hulks of Mt Bogong and Mt Buffalo, their soft whiteness luminescent and disembodied from the dark earth, floating white giants, suspended in time as well as substance.

"He wasn't Australian. He was Irish," Lew remarked.

"Who?"

"Ned Kelly," Lew answered flatly, "And further, we have to assume that had he been born in Ireland, he would have been of equally impoverished upbringing, equally oppressed by the authorities, equally determined not to stand for it, and would have no doubt still have fought his battle, in his armour, at some pub in Londonderry."

"You can't know that."

"Maybe not. But the fact remains that Kelly was Irish, his gang was all Irish, and his grievances arose largely because of a penchant for British policemen to give Irishmen a hard time. The only Australian link is a pure matter of geography."

"Is it necessary, Lewington, to shatter every illusion?"

"Just another example of the Australian inability to be Australian. We have to borrow everything from other countries, transpose it onto the Australian landscape, and pretend it's ours. Why can't we do anything by ourselves?"

But the hard night was taking its toll, and they began to yawn and strain their eyes. Lew chose a spot and they eased off the road and pulled into the trees. So tired were they that they crawled straight into their sleeping bags without even bothering to erect the tent, Lew in the front seat, Griffin sharing the back with the growling and disgruntled Monster.

"On the road at dawn," they assured each other.

The Monster gazed at where the sky was already beginning to lighten in the east and yawned its scepticism.

Indeed when the sun rose brilliantly to incinerate the clouds of dew as fast as they could rise from the ground, only The Monster was there to see it. Booted out of the car by grumpy Griffin, it stood guard over the beloved football awaiting the emergence of either human being to begin a game that paddocks like this could only cause to be a great one.

The sun gave up at nine, swamped by a mass of cloud so irksome that it could only have been dispatched by Melbourne's morning peak hour traffic. The Monster gave up at ten and was off chasing rabbits. When it returned at eleven, the hungover humans had appeared, but stumbled about so awkwardly it was best to keep a distance.

There were small matters to be attended to. The boot, for instance, which Lew had to burst open with a crowbar, whereby Griffin piled the gear in and tied it down with crocodilestraps. Lew did some adjustments on the carburettors and then they were moving again, heading out of Victoria through Albury and into New South Wales.

"We're going the wrong way," Lew decided to point out. He was hunched over the map while Griffin drove and The Monster languished in the newfound luxury of the backseat.

"Queensland's a big place, Lewington. All you do is head generally north and you can't miss it."

"True enough, Griffin. But you must remember the small degree of illegality concerning our present mode of transportation, and how the considerable risks of falling foul of the law can only be enhanced by traversing so large a metropolis as Sydney."

"You propose that Sydney should be bypassed?"

"Indeed, Griffin. A pity I know, with the beauties of the harbour and whatnot, but it's not for us. Which means we are going the wrong way."

"Then I suggest you plan an alternative."

"That I have done. Not far ahead, you ought to come upon a turnoff we can take. It should indicate Wagga Wagga."

"Oh god, not Wagga Wagga!"

Turning inland, toward the burning heart of New South Wales, and the flatlands of yellow grass with the intermittent stark white trunks of dead ghost gums, stretching away from them in every direction, lulling their minds to torpor, the Great Australian Stupor, it was called, or perhaps the cause of it.

"There's one there!"

Scaring the living daylights out of Griffin who bounced upright in the seat and swivelled his head every whichway but could not at all see what it was that was there.

"Stop the car, Griffin. Quick!"

Griffin allowed the Jag to roll to a lumbering halt, still puzzled but no longer concerned. In the face of true disasters, Lew Sigg was always cool and perhaps it was because he only ever allowed himself to panic over the most trivial matters. The engine, Griffin noticed, was blowing hard in these warmer conditions.

"One what?"

"Look at it, Griffin. It's a bewdy!"

And he was out of the car in a flash and around to unfasten the boot. The Monster went with him, sharing the excitement, while Griffin tagged along with mild amusement. All he could see was the expanse of broad flat land just exactly like all the other broad flat land they had passed through that morning.

"What...is a bewdy, Lewington?"

"Oh, Griffin. Open your bloody eyes. Look at it. A footy kicking paddock if ever there was one."

And he had the football out and was off.

It was not the most remarkable footy kicking paddock that Griffin had ever seen. It was flat and big enough and the grass was short but there were huge anthills scattered about and further over, some cows, which meant cow pats—not only messy underfoot but if it got on the ball could slur stabpasses and worse, splatter in the face when taking a mark.

"Lewington. This is New South Wales. They only play imported codes of football here."

"So we'll show 'em how."

Though there was no one to see.

"But what about the anthills?"

"The opposition, mate."

"They don't move much."

"Couldn't be any slower than the Richmond forward line."

So they tore into the paddock and raced around—handpasses, shortpasses, long bombs straight down the centre, streaking out onto the flank for the onehanded pick-up, selling the dummy to that charging anthill, swinging onto the right boot and the long low torpedo straight down the throat of Lew at centre-half-forward. And The Monster yelped with excitement as he bounded after whichever of them had the ball—a solid half-back-flanker able to take a strong mark if it could get its teeth into the lace but a lousy kick in spite of its two extra legs.

Lew soared over and anthill for a towering fingertip mark and played on, two bounces as he charged through the centre and he had Griffin on a lead in the forward pocket but the pass was wide—he got a hand to it, buttered up, and the flashing handpass over the shoulder to Lew charging into the open goal for another one to the Roos!

So they went until they were exhausted and then kept on going until The Monster shirtfronted Lew and laid him out with a twisted ankle. Griffin picked him up and helped him back to the car.

"God I needed that," Lew panted, the sweat streaming down his face and dripping from his beard onto his shirt, "All that sitting and driving—a man could go mad without exercise." Griffin, who was certain he could manage perfectly well without physical exertion, could not fly in the face of such enthusiasm.

"Well, at least it builds up a thirst for the lunchtime ales."

"That, Griffin, is why they bothered to invent the game in the first place."

They drove into the next town and pulled up outside the pub. The pub faced onto a central square with a monument in the middle of a small grassed area. That monument consisted of a statue of a WWI soldier standing with fixed bayonet on a long square column with lists of names of those from the district killed in the various wars. It was something common to most country towns but today it seemed of special interest for about it a group of people stood with their heads bowed in prayer. There was a band, in uniform, and various soldiers too. And the old men and women with their heads bowed were all wearing their medals.

"What's happening, Griffin?" Lew asked. He even seemed to want to go over and investigate.

"What makes you think I'd know?"

"Well, because you do know. About all this sort of stuff."

"Well, it isn't fucking Anzac Day, so there's still some chance of the pub being open."

He went straight to the door and pushed and it was. Lew followed along, his curiosity aroused more by his friend than the unscheduled parade.

"You don't ever march on Anzac Day, do you?" Lew said as they bought beer and moved toward the pool table.

"Certainly fucking not."

But some regulars were having a competition so they backed off and sat at the table, ready to order lunch.

"You don't ever talk about it, do you?" Lew asked.

"Of course I do. All the bloody time. Too much," Griffin snapped.

"No you don't. You talk in vague terms but you never give detailed accounts."

"I have no desire to satisfy your ghoulish demand for blood and gore."

"But here I am, on the run from the law because of this, and you, with first hand experience, refuse to tell me exactly what it is I'm running away from."

"Just keep running. Take my advice."

"But why can't you talk about it?"

"I can. I just don't want to."

"Well, I think you owe it to me."

"Do you?"

"Yes. Give it to me straight. In all the bloody, gory, boring tedium of it."

"I'm really not in the mood to tell war stories right now, Lewington."

"Okay. But later on. I want you to tell me all about it. I'm serious."

Griffin eyed him. Of all the strange moments in their relationship, this was the strangest. Lew was never serious about anything, ever, except he was now.

"Yes, Lewington. I see you are. I hardly know how to cope with it."

Lew smiled, easing the pressure, and offered a compromise.

"Okay, if you don't want to tell a story, then at least explain why."

"Why what?"

"Why you never talk about it?"

Griffin had to think long and hard to come up with an answer.

"Because you can't," he said.

*

Lunch was over, the parade had finished and dispersed and they were on their way again.

"Always nice to observe the national traditions," Griffin observed casually. It was a mistake.

"I thought we just avoided observing one," Lew mused.

Griffin sighed: "I was referring to the tradition of going to the pub for a few beers after a game of football."

That was a different sort of mistake.

"Hardly national, Griffin. Young men kick footballs and then retire for well earned ales in every country in the world."

"I suppose. The only difference is the type of football."

"More or less, and maybe the type of ale. But there's nothing particularly Australian about it, as we like to imagine."

"Except Aussie Rules. No other game like it."

"Except Gaelic Football, which it was copied from."

"They don't drink beer the way we do..."

"Europeans taught us how to make beer, and drink it."

"Their beer isn't as cold as ours."

"Because their climate isn't as warm. Griffin, you're clutching at straws. There really isn't any such thing as an Australian tradition. It's just a collection of things borrowed from other countries."

"You said that about Ned Kelly."

"Jesse James. Ben Turpin. Same person in a tin suit."

"What about Gallipoli?"

"A British force undertaking a British invasion of territory wanted by the British. It just happened that most of the British soldiers that were killed were actually from Australia."

"What about the pioneer spirit. Henry Lawson. Banjo Patterson."

"Davy Crockett. Johnny Appleseed. All that happened in North America and South Africa and lots of places. We were just the most recent, which is about as far from the first as you can get."

"What about the Aboriginal traditions. Dreamtime,

Walkabout, pointing the bone..."

"A point in my favour, not yours. The so-called primitive race of this country have a particular identity, culture, traditions all of their own. Yet we so-called advanced white invaders can do no better than eternally imitate our forebears, while trying to stamp out Aboriginal individuality the same time."

"Alright, but be fair. The white Australian culture is only two hundred years old. So we have to borrow from other countries, older and wiser."

"Who fight wars and have crooked governments and vast poverty and urban terrorists and have economic depressions invoked by sheer greed of the rich. They do everything wrong and they know it and they say so, but we don't listen to them and simply copy their mistakes. Nothing is right to us unless the Americans or Europeans do it that way. Which is why we have no traditions and no national identity worth having."

"So you think, Lewington, that we ought to go out and invent a whole new set of traditions."

"If you want to make traditions, first you have to do something that's worth basing a tradition on. We have to stop trying to imitate and do something original, something all our own, that they didn't do. The tradition follows from there."

"And what sort of original thing do you have in mind?"

"Griffin, it can be anything. Just anything at all."

On through Wagga Wagga, Temora, Barmedman and to West Wyalong, on the Newell Highway and Sydney's great metropolis passed two hundred kilometres to the east. Rearing up on this flat, thinly treed country—sheep country and good for nothing but sheep—the marvellous Riverina. In the days when Australia rode on the sheep's back, this was the undoubted spine of the country, but then the nation decided it was time to follow everyone else and bury themselves in mines—although the sheep looked utterly unconcerned.

Onward they argued through the drab monotonous landscape, and Lew didn't always have the best of it.

"Is there no end to this bloody country?" Lew murmured in a semi-somnolent state.

No end or beginning but just one bloody great middle.

Aunt Merle's Favourite

He was not going to get out of bed that morning—there was no way. Out there, he knew, what people liked to call a beautiful day was going on—already the sun had infiltrated his room—but weather wasn't everything. This day would be anything but beautiful, and he pulled the covers over his head to ensure that he knew nothing about it; already he knew too much. It was Sunday and Sunday noises were going on out there—two years might have passed since he last heard those noises, but that didn't make them any less familiar.

Outside his window, in the backyard, he could hear Wally pottering around. On weekdays, Wally would have long since departed to the flour mill at this time and on Saturday mornings, after his careful and invariably fruitless examination of the racing form, he would rush Ella off to the supermarket as early as he could. But on Sundays he would venture with the dawn into the backyard, and there he would stay all day, tending his vegie patch, the strawberries, the fruit trees—apple, apricot, peach and lemon—and mow the lawn. He would have pulled the two-stroke out of the garage already and fuelled her up, but being a respectful man, thankfully would not have started that infernal machine before he was sure that everyone in the house was awake. That made for another good reason to stay in bed—to forestall the mower racket as long as possible and therefore give his hangover a chance to fade.

Ella was also on the move, bustling about the house in the last moments before her departure to the local church for her weekly forgiveness of sins that you could be fairly sure she had not committed. The Sunday roast would be prepared first, and then she would slip into her newest dress, and the roast would go into the oven in the very last minutes before she left. The local minister knew only too well the importance of getting speedily through the ten o'clock service, for should he run overtime, most of Moorabbin's Anglican roast dinners would be well and truly on his conscience.

Right now, Ella was busy herding Michael and Narelle along which meant it must have been after nine-thirty. These days, Narelle would pilot the mission in Wally's car, slipping off her high-heeled shoes but not her hat in what probably wasn't a deliberate attempt to parody the whole thing. Driving Ella to church on Sundays was a matter of descending rank; originally

Wally had conveyed the whole family but on the very Sunday following the day Griffin received his driver's licence, Wally had passed the reins to him and headed for the backyard. Now, the army's intervention had moved control to Narelle. Soon enough, Narelle would get someone to marry her whereby Michael would have a licence and take over until eventually he found his course in life and moved away—then Wally would return to God. But he was plainly in no hurry for that to happen—for the moment, Wally was content to save his soul by horticultural means.

This amounted to another good reason to stay in bed. Several times already, Ella had gasped. "I wonder if Ken would want to come?"

"I'm sure he wouldn't," both Narelle and Michael would answer. Still, before they left, she did sneak into the room, just to see if he might be awake and penitent.

"Poor dear," she murmured. "He's sleeping all the time. He must be so tired."

He dared not move a muscle until he heard Narelle drive them off in a flurry of grinding gears.

He breathed, and sat up in the bed—it was the need for a cigarette that drove him into action. He lit it guiltily—beside the bed Ella had surreptitiously placed the very large ashtray normally reserved for houseguests, but that sort of acceptance did not take away the memory of her horrified expression when she first saw him light one up, in those initial moments of reunion at the airport.

"Of course, now that you aren't there anymore, you'll give them up again, won't you," she told him.

Of course he would. But it was only one of several such moments of shock for Ella in these last few days. There would have been another now, had she been able to see the visible effects of the monumental hangover from which he was suffering, one that was all too thoroughly deserved. He leaned back on the pillows, smoking. For the next hour, the coast would be clear; after that, he did not know what he would do.

But what could he do? What could he say? There were so many things that she just did not, or could not, understand, and even the simplest of them needed tedious explanation. On the first morning after his discharge, his initial act was to pile up his military uniform and march it outside to the incinerator for the ceremonial burning. Ella and Michael trailed after him in puzzlement.

"But you look so smart in your uniform," Ella protested. "It all looks almost new."

"They're filthy, mother. You have no idea of the muck and vermin of that place."

"What about the boots," Michael gasped. "I wouldn't mind them if you don't want them."

Reluctantly, he gave them up. "But make sure you soak them in disinfectant for a few days first, and then really layer them thick with polish."

He nodded enthusiastically, and clutching them, backed off a few defensive yards, while the fiend poured kero over the rest and set it alight.

"You could have at least waited until everyone saw you in it, just once," Ella moaned.

Just once too often, he knew.

He had been back for a week now, and must have spent an accumulative two days of that in the bathtub.

"I'm sure it's not good for you," Ella insisted.

But every time he ran the water and popped himself in, that water would immediately turn the foulest yellow colour. He stank too, beside these more normally scented people he could smell his vileness quite distinctly. It was so bad that everyone tried to pretend they had a cold and couldn't smell anything. It seemed to him that he would never again be clean; it was becoming an obsession, this sense that the corruption that had permeated his flesh would never leave it. That, at least, was how he viewed it in his more imaginative moments: the murk of his body a match for the murk of his mind. But in reality, all he wanted was to be clean—it would be a nuisance to have to try and keep upwind of everybody for the rest of your life.

Sleeping was quite another matter. The truth was that he was very tired, and spending long hours in bed, but very little of that in sleep. His exhaustion demanded sleep, but sleep itself was an object of dread, and mostly he strove to stay fitfully awake. When he slept, dead men stalked the room, explosions erupted about the ceiling, and voices he knew screeched out him in their incredible agony. Not dreams, but memories, that his consciousness wanted to quickly forget but his subconscious could not. He would jolt awake, sweating and embarrassed as he would hear Wally padding down the hallway to quietly ask through the door if he was alright, and he would know that he had cried out again in his sleep. After the first few times, Wally stayed in bed, and although no one said anything, he knew that the nightly screams that shattered their way through the Griffin household were still going on.

And the reality could be as bad as the dreams. There was the inevitable night when his blind shot up, and he found himself out of bed and down on the floor, grappling for his rifle. Everywhere he went, his shattered nerves carried that imaginary weapon with him and it only took the slightest bang—a dropped cup, a TV shootout, or someone knocking at the door, and he would have them well and truly covered.

But if all that was too be expected, there was another effect that was very odd indeed. He would be wandering along, in a crowd, when suddenly the old sixth sense that always warned him of danger would come alive. He would stop, rubbing at the tingling in the back of his neck, looking about sharply. There, somewhere in the crowd, a Vietnamese would be standing some way off, staring at him, and that look would be one of purest hatred. And then the man would turn and be lost in the crowd. On the first occasion, he gave chase, but after that he didn't bother. It happened several times in that first week, and he could not tell whether it was the same man or a different one each time, but he was always Asian, and the glare of abhorrence always the same. Those fierce, despising eyes, seeing straight though his civilian disguise. It was, of course, some trick of the mind, but such knowledge didn't let it scare him any less. Every time it happened, his senses exploded within him. In that instant, that man—those men—were real.

If the nights found him restless, the waking hours were no improvement. Each day since his return, straight after breakfast, he would take to his old FJ Holden and be gone. Each time, he had little idea of where he was going; he had gone to the mountains, he had gone to the sea, and just about everywhere in between. At first it seemed that he was just trying to get the feel of being back—heading to old familiar places to have a look around, to see if they were still there. But the truth was it didn't seem to matter much where he went. He went down to the ocean but didn't go in the water; he went to the wildlife sanctuary but didn't cuddle any koalas; he went to the zoo and didn't throw a single peanut. He went to pubs and didn't talk to any girls; he went to movies that he had already seen. It was always late when he got home, which made what was happening all too obvious. The point of these expeditions dawned on him slowly—the truth was that it didn't matter where he went because he wasn't really going anywhere. What he was doing was not staying.

After a week, all this was perfectly plain to him as he sat propped up by the pillows, smoking his second Camel for the day, and continuing to blockade Wally from his lawn mowing duties. The restlessness, the nervousness, the evasion—all of these things might have been expected. The world he had once known so well and loved had waited for him unchangingly, reliably, predictably, biding his return. It had not changed, but he had. The two years that had passed might just as easily been two hundred. The truth of it was that he really cared for these people, for this world, and so much so that he was going to have to get out of it, right now, before he turned against them altogether.

It could no longer be evaded either. The culmination of these things had arrived last night with the occasion of his official welcome-home party, which amounted to yet another predictable gathering of his innumerable uncles and aunts. His uncles were all big bald men with huge beer bellies whose idea of a party was to stand in a broad circle around a keg of beer and heartily shout insults at each other. Wally had established the beer barrel in the garage, and Griffin took what he could only regard as his rightful place amongst them and indulged as best he could in the tumultuous conversation on the inevitable subjects of horseraces, cricket, football, duck shooting and the prevailing states of their various automobiles. In other circumstances, Griffin might have been quite happy to participate in this, but his period of absence had deprived him of the necessary immediacy needed to see anything new in it—or perhaps it really was that absolutely nothing had changed. Except himself.

From time to time, one or the other of the uncles would seem to remember the reason why Wally had been good enough to provide them with all this free beer.

"Hey Wally," Uncle George guffawed at one point. "Yer better not let Ella catch that boy of yours hoppin' inta the grog like that!"

"Then she'd better stay in the kitchen," Griffin muttered.

"He's over twenty-one," Wally was simultaneously saying. "He can do what he likes, George."

It seemed that only Wally's comment was heard, which was probably just as well. Still, just to show them, Griffin tossed off the rest of his beer and promptly poured himself another.

"Teach yer ter drink like that in the army, did they? " Uncle Bill snorted.

"Bet that's not all they taught him, haw, haw, haw," chortled Uncle Tom.

"They taught me how to kick fat little runts like you to death, Tom," Griffin mumbled into his new beer.

"Pity they didn't teach you to shoot straight, Tom," Wally was more acceptably saying. "Or we mighta got more ducks last year."

"Maybe we oughta take the boy along this year, Wally," Uncle Jim was saying,"You'd be a pretty good shot by now, wouldn't yer Boyo?"

"Can't hit anything smaller than a human target," Griffin said coldly.

But even when they could not help but hear him, it had no effect.

"He's probably done enough huntin' ter last him a while, hey Wally," Uncle Arthur grunted

And they all had a good laugh about that, and then carried on talking about the sort of sitting ducks that weren't just back from Vietnam.

While the uncles manned the barrel and their offspring ran rampant in the backyard, the womenfolk by tradition clustered in the kitchen and, while striving to make the preparations for supper as difficult as possible for whichever of their number was unfortunate enough to be hostess, they would jointly transmit the complete contemporary history of every member of the Griffin family—this continually punctuated by their hyena-like shrieks of laughter, shock or amazement.

Of all of his aunts, Aunt Merle was the most dangerous, not only because being the largest she was therefore the best clutterer, nor that she possessed the most piercing shriek, nor the most tenacious grip for wrenching the tray of uncreamed cakes from a dozen grasps, nor was it because her knowledge of the family gossip was the most profound. It was all these things combined, but worst, she, unlike the others, seemed to have the power to leave the kitchen from time to time and go ravaging in the vicinity of the beer barrel. And when she did escape, the object of her mission was invariably Kenneth. To be her favourite nephew was daunting enough—to be the favourite nephew in whose honour the party was being held was utterly unbearable. Griffin spent the entire evening in mortal dread of Aunt Merle.

All in vain, for when that night she tore herself away from the kitchen and came waddling into the garage, all of the uncles moaned in despair, since, by closing in on Griffin, she was also closing in on them

"Ohhh, there you are. Oh look at you. Standing there with all the men when only yesterday..."

Oh no, not the nappies.

"...we were changing his dirty nappies, weren't we Wally."

Wally only grunted. He knew his wife had done all the nappy changing, while the other women stood around telling her how it was done.

"Look at him. Now he's just a great big cuddly Teddy-bear and you just can't help but want to hug him..."

She advanced upon him, offering a cheek suffocatingly thick with powder to be kissed. At least the beer washed that down. She slipped her arms around him and pressed him firmly against her sponginess—to touch she was like a feather mountain.

"Oh, look how tall he's grown..."

He had, he was sure, been exactly the same height for three years now

"... just don't know anyone in the family that tall. I can't imagine where he gets it from, can you Wally?"

There were several men standing in front of her who were at least one inch taller than Griffin—Wally himself was a stunted six-foot-one. But for several decades, Wally had flatly refused to speak to Aunt Merle, and he saw no reason to change that now. In any event, Aunt Merle was not a person who needed to be answered in order to find the strength to carry on.

"Why," she was saying. "If you keep growing like that, Ken, you'll go right through the ceiling. I don't know, I just don't know."

"I think I've stopped now," Griffin ventured to say. Well, he had to say something.

"Oh, I do hope so. Why, you'll be so tall soon that you won't be able to hear us when we speak."

There were a few smiles on the faces around the barrel then, contemplating the pleasures of such a state.

Aunt Merle, meanwhile, was squeezing him so hard that she seemed to be trying to break him in two at the middle.

"And now you've been off to the war. Oh dear me. Why I remember when all these boys went off. I was at the ship to see you go, wasn't I Wally?"

Wally did manage to nod.

"And Charlie, and you Ted. Oh yes, I remember And then you all came home again, just like Ken has. It doesn't seem any time at all, does it. We were all so young then.."

And the uncles all cringed because it seemed that her train of thought had taken a bad turn for them—away from Griffin and in their direction

"Yes.... all so young. But it was a great adventure, oh yes. A real experience that made us all what we are. And now, dear Ken too," and she paused to look up at him. "I suppose you can't imagine us all once being as young as you are."

There was a smile and a nudge. Griffin carefully avoided the obvious, though only by means of keeping his mouth firmly shut.

"Oh yes, well. Life goes on, doesn't it," she was saying. "You're young and then you're old and life just goes on and on..." If not so much as Aunt Merle went on. "Nothing changes," she sighed—and the sigh was a good sign. "Isn't it good that nothing ever really changes?"

That sigh meant that she had allowed the kitchen gossip to go as far as it could without her. There was another fairly general sigh from all around the beer barrel when she finally toddled off back toward the indoors.

"Bloody old bag," Wally Griffin said.

But Aunt Merle, if gone, still left her mark, which was to inspire them to begin talking again about The War. The War, of course, was the Second World War, though they spoke of it as if it was the only one in history. Griffin tried to imagine it—his own experience magnified hundreds of thousands of times: Vietnam, really, he knew, was only a very little war.

Two of his uncles had died fighting the Germans, and three more had not survived the Japanese Prison Camps. They were remembered, but not because they had died, but instead because had they not died, they would have been here now, drinking and talking like this. No one said anything about how these men had died, or why. No one said anything about what they had seen, done, heard or felt themselves. They could speak of it only in general terms—it was as if they had not really been to The War, but instead made it up as a result of having seen too many American war movies. Just as Vietnam, to them, might have seemed to be no more than a collective figment of the imaginations of several television producers. For them, The War was only a memory, almost faded, and they were no longer able to talk about it with any sense of reality at all. In truth, they had forgotten The War.

"I don't suppose its any different these days, is it Boyo?"

Uncle Joe asked him suddenly. "Same bastard sergeants and such. Just these Vietcongs instead of the Japs, and I bet they ain't much different."

"Not much different," Griffin said quietly.

"You musta had some experiences, boyo," Uncle Louie said," Why don't yer tell us some of them, Yer ain't been sayin' much, and it's your party, ain't it."

"Nar, the boy don't wanna talk about all that," Uncle Jack was sure. "Do yer, lad. Yer wanna forget it, not talk about it alla time."

"How can you forget something like that?" Griffin asked viciously.

On the whole, that was a fairly silly thing to say. There was, of course, a rancorous edge to his voice as he made that exclamation, and it was that, rather than what he said, that brought proceedings to an awkward, momentary halt. Though only momentary.

"Nar, course yer don't forget, do yer Bob," Uncle Ron said jerkily, after a pause.

"Yer never forget," Uncle Bob concurred, and even shook his head to show how unforgettable it was.

"Some of them Jap tortures. Bloody horrible," Uncle Ron said with an air of dismay.

"Absolutely bloody horrible," Uncle Al agreed heartily.

Griffin seethed: "What tortures exactly? " he demanded of them.

"Ah, you know," Uncle Bert said. "You must know about 'em. After where you've been. Those Vietcongs do the same bloody things. I heard about it."

"Tell me what tortures exactly. Maybe they aren't the same," Griffin cried. He was beginning to feel pretty sadistic, but this was important, he was sure of it.

"Arrr, you know," Uncle Don said expansively. "Hey, remember Greyman Jacobs. He got tortured by the Japs."

"Yeah. Could hardly walk afterwards," Uncle John recalled. "Bloody horrible, it was."

"Why couldn't he walk?" Griffin persisted sorely. "What did they actually do to him so that he couldn't hardly fuckin' walk."

"They bloody tortured him," Uncle Doug roared back, as if Griffin was some sort of idiot who could not understand anything.

He was fully prepared to employ all available interrogation techniques but a steadily hand fell firmly on his shoulder.

"I think yer getting a bit carried away, son," Wally said firmly.

"I'm not getting carried away!" he screeched....

"Arr, it happens," Uncle Dan was saying. "Yer get a bit excited about it all when yer jes back, but then it goes away and it's alright again."

"You jest gotta take it easy, that's all," Uncle Alex agreed.

"You'll be alright after a while, son," Uncle Mike considered.

But Griffin was not about to be alright. Though he was certainly beaten for the moment, and so headed outside for some air that everyone would have agreed he needed.

Out in the yard, surrounding a table under the rotary clothes line, was an environment to which he might have thought he more naturally belonged. There was a gathering of his mates, some from school, some from footy, some from the insurance office. His contemporaries and equals, except they all had young wives or girlfriends which he solely lacked. But given time... He had talked to each of them earlier, when they arrived, of matters of mutual interest, and found that they didn't seem interesting anymore. But perhaps they would, when he got back into things. The only surprise was how young they all looked—much younger people than he remembered, only a year or so ago.

Age was their difficulty too. The wives and girlfriends, too young to be trapped in the kitchen, and able, with their attractiveness and sexual undertow, to keep their men away from the barrel, for the time being. Now they had accumulated as a group, and he walked up to them. They told him what a great party it was, when he knew it wasn't. They chatted. He yawned.

Then one of the girls—he wasn't quite sure which mate she belonged to, confronted him directly.

"You must be glad to be back, Ken," she smiled sweetly.

"I'd have been happier not to have gone," he replied automatically.

There was a shuffling of feet amongst his mates. Tommy Granger, half-back flanker for the Moorabbin Black Arabs, expressed what seemed to be a universal discomfort.

"When they didn't draw my birthdate, I was pleased. But now, thinking about it, I really reckon I missed out on something."

"You didn't," Griffin assured him.

"I failed me medical," said Greg Taubert from the office. He looked pretty fit to Griffin.

"It must have been a real experience," the same girl persisted.

"Oh, it was, it was."

"And you were in the fighting. Like, not just back at the base all the time."

"No. I was combat duties."

"Oh? So tell me, how many people did you kill?" she asked blithely.

"I lost count after the first hundred," he answered casually.

He was ready for that. It was the stock answer he had carefully implanted in his head, just in case some moron asked the question.

And yet he said it so coldly, ruthlessly, that only a silence could follow. Then they each turned to the other and said things like. "I reckon I'll get a few games with the firsts this season."

"Don't you think Angela looks really lovely this evening."

"I think I'd go water the lemon tree."

Griffin got out of there, even though there was nowhere to go. Certainly not toward the house, where he could hear Aunt Merle and the others shrieking. He went the other way, toward the incinerator and oblivion.

In the furtherest corner of the backyard, he found someone else apparently in need of air—his brother Michael who sat on the chopping block absently stroking the family dog.

"Big brother, you are really pissed."

"I certainly fucking am "

"That's twenty-three."

"Twenty-three what?"

"Twenty-three fucks you have dropped this evening. And nine cunts I haven't been counting the bloodys and buggers."

When Griffin had been making extreme efforts to be careful about that.

"Shit," he breathed

"That's fourteen shits."

Griffin grinned: "And nobody said a word."

"Nope," Michael sighed. "And you've been smoking fags three at a time and drinking more than everyone else put together. You bloody war heroes can get away with anything."

"Except going to wars."

"I wish I could go to a war," Michael grumbled.

"You don't want to go to Vietnam, Mickey. It's a horrible fucking place."

"Twenty-four."

"I'm serious, mate. You just can't imagine how bad it is there."

"That bad, huh?" he said sarcastically. "Funny it doesn't show."

"What am I supposed to do. Run around tearing my hair out?"

"You could tell me about it. Nobody around here ever tells anyone anything."

"These things are hard to talk about. It's just completely impossible to describe something as disastrous as a war to someone who's never experienced anything like that."

"You got wounded. Tell me about that."

"It was nothing. Just a scratch. I showed you the scar."

"And you don't really remember how it happened."

"That's right. It's the truth, really. What do you want me to do? Make up some gory story to give you all nightmares?"

"Be better than trying to convince us that you got shot and failed to notice."

"I wasn't shot. It was..."

"Just a bit of shrapnel. Yeah I know."

"That's all there is, Mickey. Really."

"You came back early. The rest of your outfit is still there. Why? You haven't explained that."

"I just..." he began, but stopped short. Only minutes later, he was doing the same thing that he had berated his uncles for doing. He sighed: "I had a sort of breakdown. Can't explain it really. I just stopped functioning. So they sent me home."

"Why did you have a breakdown? What caused it?"

"Nothing specific. Everything just built up on me, and I stopped coping..."

"Coping with what?"

"Jesus, Mickey. How can I explain. The context just doesn't exist. I just..."

Just what? Shot friends? Blew children away? Drooled over splattered corpses? Drank too much? It wasn't anything in particular. It was all of it. Anxiety neurosis, the doctors had called it.

"...It was just an attack of anxiety."

Michael's expression only grew cold at that lame effort. "You went away a kid like me. You come back older than any of them blokes in there. Just an attack of anxiety, you say. That doesn't tell me anything. You're no different to them in there. How's anyone supposed to know about wars if no-one talks about it."

"Alright. What do you want to know?"

"How many people did you kill?"

"All by myself, unassisted? None."

"What do you mean by unassisted?"

"In the jungle warfare, the usual situation is a bunch of blokes all firing into a patch of jungle where they reckon a bunch of other blokes are firing back at them. People end up dead, but you usually just can't tell which holes you put in them personally. It's a team effort. Everything is shared, including bodies."

"How many then. Assisted."

"Depends on how you count them. A dozen maybe. More, if you count possibilities. Hundreds, if you count airstrikes and artillery that I was partly responsible for bringing down on them."

"So you don't really know?"

"Not really."

"You don't really want to know?"

"Not if I can avoid it."

"So what's the hassle. It's a job. You did your job. Where's the big deal? Why did you have a breakdown when all the others didn't?"

Griffin let out a long sigh. He thought about saying what he had to say next. Somehow he knew that the words, once spoken, would tarnish his life irreparably for all time, in the eyes of his brother, and the world. To speak it was to diminish himself, for eternity.

"Mickey, some of them—some of the assisted kills in which I figured prominently, or more prominent than anyone else—some of them were children. And some of them were other Australians."

To that, he shrugged. To that, he could actually shrug!

"So what. That sorta thing happens in wars. I've seen it in movies. On telly. You can't help things like that happening in wars. They're like that."

"They're not like that. Mickey, the world isn't the way you see it on television."

"Now we're getting to it. How is it not? Tell me what the hell they did to you."

Stopped again. Weakening everything with words, of which there were none in the language that could possibly hope to express it.

"Mickey, you aren't getting it. The problem isn't what they

did to me. It's what I did to them. You become a monster, some sort of primeval hunter-killer to which the most abominable things become normal, natural. You go along with it, even enjoy it or at least get stimulated by it. Then I come back here and I'm supposed to behave what they call normally. Sorry, we've changed the rules again. That isn't okay anymore. You gotta do this instead. But this isn't normal. The Beast, soaked in the blood of others, savaging through the jungle. That's normal. And this, all this...civilisation. All this around you is bullshit. And when you've actually experienced being the crude, basic, primordial, instinctive monster that we all really are, then the bullshit becomes too hard to swallow."

"Sure. Okay. But you do swallow it, like them in there. Like you were doing to me a minute ago. And then it's all okay. Did you really go there and do all that for no better reason than so you could continue swallowing bullshit along with the rest of us? *The beast within us*. They talk about that in sixth grade. In church even. You aren't telling me anything."

"Jesus, what did I have to do? Get my fucking head blown off?"

Michael was walking away in disgust, leaving Griffin with a head that, if not exactly blown off, was anything but intact.

But then it was supper time and the three factions of the party converged upon the kitchen to jostle for best positions around a table sagging under the weight of things that had to be dunked in tomato sauce or left great icicles of whipped cream clinging to upper lips, all of which gladly made conversation impossible. This pause, though, could only be regarded as something of a prelude to disaster, for immediately supper was devoured, it would be time for the next door neighbour, Mr McKenzie, who was a member of toastmasters, to demonstrate his skills and stand himself upon a chair, delivering for the delight of all the official speech of the evening.

"Ladies and Gentlemen, boys and girls," Mr McKenzie began. It was probably that 'boys and girls' line that did it, for he looked with a huge smile toward young Michael when he said it: "It is my pleasure to say a few words on this auspicious occasion. As you all know, we are gathered here this evening to welcome home from distant conflicts our dear, young friend Ken, who as you all know, has just returned from Vietnam..."

"Yeah, we know," Michael said bitterly.

He was facing Griffin across the table at the time, and could be offered a smile of encouragement, while from behind,

Narelle gave him a nudge that nearly knocked him off his feet. Griffin realised, with mild surprise, that there was more than one Griffin brother who might have had too much to drink.

"... Of course, I must first say how glad we are to see him home unharmed...." Mr McKenzie continued.

"Except for a hole in the leg," Michael interjected.

Mr McKenzie, who had survived Michael's first comment without the slightest flinch, did hesitate this time for a glance at the culprit.

"...yes, well... Um... For this fact, I am sure, is a great relief to his parents, our friends, Wally and Ella, who have seen fit to raise their children in a strong Christian morality..."

"Not anymore," Michael chuckled.

To the flank, Griffin could see Wally closing in on him.

Mr McKenzie struggled on: ".... and they have produced in young Ken the fine, upstanding and brave young man you see before you now...."

"A drunken, foul-mouthed tobacco-addict," Michael laughed, and then Wally had him, by the hair from behind, and twisted his head right back. Wally's other hand slapped quite firmly over his young son's mouth, and in a flash, Michael vanished from view, dragged out to the rear of the audience.

This Griffin watched dispassionately. Mickey would get only what he deserved, but that wasn't it. When lies were told in public, the truth always led to persecution. When the gunner went down in the fight, the only thing to do was pick up the gun and carry on into the fray.

".... What young Ken has been doing has one of the longest and most famous traditions in the world behind it. I refer to the Anzac tradition, that fine tradition of our young fighting men that began with the Boer War and has continued on almost unbroken until this very day. The Anzac Tradition is the finest that this troubled modern.."

"The Anzac Tradition is a lot of bullshit," Griffin heard himself say.

"... world that..,. what ?..."

Griffin turned on the good Mr McKenzie—who probably didn't deserve it, but did, because he had troubled to open his big mouth in the first place.

"The Anzac Tradition, sir, is fucked," he growled. "Anzacs spend their lives crawling around the place pissed off their brains, up to their arses in shit, frightened silly and shooting at each other as much as the enemy."

And a deathly silence descended upon the scene, except perhaps for the gasps of Michael who, out of sight, could still be heard battling to get free of his father.

Before him now was a broad array of singularly astonished faces. And then, almost as one, their voices raised in protest, not words, but gasps and moans and mutterings. Only his mother spoke—she was standing almost right beside him. "Now, Ken. I really don't think you're being very fair to Mr McKenzie, who has...."

"Mr McKenzie is not being fair to the world in general, laying on a lot of crap like that," Griffin interrupted. He had never before had cause to speak back to her like that. "I'm sorry, mother," he added. "but it just isn't right."

"There's such a thing as common courtesy," she bit back at him. The poor woman—he could see that he had hurt her beyond imagining.

"Perhaps if I were to propose a toast," Mr McKenzie offered magnanimously.

"There won't be any fucking toasts," Griffin exploded. "Listen to me, will you. You men, you know what I mean. Over there in Vietnam, young blokes like me are killing and getting killed, and it's for no fucking good reason whatsoever..."

"Do please mind your language, Ken,!" Aunt Merle cried. "My goodness, I've never heard anything like it."

"Well, I'm sorry too, about the language, but that is the language of war. It's the only way to describe it..."

"Well, it's getting to be a dry argument," one of the uncles said. Several others agreed, and in a flash, people were shuffling out of the room.

"Ohhhh, it's all this damned drinking," Ella Griffin cried, and was in tears too. Aunts were assisting her off into the next room.

"Wait a minute," Griffin cried. "I've got more to say...."

"I think you've said more than enough," Mr McKenzie gruffed, and was off. And they all trooped off, the uncles back to the barrel, the aunts to hide in the bedrooms, the others back to the yard and the music. Until there was only Wally Griffin, and his two wayward sons.

Michael stood off a small distance, it was plain that Wally had ruffled him up a bit and he looked subdued. Wally, surprisingly, did not look at all angry.

"They wouldn't listen," Griffin murmured.

Wally just stood there shaking his head at the pair of drunken, loudmouthed morons that his sons had become.

"It isn't important," Wally said.

"It was important," he cried.

"You can't say anything important if there ain't anyone around to hear it, son," Wally said.

Griffin was sobering up rapidly, if perhaps not so rapidly as his father.

"Sorry, Wally," he said finally. "I guess I fucked up a perfectly good party."

"I'll say you did," Michael squawked.

"Shut up you," Wally growled at him, but he did not growl at Griffin, instead he was grinning. "Anyone who manages to save us from one of Macca's speeches is alright by me."

Griffin grinned. "I think it was the youngest over here who ought to get the credit for that."

Wally eyed Michael slyly. "The youngster over here will get credit for things when he's old enough to know what he's doing, and not before. Now, off to bed, laddie, before I tan your hide."

"Aw shit," Michael said.

"That's one," Griffin chuckled.

"Move!" Wally bellowed.

And Michael vanished in a flash. Griffin could laugh. Wally, his father, had all too plainly been a sergeant after all. It was strange he had never noticed that before.

For the rest of the evening Griffin sat finishing himself off. The guests were leaving in droves and you could hear them out the front as Wally and Ella escorted them to their cars.

"I understand Ella," they were universally saying. "The poor young chap. He's obviously been through a lot."

"Yes, it'll take him a while to settle down, I suppose," Ella would cheerfully answer. By now, he had at least developed the sense and anyway, lack of coherence to avoid bothering to want to comment on things like that. Everyone was anxious to assure Ella and Wally that it had been a lovely evening. He heard Ella assure Wally that she would never again allow drink in the house, before she took herself off to bed. And then, Griffin was alone.

And now it was the morning after and the time for regretting things like that. His hangover was nowhere near as bad as he might have liked it to be. After his third Camel, he got out of bed, got dressed, and headed out to the backyard, where indeed the lawnmower stood, fuelled up, ready for action. But Wally, who was over in the Vegie patch, was a patient and tolerant man, and did not rush to start it up the moment his son appeared.

"Well," he said,"I'll bet you're feeling good this morning."

"Terrific,"

"A man likes to be proud of his son," he sighed, and continued what he was doing, which was pulling up ripe carrots.

"I wasn't wrong."

"Now don't start in on me," Wally warned, pointing one of those carrots at him like it was a gun.

"You knew, all along, didn't you."

"You aren't the only bloke who come back from a war, you know."

"So you knew what to expect."

"More or less. All wars are the same. They affect young blokes the same. Some of them take a long time to get over it. Others never do."

He silently watched his father pulled up a few more carrots.

"Well," he had to ask. "What's up?"

Griffin shrugged—but there was nothing to do with someone like Wally except to be blunt and straight to the point.

"I gotta go," he said.

"Surprised you lasted so bloody long as you did," he answered without looking up. "Where you going?"

"Some friends have got a spare room. I might move in there."

"Fair enough," he said. "You leaving before or after lunch."

"Sooner the better."

"And you want me to tell your mother," and he shot Griffin an ironic look.

Pause. "Ahhh, no. I can do it, I suppose."

"Better if I do it," Wally said resignedly. "God knows what you might say to her. I already warned her, anyway."

"Warned her?"

"That you'd probably be restless. Probably not want to stay around. She even understood, sort of."

He stood up then, and was pulling off his garden gloves and walking over to face him.

"Well, what you hanging around for?" he asked with a grin. Griffin shrugged, and then started off. "Oh. You better give me the address of where yer going to."

"I'll call you. Don't know it off hand. Not far away. Be able to visit for Sunday dinner or whatever."

Wally nodded. He suspected he knew what that meant too. He held out his hand and they shook, just as they had the day

Griffin first went in the army.

Griffin went inside, grabbed his things, jumped in his car, and was off. He was feeling just a little cowardly for not waiting for the others to come home from church, and pretty hungry to know that he was missing out by choice on one of Ella's wonderful Sunday dinners. But there would be more of them, he supposed. There just wasn't any need to make a scene about it—and no need to stay any longer. He might not have known *where* he was going, but only that he *was*. For, as Wally must have suspected, those friends with a spare room somewhere simply did not exist.

Last Leg

Over the border into Queensland, two hundred kilometres out of Brisbane now and Griffin driving hard, unable to convince himself that this was other than the last leg of the journey. And still nothing said, for Lew was always a man to avoid dramatic confrontations whereas Griffin, overtly selfconscious about the melodramatics in both his writing and his life, was holding back as long as he could. But nothing, of course, would happen unless he forced it to be so. It was true that since he had been thrown out of his studies at RMIT, Lew was again vulnerable to being drafted. But there was no need for Lew to hide under the bed every time someone knocked on the front door and certainly no need for this so called escape expedition. As far as Griffin knew, the Feds didn't actively seek draft dodgers anymore. Nevertheless, it was technically true that Griffin was aiding and abetting the felon, so what sort of a turncoat did that make him? The right sort, he supposed. It didn't bear thinking about and didn't need to be thought about either. For there was another deeper reason why they were here—one that Lew still refused to face up to. Surely he did not plan to land them on her doorstep and then try to make some explanation of himself. Ludicrous!

Late in the afternoon they came down from the mountains on the sweeping curves of Cunningham's Gap and away beyond the plains could be seen the urban sprawl of Brisbane—mainly in the form of a smoggy smudge. And with that sight, Griffin could contain himself no longer—he was tired, hungry, driving mechanically, Lew lulling beside him, the Monster snoring and snorting in the back as they shot down onto the plains. Keeping his voice level and calm, and no doubt very falsely conversational, Griffin asked quietly. "Did you tell her we were coming?"

As precarious as his situation might have been, Lew could still smile and direct a sly gaze at Griffin. "Been reading my mail, have you?"

"The envelopes hissed at me when I opened the letterbox."

The old game: I know, you know I know, I know you know I know...

"Yeah, alright. So she's been writing and asking me to come and see her."

"Does she know we're coming?"

"I told her I was coming, Griffin. Though somehow I think I forgot to mention you."

"I get to be a big surprise, huh?"

"You worry about things too much," Lew said flatly.

"It gives life that little added tension, Lewington, that makes it worth living."

Lew laughed. At least he felt he could laugh about it. But then he realised he was supposed to be serious, and so rummaged around until he found a solemn tone.

"Dell," Lew said, "is a very professional and very sensible lady, and not entirely the dragon you reckon she is. She's doing very well, apparently. Making pots of money."

"Did you ever know an engineer who didn't?"

"It will all be mature and adult. You'll see."

"Lew, she thinks I'm the most despicable human being on the planet."

"Yeah, well, in any event, Griffin, she'll probably be so happy to see me that she won't even notice you're there."

*

In fact the last hour of the journey took them three, largely due to a lack of visible street signs in Brisbane's endless maze of identical suburbs—all stilted single-storey dwellings badly in need of a coat of paint. They had to stop and go into a couple of pubs to ask directions and argue over a pot or two about whose fault it was that they were where they were instead of where they ought to have been. It was long past nightfall when they located Cleveland and Lew switched from the Brisbane and Environs Map to a rather tattered letter from Dell on which, Griffin could only hope, the final street instructions were inscribed. They went down a bumpy road beyond which the moonlight glistened on the glassy waters of Moreton Bay, stretching away to a larger lump on the horizon—Stradbroke Island, Lew informed.

"Bit of an improvement on Elm Street, Lewington."

"Yes, Griffin. Dell always was one for getting on in the world."

They found the number, a low, long rather new dwelling with bay windows under palm trees that stood on the immaculate lawn, glowing orange curtains imbued with the light from within, and the water of the bay lapping only thirty yards from the front door.

"Lewington, this has to be the wrong place. It's altogether too opulent," Griffin cried.

Even Lew Sigg gazed at it blankly for a while. "I'm sure it's the right number, though," he murmured.

"Maybe its one of daddy's many assets."

"No. Hers. She bought and paid for it herself. I knew she was making money but I didn't realise she was making this much."

"One appreciates depth in a relationship, Lewington."

They rolled the Jag to a halt on the grass at the water's edge and, still somewhat dazed, climbed out. The humans that was—the Monster, less able to be astonished by material things, utterly flew out the window and was off this way and then that, overwhelmed by a thousand canine possibilities. There were frogs jumping on the lawn to be sprung upon, strange trees to be spotted, water lapping down there to cool off and lots of mud for a good roll after, and there had to be plenty of cats and possums too to be run up into the branches where they belonged. A true paradise.

Lew and Griffin walked across the narrow beachfront road toward the house, Lew in the lead, Griffin tending to hang back, and before they had traversed half the distance, the door of the house flew open, bathing them incriminatingly in light, and a silhouetted figure in a nearly transparent flowing caftan stood there, peering out.

"Good God," Dell gasped.

Lew could immediately make a pantomime of it, pointed thisthatway. "Hello, my love. We just happened to be in the neighbourhood and saw the light..."

Dell, her long sheening black hair down and eyes alight, stood on the porch, hands on hips, looming over them. "What the bloody hell are you doing here?" she demanded fiercely, to show she could fake anything as easily as Lew could, "I was sure that no one I knew would be driving a car like that...what a bomb....where on earth did you get it?...and why the bloody hell didn't you let me know you were coming?"

She towered, glaring savagely, demanding answers. Lew looked lamely at Griffin as if he hoped he might know the right reply, whereas Griffin was trying to look like he did not exist at all. And then she sprang like a panther to clasp Lew firmly about the neck, though not to do him harm, but to shower him with kisses.

"You bastard. You rotten bastard," she slobbered at him through it all.

He finally fought her off—she leaned back on his embracing forearms and smiled as hugely as she could. Griffin waited it out, looking everywhere but at the scene before him, and she did eventually seem to notice that he was there. Surprisingly, she did not beat Lew Sigg to death for bringing his deadbeat friend, instead she simply looked Griffin right in the eye and allowed her smile to fade.

"Hello Griffin," she said, very coolly.

"Hello Dell," Griffin answered, as brightly as he could manage.

"I see you brought your silly fucking dog," she then added brilliantly.

Lew and Griffin exchanged bleak glances—no way on earth was there an answer to something like that.

They stood there for a moment, while Dell celebrated her all-conquering wit and subtlety. Plainly no one quite knew what they should do next. It was Dell, finally, who broke the deadlock. "Well, I suppose you'd better come in."

"Yes," Lew said, "I suppose we had."

Walking into Dell's sumptuous house, Griffin could not have felt more like an invader. Everything was so clean and modern and untouchable, the white fluffy carpets, the stylish leather armchairs, the long orange curtains dropping all the way to the floor. Vases obviously long searched for in antique shops held freshly cut flowers, prints on the wall if not real paintings were at least the works of great artists—the one exception being a rather large and gory mess of an original by Lewington Sigg. The wooden table at the centre must have been a hundred years old before it was redressed—you could almost smell the fresh woodstain. The whole thing generally had the effect of exactly what it was—a new modern house recently obtained by an owner who immediately rushed out to buy all the right things to fill it.

It was all so clean and nice—Griffin could only shudder at the thought how Dell must have endured the grisly circumstances at Elm Street all those years, if this was where her true nature lay. How she must have hated it. And now the two travellers themselves, dirty, smelling and sweaty, standing in the midst of it all, completely defiling everything. Though Dell, gushing about in her flimsy caftan, did not seem at all concerned.

"Sit down, sit down," she cried, waving her arms at the chairs whose leatherwork bristled with horror at the thought, "I'm sorry, I don't have any beer. Would you like some coffee?"

Griffin, dying of thirst, thought it wise to let Lew answer. "Oh I suppose. Or if the pub is still open..."

"You could have some coffee first," Dell said, already attacking the percolator.

"Okay," Lew relented.

"Griffin?"

"Yes thanks Dell."

And he slithered his way into one of those armchairs and allowed himself to sag.

Dell swept across the room, again casting her arms around Lew's neck and smiling a radiant smile that Griffin could not for the life of him remember her possessing in the past. Though of course she must have.

"You both must be very tired," she was saying while the coffee bubbled, "Was it a hard journey? How long did it take you? And where on earth did you get that extraordinary car?"

Griffin was suddenly acutely aware of her American accent, a Californian accent, he knew. That was something else about her he had tended to forget. The years in Australia had once caused that accent to fade such that only strangers really noticed it—now it seemed to be asserting itself again. Perhaps she had been back home again, and no one had told him. No reason why anyone should have.

But mostly you had to try and conjure an image of this undoubtedly ravishing female in the world of Engineering—incongruously perfect, fulfilling every smarmy consultants wildest fantasies. Certainly this was not any Dell Turner that Griffin had ever known, if indeed he could have been said to have known her at all. While Lew endeavoured to answer her innumerable questions, Griffin shrivelled in his chair like a vampire exposed to her dazzling light.

Then, suddenly, she was towing Lew off toward the deeper reaches of the house, and Griffin supposed he couldn't blame them for that. Lovers, if that was what they were to be called, were after all entitled to such things.

Griffin sat, percolating along with the coffee—a bit of patience and tolerance was what he needed now. They had disappeared behind what had to be a bedroom door, and Griffin, grappling out a cigarette with sweaty fingers, looked around for an ashtray. There was none—Dell, inconsiderately, did not smoke. He silently rose from his chair and went to the kitchen where he hoped to find an old cracked saucer or an empty matchbox. Such things were an impossibility in so pristine a place, but at least it kept him close to the percolator, the bubbling of which might shut out other less palatable sounds that he could reasonably expect to begin to occur. Not that he hadn't heard it all before, on many a lonely night through the thin walls at Elm Street, but mostly he did not want to hear it now. Perhaps he was lonely and homesick already...?

"Hey Griffin, where are you?" Lew was suddenly calling softly.

"In here. Looking for an ashtray."

"Well, belay the fag a minute. Come here."

If there was somewhere he knew he did not want to go, it was the 'there' defined by 'here'. But of course he had to. He slipped the unlit cigarette back into the packet and crept back into the lounge room.

Lew stood by the door, thankfully still decently dressed. He was crooking a finger at Griffin, beckoning, luring, him closer and smiling the very strangest of smiles while he did so. Griffin advanced edgily, up to the door of the dimly lit room that, indeed, was some sort of bedroom. Lew virtually had to drag him in there, and as he looked across he saw Dell standing over in the corner, again wearing that brilliant smile he was sure he had never seen before. She exchanged a glance with Lew—they were teasing him—and then with her eyes she redirected his gaze to a different part of the room. Over there was something so completely unmistakable that he could only gape in disbelief, and, even when Lew gave him a shove to set him moving that way, he was still refusing to accept what had to be in there even though there was only one possibility. He peeped over the edge and down amid the whiteness and softness there was indeed a wrinkled head the size of a newly ripened grapefruit and a miniature of a hand on the crumpled pillow.

Knowing that his continued astonishment was making a complete fool of him, Griffin still had to look questioningly at Dell who was content with a smile that answered all his questions and was moving in to join Lew at the side of the cot. Griffin transferred his gaze to Lew, who could manage a shrug and then a wink. "I don't suppose you've met my son," Lew said quietly.

Defending Alfie Magee

The words *W.R. Keep—Smash Repairs* were painted in fading letters on the cracked plaster wall above the gaping doorway of the tired building, standing starkly fifty metres back from the highway, surround by languid hills of yellow grass and clumps of spindly gum trees. Annexed to either side were sheds, one leaning wearily on the main structure, the other completely collapsed. Two tall gums, leaning at the same angle in deference to the prevailing wind, stood like sentinels to either side of the broad dusty tarmac. Here two dozen wrecked cars were placed in neat rows, like soldiers melted by some hideous weapon before they had time to break ranks. The cars were like tombstones in a graveyard of failed journeys, the degree of rust denoting the time elapsed since unspoken tragedy had transformed a destination into oblivion, or at least a casualty ward.

Griffin sat in his car regarding the scene grimly, his elbow out the window, his eyes squinted in the intense morning sunlight. He had driven into this highway town, his eyes searching the roadside for the visage that lay opposite him now, and when he saw it, pulled off the road and bumped along the gravel to a halt opposite. Other cars roared by him like bullets, instantaneously obscuring and restoring his view, ignoring the cold warning that it offered. Every car that passed was speeding, those going north picking up speed for the long climb immediately ahead, the southbound making no obvious attempt to deplete their momentum from the steep downhill run, bravely ignoring the speed limit that began here on the outskirts of the town.

This was the place where the highway from Melbourne departed the coastal plain and ascended onto the Great Dividing Range, from the plateaus of which the whole continent opened up. That way lay the great river basins of New South Wales, glittering harbour-bound Sydney, tropical Queensland and the Great Barrier Reef and eventually Cape York Peninsula, the northernmost tip of Australia. But long before any of those places, there was the turn-off to Puckapunyal, where Griffin was headed this one last time. And this spot the halfway point of his journey, with Melbourne's smoggy blur still visible forty kilometres behind him and the whole city visible from the top of the steep hill ahead. Pretty Sally Hill—the most infamous and treacherous kilometre of road in the state.

He regarded it now. Three wide lanes each way rearing straight up the slope to disappear over the hump and reappear further on, just before going into the long wide curve at the crest. It was hard to understand what the danger was—the semi-trailers crashing down through the gears, the cars whipping by them in two passing lanes, the visibility good, the road surface excellent. Perhaps that was the trouble, that the climb or descent could be taken too fast and was too frequently and the odds of survival became appalling should anything go even slightly wrong. In the year he spent at Puckapunyal, Delta Company lost five dead and ten permanently maimed on that hill, a higher casualty rate than it suffered in the subsequent year of combat in Vietnam. Griffin didn't want to think about that—on compulsion, he saw a gap in the traffic and fired his engine, sending his own car across the highway and into WR Keep's yard.

There was a bugger-up with his discharge papers and a month after his return from Vietnam, he was required to proceed to Army Records at Puckapunyal and sort the matter out. When he hoped to be rid of it forever, here he was back in military green, his boots polished, brass shined, greens starched. They had given him some service medals but he didn't wear them and, to be less soldierly, he deliberately left his slouch hat in the car. The black patch of sweat he knew showed on the back of his shirt from the car seat pleased him too. Still, he noticed, when he walked, he was prone to march.

He heard about it on the news the night before, when the names of the victims that had been released by the police were announced. 'Alfred James Magee, twenty-two, died when his car skidded off the road on Pretty Sally hill last night...'

It took Griffin a moment to realise that he knew who that was. And so as he drove through the town of Wallan, he was on the lookout for the Holden in that unforgettable shade of green he remembered and when he saw it, he stopped. It was at the very front of the bunch of cars collected by WR Keep. Griffin parked some distance from all of them, as if he feared the dreadful disease that had destroyed these vehicles might contaminate his own. He kicked the door open and walked toward the wreck with slow strides.

The principle impact had occurred at the left front where the mudguard was ripped away, the wheel buckled under and the bonnet crushed into a V shape as if a giant had struck it a mighty blow with his fist. You could see where the paint had been sheared off and the exposed metal skin was torn and clotted with red dirt where it had clawed at the earth in a desperate bid to arrest its berserk career. The metal exposed by stripped paint gleamed in the sun and the roof flattened where it had gone over. You could see where the police had cut the door with oxy-torches to get the driver out. Beneath the car was a huge pool of oil as if the wounded vehicle had crawled here in its agony and finally bled to death.

Griffin walked a complete circuit of the car, his face lined with disgust. There was no blood although probably that had been hosed out. The steering wheel was tangled with the shredded seat and the dashboard crushed downward. From the rearview mirror clearly visible through the shattered windscreen, a small St Christopher hung on a string. It might have been the only indication of Alfie Magee's existence that was left.

From out of the shadows of the garage, a man came walking. Short and bald and dressed in filthy overalls, he waddled forward, toward Griffin, plucking at his teeth with a long stem of grass as he came. Griffin wanted to go then—just walk away before this man reached him. But it was too late.

"Know him, didja?" the man called.

Griffin was filled with denial but, because he couldn't reject Alfie verbally, had to settle for a brief shake of his head.

The man, Mr Keep presumably, was weather-beaten and stubble-chinned, and his eyes squinted at Griffin with overt doubt.

"Soljerboy, he was. Jus like you."

"Yeah," Griffin said. "There's a lot of us around."

"Half these cars belong to soljars," Mr Keep said in his staccato voice. "And there's three more yards like this one in the area, and it's the same wif them."

"I guess."

"Happened up there. Always does with the soljars. They come through here too fast alla time and it's just a matter of time before one of 'em goes. Accidents gowan someplace to happen. And up there on Pretty Sally—that's where they happen, like as not."

"Everyone knows Pretty Sally," Griffin had to concur.

"There's lotsa you soljars go back and forth to Pucka alla time and I sees 'em go by and say, one a these days... Seen this bloke lots, gowan like the powers. Knew he'd go, and he did."

"Doesn't look like a fast car," Griffin said—what he didn't say was that the Alfie he knew didn't drive or do anything else at other than an irritatingly slow pace.

"Ah, he was travellin' orright. Have a look at how he hit. He comes over the top like a bat outa hell and there's ice up there cause of the frost and his loses it and goes over and into the bank and back out onto the highway, rollin' and rollin'. Lotta traffic up there at the time and he comes tumbling through the middle and misses the lot of 'em. Sure was a lotta lucky folks up there that night."

"He wasn't," Griffin said.

"He'da died ten times with the way he hit and bounced and rolled and hit. Took the coppers three hours to get the body out. Sure made a mess of himself."

Griffin didn't answer. He didn't want to know any of this. Morbid curiosity had led him here and it was begin punished beyond imagining. Griffin started walking back toward his car, but the old man followed.

"You been to the war, son?" he asked.

"Yeah, I been to the war."

Griffin was in the car and got the engine going, but the old man came and leaned on the window, filling the interior with his pungent breath.

"Doncha reckon this bloke woulda been better off dead in the war, than to die like this, fer no good reason."

"No," Griffin said. "When you're dead, you're dead, Pop. Reasons don't make it any different."

He roared the engine and the old man backed off, and Griffin drove out to the highway, throwing spiteful dust and gravel at the yard of WR Keep. He felt sick and disgusted, and roared his car up the hill, as if just to show the old man how right he was. But was he right? Would Alfie have been better off dead in Vietnam than here? Who could say—certainly not Alfie Magee, who didn't want to kill anybody, except maybe himself. Maybe Alfie did die there. Maybe they all did. Maybe it didn't matter anymore.

As he topped the long climb and approached the bend, he could see immediately where it happened. There were black streaks of desperately grasping tyres swerving across the road surface, ingrained diamonds of crushed glass embedded between the stones of the gravel, there a white post had been knocked out of the ground and beyond a great deal of gouging in the face of the cutting.

For an instant, it flashed before Griffin's eyes—night, lights glaring wildly, the white car going over, the wide-eyed frantic

Alfie at the wheel, staring at oncoming death in horror. Griffin shook the image away and drove on, around the bend and into the hills beyond. He felt just a little bit ill. Poor Alfie. Silly little useless bugger. Right to the end...

Twenty minutes later, he was cruising into Puckapunyal. The day was hot and dusty and the wind swirled as it always did here. But for Tit Hill—perhaps the most appropriately named geographical feature in the country—and the distant larger bald lump of Mt Puckapunyal, everything was flat and yellow and brown.

The long rows of barrack huts stood back amongst the trees, the broad parade ground unsheltered to the sun and wind. Remarkably for the army, it was all rather discrete. Just the odd sign with arrows indicating the direction of various units at intersections—the unit names in that coded form that he still found not quite comprehensible. 2RTB was familiar, of course, but *3rdRE,TR,ut* was vague.

The distant shabby barracks that had once housed the Pig Battalion was now *1stSTHN,Trg,coy*. It didn't look any different. Here and there, a tank or artillery piece stood on a grassy patch surrounded by the low chain fence. Without them, it would have been quite impossible to guess what went on here at all.

Until he saw the soldiers marching... His temptation for a nostalgic run-around the place diminished immediately. There were a dozen men out there in the heat, and a Land Rover parked nearby. An officer with a cane stuffed under his arm stood, bellowing at men rigidly at attention.

Then six of the men moved in slow march toward the Land Rover and begin to remove a long wooden box. They were going through the drill, Griffin realised, for funeral honours.

There wasn't any reason to doubt that in a day or two, they would be doing it for real, at where-ever Alfie Magee was to be committed to the earth.

Griffin slowed the car at the nearest edge of the parade ground and slowly got out, plucking the wet, sweating patch of his shirt as he did so. It was hot out there but the trees threw some shade so he didn't want to bother with his slouch hat... but then he realised he was still a soldier and on an army base. He grabbed the new slouch hat they had issued him and fitted it to his head, pulling the chin strap under—it felt weirdly unfamiliar.

He checked his brass, his boots and rubbed the dust off on his calves, and then walked with all due reverence to the shade patch and stood watching.

The six men carrying the coffin had apparently arrived at the imaginary grave and stamped loudly to a halt. Lowering the box, they fumbled, sending the officer into a paroxysm of rage at which Griffin smiled—even he could see they weren't very good.

"You all look like you've got oranges for balls!" the officer was bellowing. "It's a slow march, not a fucking fan dance!"

The other men snapped their rifles at the sky but didn't fire, for the officer was too busy strutting like a rooster meeting a rival and roaring at his charges, to give the order to fire. Thank God, Griffin was smiling to himself, that all this was now in the past for him.

Almost immediately, it jumped into the present. The officer turned his way, while the men restored the pretend coffin to the Landrover and the others lowered their rifles. The officer advanced five paces, clumped to a stop and pointed his cane right at Griffin.

"You, there! Soldier!" he thundered. He was still fifty yards away but his voice was completely distinct.

Griffin looked around but there was only himself and two gum trees that could possibly be the object of the officer's rage. Behind, it was the funeral party's turn to smile, now that the officer's fury had been directed away from them, if only for the moment.

"What? Who? Me?"

He even pointed at his own chest, to complete the image of the fumbling recruit. He had fallen through a time warp and arrived at a moment exactly two years back.

'Yes, you soldier. What the fucking hell do you think you're fucking doing!"

Like all the best officer's, he did not drop the 'g' from his 'fuckings'. Griffin groaned.

"Nothing..." and then, after two years of defying real fighting officers in real situations, weakened and flinchingly added. "Sir."

"What did you say, soldier?"

"NOTHING, SIR!"

The officer, a captain by the look of him, probably CMF, probably purely administration, whipped the cane about to indicate the scene behind him.

"Do you know what this is, soldier?"

"Yes sir."

"What is it then?"

"It's a drill for a funeral."

"Yes, laddie. A funeral indeed. SO GET YOUR FUCKING HAT OFF!"

Griffin sagged inwardly as he removed the hat and then held it in front of his chest, which he supposed to be the right position. Was there no end to the idiocy? Apparently not—but the one thing he didn't want was to be charged and chucked in the stammer on his very last day in the army.

"Do you have anything better to do than stand around gawking, soldier," the officer was bellowing.

Did he ever. "Yes sir."

"Then you better get there, hadn't you."

"Yes sir."

He galloped back to the car without looking back. He knew the men out there would be laughing, as he would have been in the same circumstances himself, even before he heard the officer bellow. "AND WHAT DO YOU FUCKING LOT THINK YOU'RE FUCKING LAUGHING AT?"

Griffin drove away, glad to be out of earshot. A decent officer really, exploiting Griffin's foolish presence to relieve the pressure on his men, to give them a break and a laugh and show there were no hard feelings and maybe they would regather their wits and get it right this time. But Griffin didn't care if they got it right. The humiliation drove him forward furiously toward the Area Headquarters block. Get in there, get it done and get out of this fucking army, before it's too late, he told himself. Just one long agonising hour of bullshit and it would all be over. And that was all he wanted in the world.

He parked the car outside the Administration Block, a WW2 vintage building in yellow weatherboards and green iron roof and a long verandah at the front along which, as Griffin mounted the steps, an MP approached from the other direction. The MP gave him a hard look and Griffin hurried on, sure this was more trouble he didn't need.

"Just a minute, soldier," the MP called gruffly.

Griffin bowed his head and turned, and then saw that this improbable MP was wearing a huge grin just the way they were never supposed to. He stared, and the MP gave a mock stare back.

"Well I'll be fucked," Griffin breathed.

"Language, Private Griffin," Mick Delaney replied. "You're not at Nui Dat now, you know."

Since it was really him, no matter how impossibly, and they were apparently old friends just they way they never were, Griffin relaxed and offered a little laugh.

"I get it. This is a disguise for your next escape attempt."

"Haven't gone AWOL for at least three months, Griffin."

Amazingly, they shook hands, and then stood on the steps, for a chat presumably.

"So what's with the get up?"

"Apparently, the principle that *if you can't lick 'em, join 'em* applies."

"As the clerk said when he stapled the typist's tits together."

"It's the truth, Griffin. They reckon that since nobody knew as much about going AWOL as I did, they ought to make use of my expertise."

"The army is getting sillier by the day, Mick."

"That it is, Griffin. That it is. Which explains me, but what on earth are you doing here. I was sure you'd be discharged by now."

"This is my very last day. There was a fuck-up in the papers."

"The last Griffin fuck-up," Delaney chuckled. "Sure been a few of them along the way."

"And what about you?"

"I'll never fucking get out of here, Griffin. All time a bloke spends AWOL and on the punishment that follows adds on to your time. I won't be eligible for discharge for fourteen months yet."

"All crimes are punished, Mick."

"Yeah, sure they are."

"You realise that on that principle, you may be in the army for the rest of your life."

"Thought fills me with terror, Griffin."

"But at least next time you do a runner, you'll be able to get the credit for catching yourself."

"It isn't that funny, you know."

"Yeah, well, I'd like to stay and chat but civvy street is calling. Which way to the Adjutant's office."

"In that door. You'll see the sign."

"Thanks, Mick. Enjoy the rest of your life."

"You haven't heard the best bit," Mick Delaney said sadly. "I'm off to Nui Dat next month."

"Well, at least that'll cure your AWOL, Mick," Griffin laughed. "From Nui Dat there ain't no place to go."

"I'll find somewhere," Delaney chuckled.

They were laughing, but it wasn't funny. The position Delaney found himself in was one that filled Griffin with horror. The fact that he had brought it upon himself changed nothing. It was hard to imagine anyone spending a more unbearable year.

"Tell me, Griffin. Is it as bad as they reckon?"

"No, Mick. It's a bloody lot worse than that."

"Thanks for the encouragement."

"I'd run now, Mick, while you can, and this time don't come back."

"See you later, Griffin."

"I hope not, Mick."

You could only do your best to help.

You watched him stride away, marching rigidly in the best soldierly fashion. He was someone you never thought you'd feel sorry for, not in a million years.

Griffin went through the door into the dimness of the interior and found the sign that indicated the Adjutant's office. A clerk took his papers and told him to wait but it was only a moment before he was summoned. He stepped through the door and saw a small man with a bald head sitting behind a littered desk. He didn't look up nor stop writing as he spoke.

"Stand at ease, digger," he said abruptly.

Griffin only belatedly realised he probably should have been standing at attention and saluting and whatever. He moved his feet in a pretence and the Adjutant finally looked up.

"So, Private Griffin, is it? Then you really do exist."

"I certainly do."

"Not according to our records, you don't. Sit down, Private, and let's see if we can sort this out."

It took some time. Griffin was pleased to see that there *was* a file the Adjutant could read, although it was very thin and didn't seem to tell him very much.

"I see here you have returned precipitously, Private Griffin," the Adjutant murmured. "Were you wounded?"

"Well, yes and no."

"You have to be one or the other."

"I was wounded but it was only minor and had nothing to do with my early return."

"No mention of being wounded here..."

"I can show you the scar..."

"Show it to the medical examiner. They'll know what to make of it. So why were you evacuated early?"

"I fizzled."

"Fizzled?"

"Yeah. You know. Dropped out. Broke down. Stopped coping."

"Oh I see. I see. Tell me about it."

"I can't. I don't remember any of it. I was unconscious at the time."

"For how long?"

"Beats me."

"Private Griffin, describe for me, if you will, what you can remember of your last weeks on active service."

Griffin did as best he could. It seemed strange. Somehow it just didn't seem to be himself that he was talking about.

"I see," the Adjutant sighed at the end of it all. "On the whole, it would have been better had you been evacuated following the first injury."

"A lot of people said that."

"So, you were set for evacuation, then returned to the unit, then subsequently hospitalised under curious circumstances, not evacuated when you plainly should have been a second time, returned again to the unit, then finally evacuated. Extraordinary. And at some time during all this ducking and weaving, your records took someone at their word and made a wrong turn, which means they could be anywhere between here and Nui Dat."

"Does this help?"

"Yes. What it means is that it would be foolish to waste time trying to find your file. So I suppose we'd just better discharge you from here on the basis of the papers you brought with you and hope for the best."

"How long will that take?"

"Oh, ought to be ready by tomorrow evening."

"That long?"

"With luck. So first we'd better get you some quarters and some bedding from the Q store..."

He started writing chits furiously, tearing each off it's pad and handing it to Griffin in turn.

"...and this will get you three meals at the mess and this okays you into the Admin Company wet canteen. Now, you'll need medical and psychiatric examinations—take these to the RAP, this one to the pay clerk—do you have civilian attire with you? No? Give this to the Quartermaster to allow you to keep the uniform you are presently wearing. There are a number of statutory declarations you will have to sign, and meanwhile I shall arrange leave time and run a check to see if you have any citations or charges or other matters outstanding. Got all that?"

Carrying his handful of chits, Griffin walked from the Adjutant's office in complete dismay. He felt trapped, suffocated, compressed until the weight of a vast block of bureaucracy. It was as if the army was reaching out a long tentacle and hanging onto him, drawing him back, refusing to allow him to escape.

He stepped out onto the verandah, pausing for a moment to recall the direction to the RAP which was his next stop. From down on the parade ground came the staccato of gunfire, a volley in three distinct percussions. The firing party practicing with blanks over the pretend grave of Alfie Magee. They were going to have to do better than that on the day.

It was supposed to be his last day in the army only it wasn't anymore. Perhaps tomorrow... By ten o'clock the evening—which definitely wasn't 2200 hours in Griffin's mind—Griffin was sitting in the Admin Coy Wet Canteen, in the fartherest corner he could find, drinking beer at a rate that raised the barman's eyes every time he returned for another.

"You better go easy, soldier," he recommended at one point.

"This is easy," Griffin muttered.

He sat drinking alone and hoping desperately that no one he knew would walk in—every time the door opened he glanced that way, praying it wasn't Mick Delaney or maybe the ghost of Alfie Magee.

He knew he shouldn't have been there. He should have driven back to Melbourne and returned in the morning only somehow he just couldn't face two more journeys over Pretty Sally hill at the moment. Perhaps he should have gone to Seymour but there he was sure to have run into Delaney and got into God knows what trouble. Better to stay here, alone, systematically wiping himself out. There was a nasty taste in his mouth that no amount of beer was able to remove.

The army doctor examined him minutely and found nothing wrong.

"You seem to be in the prime of condition, young man."

"Haven't you noticed the scar on my leg?"

"Hardly serious."

"It severed the artery. I nearly bled to death."

"Well, it seems all cleared up now."

Whenever Griffin stood up, he always staggered the first few steps before his leg remembered its duty—if he walked more than a mile he began to limp pathetically—at night the numbness around the scar fought to keep him awake. Sure, all cleaned up.

He fared better with the psychiatrist who ummed at the end of Griffin's every sentence and nodded a lot, and was very interested in the fact that Griffin now smoked and drank.

"You can expect a sense of ongoing anxiety for some time and a beer and a fag will help with that. Usually, chaps like you have a lot of trouble sleeping. Lot of nightmares, that sort of thing. All perfectly normal for someone who has been through what you have. I tell you this so you won't worry about it any more than you have to. It will all go away in time. Meanwhile, you must be careful to stay out of situations that might induce anger. And you will be quite paranoid, I expect."

"What's paranoid?"

"A morbid belief that everyone and everything is conspiring against you."

"But they are!"

"You see what I mean? Best to get all this into the record while we can," the shrink smiled.

"What record?"

"Yes, strange business that. But then, since you were stuffed around so badly, it doesn't surprise me that the evidence of their folly was 'temporarily misplaced'."

"You mean someone did it deliberately, as a cover up for their mistakes?"

"Oh, now let's not be paranoid about this."

After his day of bitter bureaucracy, he found himself exhausted and since it was after six and he was tired and hungry, went to the mess for a meal before deciding his next move, after which he feel asleep and by the time he awoke, it was too late to go anywhere.

Except to the boozer for a few stultifiers. He sat in his corner, drinking and getting surlier and no one went near him.

There were only a couple of other small and relatively quiet groups that got less quiet as time passed. One was plainly a group of recruits —you could tell by their spit-polished neatness and the callowness of their haircuts. There were about a dozen of them and they were accompanied by a corporal. From time to time, gusts of their conversation blew into Griffin's ears. He tried not to listen—it was none of his business. Anyway, it was, as always, a series of complaints about officers, or one in particular, whom they called *Captain Casket.*

"Fair fuckin' dinkum, who does he reckon he is, yellin' like that.." was the sort of thing they were saying—fairly much what Sam the Sumerian said about Sargon of Akkad, Griffin supposed.

"This is a fuckin' funeral, not a ballet rehearsal," a red-haired kid burbled in mock parade ground tone.

Griffin groaned. He supposed he should have guessed who *Captain Casket* was.

"Fair fuckin' dinkum, prancing about like a bunch of fairies, shootin' at passin' sparrows, what the fuck's it all about?"

"They call it respect for the dead," the corporal offered.

"Respect? For a pissed office wallah who was pullin' himself as he drove and ran up a tree when he jacked off. What's to respect about that?"

Griffin was on his feet before he knew. He could feel a remarkable anger surge within him, arising as sudden nausea in his belly and scorching up his throat like pile. His head almost exploded in rage. He knew he bounded across the room and whatever happened next happened next. All he saw was a white intensity glaring in his eyes, like oncoming headlights.

Then two blokes had him by the arms and Griffin, hot and sweating furiously, glanced frantically from one to the other. The corporal one side, the barman the other, and they were shouting at him to calm down. Only then did he see why—the immediate vicinity was devastated, the table overturned and all twelve recruits on the floor, all entangled with their chairs, mostly looking at him in terror if they weren't complaining of their various injuries. A vast pool of spilt beer spread under them, like blood, of which, as far as Griffin could see, there wasn't any.

"You bastard," the young redhead was screaming, jumping to his feet. Although firm pinned by the arms, Griffin was able to kick the kid fair in the kneecap as soon as he was in range. The redhead went down yowling, and all the others by then had the sense to stay where they were.

"You better come outside, digger," the corporal suggested, and when he towed on Griffin's bicep, he followed. The barman saw them off at the door, through which Griffin made a final glance at the scene of chaos he was leaving behind. It was slowly beginning to occur to him that he might have been somehow responsible for it.

The corporal took him a few yards away and they paused. "You alright now, digger?"

"Yeah, sure, fine," Griffin said, although he doubted it.

They lit cigarettes, Griffin and the corporal, as if they were old friends.

"So what was that all about?" the corporal wanted to know.

So did Griffin.

"I didn't like the way they were mouthing off," Griffin said—it was the last thing he remembered.

"No reason to go 'em like that," the corporal said. "They're just dumb recruits. Silly kids. You mighta hurt someone seriously."

"Well," Griffin sighed. "They're older and wiser recruits now."

The sweat was drying all over Griffin's body and the chill was leaving his flesh. The cigarette was restoring his nervous system to normal functioning. The fog in his brain was more probably the result of alcohol than trauma. Suddenly he felt enormously tired.

"You better get outa here, digger," the corporal grinned. "I'll sort all this out."

"Yeah, thanks corporal," Griffin said, and turned and walked.

He was sore in a dozen places so it must have been a hell of a fight. He strained his brain but no memory would come. And like the corporal he too wondered what the hell that was all about. Rushing like a dragon to defend the honour of Alfie Magee. 'Wouldn't want you to hurt anyone on my account,' Magee would have said. Griffin staggered around for some time, his brain becoming no clearer, before he finally located his quarters and fell on the bunk and straight to sleep. He didn't even bother to take his boots off.

*

His last day in the army finally dawned, although not on him. Since the day before had also been his last, as had two other days over the last month, he was beginning to lose faith in the concept. He slept the sleep of a dead man and in the morning, the sunlight through the dusty cobwebbed window of the hut drew him back to life in the form of an appalling hangover.

He wandered through the ablution block and emerged damp but still with few of his senses functioning. He dressed in his uniform and went to the mess where army-issue scrambled eggs, burnt bacon and soggy toast at least formed substance at his centre-of-gravity and allowed him to walk with some equilibrium. 'Get to the Adjutant's office, get this done and get out of this fucking army, before there's real trouble,' he kept telling himself. And all the time he suspected, although hardly remembered, that some *real trouble* had already happened.

"Well, we seem to have progressed in some areas but not in others," the Adjutant informed him. "I'm afraid you'll need to stay with us for some time yet."

"I don't want to stay," Griffin said grimly.

"No, I should imagine not," the Adjutant smiled at him. "However, we have managed to establish that you do exist, and that you have just completed a tour with the Pig Battalion."

"How much longer will it take?"

"Well, there is a suspicion that your records have been removed maliciously which will need to be investigated. I truly can't promise to have completed processing you before tonight."

"I'll just sit here and wait until you've finished."

"No, Private Griffin, that won't do. Anyway, something has come up."

Griffin groaned. What he needed least of all was for 'something to come up'.

He waited silently and the Adjutant saw he could safely continue.

"There was a soldier killed in a motor accident last Friday night. A Private Alfred Magee. He was in the Pig Battalion for a time, I understand."

"Yes. The Padre's batman, as I recall," Griffin said, suspecting he was saying too much.

"Hmmm, that's right. Did you know Private Magee?"

"Only slightly."

"Oh good, that will be fine then."

Perhaps, instead of too much, he was saying too little.

"How will it be fine?"

"Well, since, as you know, the Pig Battalion is still on active service in Vietnam—in fact they are on the ship and will return in about a week—but meanwhile Private Magee's funeral services are taking place today in the town of Mansfield. About a hundred miles from here..."

"I know where Mansfield is."

"In any case, we are despatching a party to offer the family full military honours and we found that we lacked someone who knew him, or at least could represent the unit."

"Surely he made some friends after he got back..."

"A representative of his unit whilst on tour of duty is far preferable."

"I don't want to do it."

"Don't you. I see. And why not?"

"I don't want to get involved in this."

"Oh no? But it seems you already have..."

"Have I?"

"I understand there was a... disturbance... in the Admin Company Wet Canteen last night. At this stage, no charges have arisen however..."

"I'll go."

"A very wise decision, Private Griffin. And thank you for helping us out like this. The bus is down on the parade ground now. They're waiting for you."

"I have my own car."

"Since we have gone to all this trouble to lay on transport, it must be put to the maximum use. Good luck, Private Griffin. And rest assured by the time the bus returns you here this evening, your discharge ought to be fully processed and ready for you."

"Thank you sir."

The bus indeed stood on the parade ground. In fact it was almost standing at the exact spot that had the one that first brought him to this place, two years earlier, where he stood with those unfamiliar faces and heard the terrible words of Skull Braddock. No matter how unlucky they felt, Skull told them, it was going to get worse. Wise man. True words. A century of forgotten wisdoms ago.

Now he saw the recruits that formed the funeral party standing about smoking and laughing beside the bus in just the way Skull would never have tolerated. The corporal was there and so was the Captain—*Captain Casket*—he supposed. It hadn't occurred to him before that it might have been a joke. They all saw him coming and stood watching, none speaking or moving. He couldn't imagine what they might have been thinking. The captain broke off and matched to meet him over the last few yards. Griffin could not bring himself to salute—still did not remember which hand anyway, but as it happened Captain Casket reached instead for a handshake.

"You must be Private Griffin," he said with a reverent smile. "I'm Captain Cathcart. This is Corporal Barber, and the rest of our party are recruits from 2RTB that we have trained especially for performing military honours. Welcome aboard."

"Thank you, sir," Griffin smiled, pleased to know that at least one of them did not recognise him from the day before.

"You may feel free to act as your own agent, Private," Cathcart continued. "If there's anything you want or need, just say so."

"I'm fine thanks."

"Okay, corporal. Get them aboard and let's go."

Corporal Barber plainly had not forgotten him, nor had the recruits, especially the redhaired one. They only glanced his way and went onto the bus. Griffin boarded last. They all sat in a group at the front, so he pointedly made his way down to the back.

The bus took them out to the highway and into Seymour were the turn-off to Mansfield followed floodplain of the Goulbourn River all the way to its source in Lake Eildon at the foot of the mountains that could soon be seen as a blue outline on the horizon. For most of the way, the scenery was divine and Griffin leaned his aching head on the window and regarded it vaguely.

Before long, Corporal Barber made his way down the aisle and sat in the seat opposite Griffin.

"John Barber," he said, extending his hand.

Griffin shook it without raising his head off the glass.

"So you knew him, did you?" Barber asked carefully.

"Alfie Magee? Yeah, I knew him."

"Good mates?"

"I knew him."

"Sorta explains things a bit."

"I doubt it."

"Did you know him in Vietnam?"

"Yep."

"Look, they are just kids. Didn't know what they were saying..."

"I hardly remember any of it."

"You dumped the table on top of the lot of them."

"I suspected something like that."

"Anyway, they just wanted me to say no hard feelings."

"Sure. No worries."

"You know, you oughta wear your campaign medals. At least give others a fair warning."

"They've had their warning," Griffin heard himself say coldly.

Corporal Barber gave a little involuntary shiver and then

somehow managed to smile.

"Okay. Anything you need, you just say," he said as he stood and moved back down to the safety of the front.

For a time they spoke in whispers down there, and Griffin saw them giving little nervous glances in his direction. He smiled inwardly. It was amazing how easy it was to seem to be tough when people were scared to death of you.

You had to wonder what Alfie Magee would think of full military honours. Not a great deal. Griffin supposed that they would fire live rounds, when blanks would certainly be more in keeping with Alfie's reputation. He would have to remember to ask Captain Casket about that... But what about Alfie. Griffin was trying as hard as he could to feel something and nothing was happening. Last night he waded in to fight a dozen blokes simultaneously and did so with grand passion, but where was that passion now.

Alfie Magee was a silly little bugger who refused to carry ammunition on patrol and finally shot himself through the hand before someone else shot him through the head. Plainly he drove a motor car about as incompetently as he did everything else. Griffin liked him, even helped to try and protect him from officers and bullies, but in the end Alfie ran beyond their ability to protect him. And now he was dead and even further beyond help. So what? So what.

There was just simply no reality that Griffin could attach to the occasion. It was ridiculous that he was here, doing this. It made no sense. It was not part of his life. And maybe that was what Alfie knew as well, that it was all ridiculous and made no sense. Griffin knew that he had to hang on, see it through and get to hell out of the fucking army before it killed him too. Like it had Alfie Magee. For, in Griffin's mind, there was no doubt. The army had hung onto Alfie until he was dead. Was it trying to do that same thing to him?

Ninety minutes after the journey began, they rolled into the sleepy town of Mansfield. Pretty place in Autumn, Griffin knew, with the leaves all colours and the snow-capped peaks beyond. But this was late Summer and it was all dust and mosquitoes and snakes. A smoky haze hung about the town from the fires in the mountains. It was hot, and flat, and grim. It had never occurred to Griffin that Alfie Magee came from this town. He didn't know where he came from. He had never bothered to ask.

The bus had halted at a roadhouse on the outskirts of

town while the soldiers used the facilities and made their last minute preparations. They would be on a parade basis from the moment they entered the town. Griffin alone stayed on the bus which meant that the moment they arrived at the small church, he discovered he needed the leak. It also meant that, having already briefed the troops, Captain Cathcart now had to offer him a private briefing. He ventured to the rear of the bus to do so.

"The service is scheduled for 1100 hours. Then we proceed to the graveyard which is just a short way down the highway toward the mountains. Finally, we return to the RSL Hall where lunch will be turned on by the Ladies Auxiliary."

"What time do you expect us to be clear of that?" Griffin asked ruthlessly.

"Oh, by 1500 hours at the latest. We expect to be back in camp by sixteen-thirty."

"Fine," Griffin sighed.

"Do you wish to pay the army's respects to the family or shall I do it?"

"I don't know them. Better if you do it."

His options, those of his bladder and his stiff limbs, had closed by then. It was twenty-five past ten at that stage and everything hurt. Finally he was forced to abandon his refuge at the rear of the bus and face up to the world. Limping slightly when he was sure there was no reason for it, he made his way outside and decided to wander off and find a dunny. Time was refusing to pass. Only six hours to go but it seemed to be moving further away rather than closer on his day that would never end.

The church was a small sandstone affair planted amid a outcrop of pinetrees and surrounded by long yellow grass. Fire regulations, let alone respect for the dead, suggested that grass should have been cut. There was a small gravel area below the steps and there the soldiers moved with their rifles and bayonets already fixed and stood in two facing ranks at ease. It was hot and steamy and Griffin could see trickles of sweat on several of their faces. Plainly he wasn't the only one doing this the *very fucking hard way*.

He wandered down the broad main street until he came to the first pub. All about the locals moved lethargically through their morning activities, and every one of them looked him over and knew... He wasn't sure what they knew but he could see they all knew it. It was just on opening time and he was desperate for some *hair of the dog* but he knew that once he started drinking he would never stop, and end up in the slammer on a D&D instead of discharged and free.

Resisting gigantic temptation, he went to the cafe next door and ordered three cups of coffee in succession. The ladies behind the counter stared at him and whispered to each other—he felt ridiculously conspicuous in his army uniform—in such an environment it was pure fancydress—it might as well have been a tu-tu, top hat and riding boots. He felt like a freak, a visitor from another planet, weird and alien. He hated the army more than anything he had ever known.

By the time he returned to the church, the service had already begun. He crept in as much as his boots allowed and took a place in the back row. The soldiers were placed to either side of the coffin over which the priest stood, going through the motions of the service. If he knew Alfie Magee personally, he gave no sign of it. Off to the left, Griffin recognised the white-haired couple he had seen briefly once. He remembered that Magee's parents were old, more like his grandparents, from the day on the platform at Spencer Street station when they began their journey to Vietnam. Several people spoke brief eulogies. Alfie Magee was a good son of the church and the town. Griffin realised that they knew no more about him than that. They remembered a warm person, Griffin remembered someone shy and afraid of everyone; they remembered a happy person, Griffin a sullen chap: they a proud soldier, Griffin a man who deliberately made a mockery of military honour. In death, Alfie Magee had in fact gone out of existence.

The soldiers hoisted the coffin and made their way out and placed it on the gun carriage that somehow did not look incongruous in the street. They went in the bus to the graveyard, went through their routine, fired evenly into the sky and the deed was done. All the way, Griffin hung about in the background. He was terrified that someone might try to speak to him; terrified mostly of what he might reply. Old man Magee looked his way a coupe of times but that was all. Finally they were delivered to the RSL Hall. It was midday—four hours to go. Griffin passed each minute in agony.

In the RSL Hall, the ladies auxiliary had excelled themselves with a table weighed down with ham and salad and pies and creamcakes and scones and jam, all to be washed down with tea. The soldiers, like Griffin, grew increasingly desperate for a beer. Griffin supposed that he would get clean away with it, but his labour of inconspicuousness had him by the throat at that stage—instead he took a ham roll and a cup of tea and retired into the most distant corner.

The cheery ladies chatted. "Oh, it was such a nice service, wasn't it Joanie."

"Yes, Kath. Lovely service. All those nice flowers."

Griffin had seen no flowers.

When the old man entered, the room fell silent for an instant, then tried not to be silent but the ladies auxiliary remained just a little less cheerful. The old man spoke to Captain Cathcart for a moment, they looked Griffin's way and then both approached. Griffin died inwardly. This was going to be one of the worst moments of his life.

"Private Ken Griffin," Captain Cathcart was saying. "This is Private Magee's father—Mr Desmond Magee."

The man was weary and drawn. They should never have let him out of the nursing home. His face was spotted with age, and his lips cracked and his eyes had that watery gloss. Up close he looked even older than he could possibly have been. The hand he extended was shaking—when Griffin took it, it was cold.

"Ah, yes. I remember the name from Alfred's letters," the old man said. Surely he couldn't have.

"Glad to meet you," Griffin murmured hopelessly.

"You're the one they called The Bear, aren't you?" old Des Magee knew.

Oh my God, Griffin sighed.

"Yes, that's right."

"Yeah. Look, I wonder if I can have a word. In private, y'know?"

There was no way out. This had to happen and Griffin could only smile and nod. "Sure."

"Though maybe we could step over to the pub and have a beer, maybe."

"A beer would be terrific."

They only had to cross the wide road, Griffin striding beside this waddling old man and suddenly Griffin was gripped with a sense of pride. This man knew him. God knows what he knew. All around the town, people were stopping and looking. This, Griffin could tell, was a proud moment for the old man. He did his best to look worthy of that pride as he walked his soldierly walk—not exactly marching. He might not have felt it but he could certainly look the part.

They entered the cool of the interior of the pub and Des

directed him through to the saloon. As if by arrangement, all the tables were empty. Griffin headed for the bar but the old man caught his arm.

"On me," he declared—it might even have been an order.

Griffin shrugged and took a chair and soon the old man returned to two frothing pots of beer—it was exactly what Griffin wanted and needed even though the old man hadn't bothered to ask if Griffin might have a preference. Perhaps he already knew that too.

Des Magee sipped his beer and rubbed his bald head. "Been back long?" he asked lightly.

"Just a week. I'll be discharged by tonight."

"Good luck to yer," and then, after a moment's thought, added. "In that case, it was good of yer to turn up today."

Griffin almost said he was ordered to do so—blackmailed in fact—but he caught himself in time. No, that wouldn't do at all.

"Alfie was a good bloke," he said.

Des Magee scowled.

"Sounds funny, hearing you put it like that," he said bluntly.

Griffin shuddered at the thought of the sea of lies that lay before him.

"No, really. He was okay."

"I worried about him, all the bloody time," Des was saying.

"Yeah. So did my folks about me..."

"But Alfred was different. He was a soft kid and he didn't seem to be army material to me."

At least here was something he could admit to.

"He wasn't really..."

But Des was talking, not listening. Maybe his hearing aid wasn't switched on.

"All the time, I expected them to chuck him out. I thought he'd be useless. But then they gave him that Padre job and off he went to that Vietnam place. You coulda knocked me flat with a feather then. I really never expected that he'd end up there."

"Neither did we," Griffin was glad to be able to contribute. "But he got through somehow."

The old man's bloodshot eyes jerked up to meet Griffin's.

"Yeah, that's what I wanted to ask yer. How?"

Griffin tried desperately to try and think of some right thing to say. It didn't matter what, but this man was so frank and direct about his son. No lie would work. And the truth couldn't be told. There was no way out.

"Hard to say," Griffin tried. "I wasn't much of a soldier at first myself. But a place like Vietnam hardens people. Even blokes like Alfie."

"What happened to him?" Old Des asked flatly. He could plainly tell Griffin was waffling.

"Nothing bad. Nothing in particular. He just did his job..."

"Nar. Something happened. When he came back, he was all sullen, like. Wouldn't respond to anything. Lost interest in everything. Wouldn't talk about how he got wounded."

"I can tell you how that happened if you like," Griffin said. After all, who better to tell the true story than the man who made it up in the first place. But old Des made a perfect interception.

"There was some yarn about him grabbing the muzzle of a Vietcong's rifle. That was in the press."

"That's what happened..." Griffin stumbled, but he could see he wasn't going to get away with it. The old man gazed at him sternly.

"Look, I was in Tobruk, mate. I know what happens. There was plenty of blokes shot 'emselves through the hand. All the ones that had enough imagination not to shoot 'emselves through the foot. Always the left hand. Point blank. You know what I mean?"

Griffin bowed his head. There was no escape now. A war was a war—it was foolish to think he could put one over this wise old man. Griffin rubbed his eyes until they were blurred, bit his lip until it hurt, but there was no way out.

"Alright," he sighed. "It was just the way you imagine. Alfie was useless. There wasn't anything that he was good at. He was the most unsuitable combat soldier in history. But that was the point. He went out there and did the job, despite the fact that he was scared to death and so bad at it. That's what real courage is. You ought to know that. It isn't the fearless or the tough guys who are brave. It's the ones that do the job despite being in a state of dithering panic at the time."

The blotchy old head nodded ruefully. "Yeah. I can see that. But he still shot himself, didn't he?"

Griffin began to feel his own resolve steeling. He was going blow for blow to the death with this brave old digger.

"He had to. He knew he was a liability we couldn't afford. He did it to spare us the trouble. It was an act of courage, not cowardice."

"Hard to believe."

"Believe it."

"Okay, but how was he such a liability?"

"What do you mean?"

"I mean, why was he such a liability that you thought you might have to shoot him?"

Griffin regarded the old man. There were tears in his eyes although maybe they watered all the time. Well, he'd put poor Alfie in it now, and once again there seemed to be no choice but to finish him off.

"He refused to carry any ammunition."

It must have been a remarkable experience, to reach such an age and finally hear something you'd never heard before. The old man shook his head to clear it but he still could not overcome his disbelief.

"He what?"

Griffin explained in firm patient tones. "He went out on operations with an empty weapon."

"My God. Why?"

"He said he didn't want to kill anybody."

Only the father of Alfie Magee could have known it was true without evidence.

"He did that?"

Griffin nodded. "Yeah, Mr Magee. He did that. Right from training, he told them so. I don't want to kill anybody, he told them. They didn't believe him. But that was his conviction and he stuck to it."

Des Magee laughed, shaking his head in mingled disbelief and joy.

"Well, I'll be buggered. You're not bullshitting me, are you?"

As if anyone would have dared at this stage. "No, Mr Magee. That's the truth."

"But hang on a minute," and his eyes narrowed with suspicion. "If his rifle wasn't loaded, how'd he shoot himself?"

"Because that one time, when he went out on picket, he swapped weapons with me. After he was shot, I swapped them back again and cleaned my weapon. That's what forced them to believe his story. The bullet that got him must have come from an enemy weapon because there were no bullets in his own. They had no choice but to believe it."

The head shaking continued, accompanied now by a wry smile. "You did that for him."

"Sure. I suppose had I thought about it at the time, I would have realised why he switched weapons. But if I had, I wouldn't have stopped him."

"My good God, how amazing."

"At the time it seemed perfectly normal. A place like Vietnam is like that."

Old man Magee sat, wiping his eyes on a tattered old handkerchief. Even Griffin could feel a small amount of emotion wandering around in the depths of his belly. He waited for the old man to recover himself sufficiently to speak again.

"There I was, thinking he'd done somethin' wrong, somethin' pissweak. I thought he was a gutless wonder for a son. I though maybe he found out about himself what I already knew. I thought that was why he was so depressed and didn't care about anything in the end."

But in the end, it was only when he spoke the words that Griffin finally realised what it had all meant.

"No," Griffin said. "Alfie Magee was the bravest man I ever met."

In Praise of Womankind

Emerging from a heavy brain-numbing sleep into some sort of half-waking condition, Dell suffered a fractional moment of panic in realising that she was alone in the bed: as if it had all been dreamed. And well it might have been. During the night, little Cabel had cried and, dragging herself wearily from the bed, it hadn't occurred to her to dispatch Lew Sigg instead. Lew would never, she was sure, adjust easily to his fatherly responsibilities and would probably have dropped the poor little bugger anyway. But now she was alone, or so it seemed. No—Lew was out there somewhere, shuffling around. She did not want to roll over and see what he was up to: that, like all things about Lew, would reveal itself in time. He must, she concluded, have risen this very minute, disturbing her in the process. She remained, coiled up under the blankets, assuring herself that she was exhausted, and hoping that sleep would return. Which, since Lew was awake, she knew was fairly unlikely.

"Hey Griffin, you there mate?" she heard him call.

His voice, as always in the mornings, was rather croaky and inaudible.

She remembered then that they had smoked his last cigarette in the course of the night—she had given up long ago but there was something about a post coital smoke that lay outside the realm of habit. This, then, was the old familiar sponge-one-off-Griffin-in-the-morning scene. In a night when the past constantly bumped against the present, this was the heaviest collision, perhaps even nearly fatal. Lew, she assessed, was just outside the bedroom door on the landing above the few downward steps to the living area of the house. She could easily visualise him, leaning on the rail, either naked or wearing her most feminine robe, perplexed expression willing to wait forever until Griffin answered.

Griffin, who never seemed to sleep, would have been up and about for hours and of course well equipped with fags. He was one of those people so dependent that he always kept plenty around—to be on guard against running out was a central issue in his life.

"Who's cooking breakfast?" Lew then demanded, and beyond his throaty utterance, she could hear what was certainly the crackle of the frying pan and bubble of the jug.

"Not breakfast. Lunch," an amused, patient voice replied, as thick and grumbly as Lew's but Griffin's voice was always like that.

"Lunch?" Lew muttered in confusion, and no doubt peered at the wristwatch he didn't wear and the wallclock that didn't exist.

Lunch? Dell thought grimly. It was just as well that she had arranged for Esther—who looked after the baby when she was away—not to bother to come until lunchtime. She had planned a good sleep-in even before this extraordinary justification for it arrived bedraggled on her doorstep. There was a meeting with Holyrood and the Council Conservation Group at two—she didn't have to be at work until then and was thankful for that. Only, she might already be running late. If Griffin was cooking lunch then it had to be one. Griffin was one of those people who always did particular things at particular times. He probably even brought his bloody typewriter with him.

In the night, Cabel had cried and, forgetting all else for the moment, she had gone naked down the hall to attend to the infant. That bloody awful dog lay there, and the eyes that glowered at her might well have been the perving ones of Griffin. She thought about returning to the bedroom for a robe, suddenly feeling very foolish for that. It was her house, after all. In the end she compromised wrapping a spare blanket about herself, trying to convince herself it was really because it was cold. The dog lay, quite unimpressed by her show of modesty. She contemplated giving the brute a good kick, although sorry experience had taught her the futility of that. The Monster, reading her mind precisely, silently wrinkled its nose and bared its teeth. By then, Cabel had settled again and with a sigh of defeat, she returned to bed. At least, she supposed, one of the three invaders wasn't afraid to let their true feelings show. The Monster, she knew, probably hated her most of all because she was in some way responsible for him being called that silly bloody name in the first place.

Now, she could hear Lew calling. "Got a smoke for an old digger, have yer, matey?"

There would be the whiz of the packet flying through the air and the plop if Lew dropped the catch—yes, he did. God didn't anything change? If she didn't know this was her house at Redland Bay, she might have been right back in Elm Street and this a replica of every other morning of the four years that she had shared it with them. Deciding that it might be better not to go too far along that line of thought, she snuggled deeper in the blankets in the vain hope of just another few minutes sleep.

Lew came padding back into the room: she heard him trip on something, caught the whiff of cigarette smoke. He stood at the foot of the bed and plunged his fingers into his hair, the nails scraping audibly on the scalp, dislodging dandruff on her new carpet. She could hear him stretch and yawn— what she was really doing was bracing herself for the onslaught she knew was about to begin. If Lew Sigg was a pleasure and a relief to go to bed with in the evenings, in the mornings he was only a pain in the arse.

"Woman," he gruffed at her harshly.

Advancing around the bed, he kicked something—her hairdryer perhaps—and there was the cracking of an toenail causing him to yelp and hop and finally topple onto the bed.

"Bloody junk all over the floor. You used to reckon I was the one who made all the mess. Look at all this!"

She knew she wasn't the tidiest person in creation, but still it hardly constituted the abominable mess he had created in their room at Elm Street where a partly dismantled motorcycle was regarded as an item of furniture secondary only to the bed, not to mention the wardrobe that contained his beer-brewing equipment, for course all of his clothes belonged on the floor. She could wonder, these days, how she had possibly survived such monumental disorder. But now, for revenge apparently, Lew strode across the trampoline of the bed and stuck the blind, causing the nuclear fission of daylight.

"Shit, Lew!" she cried, her fingers flying to her eyes to prevent them being burned from her face. He dropped onto her, encompassing her blanketed form between his limbs and torso.

"Arise, woman, and greet thy lover."

"You shit, Lew. It's all right when you want some sleep. All of importance is waived when Sir Golliwog desires his forty winks. But when he's awake, everyone's awake."

Triumphantly he poked his tongue in her ear and she escaped under the blanket with a giggling trill.

Her muffled voice yawned out at him. "What on earth are you doing awake so early, Lew? I'm sure its not afternoon yet."

"Hunger, woman. The need for sustenance. I pain for nutrition."

"So go get yourself some bloody breakfast. All I pain for is sleep."

"Slovenly bitch. After hours of drawing forth a man's energies, she refused to aid in his restoration. Ahhh, the cruelty of womankind is immeasurable. I don't know why I put up with you."

"Pity, pity, poor little Lewie. Money, food, sex—you don't ask for many things, lover, but you surely ask for them in excess."

He bounded again on the bed, this time wrenching away her protective layer of blankets. The springs spronged, some never to recover.

"The talons of evil bared," he roared victoriously, "The root of all evil shrivelling in the light of day."

"If you'll forgive the pun," Dell moaned, "And I'm not shrivelling. Those are goosebumps."

"Shrivelling! Shrivelling!"

"Freezing!" she cried, "Shit, Lew. Don't you ever feel the cold?"

But Lew, the world's greatest dramatic actor for the moment, was in full flight. "Ah-huh, the perfect ploy. Aimed at the goodness and kindness of my belaboured heart. To draw me near with the sumptuous lure of its warmth and so enclose me in the trap..."

"I'm getting angry, Lew..."

"...but I shall not be smitten. I shall not falter in the course of truth and righteousness..."

He would have risen to his feet, finger upraised, but the bedsprings baulked at the task.

"Alright, Lew, alright. I'm getting up."

And would have too, but he dived and his hands gripped her biceps and pinned her back.

"The vanquished foe tries to slither away but I shall not allow it. Undaunted and ruthless, lest it be given time to lick its wounds and return with strength renewed..."

"Lew, I'm freezing to death..."

She was too—even shivering for effect. He freed her and she rose onto one elbow, gazing reflectively, as he did, along the length of her lithe brown body. He reached for her—he had a fixation about grabbing her breasts which annoyed her because there was so little to grab. But Lew, though he thought her self-consciousness was absurd, was never game enough to tease her about that. And, right now, she found she had no objection. He was shedding his orange jockettes and outstanding for things that she might have resisted but wouldn't have minded.

"Lewington?"

It was not her own muffled voice that called as he spread her back on the bed and plunged into her excruciatingly. It came from beyond and below. Heedlessly, Lew pressed deeper and she arched her back in appreciation, fingernails scratching along his flesh.

"Hey Lew, You there?"

And closer now—the clump of shoes was right outside the door. Lew paused, frowning in confusion and she could feel his hardness depleting.

"That you, Griffin?"

And who else might it have been? There was always, Dell was sure, something very sinister about Griffin's sense of timing.

"Don't come in," she had to say because Lew would not have thought to, and Griffin might well have barged in on them otherwise.

"Sorry. Am I disturbing?" Griffin asked through the door. With a mischievous smile, no doubt.

"Only a little," Lew said, "What's the problem?"

So Griffin remained doubtfully but thankfully behind the door. His brief silence conveyed his embarrassment, or envy.

"Ahhh, I was just cooking some bacon and eggs and stuff. Thought you might like some."

Dell, impaled on a sausage, was doing some frying of her own. Lew's belly rumbled expectantly, although a mere glance at her face put an end to that.

"No. It's alright. We'll eat later."

"Okay," Griffin said, sounding alone and disappointed.

Had it been anyone else, Dell momentarily reflected, it would have been an offer too good to refuse. She was so very hungry. But it was Griffin and that was that. Out there came a shuffle—if not exactly staying, neither was he going away. But then he never did.

"Ummm, I was just going to the shop. Do we need anything?"

"Milk," Dell whispered to Lew.

"Milk," Lew echoed on relay.

"Yeah. Getting some of that."

"And fags."

"Them too."

And still didn't go.

"Ummm, which way is the nearest shop."

And Dell sighed, knowing she was going to have to answer

that one herself.

"You go back the way you came in last night and take the second left. Keep going up the hill—you'll find it."

"Okay."

"We'll be up shortly," Lew called, "And go check out the local. Alright."

"Fine. No worries."

He was shuffling away now, tripping on something, and they lay there without moving, both listening to his movements until he finally reached the mental safety of the outside world.

"Hey Monster, come on. Let's go," they heard him call.

At least he walked, which would give them more time, but time had already run out.

And so, because Griffin had ruined everything, Dell said. "I hope you're not planning to spend your whole time here in the pub."

Lew made his own escape across the sagging mattress.

"Never. Anyway, we have to get that car in order. I'll get started on it today. Later."

"What do you have to do?"

"Get it registered mostly. Which might take some time. Got some minor repairs to do first."

There were certain things in the world that were all too predictable.

"Do you mean to tell me that you drove all the way up here in an unregistered car?"

"That's why we made the trip. We weren't able to register it in Victoria."

"Oh," she said, and decided that she could look angry about that, "For a moment there, I was thinking you might have come to see me."

Lew squatted in the corner, playing with some fluff he pull out of his navel.

"Now love, there's no need to be sarcastic."

"I should have known..."

"Well, what's the problem. I'm here, aren't I?"

A performance was plainly in order and Dell jumped up and started to stalk about the room, throwing her arms around and slanting her tone toward that fiery Latin woman that she might have been but wasn't.

"It's all the bloody same to you, isn't it, Lewie. It's all cars and motorbikes and pubs and there just isn't anything else that's important. You're slipping into an abyss of conformity,

Lewie. You have no scope, no latitude. You can't adjust. Next thing we know, you'll be working a steady job and paying your taxes."

"You're crapping on," Lew said, although that last thought made him cringe.

And continue to crap on she would—there had to be some small pleasures in life.

"And you drag your bloody mate to make sure you have someone to go to the pub with. I don't know why you bothered to leave Carlton."

"Because I had to stay a step ahead of the Commonwealth cops."

"They aren't still looking for you."

"Cors they are. Blokes go to gaol every day..."

"Why would they be bothered with a dolt like you?"

"For the same reason you wanted me to father your child."

"I may become offended."

"I wish you would."

"You want me to get angry, don't you."

"Yeah."

"Why."

"Because you being shitty and sulky is easier to take than you crapping on. A bloke comes a thousand fucking miles to see you and all you do is yell at him."

"You came to register a car. You said so."

"Yeah, that too. But also to see you."

"Then explain to me exactly why you brought Griffin along."

"Because its his fucking car!"

"There are other ways of getting here, you know."

"Yeah, but the Commonwealth Cops watch the stations and airports, you know that."

"You could have hitch-hiked."

"Fuck you, Dell. It's just how it turned out."

She glared at him, conjuring up as much anger as she could muster. "You know, Lew, I feel used. You're just here so that you'll have somewhere to go when they kick you and Griffin out of the pub every night. You don't care about me. You don't care about our kid. Just a gut full of grog and somewhere to poke your dick when you stagger home. That's all it means to you, isn't it."

"What else is there?"

"There are other things to life than pissing on all the time."

"We won't be pissing on all the time. We got things to do."

Dell could afford to smile, because she knew she was winning.

"That, Lewie, is something to be seen to be believed."

And she even turned her back on him to show how ludicrous it was.

"There's no fucking gratitude in this world," Lew muttered.

She was dragging on her bathrobe and getting things ready for the bathroom—she would be late for her meeting at this rate.

"So tell me, Lewie. How long do you plan to stay?"

"I don't know. As long as it takes."

"That's no answer. If you don't know, guess."

"We have no idea how long it will take..."

"We! Yeah, I get it. What do I have to do? Ask Griffin to get a straight answer."

"We really didn't make any definite plans."

"You never do."

"I thought I might check out see what you were up to before making any plans," he said, when it was far too late.

"I bet."

"It's true. I really haven't decided how long..."

"But you will be going back eventually."

"Not necessarily..."

"I'm sure Griffin will see that you do..."

"Griffin didn't want to come in the first place. I conned him into it."

"A sort of insurance, hmmm?"

"Look, love. My options are open. I'm thinking about staying..."

"Very thoughtful of you."

She was walking out of the room, leaving him hanging there.

"Where you going?"

"To have a shower. I smell and so do you."

She marched down the hall and he tagged along, no doubt wearing his perplexed expression. It was a lie, of course. Lew Sigg, like no one else she knew, truly had life figured out.

"As a matter of fact," he was saying, "Oh smart-arse all-knowing creature, I do plan to check out the possibility of transferring to Queensland Uni while I'm here."

She could laugh at that. In all probability, the idea had not entered his head until that moment.

"With your record of droppings out, failures and campus disruption, I'm sure they'll be delighted to have you."

But she noticed the idea did give her a raft to cling to.

"It's worth a try."

"Oh, it is, it is. And tell me, how will you live? Not off my money, I can assure you. I've already invested enough in your dubious future, thanks very much."

"I'll get a job."

But he could not avoid flinching as if in pain when he said it.

She laughed outright—the argument had taken an all too familiar course now—they were on their firmest ground.

"What? Who? You? Lew, honey. You are useless. There isn't anything you can do that anyone is likely to pay you money for."

"I can drive taxis."

"They don't give taxi licences to people on the run from the law."

"Bullshit. They give 'em to anybody."

She was laughing as she reached into the shower and turned the water on, and he followed her, almost aimlessly, under the cascade.

"What's so funny about it?"

"Lewie, you can barely find your way around Carlton. You'd never have found your way here without Griffin. You don't know anything about Brisbane. You'd run your little taxi into the river on the first day."

The water came from the showerhead in sporadic bursts and as the steam rose, Lew stood by her in the pretence of washing her back but he allowed his hands to roam freely.

"Bloody hell, Lew. Don't you ever cut your fingernails?"

"My manicurist got pregnant."

She put a hand in the middle of his chest and shoved him back, almost causing him to slip over. It would be just like him to break his neck in her shower.

"Lew, give me a bit of room, please. I'm freezing."

"You've got a whole bathtub full of room."

"But you've got all the bloody water."

If it wasn't water, it was blankets.

"I'm dirtier than you are."

"You're not wrong. I smelled your feet last night. What a pong."

"That's why they're put so far from my nose."

"Lew, you don't have to shampoo your entire body."

"Why not? It's got hair all over it."

"But its my shampoo and expensive stuff."

"You don't want me to get dandruff in my chest and pubics,

do you?"

"No. It'd choke the fleas."

"Soap makes me itch."

"That's one way of getting some life out of you, I suppose."

And she got out of the shower and dried herself down.

"Do you have to pick shit out of everything I do?"

"Only because you do everything so badly."

"Is that right?" and he might have been hurt too, "Well, in that case, why don't I just piss off and leave you."

"I pissed off and left you, remember?"

"Well, you can piss off again."

She was pulling on her robe, and leaning forward, presenting her chin, daring him to hit it.

"It's my house, honey. And you can piss off any time you like."

And reaching deftly, she flicked off the hot water and fled in raucous triumph.

"Bitch," his teeth rattled after her.

The next thing she had to do was check on little Cabel—he had been so remarkably quiet for hours, and anyway, she needed to make sure he was ready for Esther, who would arrive any moment now. She crept into the room. The child lay awake, playing happily, unperturbed by all this nonsense. Dell picked him up and her hand automatically felt the nappy. She looked at the child and frowned. "What's up, kiddo. Waterworks broken down?"

She looked around grimly. Things had changed. Over there, someone had placed a wet nappy on the bucket—someone who might not have known what else to do with it. The one the child wore, she saw, had been attached rather clumsily... God, Griffin, of all people. It couldn't be. What would that idiot know about changing nappies..? But of course he always thought he knew everything...

Grimly, she unclipped the nappy and took it off disdainfully. It was time to bath the child anyway. And if the fabric was not at all wet, still she carried it away as if it was contaminated.

Bloody Griffin. Surely then, nothing was sacred after this...

The Bucket

The city could be a beautiful place. Viewed from here, a broad window on the twenty-sixth floor, such a sentiment was easy to believe. At that height, the broad expanse of Port Phillip Bay was offered, the wide arc of the bayside suburbs all the way to the horizon and it was amazing to see just to what extent the inner city was benefited with parklands. Over to the left around the river mouth were the docks and the intensive industrial suburbs but even those, on such a brilliantly sunny day, possessed a cruel grim beauty when taken in as a vista from such a great distance. Closer in, the River Yarra snaked right by the sheening office towers, laced with bridges. The traffic and the trains seemed to drift along, unhassled and unconcerned. Distance, at such a time, could be invaluable.

Distance was what he needed now, for he only had to turn himself through one hundred and eighty degrees—a simple task in his castored swivel chair—and the illusion would be completely shattered. As it was, he did not even need to turn, for he could hear their voices, and that was bad enough. The illusion was just that—an illusion. The city was a truly ugly place where ugly people lived.

"They moved in three weeks ago," Telford was saying, reporting, whatever. "About seven women and maybe ten children. Usual types—funny clothes, long hair, beads, some even have tattoos. Real bunch of freaks."

Freaks. Had he swivelled in the chair, he would have seen freaks alright. Five fat bald men in business suits, and one in a uniform. Four of them had ulcers. Three had a heart condition. All had high blood pressure. They ate and drank too much at daily business lunches, non-smokers chuffing fat cigars afterward, and carried Quick Eze in their pockets to relieve the subsequent indigestion. Yet all of them aspired to positions of greater pressure, greater responsibility. And they called other people freaks.

"They put up banners—didn't try to hide the fact they were there, but that's how they operate. They welcome the complaints, the publicity."

Now Telford was a nice man. In his early fifties, he had a wife and three children, a good job and as departmental manager, was moving nicely up the line. He was a gentle soul, thoughtful, generous and kind. He was the sort of man who gave up his seat on the tram to old ladies, who would never have considered starting up his motor mower before midday on a Sunday. He supported local charities, he tried to use his spare time beneficially to the neighbourhood. His wife gave friendly, decorous parties, and they kept their garden in excellent order. Telford was a good man.

That was what Griffin found most sickening of all. It was a nice man, a friendly man, a good man, who was saying these monstrous things.

"We've done all we can. We tried to negotiate with the Squatter's Union, but you know how impossible they can be. We've given them more time than we were required to by law. We have asked the Housing Commission to do what they can. All in all, we have bent over backwards for these people, tried every avenue, without result."

All quite perfectly true, for Telford was a very honest man as well. They had approached the appropriate bodies and shown every reasonable consideration. It had been Griffin himself who had done most of the approaching and negotiating and considering. They had bent over backwards, trying to make a deal with the squatters. They had been met solidly with unheeding defiance. All true. Everything possible had been done.

Like hell it had.

Telford was a good and honest man, but he could not see beyond the end of his garden. He had a nice house. There were other people in this city just as good and honest and hardworking as he was, who did not have anywhere to live. Out there, a band of women were trying to change all that, to make it fairer. Telford simply couldn't see it.

This was a wealthy society. Most people lived well, some rather better than well. There were plenty of houses. It was just that some people had two and others had none. In such a wealthy society, that was inexcusable. But it was also worse than that. Here was a government department, which possessed almost a hundred houses. No one lived in most of them. They weren't meant to be lived in. They were intended for property development. Out there, a bunch of ragtag women thought that in a city where there were homeless people, there might have been something basically wrong with that.

But Telford saw nothing wrong. It was business. That was that.

"They have made the usual list of demands for housing,

free rent for the poor, that sort of thing. Quite ridiculous—they really don't expect anyone to meet their demands. They just want to make trouble."

True again. They did not expect their demands to be met. They hoped they might, prayed they might, dreamed they might, begged that they might, but they did not expect it. There was no reason why they should. There were enough houses but the people who needed them weren't allowed to live in them. It was shameful. It was disgusting. And because of that, they wanted to make trouble, so others might see how shameful, how disgusting, it was. But no one was looking. Not even the good honest people, like Telford.

Griffin swivelled in his chair now, and faced Telford and the other men. The time had come...

"Therefore," Telford was saying. "We have been obliged to arrange for the police to remove them, at 10am on Thursday morning..."

"Nobody's tried talking to them," Griffin said grimly, loudly, resoundingly.

All eyes turned upon him.

"Nobody has been there and just asked them to leave, politely, quietly," Griffin added, in case they had not heard him the first time.

No one answered. The important gentlemen all looked at one another. Some of them wondered who this young man was that had spoken, interrupted, and what he was doing there.

Telford and the GM knew why he was there. He, Griffin, was the one who located the appropriate property for the new car park in the first place, he had sorted out the leases. This was his project and it should have been him who was organising this operation—the final tidy up before the demolition could begin.

Telford was a Korea veteran, the GM a former World War II fighter pilot, and they had taken Griffin into the department because they understood what he was going through. No one else wanted him, even though by law his job had to be kept open for him throughout the two year's of the fulfilment of his conscription obligations. But they understood, and had taken him on and nurtured his career because they knew what it was to be a veteran. It would take him a long time to settle down, and he would be difficult until then. Difficult, like he was now. The best thing to do was to ignore him at times like this.

The GM simply looked away, toward Telford, and nodded.

"There isn't likely to be any trouble," Telford continued as if Griffin had not spoken. "The police assure me that it will take no longer than twenty minutes to remove them. It will be a surprise attack, to try and minimise the media activity. I see no problem."

When he said that last bit, he looked directly at Griffin. Griffin saw there was no reason to say anything further. What else could he have said?

He went there that very afternoon. He simply walked out of the office without giving any explanation of himself, but that was not surprising. He was a responsible Property Officer, Class 2, and had worked for the Department of Construction for nearly a year. It was expected that he should tell someone where he was going when he left the office, but it didn't really matter if he didn't. So he didn't, for the first time that he could remember.

There had been no place for him at the insurance office, but he didn't care. He felt the need to find something better to do with his life anyway, even if he couldn't think of anything in particular for the moment. As a result, the government were required to pick up the commitment for his re-employment and he was invited to sit for a Public Service exam. Since it was at about grade six level, he managed a pass and before long was instructed to present himself at the Department of Construction where there was a vacancy for a junior clerk. He was soon shuffled up the line to his present more responsible position, simply because two older members of the department retired and all promotion was on the basis of seniority. He was on the way up, before he had time to think about his ambitions, or even if he had any.

He drove his own car, losing money by getting it out of his regular all day carpark in Cardigan Street and went out along leafy Flemington Road and Mount Alexander Road, then Keilor Road to Airport West. There, in the residential district opposite the airport, he pulled up outside the new computer building that they were erecting for the Department of Aviation, and where, due to a change in the uniform building code, the Department of Construction was required to provide thirty extra car parking spaces.

The house in question was large, prominent in the street but very rundown. It was run down because of an instruction Griffin's predecessor had received from Telford, ordering that no new tenancy be offered on the house. Three years ago. Now, a banner hung across the front verandah. SQUATTER'S UNION

HOME FOR THE HOMELESS

TURN EMPTY GOVT HOUSES OVER TO THE POOR

Like the man said, no one was trying to hide anything.

Griffin got out of his car and walked some distance up the path toward the porch before he noticed that in fact there was someone sitting on the step. It was a woman with a shaven head and tattoos, in rough jeans and a blue work singlet, and he might have mistaken her for a man had it not been for the very obvious indication of femaleness in that she was feeding an infant at her breast.

At that moment, Griffin might have wanted to beat a retreat back to his car, for he never knew how to conduct himself when confronted with such open displays of biology. But he had come too far, and so forced himself to walk boldly up to the woman, trying as hard as he could to divert his eyes from what many would have described as one of the most beautiful sights in the world.

"G'day," he said cheerily.

The woman, younger than he had at first realised, squinted up at him, looked him up and down, noting carefully his polished shoes, jacket and tie, conservative haircut, and then smiled cheekily. She took her nipple from the baby's mouth and then cupped her hand under the breast, lifting it slightly upward toward Griffin.

"Hi," she said gruffly. "Want some?"

Griffin tried to look everywhere else all at once.

"Um. No thank you."

To his considerable relief, the woman now slipped her breast back inside her singlet, which took it only minimally from view. Somehow, the infant slept.

"Well, what do you want, then?"

Griffin could not have felt more uncomfortable. This was not the way he had planned it. Faced with this neanderthal woman, he could not find the words to explain himself. Really, he had hoped for someone more civilised to speak with.

"Arr, my name's Ken..."

"Congratulations."

"...and I...er..wondered if I could have a word with you and the other ladies inside."

"Depends. Who are you?"

"I'm from the Department of Construction."

"Piss orf."

"Look. I just want to have a short chat with you and your... friends."

The woman now stood, cradling the baby in her rough hands. She was looking beyond him, as if seeking out clues to whatever sort of trap this might have been.

"Maybe we don't want to hear it."

"I won't bother you. I'm alone. I don't have any documents to put to you nor threats to make. Just a chat, that's all."

"I told you. We ain't interested."

"I thought you people believed in communal decision making—not one person deciding what the others ought and ought not to hear."

The woman was stumped. So was Griffin, who completely astonished himself by coming up with that. There was a moment while she ran her mind through his words, but plainly there was no way out of it for her. So she half-turned her head towards the flywire door behind her.

"Hey gang, come out here and get a load of this!"

In dribs and drabs they began to emerge. There were seven women and about ten children at all ages from the infant up. Of the women, two seemed perfectly normal middle-aged mums, two were young girls plainly forced into early motherhood, and the remaining pair were very freaky-looking students. One of the latter was obviously the leader of the bunch—a tall creature with long unbrushed red hair, clothes patched and hand-painted, face with stars stuck on it, but under it all, even Griffin could detect, might have been a fairly good looking woman.

"What have we here?" this latter one said, in what seemed to be a clear American accent.

Griffin could manage to smile at her. "G'day. I'm Ken Griffin, Department of Construction, and I..."

"Break out the tar and feathers," the American said laconically.

Griffin laughed. Good one that. Then he noticed no one else was laughing. He stopped.

Now the tall American descended the steps to stand directly in front of Griffin. She met his gaze at the same level.

"Don't worry, sisters. He's just a lackey from the oppressive bureaucracy come to offer us the latest official lies."

Griffin wondered about it. Could it be that only Americans were able to say things like that spontaneously? Did that cause their prominence in civil disobedience matters? Was it some contorted CIA plot? Or was it just that they really were a more advanced civilisation and therefore better equipped for such activities than their homebred counterparts?

"Aren't you afraid you'll be raped or somethin', Lackey," one of the others uttered crudely, as if to try and confirm that last theory.

"I just want to talk," Griffin was saying lamely.

"Who's pulling your strings, Pinocchio," the tall American asked sharply.

"Nobody. My idea."

"He even has ideas," the American said, in what might have been genuine surprise. "I bet they don't approve of that in the Department of Destruction."

The other women thought that very funny and all chortled variously. Even Griffin found he had to strive to suppress a smile.

"Don't you even want to hear what I have to say?"

"Sure not to be anything we haven't heard before."

"I'm trying to help you people."

"Conscience getting to you, Pinocchio?"

"No. I just want to be fair!"

As the argument proceeded, Griffin was becoming quite irritated, but the American girl countered that with a cold deliberate anger.

"Fair? Listen to me, Pinocchio. There are thousands of homeless people in this city, and there are thousands of empty houses that they could be living in. The government owns a great many of those houses, but they want to keep them unoccupied so that they will run down, become worthless, uninhabitable, and then they can knock them down and turn them into car parks. While mothers and their babies are left out in the streets. And you are working for them, helping them, and yet you say your conscience isn't bothering you. Then I say to you that a person with such a lack of feeling is unlikely to be fair to anyone about anything."

It was quite a tirade, and left Griffin floundering, battling desperately to find a way forward.

"It's not me who's doing this to you..." he protested defensively.

"You're taking their money and doing what they tell you."

"But I don't approve of it."

"Then stop doing it!"

"If I stop, someone else will simply take my place. Maybe someone less considerate."

She could smile at that. For such an outrageous looking creature, she had amazingly straight teeth. Too straight, too even, too clean and perfect. It tended to spoil the whole effect, whatever that was.

"Pinocchio, Pinocchio—that's how every running dog henchman of the Capitalist Masters justifies doing their dirty work for them"

From the other girls, there was a pronounced murmur of agreement. Griffin could not restrain a final outburst.

"Aren't you even going to listen?"

"I can't promise that we'll listen," the tall American smiled. "but okay, go on, say your piece."

Except now he could not remember it for the life of him. Told to speak, there did not seem to be a word in him. Griffin ummed and ahhed and they all sat before him like expectant little puppies, wearing bemused expressions. When a cool controlled discourse was required, instead he had to force out the only words he could find.

"On Thursday morning, the cops are coming to forcibly evict you..."

"We know that!"

"Do you mind? Well, you've been handed notices and been given ultimatums and been threatened and there's been negotiations with the Squatters Union, and all that..."

"Yeah, yeah. Yeah, yeah."

"...but...well...it seemed to me that it wasn't being done right."

"No argument there."

"I mean, no one actually approached you. No one has come along and said, look, thanks for looking after the place but it is our property and we need it now and so will you be good enough to pack your stuff and leave. Thank you."

For Griffin, there was such relief at getting it all out that he barely noticed at first the way they all stared at him. Even the tall American had a mask of pure astonishment on her face, her mouth open but unable to produce words as she turned, to her friends, back to Griffin, to her friends, neither knowing which to address nor what to say. Finally, she, rather like Griffin, managed to find something to blurt out.

"And that's it?"

"Yes. That's it. I just thought that someone, nicely and politely, ought to ask you to go, before people start calling in cops and all that."

Confirmation only deepened their amazement. Heads were bowed, being shaken. Finally, the tall American singled out the girl with tattoos.

"Ahhh, Carole. I think you know best how to handle this."

Carole nodded, offering what she but no one else would have called a smile, handed her baby to one of the others, and disappeared into the house.

The tall American seemed to need to sit down, taking Carole's place and clasping her hands between her knees as people do when they are trying to show they are being reasonable.

"Alright, Pinocchio. I see now that you are probably a genuine victim of the collective guilt of the silent majority and I suppose that you really believe you are doing the right thing, but I have to tell you this: you are a complete idiot!"

Griffin didn't know the answer to that, but then perhaps complete idiots weren't supposed to.

"You've misunderstood us, Pinocchio. You've managed to misunderstand everything with a completeness so rare it might be called an art form. When an innocent person is condemned to death, it does not make them feel at all better to know that the executioner is a polite and friendly fellow."

"I just thought.." Griffin began.

"Give up thinking, Pinocchio. It doesn't suit you."

And she turned toward the door.

"Give him our answer, Carole."

Carole came through the door abruptly. She was carrying a bucket of water and with perfect timing, she immediately hurled the contents over the disbelieving Griffin. While they laughed, he stood, astounded, saturated, looking down at his soaked suit wide-eyed. Amid the laughter of the women, the tall American stood now. "It was nice talking to you, Pinocchio, but you bored us. Now be a nice fellow and go away."

Griffin did not know what to do. He looked at the water dripping from his sleeve, touched the sogginess on his lapel, and looked at her with utter dismay.

"There was... I didn't..."

The American stepped closer, jutting her jaw toward him as if inviting him to hit it, but he had no strength left for anything like that.

"Go away!"

She might have been ordering a dog, such was her tone, and Griffin did stumble off a few paces, pause, look back pleadingly.

"Go away! Go on! Git!"

And so their laughter chased him all the way back to his car.

Griffin swung the car through the heavy traffic, turning into thronging Queen Street where the legions of commuters were making their way toward the stations, and there, as always, stood Karen waiting at the kerb. As he often did, he observed that she was the prettiest girl in the whole street, in her smart blouse and tartan skirt, her hair neatly brushed, handbag over her shoulder, jacket over her arm. As she skipped her way through the traffic toward him, she must have incurred many an admiring glance, and it always made him feel good for those observers to see it was his car into which she got.

"Hi, handsome."

"G'day, Sweetie."

As swiftly as a viper, she leaned across the seat and kissed his cheek, but having touched him she then pulled back, frowning slightly, although on her a frown amounted to no more than a sexy little pout.

"I didn't notice it rain today."

"It was only a brief shower."

Karen Kerrigan had one of those Irish accents from the north counties, always high pitched and full of expectation, in every tone expressing her delight and surprise with the world and all its doings. And it was probably for the best that she was so pleasant to listen to, for she did tend to talk quite a bit.

"How was your day?" he asked, to encourage her, not that she needed it.

She perched on the seat rather than sat, her legs under her, knees erotically protruding toward him, but for all that was able to get the seat belt on. But she was a very small package.

"The boss was away. He left me such an enormous pile of typing. I wasn't able to get through it all, but with a wee bit of luck I'll put it away before he arrives in the morning. Given to being late is the boss."

Griffin nodded. Now it was his turn to tell her of his day, since their conversations were always democratic. He replaced the normal with a silence and she, who knew his every mood, had no trouble spotting that one.

"Well, then. Did absolutely nothing happen in the world of gigantic erections?"

He tried to laugh, but the remark deserved more than the strangled gurgle that he offered it.

"Not a lot."

But he would tell her. She knew that. It was just a matter of time, and she set about passing some of that.

"Are we doing anything on Thursdee night?"

"Not that I remember."

"Some friends of mine are goin' to O'Connells. Havin' a bit of a singsong, yer know. Should be fun."

"Folkies, hey? Rough place, O'Connells."

"Not when the folkies, as you call them, are there. They're an alright bunch, really."

"I didn't realise you were keeping up contact with that lot."

She chuckled. "Jealous old thing. It just happened that I ran into Julie O'Dea in Myers at lunchtime. She told me it was on, okay?"

He supposed it might be okay.

There was the briefest silence—something was brewing. He glanced her way and saw her look of expectation. There was something else he had to tell her—but not before she prompted him. It was a game they played—teasing each other to the limit.

"Well," she finally had to ask. "Did you get it?"

"Get what?"

"Oh Ken, you know..."

"No. What?"

"The lamp."

"What lamp?"

"The sale at McEwan's, remember? That lovely little frilly one. You promised to pick it up today."

"Oh shit, I forgot."

"How could you forget? We spent all day Saturday looking for the right one and all day Sunday figuring out that we could afford it."

"Seems such a long time ago."

"Oh, Kenny. It would have gone so well on that side table..."

But then she realised. He simply wasn't apologising enough. She eyed him darkly from under her meticulously plucked brows.

"Ken, it just isn't fair to tease me about something so important. You know how much I wanted it."

"Who's teasing?"

"You are. You can't fool me."

"Oh no? I just did, didn't I?"

"What do you mean?"

"Of course I got it. It's in the boot, goose."

There was a wail of delight and she threw her arms around him and kissed him on the cheek in her excitement.

"Oh Kenny, you are such a darling," she cried and wanted to kiss his lips, right there in the middle of the South Eastern Freeway. Other motorists would need to look to their own defence for a moment. But then she withdrew, touching the shoulder of his suit and again frowning at her damp fingertips.

"You are really wet through."

"You think I haven't noticed?"

"But how do you get soaked to the skin sitting in an air-conditioned office all day?"

"By making the mistake of leaving it," he said.

The Crab Hunters

On the whole it was not too difficult to understand Dell's misgivings about the Redland Bay pub for there could hardly have been a more salubrious place to idle away endless hours. You could sit out on the broad patio as almost everyone did, languishing in the brilliant sunshine, drinking cold beer and gazing out across bay waters to the long low flank of Stradbroke Island dominating the horizon. Only a few kilometres to the south began the cluttered beaches of Surfer's Paradise with its gaudy buildings and choking congestion, a pathetic imitation of Honolulu or Miami, which wasn't too surprising since it was the work of American developers, before they and it were swamped by the Japanese. Only a few kilometres to the north began the suburbs of Brisbane, grim and industrial, the beaches thick with gritty workers desperate to cool off from the torrid effort needed to labour in sub-tropical heat. But here, halfway between, was a no man's land, quiet and tranquil, populated only by locals and a few drifters like Lew and Griffin. It was too far away for the workers and offered too little for the tourists—in other words, it was perfect.

The vehicular ferry provided them with the focal point of their lives, since there was absolutely nothing to do except watch it chug its way back and forth between the terminal which lay happily out of sight around the next headland, and the small town of Dunwich, faintly visible out on Stradbroke. The ferry made the run in forty minutes and was visible all the way, weaving around smaller islands and sandbars, following the indirect line of buoys that marked out the channel. Lew and Griffin found that they could watch its meandering journey back and forth for days on end without the slightest indication of tiring of it.

The only real effort involved was remembering whose shout it was.

"We must, Griffin, load our splendid vehicle onto that little ship and head over and explore the wonders of Stradbroke Island."

"Feeling the allure from across the waters, Lewington?"

"They have, I'm told, a very fine pub out there, at Port Lookout on the ocean side of the island."

"It would have to be fine indeed to be better than this."

"A marvellous view, they tell me, across the strait to Moreton Island, which, you may not know, happens to possess the highest sand dune in the world."

"Truly?"

"So tall in fact that they call it a mountain. Mt Tempest, over nine hundred feet."

"Extraordinary. But I was always under the impression that impermanence was a vital feature of a sand dune, by definition."

"That's right. Apparently, it doesn't usually appear on maps for the very good reason that no one ever knows exactly where it is."

This conversation, always with social or geographical variations, they had several times a day, although they had not got around to doing anything about it yet.

"Dell has Thursday off. She has, I understand, a meeting in the evening but is free for the day. Perhaps we'll go then."

"Yes Lewington. Although perhaps it would be wise for you and she to go; alone together so to speak. I should stay here and hold the fort."

"Griffin, what an old romantic you are."

"That was not the reason behind my suggestion, as you well know."

"I was under the impression that relations between you two were on the improve. Not one violent clash has reached my ears to date."

"Verbal conflict is difficult when there is no conversation."

But such things were best ignored under such circumstances, and conversation on the subject wisely kept to a minimum. Just to sit in the sun, that was all a man needed, and should the sun become too hot or else the predictable evening downpour arrive—for the wet season lingered on beyond its time—there was in the bar a most excellent pool table that could be resorted to.

The island shimmered welcomingly, blue-green for most of the day, purplish under the rare cloudcover, pink running to deepest reds and oranges in the sunset glow. It was long and low, broken only by a huge ugly scar that lay midway along its broad flank where the sandminers were at work, gouging out minerals—rutile, zircon and titanium—for export to the United States or England where, presumably, someone had a deadly purpose for them. It would need to be—you could almost feel the pain of the great wound in the landscape from where you sat. It was better, always, to direct your eyes to the gentler aspect of the vista.

Yes indeed, a fine pub. Amongst the very finest of their experience.

It was perhaps in line with Lew's Cro-magnum appearance that he should prove to be a hunter-gatherer of primeval skill. He was given to sudden fits of enthusiasm for such activities several times a day which would last for about three seconds. Restrain him for those three seconds and he would quickly relapse into the more natural activities of sitting and drinking and talking or, at worst, the rigours of a game of pool or darts. But if loosed in those critical three seconds, he would be off and once off, was quite unstoppable. You needed only to indicate some sharp rocks exposed only when the tide receded and he would go clambering about, cracking oysters from the rocks, oblivious of being doused by occasional large waves. For hours, he would chip away madly with half a brick or a large stone, gobbling some immediately, hurling others to Griffin, and all the while shouting his enthusiasm—what he lacked in organisation he made up for in fanaticism.

"There's hundreds of them down here," he would soggily bellow when the tide finally forced him ashore again. Twice he very nearly drowned, and anyway usually returned lacerated from being buffeted against the rocks.

"We must get a better tool, Griffin, and return to this place."

This he had said of at least ten places within walking distance of the pub but they had returned to none of them.

*

They had taken time off from watching the ferry a few days before and arrived bright and early and beaming with optimism at the local police station in the not to substantial town of Cleveland, and set their attempt to register the Jag in motion.

"No worries," the large redfaced police sergeant behind the counter smiled, "Just let me see your roadworthy."

"Our what?" astonished Lew said to the policeman.

"Our what?" astonished Griffin said to Lew.

"Its a new regulation," the sergeant told them cheerfully, "Just passed a month ago. You have to get a certificate of roadworthiness from a registered mechanic before any vehicle can be registered."

"I see," Lew sighed.

"I see," Griffin growled.

But if Lew felt himself disgraced over that little mishap, Griffin eventually found he could laugh about it.

"I must say, Lewington, that it has been a most pleasant trip, even if undertaken for no good reason whatsoever."

"Bastards," Lew muttered in disgust, "They changed the law just to make things difficult for us."

"I should imagine, Lewington, that is precisely why they did it."

But now, in these idle hours, Lew was troubling to think it through again.

"Are you suggesting," Griffin said helpfully, "that there might be some other part of the country where the law hasn't been altered yet. The Northern Territory or Tasmania. We could whiz off there next, perhaps."

"No, I'm sure not, Griffin," Lew said, horrifying Griffin by taking his suggest seriously, "The banana-benders are always last to do everything. If they have the law, we can be sure everyone else does."

But his optimism could never be dampened for long. "What I am thinking," he went on, "is that it might not be as difficult as we thought to get a roadworthy certificate."

"Is this a joke, Lewington? Have we got to the funny bit yet? Do I laugh now?"

"No, really. I'm serious."

"Lewington, the car is fucked."

"It got us here, didn't it?"

"And polluted most of the east coast of the nation doing so."

"But it got here. It goes. Ergo, it is to some degree roadworthy. Anyway, we have no alternative."

"Yes we have. We can put the car on yonder ferry, have a drive around the island, on the way back accidentally allow it to slip off the ferry into the depths of the channel and hitch-hike back to Melbourne."

"Good God, Griffin. You animal. You absolute savage. How can you even think of so foul and barbaric a deed."

"Desperation, I should think."

"Let's consider the less drastic solution of getting a roadworthy first."

"I'm not convinced it is less drastic."

"No, look. I'm sure of this. The folk up here do everything at a slow and sloppy rate. They are simply not as efficient as their counterparts down south, mechanics, I should think, included. So we find some little out of the way garage where the bloke's dumb or illiterate or both, sink a few beers into him and get him to sign."

"Oh, come on, Lewington. The bloody car is fucked. Hardly any part of it works properly. No one is going to give you a roadworthy for the very good reason that it is not a roadworthy car."

"You see. You expect everything to make sense. The one thing you, of all people, ought to know is that governments never make sense unless you are able to reveal the underlying corruption that informs their decisions. Apart from certain southern US states, Queensland has the most corrupt government in the world. Populations always get the government they deserved. Ergo, Queenslanders are eminently corruptible."

"You are suggesting crime, Lewington. Bribery."

"To put it crudely."

"Is there a stain of the mafia in your ancestry, Lewington?"

"Probably something to do with my Catholic upbringing."

"Are you a Mick?"

"I was."

"Lapsed, I pray."

"Collapsed is rather more like it, Griffin."

They could discuss it indefinitely. In such circumstances, nothing could have been more prefect than to make plans and subsequently do nothing about them. There was plenty of time. At one stage they did consult maps and telephone directories looking for likely garages but since none were clearly indicated as being staffed by corruptible or short-sighted mechanics, that was as far as it got. Mostly it was better to pass the time drinking, and otherwise sucking watermelon or eating freshly plucked oysters, lobster or crab, most of which you suspected had been produced within visual distance. Sitting in the sun.

"This is almost as good as the crab we cooked ourselves," Lew remarked over lunch, sucking the morsels delightedly, "And to think these Queenslanders eat like this all the time. Fantastic!"

Griffin was sure Queenslanders usually ate sausages or roast lamb just like everyone else, but it would not have been to the spirit of the occasion to say so.

"I must say, Lewington, that you cook a great crab."

"Yes, Griffin. We must catch another and do it again."

"You can catch another, Lewington. I shall be delighted to watch you do so from the beach and enjoy the ensuing meal afterwards."

"Griffin. Can it be that your spirit of adventure has been dampened?"

"Not funny, Lewington, not funny."

*

The crab hunting episode was, by necessity of its complexity, a less spontaneous operation, but otherwise lacked none of the Lew Sigg informality. It needed only for Dell to mention that there were excellent mud crabs to be had from the bay waters right outside the front of the house to send Lew, at first light, tearing apart someone's wire mesh fence and reconstituting it into what he informed Griffin was a crab pot. What it looked like to Griffin was one of those wire baskets you used in supermarkets to gather supplies, except for the long nylon cord attached to the top and the piece of left-over rump steak secured in the middle.

"Should there not be some contrivance for trapping the beast once it takes the bait?" Griffin asked when he should have known better.

"No. Not necessary, Griffin. Well, real crab pots do, I admit. But crabs are such tenacious creatures. Once he gets his clippers into the meat, he just won't let go. When we pull him in, he'll still be there trying to drag it off to his lair and refusing to face the reality that it is our lair he is destined for. So we just drop the pot in, wait until dusk when they come out to forage and pull it in, and there's sure to be a big crab in there, fanging madly and not for a moment suspecting its capture. Easy."

"Dusk? Then why drop it in so soon. It gives them all day to devour the meat."

"No, they won't eat it until they get it to their lair. The only thing that will make a crab give up trying will be a bigger crab scaring it off and taking over. By evening, we ought to have the biggest bloody crab in the bay in there. A bewdy!"

Dell was even able to provide a small aluminium dinghy to facilitate this operation, much to Griffin's distress.

The water was as flat as glass when they rowed out about fifty yards from the house and put the basket over the side. With a buoy—in fact a plank torn off a neighbour's fence—Lew marked the spot and they rowed in again.

Thereafter they could sit in the pub all day, waiting for sundown, and even feel productive. But later in the afternoon, in the way that never happened any other day—rainclouds closed in and the wind sprang up, harrying the waves on the bay to quite startling heights. They were forced, toward evening, to contemplate the issue over the pool table—Lew was so concerned about it that Griffin won five games straight.

"Perhaps we should leave it until tomorrow, Lewington."

"No, no, Griffin. The very thought of some juicy crab gnawing away thankfully at our meat, just waiting for us, right now, is more than I can bear. We must go."

And go they did, huddled against the wind, Griffin complaining bitterly all the way but Lew remained steadfastly determined. They were almost capsized twice just carrying the dinghy to the water's edge.

"You're crazy going out there in these conditions," Griffin yelled above the wind.

"You don't have to come with me."

"Sure I don't," Griffin heard himself say, and much to his own amazement, "To stand helplessly by and watch you drown is as horrible an experience as I can imagine, whereas I won't give your wellbeing the slightest thought if I'm sharing the danger myself."

"I've often wondered, Griffin, at the dividing line between heroism and madness."

"Heroism is a state of temporary insanity, Lewington."

"Still it does manage to win wars."

"That's because wars themselves are madness."

Griffin was not one of the world's great seafarers—he tended to flail rather uselessly with the oars while Lew shouted inaudible instructions from the stern. The only real advantage in rowing was that he had his back turned to all the dangers and couldn't see how much trouble they were getting into.

"Go past the marker and then we'll drift back onto it with the tide and I'll grab it and haul it in," Lew declared.

With his eyes full of salt and spray and the wind whistling in one ear and out the other and his stomach surging up and down in inverse relation to the rest of his body, Griffin had no chance of following such instructions. Soaring up onto the crests and down into the toughs where the waves seemed ten feet high, Griffin strove to keep the prow pointed into the weather, just the way he'd heard about in movies, but somehow the uncooperative waves seemed to come from all directions. He refused to think about how he always got seasick, that he did not know how to row a boat and worst of all, that he was a lousy swimmer. But somehow, while he waved the oars erratically, they did seem to achieve the desired effect. For far too long, they rocked and wrenched about, Lew becoming increasingly frantic, until suddenly he reached over the side and jubilantly displayed the plank with the cord still attached. The moment of truth had arrived.

Several things happened at once. Lew, hauling the basket in, was obliged to stand in order to prevent the basket from being too far tilted when he pulled it over the side. He twisted so violently to maintain his footing that he put too much strain on the buttons of his shorts. Suddenly, surreally from Griffin's point of view, Lew's shorts dropped to his ankles. Probably totally hysterical, Griffin laughed so much that he lost one of the oars and only a mouthful of water could halt his mirth. But Lew, heedless of modesty, was roaring. "We got one. We got one."

Whereby indeed the basket cleared the water and one very fearsome large orange crab was added to the crew of the boat.

This advent put a new light on everything. The crab, suddenly realising it had run out of ocean, relinquished its hold on the meat and decided to chomp the nearest large object, which happened to be Griffin. As he reared back from those huge and getting huger pincers, the remaining oar dug in. Lew was after the crab but his halfmast shorts tripped him and he sprawled in the bottom of the dinghy. And just then they were hit broadside by a huge wave. Needless to say, over they went.

Griffin hit the water with a clear understanding that he would now drown. He knew the reason most people drown is due to panic and in water, Griffin was panic personified. Added to that was the fact that as they went over, the oar gave him a nasty crack on the head, and further the knowledge that there was a large crab of very unfriendly disposition in the vicinity but mostly that his mouth, nose, ears and eyes were all full of water, all meant only one thing to Griffin. He was doomed.

He hit the bottom bum first, where he launched himself upward in a desperate bid to reach the surface, when he discovered that his arms, making a frenzied imitation of swimming, were in fact flailing in midair.

Air?

Safety?

When he was sure his backside was still contacting the bottom? It was true, for at that point, the water was only three feet deep.

The critical information that had thitherto escaped his

attention was that due to the excessive murkiness of the water—itself the combined effects of the Stradbroke mining operations, the dredging of the channel between and the outpourings into this strait of the urban-coursed Brisbane River—there had been no clue to the shallowness. In a state of revelation, Griffin stood himself up, the waves crashing harmlessly against his back, the half-submerged boat bumping against his thigh, staring at Lew Sigg in an shared amazement.

"You fucking tried to drown me, you bastard!" Griffin roared at him.

But Lew, by then, had other problems—something unexpected seemed to be happening to his shorts which at present were awash and about his ankles.

"Shit!" he cried and plunged downward and began a frantic struggle in the shallow depths. For the crab, plainly as displeased with Lew as Griffin was, had launched a counter-attack and in its confusion, was venting its rage on those troubled shorts. Lew seized upon the creature's back and tore it free. "We got the bastard. We got him!" he shouted jubilantly, waving the trophy high over his head while the berserk crab continued to savage the tatters of his decency.

"Stick it up your arse," Griffin bellowed back, "You're fucking insane, that's what you are." Another wave hit him in the back as he set off to wade over the sharp rocks to the shore.

"Hey, come on, Griffin. Give us a hand, will you?"

"You bloody maniac. Solve your own fucking problems."

"Here. Grab the rope and tow the boat in with you. I gotta hold this fucking thing."

"Hope it rips your fucking arms off."

Griffin, with his back turned as he struggled away, could hear those pincers snapping angrily in the air. He wasn't tempted to look around—he looked only toward the distant dry land and surged onward.

"Then you carry the crab and I'll get the boat."

"It's your fucking crab, you carry it."

"Well at least come here and pull my shorts up so I can walk."

"You tried to murder me. Pull you own fucking shorts up."

He was walking, lurching, staggering, battered by waves, sinking in the muddier sections, and had thoughts only of reaching the shore and safety.

"You can't leave me like this!"

"I'll never forgive you for this. You tried to drown me."

And Lew was left adrift, yelling for aid, suffering indecent exposure, clutching the snapping crab, clutching the rope to which he hoped the upturned boat was attached, abandoned to sort out his own wicked contrivances.

He would, Griffin later reflected, have to ask Lew, when an appropriate moment arose, just exactly how he finally got himself, the crab and the boat (though not the shorts) ashore. But Lew was good at things like that—he had even recovered both oars but then, considering Dell's likely reaction to loss of boat or oars, you could only suppose there had been no choice. And, he had to admit, when the crab was served that evening, they dined so splendidly that it might well have been worth it in the end.

"How did you cook it?" Dell asked, for she had been absent at work while the adventure had taken place.

"Just chuck in some onions and boil her in the shell," Lew said proudly.

"Surely you have to kill them first," Dell said with a shiver,

"Don't you stab 'em between the eyes or something?"

"Only if you want to risk losing a few fingers."

Apparently they had even bigger crabs in America but not anywhere Dell had been. Like any visitor to a foreign country, she had made her own previous attempt at this.

"When I cooked one," she said, "It scraped and scratched in the pot for hours. It was awful. I couldn't stand it. I never tried it again."

"No love," Lew was patiently saying, "They die the instant you drop them in the boiling water."

"Oh?" Dell gasped, "I see. You should boil the water first."

The hunter-gatherers stared at each other in horror—plainly the wonders of modern engineering did not extend themselves to being merciful in the cooking pot. Lew regarded the morsel presently on the end of his fork ruefully. "Crab, you might be being eaten, but you don't know how lucky you were."

But if the crabs and other creatures might have suffered, the same could not have been said of Griffin and Lew. They could, they knew, have sat it out in the Redland Bay pub for the rest of their lives without regret. Except Lew was getting itchy feet.

"Be a nice change of scenery, over at the Port Lookout pub."

"You really think we'll go, Lewington?"

"Perhaps, Griffin. Hard to tell. You're such a stick-in-the-mud. You can be hard to move at times."

"I like to stay where I'm happy, Lewington."

"Actually, I'm surprised I got you this far. I feared you might not be able to breathe the air outside Carlton."

"When you've lived for a year in a tent in a place subject to mortar attacks and from where weekly you rode out in helicopters to land in combat zones, the need to run off pursuing adventurous activities is somewhat diminished."

"Yes, I can see how it might be superfluous."

"Still, if we don't go, it is pleasant sitting here thinking about it."

"Life is becoming incredibly simple, Griffin."

"Incredibly simple, Lewington, incredibly simple."

Heritages

There were places that Karen Kerrigan could take him. It was she who found them tickets to concerts, who received all their invitations to parties. It was she who arranged picnics and other outings. It was she who took him to O'Connells Pub.

In fact, she had been there before, and more than once. In some strange way it came as something of a shock to realise that she had a past, an existence before he met her. There was England of course, although she barely remembered it, and school, and home, and that was all she ever spoke of. But O'Connells was the place where she had once gone every Thursday night, looking for love, he had to suppose.

It was curious to think about. Throughout the entire year they had been living together, she had never mentioned that corner of her life. She had forsaken all of her friends for him. When she said that he was all she needed or wanted, she really meant it. He found it just a little difficult to cope with that. Nevertheless, on the nominated Thursday night, he happily drove her across the city to Carlton where, he had learned, lurked student radicals, junkies and half of Melbourne's underworld. The pub itself was in the very depths of Carlton, down past the university and into the side streets, a shadowy and rather gothic looking place complete with gargoyles, tower and buttresses.

But it was popular alright. Although early in the evening, the bar was crowded and full of cigarette smoke. All of the men were bearded and wore shabby clothes, all of the women wore secondhand tops and patched jeans and had plainly lost the art of brushing their hair. Griffin cringed in his cleancut conservativeness—fortunately she had managed to talk him out of wearing a three piece suit and tie, but even his sensible trousers and cardigan made him look pronouncedly out of place.

And more than he realised, for as Karen led him through the throng to the bar, easing their way past this shoulder and that, Griffin observed that everyone seemed to be speaking with distinct accents. Because he had never been able to tell the difference between Irish, Scots and the other extreme British accents, to him they all sounded the same.

Karen knew the barman.

"Long time, lassie," he smiled at her, a freckled redhaired blob of a man.

"Hi, Mack. This is my friend Ken."

"G'day," Griffin answered. His own Australian accent could not have been more prominent. Nearby drinkers even turned to look, on the basis of that single word.

Mack immediately plonked two frothing beers on the bar, and waved a hand while Griffin fumbled for his wallet.

"Visitors always get the first one on the house. It's a tradition here, laddie."

"Ah, thanks mate," Griffin said, feeling as though he had just arrived from another planet.

"Like to make outsiders feel welcome," Mack said and was away to serve other customers.

When he might have wanted to head for the flanks, Karen was towing him deeper. On the far side of the room was a small rostrum on which a shabby young man was singing a song, or some semblance of one. There was no accompanying music although those around him did have instruments and the song was rendered in a straining, guttural voice and in such Gaelic brogue that Griffin could not understand a word of it. A ballad, surely, of some ancient war in kilts, for the voice did carry the strain and struggle of warfare imbued in its throat-wrenching tones. Griffin was guessing—it might equally have been a lament of lost love, or even the enthroned dirge of a man with bowel problems.

Karen was swamped by friends. "Ken, this is Sally and Kerrin and The McKane. Folks, my friend Ken."

But they were all too busy embracing her and whooping welcomes to take much notice of 'her friend'.

"G'day. Glad to meet yer."

Then they all stared.

"Not from the old country, then," The McKane accused him.

"No...not me. Born right here."

"Well, never mind lad. Here's to yer anyway."

It wasn't easy to get her alone.

"I feel like a foreigner."

Karen chucked. "Well, you are likely to be the only dinky-die Aussie in the place, if that's what you mean."

"I think I'm suffering chronic xenophobia."

"I wish you'd speak English."

Griffin wished he could too. Or Irish, or Scots, or Welsh, or whatever.

Or American, he suddenly observed. For in a gap through the crowd, he spied a bunch of multi-hued hair that was all too familiar. The tall American was over there, laughing with friends. Griffin ducked.

"No need to be scared," Karen tried to assure him. "They won't hold it against you."

He could at least be thankful for that.

That made the third time in a week he had seen her, and the train of coincidence began to worry him. The second time had been on television, when Griffin had watched the news reports of the clearing of the squat. There she had been in all her colourful glory, fighting back fiercely as four burly policemen tried to carry her out. They had no easy time of it and, unless he was mistaken, had managed to land on one of those policemen a blow that he would remember for some time to come. The newsreader had informed him that only one woman had been arrested, and there was not the slightest doubt which one that had been. Now she stood on the far side of the bar, talking to a rough looking character she might have picked him up in prison. She was out on bail, Griffin happened to know, and apparently had taken advantage of the matter to haunt him further.

Someone who was named O'Something or McSomething advanced and engulfed Karen in a giant hug. Griffin wasn't sure that he ought not to put a stop to this sort of thing.

"Kerrigan, Kerrigan, I'm thinkin' it's been too long, girl. Where you been hiding?"

"Deep in the suburbs," Karen laughed.

"And will you be giving us a tune, girl."

"Oh no, it's been too long," Karen said demurely.

Griffin stared at her: "Tune?"

She waved him off with a tiny frown. This was getting very complicated.

"Ah, come on, girl. Be a sport. We've all been deprived of yer melodious fingers far too long."

"I doubt those fingers will be able to find the way..." Karen sighed dubiously.

"What sort of tune?" Griffin burst in again. He was beginning to realise that this girl he thought he knew all about was in fact a total stranger.

"See. Yer fella-me-lad needs educatin'. Come on, how about it."

"Oh, alright then," Karen said, giving in with hardly a fight. At least that was familiar.

"What's he talking about?" Griffin demanded.

Karen flashed him her most reassuring smile.

"You'll see."

From behind the bar she obtained from Mack a long thin black box, the contents of which, when she assembled them deftly, was unmistakably a flute.

"Can you play that?" he gasped at her. She handled it so skilfully, the question was plainly idiotic.

"No," she laughed. "It's just a magic wand to drive away evil spirits."

And she waved it at him menacingly.

The Evil Spirit backed off, and could only stand like a fool while she moved away toward the rostrum, or stage, he supposed. It annoyed him that she had kept secrets, but all the more so that he was reacting so badly to the discovery. It gave her an allegiance with them that might have been stronger than he realised. He could feel his alienation intensifying.

She joined the musicians on the stage and, mid-tune, added the lilting tones of her own instrument. The notes floated softeningly over the room as her fingers danced along its shining extent. With her long hair and shapely form, Griffin realised that she might have fulfilled every fantasy of every man in the room. Worse still, she could really play the thing, and soon the other musicians left her to a solo which, as far as he could tell, was utterly flawless. Her eyes glowed as she played, and they were always looking at him, seeking, as always, his approval. He did everything he could to get a smile onto his face, striving to shed his foolish insecurity, his petty obsessiveness. She was their fantasy, but she was his woman. He decided it would be more appropriate to be proud of her, and promptly was so. He had been feeling intimidated by these people, but he suddenly saw that they were the strangers. His whole heritage might have risen from their kind, but he was the end result, and something quite apart from them now.

Satisfied that he now had things under control, he gulped his beer down and went to the bar for another.

"Oh no. Pinocchio's escaped his strings again."

So intent had he been on watching Karen that he had not noticed who was right next to him as he bellied the bar. It was as if, in this mad American, he had loosen a monster who would haunt him for eternity.

"G'day," was the best thing he could find to say.

"In the enemy camp twice in one week. You really are heroic."

"It's all an accident, I promise you."

"Yeah, sure—co-incidence has a way of having accidents... two pots thanks Mack... suit dried out yet, Pinocchio?"

"I suppose I deserved that."

"Guilt is a terrible thing."

"Nothing to do with guilt."

"Oh no? And I don't suppose you know anything about the mysterious person or persons who bailed me out."

"The Department of Construction, as a matter of fact."

"Well, no doubt they'll understand if I don't express my gratitude."

"Actually, they don't know about it yet."

"Come again?"

"I put it through on a purchase order against Departmental running expenses."

It floored her, as he hoped it would. Except he never really excepted her to find out about it. She stood, staring, spilling her beer, caught short for the first time in her life, he liked to imagine.

"Shit," she uttered. "God damn it. I should have bloody known."

"I carefully arranged it that you didn't."

"Good God, why? Did you expect to earn my gratitude or something?"

"No. Never expected to see you again."

"Then why, fuck it."

"Just a matter of common decency."

She took a gulp from her beer and dumped it on the bar, shaking her head in dismay.

"I gotta take a leak," she uttered. "Watch these beers for me, will you?"

"I'll guard them with my life," Griffin grinned.

"Somehow, I know you will," she groaned and pushed through the crowd away from him.

That left him stranded. Griffin looked around, hoping Karen might reappear and rescue him—from himself if nothing else. Instead he saw he was face to face with a giant Golliwog. It was a vast blob of black curly hair, a dark face gleaming with sweat, a matted beard and rather milky eyes that seemed to float in his head, never really able to focus precisely.

"Bloody Griffin, as I live and breath," it said.

Griffin stared. There was nothing at all familiar about this person, he was certain. And then not so certain...

"Lew?"

"Of course. How could you fail to recognise me?"

"I can't imagine."

"Still not wearing your glasses, I see," Lew Sigg grinned, rather more, Griffin suspected, at the memory of the night the comment brought with it. Griffin could not help chuckle himself.

"No. I still don't need them."

Lew reared back in mock shock at the implications of that.

"So, I guess you didn't get killed in Vietnam."

"No. Everyone who shot at me missed."

"You mean you really went there?"

"Yes, I was there. I only got out a few months back..."

"God, don't say it so loud. They'll lynch you as a CIA spy in these parts if they find out."

"I doubt it."

"But don't worry. Now that you're with me, no one will suspect."

"I don't care."

"You will if they find out. Who's beers are they?"

"Some Yank sheila..."

"Oh yeah. I saw you talking to her."

"I'm just minding them."

"There are better things to do with her than mind her beer," Lew said and licked his lips.

For a brief moment, Griffin considered the consequences of allowing this mad Golliwog thing to steal the wild Yank woman's beer. It was completely intolerable just to think about.

"Let me buy you a beer, Lew."

"For old times sake."

"I don't think we have any old times worth remembering. Let's make it the future."

"I'm not sure if we have too much future either."

Griffin ordered the beer and the American woman returned, reaching past rudely to grab her drinks.

"That sure is some hairstyle you got there, Mary Lou," Lew said in her ear.

"Piss off creep," the American spat at him and shoved her way through to safer ground. Griffin was delighted that she didn't bother to thank him.

"Well, that went well."

"I think she liked me," Lew drooled at her departing back.

"No, she says sweet things like that to everyone."

Lew shrugged and took a firm gulp from the beer Griffin handed him, and looked about to leave in pursuit of the woman, but then paused and regarded Griffin with sudden deep seriousness.

"Griffin," it said again, with great assurance. "Have you ever considered the significance of your name?"

Weird. Griffin shivered, but who could resist the bait.

"Why's that?"

"Griffin. Or Gryphon actually. Fabulous creature of Assyrian mythology. It had the head of an eagle and the body of a lion."

"Truly."

"Which, no doubt, must be very confusing for you."

"Well, it would be, wouldn't it."

Lew looked at him curiously. Then his demeanour completely changed.

"Yes. I think she really liked me."

"Let's say she likes you better than she likes me," Griffin grinned.

"I think she's had enough time to regret her error. Back in a minute."

And he was gone. Griffin stood, staring in astonishment at the receding back as he pranced away, seeking new victims to torment with mythical names. Now that he knew just how freaky a freak could be, Griffin began receding into a corner himself.

Soon, if far from soon enough, Karen was back at his side.

"Did you like it?"

"Impossible not to like."

"I was a bit rusty..."

"You're very good," he said, even though he would not have known good flute playing from bad. "But you might have warned me."

She cringed. Most of all, she wanted only his approval.

"I wanted to surprise you."

"Girlie, you certainly did that."

She wanted to introduce more people. She dragged him hither and yon and everywhere friends greeted her warmly and offered him a what-have-we-got-here expression.

"Not from the Old Country then?"

He was realising that his original error was no such thing—the Old Country was equally Ireland or Scotland, depending only on the accent, and might even have been Old Blighty herself, or indeed just anywhere that wasn't Australia. The obvious reply was to ask what part of 'the Old Country' each individual was from whereby he got a further surprise.

"The family comes from Country Cork," they might answer. Further interrogation revealed that most of these 'Old Country' folk had in fact been born in Australia, or else brought here as part of the Post-war Migrant intake when they were very young. The greater number had, actually, never been to 'the Old Country'. And neither had Karen Kerrigan, unless there were more secrets.

"You're not really enjoying yourself, are you?" Karen was sure.

"Oh, it's an interesting place. But you don't have to introduce me to everyone."

"I was just trying to make you feel at home."

Since everyone in the pub seemed to have trouble figuring out where home was, he decided to change direction.

"Look. I'm okay. You run off and play with your friends. I'll be about. I'm sure I can amuse myself."

By hiding in a corner and drinking himself to oblivion, for instance.

"Are you sure you'll be alright?"

"Truly. Go on. Enjoy yourself."

When she was gone, he could not have felt more alone.

But almost immediately, that hot beery breath was back at his ear.

"You and me, Gryphon."

Whereby Lew the Golliwog all but fell on top of him, and then stood with its body weaving precariously.

"Why...dare I ask...must it be very confusing?"

"Head of an Eagle, body of a Lion. American Eagle. British Lion. How can you possible know what you are in that condition?"

"Alright, I admit it. I don't know what I am."

"You see. Confused. Let me help you, Griffin. Where are you from?"

"You know where I'm from. We went to the same school, remember?"

"But you could have come from anywhere before that."

"Do I need to be 'from' somewhere?"

"Of course you do. Everyone in this place is 'from' somewhere."

"True. As it happens, I'm from Melbourne."

"The one in Wales?"

"The one in Australia."

Lew looked so astonished at this news that it's milky eyes bulged, and then suddenly narrowed, darting right and left.

"You know something? So I am."

Griffin thought about it. There was no doubting the Australianness of Lew Sigg's accent, even if he looked like he came from Venus.

"Incredible."

"It is," Lew colluded dramatically. "Think about it. In this pub, two people from the same home town. Small world, huh."

Finally Griffin had to laugh. Lew shared it briefly, but then nudged closer. "Listen. As far as I can tell, it's you and me against the rest of them."

"Against?"

"Of course against. Haven't you noticed. All these strange accents, all these strange rituals. Don't you see what they are?"

"Subversives."

"Exactly. Isn't it obvious? First there were the abos, and then these characters' ancestors came along and took the country off them. Now there's us Aussies and here they are again, taking over."

"And where, exactly, did these Australians come from, may I ask?"

"Same place as the abos. Australia. Where else would an Australian come from?"

While Griffin's crumpled brain strove to unravel that little lot, Lew gulped its beer with jubilation, and then leaned again, eyes narrowed with distrust.

"Look," he said. "It's up to us. They're trying to swamp us with their traditions. We gotta show them that we have traditions of our own."

"You're suggesting we get our swags and sit under the nearest coolabah and burst into Waltzing Matilda?"

"Better than that. I got a plan. But you've got to help."

"What's the plan?"

"You'll see. I'll fix 'em. But then they'll be after me. You gotta make sure they don't get me."

"What's the plan?"

"I know you will. You and me, mate. Aussies. You'll come through for me when the shit hits the fan."

"Fair dinkum and true blue."

"Right, be back soon."

In a flash, he had vanished out the door.

Bloody Lew. He'd always been as silly as a snake. Griffin stood holding his drink and contemplating the sorrows of allegiance. He was wondering if perhaps he might come to a similar fate himself were he to hang around a place like this long enough. But it was a matter of traditions, of heritages. Whatever it was that had become the Australian character had arisen from people like these but then carried on to become something quite distinct, almost unrecognisably different. And yet that difference did remain hard to put your finger on.

"How's it going?" Karen materialised into his thoughts to ask.

"Oh, fine, fine."

"That bad, huh? Who was that you were talking to."

"The Golliwog?"

"Yes. Funny fellow."

"To put it mildly... His name is Lew..."

"I must admit I was wondering what you and he to might have found in common."

"We come from the same city."

"Really? Which city?"

"The one we're standing in right now."

Karen laughed, though it was a disappointed laugh: "Here I am, dragging you out for a multi-cultural experience and the only person you can find to talk to is another Australian."

"Well, it seems to me that all the Scots are talking to Scots and all the Irish are talking to Irish."

"I suppose," she sighed, all the more disappointed. He was even beginning to feel like a disappointment to himself.

"Actually, Lew and I were at school together," he had to admit.

"Ah, an old friend then?"

"We were never really friends. We just occasionally tormented the same teachers."

"I can imagine. He looks a real ragtag."

"Yeah. I know. He doesn't seem to have changed."

"I shudder to think. Look, we can leave if you want," she said suddenly. He looked at her. She obviously didn't want to go anywhere.

"No," he said, suspecting a truthful statement for a change. "I have a feeling something is going to happen."

Without the foggiest idea of how right that might have been.

It began with a sudden commotion over the entrance. People were milling and gasping and shrieking and in the middle of it all could be glimpsed a fuzzy-wuzzy head with some strange arrangement of feathers attached. Heavy grunting cries seemed to arise from under those feathers.

"Good grief," Karen said, on tip-toe and craning. "What's going on?"

"Can't imagine," Griffin said, but as she towed him in that direction, he had a horrible suspicion that he knew exactly what it was.

They thrust their way through people buffeting and pushing as they tried either to get closer or else make their escape. There were shouts and cries of all kinds—anger, amazement, delight, horror, but the loudest cries came from the centre of the throng and of course at the centre was his newfound ally, the mysterious Lew Sigg.

"Oh my God," Karen was gasping mirthfully. "Isn't he a crazy one?"

Brave, was what Griffin would have thought.

For the most part he was naked, although for the sake of decency he had bothered to tie a piece of cloth about his waist. Otherwise his brown body was covered from head to foot with long stripes of white and yellow and red, applied thickly and roughly. He had tied a band about his head and into it poked a line of chook feathers. He strutted about emphatically, and then would suddenly draw himself into a stock-still pose, then contort again, stamping his feet and editing throaty grumbles interspersed with fearful warcries. At times he waved imaginary spears at onlookers, his face twisted into the most malevolent expressions, suddenly rush at someone terrifyingly, stop, retreat, poise, twist, and strike again.

"It's a corroboree," Karen cried delightedly.

"And to think I forgot my didgeridoo," Griffin mused.

The general reaction to this carry-on was mixed. There were those who, like Karen, were enthralled by this creation and clapped and cheered and stamped their feet in time with the frenzied movements of the dancer. Others stood with their mouth gaping in astonishment, while there were others still, perhaps a majority, who were outraged at this abuse and mockery of their traditional ways and called for someone to get the police or men in white coats to take the interloper away. Mack was behind the bar, gasping that no one could do what Lew was plainly doing. The jiggers and musicians were obliged to curtail their time-honoured activities and could only stand and watch in dismay.

"He ain't even an abo," someone roared, and that was the signal for attack.

"Grab him," others called and they tried.

But Lew had lost none of his schoolboy agility and eluded them or almost did. Someone grabbed his loincloth and whipped it away from his body, which induced the rather shocking realisation that Lew had omitted to daub his buttocks and private parts. Desperately, and so very vulnerably naked, he raced for the door with several of the more outraged individuals in pursuit but Lew got there first and slammed it in their faces. The door was only a few feet wide of Griffin who, with two quick paces, got there second and then did nothing. Hands and arms grappled all around him and they pulled at the door but Griffin got all tangled up in that such that it was at least fifteen seconds before they managed to get him out of the way and through the door. Griffin, flattened against the wall, apologising furiously for his oafishness, allowed the stampede to thunder by into the street and then followed along. He was fairly certain that his patriotic role wasn't completed yet.

Out on the street, they were calling for blood, in scurrying twos and threes, going this way and that, but there was no sign of their tormentor. Griffin contemplated the scene. Across the road was a row of houses with some fairly dense foliage in several front yards: in the available time Lew could not have got any further than that. The vigilantes thought he was in the park further down the road, or the network of lanes behind the pub, but the Australian Army had invested a lot of time and effort to teach people like Griffin how to find fugitives. He crossed the road and immediately saw amongst the parked cars a white Holden with a dark smear on the mudguard—as he went by he surreptitiously removed it with his handkerchief. The hunters were beginning to slow down, knowing they'd lost the scent and starting to think, so he needed to move carefully. He found a wrought iron fence where more pigment gleamed and stood there, still and silent. The rustle of movement and breathing in those bushes were almost indiscernible, but enough.

"Stay there, mate. You'll be right," Griffin said quietly.

"That you, Griffin."

"Just keep quiet. I'll keep them away."

The angry Celts were giving up and trooping back into the pub and only the most determined of them continued the search now. Griffin leaned on the fence and lit a cigarette and watched calmly.

"Hey laddie. You seen a chappie wit nought on?"

"Yeah. He went around the corner up there."

Eventually the allure of music and beer drew them all off the street, although it took rather longer than either Lew or Griffin would have liked. It wasn't the warmest of nights, being midwinter, and Griffin could clearly hear Lew's teeth chattering in there. Then Karen came out looking for him and crossed the road to his side.

"What are you doing here?"

"Just getting some fresh air."

"You aren't really enjoying yourself."

"On the contrary, it's great. I'll be back in shortly."

"Don't you go catching a cold now."

"I won't. You go back. I'll be there in a minute."

Karen went off to rejoin her friends, rather surprised to have learned that she had got mixed up with a fresh air freak.

They waited.

"You having it off with that little sheila, Griffin?" Lew asked from in the bushes.

"Mind your own bloody business."

"Sexy little bit of vagina."

"You want me to tell those blokes where you are?"

"A warm and wonderful woman."

"That's better."

"And I couldn't give a stuff if they find out where I am."

"Very brave of you."

"Why should a man have to run and hide because he upholds his traditions?"

"Are you an aborigine, Lew?"

"No. I'm Australian, and so are they. We ought to share everything."

Since he could think of no answer to that, Griffin lit another cigarette. In the bushes, he could hear Lew standing and slapping his flesh for warmth.

"Listen to those bastards. They think their heritage is the only one worth having."

"I suspect they thought you were taking the mickey out on them."

"Who cares? I showed them."

"That you did."

"I think I'll go back and show them again."

"You must live near here to have got into that get-up so speedily."

"Just up the road there."

Griffin took off his coat and handed it to him. "Put this on and I'll get you home."

"No. I'm gonna show 'em again."

"You won't, you know."

"You wouldn't try and stop me, would you, Griffin?"

"I think you made your point."

"Listen to 'em. They've forgotten it already."

"Somehow I doubt they ever will."

"I'm gonna show 'em again."

This sort of dispute might have gone on indefinitely, had not Lew decided all reason had failed and jumped the fence. Griffin pounced and got him in a bearhug but Lew writhed and squirmed frantically and that coating of pigment—which proved to be oil paint—gave him the slipperiness of an eel. Griffin had no choice but to take his legs out from under him and they went down on the pavement and struggled for a while until Griffin got him pinned.

"I'll show 'em! I'll show the bastards!" Lew was bellowing, but his breathing was beginning to rasp and Griffin pushed a knee into his chest to silence him. The night was cold, the pavement was wet and lights were coming on in several houses. And in the distance came a wailing that only might have had something to do with them, but certainly would if they allowed it to arrive and witness their present circumstances.

"Shit. Cops," Griffin gasped.

"What's happening out there?" someone called from their front step.

"Let's get outa here," Lew gasped.

They were on their feet and running and Griffin passed him the jacket to pull around him—it was now heavy smeared with paint anyway. Fleeing into the night, his clothes multi-hued, with this madman. They found the house—a small single terrace in terrible decay. Griffin found the front door open.

"Is there someone home?"

"No. I just didn't have anywhere to put the key. Well, nowhere decent at least."

"You'll be safe now."

"Hold on. Come in for a drink. There's something I want to ask you."

"About what?"

"You went to Vietnam. I didn't. Remember?"

"You were smart. I was dumb."

"The cops are looking for me. I'm threatened with gaol."

"Even in gaol, you'll be winning."

"You must come in and explain. Tell me why. My whole life hangs on it."

Drawn on by Lew's sheer energy, Griffin entered the astonishing junkheap that was the interior of the house. Lew hurled rubbish out of chairs and offered a flagon of wine. Griffin sat in great discomfort, while Lew dragged on a pair of paint splattered shorts.

"Look, Karen will be wondering..."

"Okay. Make it short and sweet. Wouldn't want to keep the young lady waiting."

"There is no short and sweet. It's all far too long and complicated."

Lew sat cross-legged on the floor, took a great gulp from the flagon, and then stared, wide-eyed, waiting for enlightenment. Griffin lit a cigarette. It was a ridiculous situation, and impossible.

"Come on," Lew said. "Will I be better off being buggered nightly by wardens at Pentridge or should I give up and got to Vietnam. Yes or no."

"I told you. Better off alive and buggered than dead and fucked."

"But I might survive. You survived. Lots of blokes survived. It's a fair gamble."

"No it isn't."

"Well why not. Give me one good hard reason why not."

Griffin realised the answer was to stop thinking and say whatever he said. He emptied his brain and opened his mouth and the words began suddenly to flow.

"Lew. Think about war stories and movies and such like."

"You aren't going to tell me it's like that."

"No. Nothing like that. But remember, in those movies and stories, there were the sorts of things that Biggles and John Wayne did, and, on the other hand, there were the sorts of things the Rotten Nazis and Dirty Japs did."

"Yeah. Good guys and bad guys."

"In the other wars, we were always able to perceive ourselves as on the side of good. In Vietnam, we were the bad guys. What we were doing was wrong, and we knew it."

"Isn't that a bit simplistic?"

"Sure. But it's also true. We were behaving like the Rotten Nazis and Dirty Japs."

"Shit. Where are the good guys?"

"It soon became apparent that the people behaving like John Wayne and Biggles were the Viet Cong, whose heroism we were often forced to admire. There was no doubt that we were the enemy."

"But surely wars are always like that..."

"Are you sure? Our existence wasn't confined to inflicting brutality on the local population, but also upon ourselves, sometimes by accident, other times with intent. Brutality became our way of life at all levels. I don't mean atrocities, although they followed. I mean attacking civilians and treating them as enemy—we were an occupying force. I mean rounding up citizens and putting them in camps (that we weren't allowed to call Concentration Camps), then burning their villages and destroying their property. I mean fighting and killing women and children. I mean approved vandalism, random searches and interrogation, and general harassment of the community. They were terrified of us and rightly so. We also did almost all of our killing from ambush, which is hardly the spirit of the Anzacs. There was also rape and brutalisation of the locals. We soon knew who we were."

"But surely you were just following orders."

"Doing these things under orders is one thing. Enjoying them is quite another. We loved the power of brute force and armed superiority. We carried out these actions with great glee and a lot of bragging. We were hooligans with a licence to kill, just like the IRA and PLO."

"And that's it?"

"That's it, Lew. So buy a jar of Vaseline and go to Pentridge. It might be tough, but at least when its all over you'll be able to sleep without waking up screaming and soaked in sweat every night."

"Is that what happens?"

"I don't think I'll ever sleep properly again, Lew. And now I've got to go. Before Karen gives up on me completely."

"Sure," Lew said. "I guess you need all the help through the night that you can find."

"See you again sometime, Lew."

"Maybe at O'Connell's next Friday."

"I might be there. I doubt you will be."

"Ahh, I'll square that away. And anyway, now you know where I live. I want to hear more about this."

"See you Lew."

He walked back to the pub, wondering how the hell he was going to explain all this to Karen. As it turned out, Karen was pleased.

"Looks like you found a new friend then," she said.

"And old friend, actually, that I never knew I had."

"It's still hard to imagine what you have in common."

"He owes me his life," Griffin said.

Lady on the Far Side

Griffin stood, drinking a beer and contemplating the weather. The beer was cold and the weather was warm and both were wonderful and neither had required contemplation until half an hour ago. Standing out on point, high on the cliff, he was been watching the surfers ride the wild waves toward the rocks below, and sometimes the porpoises plunging along with them, showing how easy it really was. Further around was the long stretch of ocean beach, the sand crisp and white and doted with sunlovers, baring their flesh to the cosmic rays. Dell, Griffin knew, was amongst them somewhere although from his present great height it was impossible to discern which of the brown prostrate figures she might have been. On the other hand, Lew could not have been more prominent—he was out there doing porpoise imitations with frenzied abandon, his golliwog head now a huge black shag.

The towering crag on which Griffin stood was called Point Lookout, the northernmost tip of Stradbroke Island, jutting audaciously into the Pacific Ocean, arrowing the United States of America, just over the horizon and half a world away. Directly behind him, above the beach, stood the Point Lookout Pub, from which Griffin decided he had strayed far enough. Beside the pub, he could clearly make out the great grey blob of the Jag. Between each of these locations, a soggy black and white object raced madly, to surge the waves with Lew, across the beach to spray sand and water over a furious Dell, up to the point to ensure the master was still immobile, down to check out an interesting bitch waiting for its owner on the steps of the pub, out to the car park to make sure none of his responsibilities had run out on him. The Monster was having the time of his life. Griffin decided Point Lookout was the most perfect of places.

And then it wasn't. It all changed in a matter of minutes. Out there, the sky was brilliant blue and completely clear but for with the dazzling sun directly overhead and the occasional silver glint of a plane descending into Brisbane Airport. The water beyond the reef was glasslike and deepest blue and the big ships nosing through the straight between Stradbroke and Moreton Islands heading to or from the mouth of the Brisbane River seemed to glide along, barely touching the surface. The horizon was as sharp as if the work of an expert draughtsman.

The air was warm and soft and caressing. A perfect day.

One gulp of beer later, it was all changed. First the horizon reduced to a greyish blur and then disappeared altogether. Then white tufts of crests appeared on the distant waves. A frivolous zephyr danced in his hair, and then fled, and the breeze that followed immediately had a sense of purpose about it.

The sun began to turn grey and although the sky remained cloudless, it began to lose its blueness and the sun notably depleted in intensity, as if an invisible screen had been drawn about the earth. Then, finally, the clouds did appear, massive great billows of them, way out over the Pacific but obviously rushing straight at Point Lookout. Maybe, Griffin mused, he had misunderstood the name, and it was in fact three words, not two.

Things began to happen. Down on the beach, every brown figure stirred simultaneously and began to grab items of apparel, gazing in puzzlement at the brightness and blueness, baffled by the sun's betrayal of their adulation, for the headland obscured the approaching turbulence from their view. The Monster was suddenly there, at his feet, staying close, the wind creating disconcerting ripples in his fur. Every board rider suddenly discovered his waves had disappeared and with frantic glances over their shoulders, began to paddle ashore. The porpoises had vanished back to the depths. Over at the lifesaver's pavilion, a man was hoisting the red warning flag up the pole but his effort was belated since the word had already spread to the bathers and they were universally swimming through the increasingly chilled water to the shore.

"I think, Monster," Griffin said, "It's time we were moseying along."

And man and dog headed back along the point toward the pub. They had covered only half that distance when the first huge clap of thunder sounded. This sent The Monster scurrying for cover but Griffin strolled on, refusing to be intimidated. The climate offered the more persuasive argument of huge droplets of rain when he was still twenty yards distant, and he had spent enough time in the tropics to know what followed. Conceding that Monster had judged the matter better, he bolted, and only just got under the shelter of the veranda when there was a great whoosh of air and a dense curtain of water fell upon the scene. The thunder of its impact on the hot dry earth was a rival for that of the aerial variety that could now be heard all around. Every drain and hollow was already flooded. It wasn't like rain, more like something dumped from a galactic bucket.

No one arrived before him, although there were a number of regulars in the bar who never left. They stood nodding and grinning.

"Jeez, she's comin' down a bewdy."

"Yep. Cyclone off Rocky. This'll be the tail."

"Bloody cyclone, hey? Might last days."

Griffin nodded. In Queensland, unlike Melbourne, the very predictable weather made everyone expert.

He ordered two pots of beer and one brandy and dry and headed over to a table by a huge window to watch the show. Already it was oppressively humid in the bar and the window was steaming up and his ears rang with the chatter of rain on the iron roof as he sat down and amusedly lit a cigarette, gazing calmly at the wall of water deluging outside. The Monster, not slow to take advantage of the confusion, had slipped inside and with a total lack of regard for nature's wonders, was curled up under the table and shuddering fearfully at each thunderclap.

Out in the greywhiteness, murky figures began to appear as the people came running, protecting themselves from the downpour any way they could. They came in bathers and towels looking more saturated than they ever did emerging from the ocean, while those more completely clad were all the more soggy. They stood, panting and ripping, saying things like 'Shit where did that come from?' and 'Thought I was gonna drown'. They shivered, their flesh covered with gooseflesh and droplets. A very dry Griffin nodded and sipped his beer.

One batch gushed Dell upon him, wearing a blouse so adhered to her skin that modestly necessitated she clutch her towel to her breasts. Otherwise, she only wore a bikini bottom and a very sour expression. Her hair, normally so shining and flowing, was plastered all over everything above her armpits as if a giant black anemone had attached itself to her head. She glanced momentarily in the direction of Griffin who offered the faintest of smiles and the slightest of waves but she did not respond, instead looking amongst the soppy heads and bodies, undoubtedly seeking Lew Sigg. The steaminess of the bar was now filled with the babble of voices excited and annoyed as they sought out means of drying themselves or comparing their wetness. But there was no Lew Sigg.

Thwarted, Dell approached and sat at the table.

"Is this mine?" she asked, pointing to the brandy and dry.

Though it was hardly likely to be otherwise, Griffin

sidestepped all smart answers and only nodded. Dell, in turn, restrained herself from demanding coffee or tea or beer or just anything other than what he had bought her. She sat down, took the desperately needed brandy at a single gulp, and regarded the empty chair between them.

"Lew hasn't come in yet?"

"No. He was halfway to Moreton when the storm hit."

"I hope he's alright."

"He'd better be. I've already paid for his beer."

Dell offered that the disparaging look it deserved.

But if the empty chair would remain between them for some time yet, it might just as well have contained Lew Sigg. Somehow, they always arranged themselves with him in the middle. And if he divided them, so too did he keep them from each other's throat. Now, bereft of Lew, they allowed the storm to do their talking for them. After a while, he might even have shared her anxiety if that was allowable, for even the most intrepid surfers seemed to have scampered in by then, laughing and bragging about that terrifying last wave to safety.

"Something must have happened to him," Dell could finally not resist saying. She was, by then, a fitful ball of tension.

"Not like him to let his beer go flat," Griffin said, because that was how he understood his role.

"This is serious," Dell snapped at him, "He might have drowned, you know, and all you can do is joke about it."

"I could go into a panic, if you think it might help."

"Oh, shut up, Griffin!"

Then, as he glanced about hoping Lew might have found some other entrance, he saw some people pointing out at the wall of rainwater and beginning to laugh. He knew, even before he looked, what that would be all about. Out there in the grey-dark world of what might have been a giant aquarium, a dark silhouetted figure could be discerned from time to time, dashing about madly, appearing and disappearing as the swirls of the downpour fluctuated. A ghost, it might have been, of a slaughtered sunny day. The figure darted this way and that and then would stop in a dramatic pose, remaining utterly motionless for just a little longer than you expected, then race around until a new peculiar pose stopped the frame again. It might be an emu bobbing worms from the earth, a frog about to leap, or a man about to spear a crocodile. At other times, he raced in circles with arms spread like a boy playing a game of dive-bombers.

"What the hell is he doing?" Dell breathed, but you could feel the anxiety draining from her.

"Corroboree. A rain dance, I should think."

"I think we have enough rain already."

Painfully—there were times when Griffin could physically feel her mental anguish—she jumped out of the chair and strode across the face of the delighted audience and out onto the porch. The performer continued to rush about and the lady, no less a performer, stood with her hands placed fiercely on her hips. When Griffin would have thought it impossible, her voice could be clearly heard above the clatter of the rain, the thunder and the laughter.

"Lewis! Get in here this minute!"

Under the table, The Monster was looking for where to get into. Out there, that other hound paused with its imaginary boomerang unlaunched, gazing at her in bewilderment. No less sensitive to her tone of voice, he dropped on all fours and ran to her, and then cocked a leg to piss on the verandah post. She kicked him in the ribs. Immediately, Lew jumped to his feet, grabbed her, and delivered a very soggy kiss on her astonished lips. Finally, she towed her waterlogged escapee back into the pub, to the roars of laughter and applause from the audience. Lew stopped to take a couple of bows while Dell stalked on and dropped in her chair, her face gleaming with embarrassment, anger and a few other things that she definitely would not have admitted to.

Then Lew was there, sitting between them, dripping over everything, and held up his beer in a toast. He drank, and scowled. "This bloody beer's warm," he muttered to Griffin in horror.

"I didn't realise you were such a slow swimmer," Griffin sighed.

Lew gulped the beer down, grabbed Griffin's empty glass, and was all set to make his escape to the bar.

"I'll get another," he said confidently.

Griffin knew he would never make it.

"Must you invariably make a fucking clown of yourself," Dell savaged at him. Lew sighed, and halted, and handed the two empties to Griffin as he sat down again. Griffin was only too happy to buy twice in a row.

He took as long as he could manage at the bar, but returned to the table with the drinks far too soon. The brandy he placed before Dell was no sort of peace offering. As far as Griffin could tell, they had not spoken a word while he had been away. Maybe both thought they needed a witness.

"Remarkable turn in the weather," Lew said, to Griffin mostly.

"Absolutely astonishing," Griffin concurred.

"I just couldn't resist offering an expression of my appreciation of the awesome forces of nature," Lew added bravely.

"And making fools of the rest of us," Dell snapped.

"Leave me out of this," Griffin murmured.

"Some of these people know me professionally," Dell was saying, jerking a thumb at the soggy mob in the bar, "And you make it very embarrassing for me."

"They weren't embarrassed. They enjoyed it. Didn't you hear them?"

"People always laugh at idiots."

Griffin, however, was harbouring the key to the solution to all this. The best way, he knew, of diverting Dell's anger was to find something to make her even angrier. She, eternally, sought out the jagged edges in life to lacerate herself upon.

"While I was at the bar," he said, "I happened to pick up some interesting data concerning the current meteorological phenomenon."

"I don't need a fucking weather report to see its raining," Dell seethed.

"More than raining," Griffin pointed out, "A cyclone coming in from the Coral Sea, presently crossing the coast below Rockhampton. Gale force winds and torrential rain are expected to continue in the Brisbane area for some considerable time. With the result that the captain of the vehicular ferry, in the interests of public safety, has decided to discontinue the service until such time as the storm has abated."

Dell turned on him in a fury, as if the weather was also his fault. "They can't. I have to get back. I have a crucial meeting at seven o'clock tonight."

"They have," Griffin said.

"You haven't," Lew added.

Dell jumped to her feet: "I've put weeks of work into this. I won't let it be fucked up by something as silly as this!"

And she marched off in search of a telephone.

"Life is such a panic to her," Lew sighed as he watched her elbow her way through the crowd.

"She doesn't do much the easy way," Griffin had to admit.

Her return was not speedy, for which they might have been thankful. There were amongst the sun-seekers of Stradbroke, quite a number who found this sudden dislocation from the mainland disconcerting. Their efforts were to prove to be in vain for the storm had upset the telephone lines and there was no way of getting through. Dell and thirty others remained standing in a queue at a dead telephone, clinging to the supposition that the problem might be speedily fixed. One by one, they gave up and she was soon at the front of the queue which only meant she was doomed to be the last to give in.

Meanwhile, Lew and Griffin were left free to discuss the situation more realistically.

"You know, Griffin, it has long been my ambition to be trapped indefinitely in a pub just like this one."

"The connotations are rather striking, Lewington, provided the storm lasts."

"Oh, let us pray that it will."

"If not, perhaps further rain dances are in order."

"I'm sure that can be arranged."

"But of course you realise, Lewington, that this dramatic turn of events does rather upset our own plans."

"To some extent but then, Griffin, if we don't leave tomorrow, then the next day will be perfectly adequate."

"We are fortunate, Lewington, to possess such flexibility."

For at last they did have a plan, if only because one had been forced upon them. Quite surprisingly, Lew's plan for the Jaguar had gone much as expected and they had found a mechanic who ran a tumbledown garage in a small town not far away. He had listened to their story without emerging from under the old Ford he was working on and when he finally emerged, he looked at the roadworthy documents only long enough to put one very black thumbprint on them and, passing them back to Lew, began rolling a very greasy cigarette.

"Fill 'em in yerself," he told them, "Ain't got time fer that sorta bull. I work on cars, I don't write about 'em. If I did, I'd work fer the papers."

"Don't you want to see the car?" fool Griffin asked quietly.

"I can see it from here. Good looking car. How's it run?"

"Terrific," Lew cried before Griffin could say anything else.

"Then yer don't need a mechanic, do yer," he declared and crawled back under the Ford.

So the Jaguar added to its other distinctions the official condition of roadworthiness and they drove straight to

Cleveland Police Station. The sergeant paid little attention to either them or the car but spend most of his time ruffling Monster's fur.

"Usta have a dog like this one," he said, "Bloody great dog." And signed the appropriate forms.

"Got a screwdriver?" he asked Lew.

Lew was obliged to admit it—it was the one they used to open the bonnet but the sergeant had a different plan.

"You gotta remove them Victorian licence plates and hand 'em to me. You get the new Queensland plates in two weeks. You get a letter tellin' you to collect 'em in the city, bring 'em here and fit 'em under my supervision. Okay?"

It was anything but okay.

"Two weeks! What do we do about licence plates until then?"

"Nothin'."

"You mean we can't drive the car."

"Sure ya can. Means every copper that sees ya'll pull ya over, but the bit of paper says its okay. As long as ya don't cross the border, of course."

Two weeks. The words churned in their respective stomachs as they drove away in their illegally legal car.

"I'm not convinced, Lewington, that I will survive two weeks of life with your one true love."

"It does sound unsatisfactory, Griffin, but I do have a suggestion."

"I've come to fear all of your suggestions mightily, Lewington."

"Since we have two weeks to kill and can't leave Queensland, we might as well look the place over."

"Look the place over where, exactly?"

"North did seem to have some momentum. Let's go to Cairns."

Just down the road, turn right and straight ahead for a thousand miles.

"Cairns, Lewington, is the same distance from here as Melbourne."

"Just a comfortable two weeks, there and back."

"What about Dell?"

"I doubt she'll be able to get away."

"I meant, how are you going to tell her?"

"Well, Griffin, remember your suggestion of a day trip to Stradbroke?"

"My suggestion?"

"Yes, that one. I thought, if you could bear it, we might take Dell along. Nice little outing for her. Soften her up for the blow."

"It would be even softer if you left me behind, Lewington."

"No need to go that extreme, Griffin."

But now the forces of nature seemed to have intervened to temporarily thwart their plans, if not so much as they might have thwarted Dell, who continued to struggle to get a long distance call that seemed to be getting further away all the time. Sitting it out in the Point Lookout Pub, watching the flashings and thunderings and outpourings of the storm, Griffin suddenly thought to ask. "When are you going to break the news to Dell, Lewington?"

"Believe it or not, Griffin, I already have."

"I don't believe it."

"How could you doubt me, Griffin."

"It possibly does explain where this incredible storm came from."

"As a matter of fact, she took it very calmly."

"Dell and calm are two concepts that cannot be used in the same sentence, Lewington."

But even as he said it, the penny suddenly dropped, and he turned and saw Lew's face wearing a very dubious smile indeed.

"Lewington, did you make a deal with her?"

"Griffin, whatever can you mean?"

"I'm just wondering, Lewington, how many times the same soul can be sold."

As the afternoon proceeded, the scene in the pub began to fall into conspicuous decay. In the tight, oppressive circumstances, the beer forcibly consumed was taking its toll. The rain began to ease a little and Lew borrowed an umbrella to scamper to the car and bring back dry clothes. Telephone contact with the mainland remained unsuccessful.

"We should go to Dunwich and wait for the ferry—so that we can be on the first run," Dell suggested. Dunwich where, she knew only too well, there was no pub. And anyway, their place on the ferry was firmly booked.

"Don't like it," Lew murmured, "The road will be a quagmire—bad enough without the rain."

But the drunks were becoming belligerent and falling over things. More beer seemed spilled than guzzled. Dell, in complete disgust, departed to wait in the car.

"No sense of humour, that woman," Lew sighed.

"She does seem to take the world a little more seriously than it deserves," Griffin thought.

Options were closed, of course, and they went. Anyway, the word was that the ferry service would resume in two hours. But no one seemed to care anymore.

"Maybe we shouldn't tell her," Lew said wickedly.

"There is a limit, Lewington."

"I suppose. But it was fun while it lasted."

They finally trooped to the car, taking their things with them—sleeping bags for instance, which Lew had brought in on the off-chance they might have to sleep in the pub.

"No one else is leaving," he muttered in disgust.

They climbed in the car, Griffin in the front because Dell was already sitting in the back and refused to move—it meant she shared the seat with Monster—neither looked too happy about it.

The Jaguar slipped and slid along the muddy road for about three miles and then suddenly they began to slow down. Lew, realising he had no power, spied a hollow on the right side of the road and eased them into that.

"Oh no," Dell moaned, "What now?"

Out in the residual drizzle, Lew and Griffin leaned over respective mudguards, peering under the bonnet.

"We seem to have water instead of petrol," Lew pronounced.

"Lewis!" Dell shrieked, "I have just an hour and a half to make that meeting. Everything depends on it. And it will take that long to get home as it is..."

"Won't take long," Lew lied self-defensively.

Further investigation revealed a blockage of the overflow from the lefthand petrol tank filler recess. The rainwater had come with such force that it had filled the recess and unable to escape through the overflow, had instead forced its way into the tank. They could run on the right tank—for such a car had two—but first they would have to clear the carburettor and fuel pump system of water. Lew stripped the former down, Griffin left to the lesser tasks of clearing the blocked over flow and draining the fuel pump and lines.

"How bloody long is this gonna take?" Dell demanded, for she had ventured out to supervise the job.

"About an hour, if the rain holds off," Lew pronounced.

"Well fuck you," Dell exploded.

She was dragging her things out of the car and slamming doors and then stormed off to stand on the other side of the road.

"What are you doing now?" Lew asked her.

"I can't afford to piss around here all night," she seethed, "I'll hitch-hike to the ferry and get myself home."

And because neither male saw any reason to dispute that idea, she glared at Griffin. "I don't know anyone else who would be so stupid as to buy such a heap of junk in the first place," she added.

Because he didn't either, Griffin kept his head down and continued poking the wire through the overflow pipe.

So they remained for an hour, a veritable state of siege. Lew at the front, stripping the carbie with nerveless fingers, carefully laying the bits out on the front seat, Griffin underneath in the mud, draining things and Monster with him because it was warmest near the exhaust pipe and Dell across the road with her thumb stuck out. Although only twenty feet away, she could not have looked more isolated. Griffin felt sad for her, the way she bumped and jolted her way through life, het up by issues that would be forgotten tomorrow. No one offered her a ride. The few cars that came by didn't pick her up. One sprayed her with mud, one stopped to see if Lew needed help but was already overloaded with passengers, two girls in a mini slowed down and one called to her. "You want a ride, love?"

"Yes," Dell answered, scampering toward them.

"Hope you get one," the girl laughed and also sprayed her with mud as they raced away.

Dell, adamant, defiant, proud, showed none of the misery she was plainly suffering. That she remained so hopelessly attached to someone as inappropriate as Lew Sigg only added to her absurdity. She was a tough lady, Griffin knew, and when she decided something she never gave in. She had, long ago, decided Lew was hers and so it would be. She would never give in. And when they returned from Cairns, assuming they got there, she would prevail. Or so it seemed. Griffin could only wonder what on earth 'd do with him once he was hers.

And it was not without guilt and sympathy that Griffin watched her, when Lew declared the repairs complete, troop back from her idiocy across the road and climb wordlessly in the back. The engine sparked to life and she allowed them to carry her battered but hardly beaten pride on the remainder of the journey back to where she all too obviously belonged.

Lew's Alternative

Lew was sitting on a stool by the bar and guarding another for Griffin and had even ordered a second pot of beer when Griffin walked in. Both were accepted gratefully.

"Terrific day," Lew grinned. Out there it was grey and bleak and rather cold but Lew wasn't talking about weather because he never did.

"Appropriate to the occasion," Griffin said as he hauled off his coat and long scarf and beanie, all in the proper blue and white of the Kangas. Lew wore no such identification although the same team shared their support, but then maybe Griffin wore enough for both of them.

"Maybe the Kangas won't show up and spare themselves the embarrassment of another massacre," Lew suggested.

"Now Lewington, that is hardly the right partisan spirit."

"Enthusiasm dampens when there isn't any hope."

They met in this pub because it was the nearest to the football ground. All around them, confident Tiger supporters were there in their yellow and black, whereas the blue and white was rare. Plainly, most Kangaroo supporters shared Lew's pessimism and decided their time might be better spent in the garden or painting the spare room.

"Perhaps there'll be a miracle," Griffin suggested.

"I seriously suspect, Griffin, that God, if he existed, would discern any spiritual advantage from lending a hand to a bunch of second-rate so-called footballers."

Griffin understood. He was sagging himself, he knew. Just to glance around the bar at the Tiger fans sneering with delight at the inevitable was sufficient deterrent. But he could tell too that Lew had something else on his mind, though he didn't ask about it. He didn't need to. With Lew all was invariably revealed but only when he was good and ready.

"It's gonna be a boring game," Lew said cheerlessly.

That had something to do with it.

"Do I detect, Lewington, a certain reluctance to participate in today's fixture."

"The spectre of doom does seem to hang over it."

"Such a grey day isn't much good for anything other than watching football."

"That's my point, Griffin. Maybe there are alternatives."

"You have some other plan."

"No."

Now that had to be a lie. Lew would never have offered so simple an answer unless it wasn't true.

"Okay, Lewington, who is she?"

"Who's who?"

"When a bloke looks as miserable as you do, there has to be a woman in it somewhere."

"Nothing to do with it," Lew snorted.

Another simple answer.

And maybe Lew realised it himself, when he turned and looked slyly at Griffin and asked. "How is the lovely Karen, by the way?"

"Fine."

"No better than fine, hmmm?"

The simple answer difficulty was something they shared.

"Well, we had a big fight just before I left."

"There you are. You have woman trouble and you don't look miserable. Blows your whole theory."

"I feel miserable."

"That was apparent in your false cheery demeanour, Griffin. I take it you haven't proposed marriage to the unfortunate girl yet?"

"What's that got to do with it?"

"Whatever the fight seemed to be about, Griffin, that's what it was really about."

"The matter wasn't mentioned."

"I see no reason to change my response."

"What makes you think we're thinking about marriage?"

"You aren't. She is. That's all a woman like her ever thinks about. And you have been together an appropriate period of time."

"As a matter of fact, we were arguing about the idea of living together. Two cheaper than one and all that."

"There you go."

"Marriage was never mentioned."

"Very shrewd of her."

"She's the one who wants to take up shared domestic arrangements. I'm the one who isn't sure."

"And what, Griffin, do you suppose is holding you back?"

"Nothing is holding me back. I just don't feel... ready..."

"Then perhaps you should broaden your horizons, Griffin."

"Steady on, Lewington. Karen, who likes to think she's a friend of yours, might not appreciate you plotting against her like this."

"I wasn't actually referring to Karen..."

"Oh, I see. The topic of conversation changed without me noticing."

"No, Griffin. Still the same topic. I'm trying to help you out here a bit."

"Why bother to change things?"

"Tell me, Griffin. What do you think of the war these days?"

"I try not to think about it, Lewington."

"Still having the nightmares?"

"Not every night. Look what is this..."

"Loud noises still turn you deathly pale, I notice."

"Lots of people scare easily."

"Whenever you hear a helicopter, you go hunting the sky for it."

"Lots of blokes are fascinated by aircraft."

"I've seen you almost get run over because you wandered obliviously onto a busy road while watching a chopper pass over."

"I just like to know where they're going."

"You still break out in a sweat every time you walk in a crowded room."

"A touch of claustrophobia..."

"Face it, Griffin. It still bothers you. And it still bothers you a lot."

"It is supposed to take some time to recover from these things, Lewington."

"It has been some time."

"They think it's just normal war veterans."

"Does this state of normality happen to have a medical name?"

"Anxiety Neurosis. And before that Battle Fatigue. And before that, Shell Shock. All the same thing, depending on which war you attended."

"So the situation hasn't improved since the First World War."

"Very detailed studies of Vietnam veterans are being conducted, I understand."

"So why not do something about it yourself? The best defence is a good offence. Why not take to the problem nose on?"

"Are you suggesting I go back to Vietnam?"

"No, Griffin. You are so out of touch. Don't you read the

papers? Vietnam isn't where the war is happening anymore."

"Don't tell me the domino theory really works."

"No, Griffin. Here is where it is happening now. In the streets. All around you."

"You're talking about the demonstrations."

"Sort of."

"I'm not interested in that sort of bullshit, Lewington."

"What you are saying, Griffin, is that you don't want to know anything about it."

"I didn't know you were interested either."

"I'm not. I just thought it might be better than watching the Roos get another hiding."

"You must be joking. All those people waving banners and chanting and yelling at people."

"Isn't that what we'll be doing at the footy?"

"It isn't the same. Footy's fair dinkum."

"And trying to stop a war isn't?"

"It would be if they had some sort of chance of success."

"More chance than the Kangaroos have of beating the Tigers."

"That's true."

Lew faced him, front on now, trying to make a real issue of this.

"Look. You'd like to see the war stopped and conscription abolished, wouldn't you?"

"Sure, but..."

"Well, people are out in the streets trying to do that."

"Students, and left wing whackers, are out in the streets, Lewington. The people are still in their houses, watching it all on television and tut-tutting them as troublemakers."

"Yes, television. That's the key. Nightly they are seeing how dreadful the war really is, and they are also seeing people in the streets saying it ought to be stopped. And..."

"All the time the media is telling them that the war is just and look out for the Yellow Hordes coming over the hill and the falling dominoes and what right do these commos have to block the city traffic."

"No doubt about that, but the images matter more than the words."

"Being a painter, you'd have to believe that, wouldn't you."

"They are seeing the images and they are the ones who elect governments. And the politicians are becoming worried..."

"Lewington, I've heard it all before. Nobody takes these

student uprisings seriously."

"It's bigger than that, Griffin. Much bigger. There have been massive rallies in America..."

"Is it entirely necessary to follow the Americans everywhere they go? That's how we got into Vietnam, remember?"

"Before we were cheap plastic imitations of Americans, we were even cheaper imitations of the Poms. That is a fact of life. It doesn't change the reality that we have to get out of that war."

"Americans can fly to the moon, and they can get out of Vietnam any time they like. They don't want to. That's the problem."

"The politicians and businessmen don't want to, but the people do. If all the people get together..."

"The people are not going to get together."

"But it's worth a try, isn't it?"

"It's a waste of time and effort."

"So is watching the Kangas get clobbered."

"I have to agree it will be a terrible game. Maybe we could go to one of the other matches."

"Maybe, Griffin. But I'd rather go to the demo. And I think you should too."

Griffin knew he was being worn down by sheer persistence and weight of argument. It was time for a change of tactics.

"Okay, Lewington. I'll go but only if you are completely honest with me about this."

"Aren't I always?"

"No. So who is she?"

"Who is who?"

"The woman you hope to encounter there. The truth or else I won't go."

"But you will go if I confess."

"Yes."

"The most gorgeous and interesting creature I ever met."

"I knew it. You almost had me believing all that moral bullshit for a while."

"Griffin, are you suggesting that I would drag you along to something like this merely to resolve my carnal desires."

"No doubt about it."

"I'm aghast, Griffin. It will be a valuable experience for you, honestly."

"I doubt it. I'd really rather go to the footy."

"No you wouldn't. You want to go now. I've aroused your curiosity. You have to go if only to prove how wrong I am later."

"I'd be out of place, Lewington. The short hair. I still walk like a soldier. They'll think I'm some sort of spy."

"You'll be with me so they'll know you're okay."

The Tiger fans were off to the game and the factory workers back to the job.

"Fuck you, Lewington. If you get me into trouble..."

"It'll be okay, really."

Experience had already taught Griffin that this was the most ominous statement of all.

The marshalling point was in the Treasury Gardens, just a twenty minute walk through continual parklands from the MCG. There was a sizeable crowd gathered, by no means as unruly as the football barrackers they had left behind. In number, they looked about the same as an infantry battalion, Griffin cynically guessed. The police would count 500, the organisers 2000 and both would be lying to approximately the same degree.

They stood in clusters and groups under their various banners, more or less listening to the speaker on the rostrum. There was a stiff breeze and he could not be heard distinctly as Lew and Griffin moved amongst the masses. At least no one seemed to particularly notice that there was an unbeliever in their midst. In fact Griffin could feel his conspicuousness fading—there did seem to be a greater diversity of people than he had expected.

To be sure; there were the student political factions at the centre. Amongst their innumerable banners he spied a North Vietnamese flag that he was surprised to find offended him. To dispute your own government was one thing, to support a foreign one against it was quite another. As his prejudices surged, Griffin restrained the urge to walk over there and punch someone. He remembered the little men in the jungle with their rifles and black pyjamas who could live on a handful of rice. He might have shot at them, but he would never have offered the insult of a punch in the nose. Such was the perverse logic of warfare, and these people strove to introduce that logic into civilised society. They looked about as silly as that sounded.

But that was far from the whole story for the radicals were only a small proportion of the crowd. About them gathered a much larger group, still young mostly, bearded men and women in hippy clothes, but they were older, sitting on the grass smoking cannabis openly, while many small children played about them. They really did have flowers in their hair and greeted each other with the peace sign. But beyond those and by far the majority were people who seemed to have no common uniform or allegiance. Most of them looked as embarrassed by the inner circles as Griffin was, but they were plainly all types. Over there, some pensioners, nearby families from the suburbs. There were middleclass people in smart clothes and ruffians from the western suburbs. And there were a lot of just plain folk, the sort you might have expected to usually watch such things on television—now they had come to see what it was really like, maybe even instead of going to the footy.

Lew, of course, was looking smug while Griffin took all this in. What surprised him most was how quiet they were, even though the badly placed amplifiers offered them little chance of hearing what the speaker was burbling.

"You want to move closer so you can hear," Lew asked quietly.

"Nar. He'd just be sprouting that same bullshit you were dumping on me," Griffin said, though with a grin.

"It's just to get the crowd in the right mood for the event."

"Revvin' 'em up for the big game."

"Will you get your bloody mind off football."

"But the Roos might be winning."

"The game's hardly started."

"Sometimes they get the first goal."

"Then wait for the opposition to kick ten before they get another. Forget the footy, Griffin. This is really happening."

Things that were really happening, Griffin knew, were the scariest of all.

The crowd was growing as restless as Griffin felt, but all of a sudden he was more restless still. Through the crowd, he spied that American woman with the crazy hair from the squatter's place, and she seemed to be heading his way. She was wearing dufflecoat, tatty jeans, and her hair was now dyed orange and long and straight—still she was the very picture of the questioning generation. Griffin supposed he should have expected her to be there, but he didn't expect her to walk right up to them, wearing a rather curious smile.

"Oh good, you made it," she said to Lew and Griffin was floored when she kissed his cheek, but he was then flattened completely when she turned her gaze to him.

"And you, Pinocchio. Amazing."

It was, at very least, that.

"He told me we were going to the football," Griffin said, as if he needed an excuse and all the more needed to blame Lew.

"Yes, that's what he told me," she said.

Lew, because the whole situation was getting too confusing for him, tried to introduce people who seemed to have already met.

"Griffin, meet Dell. Or am I to assume..."

"Sort of..." Griffin sighed and didn't want to explain.

"Pinocchio has a strange habit of turning up in places he doesn't belong," Dell said coolly, and that American accent could not have been more prominent.

"His name is Griffin," Lew persisted.

"Ken, actually..." Griffin said.

"So what misguided purpose has brought you here today, Pinocchio?"

"I'm here taking names and addresses for the CIA."

Dell looked perfectly happy to believe that.

It was all too much for Lew. When Dell took his arm and tried to tow him away, leaving Griffin behind, he dug his heels in.

"As a matter of fact, Dell," he said as seriously as he ever managed. "Griffin has more right to be here than any of us."

"Is that so. Do you mean he really is being paid for it?"

"It happens that he is a Vietnam veteran."

It did at least disrupt her momentum. Ding-ding Dell was obliged to look upon Griffin with renewed interest.

"Bursting with moral outrage, I would hope."

"Something like that," Griffin said, genuinely embarrassed.

"Well," she sighed, finally willing to compromise. "I suppose that anyone who can instil a moral conscience in Lew Sigg can't be all bad."

Who had instilled what in who? But, fortunately for them all, the demonstrators were shuffling about and getting ready to move off. Griffin was thankful for something more substantial to follow than such lines of thought.

The Shadow Minister and other celebrities led the way and the leftwing activists with their banners and chants quickly fell in behind. 'Stop the War' they chanted and then the variant: 'Australia Out: Of Vietnam. Out. Out. Out.' The rest of the crowd, which was increasing rapidly, shuffled along behind in a quiet orderly manner, and Lew and his two best friends were placed at the head of these. The air was damp and heavy and the chants sounded hollow and distant—it would be better when they reverberated amongst the taller city buildings.

The column marched out into Spring Street, past Parliament House and turned into Bourke Street. It was, Griffin remembered, the same route that had been followed by the Pig Battalion two years earlier on its final parade before departure to Vietnam. To the tune of Waltzing Matilda, the battalion had marched with bayonets fixed and slouch hats at a cocky angle, their boots tramping on the tram tracks, men supposedly on the brink of glory. The only murmur of protest in those days were a small bunch of mothers, quietly standing at the corner of Swanston Street with their 'Save Our Sons' placard clutched to their wounded breasts. The soldiers had stepped out. swinging their arms to regulation height, their rifles locked in at their sides, and even if those rifles were empty still they brought the city to a standstill for an hour as they marched to board train and ship for the glorious shores of Vietnam.

Today the parliamentarians hid in their offices and the only onlookers were the row of policemen to either side and the television crews. Saturday was the only day on which the organisers could get a permit for the march and the shops were closed, the city all but deserted, and those in the pubs saw no reason to step outside. In turn, the marchers lacked the impact of the soldiers as they straggled along in uneven pace and disorderly ranks on their silent running shoes. And the only dissent occurred again at the spot where the ladies from 'Save Our Sons' once stood, only this time it was a small bunch from the Australian Nazi Party.

"Well, how are you coping so far?" Lew had to ask.

Griffin decided his sentiments ought to be shared.

"I marched here once before. I feel like I'm in a new battalion, off to fight a battle in the same war. Only I seem to have switched sides."

Indeed, directly ahead, the Vietcong flag fluttered.

"This isn't a war," Dell insisted adamantly. "It's a peace demonstration."

Griffin shrugged. Nearby he spied a marcher with a transistor radio pressed to his ear and darted over.

"What's the score?" he asked anxiously.

The Kangaroos weren't even nearly as far behind as was expected.

The marchers turned into Swanston Street and headed over the bridge and out along StKilda Road. That way, Griffin knew, lay the US Embassy. The police plainly knew it too.

"God, there's a lot of cops." Dell breathed.

Griffin smiled: "Not as many as you think. You're seeing the same ones over and over. As we pass, they get bused around to the front of the line again."

"Wouldn't it be more sensible for them to simply march along with us?" Lew asked.

"No way," Dell declared. "They're scared some of them might get inspired and start thinking for themselves."

"The real reason," Griffin pointed out soberly. " is because if they march with us, it will make our numbers look greater on television."

"But they're wearing uniforms," Lew cried. "Surely they don't think the public to be that stupid."

"Television producers do," Griffin said. "And so do policemen. And they might even be right."

Dell gazed at him with a puzzled look: "For a first timer, you sure seem to know a lot about this, Pinnock."

"Standard army tactics," Griffin shrugged.

"I wish you'd stop comparing this to an army parade," Dell snorted.

"And to bloody football games," Lew concurred.

"Some things are just too obvious," Griffin sighed.

The police had decided to block access to Albert Street, a short way down from where the US Embassy was located. The march was halted and the police and protester lines stood in bland confrontation. Prelude to battle—Griffin realised for all his combat experience, this was the first time he had stood in the ranks of a massed army facing the equally massed enemy across the battlefield.

But it was hardly a time for philosophical meditations, for the mood of the day was rapidly changing. What might have started out as an afternoon stroll was now definitely nothing of the sort. The protester's voices began to grow sharper and more urgent, their cries of anger exploded like flack above their heads. They flapped their banners fiercely, chanted savagely, thrusting forward and back, intimidating the stoic police lines. Behind, the cavalry—mounted police—were assembling, while at the front the order came to draw batons. Elsewhere, Griffin was sure, there would be detachments with tear gas and fire hoses. No longer did the police stand calm and detached—now their faces began to show the strain and they began to react and respond. Tension rippled through the ranks on both sides.

Now an amplified voice urged the crowd to disperse, that they could not proceed this way, to move peacefully on, but the people began to shout to drown him out.

"Come on, let's get to the front," Dell breathed in their ears.

"You'll get arrested again," Griffin warned.

"The fines just add to the government coffers," Lew agreed.

"This time I've got a little surprise for them," Dell said, and plunged her way forward.

"That," Griffin said with a certain admiration. "Is one wild lady."

"Don't I know it," Lew breathed. "Come on. Let's go."

They pressed through as far as they could, but now everyone was jostling and lurching. The cries became more urgent, a scuffle broke out on the flank, and that was the signal for the police to make their move. They seized upon the more troublesome militants at the front and started to drag them away. The crowd surged into the vacuum and the police retreated.

"This is getting out of hand," Griffin said, but there was no way back now. Dell had forced her way to the forefront, calling the police 'pigs' and 'fascists' until she drew their harried attentions. She stood, jaw jutting with determination as two policemen grabbed her, and there was a bit of a struggle. Two more closed in to try and subdue her and then, suddenly, there was a sharp crack and a huge pink cloud blossomed. Several pink policemen came staggering out of the cloud.

"Bloody silly woman," Lew cried, and was off into the pink cloud in the best Galahad manner.

The mounted police eased on the reins and the grey horses began to move forward, steadily, still in a line. Griffin saw he could not escape their path even if he wanted to. He looked up at the policeman's expressionless face as the horse and rider loomed over him, then the crowd shoved him right up against the hardness of the animal's chest. With no way around, he ducked under the belly of the horse which began to snort and rear and as he came out the other side, they was the thump of a baton coming down on his shoulder, another blow to his back and then he was clear. The mounted troops ploughed into the crowd, the riders swimming in a sea of angry faces, lashing downward with their batons left and right. People went down beneath those hooves ringing on the asphalt.

The wall of human bodies slammed Griffin onward. Hands were clawing at his face and his legs. There were screams of pain that took him back to the dreadful battle in the storm and he knew he was sweating with fear. Then, he had not been afraid. He was fighting back and in control. This was only chaos. He clawed furiously to get himself out of this mess of people and away. Finally, he saw the bobbing black curls that had to be Lew and plunged through the bodies to his side. Lew stood in the middle of that pink patch, looking around.

"Where's Dell?" he shouted at Griffin.

Fucking heroes—dickheads to a man.

Clear of the mob, this was a scene of more individual combat. There were at least twenty scuffles each with several policemen striving to control a protester, wrestling them to the ground, laying in with their truncheons. On Lew's own face there was blood but more than that there was desperation as he looked all around, his eyes blinded by the tears caused by his pain.

"Shit that hurt," he gasped. "What hit me?"

"Next winner of the Melbourne Cup," Griffin answered," Come on, let's get out of this."

"Where the fuck is Dell?" he wanted to know, one maniac in search of another.

"I can see her, over there," Griffin said. At least, he could see a pink blob that might have been her.

Police were closing in on them, batons raised, heading for a place where a riderless horse glided through the throng looking for all the world like the Loch Ness monster. Griffin, as they went, towing Lew who was still bobbing up and down as he searched, discovered he was limping himself. Looking down, he saw his jeans were ripped open and blood showed on the thigh that had nothing to do with his skinned knees and elbows.

"You alright?" Lew finally decided to ask.

"The fucking horse kicked me," Griffin realised belatedly.

"I think a building fell on me," Lew said.

"Remind me to cancel my subscription to the pony club," Griffin snarled.

Finally, Lew spied Dell, which wasn't difficult since she was completely doused in pink paint. Unfortunately, that also made her more easily identifiable to the police who were dragging her flailing form toward a divvy van.

"Mad woman," Griffin muttered.

But then he fell, for he lost his sole means of support. Lew was off, charging madly into the fray. The police had the doors of the van open and were battling to thrust the fierce figure of Dell in when Lew arrived, only adding to the confusion. He achieved nothing other than managing to get himself thrown into the paddy-wagon along with his beloved.

Griffin stood on the kerb, well clear of the battlefield now, and pressed his hands into his pockets. He shook his head in dismay at the way Lew had squandered a perfectly good rescue. The hectic battle was reduced to skirmishes, the crowd was dispersing and police vehicles rushed from the scene, sirens wailing, while incoming ambulances took their places. Hands still in his pockets, Griffin strolled away and soon picked up a tram that would take him home.

Later he would learn how that paint bomb was rigged—Dell, it emerged, was an Engineering Student—they didn't make them like they used to. Later too he would learn that Dell had a rich daddy who could, probably quite begrudgingly but lovingly, pay fines and good lawyers to sort out little difficulties like pink policeman. At least for the moment, her hair was all one colour. Before that, he learned that the Kangaroos had staged a miraculous fightback and run out winners by three points in the thriller of the season. "I told you we should have gone to the footy," would be the next thing he would say to Lew when they finally caught up.

He sat alone in the pub, watching the footy replay on television, and after that another replay on the news, of a crazy mob of mad people trying to unseat a mounted policeman from his horse. He saw nothing familiar, no one he knew. Fifty had been injured, thirty arrested, and everyone interviewed wanted to agree with the reporter that it was a disgrace to the city. The Police Commissioner knew that violence and peace demonstrations were synonymous, the organisers knew it was all the work of rightwing agitators planted in the crowd by police. Griffin watched it all dispassionately, made some phone calls and arranged some money, leaving a message for Karen with the barman, and set out for the City Watchhouse to bail his favourite pair of miscreants out.

The Gladstone Glide

They had left Dell's place at Redland Bay on the morning following their return from Stradbroke Island. Dell had to be at work early and had to take the child to the welfare centre first—all that happened before Griffin was awake.

"We are not, are we Lewington, making a cowardly escape behind Dell's back?"

"Good Heavens no, Griffin. How could you think such a thing?"

"I wonder what it is, Lewington, that people who have no souls sell to the devil."

They raced up the highway on the first leg of the adventure, heading north and out onto the flat country where the towering sentinels of the Glasshouse Mountains reared emphatically out of the wooded plains. Gigantic moon rockets, cleared of their service gantries, waiting through erosive millennia for the blast off.

"No, Griffin. You're getting too technological. They are Neanderthal church spires."

"Ah, Lewington, don't be so prosaic. Don't you feel the excitement of them?"

"I'm watching the road, Griffin, like any good driver should. But yes, they are rather imposing. Almost a match for Monument Valley in Utah."

"Except you trade Utah's reds and oranges for our drab green and drabber grey."

"I wouldn't be the one to regard that as inappropriate, Griffin,"

Thundering northward, northward through the shimmering midmorning heat. It might have seemed that they had stagnated in Brisbane in their lethargy, so intense now was the feeling of freedom. The patchy black asphalt of the Bruce Highway flashed beneath the old car as it hummed with pride at the achievement of a roadworthy certificate which, if ill-gotten, was still well deserved. They whizzed through Beerwah and Landsborough, the low mountains to the left, the deep forests to the right and beyond those forests, to be sensed rather than seen, the Pacific Ocean. This they could tell not only from the map but also the flocks of drifting seagulls.

"We should cross over to the coast road," Griffin proposed, consulting the map with avid concentration.

"Is it much further?"

"No. Ten miles wide to Caloundra then we run parallel up the highway to Noosa Heads. The Sunshine Coast—magic place, they tell me."

"Sounds good to me."

And the Monster, murmuring sleepily in the back, made it unanimous.

They veered off the highway and sped across the sunny plains to where the Pumicestone Channel divided Bribie Island from the mainland. They came upon a world of towering white hotels, intricate electrical lacings of neon signs and bikini-ed girls wandering around the parking meters.

"Looks a bit commercial to me, Griffin."

"Bloody near as bad as the Gold Coast. Fucking American developers—gawd what a mess they make."

So they fled Caloundra and stopped at a place called Dickey Beach for lunch.

There they found the wreck of an old iron ship that gave the place its name—the SS Dickey lay on the beach, merely a rusted skeleton through which the surf gushed in and out of its exposed rib-cage. They scrambled about it for a while, playing pirates—Griffin was Captain Hook, the Monster a non-ticking crocodile and Lew a hobbling Long John Silver, speaking only parrot as they duelled on the remnants of the deck. After a while, they sat on the beach with a well-earned beer and contemplated the horror of men trapped and dying in the debris. The old ruin creaked and groaned as if praying for a miracle or perhaps a tidal wave to wrench it free and whisk it away to Davy Jones Locker where it belonged.

And onward in the afternoon, following the flat coastline with its broad beaches, through Maroochydore and Mudjimba and Coolum Beach. This fifty miles of sand and surf must once have been idyllic but now escaped chunks of suburbia marred every prospect. The only things worth looking at were the girls who offered tantalising flesh in abundance but you could tell from their tolerance of the surroundings that they would have nothing to say worth hearing. The creation of these beautiful beaches might well have been Nature's greatest mistake for the overwhelming temptation they offered man to mess them up.

"We might stay away from the coast for a while, Griffin, if it's all like this."

"Yes, Lewington. We can only hope it's less disastrous further on."

And finally they came to the last of it, these resorts they had scurried through without stopping. The town of Noosa Heads, they discovered, was the favoured hangout of the board riding fraternity, but there was a decent pub, even if overcrowded by the young and muscular blondehaired men and their lithe deep tanned girls.

"God, Lewington. I thought the surfing craze died out a decade ago."

"At least you have the right hair-colouring, Griffin," Lew said ruefully.

In that vast beer hall, these juvenile relics of a forgotten age danced to thundering music in flashing lights, their surfboards parked in racks along the walls. They lived in an era that had passed when they were five years old, wearing wetsuits as if they were their only clothes, drinking and laughing and dancing to The Beach Boys, Jan and Dean and at a pinch, the Bay City Rollers. In another room, they found a pool table and soon found these lads had also missed out on the fundamentals of mis-spent youth—Griffin and Lew held the table as a doubles pair all night, swilling the beer each win secured them and finding they did not speak the same language as these people.

"I feel like I've just dropped in from the Jurassic Period," Griffin remarked.

It was a reflection that was to be underscored beyond his imaginings sometime later in the night when suddenly a young girl with straight blonde hair and the skin peeling off her face stood directly in front of him.

"Do you know you look just like Charles Darwin?" she said. He was feeling more like one of his primate ancestors at the time, but nodded. Lots of people said that, although not usually under such circumstances.

"Come on, dance," she said and towed him into the throng by the hand.

She danced to the wild music without hardly moving while Griffin wobbled this way and that, several times wondering if it was still the same girl in front of him, but when the music stopped, she advanced and stuck her tongue down his throat and, apparently finding that satisfactory, took his hand again and lead him outside and down to the beach and they lay on the sand.

"Are you sure about this?" he asked her.

"I have a father figure fetish to work out," she declared.

He was about to be mortified by that insult but right then she rolled him over and sucked him into her and biology dominated for a while. At the end of it, she stood, a glorious figure in the moonlight against the backdrop of the glistening sea as she wriggled back into her bikini bottom and paused to smile and kiss his cheek before she ran off.

"Thank you," she said primly, "That was just what I wanted." Since he had no energy left to chase her, he flopped on the sand and completely forgave her for the cruellest thing that had ever been said to him. He never saw her again.

But if his pride was damaged beyond repair, he realised that the act had been as necessary for him as it had apparently been for her.

He returned to the pub and found Lew and eventually the champions retired with a goodly supply of bottles and sat on the sand, just a few yards from the scene of Griffin's glorious moment, while the surf grumbled at them and called alluringly to the young men in the town behind them.

"You dirty bastard," Lew grumbled, "You got your end in, didn't you."

"I admit nothing."

"None of the bitches would talk to me."

"You got your share back in Redland Bay. This squares the account."

"What, who, Dell? She doesn't count."

"I'm sure she'd be delighted to hear that."

"You are comparing true love and devotion to lust and debauchery. It isn't the same."

"True what and what?"

"It isn't fair, that's all."

They finally fell asleep, alone on the warbling beach, without need of covering, Lew in frustration, Griffin utterly content. Quiet, easy, undisturbed.

A piercing scream knifed through Griffin's brain—in the instant he was awake he was sure the old nightmares had returned, but the cry had not come from him. It was from a distance, out on the water. He stared in astonishment—a scene of chaos had overrun their quiet beach. It was barely dawn and already the sand and water was besieged by hosts of the young blonde men. The sea was speckled with them, their bobbing heads pushing boards outwards while each respectable incoming wave was picked up by a dozen or so board riders, all waving their arms and uttering wild war cries.

"God, Lewington, we've been invaded."

"Yes Griffin. Maybe what they told you guys about the

yellow hordes was true."

"I don't think I want to stay here anymore."

They drove out to rejoin the Bruce Highway at Cooroy which took them inland through peanut country.

"Peanuts is right," Lew muttered.

"Whatever you mean by that, I agree," Griffin replied.

They wound through deep forests and over mountains and out into valleys spread with pineapple plantations. And all long the road now, there were cane toads, huge and fat in their assured prosperity, croaking and jumping into the path of the car, heedless of the warnings of their many ancestors whose squashed bodies formed an almost continual patchwork on the asphalt.

"Don't they do anything in small numbers in this part of the world, Griffin?"

"Queenslanders dream of Texas," Griffin sighed.

But then light gleamed in Lew's eyes. "You know, we could get a truck, Griffin. You could just walk along the side of the road, pitching these chaps in. We'd fill it in no time."

"Why on earth would anyone want a truckload of cane toads?"

"To sell the legs to French Restaurants. There's a fortune, just begging to be made."

"I believe they're poisonous, Lewington."

"...it'd be a pushover. We'd corner the world market..."

"Lewington, you can't eat them."

"They're a delicacy, Griffin. You might not like them but others do..."

"The skin is poisonous. A danger to human health."

"So, we'll skin 'em."

"Lewington, I don't want to make my first million skinning cane toads."

"I suppose it would be a little inglorious."

"But otherwise, a great idea, Lewington."

"It remains a land of opportunity, Griffin."

They headed through Gympie where stood a colossal forty-foot pineapple to amaze the tourists.

"Bugger the tourists. It amazes me."

"I think your amazement is not of the variety the locals are seeking."

Onward through innumerable small towns, rolling over undulating plains, and the Monster stirring in the back in his never-ending sleep, growling faintly, lethargically, at the monotony of the continuum.

"You know what Australia is like?"

"No."

"The rest of fucking Australia."

And it might have been true. These hilly plains and forests they intermittently passed through were no different to those a few miles out of Melbourne—those distant mountains, so blue and flat, were still the same Great Dividing Range they had crossed in the first hour of the journey, three weeks ago. The further you went, the more the country went on and on, until everywhere seemed to be nothing other than distant from everywhere else. Even the weather didn't change—that at least contrasted Melbourne—but the difference was that there was no difference.

"You don't seriously want it to rain, do you Griffin?"

"I'd just like it to prove that it can."

When it did, the rain fell in a downpour for three minutes and five minutes later the sun was beating down again and everything as dry as it had been before.

"You happy now?" Lewington snorted.

"No wonder they have trouble making decent beer here."

"Snake!" hawk-eyed Lew shrieked.

Griffin caught a glimpse of the wreathing coils on the road and swerved—never sure whether he was trying to hit or miss it—and then jumped on the brakes. Before the car stopped fully, Lew bounded out, emitting a gutsy war cry as he searched the boot for weapons. The prey, black and looping, slithered toward the verge. The football was the first item to come to hand and Lew let fly, success marginal, then Monster was off, yelping excitedly, but chasing the football, not the snake. Lew finally got there with the cricket-bat and managed to pin the head down, reducing the body to coils of thrashing confusion until Griffin arrived with jack-handle to finish it off.

"What a ripper!" Lew declared, picking it up behind its crushed skull. The Monster, football dangling by the lace from its mouth, found the reptile a grave disappointment. But it was at least five feet of black snake with red undermarkings. Lew wrapped it carefully in a plastic bag and stowed it in the boot.

"Makes the whole trip worthwhile, Griffin."

"I suppose."

Somewhere above Maryborough and pushing through the midday heat, the old Jag was blowing hard and they kept their eyes on the temperature gauge.

"Most commercial cars would be boiling in these conditions," Lew muttered hopefully.

"As am I, Lewington."

They came thirstily to a place called Apple Tree Creek where there were no apple trees and no creek but there, the map told them, they turned off the highway and headed for Bundaberg.

"They drink rum there the way we do beer, Griffin."

"Gawd, Lewington, we'll be dead in a week."

It proved to be an optimistic estimate.

What happened in Bundaberg will never be fully clear to Griffin. It was Sunday morning and they arrived in the last hour before the pubs closed at one and they found the locals extremely friendly—malevolently friendly—so friendly in fact that they were invited to share a bottle or two of the sweet and powerful extract of the local sugar while joining them for the afternoon at the Farmer's Club. This establishment proved to be a huge shed wherein an on-going illicit two-up game was indulged.

The oppressive heat in the tightly sealed shed and the sickly smell of two hundred sweaty armpits and the third bottle of Bundaberg Rum combined to prove too much for Griffin who retired early in the event. Outside, he found the fresh air no less hot and oppressive and so evicted Monster from the backseat of the Jag and there fell into a grim headspinning sleep.

He had a dream that someone was rolling him over and going through his pockets and in the dream, that someone was Lew Sigg.

Then he awoke in a lather of sweat to find Lew—definitely not a dream apparition—making a frantic entry into the driver's seat.

"Quick, Griffin, wake up. We must escape."

Under the circumstances, escape seemed quite possible without Griffin waking up and so he determined to remain asleep.

"Hey Monster, get in here!" Lew yelled, a command instantly obeyed with the result that Monster, springing through the window, landed right on top of Griffin. Lew lurched the old car onto the road.

Griffin, having sorted out which bits were himself and which were canine, sat up in the backseat, looking around.

"Do I detect, Lewington, that we are making an unexpected departure?"

"A hasty one, not entirely unexpected."

"Can it be that you've sullied our reputation again?"

"Not me, Griffin. Them cow-cockies cheat at two-up."

"How can anyone cheat at two-up?"

"I don't know but they did."

"From which I construe that you lost."

"Worse than that, Griffin. Major gambling debts have been incurred."

"To what extent?"

"Fifty bucks approximately. It was all very confusing. I excused myself on the pretext of call of nature and hopped over the back fence."

"God, Lewington, how degrading. I insist you turn the car around and we go back and settle this like gentlemen—I possess adequate funds."

"No you don't," Lew sighed.

And he hurled Griffin's empty wallet over to the backseat.

"You fiend! You've blown all of our money!"

"At least until the banks open tomorrow. I'll pay you back then."

"You will too."

"I just needed one more throw. My luck could not have continued so badly any longer."

"But Lewington—we were supposed to use that money to buy supplies in Bundaberg. We have nothing to eat, drink, smoke. How will we survive?"

"Our first step to survival will be to create considerable distance between ourselves and that evil place."

"Evil, perhaps, but it cannot be denied they make a mean rum there."

"A mean rum, Griffin, a mean rum."

They were back on the highway and heading north, smoking their last cigarettes, burning the last of their petrol.

"We're gonna run out."

"I'm sure we'll have just enough to reach Gladstone."

And soon, ahead of them, the murky grey smudge of pollution above the grim industrial town could be seen, closing in about them along with the night.

"I think we'll make it," Griffin said confidently.

The engine immediately spluttered and coughed.

"You have the uncanny knack of saying just the right thing at just the wrong time, Griffin."

"Switch to the other tank, Lewington."

Lew switched and the engine spluttered and died.

"Ooops."

"No, Griffin, it takes a moment for the second tank to cut in."

Almost surreally, they glided along the highway in the sunset, the silence weirdly unnatural.

"The needle is dead on empty, Lewington."

"Hmmm, it doesn't seem to be happening as I suggested, Griffin."

"Still, this is a rather nice sensation, Lewington, whizzing along in the cocoon of silence like this. Like being in a submarine."

"You've obviously never been in a submarine."

"I'm sure you haven't either."

"No, but a cousin of mine was and he said that they are even noisier than surface ships, which are very noisy."

"Oh, alright then, a space ship."

"No, Griffin. Noisy too. Haven't you seen 2001."

"When they were adrift, with engines failed."

"It worries me that someone with so defective an imagination has literary ambitions, Griffin."

"I'm on holidays, Lewington. Worrying about things like that is what I'm on holidays from."

They switched back to the original tank but after a brief burst of life, the engine cut out again.

"What's the point of having two bloody petrol tanks, Lewington, if you only fill one of them."

"Gawd, who has that sort of money? Do you realise how much those two tanks hold?"

"Not enough to get us to Gladstone, apparently. I suppose we ought to look for somewhere to camp."

"Does sound a wise move, Griffin."

They were on the outskirts of the city, not that it mattered. They glided along, momentum gradually decreasing, and they wc crossing a long curving bridge over a wide river bed. At the end of it, they saw a small reserve which, the sign said, had been provided by the Lion's Club. They turned in, bumped a short way across the gravel, and stopped.

"What a bummer," Lew complained.

But their situation was even worse, more desperate, than mere lack of petrol, as they soon discovered.

"Got a smoke, Griffin?"

"No, Lewington. We just smoked my last two, remember?"

"There's got to be something unsmoked around here somewhere."

Frantically, they searched the car and although they came up with no cigarettes, the exercise was not a total loss. There, under the seat, they discovered an overlooked bottle of Bundaberg rum.

"I think, Lewington, that I hid it there this afternoon in the hope that I might never find it again."

"You are a man of remarkable fore-sight, Griffin."

"If my mum was here right now, I have the feeling that she would find a way to whip up a splendid dinner for both of us."

"Even with no raw materials?"

"There was always nothing in the cupboards or the fridge, she always said, but we always got dinner."

But even as Griffin said it, the idea glowed in Lew's eyes.

"Of course," he cried.

He sprang to the car, throwing things about and in a flash he was down at the bank of the river. Leaving the bottle perhaps in the hope that someone might steal it, Griffin followed. He found Lew on a huge rock overhanging the water, busily skinning the snake.

"My, Lewington, what a multi-talented man you are."

"Pretty easy, Griffin, except for the head."

"What do you plan to do with it?"

"I thought I might stretch it and put it on the wall in Elm Street."

"It'll clash with the mouse skins."

"I'm sure it will be complimentary."

Soon, Lew was rolling up the skin and slipping it carefully back in the plastic bag.

"I suppose, Lewington, that this is therapy to take your mind off hunger."

"Not at all, Griffin. It is the solution to that problem."

"I feared you were going to say that."

"Look upon it as a five foot sausage, Griffin."

"Are you sure about this. Maybe only certain types of snake are fit for consumption."

"You know, Griffin, sometimes I suspect you have no respect for your national heritage."

"There are some ways in which such respect is dubious. What about the poison sacs and things?"

"I chucked them in the river so the Monster wouldn't make any mistakes."

"A noble sentiment, though a bit rough on the fish."

For all that, it sizzled rather unimpressively in the frying pan, like twisted, fleshless fish. They flopped it from pan to plates and sat on logs, holding the sections in their fingers, stripping the meat away from the ribs with their teeth.

"It tastes like tasteless chicken," Griffin decided.

"With just a hint of tasteless pork."

"A spot of garlic might have helped."

He was really thinking tomato sauce.

"My God, Griffin. It would utterly destroy the natural flavour."

In the end, when most of it was devoured and the remains offered to a deeply offended Monster, it only served to remind them of their hunger.

They sat and passed the bottle back and forth.

"I'm only thankful the bottle is not wrapped in a paper bag, Griffin."

"Yes, Lewington, I agree that my own self-image is suffering under the implications of this incident."

And all the more so when they strove to roll cigarettes using newspaper and tea leaves, tree bark, dried grass—none of which proved sensibly smokable. Although the tea leaves offered a promising light-headed effect...

"I now know why aborigines don't smoke, Lewington."

"And why they are so thin, Griffin."

"The lack of cigarettes is making me hungry again."

"Perhaps we should have strung some fishing lines and used the snake for bait."

"I suspect the fish would find it no more nourishing than we did."

Sitting in the dark, the inactivity as nerve-wracking to them as the deprivation.

"Remember Burke and Wills," Griffin sighed.

"I'm trying not to."

"Their last days must have been something like this."

"Far from it. Besides, Griffin, the old explorers all fell to eating their animals to survive."

And he gazed evilly at the Monster.

"There is also some record of cannibalism, Lewington."

"Surely they ate the animals before taking to each other."

"You touch my dog, the sequence may be reversed."

"You fed him so well, Griffin. I'm sure he would be tasty."

The Monster, knowing he had the sharper teeth, remained calm. When Lew dived for him, Griffin intercepted with a fearful head butt and they rolled in the grass, fighting mad, the Monster snapping at available hands and feet. Nature red in tooth and claw...

Gladiatorial

Summer put up a ferocious last-ditch stand with a searing gusty day in mid-autumn that sent temperatures soaring to record heights, vast multitudes flocking to the beaches, bushfires raging through the hills and Griffin into the pub on the way home from work.

"I've done it," Lew Sigg said.

"I have news," Griffin said.

"What I have done is far more important than any news you might have, Griffin."

"I doubt it, Lewington, but go on."

"I'm in."

"In? Good God, not the army. You couldn't have..."

"Army? Heavens no, Griffin. My God, what a horrifying thought. That you would dare..."

"Sorry. It was just the first thing that came to mind."

"That you could imagine that after four years of unerringly dodging the draft, I would even contemplate..."

"I'm sorry, Lewington. I didn't think."

"Actually, that does have something to do with it."

"What does?"

"The army."

"I think I'm confused."

"Let me explain."

"I wish you would."

"I got this letter."

"From the army?"

"Yes."

"They like you."

"They do."

"And they want you."

"They do."

"And were they friendly about it?"

"Oh very."

"Not like the army I knew. What did they want?"

"They wanted to know how my studies were going."

"What studies?"

"Well, that was how I eluded them in the first place. Fulltime students aren't eligible for the draft until they complete their studies."

"Correct. Only you dropped out three years ago."

"Quite true. Until today. I've dropped in again."

"Dropped in where?"

"RMIT. Course begins next month. Fulltime Architecture."

"Architecture. I thought you were doing Art?"

"I was. None of the Art courses would have me back."

"Lewington, Architecture takes years. Decades for dumb-bums like you. How will you live?"

"On my wits."

"You mean you'll starve to death."

"Griffin, I'm not planning to do the course. I'm just going to stay enrolled in it."

"I see your point."

"And it will keep the grubby hands of the army off me."

"Sure. But how on earth did you convince them to enrol you?"

"I told a great number of lies."

"And they believed you?"

"Hardly at all. But there is a limit to just how much a person can disbelieve in one day. I told them more lies than that."

"But what happens when they find you out?"

"How can they? They don't have a single fact to work with."

"I suppose not."

"But you said you have news, Griffin."

"Yes. I think I've found us a place to live."

"I didn't realise we were looking for somewhere to live, Griffin."

"A chap from work. His mother owns a house she's willing to rent cheap."

"You know people who own houses?"

"I checked it out today. Excellent house. Double storey, lots of room, in Fitzroy. It'll be perfect."

"Perfect for what?"

"Us. To live in."

"But I already live somewhere. And so do you for that matter."

"You did express dissatisfaction."

"Did I?"

"Well. Dell did."

"Only constantly."

"You should hear some of the dreadful things she said about the place."

"I admit it is an easy place to say dreadful things about..."

"And Podmore Street is too small for me."

"It seems just the right size for you."

"But not for me and Karen."

"Griffin, are you finally going to make an honest woman out of her?"

"No. But we've been trying to persuade each other to move in with together but at present there isn't enough room."

"What does she think of this, Griffin."

"She prefers not to think about it."

"Actually, I find it hard to believe a bloke like you wouldn't have married a sheila like her a long time ago."

"Yes. So do I."

"What's wrong with her?"

"Nothing. She's perfect."

"She's too good for you, Griffin."

"She's too good for everyone, Lewington."

"So now she's thinking about becoming a little less perfect and living in sin."

"I believe you've grasped the essentials."

"Not a bad idea. Try and annihilate your nuptial reluctance at point blank range."

"I guess."

"Pretty good trap, Griffin. If you don't fall for that one, you never will."

"I'm not enjoying this subject, Lewington."

"I can see that."

"In any case, I need somewhere with enough space for me and Karen, just in case she sees the matter favourably, and Dell refuses to live in that hovel of yours."

"Who told you that?"

"Dell did."

"When?"

"Well, actually, she didn't. She told Karen. Karen told me."

"Griffin, our bloody women are plotting against us."

"A harsh view, Lewington."

"But true."

"In any case, this is the answer."

"Explain to me how its the answer, Griffin."

"Great house. Good location. Elm Street Fitzroy. And its cheap."

"How cheap?"

"Sixty bucks a week."

"That doesn't sound cheap."

"Thirty bucks each."

"I can't afford that, Griffin."

"But you and Dell can."

"If she will."

"Karen says she will."

"Griffin, when did this collusion between our respective wenches take place?"

"I don't know. It is kinda hard to imagine, isn't it."

"I wouldn't have thought they had anything in common."

"They haven't."

"Except us."

"Which I suppose is why they have nothing better to talk about than make plots against us."

"Which, Griffin, makes me wonder at the wisdom of putting them in the same house together when perhaps we ought to be keeping them apart."

"Lewington, you are paranoid."

"Four years as a fugitive does that to you, Griffin."

So they came to the house in Elm Street. Griffin took up the lease, moved in first and took over the large upstairs room at the front with its balcony overlooking the factory wall opposite. He took a day off and fixed his room up, and then got the kitchen and lounge into the best order he could, and waited for the onslaught. Lew had moved his meagre belongings in first and then went off, seeking Dell.

He knew it would be difficult. Karen had an Irish Catholic mother who was still alive and alert to her daughter's wellbeing, and Karen was not a person to tell her lies. Not that there weren't lies of omission—after all she slept three nights a week at Podmore Street and he three at her flat—the seventh night, Monday, she insisted on being allowed to wash her hair and do 'other women's stuff', as she put it. But to live together would mean a formalisation of the arrangement and, as she said, she would hardly be able to talk to her mother at all if she couldn't mention where she lived. Still, she confronted the occasion with enthusiasm, even though she referred to it as 'his' new home and it seemed she was merely establishing her visitor's rights.

"Where are the elms?" she asked, scowling at the overgrown forecourt. "You can't call it Elm Street if there are no trees."

"Asphalt Street would lack the same appeal," Griffin offered hopelessly.

"What appeal?" she wondered.

Somehow, while she was there, what had appeared to him to be paradise diminished and became grotty and decrepit in his eyes. Perhaps it was her pink twinset and tartan skirt that seemed far to neat and clean for such an environment. The carpet in the hall and on the stairs was threadbare, and if Lew's paintings covered the worst holes in the plaster on the walls, still there was a limit to how much canvas and oils could do.

"It's very old," she declared as they entered. "And look at all the cracks in the walls."

"A bit of filler and a lick of paint will fix that," he assured her.

"Lew did these?" she asked. "He's very good."

"Yeah," Griffin decided. "When he isn't being serious."

In the kitchen, he sat her down and put the kettle on. Lew had been and had failed with the dishes. Karen wanted to roll her sleeves up and get into them but he managed to hold her back.

"You can't just walk straight in and start washing someone else's dishes," he assured her. She sat and pouted. And then she noticed the funny things on the wall. There were about a dozen of them, wire frames bent to a circle about the size of a hand and small grey strips of fur stretched inside them. She touched one, thinking them another of Lew's creations, which indeed they were.

"What sort of fur is this?"

"Mouse," Griffin was fool enough to admit.

With a shriek, she leapt out of the chair and cross the room, holding her contaminated hand away from her body.

"Oh god, that's horrible," she cried.

"He does it as a warning to others," Griffin blabbered hopelessly.

"Can't have worked very well. There's so many of them," and she was looking around her feet for more.

"Yeah. Lew reckons if he can get enough, he can make a coat and sell it for a fortune. Only mouse skin coat in the world..."

"Is there somewhere I can wash my hand?" she asked him bleakly.

The night was hot, steamy and oppressive, even with the big double-windows open to admit the breeze across the balcony. Not that there was much breeze—the looming factory wall opposite saw to that. Griffin sat at his desk gazing out at the bleak scene opposite. It was that wall, he knew, that made the rent so cheap. And the cracks in the walls and the floorboards that creaked and bounced and the prehistoric kitchen and bathroom arrangements. Karen might have turned her nose up, but it was a truly magnificent house, close to the magic nightlife of Carlton and Fitzroy, walking distance from his office in the city, a park just down on the corner, and so much room to do things. Even the wide ranging junk accumulated by Lew's broad interests would never fill it.

Where the hell was Lew? On such a hot night it wasn't hard to imagine that he might have got stuck in the pub, but really, he should have been here. Maybe his charm and persuasive powers might have done wonders with Karen that his own fumbling attempts at explanation never could have. Not that he had given up on her yet—Karen was always one who needed to be eased into new circumstances slowly. She had chased after him in the first place, abandoning her previous boyfriend in anticipation of success and had constantly declared that she wanted him, yet it had taken him two months to establish their relationship and three more to finally lure her into his bed. He remembered the interminable nights of friendly persuasion with a shudder. He'd hate to have to try and talk her into something she didn't want.

In the end, he gave up on Lew and stripped and was heading for the shower when he heard the grumble of the motorcycle down in the street. He rushed back and leaned over his desk to peer out the window—yes, two people were dismounting in the dimness down there. Pulling his head out of the helmet, Lew looked up to see Griffin at the lighted window. Even in the poor streetlighting, he could see the teeth as Lew grinned.

"Hey Griffin. You there?"

"Come on up—the door's open," Griffin called back.

"Told you it's a great house," Lew was insisting down there as they came through the gate.

"What a horrible street," he heard Dell saying.

Lew did seem to be dragging her as they passed under the balcony and out of sight toward the door.

Griffin remained where he was for the moment, leaning on his desk, lighting a cigarette, looking around. Somehow he regretted he had not made more effort to get the place in better order. He had lived on hope with Karen, unsuccessfully as it turned out, but in any case no delusions were likely to be adequate under Dell's critical eye. Now, as he heard their footsteps ringing on the stair, he felt nervous, bedraggled, unprepared for this... Shit! He wasn't even dressed.

He did manage to get a towel around his waist before they invaded his room. They burst in—juxtaposed to his vulnerable nakedness, their leather jackets and suchlike could not have looked more imposing. They might have been alien assassins, come to finish the prisoner off.

"Just look around you," Lew was saying. "A truly great house. So clever of Griffin to find it. An utter monster of a place."

Behind him, Dell did seem to be finding it monstrous.

"I'm sorry I'm not dressed," Griffin was babbling. "I did bring clothes... I was just about to have a shower..."

And wondered all the time why he thought he needed to explain himself.

And Lew was off, rampaging into every room, flashing lights on and glancing around.

"This is excellent," he insisted. "Just the thing. So much room. Think of the parties we can have."

Griffin and Dell tagged along behind, both feeling equally abandoned.

"These old places are so hard to keep clean," she commented.

"It has a big backyard," Griffin offered hopelessly.

Plainly, Dell needed to be convinced and Lew was trying to do so by sweeping her along on the wave of his enthusiasm. Only Dell didn't seem to be near the water. Finally they had completed the loop and were back upstairs and in the room they would occupy. She liked the view out over the rusty roofs to the city skyline. She liked the space. She liked best of all the extra room for herself where she could work undisturbed. A dunny and bathroom upstairs, as well as the one down and out the back—that seemed to please her as well. When she checked the flush, Griffin knew there was hope.

Finally they were returned to his room, which if a clutter of boxes, at least offered places to sit.

"It will be better when..." Griffin began and then realised he didn't know how to end the sentence because it was going to refer to Karen's domestic touch.

"So there'll just be us three and Karen," Dell said, for she was good at reading minds.

Griffin was about to say something disastrously honest but Lew cut him off.

"Yeah. We four can handle the rent easy," Lew cut in.

"Where is Karen now?" Dell asked obscurely. Griffin wasn't sure if she meant physically, or addresswise, or what.

"Um... not here...She had to...go..."

"Pity. I was looking forward to seeing her again."

"Here she is," Lew cried. He had found her picture on the desk, and hugged it to his belly. "Bloody gorgeous, sexy creature."

"Unhand that woman," Griffin threatened.

"Sexy little thing," Lew cried ecstatically. "Makes me horny just to look at her."

"Put it down, Lew," Griffin said coldly.

"You're disgusting, Lew..." Dell said in a very unconvincing fashion.

"Cors I'd rather have the real thing..." Lew leered and kissed the photograph full on.

"Oh Lew, you're being a bore," Dell protested.

"Put it down, Lewington or I'll chuck you out the window."

Griffin said it with such menace that indeed Dell drew back, out of the line of fire.

"Listen, I'm getting horny, reading this..." Lew was gasping.

"I shall say it just one last time," Griffin said.

Dell was about to do something positive to intervene but it was already too late, for it would never be said that one last time. Lew let the pages flutter in the air and bolted but with the cry of a Watusi warrior, Griffin brought him down in the doorway with a rugby tackle. Dell screamed and dived for cover, and then winced at a sickening thud as they hit the floor and tumbled, the one over the other.

"What the hell are you doing?" she shrieked as she followed, and then. "Look out," as their interlocked forms propelled into the empty air above the top step of the stairs. In any event, her efforts were drowned out by the shrieks of delight, pain and anger that emitted by turns from the two combatants as they crashed from one step to another. There seemed to be arms and legs flailing everywhere, all the way to the bottom. "I'll kill you, you bastard," and "You'll pay for that," were the sorts of things they grunted at each other, along with other less intelligible utterances. Even the cries of genuine pain were broken up by gurgles of laughter.

Mortified Dell trotted down after them, her stomach churning at each of a dozen thumps of flesh against hardness before they hit the hallway at the bottom. Along the way, Griffin lost his towel and Lew had it and it became the object of the dispute. On their feet again, they locked together in a fierce test of strength—leather straining against skin, a pink Roman gladiator and a golliwog Viking warrior. Lew's face was impossibly red, Griffins body glistened all over with sweat, and finally they broke and Lew fled with the towel, Griffin in roaring pursuit.

The battle ended in the outside bathroom, the shower gushing cold water on them both, naked Griffin caring less about the soaking than fully-dressed Lew, and in repossession of his towel and modesty, the former was claiming victory. They returned, dripping, to confront Dell who, throughout the battle had passed through her full range of emotions, and had settled finally for anger.

"You pair of fuckwits, have you gone mad?" she shrieked.

"I think I broke my leg," Lew declared and started limping.

And this inspired both to examination of injuries.

"Got you a bewdy there, Lewington. See, I've drawn blood."

"Look at that bruise, Griffin. You'll feel that tomorrow."

"You're both queer, that's what you are," Dell gasped.

Lew, to comfort her, offered a soggy hug.

"Oh, my love, what a drag you are. A simple test of manhood. There's no need to bring in complex social issues."

"You call that manhood. It's not even adult..."

He closed in on her.

"Get away from me, you horrible wet thing."

But her anger was fully expended now. She had been angry mostly because they had managed to scare her so badly —in the end they all knew that what she felt most was left out.

Griffin, shivering now, went by her, his hand lightly touching her shoulder as he went by.

"At least we know the outside shower works," he smiled gently.

"Unhand that woman," Lew declared.

They glared at each other and it might have been on again, had not Dell thrown herself between them.

"One of you could have been seriously hurt," she snapped. "Now stop it."

Griffin passed on and headed up the stairs to dry and dress, while Lew imitated a soggy Dracula and sent Dell screaming out of the house.

"If you think I'm going to live in this bloody madhouse, you're out of your fucking minds!"

Storm Journey

The sadistic morning sun found a gap in the gumtrees and sent a savage sliver of light through the windscreen to strike Griffin right between the eyes, scorching his brain and incinerating his dreams in a blinding explosion of consciousness. He discovered, to his complete dismay, that he was still alive, or partly so. There were his legs, for instance, one over and one under the steering wheel with his knees twisted to impossible angles and the gearshift doing terrible things to his thigh. In fact every bone in his body seemed broken, most notably that section of his back where the window-winder had spent the night making a relief impression of itself in his flesh. The rest of him was numb but that was alright and anyway, it was only because of the pain that he could tell that somehow he had survived again.

With a series of grunts and groans, he set about the enormous task of manipulating himself into a more humanlike position but eventually that proved far too complicated within the confines of the front seat of the Jaguar. He realised that he must vacate the car first, and sort himself out on the ground. Carefully, he reached back over his head and got hold of the door handle and finally achieved air and space. At that instant, the Monster, who was luxuriating in the backseat and might have been busting for a piss for hours, seized the opportunity to bound over and out of the car, heedlessly trampling his human being in the process.

"You useless, fucking mongrel!" Griffin croaked, but the Monster was already off to explore the trees and was not even slightly interested in the opinions of Homo Sapiens.

Contorting excruciatingly, Griffin dragged himself backwards along the seat and it was only when, clinging to the door, he was half in and half suspended that he realised there was no way to avoid falling flat on his back. He clung on grimly, quite stuck, and might almost have convinced himself that he did not feel half as bad as his predicament suggested. Then his head fell on the ground and shattered in a thousand pieces and his body sagged hopelessly after it. He lay moaning, his back on the dirt, feet on the seat, and eyes closed to spare them from the dazzling sunlight. A kookaburra thought that was pretty funny—Griffin glared into the trees and marked the creature for the breakfast menu but it chuckled on undeterred. Still, it was humiliation alone that eventually got him to his feet.

The first thing he needed was a cigarette, but of course there were none of those. He looked hopefully at his watch but it wasn't yet nine. At least an hour before the banks would open and allow anything to be done to ease the constriction in his lungs—was there no end to this madness? Leaning on the car, he surveyed the scene. Ah yes, the bridge, the river, the small reserve with a sign that said picnic facilities were provided by the Gladstone Lion's Club. Slowly it was all coming back to him.

There was a body lying over by a fallen log—it was hard to tell in places which was which, but the clothing suggested Lew. Just like Sergeant Kennedy, shortly after he finished his polite conversation with Ned Kelly. Griffin began to cough—deep and throaty—he would have to get a fag from somewhere—and staggered over to explore the remains of what had once been a friend of his. Lew was alive—his belly rose and fell and his flesh showed goosebumps from the chill of the dew that had settled on him as he slept. Cruelly, Griffin nudged him with a tentative foot.

"Good morning," something deep within his body reverberated.

Lew sat up carefully, plainly going through the same orientation process Griffin had a few minutes earlier. He scratched his head frantically—bits of bark and leaves had become entangled in the incredible pile of knots that was his hair.

"Which of us, do you suppose Griffin, was sober enough to drive us to this spot?"

"Had to be Monster."

That solved to his satisfaction, Lew curled up and went straight back to sleep. Obviously, it was going to have to be Griffin who would extricate them from their present predicament. His brain and body were running on nicotine cravings alone. He went back to the car and found his bankbook and collected the jerrycan from the boot, and leaving Monster in charge, walked up the slope and crossed to the other side of the highway. There he remained, waiting for a ride. Stranded. Opposite the Lion's Club reserve near the long bridge on the road into Gladstone—three hundred miles up the coast from Brisbane.

A huge old Dodge came trundling along and picked him up. His benefactor was a grisled old farmer who spied the jerrycan at his feet.

"Run outa gas, didja?"

"And everything else."

"Look like yer had a hard night, mate."

"I've had easier."

It turned out to be less than a mile to civilisation, although it might just as well have been a hundred.

*

These then were the badlands—barren, monotonous, scrubby, flat, dismal. No one lived here and no one would want to, on the inland run between Rockhampton and Mackay, a scruffy tract of country, normally dry. Normally... but at the moment it was a scene awash with torrential rain as they drove through the late afternoon, Griffin at the wheel, quiet and concentrating in the poor visibility. Another cyclone, they had been told, was moving in and rain tumbled incessantly, hour upon hour, mile upon mile, from a drab grey sky that was as featureless as the land beneath.

Lew had fallen ill after Gladstone and was still suffering the effects. It might have had something to do with Bundaberg rum, less probably something he ate but they called it Blacksnake's Revenge. He had been violently ill for a time, necessitating numerous stops by the roadside, but he refused a more permanent halt and suggestions of medical assistance. Now, it seemed to have passed through him and he flopped about in the passenger seat, sleeping it off. Griffin could not have felt more alone. Everything within him wanted to turn back now, but neither would have had the nerve to suggest such cowardice. They were the heroes of the story and heroes could never turn from their fated course. They could only go forward...

"Forward," Lew murmured in his sleep.

In the deluging rain there was no point stopping anywhere. They did pause briefly in Rockhampton, but Lew was so ill that he could not be enticed into any of the pubs. Nor the hospital.

"Do you suppose that this is some sort of divine retribution?" Griffin asked at one point.

"For what?"

"Running out. On Mother and child."

"Yes, Griffin. I can just imagine Dell back there, whipping up evil spirits to pursue us."

"Don't you feel a little but bad about that?"

"No. I just feel bad."

And now in this barren country there was even less to stop

for—you could only drive on and on, into the darkness, toward Mackay and the only interest those sudden narrow bridges that would materialise treacherously out of the wall of rain, and the ploughing through the sections of the road that were flooded. The rain sliced through the headlights in illuminated slats—night had not fallen but simply added to the darkness. His back ached and his peering eyes were straining from hour upon hour of bulging out of his head and he strove to discern the true nature of the distorted images constantly composed fitfully on the watery windscreen. Water leaked in on them everywhere but through the sunroof mostly. It was a world soggy, miserable and blearily constricted.

At last he could see the lights of Mackay and if it was all flat and open and studded with neon-lit petrol stations and motels, still it was a warm relief after the arid void before. At the first place they came to, long before entering the town, they stopped for hamburgers, coffee, cigarettes, dog food and petrol. They could want for nothing, almost...

"Don't suppose you feel like a beer," Griffin said hopefully, perhaps cruelly.

"No," Lew sighed, and might almost have wept to admit it.

"We only passed two or three pubs."

"We'll get 'em on the way back. You could have a beer without me."

Griffin gasped in complete horror.

"If you can live without it, so can I," he said stoically.

"I'm not sure if I am alive."

The whole basis of their existence seemed to be dissolving in the rain and wind.

Lew could not even manage coffee or food but Griffin could see he was improving and restrained suggestions of doctors and hospitals out of fear of becoming a nag. Thunder erupted all around them—the sky seemed just a few feet overhead—you could have believed there was enough rain in those clouds to continue forever, unceasingly, the beginning of the cataclysmic end of the world.

They drove through the deserted main street of the town.

"You want to stop here?" Griffin had to ask.

"God, what for?"

He was right, Griffin knew. A warm dry hotel room would have been just too cowardly after such hardships. It had become a test of strength against the elements themselves and they were committed to press on. They pressed on, cruising out past billboards that assured them Mackay was a picturesque place of sunshine and sugar cane and pineapples. Population, 28,000 very wet people.

On the run toward Proserpine, the road became narrower and even more dangerous and Griffin could feel his reflexes slowing, his mind less able to predict the curious visions of obstacles—great potholes, missing sections of road, tight bends, fleeting silhouettes of unidentifiable animals—that would suddenly spring at him out of the night. Lew insisted that he was getting better, even offered to drive but was now sleeping again. Griffin himself barely existed in this tightening claustrophobic world of isolation. He smoked cigarettes end for end and drove on—if he stopped or complained of his exhaustion, Lew would want to take over when he was plainly in no condition to do so. Griffin hunched over the wheel, eyes staring desperately ahead, several times burning his fingers when cigarettes burned down to the butt as he continued to grip the wheel. He was down to his last skerrick of energy, through what had long since become an endless night.

On the straight empty stretch beyond a place called Bloomsbury, he found the rain easing somewhat. It must have been about two in the morning and he saw something on the highway ahead that seemed to be a fire, in spite of the rain. He shivered, sure he was hallucinating—but slowed down all the same as he approached the black shape on the highway, indeed flickering with flames. As he drew nearer, it became what he suspected—a sedan with all doors open, in the middle of the road, low on burst tyres, flames licking inside and out. He stopped the Jag a few yards back, as if he feared that they too might be infected with that fiery, fatal disease. Lew woke.

"What's up?"

"Have a look."

Dread was a small spiny creature crawling about his stomach as they got out of the Jag and walked through the rain toward the wreck. It had been a recent model Holden but now the entire rear half was gutted, the body blackened with blistered paint, the tyres ruptured, the crumpled gory innards of the seats disgorged. Plainly the petrol tank had exploded. Fearfully, they searched about but there was no trace of the occupants. No one, it seemed, had died a blazing death here.

"Fucking strange," Lew murmured.

"I guess the driver hitched to town..."

Leaving his car abandoned, scuttled, like a phantom ship

of legend, in this open land, blocking the middle of the road. It was like some sort of warning, a sign, an omen, something spiritual. You could not believe that it might have belonged to someone...

"You surely get some strange ideas, Griffin."

"Let's get out of here."

Not far down the road, police and a tow truck were on the way but Griffin would know nothing of that for a long time. Lew was first back to the car, heading for the driver's side.

"Hey! Where you going?"

"I'm better now."

"You don't look better," Griffin said grimly, and he didn't either—pale and drawn.

"Perhaps not, Griffin, but I certainly don't look as bad as you. You're rooted."

"But healthy."

"But cactus. Whereas if a little indisposed, I am nevertheless rested. I'm driving."

Griffin could feel the last of his strength drain away. Suddenly he was so tired he could not speak, much less argue, He crawled into the passenger seat and was asleep before Lew started the engine.

He awoke beyond dawn, and they were passing through a small rain-drenched town—Ayr or maybe Brandon—spied briefly through the swishing windscreen wipers. Griffin stirred from a bleak, blood-draining sleep, joints stiff from the chill, his mind haunted by ghosts of incinerated cars and charred bodies that couldn't be found. He stretched and yawned, but there was no escaping the knots and aches from heedlessly sleeping in uncomfortable positions.

"Where are we?"

"Does it matter?"

"Not a lot."

"Be in Townsville in an hour."

Townsville—last night it might have been on another planet.

"How do you feel?"

"Nowhere near as bad as you look, Griffin. Do you know you're more active when asleep than when awake."

"I had this nightmare—about how I went to sunny Queensland and it rained all the time I was there."

They rolled on into Townsville, onto the busy thoroughfare of Flinders Street, beneath towering Castle Hill on the rocky crag of which someone had painted a fifty foot effigy of the stick-figure saint motif. They stopped for breakfast in a cafe but the rain kept on despite the portly lady who told them that the cyclone had broken up while still out to sea. Bacon and eggs, coffee, cigarettes and the lady had some nibbled T-bones for The Monster. And the pubs would not open for an hour yet.

"How far are we from Cairns, Griffin?"

"About five hours. Bit over two hundred."

"We could be there in time for a counter lunch."

But in fact they were not, for they stopped at every pub along the way for beer and games of pool and darts. The weather had wrecked the world—interesting locals all stayed home and the tourists had scattered. They passed the point where the speedometer told them they had come 2000 miles—Melbourne seemed much further away than that. The promised counterlunch took place in Innisfail, which might have been a pretty place too look at were the world not so wet and grey. The huge Atherton Tablelands closed in on them from the left, their tops shrouded in heavy mists—while the grim flat ocean lay to the right. They plunged from banana plantations into dense tropical jungle and out onto lush green plains.

"We could spend some time in these places, looking at the sights, Lewington."

"They'll still be there on the way back."

"Perhaps the weather will be better."

"Why do I find that so hard to believe, Griffin?"

"Experience, Lewington, sheer experience."

If there was one good thing about the sizeable fishing port of Cairns it was that under these cyclonic conditions, there were many comfortable pubs. They arrived toward nightfall and visited them all and the night vanished into a damp haze. At morning, they found themselves parked down by the beach, wrapped in soggy sleeping bags, Lew in the front, Griffin and Monster in the back. But the rain had finally stopped.

"Well, Lewington, what now?"

"Here we are, at our destination. Glorious Cairns. Who would have thought this old bomb would have got so far."

"An extraordinary achievement, Lewington."

"And the weather is clearing."

"Yes. It should be a nice trip back."

"Yes, Griffin. And when do you think we should embark upon this return journey?"

"I can see no reason why we don't start immediately."

"No reason at all, Griffin. No reason at all."

"Except..."

"Except what?"

"Well, in fact the end of the road is Cooktown. Couple of hundred further on."

"Rough road conditions, they tell me. Probably impassable after the cyclone."

"Probably. But it is as far north as you can drive in this country. Think of it."

"We'd be pushing our luck, Griffin."

"Pushed luck is the only sort that offers satisfaction."

It was ridiculous, really. The old car, their battered selves, the hard road, to go all that way with all that risk just to turn around and come back again. Silly. Absurd.

"Cooktown, hey?" Lew said thoughtfully.

Final Morning

When he left the house that final morning, his departure coincided with the pre-dawn light. It was the coldest time of day of the coldest time of year, and as he opened the front door and stepped out, a gust of icy air engulfed him ruthlessly, biting through his coat and scarf, rattling his teeth and causing him to gasp out a miniature fog of his own. Out there, all was dark and damp, and the frozen dew that coated Karen Kerrigan's pink Volkswagen might well have been a warning to fools to venture no further. The new Ice Age was coming and everyone knew it except Griffin—at this time of morning a somnolent still hung over the city as if everyone else had the sense to stay huddled in bed for a few more hours yet. But not dumb Griffin, who carried on regardless, and it was no comfort at all to know that this would be the last time, the final morning, that he would be required to set out for work at such a ridiculous hour. Tomorrow, he could smile, but today there was no choice but to face it bravely and head on out there. His lips were blue and stiff and could not have smiled anyway. The door clicked shut behind him, and he suffered a moment of panic that he might yet again have forgotten his keys and locked himself out. Each of them had managed that trick several times, except Dell who never did anything wrong.

To stride it out along the footpath was the only way to combat this sort of cold—hands pressed deep into pockets, chin tucked into scarf, shoulders hunched forward. He marched along the uneven footpath heading toward the damp wash of yellow street lighting where Elm Street's dark dreariness ran into the wide arterial expanse of Nicholson Street. He strode past the narrow terrace houses, identical to the one where they lived, and again refused to think about the sensible people in them, keeping warm. He had left Karen in the bed, a tiny lump in the clutter of blankets, devastated by sleep. "Don't wake me," she pleaded. "Please don't wake me. I'm so tired."

He kissed her lightly before he left—she offered no response. Since would be another two hours yet before she would be required to rise, he could not bring himself to hate her for it.

Arriving at Nicholson Street, he slowed his pace. There was now some sign of life—other unfortunates like him. A tram rumbled its way up the rise toward him, tailed by its impatient bottled-up entourage of cars awaiting the chance to sneak by. There was the paper van pausing outside the newsagent farther down the road, and the thump of the bundle of morning papers on the footpath, hastily discarded as the van raced on. The milkman was not to be seen when he might have been expected—perhaps it was too early even for him. There were cars moving—the harbingers of the clutter of peakhour traffic that would soon follow, but he looked both ways and there was not another pedestrian to be seen. When he might have been disappointed, he decided instead to be proud of that. He could afford to be optimistic—the world seemed to be running in his favour these days.

Karen, being Karen, had never actually made any decision about moving into the house. She liked the place well enough—was quite thrilled by it all as he showed her around that first day, and knew that she would like to live there. She got along well with his two friends Lew and Dell with whom he shared the rent. The symmetry of two couples in joyful occupation was enticing to her—it gave a sense of security of tenure that she badly needed. But there was her mother, who was old, and Catholic, and would never understand. Griffin was, for a change, sensible enough not to press her about it—he made little comment, and simply left the option open. Karen had never in her life been called upon to make a decision about anything, and so instead muddled around in the middle while he was almost unbearably patient and understanding.

The traffic was clear, and he marched his way across Nicholson Street on a broad diagonal heading toward the corner of Carlton Street. Ahead of him, beyond the trees, loomed the great pink dome of the Exhibition Building—a papier-mache replica of Michaelangelo's Europe—that was the symbol of a colonial city that had once aspired to greatness. This was the site of the extravagant World's Fair of 1880, when Melbourne provoked a grandeur in the dizzy days of prosperity that followed the gold rushes, until corrupt governments and crooked property developers shattered the economy and induced in the city a depression all of its own, sandwiched between those other great depressions suffered by the whole world for similar reasons. Beyond the trees too could be seen the enormous glass and steel towers of the Central Business District, some of them still topped with giant cranes, to show plainly that the lessons of that great disaster had not been learned, that they were still at it, in this city that had still not fully recovered from its previous sudden, dramatic, decline.

Reaching the park, he slowed his stride. If there was a good thing to be said for the medieval monstrosity that was the Exhibition Building, it was that it had also provided these parklands. There were two in fact, lying to the north and the south of the great structure. The one to the south, nearest the centre of the city, was adorned with fountains and manicured lawns and trees placed in straight rows amid plantations of flowers. There, city workers could come to sit on sunny days and eat their lunches, beside attractive beds of flowers, loomed over by the best aspect of the old building. Organised picnics, secular festivals, visiting schoolchildren and political gatherings were the activities of this region, along with the imported swans and ducks that drifted on the pleasant ponds. That part of the park was very much favoured, and therefore of no interest to Griffin whatsoever. His domain was this northern section, which, in spite of obvious attempts to make it match its glamorous southern counterpart, was quite a different proposition altogether.

Walk along any of Melbourne's interminable network of suburban streets, and should you look into the yards you would see an elegant monotony of well-tended lawns and shrubs and gardens at the front, but you needed to take to the back lanes and peer over the fences if you were to learn anything of the character of the occupants of any given house. So it was here. The southern section of the Carlton Gardens was the front yard and this rather scruffy northern section the back. At first glance, it was little different, although it was rather obviously encroached upon by tennis courts, car park and kindergarten, and there were no fountains here, nor garden beds. Though it was doubtless maintained by the very same council workers, somehow their efforts were less successful here—the trees seemed to grow less straight, the grass less evenly. In the front, people politely promenaded, here they kicked footballs, there they sat delicately on the grass, here they stripped and sunbathed, there they strutted pedigree dogs on leads, here they turned their mongrels loose for a run. The public dunny at the front was an engaging structure in bluestone beneath a lattice of flowering ivy where the paper supply was always kept up, in the back yard the dunny was a monstrous brick veneer and concrete place, the haunt of homosexuals, SP bookies and drug dealers where several people had been knifed and the only paper was abandoned Form Guides. In the front the benches were architecturally designed for those sorts of people whose clothes were too expensive to be placed in contact with nature, in the back the benches were regulation council issue and utilised as home and bed for the innumerable old men who came in their gaberdine coats with their bottles of McWilliams Sherry and methylated spirits indistinguishably still wrapped in the brown paper bags.

Entering the park to cross on the diagonal path, Griffin could feel himself transformed immediately. Ostensibly, he was still a young man walking along on a very cold morning with his hands pressed into the pockets of his coat but whereas before he huddled desperately, now he had loosened up and, having slowed his pace, was rather more the aspect of one taking a pleasant stroll. He could feel it himself, and was suddenly alive, alert, and somehow more awake than at any other time of day. He never ceased to wonder at this, and knew that somehow, it was very important.

These days he was always tired. In the recent months he found his life completely controlled by the jangling little alarm clock that Karen had given him about a year ago to signify the occasion of his promotion to the position of office supervisor.

"You're on your way up," she told him proudly. "You can't afford to be late anymore."

If he might have been less pleased by such a prospect than she, the fact remained that he would have been dead without that little clock. Every morning at precisely six-forty five, the clock jangled and found Griffin still desperately asleep. His metabolism never seemed to learn. In the evenings, he had a few beers in the pub and usually Karen met him there. Frequently, Lew did to. Late at night, Karen would retire and Lew would suggest just one more for the road. Except they weren't going anywhere. Except for the nights they spend the whole evening in the pub. Somehow, he always intended to go to bed just a little earlier than he eventually did—he would protest when Lew would open another bottle but not stop him, not refuse to drink. Lew, of course, did not have to be up early in the morning. Somehow, Griffin was always short of sleep and was caught in a bind that ought to have been easy to escape but wasn't. The less willpower you needed, the harder it was to find.

He was not the first man in history to like a drink, but the truth was he didn't like it much—he just did it. He had never been much of a drinker despite the solid reputation that his father had in that regard, and his mother blamed the army for that, as she did with the son, but that wasn't exactly true. At

Nui Dat, in the three day breaks between operations, there were always pretty solid two-night binges in the Delta Company boozer, and he drank himself as silly as the rest of them, but that was the way it was, back then. In the first year out, he drank very little—just at parties and business lunches, but then slowly he began to drop into the pub for a couple after work, at first occasionally, then regularly, and then the couple became a few and the few extended to closing time, and suddenly he was in the pub every chance he got. He went to the pub for lunch, and then morning and afternoon tea breaks, and stayed longer and longer. Now that he was the Supervisor, no one checked up on his hours as he did for his staff. He exploited this hypocrisy without conscience, and then he had just one more before returning to work, and then one more...

Plainly it was getting out of hand, but he refused to think too deeply about that. It was the speed with which this alcoholism had overwhelmed him so completely that was frightening. Sober one day, a habitual drunk the next and it was getting worse. Not that he couldn't control it, of course, but he didn't want to control it. He simply didn't care. Some mornings he found himself sitting on the steps of the pub waiting for it to open, other times he awoke without knowing where he had been. He took booze home and drank with Lew deep into the night and wasn't sleeping anymore. All he did was drink. He peered at the world through the alcoholic haze and was truly amazed that he had come to this so swiftly. And Karen worried, and he knew she worried. Once they did things together—now she did them while he waited for her in a pub somewhere.

Throughout it all, he was constantly aware—at least at those times when he was aware of anything—that there was something going wrong with his life. All this drinking, this ceaseless alcoholic swill, was not the problem in itself. Something was causing the drinking, of that he was certain. The question was, what? He was fit and strong and lived in a nice house with good people, he had a good job that he actually liked despite his increasingly rare appearances, he had a pretty girlfriend whom he loved dearly and who loved him and soon they would be able to afford to buy a house and get married and have kids... He even had a car that never broke down. So what the bloody hell was the problem? Sure, there were the nightmares, but the army psychiatrists said they were normal and to be expected. They would go away in time, he was assured, and it was true. Most nights, he was too sozzled to dream, and too hungover in the morning to remember anything anyway. No doubt there were murky things going on in his subconscious that he kept repressed by keeping himself numb, but wasn't that true of everybody? According to Freud, certainly. Despite her Catholic background, Karen Kerrigan had opened up to him completely, and was delighted to offer him the use of her body for whatever he wanted, whenever he wanted. No, it wasn't anything like that. It had to be something else. But, plainly, there just wasn't anything else.

His life was perfect and that perfection was somehow causing him to spontaneously self-destruct. What the bloody hell was going on?

There was the decisive occasion a few weeks back. He awoke suddenly from a ferocious blood-draining sleep to find her sitting on the end of the bed, gently caressing him back to the land of the living. Or only just.... He realised that he was lying on the bed fully clothed, sweating awfully, his body exhausted from the effort of such sleep.

"Are you alright?" she asked him, frowning somewhat.

"Cors," he answered roughly, or tried to—someone had poured clag down his throat while he slept and made speech nearly impossible. Every part of his body seemed cramped, sore, and in the wrong place—his head ached, his stomach felt like someone had been playing football with it, his ears rang, his tongue seemed far too large for his mouth....

"Yeah, I'm alright," he said, more successfully this time. He was erect too, he noticed.

She had noticed too.

"Who's the lucky girl? " she asked him tartly.

Of course, she was probably hoping that he had been dreaming erotic dreams, and about her, but he could only remember fitful, frightening, intangible images, definitely unsexual. The erection was a mystery, and anyway, declining now. He moved himself awkwardly into a sitting position—millions of micro-lumberjacks were sawing their way through the forest of his hair and he clawed at them frantically. But such violent action only served to induce a coughing fit, deep and spluttering and chesty—dragging his lungs with barbed-wire nets. Trying to be helpful, she belted him on the back, driving the spikes through. Feverishly, he went for his own, surer if more barbaric cure—a cigarette—and once he had grappled with that, the urgency enhanced by his shaking hands, and got it alight, he seemed to be more or less back in one piece. Though she didn't think so.

"Shit you're a mess," she bit at him.

And she bounced off the bed to cross the room and sit at his desk and glowered at him with annoyance. Hunched on the bed, his hair standing on end, clothes dishevelled, pale, shaking, smelling, gazing at her vaguely through the drifting cigarette smoke that seemed to have filled the room at a single puff, he could not think of an answer to that.

"Why don't you marry me so I can look after you properly," she said with sheer malevolence. Nowhere in the world was there an answer to that, and he did not attempt one. Then she relented with a sigh. "What have you been doing to get yourself in this state?" she asked instead—the same question, turned inside-out, just like he was.

"I'll be alright in a minute," he managed to murmur.

"Been drinking all day with Lew, I suppose."

"No," he said shortly, but that was a lie. "Just for an hour this afternoon. . ."

"Or two. . ."

"No. I was at work..."

"Kenny, it's not night. It's morning?"

That confused him for a moment. He was sure that it was also morning, last time he remembered.

"I'll call them and tell them I'm sick."

"I'd better do it for you."

"You don't have to do my lying for me."

"I'm not so sure it's a lie."

On the whole, he might have preferred to have gone to the office, explaining to the boss that he had been kidnapped by aliens for 72,000 light years along the way, which might not have been true, but felt like it was.

"Look," he was saying. "I'm alright. I was just tired—I got my sleeping time a bit mixed up."

"Just a bit. . ." she began, but she could not persist with such cruelty—Karen was never one for the knife.

"I'd better have a shower and get going," he said abruptly.

And he was off too, but she jumped up and intercepted him in the middle of the room, catching his arm first, then wrapping her arms around him. She gazed upward into his eyes, her own eyes sad, pleading.

"I'm sorry," she said, and meant it too. "But you do worry me. You're running yourself into the ground."

"Rubbish," he said curtly, but then he could smile down

upon her: "But it's good of you to care."

And he kissed her lightly.

In fact, he found his stomach was acting strangely, and was in a bit of a hurry. With a show of bravado, he launched himself away from her and headed for the bathroom. Or in that general direction... just two paces out the bedroom door, and suddenly he was reaching for the bannister at the top of the stairs that was right there and yet miles away. The floor jumped up and slammed him in the face and there was an enormous explosion in his head...

For some idiot reason, he was pressing his face against the carpet, and his nose was crushed and seemed to be bleeding. Karen, and Lew, who had appeared magically, were clawing at him, but he fought them off.

"What happened?" they were asking him variously.

He knew then exactly what had happened.

"I just passed out for a moment," he said.

"Come on," said Lew. "Let's get him back to bed."

But that wasn't where he was going. Partly with their help and partly with the aid of the bannister, he was on his feet, if rather uncertainly.

"Gotta go to the dunny," he muttered, and shrugged them off, reeling along the hall and into the bathroom and, locking them out, just made it in time. They hovered outside the door.

"Are you alright in there?"

"Sure, sure. Fine, fine."

The sweat poured out of him, amongst other things. He was pleased to be only semi-conscious while such vileness was being ejected from his body. But the sweat made him cold, and he was shivering all over—still, when he stood and flushed the mess away, he was able to walk out of the bathroom again under his own power, and smile at them as he came through the door.

"What's the problem? " he asked brightly.

They stared at his pale face and wet hair, his vague eyes and the blood from his nose, and he allowed them to steer him back to bed.

"I'm sick," he said pathetically.

He was too. The next day was Friday and Karen stayed home and drove him to the doctor. He had the flu, like anybody else might have, but there was more.

"Do you suppose," he asked. "that there's something else wrong?"

"Do you have other symptoms?" the doctor asked.

"Aren't these enough?"

"In spite of your present illness, you seem quite strong and fit to me."

"I mean, do you think that might be something that caused my condition in the first place."

"Psychosomatic, you mean?"

"Yeah."

"No. You definitely have a virus. You have slight congestion of the airways and a slightly enlarged liver. Cut down your smoking, drink a bit less and take two of these every four hours and you will be one hundred percent in a week or two."

"Week or two?"

"You do seem to be a bit run down. I'll give you a certificate for two weeks. Get all the rest you can. And you'll be fine."

The one thing he knew for sure was that he was not going to be fine, in two weeks or any other time.

There were pills to be picked up from the chemist on the way home.

"You see you take them," Karen said, enjoying her newfound position of power. The treacherous medico, not trusting him, had troubled to pass his condition onto her. Karen was not the sort of person to say 'told you so'- she just smiled a very jubilant smile a great deal.

For all that day and over the weekend, he remained in bed while she fussed about him. Mostly he was sleeping, but otherwise he was constantly aware of her. She cleaned everything, brought him meals and pills, made the bed around him at least twice a day, fluffed up his pillows. Karen, he knew, was having a wonderful time looking after him like this; so much so that he suspected she secretly wished he would stay sick forever, though he would never have been so cruel as to suggest such a thing. She even tidied his desk, filing and arranging all the papers. He would never be able to find anything again. On Monday, he forced her to return to her job, but she left late, returned early, and even whipped home in her lunchhour to make sure that he was alright. By Tuesday, the worst symptoms began to pass, but he promised her he would do what he was told and stay in bed.

On Wednesday, he could stand it no longer. Something was going on—he knew it. He felt the stubble on his chin—no, he had been washed and cleaned enough these last few days. From his desk he took a pad and pen and sat up in the bed and began to write.

"What are you writing?" Karen asked, when she caught him at it.

"A story."

"What about?"

"Vietnam."

"How interesting. You never talk about it."

"No. But maybe I can write it down."

"Can I read it?"

"When it's finished."

On Thursday, he finally managed one page, done in stages at five attempts, his persistence amazing him. By Friday his strength was returning and he did three more. When Karen came home to fret about him, he dragged her into the bed with him.

"My! You are getting better."

But she had to stay on top and do all the work.

"And you need a shave," she murmured eventually.

"Maybe," he said.

Over the weekend, he sat scribbling in the bed while Karen bustled about him, cleaning, tidying, bringing him things. He wouldn't let her touch the sheets of paper littering the bed.

"This is turning into a very long story," she said.

As she fussed about him, she had abandoned wearing knickers and whenever he became erect, which was very often, he could pop her straight on it unhindered and she would wriggle in her delightful way until they had both come.

"You are supposed to be resting."

"This is resting. I've never felt so rested."

Other times she used her mouth, but if that silenced her playful complaints, it was a just a touch too stimulating for one in his condition. As he had suspected, the perfection of his former life had been a total illusion. This was what perfection really meant. It was all a monumental effort, and he wallowed in it, and all the more so because he could see that Karen was enjoying herself so much.

By Sunday, largely due to his continual nagging, she did allow him out of bed for a while.

"We'll go for a walk," he said. "Down to the park."

"Don't be silly," she said scornfully. "It's too far."

"Rubbish. Just around the corner. I need some fresh air. You can't imagine how hard it is, cooped up like this all the time.."

It was a beautiful sunny day, and if she might have felt that her prisoner was escaping, she could not argue that the sunshine might do more good than harm. He started off with great enthusiasm, but found that as they progressed along Elm Street to the corner, he did have to lean on her a little. But once they had crossed Nicholson Street and entered the park itself, he found his step lightening.

"They ought to change the name of this place from whatever it is to Griffin Park," Karen said with a smile, for she was trying to be cheerful about the expedition. "You come here so often."

"Yeah, I like it, for some strange reason."

Even he could see it wasn't much of a park—just a few acres of definitely urban property upon which someone had forgot to build the multi-storeyed commission flats and so allowed the encroachment of trees and grass and birds, all of which paid no rent. Karen was looking around, screwing up her nose slightly. It wasn't even a pretty place: every way you looked you could see the ugly buildings glaring enviously from outside its bounds—the huge towers of flats and office blocks, chimneys arrowing the sky, cars, trucks, trams, buses, all sorts of bikes, bumping and beeping around the perimeter roads. It was no sanctuary for natural things, no world of isolation—only a scruffy, polluted place where, if anything, the greenery only served to emphasise the gruesomeness of city life.

But Griffin liked it. And because he liked it, she would have liked to have liked it too, but could not. She supposed that it required the peculiar sensibilities of someone like Griffin to obtain rewards from so uncompromising a place.

"I've made a decision," he said. Here, on his home ground, he was going to drop a bombshell on her. They sat themselves on the grass, and she waited for it.

"What decision is that?" she asked nervously. It occurred to him, with a sudden shock, that she would have no idea what to expect. Perhaps she suspected that he was about to propose—to offer to marry her as a reward for the devotion to the cause that she had shown him this recent week. Realising that, he knew he would have to break it to her gently.

"Being sick has had its desired effect," he told her. "I might not have seemed to have taken what the doctor said seriously, but I do know it's true."

She thought about that. He realised again that it would not entirely dampen the primary thought in her mind.

"You are rather bad at looking after yourself," she told him, to try, perhaps, to keep the conversation in line with her thoughts.

"I'm not going to shave anymore," he said.

She smiled, and if there was disappointment in that smile, there was also relief.

"Don't be silly," she said. "You look like a bloody porcupine."

"Presumably this will eventually turn into a beard."

"Hmmm, yes. I can see how it might look."

"Think you can live with it."

"Might be alright. And you can always shave it off, if it doesn't."

"Don't tempt me, Delilah."

"It was Samson's hair, not his beard."

"Principle's the same."

"You seem to be taking this decision very seriously."

"It is serious. First thing every morning, a man stands in front of a mirror with a razor in his hand deciding whether or not to cut his throat. The experience keeps him subdued for the rest of the day."

"What are they going to think about this at work?"

"They won't like it at all."

"So?"

"They can lump it."

Her face struggled then to divert a look of fear. In those words, everything she dreamed of was threatened. His job, their security, the continuation of their saving toward their house, aided of course by his eligibility for a War Service Loan. All of it, suddenly menaced by this whim. She struggled with it for a moment and he watched her do so, feeling dreadfully cruel. But she got through it alright, as Karen always did the minor thumps and bumps of life, with a smile.

"Men with beards do look—stronger somehow," she managed.

"Scratching at your face with a razor every day. It's ridiculous. The bullshit begins there."

"You ought to see some of the silly things we women have to do to ourselves."

"You should stop doing them."

"No chance. I'm not going through the rest of my life with you calling me 'Hairylegs'," she laughed.

But he was not watching her anymore—suddenly something beyond had caught his eye. It might have been by way of necessary distraction. She looked around too. Over there, an old man was staggering along the path, a disgusting ancient creature with his bald and grey-bristled head wobbling even more than his body, filthy decrepit clothes hanging disjointedly from his weaving frame. They could almost smell the metho from where they sat.

But there was nothing significant about the old man that Karen could see. He was not even the only person on the path at the time since people commonly used it as a short-cut—and such men, anyway, were quite common in this part of the city. But it was the old man, Karen saw, that Griffin was watching so intently, and even as he did, almost as if Griffin had used some secret power to will it, the old man took one more step than his alcohol-soaked brain could comprehend and spilled forward onto the path.

"It's pitiful, people like that," Karen was saying.

"Yeah, poor old bastard," Griffin murmured, and with that, he stood and started to walk toward the fallen figure. A woman, pushing a pram, and several school children, walked right past the collapsed figure, averting their eyes as Griffin approached. Karen, feeling quite thoroughly deserted, got up and followed along.

"Arm oorite! Arm oorite," the ancient voice croaked and Griffin leaned over him. Some people had stopped to watch now, suddenly interested, and the schoolchildren were coming back, for it was then plain that blood was spurting from a gash on the fleshy dome where it had struck the edge of the kerb.

Griffin squatted there, administering his fingers to the wound to try and staunch the flow of blood. There was a lot of blood—Karen felt suddenly quite nauseous, but it was also noticeable that as Griffin attended it, the flow began to stop, if not before a certain amount of it had splattered on Griffin's shirt. He glanced up then, and spoke with an authoritative tone that Karen had never heard from him before.

"Karen—run down to the telephone box and call an ambulance—quickly now."

As much bundled along by the sheer force of his tone as she was by being pleased for an excuse to be elsewhere, Karen ran down the slope toward the telephone box at the corner of Nicholson Street.

"Wadda yer doin' ter me," the old man was protesting at Griffin when she got back. He was struggling, rather feebly, and both men looked rather pale and sweating.

"Wadda yer doin' ter me?"

With one hand, the old man was trying to seize Griffin's wrist, though he had nothing of the strength required for the task.

"Take it easy, Pop. It's alright."

"Ain't got nuffin ter pinch. Yer can't pinch nuffin from me." Karen was noticing how bad the old man smelled, as if the puncturing of his skin had freed the pungent odours of rot from within his body.

The small crowd that had gathered was losing interest now that Griffin had halted the flow of blood and so ruined their day. Newcomers stopped for a moment to peer, but soon continued on. And soon the wail of the ambulance could be heard, and Karen went down to the road to direct the ambulance men and their stretcher to the spot.

"Quite a nasty wound," the ambulance man said. "Good thing you stopped the bleeding. You medical?"

"Army," Griffin said, with the reluctance of one realising that the two years might not have been entirely wasted after all.

"Well, we'll fix him now," they said, and loaded him onto the stretcher.

"Ain't goin ter no horsepiddle," the old man protested, and struggled vainly, hopelessly, in the terror of facing his readmission to the world. All that effort had tired Griffin badly. When the ambulance was gone, he happily allowed her to walk him home.

"You got blood on your shirt," she told him.

"It'll wash off," he said. She walked beside him, nuzzled against him, warmingly.

"You're a good man, Griffin," she said emotionally. "You didn't have to help him. You make people like me, who stay away from such things, feel rather disgusting."

"It's best to stay away, if you don't know what you're doing," Griffin said, and then he smiled. "Anyway, I look upon it as an investment in the future."

"How's that?"

"One day, that old man might be me."

She could not contain her horror at such a thought.

He squeezed her: " Joke, Joyce."

"It isn't funny," she said grimly. And Griffin decided that was quite enough for one day, and went back to bed and stayed there.

And now he walked the park that final morning, his hands pressed into the pockets of his coat, taking his time, gazing upward at the exposed nervous systems of the barren tree branches against an almost lightening sky fading into that yellow light that always hung over the city at night, he felt an inner calm, a sense of achievement, a sense of purpose in his life. When he reached the very spot where the old man had fallen, he paused to contemplate it. That was the real moment of decision. That was when he knew which way he was to go, whatever the cost.

There were two old men in his mind at that moment. There was his father, Wally Griffin, sitting out his time in front of the television, too exhausted from his day's labour for anything else. His house was paid for, his kids visited on Sundays, his wife continued to complain about everything he did. He was probably happy, surely had peace of mind. But was he really any better off than the old man who fell here; who, you could presume, had risked all that and lost. The point was that there wasn't enough difference between the winner and the loser to make the effort worthwhile. Both men were doomed, utterly subdued by life, but the old man who fell had put up a fight somewhere along the line. He had said 'no, I'm not going to play the game your way.' Neither would Griffin. And if he ended up in the gutter, so be it. The job was to make his own life, and not simply accept the one they offered. The only question remaining was what form that life would take.

The second week passed, and his face had ceased to look like a worn-out dunny brush and instead was a definite beard.

"And a very handsome one too," Karen Kerrigan said bravely.

On the first day back at work, the Departmental Manager let it pass with a smiling aside.

"You seem to have forgotten to shave today."

On the second, he was reminded of the Public Service regulation which allowed the growth of moustaches within certain guidelines—nothing below the lip, nothing extending beyond the contour of the face. The same rules they had in the army. It took a week before he was finally summoned before a disciplinary committee and informed that if the beard was not removed within a week, he would be obliged to tender his resignation.

He put the matter before the Clerical Officer's Union, who after trying to talk him out of such reckless action, finally offered their support. They wanted him to tell lies about skin rashes that prevented his shaving, but he refused. They wondered if there might be some religious sect he could claim devotion to, but he would not. Finally, the wheels of the forces that decided the Public Service regulations regarding an employers right to control the growth of facial hair on employees where safety considerations did not apply, began to creak. The week passed and he did not tender his resignation. He was quietly replaced as Supervisor, and returned to the disciplinary committee. He was removed from the public areas. But, around the building, he noticed others beginning to show heavy five o'clock shadows.

"Don't you think this has gone far enough?" Karen Kerrigan asked him, just as everyone else seemed to ask him.

"Don't you like it," he said, but he stroked his beard to direct the emphasis to specifics.

"Tickles a bit, but, yes, I like it. But I don't like what it is doing to you."

"The beard isn't doing anything except growing, as all beards should. It's me, the chap behind the beard, that's doing this."

"But what the hell are you trying to prove?"

If only he knew.

Now he reached the end of the park and the pedestrian lights on Rathdowne Street. The traffic was on the move and he waited, not pressing the button although his over-trained instincts wanted to. Instead he sought a gap and crossed. They couldn't make him press the button to change the lights. If he wanted to take the risk, that was his choice. No one could make him do anything.

Today he would work until five and then be finished with the Department of Construction, and the Public Service generally, forever. They had demoted him as far down as they could go, and moved him to a small room in the basement, out of sight. It was said that it was almost impossible for anyone to be fired from the Public Service, but he managed to be the exception. Along the way, they had tried to talk him into staying, offering more money, better position, more civilised hours, if only he would condescend to shave. But once he had made the decision, there was no turning back.

Of course, he had been careful not to mention their offerings to Karen. It was hard enough, he knew, for her to be brave about this. Their offers, generous as they might have been, did not even tempt him slightly. It was as if, in the making of the decision, vaguely in the midst of those days of ill health, he had transformed himself into a different person altogether. He felt changed, felt different, he felt pleased with himself. The directions of his life had always been of necessity, had been chosen for him, up until now. This time, he offered no excuses, and would have no-one to blame but himself. He had chosen this direction for himself, and whether it worked out or not, he knew already that he would never regret it. It was the first step to becoming a person that he could relate to as himself, rather than one constructed by his environment. Almost accidentally, he had stumbled upon what it really meant to be alive. So he walked the park to work that final day, and when that day was ended, so too was a part of his own very existence. And it was not at all insignificant that, the following morning, the man carried his razor away with the garbage.

The Cooktown Trick Shot

At the very stroke of one, for as long as anyone could remember, Charlie Manchek came in through the frosted-glass door of the Cooktown Hotel, deposited his sack of partly delivered mail behind the door and, still squinting from the bright sunlight outside, walked across to where a freshly poured beer awaited him at the bar. At the time, Harry Waters—the licensee—had returned to his glass-washing duties in this brief hiatus between those customers who went to lunch at twelve and those at one—in fact the one-to-two period was far quieter for few people worked businessman's hours in such a town. Harry Waters was a rotund, stunted man who, they liked to joke, almost had to stand on tip-toe to see over the bar. He glanced over at Charlie the postman—who was fully three inches taller—and was not unhappy to see there were no letters for him, except that it might have deprived him of his daily complaint about bills.

"Nuthin terday, Harry," he was assured.

"Good thing too. Only ever bills when it is," Harry answered, and felt decidedly better then.

Charlie Manchek, on these hot days, always took his first beer at a single gulp and Harry broke off his glass-washing to pour three more—one for Charlie and the other two for Teddie Thomas and Willie Briant who always shared Charlie's round and could be seen crossing the road from the Caltex Garage where the former was the owner and the latter the chief and only mechanic. This visual aspect of the street was in fact a new perspective from the Cooktown Commercial Hotel for the windows had originally been frosted glass to spare the passing ladies the sights of horror within, but now that age was past and as each window was broken—usually by means of someone being thrown through it late on a Saturday night, Harry replaced it with clear glass. It looked better, gave more light, and offered the view of the street which was a matter of eternal interest. There were only two frosted panels remaining and there was an unspoken understanding that if anyone happened to be thrown through either of those rather than the clear panes, the usual property damage prosecution might well be overlooked.

Now it was exactly one minute past one and Teddie and

Willie could be seen crossing the road out there and Harry poured their beer in advance—not that he actually needed to look to know they were on their way.

There were five other men in the bar at the time: Fred Graham, a retired meat worker who always stood in the corner with the best view of the television set and four farmers further over who came in once a week to settle with the bank and have a few—Joe Cameron, his son Roy, boss-cutter Jack Leeson and plantation foreman Clarey Best.

"G'day, Charlie. What's new around town?" Clarey Best called, since the postman was the best person to know such things.

"SFA," was Charlie's standard answer and he gave it now, then grinned and added, "I hear you got the truck bogged again last night."

"Right up to the fuckin axles," Clarey grumbled, "Fuckin thing's still there."

But he was able to brighten when he saw Teddie Thomas enter. "Hey Teddie. When're yer comin ter drag the Inter out?" Grey haired, wrinkled Teddie Thomas, in overalls smeared with grease they reckoned was five years old because it was that long since he'd last been under a car, offered his usual good humoured smile.

"When you get outa the pub and come and give us a hand, Clarey."

"I been waitin all fuckin morning fer yer, Teddie. A bloke's got fuckin work ter do, yer know."

"You blokes wouldn't know what fuckin work was," Teddie grinned, "You got all them machines do it for yer. Not like in the old days. Ain't that right, Charlie."

"What's that?"

"These blokes wouldn't know what work was."

"I'm a postman. What would I know about work?"

"Ain't like it was in the old days, but."

"Thank fuck for that," old Fred Graham said.

Young Willie Briant, always a walking swamp of grease, eyed the pool table hungrily. It was a new large table with its smooth mantle of green felt.

"Anyone for a game?" the pimple-faced youth asked excitedly.

When no one bothered to answer that, he looked down the bar toward Fred Graham.

"Hey Fred, how about a game of pool?"

"Savin meself for Satderdee night," Old Fred croaked.

There was a pool competition on Saturday with a dozen bottles prize and wily Old Fred won it more often than not.

"How about some practice, then."

"Don't need no practice to clean you up, Sonny-Jim."

"Aw shit!"

And as almost always was the case, Willie had to content himself with beer and conversation.

"Busy mornin'?" Charlie Manchek saw fit to ask Teddie Thomas.

"Dead quiet mate."

"Cept for that woman," Willie Briant put in excitedly.

"Arr, shit yeah," Teddie remembered, "This bloody woman comes in with steam blowin' everywhere—bloody Datsun Jap crap—cracked the head wide open, she did. Broke the fan belt, yer see, outside town and saw the steam so she reckons she drives as fast as she could before she runs out of water. Silly bitch. Fucked her car completely. Then she complains because I tell her that I can't fix it before lunchtime. So she's back in the car—gawd knows how she got it gowan—and roars off flat out. Reckoned she'd go to the Shell place down the road cos she didn't like the service here."

"People like that shouldn't be allowed to drive," Harry Waters said—he hadn't owned a car for twenty years.

"Arr, they can have her. We got plenty of work on."

"Didn't like the fuckin' service," Willie Briant echoed, "Rooted her fuckin' car!"

The conversation drifted on to the inevitable subject of the racing at Warwick Farm, a matter which all were able to comment on and no one agreed on anything, which was the way they liked it. Then suddenly the predictability of it all was altered when Roy Cameron, who was gazing idly out into the street, interrupted with an expression of surprise.

"Hey. Have a geek at this!"

This was a huge old grey car, battered and rusted, pulling in to a parking spot right outside.

"Hell of a car, that," Jack Leeson said, "One of them Pommie jobs, ain't it? Bentley."

"Nar," said Clarey Best, "It's a Jaguar."

"Can't be," Jack replied, "Too big fer a fuckin Jag. Hey Teddy, what sorta car's that?"

"Jag," Teddie Thomas pronounced flatly, "Mark Seven."

"See. Told yer," Clarey Best chortled.

"Too bloody big fer a Jag," Jack muttered.

"Shit," Charlie Manchek then observed, "She's blowin' a bita smoke."

Teddie Thomas continued to shake his head: "Arrr, she's an old car. Burn a bit of oil, leak a bit. Good cars but. Keep goin'."

"Hey, it ain't got no licence plates," Willie Briant noticed, "It ain't even registered."

"Yes it is," Teddie sighed—to be the font of all knowledge was wearisome sometimes, "Got a current sticker in the window. Victorian sticker at that, by the look of it."

"Jeez, come a long way."

"Bloody Victorians," Harry Waters muttered, and they all grumbled in their shared hatred of the southern state, even though it was a thousand miles away.

"Look like fuckin Victorians too," Fred Graham added and all present laughed at that.

The simple fact that all the men in the pub were short-haired and clean-shaven with the exception of Fred Graham's perpetual stubble was enough to make the two young men who got out of the car distinctive. In this part desert part tropical climate, beards were rare and never the abundant growths of these two characters. One was a large fellow of ponderous movements, his hair and beard yellow and shaggy. The other was thinner but taller, very well built with lithe movements and his head completely engulfed in hair and beard of tight black curls.

"Couple of bloody pirates," Harry Waters said, but the resultant laughter died quickly when it became plain that the pirates were coming into the bar.

Meanwhile, the rural contingent were taking even greater interest in the third occupant of the car, a shaggy medium sized dog that bounded for a moment between the two humans.

"Must be country boys," Roy Cameron said, "Look at the dog."

"Ain't no country bloke ud have a dog like that," Joe Cameron told what he regarded as his idiot son.

"It's a sheep dog. Some sort of Border Collie."

"Too big fer a Border Collie, son. And they don't have long hair like that."

Roy Cameron was not about to give in to what he regarded as his idiot father: "Have a look at the spots on his legs and nose. Queensland Heeler spots."

"It's a bloody mongrel, son."

"Yeah. But it's a sheep dog mongrel."

"Prob'ly as silly as a sheep," Joe Cameron said and general laughter made that the final word.

Confronted with all this laughter, coming from both fronts, the two pirates, on entering, might have regard this a very cheery establishment indeed. They immediately divided their forces, the yellow-haired fellow diverting to the pool table while the dark-curly chap continued on to the bar.

"Two pots, or middies, or whatever you call them in this part of the world, please," the dark curly chap said in a slightly cultured tone that marked him all the more alien.

"We call 'em beers here, mate," Harry Waters smiled.

The balls rattled while the yellow-haired one set them up on the table.

"Call," he said and flipped a coin.

"Heads."

"You lost. I'll break," yellow-hair declared in his gravelly voice and immediately pocketed the coin without allowing his opponent the slightest opportunity to confirm the outcome. Willie Briant gasped at this blatant breach of etiquette—there'd be a fight for sure if someone tried that during the pool comp. But dark-curly offered no protest. Strange folk, these Victorians.

The two regular contingents went back to their more normal conversations for a while—about racehorses and television programs and fertiliser—with only the two youngest members of each group taking any further interest in the strangers. Roy Cameron was observing that the silly-as-a-sheep dog was now sitting patiently beside the old Jaguar, waiting obediently for the return of the humans. He would have liked to have pointed this out to his father: in fact Joe Cameron had already noticed and wanted to go out there and move the bloody mongrel, just to prove the point. Roy got his chance between the first and second game as the victorious yellow-hair waited for dark-curly to set the balls up again.

"Hey mate," he called, "Does yer dog always sit waitin' fer yer like that?"

Joe could have killed him, or more likely the yellow-hair when he answered.

"Always."

"How'd yer train him?" Roy asked triumphantly.

"Didn't. Taught himself. That and a few other things."

"Yer musta had to give him some trainin'."

"Nope," yellow-hair grinned, "If I was half as good at being a human as he is at being a dog, I'd be a millionaire by now."

Joe Cameron could only seethe while the others laughed, while Roy sipped his beer in jubilation, knowing he had the upper hand now, at least until they got home.

Willie Briant, meanwhile, was absorbed in the progress of the pool game and seeing these were both pretty good players. He'd have liked to have challenged one of them but they did seem to be engaged in some private grudge-match. In the regular pub pool comp, either would have acquitted himself well. And this did not go generally unnoticed—when dark-curly played a couple of remarkable shots during the second game, most of those present decided the contest was worth a glance from time to time.

As the second game progressed, it became evident that the two players were not so evenly matched. Dark-curly was rather more their style of player, a player of clever if risky shots and his agility had a deftness that his well-muscled frame suggested as he moved smoothly about the table, playing improbable but often excellent shots with cool confidence. He maintained concentration at all times, speaking soft precise sentences when he commented on the game.

"You'll not get out of that, Griffin."

"I'll do so without effort, Lewington."

"You confuse your fantasies with reality, Griffin. My every ploy has thwarted you so far."

"I merely await your offering a worthwhile challenge, Lewington."

Yellow-hair went about the game altogether differently. Lacking his opponents dexterity, he played a game of cunning and confusion, always forcing Dark-curly into utilising the best of his skills. His attitude was rather more loose and casual—he talked most of the time, making jokes, making noises and laughing all of which was obviously part of the strategy. He seemed to play his shots carelessly but still somehow managed to keep Dark-curly bottled up. Indeed, all spectators were delighted when the latter suddenly broke loose with a brilliant shot and won the second game.

"That was a most fortuitous double, Lewington."

"Luck was only the slightest of factors, Griffin."

"I remain confident that your intention and outcome with the green ball were not the same."

"My intention, Griffin, was to win and this I have done, as you see."

That was something else—the odd way they spoke. Plainly

it was some sort of ongoing joke. Willie Briant remembered reading seeing old stuff like Sherlock Holmes and Dr Watson on television—it was the funny way those folk addressed each other. In this environment, it could not have seemed more alien.

In the third game, the discrepancy began to manifest itself. Dark-curly got away to a great start sinking three balls, leaving Yellow-hair little means of suppressing him—he miss-cued a snooker shot and Dark-curly removed his remaining colours to be on the black with a six-ball lead, and the black itself set close to the pocket. Yellow-hair grinned broadly. "You think you've won this, don't you Lewington."

"I certainly have. Do the gentlemanly thing and concede."

"You think so only because you haven't seen my next shot yet."

And it had to be said that considering his past efforts, yellow-hair might not be so easily beaten. He played his orange ball—the least likely of his possibilities—with a shot light as air, and the ball rolled gently to squeeze its way between the black ball and the cushion and finally position itself right on the brink of the pocket. The white he left way up the table such that dark-curly could not play the black without risking the illegal sinking of the orange.

"Nar," said Clarey Best, "He'll just knock the orange in and give away two shots. He can spare 'em."

"He oughta play the black down the table with the double shot," Joe Cameron thought, "Play it safe."

"Not this fella," Jack Leeson considered, "I'll bet he takes up the challenge."

"Fool if he does."

Fool or not, that bet, had it been taken, would have been a safe one. Dark-curly looked across at Harry Waters.

"What rules do we play in this pub?" he asked quietly.

For the rules of pool vary from place to place and you always had to play by the rules of whatever pub you were in at the time.

"Down the table. One on the black. No foul snooker. No loss of game unless the black's down," Harry said mechanically.

Dark-curly nodded and moved around the table, lining up to try and play the black past the orange—a dangerous manoeuvre to say the least.

"It's never been done, Lewington," yellow-hair said.

"It hasn't been done yet."

"Chewy on your boot."

This shot required even greater delicacy than had the previous and it was executed to perfection. The white kissed the black lightly, and somehow it squeezed the orange away from the pocket a fraction and settled itself on the brink. A ripple of excitement passed through the onlookers. Yellow-hair had been outwitted at his own game.

"I've got you now, smartarse."

"He who counteth chickee before hatchee gettee egg on facee."

Yellow-hair was still grinning as he leaned across the table to line up his red ball, pausing only an instant to concentrate on the shot.

"He's gunna try and knock 'em both outa there," Harry Waters said, predicting the obvious.

"Can't be done," Teddie Thomas was sure.

"Has ter knock the black in," Charlie Manchek knew.

But the shot as played was not what they expected—instead of fast and hard to smash the black and orange balls away from the troublesome pocket, Yellow-hair played at an incredibly slow place. The red ball rolled gently, inexorably, and for a moment seemed that it would fall well short. But instead it oozed up to the orange ball and nudged in beside it, a hair from touching the precarious black. It took a moment for the implications of this to dawn upon the spectators.

"You animal," Dark-curly breathed.

For suddenly, they could all see, Dark-curly's position had become diabolical. The red and orange balls completely blocked his path to the black, and further, just to breath on either ball would surely send the black toppling illegally, fatally, into the pocket. Yellow-hair walked from the table chuckling with elation.

"Get out of this one, Lewington, and I will heartily agree you are the greatest player in all history."

Still the onlookers stared at this, the most subtle and cruel blow ever struck on a pool table that they had ever seen.

"I reckon he's fucked," Joe Cameron declared.

"The dirtiest, lowest trick I've ever seen," Clarey Best muttered.

"Maybe," said Old Fred Graham, "but oh, so, clever."

"Has to be a rule against it," Roy Cameron decided.

But there wasn't—it was merely the most wicked of contrivances. In his anger, Dark-curly stalked a complete circuit of the table, but there was only one option, apart from conceding defeat and he wasn't about to do that. Deftly, Dark-curly shot Yellow-hair's blue ball into the nearest pocket.

"Two shots to you, Foxy," he snapped.

His plan was obvious—he would illegally remove Yellow-hair's remaining balls from the table, hoping to force penalty shots that would oblige Yellow-hair, rather than himself, to be obliged to solve the riddle of the black ball and its two intimate guardians. Yellow-hair, looking unconcerned, calmly dispatched his maroon and green balls, then missed twice on the purple. Dark-curly reached with the butt of his cue and tapped the purple into the pocket.

"Two shots to you," he seethed.

"I must say I do appreciate all this assistance, Lewington."

Dark-curly was too enraged to speak.

Now, but for the three balls locked together in the corner, only the yellow remained and when the onlookers expected otherwise, Yellow-hair calmed played it into the pocket. With two free shots remaining, it seemed he would now have no choice but to play his orange or red ball.

"He's buggered it up," Willie Briant assessed.

"No he hasn't," Fred graham said wisely.

For, lining up his next shot, it was plain that yellow-hair was taking not the slightest notice of the three balls locked together down the table. Instead, he played the white ball the other way, out into the middle of the table without hitting anything or even intending to.

"Oh dear, looks like I missed," Yellow-hair grinned. "Your shot, Lewington."

Dark-curly fumed, his face red as fury and his milky eyeballs striving to burst from his face.

"You can't do that! You've have to attempt to hit your ball."

"No such rule. Correct, Mr Bartender?"

"That's right, mate," Harry Waters replied dryly.

Seeing the genius of the move, Fred Graham nodded knowingly, while Willie Briant even saw a way it could have been improved on.

"What he shoulda done was shoot the white ball in the pocket," Willie breathed, "Then the other bloke has to play a double shot down the table. Makes it even more impossible."

"Nar," Fred Graham smiled, "He don't wanna make it impossible. He wants ter dangle the bait."

Hearing this, Dark-curly calmed a little, squinting evil eyes at Yellow-hair who wasn't making a very good job of trying to appear modest. Dark-curly leaned over the table and fired the white ball into the pocket, fetched it when it fell into the tray below and spotted it.

"Two shots to you, Griffin."

Yellow-hair, unable to rid himself of a smug grin, leaned and again played the white gently into the middle of the table.

"Bugger. Missed again."

Dark-curly raged.

"I can do that again. We'll be here forever."

"Why not? I'm a patient man."

"We're deadlocked. Stalemate."

"Perhaps, Lewington, only since I was doomed to lose the game anyway, I'll obviously be delighted to settle for a draw."

"Okay, it's a fucking draw."

"And a moral victory to me for forcing the draw from a losing position."

"There's nothing moral about this, you cunt!"

"I'm sure you will be haunted forever if you don't attempt to win the game, Lewington."

"I'll take the fucking balls and stuff 'em down your fucking throat!"

"That's one way out of it, I suppose."

"You fucking smart bastard..."

It seemed as if the threat would be realised as Dark-curly, fists clenched and shaking all over, lurched forward wildly as if to seize the three troublesome balls. He roared like a tiger with his teeth bared—he might even have been frothing at the mouth. The onlookers reared back, seeing violence imminent, but Yellow-hair stood his ground and with a quick movement, raised his pool cue and lashed it like a whip, cracking it sharply on Dark-curly's black curls. The sharp thwack! echoed through the bar and for a moment, time stood still.

Willie Briant, closest to the action, tried to position himself behind Charlie Manchek who in turn clutched his beer to his chest for fear of spillage. Teddie Thomas groped for the big shifting spanner that he had been forgetting to slip into his back pocket for years now, while Fred Graham thought it might be a good time to go for a piss. Harry Waters wondered how he might protect his windows: Joe Cameron prepared to launch himself into the fray but was pleased when Clarey Best held him back by the arm: Jack Leeson remembered the great fight over a pool game that had ended in an all-out brawl and waited his chance to tell the story: Roy Cameron thought about rushing to let the dog in with the hope the animal might know some way of controlling these two maniacs. So they remained, everyone there, locked in a freeze-frame for what seemed minutes but was probably only a split-second.

The Dark-curly chap stood, half-crouching, his face livid, primeval, slowly turning his cue toward his adversary—what seemed to be about to happen was a hustler's sword duel. But Yellow-hair laughed lightly, his eyes alight with joy and he said softly. "Come on, Lewington. Stop pissing around and play your fucking shot."

Dark-curly stood his ground for a moment more and then slowly straightened his posture as the heat diminished on his face. With a toss of his head, he hoisted the cue into a standard bearer position and marched, three quarters of the way around the table, his expression of proud arrogant defiance. Without hesitation, he took up position and played the white ball, striking it very low with a fierce blow such that it sprang in the air, flew across the table, hurdled the red and orange balls and came crunching down on top of the black, ramming it into the pocket. The spectators caught a breath of awe to see that neither red nor orange had been touched but the white ball, ensnared in its own momentum, bounced up again and off the table to crash on the floor, the sound of its rolling on the lino underscoring Yellow-hair's victory.

The two players watched it until it was stopped, and then the victor turned to the vanquished with a grin of pride. "That was a breathtaking shot, Lewington."

"And a moral victory to me."

"And a real victory to me."

"A most satisfactory outcome."

"We must drink to it."

"Bar-tender. Two pots or middies or whatever you call them."

"On the house, boys," Harry Waters was shocked to hear himself say involuntarily.

The beers were provided, raised in toast to each other, gulped down.

"A terrific attempt, Lewington, but no way could you have kept the white on the table."

"I'm sure that with enough backspin on it, it could be done, Griffin."

"Not even against a cyclone, Lewington."

"The laws of aero-dynamics still offer modern science grey

areas, Griffin."

They thumped their empty glasses on the bar, marched out side-by-side and, greeted by the tail-lashing dog, climbed into the Jaguar to drive away.

In the bar, the locals one by one began to breathe again and then they pointed at the white ball still lying on the floor, the door, the cross cues lying on the table that were not covered with blood. And they began to wonder how they would be able to get those who missed the action to believe such a story was true. The two strangers drove out of town, disappearing as if they never existed, leaving only their legend behind.

Jim Cairns' Thousands

Ramsay, the Distribution Manager, was going to be his problem. Harry Trimble, the Foreman, was a good bloke but not much chop when it came making decisions; he would frown and mumble and scratch his earlobe and finally decide Griffin ought to talk to Mr Ramsay. All Griffin wanted was the afternoon off, but Ramsay, who would know why, wasn't likely to come at that. Griffin would be reminded that there were a lot of orders to be got out and that it would not be so bad if they weren't so far behind. Griffin would need to avoid pointing out that since the company was too stingy to employ the two extra men they needed, they would always be behind. He had been working here as storeman and driver for just a few months and his position was anything but secure—it was, anyway, his third job in a year.

Usually he was out in the van, making deliveries around the bookshops and picking up from the wholesalers and the office politics and presence of bosses were little trouble to him, but when the mail orders got too far behind he would remain in the store to help out. That was the unfortunate part—had he been out today he could have just parked the van and taken the time and probably got clean away with it, but he was not. He was here, in the store which was in the basement of the publishing house and he needed to get upstairs and past the offices to make his escape. It was not going to be easy.

As the morning passed, he contemplated various schemes—lies about dental or medical appointments, dead grannies or sick girlfriends. Ramsay wasn't likely to be fooled.

It was May 8th, 1970—Moratorium Day—which the newspapers had propelled into history in advance by calling it the greatest disaster in modern Australian history even before it occurred. But Dr Jim Cairns, a pacifist and powerful political figure, had put out the call that the people should occupy the streets to show their opposition to the Vietnam War and all manner of unions and community groups had openly declared their support. In their editorials, the press had warned grimly of the traffic chaos that would result, of anarchy and political suicide by Gough Whitlam and his Labor Party of which Cairns was a senior member. They shrieked frantically of how one small militant minority group or over-zealous policeman might precipitate disaster. The Government cried hysterically that this was proof at last that the society had been subverted by a handful of Communists. No-one, they were sure, had the right to bring commerce and industry—not to mention the traffic—to a standstill, even for a couple of hours. As evidence they published figures of what the financial loss would be, a figure that grew by millions every time it was printed or spoken.

At the end of the day, that Government would be doomed and Whitlam and Cairns set soaring irrevocably toward national leadership, the economic loss would be insignificant and the traffic rolling unhindered again; there would be no violent outbursts, and when it was all over and done, the media would rewrite history as only they can and claim that it was their efforts most of all that pulled the Australian troops out of Vietnam and brought an end to that war.

In the hour after the lunch break that monumental day, Griffin fretted that his chance of playing his own minuscule role in making history was in the direst jeopardy. Desperately, he had sought the support of his workmates, but it seemed that even if the city was brought to a standstill, J Ramsay Publishing Agents would battle on alone.

"It's just a bloody mob of red-ragger troublemakers," declared Lance Peters, a jovial rotund fellow, who had stood at this bench packing books in boxes for eighteen uninterrupted years now, and saw no reason for that to change.

"The Labor Party ain't gonna win any votes doin' things like this," said Louie Johnson, whose fifteen working years had been spent in the mines until his lungs gave out and forced him to take this lighter work.

"Jim Cairns is a dickhead," was the best Joe Bailey could offer, a young man who had once been a tough in the northern suburbs and now firmly believed that he could liberate himself from this mindless job—and his family of wife and three kids from the dreary commission flat life they endured—via his efforts in off-course betting shops and the purchase of lottery tickets.

"They'd take the time out of me pay—can't afford that," said Daryl Holborn, the seventeen year-old message boy who did the same work as the men around him and was paid half as much because of his junior age.

Griffin didn't trouble to argue much with any of them. There was a large table in the centre of the store and they stood about it, day after day, checking the invoices and packing the books into boxes in accordance with the orders. Griffin wondered how they could do it—he would have gone mad in a week had he not been able to escape most of the time in the van. But they worked on, complaining all the time to Griffin and each other, but never to Mr Ramsay who sat in his office upstairs and would come down twice a day to make sure they were all hard at work. Each of these men, Griffin knew, voted for the opposition—the Labor Party of which Jim Cairns was a prominent member. All of them agreed that the Vietnam war was a terrible thing that ought to be stopped. But all of them were staying right where they were today.

"Bloke's gotta think of his job," Lance Peters said grimly. "Old Ramsay votes Liberal, yer know. He ain't gonna like any of his staff gettin' mixed up in somethin' like this."

Every day, Mr Ramsay descended from his lofty office perch to assure himself that none of his staff was late back from lunch. Griffin awaited this appearance like a vulture.

Harry Trimble, the foreman, had the task of pulling the books from the shelves in the main part of the store in accordance with the orders and stacking them on the bench for the rest of them to pack. He was a grouchy, aging fellow who would soon retire—an event that Lance Peters had awaited for these eighteen years. But Harry had been pulling out the orders for even longer than Lance had been packing them. Griffin carefully stuck what might have been his last label on his last box, certainly for today, perhaps forever, and looked across at Harry's stooped and grizzled form as he stood on a crate over by the shelves, piling books onto his outstretched arm.

"I'll be off in a minute, Harry," he said quite loudly.

The other four storeman went right on working, while Harry lowered his pile of books onto the bench and gazed at him steadily:

"Yer goin' then, are yer?"

"I certainly am."

Harry shook his head in dismay: "Mr Ramsay'll be down in a minute. You better get his okay."

"I was hoping you might do that for me, Harry."

"I can't say what yer can and can't do, son. Yer better talk ter him yerself."

"I will," Griffin said, quite malevolently.

Harry looked very sad—so did Lance and Joe Bailey. There was going to be disruption in the store of J Ramsay Publishers, and disruption was something that they could only look upon fearfully. Harry was off to get some more books, but then halted, and looked back.

"Yer don't look ter me like a bloke who'd get mixed up with them sort," he said sadly.

"This isn't your average demonstration, Harry," Griffin said," I don't usually have anything to do with protesters in the normal sense. But this time is different. Them sort, as you call them, are going to be people just like you."

"Bloody troublemaker, that Cairns," Joe Bailey said.

"Just a man doing what he believes in," Griffin said. "And I happen to agree with him this time."

"I reckon it'll come out of yer pay," Daryl Holborn warned.

"I couldn't give a fuck about the pay," Griffin gritted.

"It might be worse than that, son," Harry sighed. "It could make for some trouble."

As he said that, his voice quietened, and you could hear the clump of footsteps coming down the stairs and into the store. Harry looked that way nervously—Griffin feared that he was wearing one of those defiant-young-man expressions that he deplored on the faces of other people. The other four jumped heartily into their work, but Griffin continued to stand still, and so did Harry, such that when the grey-haired and grey-suited figure of Mr Ramsay appeared, he had cause to say. "What's going on?"

Ramsay, a middle-aged, middleclass business and family man, was probably in reality a gentle soul, but not when he came into the store. He had that aloofness, that slight disdain, slight embarrassment, that businessmen often display when obliged to mix with the workers. It seemed to Griffin to be the same as that other awkwardness that civilians showed when amongst soldiers, trying to look powerful and superior when in fact they were scared stiff. Mr Ramsay never had direct confrontations with his staff—he always spoke to or through Harry Trimble, and when there was disruption amongst the storeman, Mr Ramsay would leave and immediately summon Harry to his office upstairs where, from that lofty, secure position, the course of disciplinary action would be decided.

Therefore, it was of Harry that Mr Ramsay made his demand to know what was going on.

Harry looked at Griffin: "Tell him."

"It's necessary for me to take the rest of the afternoon off, Mr Ramsay," Griffin said bluntly.

Mr Ramsay offered Harry a rather puzzled expression. "There's a lot of work on, isn't there, Harry?"

"That's right, sir."

"Then I'm afraid we can't spare him unless he has a very good reason."

"I feel morally obliged to take part in today's moratorium march," Griffin said from his distant flank—it was rather like talking back to a television set.

"Well," said Mr Ramsay. "I really don't think we can spare him for that sort of reason, do you Harry? I mean, if it was something important perhaps it..."

"This is important," Griffin grated.

"...might be a different matter. Don't you think Harry?"

Harry Trimble, of course, was put on the spot and didn't know what to say.

"The request should be denied, don't you think, Harry?" Mr Ramsay persisted.

"It is not a request," Griffin said firmly.

Harry looked across the bench, his face a shattered ruin of dismay.

"I believe that Mr Griffin is going...sir," he told Mr Ramsay. "Whether he has permission or not."

It was said as if a death sentence. The condemned hastened to assure Harry Trimble that his assessment was correct.

"That's right, Harry. I have to go."

"Well," Mr Ramsay uttered in a shocked voice. "Perhaps you'd better come up to my office and we'll discuss it there, Harry." Harry Trimble groaned the groan of any man who could see plainly that he was caught in the middle.

"No, Mr Ramsay," Harry said in a respectful voice. "It ought to be discussed here."

Mr Ramsay nearly collapsed right there on the spot.

"Well, I really don't think..."

"Mr Ramsay," Harry said, suddenly lapsing into a monotone. "As the company's representative of the Storeman and Packers Union, I am afraid that I must apprise you of the instructions that I have received from my Union in regard to this matter."

"Instructions?" Mr Ramsay gasped in horror. His worst nightmare, clearly, comprised instructions to shop stewards from unions.

"Yes sir," Harry said ruefully. "The Storeman and Packers Union has instructed all shop stewards that if any members of that union are disadvantaged on account of their taking part in the Moratorium March, the company responsible is to be declared black. I'm truly sorry, Mr Ramsay."

"You wouldn't do that, would you Harry?" Mr Ramsay wailed.

"I'm afraid I would have no choice, sir," Harry said.

At the mention of that magic word 'black', the other four storemen immediately stopped packing books into boxes and stood as if paralysed. Mr Ramsay looked as if he was about to burst into tears, while Harry Trimble, his mentor, seemed even more distressed. And Griffin was making a mental note right then that it might well be a good idea to pay his union dues as the first possible opportunity.

"Well," Mr Ramsay was saying as he emerged from his state of shock. "Surely that would be extreme action to take, Harry, over so trivial a matter."

"My union does not regard it as a trivial matter, Mr Ramsay."

"Well. I see. I gather then that you are being compelled by union blackmail to take part in this outrage."

"Union members are to decide by their own conscience whether they take part in the march or not, sir, but the instruction about disadvantaging staff on the basis of their beliefs is quite clear."

Mr Ramsay squirmed and frowned, but it was plain to him that his staff was in a state of open rebellion:

"And are you all going then?"

"We are about to have a stop work meeting to decide that, Mr Ramsay."

Griffin blinked. No-one had mentioned that before. But Harry, now that he had made a stand, had plainly decided that he should go through with it.

"Well. You'd better do so then."

"I must respectfully ask that you leave the room while the meeting takes place."

"I can easily have you all replaced you know," Mr Ramsay suddenly flared—this final insult was too much.

"Then I would be obliged to report the matter to the union, sir."

Mr Ramsay sighed defeatedly—he had also turned extremely pale and indeed looked so distressed that Griffin feared he was going to have a heart attack on the spot.

"Well, Harry. If that is the case. I trust that you will report the outcome of the meeting to my office."

"Immediately that the decision is taken, sir."

And Mr Ramsay looked more than pleased to be able to get out of the store and its new hostility and to the safety of his office where such ruffians would never dare tread.

Harry Trimble therefore moved across to consult with his members, standing before the bench and placing his hands firmly upon it: "Right, lads? What's it to be?" he asked.

"Well you already know my view," Griffin said self-evidently.

"Only too well," Harry said with faint disgust.

"I must say, Harry," Griffin grinned. "that I appreciate your support in this."

"I didn't have no choice, did I?" Harry grunted. "Gotta follow the union's instructions."

The other four storemen were all looking from one to the other, and frowning, and wondering if it was all true, and none of them wanting to make the first move. Lance Peters, in his seniority, decided to speak:

"So that's right, is it? We got the afternoon off if we want it."

"That's right."

"Yer didn't tell no-one this," Louie Johnson puzzled.

"Wasn't important til now."

"And we get paid for it," young Daryl wondered.

"No lad. It's just like a strike or stop work meetin'," Harry smiled at him.

"Still, pity to waste it," Joe Bailey thought.

"Well, what's the vote. In favour of following union action?"

"Aye," they all cried.

And smiled at Griffin, the hero of the revolution.

It took a bit of sorting out and Griffin stood around waiting. He was already late, but past experience had taught him that it was best to avoid getting to these things too early and having to wait while the crowd accumulated. Harry Trimble went upstairs to announce the decision to Mr Ramsay, and the other storemen busied themselves packing up for the day.

And then the six rebels of J Ramsay Publishers all walked together out of the store and into the lane that led up to the main street.

"Good on you, fellas," Griffin beamed at them as they went.

They all looked at him rather dubiously, and indeed he quickly learned why, for when they reached the corner and he turned himself toward the other side of the city where the march would begin, they turned the opposite way.

"Hey. Where you going?" he called to them.

"To the bloody pub, of course," Harry called back.

"Enjoy the demo, mate," Joe Bailey laughed.

"We'll be watching fer yer on TV," Lance Peters guffawed.

"Slug a copper for me," Daryl Holborn laughed.

Dismayed, Griffin went on, alone.

As he walked across the city, Griffin already began to feel the strange sensations that prevailed all about the city that day, long before he reached his planned destination. The city itself, usually bustling with traffic and business people hurrying about, was today as eerily quiet as a Sunday. There were still vehicles and people moving about, but they were fewer than would be otherwise expected, and they seemed to move cautiously, warily, as if unsure of their destination. There was a tension that hung in the air like a thundercloud, an air of menace and apprehension.

The city was by no means at a standstill, as Cairns had suggested, but it was tending to creep along very slowly indeed. And then he could hear them—the grumbling thunder of their voices rumbling in and out around the tall buildings, and the tramp of thousands of feet like an earthquake in the distance. The first real signs of it all occurred when Griffin reached Swanston Street, the main transverse artery of the city. What he encountered was the most massive traffic jam he had ever seen. Looking down the hill, he could see plainly that Bourke Street, where the marchers would go, was completely blocked off, and at the intervening intersections, police were trying to undertake the task of re-directing the cars and trucks and buses right and left, though their cause was plainly quite hopeless for the cross roads were equally choked and halted. Down the centre of the street, like a barricading wall, the green trams stood nose to tail, abandoned by crews and passengers alike. There were a lot of people here, on the footpaths or oozing through the cars like toothpaste from a tube, and all of them were headed one way, down the hill toward the multitude gathered at Bourke Street. The march was clearly underway, and he turned and went with them to join the ranks.

But if there was chaos in Swanston Street, it little compared to the sight that Bourke Street was when he arrived. On either side of the broad commercial centre of the city, the policemen were lined up and stood placidly, and behind them great armies of spectators milled about, watching, disapproving or perhaps contemplating the taking of the plunge. He eased his way through, past a uniformed shoulder and stepped out into an astonishing scene. From this point, Bourke Street climbed gradual inclines in both directions and about a mile of the wide road was visible.

Or completely invisible perhaps, for it was utterly filled by a great ocean of human faces and bodies, and all of them sweeping along slowly in the same direction like a mighty tidal wave. Over their heads innumerable banners flapped and waved and there was the thundering burble of their voices, that was in fact only one great voice, the voice of a giant. A sky of people like the stars, or a beach perhaps with people sand and their pebble faces. It was one of those moments when you were shatteringly aware of the enormity of the great hordes of human beings in this world, and your own singular insignificance amongst their vast onslaught.

Griffin decided to stop gaping in disbelief after a moment, and so turned himself to become a further part of it all. It was hardly to be called a march in the true sense for they tended rather to shuffle along slowly, and stand about halted for most of the time. Just looking around him, Griffin could see that these people were all sorts, just exactly those same people you might see walking about the city or its suburbs at any time, and the only difference was that at this moment they were all walking in the same place at the same time and in the one direction. Just within Griffin's immediate visual range there were people here of every kind that the city possessed. There was a priest, there a couple of the smart young Italians from the Brunswick coffee lounges, there a group of overalled wharfies, housewives, office workers, schoolchildren, even a couple of sailors. Demonstrations had come a long way, he realised, from the TV images of angry young students besieging the US Embassy.

There was none of that anger here. These people were chatting to each other, smiling or laughing, or just wearing that vague blank expression that people do as they walk the streets at any time. There were organised chants arising from this part of the crowd and that, and some would joining in heartily, some laughingly, most murmuring along self-consciously, many staying silent. They just stood around and walked along when a gap opened up ahead, but in fact they weren't doing anything in particular. All they were really doing was being there.

Griffin looked about at the faces—old men chugging on pipes, small girls licking ice creams. He looked at the banners of rotary clubs and cricket teams. 'I wish there was a war and nobody came': 'War is over if you want it': 'For God's sake Gorton get us out of this mess!' The shuffle of feet and the single voice, and then, as if magically commanded from somewhere when for such a hoard it could not have been, a deathly silence descended upon the scene. People looked around, edgily, uncertain, and then the voices rose again. That silence, realised, was even more frightening than the roar. And then the wave changed its flow, and ahead people began to sit down, right there in the street. A great ripple of descending bodies, and he looked around and spied a nice flat piece of roadway between the tramlines and placed his backside upon it. And they began to sing in mumbled, off-key voices—'We shall not, we shall not be moved'. The policemen to the flanks remained standing, their faces sad rather than dispassionate. It was pretty plain that they were not about to try to move anyone, and that they could not have anyway. Griffin wondered if any of those policemen might have liked to disguise themselves in civilian clothes and join in—certainly right then what the face of authority looked most of all was left out.

Sitting down on the hard asphalt is probably the truest test of any dissident's devotion to the cause, and Griffin soon felt the sharpness in his buttocks as he sat in the small space available between the other bodies. At first, he was whimsically concerned about piles, but then his right leg cramped in the thigh muscle. There being no circumstances under which he could straighten his leg, and neither could he stand for if he did, they would plainly expect him to make a speech or read some poetry, as other people, who were standing, were doing, though all of them mumbling or too far away to be intelligible. Right in front of him, two girls were discussing someone's new boyfriend in giggling tones, the man to his left had his nose firmly implanted in the race guide, and to the right three uniformed schoolboys were busily pummelling each other to oblivion. The person immediately behind leaned on Griffin's back for support and Griffin shared the weight—an intimate moment shared with someone that he never saw. To his right, a woman in a black business suit sat on her briefcase showing excellent legs, and when she caught Griffin's admiring eyes, smiled and said. "The crowd is very well behaved."

"Even the coppers," Griffin grinned back.

Otherwise, all about were the vague, vacant faces—like on crowded trains and trams or in ticket queues, these people coped with the presence of too many other people in too close a proximity by trying to pretend that everyone else was not there. And then, at last, the human tidal wave surged up again, and somehow Griffin gathered his legs under him—the pain in the right one had completely numbed the muscles to uselessness as revenge for being ignored—and stood himself more or less upright as those all about him were doing. To shuffle onward, apparently, toward gatherings at the City Square where speakers would tell them once again what they already knew—why they were there. Griffin moved along with them, this enormous army that had no weapons and needed none—the fantasy of Christians and Communists alike. So many people, cluttered all about him and not one had he seen before. A hundred thousand people gathered where no-one sold tickets and no-one would perform. This time, in this city of spectators, they were the performance themselves.

And then, it all changed, and later Griffin, trying to pinpoint how it happened, what came over him, would be left only with an impression of suddenness. As he walked, he was instantly aware of that strange sensation—his whole body was suddenly possessed of a strange calm that tingled its way all over him. For a moment, he was puzzled—but in reality he knew exactly what that feeling was, though it was a long time since he had last... In Vietnam, as they had crept through the jungle with their guns, they had known well what it meant when that strange calm overtook them—it was a sort of sixth sense, a forewarning of imminent danger. Often, all would seem safe—there would be no clues for the other more normal senses of eyes, ears and noses. It was a strange feeling, in itself without menace or fear—just an unusual calmness, almost a tranquillity and an exquisite tingling feeling in the nape of the neck. It was the kind of feeling that you would dismiss as nonsense when those you knew it told you of it, and would utterly ignore, or fail to recognise, when first you experienced it yourself. If you survived, it was a mistake that you never made again.

And this was the feeling that overtook Griffin now as he walked in the crowd. His skin was alive, goosepimpled with dread, and inwardly he could feel his stomach contracting into a tight ball. Sweat dripped from his brow. Fear engulfed him as he swung around, and saw immediately what he expected. There, only to be faintly glimpsed through the crowd, stood that small Asian man, but that man was glaring straight at Griffin with a look of purest hatred. Even though the crowd moved around him, the man stood still, his eyes glowering his disdain. Griffin turned, heading after him, knowing all the time it was futile but what else could he do. He shoved his way across the line of marchers heedlessly, bearing down on his tormentor. Just past these three people and he would have him and he pushed shoulders aside as he went, and then, suddenly, they were face to face.

It shocked Griffin that the apparition had not vanished as it always did in the past—he halted, staring. The face looked back at him ruthlessly—he knew the face, knew it and yet did not...

"Who are you!" he demanded.

He reached out to grab the man by the shoulders, but even as he did, to his complete horror, suddenly half of that face exploded in an eruption of blood that left an appalling open wound, a hole the size of half that face, a giant red angry eye that flew at him. And as that happened, the air above him roared with thundering detonations of flack. Hurtled so suddenly into an almost forgotten nightmare world, Griffin reeled away, involuntarily shielding his head. The mortars fell, erupting all around him, and Griffin surged through the bodies around him, running for his life.

He ploughed his way through the people, blindly at first. Already, his brain was trying to tell him that he was a fool, that he had imagined it, but he could not look back, could not stop, didn't want to... He saw a woman fall and only vaguely realised that it was his own fault. He immediately rammed straight into a man—a large labourer with his overalls still plastered with cement.

"Hoy, whadda yer doin'?" he gravelled at Griffin.

Griffin dodged around him, and picked his way through a Italian woman's entourage of children; just that day the Roman Catholic Arch-bishop had warned his flock not to go for the demonstration would surely result in children being trampled in the streets—now the woman saw it was true, and screamed. Committed now, Griffin charged on. Hands grappled him but he fought them off—ahead he could see that alley that ran down beside Coles Store, and headed that way, shoving his way through the backs and shoulders and bellies of the innumerable people blocking him from his supposed sanctuary.

"Just a minute...hey, look out..get him'" people were yelling, as shoulders bumped against chins and elbows collected faces.

"Get him out of here," someone yelled. "We don't want his sort here'" Hands seized him, heightening his panic, but then two policemen descended from the flank, and grabbed Griffin by the arms to drag him clear. At first, he thought that he had been rescued—then he realised that it amounted to no such thing. The cops threw him against the wall, and pinned him there.

Completely against his nature and instincts, he let his body relax and when the policemen, of whom half a dozen now surrounded him, felt his muscles slacken, they released him. He stood, calming himself down, straightening his clothes, while the policemen gazed at him from either side in that usual dispassionate manner of the law.

"This is a peace demonstration, laddie," one of them said. "What do you think you're doing?"

"I was just trying to get out of the crowd," Griffin offered vaguely.

He was thinking about telling the truth—a story about apparitions and people trying to murder him, but he had seen enough Alfred Hitchcock movies to know that never worked.

"You got something against peace, have you laddie?"

"No. No..." and then he realised there was a more probable way to explain himself.

"I suffer from claustrophobia..."

"A hundred thousand people out there, laddie, and just one idiot has to try and turn the whole damned thing into a brawl..."

"Truly. Claustrophobia. I just got overwhelmed and panicked."

To judge from their expressions, he might well have done better with ghost stories. They looked at each other dubiously, and then at the crowd. There was no trace of anything going on out there now that Griffin might have been guilty of doing, although the faces that trooped by did gaze at this troublemaker in the hands of the law who plainly might have turned their gesture of peace into a disaster.

"Claustrophobia, hey? Well, if that's true, what the hell were you doing out there in the first place," the policeman finally said, when it was plain that Griffin, left waiting beyond endurance, was not going to break down and tell the real story, "I thought I'd be alright."

"Get out of here, laddie, and don't come back. Your sort aren't wanted here."

It was three years since the chopper winched him out of the jungle and they put him on a champagne flight back to civilisation. Three years wasn't enough—plainly they should have left him in the jungle where he belonged.

He needed a beer desperately—he was still shaking all over, though probably more from the waking nightmare than the reality. He stopped at the first pub he came to and went in. In the bar, everyone was watching the television set above the counter where the scenes from just a few streets away were being shown. The crowds, the banners, the police—even on the small screen could not diminish it's awesome reality. Griffin went to the bar and ordered a beer, keeping his eye on the video screen. It was strange—banished from his own life and forced to watch the rest of it go by on television. The cliental of this establishment were mostly businessmen in smart suits, with the notable exception of the redfaced ragtag who had just walked in. They all watched the scenes in quiet astonishment. The announcer was at pains to point out that so far there had been no trouble. Almost no trouble, Griffin thought—if only these people knew the monster who had nearly ruined it all stood now in their midst.

Directly in front of him sat a pin-stripped gentleman upon a barstool, with his prosperity bulging within his silk shirt and his polish reflected upon his bald dome. This fellow turned to the barman, jerking his thumb toward the television set. "Quite terrible business, this," he remarked.

The barman, regarding Griffin, was sensible enough to do no more than nod.

"Just a lot of malcontents and dissidents and the whole thing is set up by the communists. I'll wager most of them are being paid."

The barman eyed the massed scenes on the video. "I don't know that anyone would have that much money," he commented. "Who do you suppose is paying?"

"We are," the pin-striped gentleman knew. "The tax-payers. That's who."

"How do you figure that?" the barman asked.

"Well, they're all on the dole, aren't they? Bloody lot of spongers, parasiting off the community."

"Unemployment must be worse than I thought," the barman remarked. "How do you know they aren't all workers."

"Because if they were workers, my friend," Pin-stripe said. "Then they would be at work now, not out there blocking the traffic."

"Just like you," the barman grinned.

At which point, Pin-stripe lost his temper, and his affected accent along with it. "Listen pal. I pay my taxes. I'll be buggered if I'm gonna let a bunch of commo fanatics disrupt the whole bloody city."

But the barman had had his fun—anyway, there were other customers waiting. Pin-stripe swung in his seat—other men in the bar were laughing, or nodding, or taking no notice.

"Bloody lotta spongers, that's what they are. Be the ruin of this country, letting the commos get away with this."

At this point, Griffin was standing directly behind the man, looking down on him while he ranted. It was clear the supreme sacrifice needed to be made. He held his beer high in a toast to the television screen, and gentle overturned it, pouring the contents on Pin-stripe's head.

"Have one on me," he said, and turned and walked quietly out of the pub.

The Cave

Townsville, Queensland's second largest city, lying 700 miles north of Brisbane on the sheltered edge of Cleveland Bay. It was sheltered from the might of the Pacific Ocean by the huge lump of Magnetic Island which lay walking distance offshore if you wore JC boots. Less endowed people could catch the passenger ferry from the terminal in Flinders Street, and chug their peaceful way out through the mouth of the Ross River, past the low extent of the Western Breakwater which might have been the biggest parking lot for fishing and pleasure boats in the country, and then enjoy a half hour surge through the waves to the island itself.

The landing place is a small jetty at the end of Bremner Point, a half mile peninsula dividing Geoffrey and Alma Bays. The peninsula itself comprised a vast litter of massive rounded boulders that almost appeared to have been dumped there by the fashionable spaceman-gods for no better purpose than to allow subsequent human developers to build a road along the southwest side of the point to the tourist centre of Arcadia at the landward end of the peninsula. Arcadia is a tiny town with a log-walled pub, plenty of palm trees and little bamboo motel rooms for the tourists. The grounds of the resort were kept in immaculate order which gave it all the appearance that Nature was being disciplined by the middle-aged mums who came here from the cities for their holidays.

Right in the middle of the tourist resort stands a giant Moreton Bay Fig tree and under that tree is a table whereat people like Griffin could sit and have a beer in the shade and lazily gaze out over the northwest flank of the peninsula and Alma Bay. And the person most like Griffin, being Griffin himself, was doing precisely that, although it had to be admitted that there was an added attraction out there to hold his interest. Every so often, way out amid the jumbled monoliths of Bremner Point, the lean agile figure of Lew Sigg could be seen, scrambling up or down, leaping from face to face, making his arduous and somewhat perilous way out to the point.

Lew was a victim of a morality that few, least of all Griffin, would have expected of him. They had spent the night in a cave amid the rocks: this cave too could be seen from where Griffin sat for it was only thirty yards away. It was the very shortness of this distance, plus the numbing effects of a hangover following a very uncomfortable night, and further, one could only suppose, the knowledge that the bar would not be open for at least an hour yet, that prompted Lew to those fateful words.

"It would be, Griffin, just altogether too decadent, I'm sure, to rise from our sleeping place and merely stagger this few yards back to the pub."

Griffin could not quite see what the difficulty was.

"I can suffer the moral decay involved, Lewington."

"But just hours ago, Griffin, we were sitting right there, drinking, talking to those women, living the high life. Surely we can do better than simply awaken and creep right back to the same spot."

"I think my difficulty is your present usage of the word 'better'."

"I think we owe it to our self-respect to take the long route, around the point."

"I have no such debts to my self-respect, Lewington."

He staggered the thirty yards and took up his place at the table and The Monster, in absolute agreement with his Human for a change, moved from his sleeping place on the beach to curl up under the table at Griffin's feet. By then Lew was gone, which meant clambering over the boulders out to the point and back again along the road. The further Lew went, the more Griffin was delighted with his decision.

For no sooner had he sat down and Lew disappeared over the crest of the nearest boulder, than the waiter appeared out of the shadows.

"Would sir like something?"

"A beer would be nice."

Good waiters are able to avoid the slightest look at disdain at such moments.

"Well, sir, I'm afraid the bar isn't open yet, but I'll see what I can do."

He did perfectly. Lew would not be pleased to hear about this when he returned.

"Can I recommend the Eggs Benedict, sir?"

"Perhaps when my guest arrives. He appears to have been delayed by some silliness."

They had not stopped long in Townsville. Just a drive up to the lookout on Castle Hill.

"I can see a lot of promising pubs, Griffin."

"I think I'd rather keep moving for the moment."

"We promised to see the sights on the way back. Take our

time, remember."

"This is a city, Lewington, like any other. There are innumerable better places to stop."

"Just one day. We are weary from our travels."

"That island out there looks interesting."

"You think it has a pub."

"It does."

Griffin knew it had a pub. Once he had received a post card from there. She was probably sitting right here, under this tree, at this table, when she wrote it. It was the last postcard, though neither of them knew that at the time. Next came the letters explaining why she would never leave Townsville. As far as Griffin knew, she never had. Karen Kerrigan, except she wasn't named Kerrigan anymore, lived here somewhere. In the city, married to the town clerk, with a couple of kids. Happy ever after.

He wondered if Lew knew that was why he didn't want to stay. Only once had he ever indicated that he knew where she had gone. A year later Dell had gone similarly.

"Our women have a habit of going to Queensland and not coming back, Griffin."

Griffin had not known the answer to that at the time. He still didn't.

In his mind there was a picture of running into her, in a shopping centre, loaded with purchases, wheeling a pram, looking happy. Polite chat. Old friends. The thought was unbearable. What did you speak about when you had already said everything you had to say to the only woman you ever loved. Griffin sat, hangover mellowing melancholia, waiting for Lew.

It had been a tough night in the cave where they had taken refuge because someone suggested the threat of more cyclonic rain. This had gone the way of most weather predictions. But it was against the law to sleep on the beach or anywhere else on the island for which you didn't have to pay a small fortune to the local authorities and there were inspectors who prowled and made sure all possible profit was obtained. The cave was free accommodation, unless you wanted to count the price of a body bruised head to toe.

The cave was not so much a cave as a gap in the boulders, a niche beneath a colossal monolith that might have weighed hundreds of tons and which, instead of resting on the ground, was wedged between huger boulders to either side. Here was the lair of nasty green ants and many spiders but fortunately no snakes. You needed to be far from sober to find the nerve and will to crawl in there, huddled in their sleeping bags trying to gather a fair night's sleep on a rough basalt floor that sloped thirty degrees down toward a twenty foot drop into the surf and rocks below. Lew, the more restless sleeper of the two, had clung to Griffin all night, while for the latter, it was almost a relief to find the nightmares overshadowed by reality.

"A most remarkable abode, Griffin. How did you find it?"

"I came upon it earlier in the day, while you were looking for oysters."

"This must be an extremely large rock that forms our ceiling, Griffin."

That ceiling, as they lay there, was about three inches from their noses.

"An absolute monster, Lewington, and, you might observe, held up there by very little indeed."

"Yes, I had observed that. We can only hope that this will not be the night when it will finally come crashing down after all these centuries, as, by all appearances, it inevitably must."

"I doubt that it will come crashing down, Lewington. The supporting rocks will simply grind a little as they move apart and our roof will drop into the gap with a swift, dull thud."

"No ear splitting cracks?"

"No. Just a dull thud."

"No thundering cascading avalanche?"

"Just a gentle resettling of stone."

"No final desperate screams from us?"

"Not even the squelching of our bodies."

"Just thud and we will be something not unlike the jam in a lamington."

"You put jam in your lamingtons?"

"My mother used to. I hated her for it."

"And rightly so. But I would like to think, Griffin, that at least a hand or foot might be left sticking out, so that someone might know we passed away here."

"Maybe a trickle of blood, to be washed away by the rain."

"Just a dull thud, huh?"

"Pleasant dreams, Lewington."

"Pleasant dreams, Griffin."

In the morning, it was only marginally pleasing to discover that the boulder had not moved in the night, certainly their aches and pains suggested otherwise. Even now, waiting for

Lew to return from his heroic expedition, Griffin could feel the hardness of the stone as surely as if it was still in contact with his body. He could only thinking ruefully of how it might have been different. There had been two secretaries from Sydney named Judy and Judith—it was never clear which was which—who most certainly had excellent beds and other warmths and comforts to offer had they been given the slightest encouragement. But Karen Whatever, nee Kerrigan, had locked herself in Griffin's mind and he wasn't in the mood. Not that it mattered—Lew could have secured the situation for them both had he kept his mind on the job. Lew had a fine way with women when he wanted—he had the confidence to fondle a girl before asking her name, to offer sex before a cigarette, but it was all done in the Lew Sigg flamboyant, irreverent, irrelevant manner—never lecherous or sly, always direct and open, if a little hasty.

"I thought them a little dull anyway, Griffin," Lew had declared after the young ladies took themselves off to their warm inviting but uninvited beds. He was always a sore loser.

"What a waste," Griffin could only sigh.

"There'll be more of them, Griffin."

"But not when so desperately needed."

"Maybe next time, Griffin, you'll be careful not to point out to a girl that she's cross-eyed."

"I think you tearing her new dress really did the damage, Lewington."

"The one you miss out on, Griffin, is the one you never catch up on."

"Nar, Lewington. Women are like missing a bus. There's always another one coming sooner or later."

Usually later.

Down toward Bremner Point, he could see Lew coming back, covered in dirt and with a couple of blood patches, sweating furiously, limping a little, the knee out of his jeans. But all of that was dominated by his jubilant grin. Griffin solemnly ordered two more beers, while The Monster came out from under the table and bounded down to give Lew the official canine welcome. Griffin watched the scene and could not deny a certain envy. Because dogs never concerned themselves with being dignified, therefore they did everything with dignity. Even showing naked feelings or shitting on pavements. Griffin sighed. If that was the sort of mood he was in, he hardly dared speak.

Lew and the waiter arrived simultaneously, and the red-faced former gulped and handed both empties straight back.

"Two more if you please, my friend," he beamed, offering money.

"Might I recommend bacon and eggs and toast and coffee?" the waiter said to cover his embarrassment.

"Recommend away. Oughta be time for breakfast in about an hour or so. Meanwhile, two more beers, thanks."

He sat down.

"Very thoughtful of you, Griffin."

"Very intrepid of you, Lewington."

"Don't you get the feeling you could stay here forever?"

"No, actually."

Lew was silent for a time, gazing, as Griffin was gazing, as The Monster was gazing, out toward the horizon.

Lew said: "You still miss her, don't you?"

"Miss who?"

"Shit, Griffin. It's been two years. Get over it."

"Go stick your head in a bag."

"You don't plan to drop in and say hello while we're here, then."

"Nope."

"Pity. Be nice to see how old Kazza is getting on."

"She'll be getting on the way she always got on, Lewington. Just fine. People who love the whole world and everything in it are like that."

"Is that how you saw her?"

"That's how she was."

"The only thing I ever saw her loving was you, Griffin. Beats me how you let her run away up here."

"You oughta talk."

"I am possessed by a she-devil. It isn't the same thing. Karen was the love of your life. You'll never get over each other."

"I'll get over it."

"In three years you haven't paid the slightest attention to other women. When she left, you replaced her with a dog."

"She'd be thrilled to know that."

"She'd love to see you, Griffin. I know it."

"I don't want to just see her."

"Oh."

"Yes, oh."

"Well, if that's how it is, maybe it is best if you stay away. Perhaps we'd better get you out of here, before you completely dissolve."

"After breakfast, Lewington. There's a limit to how many people I can disappoint all at once."

"Fine," Lew said, clapping his hands on his knees, "Breakfast, and then away into the sunrise."

"Suits me."

"I reckon maybe we'll go inland for a bit."

"Inland sounds fine."

Lew stood, looking around anxiously. "Waiter, come forth. All your wildest dreams are about to be realised."

The Postman

There was an old woman who stood every day, by the front gate of her tumbledown house in Drummond Street, waiting for the postman. She was the terror of the street, a horrific old creature bent and twisted by uncounted maladies, her lips and chin salivated, her eyes so bloodshot you could feel them burning just to look at her. She had no body to speak of, just a lump inside what daily appeared to be the same shapeless floral dress, as wrinkled as her face, as faded as her life. The only mail she ever received was her fortnightly pension cheque but she waited no less enthusiastically on all the other days, and it was plain that there was very little in her life other than the passing of the postman, and her cats. She kept several dozen cats and they were everywhere, along the fences and verandah, the threshold and the window ledges, all over the front yard; a tapestry of constant surreptitious movement. Every one of the cats was mangy and diseased in some way, missing paws, festering eyes, great patches of fur torn of fallen away. Her front door always stood open and they could wander in and out freely—you could only shudder at the thought of what it must have looked like in there.

Every morning after the postman had passed by, the Carlton Catlady would get out her shopping jeep and waddle off down to the butcher in Rathdowne Street who would provide her with a huge bag of liver and other offal. She would then proceed about the area, and most of North Fitzroy as well, feeding the vast multitude of stray cats that roamed the car parks and abandoned factories of the region, and bringing home any maimed or ill creatures she could find. You would often see her doing her rounds, and if you did, the sensible reaction was go some other way, not only because of the smell of the offal and the woman, but also because having trapped someone within vocal range, she did not let them escape very easily. You could be, and justifiably would be, rude and walk away midsentence, but here the postman was doubly disadvantaged. She seemed to feel an affinity with the postman who walked the same rounds she did, and anyway he was obliged to pass right by her house and exchange daily banalities. And he could not be rude and walk away for postmen were not allowed to be rude to the public: any complaint to the postmaster in that regard was taken with the utmost seriousness.

It was a cold midwinter day and by the time the postman reached the catlady's house, the sun was only beginning to make frail inroads into the overnight fog. The chill hung in the leafless trees and glistened forbiddingly on the grass, and the catlady stood shivering in her floral dress—plainly she did not own a coat or else she would have been wearing it—although she had pulled about her shoulders a bloodstained cardigan, or at least those parts of one that the moths had not dispensed with. Her breath hung about before her face in foggy gusts, as did the small ones of the drifting cats, and the postman came plodding along, his white exhalations all the larger for his effort since it was near the end of his round. She could see him coming from the end of the street, and would try immediately to catch his eye, though he was still out of hailing distance. The postman saw her there and groaned, as he did every morning, and secretly hoped she would have a heart attack before he arrived, although only because he knew there was little chance of that. People like her lived forever.

This particular postman, who had been on this round for four months now, was plainly a trouble to the catlady. He didn't look like a postman, she thought. The postman knew she thought that because she always said what she thought; the trouble was that she thought the same things every day and said them as if yesterday and all the days before that had never happened. When he was about five houses away, she called to him. "You don't look like a postie."

The postman tried very hard to smile. "I'm bringing the mail, aren't I? I must be the postman."

He slipped letters into the Jenkinson letterbox as if to prove the point, and reluctantly moved one house closer.

"But you ain't got no uniform. All the other posties had nice blue uniforms."

It was true. He wore jeans and a windcheater and sneakers, and the only real indication of his place in society was a PMG armband he only just tolerated and the sack of mail over his shoulder. He didn't even have one of those red bicycles—there were too many street obstacles along this route and it was easier done on foot.

"I don't like uniforms," he said.

"And the beard," she called, just as loud though he had reached the house next door, "None of the other posties had a beard."

"It's a new regulation," the postman sighed, "Beards are

okay for government workers now."

He moved along to pass her house now—it was not pension day and there was nothing for her. As he went by, she picked up one of her cats that wandered along the fence and held it protectively, as if it had something to fear from this strange so-called postie. As she did so, he sadly observed her rounded shoulders, littered with dandruff and the grey hairs that fell from the few remaining tufts attached to her scaly mottled scalp.

It was now the time when the catlady usually said something out of the ordinary, normally about the state of her cats; that one of them had got better or died or run away, calling it by name; or else there might have been an air crash or local motor accident that she could say was terrible.

"Terrible. Them kids fighting in the streets," she remarked.

The postman had heard nothing of this. "Yes. Terrible," he always said.

"I felt sorry for the horses, stuck in that mob. They oughta lock 'em all up, don't yer reckon."

"Cruel to lock up horses," the postman said absently, and then flushed as he realised that he had misunderstood. Forced to think about it, he recalled that yesterday protesters had once more besieged the US embassy and the mounted police had charged straight into the crowd to disperse them. Some of the protesters had rolled large ballbearings under the horse's hooves. None of the horses had fallen, but it had forced the event to the head of the daily news. No one seemed to notice that where once they had been hundreds, now they were thousands.

"Lucky no one was killed," he finally said.

"They all got beards, just like you," the catlady said suspiciously. "You ain't one of them, are ya?"

"No," the postman said. "I'm not."

The truth was that he had not been there, despite pressure from Lew and Dell. It was all part of the war and he no longer wanted to be a part of it. The nightmares were getting worse, if anything. He wanted to leave the war behind, instead it had followed him home and stalked the leafy suburban streets. To be sure he shared some sentiments with the anti-war protesters—they wanted the war to end, they wanted the troops brought home, they wanted conscription abolished; as such, for him, they were about four years too late, and he had no argument with any of that. But they waved Viet Cong flags and called the soldiers murderers. He had put his life on the line for them and they responded by spitting in his eye. No, for sure he wasn't one of them.

"You look like you might be," the catlady persisted.

"There's enough pain in the world," he said, knowing where that would lead.

By now he was two houses past her, and steadily moving away.

"Yairs," she said, "The cold gets inta me hip these days something awful."

The catlady always welcomed the chance to mention her hip, and there was nothing to be gained by making things hard for her.

"Summer's coming," the postman said, and could smile, though mostly because he knew that once he was clear of the next house, he would be out of her vocal range.

"Not very friendly, are yer," the catlady said sulkily. "Not like the last fella. He usta stay and talk a while."

"Have to get on," the postman said, "Lot of other people waiting for their mail. See you tomorrow."

"Goodbye postie," the catlady called, and would continue to stand by the gate until he turned the corner and was out of sight.

The catlady not withstanding, this was the best job he had ever had and he thoroughly enjoyed every minute of it. It meant rising at five and to work by six but now that the weather was improving and the nights shortening, that was bearable. He walked in and joined the other three postmen at the bench and spent the next three hours sorting his mail into streets and numbers and bundling it all into the sacks and then was ready to go. Out into the streets, heedless of the climate—that was the best thing.

He walked the streets in the sun or the rain at just the same pace, easy and loping, and when he returned the empty sack to the post office and the rest of the day was his. If he hurried, it could have been over and done with by eleven, but he never hurried. He enjoyed strolling about the streets too much to rush it, pausing to observe the activity in the area, enjoying the free beer they offered when he dropped the mail into the Spread Eagle Hotel, absorbing the songs of the birds in the trees through his flesh, sucking the sharp fresh air. This was great—it was something he might have paid money to do, so much did he revel in it. That they paid him was simply a bonus.

Though his freedom was earned. Each morning in the

claustrophobic post office, he faced his array of pigeon holes that mimicked the streets of his round, sweating and agitated as he flicked the letters into the right hole. The constriction might have devoured him, had he not known the freedom that lay at the end of the task. There were the other postmen, doing as he was doing, and wanting to pause and chat, take a tea break, a smoke-o. He just hurried through it, anxious to get out there and into the part of the day he loved most. There was too the intimidating eye of the boss—the postmaster—who was a good bloke, fair and understanding, but that didn't make him any less of a boss. Griffin always looked away from him, dreaded his eyes, feared his words. "Um...Grif, I don't want to hassle you, mate, but there's been a wee bit of a complaint."

He bristled... he did his job well and no one had anything to complain about. He knew it. Roy, the postmaster, was so awkward and apologetic that plainly he knew it too. But he was the boss, and bosses had to do things like this; just to show they were the boss of something.

"Bloody Amess Street again, I'll bet," he muttered.

Roy nodded. "Yeah. They reckon their mail comes too late."

"They get their mail at the same fucking time every fucking day, Roy."

"Now Grif, calm down. Take it easy. Have a look at this. What if you do Amess up from Fenwick Street instead of down from Park Street. That'll put it into the first half of your round, instead of the second. Won't muck you up at all."

It wouldn't either. Griffin had actually thought about it himself and saw there was nothing wrong with the idea, except that it would mean the people in Amess Street got preferential treatment over those in the parallel streets, and why the fuck should they? But mostly, he resented the fact that Roy was interfering with his round. It was his round, for him to do the way he wanted. No one needed to poke their nose in.

"Tell them to get fucked, Roy."

"Come on, Grif. Better for everyone this way."

He did it, eventually, and every morning felt the sting of pointless authority as he turned from Fenwick into Amess.

"Bastards," he always muttered.

But it wasn't Roy's fault. Roy was a good boss, the best—not like some of the other pricks he had worked for. There had been so many jobs and so many bosses. And sooner or later, they all had to try and assert their authority over him, and it always ended the same way.

"You gotta learn to control that temper, son."

"Go stick your head in a bag, you finicky old dickhead."

And stalked off to the pub.

He had been a couple of clerical jobs first, which always went the same way—arguments with the boss leading to more and more time in the pub until there was only the pub and no boss and no job. That was what he needed—a job without a boss, and outside, away from walls that made him sweat. In small rooms and on public transport, he invariably sweated and felt on edge, irritable, wanting to hit someone.

"You have a serious case of claustrophobia," the doctor had informed him.

"What's the cure?"

"Stay outside."

This then, the postman job, was functional for him. Outdoors, working alone, provided each day he got through those few hours of confinement and Roy's comments. And now Roy had moved on, posted to the bush and a new bright young postmaster was taking over. Griffin had sighted him only briefly that morning—he looked sharp and brash and zealous—the worst kind.

"But what causes the claustrophobia?"

"All combat veterans suffer from it. No one knows why. No doubt some sort of paranoid reaction."

No doubt.

"You ought to do something about those nightmares," Karen Kerrigan said. It was only now that she spent every night at Elm Street that she had come to realise that what she had thought to be an occasional event in fact happened all the time.

He was adrift, he knew, and floating away from his own life. Karen stood sadly watching him go, helpless to aid him. When he left the Department of Construction, she had accepted it. She worried though about how it would affect their savings. He got a job as a cleaner—just until something better came along, he assured her, and did fine for a while. But he was so efficient that he did the work in half the hours allotted and so the boss tried to cut the hours. Griffin emptied the mop bucket on his desk. Then he became a storeman, out back in an electrical goods wholesaler. It didn't last. The foreman was a man who liked to give orders. Griffin would have done anything if asked but could not respond when being told. The power within him surfaced in fury and the strove to control it as long as he could. The foreman seemed to notice the conflict and played on it. He got a broken nose for his trouble and Griffin returned to the employment classifieds.

With each blow, Karen saw her dreams slipping further from her grasp, but she was loyal and stuck with him.

"You've been unlucky," she assured him. "I know you'll come through in the end."

All of their friends were married and had moved off to the suburbs, were having kids, establishing their lives. All of them had done so after shorter relationships than Griffin and Karen. She was plainly feeling that they were being left behind. In the end the matter became so pressing that she actually decided upon confrontation.

"I have to know," she said one night, "when you are planning to marry me."

It hit him like a body blow—he hadn't expected that it would. His whole system crumbled at the thought, as if she was some vile creature menacing him, instead of the woman he loved—utterly adored—and who he knew to be the sexiest, most desirable and most decent person he had ever met. He tried to cover his initial revulsion to spare her feelings and later wondered if she had could really have failed to notice as completely as she pretended to. His head almost exploded such was the heat his bloodstream generated into his brain. Nausea swept through his stomach. It was fortunate that he was sitting down at the time but otherwise he might well have fallen, fainted, for sure his knees would have given out.

Quickly, he patched himself up and tried to answer sensibly.

"Well, we're not quite in a position to, at the moment."

"We were. And anyway, we can manage. I make enough for us both to live on and I'm sure you won't stay unemployed forever."

"I know. But I'd just like to be... a little more... settled..."

"Aren't you sure?" she asked him pointedly.

But he was. He was sure. He did want to marry her, live with her, have kids. She was perfect, it was perfect. *What was wrong?*

There wasn't any doubt that he adored her, nor did he even think of other women. She loved him hopelessly, blindly, completely, he knew. He wanted her, forever, to be his and he to be hers. It was all there, waiting for him to reach out and take it to his bosom. Yet he cringed away in revulsion at the idea and even though he recovered immediately and made light of it, still he knew she had seen it.

It was then that he knew that he was, quite wantonly and

deliberately, destroying his own happiness and hers only incidentally with it. In the night when she touched him, he remained unaroused and had to force a thousand sexual fantasies through his brain to accommodate her. But then even the sexual delusions failed him and he had to reach deeper. He thought of blood and murder of the most vile forms he knew and *that* worked. Instead of making love to her in his mind he was killing her. The nightmares from the war had gone and been replaced by this intentional fantasy that only he, a haunted man, could have conjured. He knew he was going insane. Why don't you go away, his brain tried to telepath to hers, and find someone worthy of your love?

He examined it with great care. As her hands touched him, before he began to use the fantasies to respond, what was he really feeling? The warmth, the touch, that would have, should have, aroused the most impotent man. The desperation to give her what she wanted, a frantic need to have himself inside her that almost drove him crazy. Yet his penis remained unmoved. How? Why? He searched beyond the touch and the sensations, lying still, pretending to be asleep, striving to see beyond his desires and carnal needs to the derangement at his core. And when he saw it, he knew it immediately. It was like seeing someone familiar far off in a crowd, a glimpsed face unmistakably who it was, yet so distant, apparently uninvolved, like background radiation. Far away but everywhere. He recognised it from that nights in the jungles of Vietnam, the quiet nights when it was too quiet. It was fear.

He knew then that it wasn't her he was afraid of but himself. He knew the monster she was wanting, thinking him a loving creature, not knowing the killer within him, the man who felt the exhilaration of destroying another man's life and never forgot it and never felt that good again. And when she asked what was only a fair question and he reared back in revulsion, he knew it was not her he was repulsed by—that wasn't possible for there was nothing repulsive about her. It was himself.

The new postmaster, whose name Griffin had been careful not to remember, wanted to see him when he got back. Griffin was not at all surprised.

"There's a complaint," he said, staying seated, his eyes dark as if some horrendous crime had been committed and he was about to reveal it. Instead, there was a single letter. "You delivered this to 644 Rathdowne Street, but the correct address is clearly shown as 644 Drummond Street."

It was the sort of error every postman in the world made at least once every day. When parallel streets had identical number systems, it was nearly impossible to always get it right. Griffin had been through this scene enough times to know how it went. This was just a trivial gripe to add weight to the more serious but probably less justifiable matter that followed. He clenched his fists at his sides, gritted his teeth, and waited for it.

"I see here that you received your instructions to go and be measured for a uniform when your probationary period ran out two months ago. You don't seem to have responded."

"No," was all Griffin said.

"Why not?"

"I don't like uniforms."

"Regulation 34 states clearly that a postman must wear the appropriate uniform provided."

"At the discretion of the postmaster," Griffin added coldly.

"My discretion."

"Roy's discretion."

"Well, it's changed."

"It can't change."

"My postmen wear uniforms."

"I never wear uniforms."

"Then you should have realised that before you took the job."

"I did. I told Roy of my aversion to uniforms and he said it would be alright."

"I say it isn't. You look really scruffy. A disgrace to the service, with that beard and all..."

"There's no regulation about beards."

"There used to be, but they changed it."

"I know."

"Well, I am in charge now, and I say proper uniforms, and no beards. What do you say to that?"

"Go fuck yourself, since that's what you seem to be good at."

"What!"

"You are the sort of mindless dickhead that can't leave something that works alone. You have to put your fucking mark on it, leave grubby little paw prints, and fuck everything up for no better reason than to show how important you are."

"You can't speak to me like this!"

"You asked my opinion, and it's the only way idiots like you can be spoken to."

"You're fired. Get out."

"I wouldn't want to work for an arsehole like you anyway."

It was the best job he ever had. Three glorious months of bliss, most of the time. He knew the way the world worked well enough by then to be content with that.

Parting Scenes

It was not actually true that Karen had gone away to Queensland on a holiday and never returned. Two months later, she returned to the south to officially farewell her old life—and Griffin along with it—and perhaps to completely reassure herself that she wanted her brief holiday romance to last forever. First had come the postcard that hinted she may be delayed, when he knew her three weeks on the Barrier Reef was a package tour because he had helped her arrange it himself. Details followed in a letter that still seemed wet from her tears as she wrote it, arriving the day before her travelling companion—Margie from her office—returned alone and came around to 'see that he was alright'.

Was he alright? Did he know? For certain, he had felt strange but then he always did. There was, to begin with, a certain sense of pride in the independence she showed so uncharacteristically and the deft manner in which she handled the details in what was undoubtedly the greatest crisis of her life. She telephoned her employer to inform him of her resignation, and several other friends to spare Griffin the need to talk about what he might not want to. There was too a sense of relief—he genuinely hoped it would all work out for her with this new man. He was shedding a sense of guilt that had been building up over time that he was tying her up, wasting her time, when he knew that her dreams were not going to be realised with him. She needed to assert herself, she needed a new chance. Someone once said: if you love something, set it free. If it comes back, it's yours forever; if not, it never was. So he let her go. He never really expected she would have the nerve to leave him, to go her own way, and certainly not without his permission.

He felt nothing. That was the truth. Yet he cared. He loved her. She was his and someone had stolen her. It didn't make sense.

There was a time when they both worked in the city and the Exquisite Coffee Lounge was where they often met for lunch. It was still there, unchanged, and it was here that she summoned him on her encore visit. He approached the scene of their last rendezvous with staggering trepidation. He didn't want to see her again and be reminded of what he had so foolishly squandered. He had almost convinced himself that she had never existed—now he feared that when he saw her he might crack and the emotions, presumably bottled up within him, would flow. The embarrassment would be unbearable. He didn't know what he would say to her. At this place, the Exquisite—grubby little hole in the wall—why there? To maximise the nostalgia? Certainly not for the food which was terrible. His tastes had improved since the days when he found it's mass-produced rubbish satisfactory. Everything had changed except that. He didn't need it.

"But the coffee's good," Karen said, as he scowled at the menu.

Griffin was fairly confident that the coffee would be awful.

She wasn't at all as he expected. She seemed older, wiser, sharper—perhaps she was. And gloriously beautiful with her flowing red hair and bright eyes. She even wore a neat little frock that offered the world the curve of a cleavage, a sight her prudishness had reserved solely for him in the past now made available to the whole world. Plainly it was to best show off her tan. But her smile dazzled in the way it always had—it was just that it was no longer directed completely at him. Had she changed so much or had he forgotten her already and slipped into selective memory. She had been eighteen when he met her and was twenty-three now, but his memory had chosen that initial, bouncy bright child as his permanent, standard image of her. Little wonder then that she seemed to have outgrown him in just two months.

But there was the old Karen too. She upended her purse on the laminex tabletop and shuffled her way through the coins as if trying to master a sleight-of-hand trick. He realised that what she was really doing was not looking at him and trying to be as brisk and busy as possible. Was she too shocked by his real appearance—were her memories of him no less deluded?

"Two cappuccinos, Vince," she said to the waiter, "And do try not to spill all of them in the saucers."

There was a self-confidence about her that was entirely new. Vince, grinning when Griffin thought he ought to be insulted, took the money and departed. Karen Kerrigan watched his bum as he walked away. Griffin was disgusted, but inwardly he knew that this small exchange with Vince—obviously she came here more often than he knew—was his first experience of a piece of Karen that did not belong to him. If his dispossession was going to be a series of moment by moment revelations like this, it was going to be tough.

"Who is he?" Griffin asked, to get it over with.

"Vince," Karen said, "He runs this place."

"You know who I mean."

Karen leaned back in her chair, full on to him, and shrugged in a way that made her breasts move breathtakingly.

"Is it important?"

"No. I'd just like to know."

"His name is Mark. He's a nice guy. I like him."

"Like?"

"Love him. Just the way I once loved you, remember?"

"Yes. I remember."

"Then why torture yourself about it, Griffin. It doesn't matter who he is, as far as you're concerned."

What hurt most, amongst a great deal that hurt, was that it was the first time she had ever called him by the name that everyone else called him. In the past, it had always been private names of her own that she bestowed upon him. Now, she just wanted to be one of the crowd. And was that the truth? Did she see him as someone else entirely, someone other than the man she once loved? Did she see him now as he really was? Probably.

"I just want to make sure you're in good hands," he said with bravado.

"I'm in very good hands, thank you very much."

"I do still care about you, you know."

"Five years. A very long time, Griffin. Five good and important years mostly. I'm sure we'll both care a great deal about each other for all time to come. That doesn't change the way things are now."

"And how are things now."

"He wants to marry me. I think I want to marry him."

"Think?" What straw was this he was clutching at?

"Yes, think. I don't know why but somehow I felt I just wanted to see you one more time, just to be sure."

"Surely you aren't after my permission..."

"Not exactly. For five years, Griffin, I was utterly devoted to you. I thought I'd die without you. But suddenly there I was, without you, and not dead. It came as a very great surprise to me."

"I bet it did."

"All of a sudden, there I was, able to do things for myself, make decisions instead of waiting to ask you, thinking about what I wanted instead of what you might want."

"It had become rather difficult to tell where I ended and you began."

"What I felt mostly was free. It was a bit scary, really. Oh, I missed you unbelievably, and felt so sad to be away from you. And when I first got involved with Mark, it was still all about you. What would you think? Would you be jealous? Would you react at all? No, of course. Not good old understanding thoughtful Griffin. But I hoped you would. But then there was this new feeling. This freedom. This sense of being myself rather than some sort of appendage of you. It was amazing."

"It's amazing to see."

She smiled as if flattered, and sipped her coffee, giving him a moment to assess his feelings. There was this new weird Karen before him who had so unexpectedly developed an ability she had never before displayed—to stick up for herself; moreover, to stand up to him. When he expected that he might have been hurt, or sad, or jealous or angry, instead he found that he was impressed. This being one of his more cynical moments, he supposed that he was in love with her all over again, perhaps for the first time in about four years. But no, not quite. He was in love with a new woman who called herself Karen Kerrigan but was really someone else altogether.

"Anyhow," she said, "Here I am and I'm just fine and dandy. Which brings us to the next subject. How are you?"

"Who, me. Oh, I'm fine."

"You look terrible."

"Thanks very much."

"You've been going steadily downhill for all the years I've known you, Griffin, and you still are."

"It isn't that bad."

"Isn't it?"

There had been a number of women since then but still Karen left a gap that was impossible to fill.

"Are you bisexual?" one girl had asked him in the dead of night.

"Not that I know of."

"In your sleep you were calling out to someone named Snowy."

Sitting up in the bed, sweating and chilled, cigarette in his shaking fingers, he laughed. Though it wasn't funny. Usually the nightmares were partial reconstructions of actual incidents, but sometimes they were weird. That particular one had him staring straight down the muzzle of a weapon, he could see the rifling, it filled his entire vision.

"This one's still breathing," his own voice called from a distance.

"Finish it," Nigel said.

The muzzle-flash and detonation sat him upright in the bed, screaming.

Other times, he reacted more physically, diving from the bed to cover as the rockets hit the jungle all about him. One freezing night, he awoke to finding himself kneeling naked on the floor beside the bed.

"What are you doing out there?" a different girl had asked in puzzlement. He could find no answer that might make sense to her—still she persisted.

"You looked like you were digging a hole."

"Not exactly," he sighed as he crawled back under the blankets, "I was trying to fill one."

Even in daylight, that Asian man—the one that didn't exist—followed him around. He was outside, in the street, right now, waiting for him. Griffin hoped only that when they left, Karen would come with him, just for a little of the way. He needed someone with him all the time, just to feel safe. And now the one person prepared to be there always was going away. The fear chewed deep into his innards.

Sitting now, gazing across the chasm that had fallen between himself and Karen, he knew he could say nothing of such things. There were now parts of his own life that were no longer any concern of hers. He needed to swing the subject away from himself.

"He must be a worthwhile guy," he heard himself saying, "Even I can see the good he's doing you."

Her eyes flashed with anger—something else newly discovered: "Mark hasn't had enough time to be any influence, Griffin. If I'm changed, it's not because I'm with him but because I'm away from you."

Her words were a spear that completely transfixed his body but like all heroes, he tried to show no pain. He obviously failed, for when she saw what she had done, she closed her eyes in acknowledgment of her own clumsiness. But perhaps it was what she was waiting for, some sign of him cracking, or even breaking down, or any sort of emotion at all. In any case, she softened then. "I'm sorry. That was cruel."

"Truth often is."

"If it was as hard as it sounded, then it wasn't true. You were good to me, Griffin. Very kind, very thoughtful, very devoted. I was never unhappy when you were around. It was only when you drifted away and I began to wonder where it was all going that I became unhappy. I'm still as fond of you as I always was. I'm just not blindly devoted and I don't want to marry you anymore."

"You think we'll be friends?"

"I'd like to think so, but I doubt it. People like me don't belong in places where people like you are going, where-ever that is."

"How can you know that? I've no idea where I'm going myself."

"Griffin, you're off on some sort of journey, and however strong our feelings for each other might have been, I was just an encumbrance, holding you back. Excess baggage."

"I never thought so."

"In the end, Griffin, I lost sight of everything. Then Mark came along. He's a nice guy, good job, handsome, nice haircut, wears smart suits, quiet-spoken, church-going, lives at home with mum and dad. My sort of bloke, Griffin. With him suddenly I could see the way ahead again."

"And I wasn't your sort of bloke?"

"He's the complete opposite of you," she said and then, perhaps for the first time that day, looked him directly in the eye; "No, that isn't true. He is like you, of course. But he's like the way you were, when I first met you. You've changed. What he isn't like is the way you've become."

"Is it wrong for people to change?"

"I don't know, Griffin. Maybe you've changed for the better. Maybe not. I don't know whether its right or wrong. All I know is that it didn't suit me."

Nowhere Coming Back

The light gleamed in Lew's milky eyes as they drifted across the verdant plain that tranquilly stretched from gentle forested slopes to the glass-top sea. He was touched, for the moment, by the excitement of an untold dream beheld. A frivolous breeze, coming from friskier days in the distant blue mountains, danced for a moment in his knotty hair, easing him back into reality.

"This, Griffin, is one beautiful place."

There was a softness in his voice that many of his city friends might never have recognised, not least the one who stood beside him, and yet, glancing sideways at him, Griffin could not have denied similar feelings himself. Although not entirely. The heat haze simmered down in the valley, there were flies by the squadron, tough undergrowth on the slopes, probably millions of snakes and spiders. All sorts of cynical possibilities that Griffin might ordinarily have voiced, just to break up the emotional continuity. But he restrained himself—there was the way in which the whole vista went together that stifled his instincts, for the moment.

They had stopped in a hundred places during the return journey, for pubs, for places of interest, events of significance, anything they found along the way. But here, they had just stopped. Or, truthfully, Lew had stopped, since Griffin still did not quite see the reason for it. But Lew stood on a little knoll, like a monolith, faced into the breeze, impenetrable. Then the zephyr wearied of him and pranced off toward the ocean and its green blobs of islands.

"If I was ever to own a farm, Griffin, this would be the place," Lew said suddenly.

It was all a bit much for Griffin—he could not stifle a laugh.

"Lewington, you'd go mad in a week. Getting up at sparrow's fart to feed the chooks and milk the cows. Crawling around the paddocks in the fastest Massey Ferguson in the co-op. And it must be miles to the nearest pub."

Though even Griffin's cynicism did not come as easily as he might have expected.

"Ah, Griffin. You urban folk are too inflexible. I am familiar with the rigours of rural life, you know."

"I'm sure you loved every thrill-packed minute, Lewington. Slopping in the pigpen, lopping off the roosters head for Sunday dinner, hanging it on the rotary clothesline to drain the blood while you join the neighbours for the word of the Lord."

"I'm delighted that you understand it so clearly, Griffin. Actually, it was rather rugged. An uncle of mine had a farm near Perth and I was despatched there as slave labour for the school holidays. Worked like a dog, I did."

Griffin chuckled while Lew fought helplessly to hang on to his dream in the face of grim reality.

"Perhaps, Lewington, we'll see such a farm for sale and you'll be able to convince Dell to buy it for you."

"I doubt my life will be sufficiently long to incorporate that amount of convincing."

"Oh, I don't know. Dell is always insisting that you do something more constructive with your life."

"I suspect this isn't quite what she has in mind."

Skimming over the pockmarked roads, the mountains now pushing the coastal plain more and more into the Pacific. They drove with shirts off and the only relief from the heat was the slipstream through the windows and the sunroof. At times they cared to kneel on the seat and poke their heads out through the overhead opening, playing tank or submarine commanders. The signs of civilisation were few, most that existed were abandoned. It seemed they would go on and on like this, driving forever. Griffin wrote a poem about it on the roof of the car as they went.

"I journeyed far and lost my way on nowhere's endless track. I turned around and found my way to nowhere, coming back."

"Awful, Griffin. Too romantic. And the mood's all up the shit."

Griffin found it impossible to care.

They came upon a town the name of which they would have forgotten even had they noticed. The corrugated gravel road widened by at least a metre and there was a tumbledown store, a garage of sorts, three houses and a desperately needed hotel which they eyed greedily.

"Certainly been a long run between waterholes, Griffin."

"Yes, Lewington. I think my tongue has a gravel rash."

The pub was built of stone in the true spirit of pioneer confidence whereas everything else in the town looked like it might have been temporary a hundred years ago. The only sign of life was the vast swarm of flies on the pub verandah, awaiting some sign of movement on the part of the flywire door—certainly two dogs that lay nearby might have been long dead. The Monster, tumbling out of the backseat with his pink tongue almost touching the ground, could not find the energy to investigate the state of the local canine society. Deprived of the windy shield of the moving car, they found the air became stagnant, weighted tons and was unbreathable. As they pulled on shirts, Lew and Griffin were already soaked in sweat. Griffin crossed to a water tank and ran the tap for a moment to create a puddle that The Monster could drink from—instead the animal staggered over and flopped in the middle of it.

"That a man could swim in beer," Lew said enviously as they entered the pub.

Caricatures of the Never-Never stood about in clumps according to type—lean stockmen, squat miners, blacks with suspicious eyes. When no one could have been expected, there must have been forty men in the pub and none of them seemed much interested in wasting energy and drinking time by bothering to speak. The smell of armpits commanded the more common odours of nicotine, rotten wood around the beertaps and, since there was no wind, the bittersweet from the urinal out the back. To a man, the customers turned to observe these strangers who came in so boldly to shelter from the dust and heat.

"G'day," the barman said. He was a short fat man with a grubby sweatband tied about his bald head, wearing a bloodstained butcher's apron and a singlet adhered to his skin by moisture in most places.

"Beer," they gasped in reply.

"Good drinking day, ain't it," the barman said.

"The very best," Lew answered, "But then I suppose you have a lot of them around here."

"Yeah," the barman said, "Ain't it wonderful."

The beer was good—not watered down like in a lot of city pubs. But then, as Griffin pointed out, around these parts where the rainfall was close to zero, it was more likely that they would spike the water with beer rather than the reverse.

"I'm not sure if that's good or bad," Lew mused.

There was a pool table but several hefty miners seemed to be in earnest competition and Lew and Griffin did not have time to wait it out. Still, competitive endeavour did seem to be in order and there was an unattended dartboard and about fifty multi-hued darts on the rack beneath.

"Shall we?"

"Lets."

Although neither would have wanted to boast their skills

at that game, still they set about it with an air of supreme confidence. They selected weapons and fired away at a dartboard so perforated it was a wonder it still held together. Most of the numbers had been long since obliterated. Soon, both declared that they were winning.

After a while, an enormous bulging man in faded overalls and a battered slouch hat walked over to them, distracting them with the smell of the sweat that ran over his huge shoulders and onto his giant biceps and singlet straining to contain his massive torso.

"Hoy! Wadda yer reckon yer doin'," he grunted loudly.

Lew looked at him incredulously: "Playing darts, my friend." The giant looked glum at this answer—it seemed the reason why he had asked the question had escaped him for the moment. But it came back to him slowly.

"Bluntin' a bloke's quills, that's what," he said.

"What?"

"Quills," he said, pointing at the darts in Griffin's hands, "Bluntin' 'em."

Griffin examined the points—they seemed sharp enough.

"Are these yours?"

The ogre shook his head ponderously.

"Nar. But one he's got is."

Lew looked at his darts blankly—he had thought he was playing with a matching set.

"Oh. Sorry, buddy. Which one?"

"That one," and a huge paw snatched it from Lew's grasp. Lew remained frighteningly calm. Griffin hastily selected a replacement from the rack.

"Hoy! Yer can't have that one. That's Roy's, I reckon."

"An' that's Porky's."

"An' that's Jacko's."

"Fuck it, which one can I use?" Lew asked in escalating exasperation.

"None of 'em, mate. They all belongs to someone."

Lew glared. Griffin ducked between them and scurried to the bar.

"Is that right?" he asked.

The barman shrugged: "Sorry, fellas. Guess you don't know the rules around here."

"I guess we don't."

"There's big dart comps played here. Biggest around these parts. All them darts belong to the locals. There's a rule that no one ever uses another bloke's darts."

Lew was still looking dangerous: "We weren't hurting them..."

Griffin groaned as he was obliged to speak the obvious to the barman. "So, can we have some darts that visitors can use."

"Nope."

"You must have."

"Nar. No need. Everyone here's a local. They all got their own darts."

"We're not."

"Yeah."

Griffin sighed, walking away. Lew glowered, unsure whether to jump the bar and do the barman or take on the large oaf by him first. Griffin knew this was the moment to move along, but as it happened, Lew's problem was presently being solved.

"Hoy! Look. He's bent some ov me feavvers."

"So I'll fucking straighten it," Lew snarled, making a snatch at the dart in the giant's hand but the latter ducked away, clutching his dart to his chest as if defending a child from a savage dog.

"Hoy! Ain't that one of Geoff Ronald's quills yer got there?" The thick finger pointed accusingly.

"Hoy, Geoff. This bloke's got one ov yer quills."

Geoff Ronald was an even more behemoth character with a many times rearranged face that he now rearranged all the more into a puzzled expression.

"Eh?"

"Ain't that one of your quills there?"

"Eh? Hey! Yeah. Yeeeaahh. Watcha doin wif me quills, fella."

"Wiping me arse with it," Lew snarled.

"Now, fellas..." the barman cut in.

Geoff Ronald loomed over Lew—the antagonist immediately passed the subject darts across to Griffin and braced himself. Griffin stared at the darts in his hand and realised that perhaps he ought to be bracing himself as well.

Geoff Ronald was saying: "Ain't no one uses me quills unless I says so. And I don't remember saying so. Who are yer, anyway?"

"Mohammed Ali."

"Eh?"

"Now fellas..."

"Hoy! That ain't yer name..."

The barman, a braver man than anyone imagined, now

inserted himself between Geoff and Lew.

"Now Geoff. Take it easy. These blokes are tourists and don't know better."

"Gimme me quills..."

The huge hands groped toward the feathered ends and Griffin offered them gladly. It still might have come out okay had not Geoff maybe had one or two too many and Griffin's hand not be shaking with terror. A brief fumble in the exchanged signalled the new turn of events as the sacred objects dropped and stuck into the floor in a tight little grouping.

Such was the simultaneous gasp sucked in by everyone in the bar that surely there could have been no air left in the room.

"You bastard!" Geoff Ronald roared and his fist came racing after his words with a blow intended to dispatch Lew to the next town by air, only Lew wasn't standing there anymore. Neither was Griffin. That left the barman who was still making general pacifying gestures when Geoff's huge haymaker arrived and this he neatly intercepted on the point of his jaw. He sagged, his butcher's apron newly decorated as he slipped to the floor. The new simultaneous gasp was far more impressive than the one before.

"Hey, look. The big shit's snotted Leo."

The felling of the barman immediately divided the room into its three basic factions, each of which concluded that the matter should be dealt with according to custom. There were, for instance, allies of the barman who, all being stockmen, moved with long strides to avenge his mishap. Then there were the miners who, seeing the stockmen going after Geoff Ronald, moved in to defend their associate. Lastly there were the blacks who were not about to pass up the chance to rush in and kick the barman while he was down, along with any other white man unlucky enough to hit the floor.

As for Lew and Griffin, whom no one seemed to bother to consider as a new faction, they were completely ignored and better still, saw the way was open between them and the door. They bolted, and would have made it too, had they not discovered that the way was suddenly blocked by a new melee trying to come in through the flywire from outside. This comprised The Monster who had finally managed the energy to investigate the two apparently dead dogs on the verandah and found them anything but. Now they came after him in a frenzy of teeth and saliva and terrifying snarls, burst straight through the flywire screen in the remnants of which they became hopelessly entangled. Griffin, fearless in the face of savage teeth, seized the Monster by the tail and dragged him through. The two local beasts came after him, but then found their progress checked by a couple of reeling human beings doing a fair imitation of their own snarling and gnashing.

With the brawl blocking their escape, Lew made for the vacant area behind the bar and Griffin followed, still carrying a furiously struggling Monster. From there, perhaps, they could make it to the rear exit Lew had spotted earlier which led to the dunny out the back.

The fight was proving to be a disorderly affair. It had degenerated into groups of two men wrestling and flailing on the floor while other men stood trying to kick them or separate them or stop someone from kicking them or stop someone from separating them. All of them were shouting at once such things as Hoy! Hoy! and I'll kill you, you bastard and hit him for christsakes hit him.

Near the bar, while they paused to assess their chances of flight, Lew realised that they had come to the place where the miners were required to hang their hard hats on entry to the bar. Quickly, he slipped one on himself and popped another on Griffin's head. It was not a moment too soon for immediately a bottle came hurtling out of the erupting mass of bodies and blood and vulgarity and was far better intercepted by fibreglass than Griffin's skull. He got such a shock that he let go of The Monster, who instantly vanished looking for interesting places to sink his teeth into.

This action again opened the way to the front door and Lew shoved Griffin in that direction.

"I don't think they like us here, Griffin."

"A slip in the popularity polls does seem apparent, Lewington."

"I really do think we ought to be elsewhere."

"Elsewhere sounds very alluring right now."

Wary of flying objects and flailing fists, they made their way to the door. Lew leapt two apparent corpses and then scampered under a table, while Griffin encountered a fellow so drunk he forgot to clench his fists when punching and sent himself sprawling into the fray.

Things were little improved at their second attempt to get out the door. An aborigine sprang onto Lew's back and Griffin was unable to remove him. They discovered too that the cavalry had arrived in the form of the local policemen—not small fellows—who moved into the fray by means of cracking all available skulls with their batons. One of the first of these blows glanced off Lew's helmet and collected his piggyback rider who immediately lost interest in proceedings. The policeman decided the best plan was to belt Lew's helmet until it cracked, which it might well have had not one of Monster's antagonists, perhaps remembering many official kicks, got the constable by the calf. The distraction was the final key to allow Lew and Griffin into the outside world.

They made it to the car and only there felt it was safe to remove their hardhats. Griffin regarded his with a smile.

"Good thinking, Lewington. You got brains in there somewhere."

"Rather bruised brain right now, Griffin. The hard hat is not quite as hard as advertised."

"That copper certainly gave it a thorough test run."

"Would you care to drive the car, Griffin, and save the post-mortems until we are definitely post and not anymore mortemed."

Behind, the disturbance seemed to intensify for the policemen seemed only to add yet another faction to the conflict. Now at least it was evident why the pub had been built so substantially.

"Hey Monster, come on, let's go."

The Monster came racing flat-out from the side of the building, hotly pursued by the other of its antagonists. Griffin had the engine going and Lew wound the window down, allowing Monster to take his well-practiced flying leap into the backseat one second before Griffin dropped the clutch. The pursuer attempted the same trick and demonstrated the value of training as it hit the door frame and was sent tumbling in the dirt. Lew, Griffin and undoubtedly Monster were all laughing as they drove out of town, leaving only a formidable trail of oil fumes to mark their coming.

"Nice to visit these sleepy out-of-the-way places, Lewington."

"A pleasure to be amongst the simple folk, Griffin."

"Simple folk, simple values, simple lives."

"A joy to behold."

"Do you suppose the next town will be any different?"

"I've never really be keen on darts anyway."

"Okay. It's agreed. No more darts."

The next town lacked a dart board anyway.

Hadrian and the Monster

There was a cat named Hadrian with sufficient lack of good fortune to be temporarily placed in their household. Dell had by then completed her studies and had a temporary job with a small engineering firm and Hadrian was the prized possession of her young boss and his wife, and they left the cat in Dell's care whilst they undertook an overseas holiday. It was never clear why Dell, who hated all animals, had been persuaded to accept this obligation but in any case Hadrian arrived with all the pomp and circumstance that its pedigree demanded. Hadrian was a large furball flop of extremely valuable white Persian which, despite its name, turned out to be female. Grave dangers surrounded those times when she was on heat. Apparently not a creature of the most pleasant disposition at the best of times, Hadrian's suffering intensified when Dell, under pressure of additional workload and as part of her longterm campaign to expand Lew's sense of responsibility, passed on to him the obligation of ensuring that Hadrian was properly fed and cared for. You can imagine that it ate fairly spasmodically.

Lew immediately became excessively attached to Hadrian in just exactly the manner that you would have safely assumed he would not—you could only guess that it was some from of cynical revenge.

"Best fucking cat I ever saw," Lew would enthuse, "A veritable Doberman of a cat. Faithful, trusty, a real bone-gnawing bloodhound of a cat."

Even Hadrian, for all her aristocracy, could never have seriously aspired to such extravagant claims.

However, Hadrian was not without a few eccentricities of her own, for although a basically inert creature designed for comfort, still she had a prize-winning conspicuousness to ferment. There were times, for instance, when she would sneak up on unsuspecting human beings and, springing into their laps, sink her claws in spitefully. Visitors would twist their clenched teeth into a smile and wait for a polite opportunity to place the 'little darling' back on the floor. Lew would sit encouraging the beast to draw more blood; when she tried it on Griffin she found herself promptly despatched to a most undignified position in the waste-paper basket; Dell of course had the sense to never sit when Hadrian was in the room or, if she did, ensured she placed some appropriate obstruction on her knees.

A similar but more spectacular characteristic was her unsuccessful but, for the human usually painful and always startling, attempts to run straight up a vertical person, clawing her way to the top of their heads like a goanna up a tree. Griffin could only assume her mother had indulged some unthoroughbred dalliance with a possum, Lew that it was her recognition of her jungle ancestry, but most likely it was because all the trees where outside the house where she was never allowed to go.

For Hadrian, disoriented perhaps by territorial adjustments, was permanently on heat for the duration of her stay and therefore confined to the house at all times. Woe betide the person responsible for letting her out where the alley cats might be allowed to exert their influence of her well-planned future genetic path. As a result, Hadrian roamed the house, yowling and cavorting in the midnight hours, her refined voice so piercing that for the other occupants, sleep became a much cherished dream in itself. All protruding objects needed to be raised more than a foot off the floor to prevent Hadrian from backing onto them and sending herself into an ear-splitting frenzy. To Griffin, it seemed to be a plot by Dell to enforce a certain disciplinary order for it got that way that you just couldn't do anything without taking Hadrian's well-being into account.

There was new order in the house. When Karen had departed, the level of domesticity in the house very quickly declined, until Dell stepped into the breach and distributed the tasks manfully. Once she had thought Karen a fool to trouble with cleaning, now she seemed to continually mutter furiously about living in a pigsty. Griffin could never have imagined the sorts of threats that resulted in Lew being seen at work with the mop, the broom even the vacuum cleaner. Guilt forced him to take on responsibility for the bathroom, toilet and laundry, which in fact he had always attended to under Karen's regime when his conscience at her tireless efforts overwhelmed him. For a time, the house was tidier than it had ever been—it was a shame that Karen was not around to see it.

Then, out of this darkness, emerged new light. Griffin was just about to depart the house that day and take himself to the pub. It was Saturday and Lew and Dell had just returned from the market and were in the kitchen arguing about what objects should be placed in which cupboards. Griffin wandered down there to see if Lew might want to join him, but since Dell was in one of her more vociferous moods, he settled for an 'I'll see you there' and set off alone. Or almost did. For Hadrian lurked in the hallway and the moment Griffin opened the door, the cat made a dash out between his feet. Griffin reacted slowly—it was not inconceivable that he might have been happy to let it go but alas, no such escape took place. Hadrian halted one step over the threshold, arched her back and hissed in a manner Dell would have been proud of, and then fled back into the depths of the house. If disappointing, still it was a matter worthy of investigation.

What he found, huddled in a tiny unwanted dejected heap in the corner of the verandah, was exactly what the evidence suggested—with all due allowance for the cowardice of Hadrian. A small cringing black-and-white furry dumpling, distinctly canine. Griffin closed in on it.

"Hey, come here little fella."

It backed off, or tried to, and might have escaped through the hole in the fence had it not been impeded by an injured front paw. Still, it could growl at him pretty boldly, this pup, a whelp, so recently born that its three good legs could barely keep its belly off the ground. Griffin scooped it up and it snapped at him, but after only a few moments of being caressed against Griffin's chest, the small quivering bundle of fur stopped quivering and settled in to the plainly unfamiliar warmth. Griffin rushed back into the house.

"Hey, look what I've found."

No one was particularly interested in what he had found. Dell disliked dogs as much as she supposedly disliked cats and Lew considered that he already had a first rate mutt in Hadrian, albeit temporary.

"You can't keep it," Dell insisted, "It'll upset Hadrian."

"Yaayy, Hadrian," Lew concurred.

Griffin was left to convey the pup to his room where he could tend to its injured paw and make it a bed of disused clothing on the old armchair in the corner that had burst its stitching and he had intended to throw away a year ago. The pup decided immediately that it was in eternal debt to this benefactor and that it should follow him wherever its little legs could carry it, and later, everywhere he went. It obviously knew a human that needed a lot of looking after when it saw one, and so it was, as Humphrey Bogart's scriptwriter put it, the beginning of a beautiful friendship.

The friendship was not without its initial difficulties. Passing the local shop, Griffin spied a notice in the window.

LOST PUP FOUND
23 Elm Street

He needed to think about it for a moment to realise the implications, however, no one turned up in response so he made no comment on it. Another problem was what to call it—had it been a bitch the name would have been obvious, but it wasn't. He spend several nights afterward, running names through his mind. Nothing seemed right. But it would come, he was sure.

Another problem was Lew, who decided the advent of the pup in the household was cause for a contest of the 'my dog is better than your dog' variety. His dog was in fact poor Hadrian.

"Even pisses like a dog," Lew would breath triumphantly, "No bloody skulking in the bushes for you, hey you old dogrooter. Just straight up to the old telephone pole and zap!"

No one had seen Hadrian piss like a dog although admittedly the kitty-litter did limit the possibilities. He obtained a lead and took Hadrian for evening walks which amounted to dragging the unfortunate creature around the block. He bought her a bowl marked 'Fido' and a rubber bone and Griffin even saw him once—when drunk admittedly—trying to teach the cat to fetch sticks in the hallway. About which Dell had certain things to say.

But all that was nothing compared to the traffic flow problems that arose involving Hadrian. The pup, though less than half the size of the cat, thought the large furry object might make a fine playmate but Hadrian was all too aware of the proper relationship between canine and feline. However small it might be, that was a dog! and whenever it was near, Hadrian puffed up into a hissing, fur-flinging panic which often resulted in the nearest human been substantially clawed as she fled to higher ground. Griffin was obliged to keep the dog in his room most of the time and when he went out carried it inside his shirt with its head poking out like a joey. And it wasn't Hadrian he was protecting it from, he knew.

There was a limit to how long this situation could be sustained and so the morning came when fate permitted all five inhabitants of the house to be in the kitchen at the same time. The three human occupants were then enjoying their morning coffee, Hadrian was there by her divine right to be wherever she wanted to be, and the pup turned up because Griffin had failed to close his door properly. Hadrian and the pup rounded opposite sides of the refrigerator and came nose to nose with the result that the cat indulged its usual puffing and hissing and then darted across the room and sprang to safe ground on the window sill. The window was open, but further advance was prevented by the flywire screen.

"Leave them," Griffin said, "Give them a chance to get used to one another."

It was the sort of thing you said in order to give yourself no chance of being right, for it was apparently at that moment that the pup realised the true purpose of cats in the life of a dog and that he didn't want this irritable fluffy character for a friend after all. The pup scurried across the lino floor, narrowly evading Griffin's outstretched hands and Dell's flying boot and took as great a leap at the window sill as its little legs would permit. The sill was low and the pup could not leap very high and it would have been alright had Hadrian not forgotten that she possessed a tail and left that part of her anatomy dangling. Into this, the pup managed to sink his rapidly developing teeth. Hadrian let out a cry that paled all former efforts significantly and went straight through the flywire screen, across the yard and over the back fence. The pup fell flat on its back on the kitchen floor and then scampered away into the depths of the house in utter terror. All three humans stared at each other in utter astonishment for a valuable moment before jumping to their feet and rushing outside, but it was far too late. Hadrian was nowhere to be seen.

"Shit!" Dell seethed.

"We better go find it," Lew said, not completely unable to conceal his mirth.

"It's not funny," Dell exploded, "Go and find it now."

She herself tore off, although not out the gate to search the alleys and neighbouring backyards but instead back into the house. Lew, thinking quicker than Griffin, went after her.

Griffin found them in the hallway. Dell had her back to the wall and was holding the broom in a manner which would not have allowed it to be mistaken for anything other than a weapon. Lew pinned her arms and was trying to calm her down. And below them, huddled at the foot of the stairs, was the puppy, wide-eyed and trembling at being fought over by giants.

"You monster!" Dell was shrieking at it, "You absolute bloody little monster!"

The Stealer of Lives

It was left to Griffin to fetch the licence plates from the Motor Registration people in Brisbane—Lew went into the city with him but then shirked the final scene on the pretext that he had 'a little errand to run for Dell.' It was the morning following their return from the northern trek and not a good time for asking too many questions about things like that—all night he had heard them arguing and Lew looked unusually tired and worn. Still, Griffin knew he had to say something.

"I take it you've informed Dell of our plans, Lewington."

"What plans, Griffin."

"Will we not be in a position to return to Melbourne tomorrow morning?"

"Oh. Those plans."

"Am I to assume that she was not pleased, Lewington?"

"The trouble with Dell is that she is a highly intelligent woman who misunderstands everything perfectly."

"I find myself unable to gather a definite meaning from that, Lewington."

"A woman in anger was a creature seeking revenge for self-inflected wounds."

"I said that once."

"Yes. I know you did. You were right."

"It isn't always a good thing to be right, Lewington."

"Now I think you've grasped my meaning."

"Then how come I still don't understand."

"Don't understand what?"

"I think I'll just abandon this conversation, before it gets to its subject."

Griffin went through the bureaucracy at Motor Registration and the man finally handed him the plates and new registration sticker. Sitting on the kerb outside Cleveland Police Station, Griffin screwed the plates into position, wondering how other more normal people handled such situations. Maybe they did it the way he did. The Jaguar did not look at all impressed at its new state of illegality and the Monster pissed on a hub cap by way of baptism and they drove across the city to the pub where he had agreed to meet Lew.

All the way, Griffin felt a sense of dread. When Lew kept him in suspense, it invariably emerged that in fact he was being protected from knowledge that he would have preferred not to know. Which was fine—the difficulty always was that eventually Lew would confess all. Usually when it was too late to do anything about it. There had been mutterings, he knew, of Lew attempting to enrol at the Brisbane university. Certainly, he was sure that Dell was pulling out all stops to try and get him to stay. And why not? Griffin would have agreed, had anyone given him the chance to express his opinion. He had enough conservative respect for family values to know that a father's place was with his kid. So what was the problem? Did they actually believe that he, Griffin, had some sort of power over Lew to decide whether he should stay or go. In fact it seemed Dell did, but that was just because she always needed to blame someone for everything. She had always been jealous of their friendship and saw it as a threat and maybe it was, except that it wasn't. Lew would stay or go as he decided himself, as Griffin would. Or was he being too simplistic about it?

The tricky bit was figuring out why Dell wanted to keep Lew in any case. Surely no one could have been less appropriate to her new lifestyle. Of course Griffin, a romantic always, had a healthy respect for the power of love, especially possessive love, especially female possessive love. Was that it? Did she simply regard Lew as her possession, which no one else could have, even if she didn't really want it herself. There were people like that and Dell might have been one of them. But he would have liked to think better of her than that. Somewhere, somehow, he knew he was missing the point.

The only real question was whether Lew would return to Melbourne immediately, for surely he would stay for a while, just to give it a go. He smiled to himself as he contemplated how long he should appropriately keep Lew's room available in case of his return. Two weeks ought to be enough. A month. A couple of months would surely demonstrate the loyalty of Jonathan or Pythias. Lew would stay, they would fight furiously, she would eventually give in and send him home to Griffin. Yes, that was the most probable way it would go. For certainly, whatever Lew's plans, Griffin was heading south in the morning.

It had been a great journey, but he was longing for Carlton now—the pubs and pizza joints, friends, the erratic weather, home. The Monster too grew restless and seemed to be tolerating this nonsense. The local cats would be growing fat without him to provide their daily exercise. Who knows what evil mutts would have been spotting his telephone poles. Carlton was calling to them both. Maybe it was calling to Lew as well.

Maybe the problem was that Lew had just plain not made up his mind.

Whatever the case, Griffin mentally prepared himself for the next few hours. At all times, support Lew's fatherly responsibilities. Say nothing to remind him of home. Quietly prepare for his lone departure. It had been a great and valuable friendship and it was sad to think that it was over but over it was. You could only be stoic about it.

What he had to be stoic about first was his knowledge that university enrolment was a long and complicated procedure and he would probably have to wait some time for Lew to arrive. That was why they had been careful to pick a nice pub with a good beer garden to rendezvous in. But, as it happened, Lew had got there first.

"All done?"

"Yep. Our fine vehicle has finally gained full respectability."

"Until we drive it over the border."

"Yes. Until then."

Griffin felt a shudder when Lew said 'we'. No doubt about it. There was a point that he was failing to grasp completely.

"So," he asked, when Lew had plainly failed to honour his turn to speak, "What have you been up to."

"Oh, just a few chores for Dell."

"Okay."

"Okay what."

"Okay you can be as bloody mysterious about it as you like."

"Mysterious. What do you mean?"

"Mysterious means mysterious. You know what I mean."

"You're beginning to sound like Dell, Griffin."

"I doubt my vocal chords are up to it."

They ordered lunch and more beer and it was time for Lew to strike up a more typical conversation. Griffin waited for it and was obliged.

"Have you observed, Griffin, the new undertakings of the Labor Party, should they be elected?"

"I'm not interested in politics, Lewington. You know that."

"Politics can sometimes be relevant, Griffin."

"Only in their capacity to oppress the poor and aid the rich to line their pockets."

"You are very cynical, Griffin."

"Yes, and its politicians and businessmen who have made me that way."

"Still Labor have made a most interesting election promise..."

"Made to be broken as are all such promises. Come on, Lewington. All politicians lie, every time they speak. Their whole activity is directed at fleecing the population for as much as they can and not giving the game away. That's who they are."

"But sometimes they can have influence."

"Only pernicious. And anyway, if they do happen to change an act of parliament which is in some indirect way to our benefit, its only because the change has already occurred in the society and the law merely recognising that change. And even that only after a hell of a fight. Can we try a different subject please?"

"This is of interest to you directly..."

"None of it interests me."

"It was in all the papers."

"I don't read newspapers, Lewington."

"I know you don't. That's why I have to tell you about these things."

"Newspapers exist only to perpetuate the false impression that politicians and businessmen are relevant. It is entirely propaganda."

"Wow, Griffin. To think you were once the most reactionary person I ever knew. That was what made you interesting—a reactionary amongst radicals. You were different."

"One cannot but help be influenced by one's surroundings."

"Right, which means that occasionally, just occasionally I agree, politics can, albeit inadvertently, be relevant, as is the case here."

"You'll not convince me."

"It has to do with Vietnam."

"I'm not interested in Vietnam."

"You were once."

"I've been there, Lewington. I didn't like it much. Vietnam made me the wreck I am today."

"Therefore, you ought to be interested that the Labor Party, if elected, will bring that to an end."

"I am certain that the Australian Labor Party is able to exert no influence whatsoever over the war in Vietnam. It will prevail until they stop shooting at each other and find someone else to shoot at, irrespective of anything the Labor Party or any other foreign politician does."

"Not stopping the war. Stopping the Australian involvement in it."

"Allow me to point out to you, Lewington, that since it is

the existing government that put and maintained the Australian presence in Vietnam, and since further that the Labor Party is the Opposition, and since further further that, by definition, the Opposition must oppose everything the Government says and does, such an attitude on their part does not surprise me in the least. Indeed, they have to do it. It's the rules."

"Griffin, I have to tell you that under the weight of mass public protestation, some of which you participated in yourself, the existing Government has already withdrawn the Australian contingent from Vietnam."

"I know that."

"I'm sorry. Since you don't read newspapers, I wasn't sure if you were aware of it."

"You told me about it. Months ago. When it happened."

"Over a year, actually. But that was only half of it, Griffin. There remained young men, as you were yourself once, being conscripted into the army. And Gough Whitlam and his Labor Party have stated that if they are elected, on the very day they take office, all conscripts and indeed all those persons imprisoned for dodging the draft will be simultaneously liberated."

"I can see certain problems with this, Lewington."

"Ah huh. I can see that to be ignorant of the matter is not to be without opinion."

"The first that springs to mind is the not inconsiderable fact that the Labor Party has not been elected to govern this country since the Second World War."

"I thought you didn't know anything about politics."

"All along, you have been confusing disinterest and disillusionment with ignorance."

"The Labor Party is now led by Gough Whitlam and Jim Cairns..."

"Who were leading it when they lost the election in 1969, I recall."

"But things are different now. The public has been made angry by the lies of government, especially Vietnam."

"The Americans have elected Richard Nixon on a platform of ending US involvement in the war. It continues still.."

"Whitlam and Cairns are honest and intelligent politicians..."

"Your adjectives and noun comprise a natural contradiction."

"How can anyone talk sense to someone who is so cynical?"

"Is that what we're doing? Talking sense? About politics? Lewington, I suddenly grow suspicious."

"Suspicious. What, of who? Me?"

"This is, in fact, a real political conversation."

"Which means?"

"Which means, Lewington, that you are up to something and you are doing everything in your power to prevent me from finding out the truth."

"I think I'd like to end the conversation now."

"Fine by me."

"Okay. The conversation ends."

"End of conversation."

They sat and drank their beer and neither said anything. It had been a long time since the last time that they had run out of things to say. Griffin cracked after less than a minute and said tentatively. "Lewington."

"Yes Griffin."

"That conversation we just had."

"The one that we stopped having, you mean?"

"Yes, that one. What was it really about."

"I have, this very day, had an encounter with the stealer of lives."

"The stealer of lives?"

"Yes, Griffin. The Stealer of Lives."

The stealer of Lives. It lurked in chilly lair on the twenty-third floor, the smile on its face as fixed as that of any other reptile, the sheen of its silken suit a match for its dark scaly hide. A throwback to the age of dinosaurs when the brain served solely the purpose of killing and devouring—a hundred million years of evolution, ten thousand years of civilisation was completely squandered here. It wore thick bifocals that were obviously designed to avoid seeing things too clearly, and was completely unable to speak without a document before it, to which it could refer your attention.

"Name?"

"I just want to ask a question."

"By all means. Name."

"No, not answer questions, ask one."

"Yes. But first you must fill in this form. Then we'll answer all of your questions."

"Can't you answer the question before the form is filled in."

"No. It's the procedure. Name."

"I don't want to fill in the form. Not at least until after you've answered my question."

"Very well. If you don't want to fill in the form, I can do it for you."

"Forget the bloody form..."

"Nothing can happen until it is filled in. It's the procedure. Name."

"I don't want to tell you my name."

The Stealer of Lives, narrow snake-eyes now widened to fill the full lens of the bifocals. This bloodsucker. This destroyer of young men's dreams.

"You have to give me your name."

"I will. After you answer my question."

"How can I answer your question without your file in front of me."

"You probably don't have my file."

"You don't have a file?"

"No."

"You must have. It would have been raised initially when you filled in your eligibility card."

"I haven't filled one in."

"Then you must be in the wrong place. This is the Department of Labour and National Service. What department were you wanting?"

"This one. I'm in the right place."

"Then you must have filled in an eligibility card or else you would have no reason to be here."

"I haven't."

"Then you must proceed to your local post office and fill in an Eligibility for National Service Card. They send it to us and we eventually invite you in for an interview."

Invite... it salivated at the thought. At night in its lair it crunched on the bones of democracy.

"I don't want an interview. I just want to ask a question."

"You can't come in here and ask questions without an interview. There's a procedure. There's security. You must fill in the form so that at least we know who we are talking to."

"You don't need to know who I am. My question is of a general nature."

"Oh, I see. Then that should be fine. Just tell me your name and I'll answer your question."

"Why don't you answer my question, then I'll tell you my name."

"Because that isn't the procedure."

"Couldn't you make an exception?"

"Heaven forbid. There are regulations..."

"What if I promise, in advance, to tell you my name after

you've answered my question."

"Promise?"

"Promise."

"But what am I going to put on the form?"

"Forget the fucking form."

"I can't do that. How will anyone know I answered your question if there isn't any form..."

"They don't need to know."

"They have to know. That's what the form is for."

"Oh damn it then, put Ned Kelly."

"What?"

"Ned Kelly. It's a name. Put that."

"Is it your name?"

"No."

"Then it won't do. It has to be your name."

"Alright then. Richard Nixon."

"Is that your name?"

"Yes."

"Well, there you are. Not so difficult, was it. How do you spell that?"

"Nix as in 'nothing'. On as in 'put on'."

"Pardon?"

"N-I-X-O-N."

"Fine. Good. Nixon, Richard. Same as the US President, hmmm?"

"It happens."

"I'm sure it does."

"Now can I ask my question?"

"Address?"

"What?"

"Your address."

"You said you just wanted my name."

"And now your address."

"You promised that if I gave you my name, you would then answer my question."

"You can't have a name without an address."

"Ten Downing Street Westminster."

"Westminster? Where is that now?"

"Near Fortitude Valley."

"Fine. Date of birth?"

"You have to answer my question..."

"Date of birth. Then we'll see."

"Try seeing without these."

"What... what are you doing?"

"Answer my bloody question or I'll snap these in half. Then where will you be?"

"My glasses. Give me back my glasses."

"Sure. Soon as you answer my question."

"Question, what question. I can't see without them. Please be careful. They are very expensive to replace."

"No harm will come to them if you just answer a simple question."

"Please... please..."

"Good. That's better. Now. Tell me, good fellow. If I were to make myself available for military service, how long would it be before I actually entered the army?"

"If you what?"

"Make myself available..."

"First you have to fill in your 'Eligibility for National Service' card at your local post office."

"Fine. I've done that. What happens next."

"You get a letter saying whether or not you have been drafted."

"Right., The letter came today. I've been drafted. What happens next?"

"All the necessary instructions are in the letter..."

"But I lost it before I had the chance to read it."

"We can send you out another."

"I just want to know what it said."

"It tells you when to report for a medical examination."

"Good. And how long does that take?"

"Depends on how quick the doctor is, I suppose."

"I mean how long between the letter and the medical appointment."

"Oh, about a month, I suppose."

"And after that how long before I go in the army?"

"Depends on whether you pass the medical."

"I have. Now what."

"An interview. At which your suitability for National Service is determined."

"How long between the medical and the interview?"

"About a Month."

"And then, assuming I am suitable, what happens."

"You are advised to proceed to an Induction Centre on a particular day..."

"How long after the interview is that particular day?"

"About two months."

"Right, fine. Four months all told. Excellent. Here are your glasses. Goodbye."

"Date of birth. Sir, Mr Nixon, sir. You have to give me your date of birth. Sir, you can't leave now..."

He ducked the elevator and took to the stairs. By now the alarm would have been raised and the Federal Cops would be running from everywhere. Twenty-three flights of stairs down, footsteps ringing hollowly, if he could get to the bottom before they barricaded the fire escape door. Three strides to each landing, whirl around the bend, three more downward plunges and at the bottom in no time. There, desperately out of breath, he flattened against the wall. Get a peek outside and see if they were lying in ambush, if so charge on to the basement. The lobby is clear. They are too slow to react. Across the lobby at full stretch, secretaries and clerks staring, pointing, memorising his description for the police later. Saw a man running out of the building. A taxi almost ran him down as he bolted across the street, onto the bike and away.

At the corner he paused, to pull on his helmet and gloves and looked back. There was no pursuit. They'd missed him. And he was away....

The Drop Kick

Two and sometimes three times a day, he took the pup walking in the park. It stayed pretty close beside him in the streets but once Griffin found a bench to sit on or, on sunny days, lay down to sleep on the grass, the dog bounded off seeking adventure. Every few minutes though, it came back, just to make sure that Griffin was getting on okay. Usually he was, although not always. One day two small boys were kicking their footy back and forth in just the way the sign said prominently that no one was allowed to. It was the same sign that said 'No Dogs'. Griffin sat on the bench, watching the two boys enviously. They fairly raced around, chasing misdirected passes, running onto open goals, baulking each other. One wore a Fitzroy guernsey, the other Collingwood but they were unable to remember a Grand Final between their teams and certainly couldn't imagine one—instead they pretended to be the two clubs currently leading the competition. The pup investigated this matter thoroughly, getting under their feet until they threw stones at it. Observing their violent streak, The Monster decided his human might need a little extra protecting that day, and he did. For what happened was, in a sense, exactly what Griffin might have been hoping for. But he should have known that dreams realised only ever led to darker nightmares. The more you gained the more you stood to lose.

The boy in the Magpie guernsey was lining up the two trees designated as the goalposts from about thirty yards—maximum distance for him—while the other boy stood the mark.

"Peter McKenna lines 'em up," the kicker declared boldly.

"Yer can't be McKenna. You're Hawthorn. You gotta be Hudson," Fitzroy shouted back.

Griffin smiled. He was able to make complete sense of all this. He also knew that the kid on the mark was just trying to put the goal-kicker off. And it worked... Neither Hudson nor McKenna would have wanted to claim credit for the kick, which slewed of the side of the boot and went wide as forty degrees, out of bounds and finally rolling directly to Griffin's feet.

Griffin could not resist. The pup gave the ball a thorough sniffing and determined it was of no interest. Meanwhile, the players were arguing about who had to fetch it—the full-forward because he kicked it or the fullback for putting him off. Griffin stood and picked up the ball and truly the only sensible thing to do was kick it back to them.

"Hey. That old man's pinchin' our ball," Hudson-McKenna cried in horror.

Old man? Griffin gasped internally. Admittedly the fringe he brushed across his baldness chose that moment to fall in his eyes, and his beard might have been in need of a trim, and maybe his belly was starting to hang over his belt from all that beer... But old man! Furiously, he rotated the ball in his hands deftly, grasping it for a torpedo—he could roost those sixty yards dead straight if he got onto it alright. He'd show the little buggers. He took the traditional shuffling steps, a couple of long strides and went into the kick and the sound did tell him he'd got on it alright. But it had been raining earlier and the footing was bad and of course he had no stops, in fact nothing to prevent his leg from going out from under him and dumping him ludicrously on his bum in the mud. Jolted from top to bottom, his embarrassment at the fall was only marginal compared to the observation that his kick went high and way off course and bounced on the path, just twenty yards away. The two boys were laughing furiously as they streamed after it. He might have jumped up and murdered the little bastards had not The Monster seized the chance to pounce on his chest and lick his nose. He limped home, crippled in the dignity as much as the coccyx and even the pup had the sense to keep his distance all the way to the gate.

This was not the only incident that occurred in the park of which he saw no reason to mention to anybody. On another day, he was sitting on the grass, leaning up against a tree when he spied a large grey Mercedes drawing to a halt over in Nicholson Street. Along that side of the street, the houses were old and magnificent but since the address did not match the grandeur of the buildings, he was sure no one rich enough to own such a car lived there. Nor did they—the grey-haired distinguished-looking driver was just pausing to drop his passenger off. She smiled and waved and stepped back from the car, waiting for him to drive off. But the driver just waved back, and so she was forced to turn and walking in the front gate of the nearest house and up to the door. Finally the Mercedes did slide away into the traffic and only then did Dell re-emerge, hurrying out the gate and around the corner into Elm Street.

Griffin smiled, feeling a warmth toward Dell that he might have found hard to explain. There was nothing untoward in this. Plainly the deception had nothing to do with anything that might be going on behind Lew's back. The driver was surely only an associate—her professor or perhaps a potential employer—giving her a lift home after some professional function or other and she had found herself too ashamed to show them the abominable place in which she was forced to live. Poor Dell—even success conspired to add to her suffering.

For she had most assuredly succeeded, and was in demand for those professional and academic functions. Although Lew had not bothered to tell him, he had overheard her talking on the telephone and finally forced the details out of Lew. She had passed Civil Engineering—the first female ever to do so—First Class Honours and top student in the state, no less.

"Boy, did I show that pack of straight-laced stiff-shirt assholes. Put the lot of them in the toilet, the bloody male chauvinist pricks."

He heard her saying to a friend. And...

"That was why I took Civil in the first place. It was the ultimate rightwing conservative, most utterly fascist faculty. I was the only woman most of the lecturers and tutors had ever seen in this classes. They were really pissed off."

She went on. And...

"But what really got to them was how easily I passed everything. It was a pushover. They really are such a bunch of deadheads. They put every possible obstacle imaginable in my path to try and discourage me, or else they treated me as a sexist joke. You should have seen some of the things I was subjected to. The vile drinking contests, filthy practical jokes. Once they even took me to a brothel and had a gangbang and tried to make me take my turn with the whore."

She said. And...

"Yeah, well, now I've really fixed 'em up. Fucking shitheads. Rubbed their noses right in it."

Griffin raised the matter with Lew and it was all finally confirmed.

"I'm sure I must have mentioned it to you sometime," Lew said sheepishly.

"Not ever."

"Well, there you go."

"You realise, of course, that I'm going to have to treat her with a little more respect from now on."

"Why? She's still just the same old bitchy Dell."

"If I'd been doing what she's been doing, I'd be pretty bitchy most of the time as well."

"Did you ever think it was the other way around?"

"What other way?"

"Maybe you need to be a complete and utter bitch, just to take on something like that."

"That doesn't make it any less impressive."

"Oh no. Think about it, Griffin. Have you ever seen her build a model aeroplane, or change a light bulb, or clean her fucking sparkplugs? No fucking way. I do all that stuff for her. She isn't interested in engineering—not ever slightly. She's brilliant and would have got honours no matter what she did. She picked Civil Engineering out of sheer spite."

"It's still a hell of an achievement, Lewington, no matter how you try to belittle it."

"Then there's Daddy."

"Daddy?"

"Yeah. Her old man. She does have parents, you know."

"Actually, I'd never imagined it."

"So why do you think a Yankee sheila lives in dear old Oz?"

"Tell me."

"Because Daddy is a big wheel in one of those megaton Yank mining companies that are gradually turning this whole country into a quarry. He came out to take over a big deal in Queensland and she got stuck here."

"Oh."

"Oh yes. Daddy, it emerges, is a millionaire. Calzinc is the family business. Get it?"

"Not easily."

"So that's what it's all about, Griffin. She wasn't really showing Melbourne Uni Engineering what a girl could do. She was just a refugee with a big complex. Daddy was disappointed his son turned out to be the wrong sex and she's been trying to prove him wrong ever since."

"Have you ever met her father, Lewington?"

"Are you kidding?"

"Just wondering."

What he was really thinking about was the grey-haired gent in the Merc.

"So one day she gets to be chairman of the board."

"Chairwoman, Lewington."

"I know what I said. She's got Daddy in the pinchers. On the one hand he's too conservative to allow a woman into a senior position—on the other, she's his little darling and he'll do anything for her."

"Except accept her on her merits."

"It isn't him she really has to prove herself to, it's herself. But they only way she can do that is to get him to take her seriously. So she ran away to Melbourne—far enough to be out of his circle of influence but close enough that he would still know what she was achieving."

"So Daddy still isn't offering any jobs?"

"No way. Apparently he thinks her doing engineering is nice but not serious. She'll have to prove herself outside first."

"So the battle isn't over. It's just beginning."

"Just beginning. First she has to get a job. And, needless to say, Daddy's attitude to women is very representative of the profession as a whole."

"Yeah, I know. When I worked for the Department of Construction, I met a lot of engineers. There wasn't one of them that wasn't hopelessly conservative."

"Not a single job she's applied for has even short-listed her."

"No. You can't get where she's going from where she is now. Things have got to change."

"You got a plan?"

"I'll talk to her."

"That isn't a very good plan, Griffin. I tried it. It didn't work very well. She's too angry with the world to take advice."

"You didn't know what you were talking about, Lewington. I do."

"Since when did that make any difference."

"Like the man said, something's got to give."

"I know someone who has a full suit of medieval armour. You can borrow it if you wish. And I could have the ambulance standing by."

"Such efforts will be appreciated, Lewington."

That evening, Dell came in, scowling and throwing things and snarling about 'bastards.' Griffin was sitting in the kitchen and Lew and the pup were there though they tried to look like the weren't. Griffin could see the time was ripe if he could manage a little subtlety. Dell came in, kicking things in her jack-boots, the old pair of probable WWII vintage that she found in a disposals store were her only footwear—plainly there had been another job interview.

"Assholes!" she seethed.

She stripped off her leather jacket, the old one with flaking surface and bursting seams that she had inherited from Lew when he inherited a new one from a motorcycling acquaintance who beheaded himself on the tailgate of a semi at a hundred miles an hour on the South Eastern Freeway. Beneath, she wore a white T-shirt from which most of the oil stains had been bleached. In cooler weather, she added moth-eaten sweaters she collected from The Brotherhood, always dark colours and with frayed cuffs and collars. Her jeans, always black, were relatively new, also from disposals stores, although this pair were showing bulged at the knees and calves because of course she never ironed them. And then there was the hair—no longer multi-hued at least but dyed a very unnatural black, chopped short at the sides and standing straight up on top. All-in-all, she looked like a Luftwaffe pilot who, having been shot down more times than he needed, was in the final stages of his latest escape from behind enemy lines.

Of course, it was clearly an image she cultivated. She was never quite able to hide the fact that beneath the battered Hell's Angel disguise was a truly beautiful woman who regarded that asset as one to avoid exploiting at all costs. She deliberately bit her nails, never wore any kind of make-up, her skin combined the deathly white of arms and legs and presumably those parts Griffin had never seen with face and hands and throat furiously burnished by their exposure to the rigours of motorcycling. She exhibited pimples and blackheads and scars with pride. The scabs from her latest array of cuts and abrasions were always on open display, often with blood stains still intact. No trifling with Dettol and Bandaids for Iron Woman. Yet she was clean. She showered twice a day and seemed to spend the same protracted hours in the bathroom that all women did. Griffin found it impossible to imagine what she did in there—maybe she was renewing the black paint under her nails or rubbing yellow stain into her teeth.

It was definitely a situation that called for subtlety.

"Engineering firms are not usually in the habit of employing scarecrows," Griffin said.

"Fuck off, Griffin," Dell snarled back at him, "I'm not in the mood."

Lew, very bravely, thought a hug in her moment of sorrow might be a better strategy. He put one arm around her neck and the other up her jumper and squeezed her breast—plainly that was the way to calm her down. If it was, this time it didn't work.

"That's the point," Griffin replied, "I don't suppose you tried smiling."

"There was fucking nothing to smile about," she seethed.

"You bet there wasn't. You walk in the place looking like you've been out wrestling Brahma bulls, sneering at their furniture and fittings and with your hair looking like your vibrator had a power surge and you wonder why they don't smile at you."

"What the fuck would you know about it?"

"I used to sit on interview panels once, you know. I know what they expect and you ain't it."

"Griffin, just lay off, will you," Dell said.

"Yeah, give her a break, mate," Lew said to encourage him.

But Griffin was well underway now: "You've got no idea how conservative these people are."

"Nor do I want to work for a bunch of conservative assholes."

"But you do have to look the way the job requires."

"They take me the way I look or not at all."

"Then they won't. You're making a fashion statement which is I want to defy all fashion. Unless you want a job designing rubbish tips and train wreck locations, they won't be interested."

"I refuse to believe that appearance is everything."

"Nor is it. But it is the starting point. If you don't have the appearance, they don't bother to listen to anything you have to say."

"Oh go fuck yourself, Griffin. Look at the fucking way you dress."

"I'm not looking for a job. Think about the way I used to dress..."

"I'd really rather not, Pinocchio."

"Come on Dell. It's just a game. Play it like a game. Kid 'em along a bit. You can do it."

"Go fuck yourself Griffin."

She hurled her helmet at him but he was ready for that and took a strong chest mark. He heard her boots clumping all the way out of the house and only then did he dare smile at Lew.

"Well, that wasn't too bad, Lewington."

"No Griffin. I think it went about as well as it could have."

"Subtlety always prevails in the end."

Of course, nothing happened immediately. But that was only the first stage of the plan. There were some old things Karen had left behind, still in the bottom of the wardrobe where she had dumped them. Karen had been somewhat bustier than Dell and less muscular but Griffin remembered them remarking how they were the same size. Now he sorted through the leavings carefully and came up with some fine choices. These he put in a garbage bag and placed it out of the way in the kitchen, all but for a rather nice silky red blouse. He had to sow a button on it—army training would never be completely useless—but when that was done, it looked perfect. The day before her next interview, he was careful to drop the blouse on the stairs.

He was safely behind his door, listening, when she found it.

"What's this, Lew?"

"Oh, that? Griffin gave me some stuff to take down to the Sally bin. I must have dropped some of them."

"Where'd he get something like this?"

"Karen left it behind."

"Didn't he think she might want it back?"

"Nope. 'Left me with nuthin but a bag of old clothes to throw out', was what he said."

They were walking away, toward the kitchen, and Griffin strove mightily to overcome the urge to follow on some invented pretext.

"It's a very good silk blouse. Lovely. She really did have great taste in clothes."

Griffin's straining ears where trying to detect sounds of her trying it on, but that was impossible now. They were in the kitchen and even their voices were very muffled. Griffin crept out to the head of the stairs.

"Look. It fits perfectly."

Eureka!

"Bit short in the sleeves," Lew grunted diffidently—it was his way of being convincing.

"I can fold the cuffs back. Like this."

Griffin crept back into his room, smiling hugely, and hauled the Monster out of his chair and gave the dog a mighty hug. The dog tolerated it disgustedly.

In the middle of the night while Dell slept, an apparition of Lew appeared by Griffin's bed, carrying her jeans. Dopey, sleepy Griffin dreamed that he went downstairs and ironed them while Lew stood guard at the foot of the stairs. Task accomplished, Lew took them back and dumped them back on the floor in the precise place she left them. It wasn't much but it was something Griffin muttered to himself as he stumbled back to bed.

He didn't see the results until after the interview the following evening. Of course, he ignored it and so did she—it was probable that Griffin would not have recognised the blouse and she played it that way. It didn't get her a job but it did get her called back for the second round of interviews.

"Well, at least you're not frightening the living daylights out of them anymore."

Sometime in the next few days, Lew let on that he hadn't quite managed to take the bag of old clothes to the Salvation Army yet. She made no issue of rummaging. The tally, Griffin knew, was three other blouses, a couple of nice pullovers, two skirts, a dress, three pairs of high heeled shoes and one pair of flatties. Some petticoats and bras he had already dumped in the garbage. Dell got to work with the iron herself—at least Griffin was spared that—and on the morning of the interview, experimented with the skirts. Griffin just could not keep himself away.

"Shit, you've grown legs," he said brightly when he did encounter her.

She scowled at him bleakly.

"You bloody men, you're all the same."

"That's what makes us so easy to predict. You better practice crossing your legs when you sit down."

It was a very short tartan skirt.

"If I want your advice, I'll ask for it," she snapped.

But she did want his advice—that was why she was hanging around.

"Actually, it looks great, Dell," he said with a sincerity that could never have been believable. And wasn't. She wore the skirt awkwardly; it looked wrong with the flat-heeled shoes but who could blame her for that; she had hairy legs and no nylons but they were problems she would have to solve herself.

"Feels very exposed and draughty," she muttered.

"That, I understand, is why they invented panti-hose."

"What would you know about it, Griffin."

"You don't spend three years with someone like Karen and not learn a thing or two about the difficulties of the female anatomy."

There was a long pause.

"Actually, this happens to be one of her old skirts..."

"Is it really? Never looked like that on her," he said, and leered.

"You're a fucking sleazebag, Griffin."

Next day he found in the bathroom a new razor and a discarded pantihose wrapper—he could be fairly confident neither belonged to he or Lew.

Slowly, painfully, it was working. Lew made his own

contribution when they had a drinking party with some friends who made leather goods, and she came home with a new handbag and purse. And there was a girl named Merryl that Griffin took to the movies occasionally who, having been appraised of the matter, spent three hours with Dell teaching her mysterious things in front of the mirror. How she mastered the art of high heels would remain as much a mystery with her as any other woman. As much as possible had been done with the hair—she was ready for the front line. When she rode off to the interview in mini-skirt, high heels, low-cut top and motorcycle helmet, she was one of the most unforgetable sights Elm Street had ever witnessed.

Lew, Griffin and the Monster stood in the middle of the street long after she was out of sight.

"Don't you feel just a little bit like Professor Henry Higgins, Griffin?"

"I have a feeling Frankenstein is more appropriate, Lewington."

The Ditch at Donnybrook

There is a place where you top the rise and from that point the whole panorama of the city of Melbourne is layed out before your eyes. At night it is an ocean of yellow lights, a carpet of stars speckling toward an intense orange glow at the horizon, like a permanent sunset. This flat tapestry of incandescence, striated by a golden lattice of arterial roads, seems to go on forever. Like a galaxy viewed from outside, it grows more intense toward the centre, while off to the right flank is the giant shadow of Port Phillip Bay. It is a place to pause in your journey and take stock—the place itself is marked by a huge pine tree that stands at the end of a long straight stretch of the Hume Highway, down from the low mountains of the Great Dividing Range and arrowstraight across a wide valley and then up to the pine tree crest and there the city lights spring out of the darkness of night. It is a sight to warm the heart of any traveller.

But Griffin did not feel warmed as he stood at the edge of the highway and surveyed the scene. It only reminded him that he had come so far and was so near and yet wasn't anywhere. He knew this spot well—the nearest point marked on the map was the hamlet of Donnybrook, but that town was slightly off the highway and anyway could not be seen at all. And for all those brilliant lights down there, still there wasn't anything that he might have called a sign of life.

Turning away from the city, he looked back up the highway, the way he had come. The very straightness of that section of road could only add to his disappointment. There could at least have been a bend or some other thing that he might have blamed. Instead there was the straight flat highway, the excellent visibility, the good tarmac that gleamed in places in the light of a full moon. As good a piece of road as there could possibly have been and utterly devoid of traffic as you might expect at four o'clock or whatever time it was this Tuesday or was it Wednesday morning. All that, he decided, was something it was better he did not know, and couldn't know anyway for his watch was broken. Better it might have been some more vital part of his body.

The highway added even further to his disappointment because he could see for miles and there was not a single set of approaching headlights to be seen. That, for this road even at so remote a time, must have been a rarity, something else sent to blight him. Even if there was a car approaching there was no guarantee that it would stop to pick him up. It was cold, the dew was settling, he huddled in inadequate damp clothing with his flesh still acclimatised to Queensland's permanent heat. He supposed that, out on the highway at this time of night and looking as miserable as he did, he at least offered a sufficiently pathetic character that should some motorist come along, they could never be so callous as to drive straight by him. His harmlessness was blatant, a fine figure of tragedy, that much would work at least. Provided someone came along to observe the figure.

He had gone so close—that was the most annoying part. It was only thirty hours ago that he sat a thousand miles away in the Redland Bay Hotel, watching the ferry on its regular trek and waiting for Lew. He sat feeling conspicuously alone, gazing quietly toward the blue hilled bulk of Stradbroke Island floating on the dazzling expanse of Moreton Bay. He encouraged no conversation, refused to look to see who was about him. It was unbelievable that it had come to this but it surely had. Of course, if you knew Lew Sigg it wasn't so hard to believe.

*

It had only taken him a few minutes to pack, while Dell sat in a corner in the lounge room, looking out the window and saying nothing, and Lew, like The Monster, followed Griffin on every trip to the car and back, carrying nothing, being useless. Not saying much either.

"You don't really have to go right now, do you?" was the sort of not much he was saying.

"It is time, Lewington."

"Yes, but... surely a short delay won't hurt."

"No. But I don't see what it will gain."

"Okay. If you must pressure the situation, I'll get my stuff and come with you."

"Sure. If you want."

"Only I'll have to talk Dell around..."

"Talk her around, Lewington. Are you kidding?"

You only had to glance at the unspeaking Dell to know that Lew had left it to this very last moment to make his decision whether to go or stay, and even then he hadn't quite made it yet. When he was ready, Griffin summoned up all of his courage and went one final time into the house. On padded feet, he approached the spot where Dell sat.

"Um, Dell. I'm going now."

"Goodbye Griffin," Dell said, without looking around. He wondered if she was hiding tears—not for him of course, though from him.

"I just wanted to say thank you for your hospitality and all that stuff," Griffin added determinedly.

Still she would not look around.

"For God's sake Griffin will you just get out of here."

He got out of there.

Again Lew followed him to the car.

"She doesn't mean it Griffin."

"Oh yes she does, Lewington."

"No Griffin. It's just that there's things about me she likes and things she hates. What she does is project the things she hates about me onto you."

Griffin laughed—there was on other choice.

"It's nice to see all those years studying Psychology weren't entirely wasted, Lewington."

"No, really, Griffin. You are just an innocent bystander in all this."

"There's no such thing as an innocent bystander, Lewington. To stand by and do nothing can never be a state of innocence."

"Alright then, since you're so determined. At least a parting ale."

"One for the road?"

"Yes. I'll just tell Dell where I'm going."

Griffin sat in the car, smoking and waiting, packed and ready, while The Monster, who plainly knew where they were going better than Lew did, panting excitedly in the back. Eventually, Lew appeared, shuffling along, looking harassed.

"Um. I'll be a little while, Griffin. Why don't you go down to the pub and wait and I'll be there shortly."

"Sure, Lewington."

"Don't go without me."

As the drove to the pub, the temptation to just keep right on going was overwhelming, but somehow here he was, one hour later, still waiting. Every so often, he shook his head in disbelief. But still he sat, watching the ferry, waiting. Perhaps it was the plan that he should run out on Lew. Maybe Dell had murdered him. Maybe. Maybe. But he couldn't run out. He had to wait it out to the end.

Lew arrived, looking no less harried. Perhaps he had claimed the call of nature, ducked out the back and run all the way to the pub.

"I thought you might be gone, Griffin."

"It's hard to know why I'm not, Lewington."

"I'm sorry. Your precipitous departure has caught me on the hop."

"This is the day on which we always planned to leave, Lewington."

"And the first time in history that either of us has ever stuck to the plan."

"Lewington, were I to remain another minute, your dearly beloved would heartily dine on Ratsack. It is truly time for me to go."

"You're overreacting. I can keep her calm."

"Oh sure you can. She'll be a bloody lot calmer when I'm back in Melbourne."

"Still, you leave me in a quandary, Griffin. I was hoping you'd hang around a few days, while I sorted things out here."

"Lewington. One of three things will happen. You two will murder each other, or one will murder the other, or she'll grow weary of you messing up her life and I'll see you in Melbourne. That's all there is. But you have to stay and I have to go."

"I can't see what stands to be gained."

"Well, at least Dell will have to find someone else to blame for all your shortcomings."

"Griffin, that is very unkind."

"It's an unkind day. Just my way of severing the ties."

"So you really are going, then."

"Yes. I really am."

"Carlton is calling."

"Very loudly."

"Well, a parting ale then."

"Just one more for the road."

It was one or two more than Griffin needed and it occurred to him that maybe this was Lew's plan—to get him too pissed to drive. It would be a long journey, alone, and he was already a little pissed and a lot tired. But there was no turning back now. Lew returned with the beer and they toasted the ferry.

"Well, Griffin. This is a bit sad. It never occurred to me that we might not be completing this epic journey together."

"It occurred to me, Lewington, right from the outset."

"I envy your ability to predict fates, Griffin."

"Lewington, Dell might get a little overexcited and vocal

at times but she's a fine and determined lady and she's been hopelessly hooked on you for five years. And you have responsibilities to the child. There comes a time when reality has to be faced. I seem to remember warning you about that."

"Yes, Griffin. I recall you did. But a man can live in hope."

"If nothing else, hope."

Griffin drained his beer and plonked the empty on the table.

"Well, time to go."

"What? So soon? Another beer, Griffin. At least.."

"No, Lewington. I want to get as far south as I can before nightfall."

And he was standing to show how serious he was, while Lew glanced all about in the desperation of one betrayed.

"There's no need to rush off..."

Griffin was on the move, but to get to the car park meant traversing the bar, and Lew, in a fluster, hastily shouted to the barman.

"Two more pots, please."

"You gonna drink 'em both yourself?" Griffin asked. And although he glanced back at Lew and grinned warmly, still he kept going.

He went through the doors into the sunlight and down the steps to where the Jag was parked, the Monster flaked out under the front as if waiting to be run over. Lew, delayed by the financial transaction, trotted up behind, beer in both hands, spilling some in his haste and anxiety.

"Here, Griffin. One for the road."

Griffin, the driver's door open, allowed the Monster to pass into the vehicle before he finally took the beer and drank. Lew could not have looked more disconcerted—his face seemed to be falling apart before Griffin's eyes. And perhaps he saw he was overplaying it, for suddenly Lew seemed to relax, and patted the Jag on the roof.

"Well, Griffin. What will you do with our fine machine once you get back."

"I don't know, Lewington. I guess I'll sell it, or maybe give it away if I can find someone worthy of it."

"God, how could you. After all this. It'd be like selling your mother. Have you no respect?"

"I don't need a car in Carlton. My whole life is within walking distance, or at least in range of the tram routes there."

"But it's too good a car to discard so carelessly."

"Then I'll give it to you, Lewington."

"You can't go giving away such a fine car, Griffin. It isn't right."

"Then I'll have to sell it."

"Okay, okay. I graciously accept your fine gift."

"Consider it yours."

He had drained the last of the beer and handed the empty to Lew, getting into the driver's seat.

"Hoo roo Lew," he grinned.

"Hey, where are you going with my car?" Lew demanded.

"I'd like to borrow it, if that's alright," Griffin laughed.

"No. Sorry. It's mine. You gave it to me. And you can't have it."

"Then you better make sure you take down the licence number so you can report its theft to the police."

He had the engine going, gave it a few revs, glanced over his shoulder to make sure The Monster was with him.

"Give me my car, you bastard."

"Look out or I'll run you down."

They were moving, Lew running along beside, clutching the window frame, trying to hold it back. Griffin jerked the wheel and threw him wide and Lew stumbled to his knees on the gravel but then came up, shaking his fist.

"Come back here with my car you bastard!"

"Come and fucking try and get it, Lewington."

And with a shift of gears he was gone, and a final glance in the rear vision of Lew standing, panting, hands on hips, shaking his fist and shouting.

*

And he ran hard, down the Pacific Highway along the northern coast of New South Wales. He drove stopping only for petrol and oil through the rest of the day and into the night, paused for a brief nap near Newcastle and then pushed on with the dawn on the expressway into Sydney, striking the morning peakhour traffic onto the great arch of the Harbour Bridge. And not stopping, though he had friends there he might have visited, but straight through onto the Hume. Southward through the heat of the day and he broke a fan belt near Holbrook and was forced to rest a few hours by the river while it was fixed. On the road again at nightfall, through Albury and into Victoria, and he was beyond tiredness now, beyond exhaustion, driving with his reflexes in some sort of euphoric state and every hour took him closer to where he had long since decided he should never have left...

...To end up here, standing by the highway with his head down and his hands in his pockets, just twenty miles from his destination but nowhere really. He had no idea what happened because he was asleep at the time, and had a nightmare that the world shook and turned upside down and awoke with a start to find it no dream. There was a mad scamper as the wailing Monster tore by him and out the window and away as the Jag settled on its roof. He heard the poor dog briefly, his continual yelping in fear and pain diminishing far out across the plain and gone to god knows where.

Painfully, he dragged himself out of the wreck and tried to figure out where he was. Slowly he detected that he had suffered no major injury, except to the dignity when he saw how embarrassingly straight and open the highway was at the point where he had left it. He glanced back at the Jaguar, so tragically on its roof. Lew's Jag, he managed to grimace, so bent and battered—another promise unfulfilled. For he was sure it was all Lew's fault—had he got away when he planned he would not have had to endure this extra long hard night at the wheel. One beer too many, thirty hours ago. Alright, maybe it wasn't entirely Lew's fault.

He limped to the edge of the highway. His shin had hit the dash board and although his jeans and the flesh beneath were torn, it didn't seem broken. He was bleeding from several places on his face and had done something nasty to his arm. But that big solid wonderful car had protected him to the last, he knew, in what might have been a fatal crash in a lesser vehicle.

And what of the Monster, poor bloody Monster, who departed the scene so rapidly. Griffin could only assume that meant Monster was only frightened, not hurt, and he had probably gone for miles before he recovered his senses. Griffin was too lame to go searching for him anyway—instead he stood calling for a long time, just in case the dog was now trying to find the way back. His body trembled with shock—waves of nausea swept over him. He had eaten too little on the journey to manage what seemed like a necessary vomit. The Monster was a smart dog—he would calm down and then either return to the wreck or make his way through the city and to Carlton. Dogs did things like that, he knew, and Monster's homing instinct would have been greater than most. Griffin assured himself of this, and reassured himself. Monster was a smart dog—too smart to be lost as foolishly as this.

He stood trembling by the roadside in the dark grim night—the light of the moon vanished behind clouds. With hopelessly fumbling hands, he got a cigarette alight and breathed again. The red glow of the end was the very raft of life that he clung to. He stood waiting but no help came. He was so desperately alone. Over in the ditch, the hulk of the Jaguar lay, its wheels pointed to the sky like four tombstones on a single grave.

"Hey Monster. Come on, come here, let's go. Hey Monster, you silly fucking dog, where the hell are you," he called hopelessly into the dawn.

First Cavity Assault Unit

There was no old man in the park that day, and even if there had been, no blazing sun to boil the alcohol in his system into his brain. And had he fallen, there was no longer any kerbstone upon which he could crack his head, nor asphalt for his spurting blood to discolour. The Melbourne City Council had seen to that with a huge excavation which, in the middle of the park, seemed to serve no purpose except making mud. It was as if the old drunk had risen to be Lord Mayor and subsequently ordered that all trace of his past misfortunes be obliterated lest the newspapers get hold of the story. Although the media had long since proven itself able to sustain interest in scandals without concern for evidence.

Though it was disastrous, what the council had done here. The ugly red clay was disgorged from the earth like vomit and spread ruthlessly over a wide area of grass to be trampled in by the uncaring feet of passersby and workmen. And to this the workmen had added a litter of drainpipes awaiting connection and burial; they had allowed their machinery to rip up great tracts of grass; they had erected rusted barricades and signs in bland yellow to prevent the thoughtless from falling into the huge trench they had excavated. Even the birds were gone, driven off by the stutter of pneumatic drills and somehow although you knew one day the pipes would be laid, the hole filling and the grass replanted to seclude all trace of the sacrilege forever, still it seemed that the birds might never come back. Although today there were no workmen either; on this Friday they had abandoned the job and left the ruins open to public viewing. But Griffin was the only one who came.

The day was overcast, the sky thick with impending rain, however unwanted that might be. There had been enough rain while he was away and then more. Floodwaters lapped the towns along the Goulbourn and Murray Rivers, unseasonal downpours and early snows in the mountains that were melting already, drizzle and sleet thrust the city dwellers into overcoats and miserable temperaments. It was freezing cold, a bitter sharp edge on the wind that bit right through the clothing and stiffened the skin. Dear old Melbourne—it was good to be back.

None of it bothered him in the slightest—he was impervious to the climate as he was to everything else. Perhaps it was that his city was trying to live up to its erratic meteorological reputation solely for the purpose of making him feel welcome. He had not even bothered to wear a coat, just to show how invincible he was. It was his first day without the plaster on his arm, the stitches on his face had been reduced to just a few scars and if he walked with a pathetic limp it wasn't due to the accident but because the other day he had fallen down the stairs and strained his ankle. Yeah he could take it alright.

The letter, if it might be called that, came that morning. There was a photograph, a Polaroid actually, and a brief note in so unreadable a scrawl you could be thankful he didn't attempt a longer letter. The photograph was of a soldier in starched uniform, eyes shadowed by slouch hat, huge grin on a clean shaven face, standing straight although gladly the camera had been held at a slight angle. He was a handsome devil, no doubt about that. And he would have been totally unrecognisable, had Griffin not already known who he was.

'Get onto this, you old dog-rooter. There just isn't anybody the army can't make a man out of, hey. Dunno what you complained about really. The army's alright as long as you can pick the bullshit from the rest. But like you used to say, the trick is to pretend to take the bullshit seriously. They've even decided to teach me a trade while I'm here. They put me in the Dental Unit and taught me to drill teeth. First Cavity Assault Unit—pretty amazing hey. So what about a letter to your old fellow digger—at least some sort of word that you got back okay. Hope your looking after our car…'

He would not write back. There was nothing he could say.

There was a car wrecker near Donnybrook who agreed to take the Jag off his hands for the cost of towing it out of the ditch and away—there was no way he could admit that. And even as inventive a mind as his had no hope of making a joke of the fact that they had turned him into a dentist. A fucking dentist. Yeah, it was amazing alright.

He moved away from the excavation and found a patch of grass to lie on, ignoring the fact that it was damp and cold, lying flat on his back gazing up at the threatening sky. Dentist. Unbelievable. Of course, he would be out by now. Last weekend, the government had been thrown out of office and Whitlam had taken over and the first thing he did on the first day was free the conscripts and imprisoned objectors. Griffin knew he should have felt joy, but he felt nothing. An appalling injustice had been corrected, but that only meant they were back where they started. Older and wiser maybe, but being old and wise never made anyone happy.

You had to be tough. You had to stand your ground and show them you could take it. He had a rotten time in Vietnam and he could have blamed everything on that—Karen, the jobs, the drinking and smoking, everything. But that would be chucking it in, and when you did that you were dead. Show nothing. Feel nothing. Never let them know how much it hurt. He was a tough Vietnam veteran whether he liked it or not, and that was the only way left open to him. They might have fucked up his whole life, but you couldn't let them know that. Never admit defeat, never give in. To pretend to be the toughest man alive was the only dignity that remained. The rest was shit!

The only thing to do now was begin again, from scratch. Everything that had been was done, was over, was gone. This was the void, the vacuum, between what was and what would be. In a few minutes, he would rise and go off to begin a new life that, no matter how it went, could never be as good as what was lost. But not yet. Right now he was tired and lay on the grass and knew that if he never rose again it wouldn't matter. He closed his eyes and allowed it all to drift wherever it wanted.

She would come, her bright eyes, her warm smile, in one of her pretty dress, and kneel on the grass beside him. She'd wake him gently with a caressing hand on his chest, ease him back to consciousness, to life.

"Come on, get up. You'll catch your death here, you goose." Maybe she was real, maybe she wasn't. Either way it didn't matter. The fantasy itself was almost enough. A nice reality was only a good fantasy lost forever.

When he might have mused on such imaginings all day in the past, he was now surprised to find his mind had better things to do. Enough of this dallying around. End of rest period. The first large droplets of rain began to fall but that was not the reason that he started to head back. He had needed only a few moments in the grotty park, to refresh himself and to allow those final residual regrets to pass their way freely and be gone. He could go himself now.

He turned down the slope, across the grass toward Nicholson Street, his mind already shifting ahead of him. And then he paused, as if he had forgotten something although it wasn't about to be forgotten. Turning his face into the wind, he called. "Hey Monster, come on, Let's go."

And the dog came bounding out of the trees and down the slope to whirl in excited circles about him, and he stopped in the rain to give him a thorough roughing up. And then they went on together, crossing through the stalled traffic to the far side and around the corner into Elm Street to vanish in the great shadow of the factory wall.

Barry Klemm enjoyed an array of abandoned careers before resorting to literature. He was a crane jockey, insurance clerk, combat soldier, advertising officer, computer programmer, cleaner, stagehand, postman, sports ground manager, builder's labourer, taxi-driver, film and TV scriptwriter and radio dramatist. He has published two novels for teen-age readers, The Tenth Hero, in 1997, and Last Voyage of the Albatross in 1998 through Addison Wesley Longman and Running Dogs, a novel of the Vietnam war by Black Pepper in 2000.

www.ingramcontent.com/pod-product-compliance
Lightning Source LLC
LaVergne TN
LVHW050909080826
845145LV00001B/19

* 9 7 8 0 9 8 0 7 3 4 3 2 4 *